The Alarai Chronicles

Book One:
Exile to the Stars

Dale B. Mattheis

Ardent Publishing
Northfield, Minnesota

Ardent Publishing
P.O. Box 489; Northfield, MN 55057 USA
http://www.ardentpublishing.com

This is a work of fiction. All characters, plot configurations, dialog and incidents spring solely from the author's imagination and are not to be construed in any other manner. Any resemblance to actual events or persons, living or dead, is entirely coincidental.

Copyright © 2001 by Dale B. Mattheis

All rights reserved. No part of this book may be used or reproduced in any manner whatsoever or by any means, whether electronic or mechanical, without written permission from the author, except for the inclusion of brief quotations in a review or critique.

ISBN: 0-9705430-0-X
Library of Congress Control Number: 00-091977

Cover design by Lightbourne
Cover Illustration by Bleu Turrell

First Printing 2002

Printed in the United Sates of America

> Full-color maps, tactical drawings and photos are available free of charge at: http://www.ardentpublishing.com

*To my children, Leah, Josh and Luke.
Listed by age but equal in my heart.
Without the joy of their presence,
whether in spirit or reality, nothing
would have been possible*

Acknowledgments

The origin of Exiles To The Stars, and of subsequent volumns in the series, harks back to 1994 when I first sat down at the keyboard. Holed up in a mobile home that was short on class but long on character, I didn't come up for air until well over a year had passed. The harsh realities facing unpublished authors quickly became apparent.

While aware of the odds, I was not prepared for the chaotic changes taking place in the publishing industry. The task would have been much more difficult, if not overwhelming, without the support and input of people in my life and those I met along the way.

My daughter Leah, a talented editor and writer, was always there with helpful suggestions. She never wavered even when confronted with the very rough first draft. The interest of my two sons, Josh and Luke, never flagged and urged me on when the task seemed insurmountable.

After moving to Minneapolis in 1996, the steady support of my sister, Deanna Johnson, and her husband, Richard, made the difference time and again. My brothers, Darrell and Dennis, were always ready to listen. Doug and Deb Ogden studied the manuscript and supported me in so many other ways. The list is long.

Finally, what would a writer be without a strong editor ready and willing to debate usage? It was a long search, but one amply rewarded in the person of Linda Tetzlaff. Her comments and suggestions were invaluable.

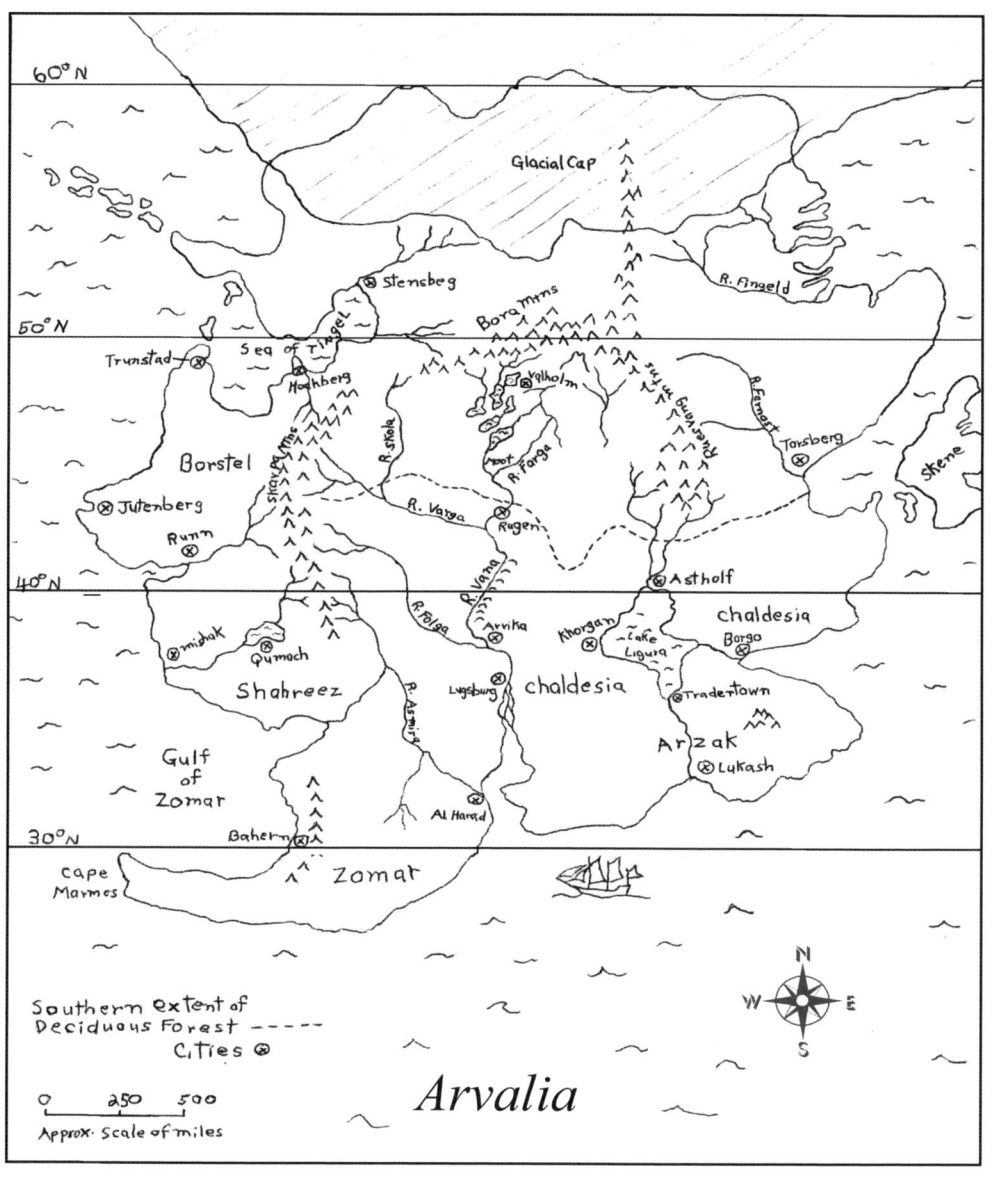

Full-color maps, tactical drawings and photos are available free of charge at: http://www.ardentpublishing.com

Table of Contents

1. An Unusually Bad Day — 15
2. Strange Dreams — 40
3. Good-bye — 49
4. Belief Dies Hard — 68
5. Battle-axe Remorse — 86
6. Horse of a Different Color — 108
7. Camelot — 127
8. Politics & Trust — 145
9. At Home on the Range — 168
10. Do or Die — 176
11. Redheaded Terror — 191
12. Worse Than Death — 208
13. A Time to Run — 225
14. Appearance Isn't Everything — 241
15. Words of Wisdom — 265
16. Go or No Go — 293
17. A Terrible Judgement — 301
18. Wolf or Human — 331
19. Forces Converge — 351
20. Revelation — 379
21. One Man's Portion — 387
22. Out of the Blue — 421
23. Guerilla Action — 456
24. Four-sided Triangle — 497
25. Denouement — 528

Prologue

Stretching north and south, Broadway glistened black. Rivulets of water curled around debris littering the street to join streams coursing toward storm drains. Many were clogged. Water overflowed curbs, leaving sections of broken sidewalk covered in deep pools. Cars passed with no more sound than the hissing of tires and click of windshield wipers.

Up and down Broadway, garish signs advertised evening pleasures. A few projected brilliant images over the sidewalk: wrestlers, nude women and men, animals and women. Most signs stuttered and blinked in the random patterns of burned out neon, casting kaleidoscope fantasies on sidewalks.

Groups of people hurried toward one tavern or the other. There were no singles visible on the street. Swinging wide to avoid an alley, members of one group muttered disgust at an emaciated figure lying face down near an overflowing dumpster. It was a partially clothed man.

Sirens blared in the distance, some nearby. To the west, the tops of Seattle skyscrapers were visible. Some ways north, what could have been a fire flickered orange shadows on clouds hanging low overhead. It was not a holiday, but a distant crackle sounded like fireworks.

A city bus with small windows and side panels constructed of armor-grade steel ground to a halt near one tavern. A bright pink and green cube suddenly flared to life over the tavern entrance. Seconds later a naked man seemed to leap from the cube and race across the street twenty feet up. A second man with horns sprouting from his head followed and impaled the first with a trident. The cube disappeared leaving a single word in crimson: Lucifer's.

The rear door of the bus snapped opened and a lone man jumped to the sidewalk. Gripping a long rectangular box, he made a dash for the tavern and disappeared inside.

Yet each man kills the thing he loves,
By each let this be heard,
Some do it with a bitter look,
Some with a flattering word,
The coward does it with a kiss,
The brave man with a sword!

Oscar Wilde

ONE

An Unusually Bad Day

"Sock it home, citizen!"

A pizza spun onto the table throwing a circle of oil. Seated at the table, a man in his twenties jerked upright off his elbows.

"Good shot. Missed the beer."

"Ready for the big time, compadre."

"What's the tempo, Paddy? Any mercenaries show?"

The waiter leaned down to wipe up the oil and also to be heard without shouting. The decibel level had a stein of beer vibrating on the table.

"One merc, Jeff. Gado came in a few minutes ago."

"Now there's a beautiful man. On his own or running in a pack?"

"Solo scout. Probably won't move until he has a quorum, but you can't tell. He's flying high and ragged. Watch your back."

The waiter hurried off through a haze of tobacco and pot smoke.

Jeff Friedrick scanned the bar and dance floor for threat. Lances of brilliant color stabbed out in psychedelic patterns to illuminate brief glimpses of determined smiles. It was Friday evening and time to blow off the stress of a long week.

Standing up to see better, Jeff felt his shirt flutter as banks of speakers slammed out a new beat. Someone gave him a shove from behind and he stumbled forward a step.

"Shove off, malcrap."

Catching himself, Jeff whirled to find a woman pulling his chair out to sit down. The woman and her two companions had shaved heads and were dressed in black costumes with high collars. Long, surgically implanted canine teeth glinted white in contrast to carmine lips.

"The table's taken, freak. Suck blood somewhere else."

With a sweep of his foot Jeff kicked the chair out from under the woman, sending her to the floor. She leaped to her feet with an oath and aimed a kick at his crotch.

Stepping aside, Jeff grabbed the leg and heaved. Arms flailing, she flew into the women behind her. They caught her and staggered backward to fall on top of a nearby table occupied by three men and a number of beer pitchers. Two of the men leaped up and began throwing punches while the third tried to save the last pitcher with beer in it.

A bouncer and several armed guards bulled through the crowd and waded into the fight. One of the women hit a guard square on the head with a pitcher, which shattered. The guard reeled back then came in low.

Picking up his chair, Jeff watched the action with the sense of a job well done. It looked to be a decent match. He caught the glint of something coming his way.

"Shit!"

Snatching up the pizza, Jeff ducked away as a beer pitcher struck the table edge and dissolved in a burst of glass shards. Grinning over at the fight, he wiped glass off the table with a napkin. A furious scream was abruptly cut off by a solid thud.

Jeff winced, but his grin broadened. "Take it outside, dildos."

An amplified voice blasted from the overhead PA system, "Hey hey, mals and fems! Here they are! Live from Twisted City, let's hear it for Lick and Swallow!"

The roar of approval was blown away when someone turned the volume up, filling the tavern to bursting with throbbing sound. Then it was gone, the sudden absence of music as shocking as its presence. The bouncers had control of the fight, and crowd noise dwindled as Jeff teased a wedge of pizza free.

An incandescent cone of light seared onto a raised platform. Audio pickups and projectors mounted around the tavern began to swivel and flex. In the blink of an eye she was there. Perfect golden body and no clothing but skin. Holding her arms up, she pirouetted.

"You going to get deep tonight? You losers good enough?"

Shouts and whistles, high-pitched and low, were drowned out by a bass line as old as burlesque. Gyrating and bumping, she was abruptly joined by an equally perfect male. Thrusting his hips in time to the music, he leered out over the crowd.

"Let's get it on!"

The music segued into a driving beat, and the dancers plastered their bodies together in a writhing mass. Leaping from the stage, Lick and Swallow reappeared on separate tabletops. Hands reached up to feel and probe, but the dancers paused for only a moment before jumping to the next table.

Someone yanked a chair from his table and Jeff turned quickly to see who it was. The dils had not gone easily into the night.

"Dammit, Carl, give me some warning! Where you been?"

Blond hair fell over Carl's eyes when he sat down. He flicked it away with an impatient twitch. "Hell of a time getting here. Damn near civil war going on out there. Cops had two blocks sealed off just south of here. What you so uptight about?"

"Paddy told me Gado's scouting."

"It figures," Carl replied with a grimace. "Friday night, and that bastard will wait until some poor slob is drunk on his ass trying to unwind." He glanced at the litter of broken glass. "I see things are getting an early start."

"Some dils tried to muscle in on our table. Managed to get themselves bounced."

"With a little help?"

Their table lit up with eye-searing brilliance and breasts were swinging in front of Jeff's face. Looking up, he gazed into blue eyes that were so real he could read the emptiness behind them. Red lips touched his, making his face tingle.

"Nice buzz, stud. Mama likes those green lamps!" Bright electronic laughter speared Jeff's ears. "C'mon, grab a tit. Probably all you can do."

"Flick off, deadhead. Show me the real thing and I'll consider it."

Whistles and applause sounded from nearby tables. A feminine voice shrilled, "Hang it on her, hairy male!"

The dancer squatted and thrust her pelvis into his face, an opalescent corona shimmering around her body.

"Ooh, little boy wants Mama."

Jeff felt a tugging sensation then raw lust as her hips moved over his head. Pushing back from the table, he growled, "Screw off. Go fuck with someone else's head."

Laughing wildly, she was gone and Jeff pulled his chair up to the table. "Those holos get any better, you won't be able to tell the difference. Damn, what crotch shot!"

"You complaining?" Carl grinned and slapped Jeff on the back. "Maybe not such a bad idea. Things might really get interesting. You know, go to your local holo store and check out a woman for the night?"

17

"I like it." Jeff tossed a wedge of pizza to Carl. "Eat up and let's move it, Norsky. Big doings at the shuffle palace."

"You got that right," Carl said, jamming half the wedge in his mouth. "I can hardly wait. Lot of talk about tonight—might have a real crowd!"

The noise level made conversation difficult and they finished the pizza in silence. Lick and Swallow had the place ragging hard. Carl slugged down the last of his beer and unfolded from the chair.

"Come on, runt."

Extracting a long wooden case from under the table, Jeff stood up. Carl topped Jeff's six feet by a good three inches and was so lanky he seemed taller.

"Where's your toothpick, Carl?"

"Out in the car. No way I was going to bring it in here."

"Good move. Hope we can make it out the door with mine."

Jeff looped the carrying strap over his shoulder and they sidled toward the door. At the bar, a man turned his head and watched them go. He was tall, and a brief flare of light revealed reddish hair. Before the spotlight moved on, odd points of light deep in green eyes gave the impression of motion although he was staring fixedly at Jeff and Carl. When they disappeared into the crowd he tipped his stein up for a drink.

"He's almost there, but it's going to be close. If only I could just say hello." He took another swallow. "But I can't."

Jeff and Carl were nearly to the door when a hand gripped Jeff's shoulder.

"Hold it, Friedrick. Running out?"

Brushing the hand away, Jeff turned to confront a rat-faced man of about his height. Gado. His pupils were pinpoints, and spittle had dried to white foam at the corners of his mouth.

"Go find a drunk, merc. That's more your style."

"Hear you won the regionals, Friedrick, but that's the way it is with you college boys—no guts for the real thing." Gado giggled and gave the wooden case a shove. "Make you feel like something to carry it around?"

"One of these days soon," Jeff replied in a coldly level voice. "Just keep showing up." He pushed through the circle of bystanders that had gathered.

"Hey now, look at him go. Friedrick's on the run. Looks like a whipped weenie dog, don't he?"

Anger flashed, stopping Jeff in his tracks. Grabbing his arm, Carl dragged Jeff along to the entrance where they stopped to zip jackets.

"Cool down, buddy. Gado isn't worth it."

"I keep coming here and I'll slice that cock sucker," Jeff grated. "He's been pushing me for months. I think it's about time for show and tell. Why the hell not? Maybe that's the only thing that counts anymore."

"We got to keep muckin', boy; keep the faith."

"Isn't anything else left." Jeff glanced out the door. "Nice night."

"What else? Cold and wet." Carl let out a snort. "Ah, Seattle. Emerald City of Dreams."

"Yep," Jeff said with a grudging laugh, "home to the starving and privileged." He put his face close to the armored glass and peered up and down the street. "Where'd you park that cybernetic chlorox bottle you call a car?"

"Around the corner, dork. You ready?"

"Let's do it. You get the door, I'll rearguard. Keep your eyes open for those dils that got bounced."

Outside, Carl checked the street in both directions and ran south. Clamping the case against his side, Jeff took off after him but stayed four or five feet behind. The only light came from a few streetlights that still functioned. The rest were dark with broken or cracked lenses. Carl dashed around a corner and Jeff put on a burst of speed to catch him.

"Let's do it quick, Jeff!"

Carl yanked his access card from a slot under the door handle. A relief valve popped, both doors shot into the roof and Carl slipped inside in one smooth motion. Jeff had to deal with the case, which slowed him down.

"Clear!"

Hydraulic pumps whined, the doors snapped shut and locks thumped home. Punching numbers into a keypad on the dash, Carl enabled the fuel cell. A low-pitched whine gradually built in volume.

Lifting free of suspension stops, the Ford leveled itself while Carl's fingers flew across switches on the dash. An orange display materialized low on the windshield and a red light blinked rapidly, accompanied by an electronic voice.

"Reset, please."

"Rapid sequence reset, feature Capitol Hill and University District."

A map of Seattle scrolled across the heads-up display. Icons sprang to life at several locations.

"This is the Police Information Network, Friday evening, Twenty-one March, 2025. Citizens are strongly cautioned to remain indoors. Civil unrest is reported on Capitol Hill off Broadway, intersections Roy and Aloha. Aurora Avenue has been closed at Greenlake, fire…"

Lifting his finger from the PIN switch, Carl pulled out onto Broadway. "Civil unrest, my ass. What they mean is riot."

After a period of tense observation that revealed no threat, the men relaxed.

"I've been meaning to ask about that sword of yours for some time, Jeff. How about some history? Seen a lot of sabers in the fifteen years I've been around fencing, but have yet to come across one that gives me the same sense as yours. It seems regulation normal, but every time I handle it I come away wondering if it's a saber at all. The balance is exquisite. In the two years we've been knocking around together, you haven't said a word about it. What gives?"

Jeff considered the question while Carl wove the Ford around deep potholes and patches of glass that littered the street.

"Probably haven't said anything because it's just a normal part of life. Had that sword since I was a kid." Jeff examined the sidewalks and street with intent concentration, then chuckled. "In fact, now that I think about it, I feel naked when it isn't with me."

"Might look a little funny if you brought it to your classes," Carl responded, throwing a broad grin at Jeff.

"Yeah, but damn, what a teaching tool."

Releasing a snort of laughter, Carl intoned, "What? Your paper isn't done? Off with your head!"

Blurred figures running across the street a block ahead caught Jeff's eye. "Hang a right, Carl. Don't like the looks of that." Blue and yellow lights suddenly strobed the night, quickly followed by a muted popping. "Shit! That's gunfire! Make it quick!"

Nearly past the intersection, Carl flicked the steering yoke hard over and the Ford lurched around the corner, gyros whining protest. Half expecting a setup, they quickly checked out the street. Empty.

"Things get any worse," Carl muttered, "and it'll be worth your life to drive after dark."

"What do you call this scene?"

"You've got a point." Carl glanced at the rearview image suspended in the holograph unit. "Okay, I think we're clear. So the sword has been handed down in your family. How old do you think it is?"

"It's been in the family for a long time but Grandad didn't know a lot about it. He thought maybe 200 years or so. It's not a classic cavalry saber—simply not heavy enough—and it never rusts. Can't figure it out."

"Has to be carbon steel."

"Given its age, what else could it be?"

"Beautiful workmanship. Bugwit's saber looks like cardboard in comparison."

"Hathwaite's saber? I think he picked it up in a costume store."

Carl turned left and they continued north, a high stone wall set with razor wire on top bordering one side of the street. He eased the Ford as far as he could to the opposite side of the street when they approached a gate set in the wall.

"Haven't been this way in a long time. Don't like this place anymore now than I did then."

"San Quentin."

"Yeah."

The gate was protected by concrete abutments and by three guards in a blockhouse. "Man, I think those suckers are packing military rifles," Carl pressed down on the accelerator, "but they aren't military."

As they passed the gate, a red dot suddenly appeared on the side of Jeff's head. Carl caught it out of the corner of his eye, floored the accelerator and the Ford shot away.

"Had you pegged solid, boy. That was just a warning, but you only got one head to lose. Wouldn't you just love to live there?"

"On our salary? Those residential enclaves take real money to get into." Jeff shook his head. "Even if I had the money, not a chance. More like a warren of terrified rats than a community. When it hits the fan, they won't last an hour."

Carl tapped the brakes. "Here we go."

After rattling across the ancient Montlake Bridge, thankful as always that it had not collapsed, Carl pulled into a secure parking area next to the university gym. On their way across the lot, Jeff counted vehicles.

"The rumor mill was right on, Carl. Will you look at all the cars!"

Entering a smaller annex near the cavernous main building, the ring of steel on steel greeted their ears. Once through the vestibule, the musty smell of sweating bodies past and present intermingled with echoing profanity and laughter.

They took in the scene and looked at each other with delighted grins. It really was a packed house.

"Tell you what, Jeff," Carl observed with a big grin, "I think Bugwit is going to have his hands full tonight. I mean, how is he going to impress everyone at the same time? This is going to be fun."

"For sure, but I keep hoping just once he won't brag about that fellowship of his in Warsaw."

Carl halted abruptly and looked at Jeff with mock horror. "Are you questioning his pilgrimage to the mecca? Tell me it isn't true! Why, everyone knows that makes him the resident saber expert."

"Well, it's a dirty job," Jeff said with an appreciative snicker. "I guess it does take a dickhead like Hathwaite to fill the slot."

Dodging around a man and woman fencing with intent concentration, they entered the main throng. Along the way, Carl threw Justin Hathwaite a derisive grin.

A willowy man with patrician features, Hathwaite wore snug breeches tucked into cavalry boots complete with spurs. Surrounded by a coterie of men and women, he sneered briefly in return.

Chuckling at Hathwaite's response, Carl said, "And Jorgenson scores ten points. It's good start to the evening, ladies and gentlemen."

"Yeah, maybe," Jeff replied. "You and Mike have been needling him pretty hard the last couple of weeks, buddy. With a crowd like this, it might not be a good idea to push him."

"Pretty hard to do, my man," Carl said. "You're holed up with George for a good share of the evening and miss the crap that jerk hands out. Not sure why, but your name seems to come up a lot when he's holding court on everyone's shortcomings. Probably because you won the regional competition and he barely made the cut." Carl laughed explosively. "And those spurs! God save me, I can't resist it!"

They exchanged greetings with members they hadn't seen in awhile, and made a point of saying hello to the new faces as they moved around. Jeff turned to speak with Carl but his eyes never got there. Facing him was a slender, black-haired woman holding an epee.

"Sarah."

"Jeffrey."

Other than an upwelling of residual pain, he felt empty of emotion. Two years, endless fights with bitter words that accomplished nothing, but fights that over time became an emotional killing ground. Neither spoke. Every word had finally been expended during the death throes of their relationship.

Although several months had passed since the final parting, strings of attachment that owed nothing to intellect had not entirely dissolved, and their eyes conveyed volumes of condemnation.

"Don't waste your time with losers, Sarah." Hathwaite sauntered over and tugged her toward his crowd. "Let's get some action going."

"Why him, Sarah?" Jeff felt like a partially healed wound had been ripped open with fingernails. Of all the men on campus, or even in the club, she had wound up with Hathwaite.

"He knows where he's going, Jeffrey. He's going to be someone and wants me to go with him. It's a refreshing change."

"Are you dating him to get back at me?"

Sarah turned her back to Jeff and took Hathwaite's hand. Looking over his shoulder, he winked at Jeff.

A hand came to rest on Jeff's arm. "Let it go. They make a pair."

"Thanks, Carl. Took me by surprise."

"Doesn't it always?"

"Too many times."

"Yeah. Aren't you supposed to meet George?"

"I'm late. Thanks again."

Jeff changed into sweats and hurried to meet his instructor, a saber master. The confrontation with Sarah had faded by the time they decided to take a break and cool down. While fencing they had been talking about more than the fine points of technique. George Greely couldn't remember feeling so frustrated.

"All right, all right! You won't compete in the nationals! But let me tell you something, Jeff. If you want to take your skill farther, at some point you're going to have to go up against other real talent. You're good, real good, but you'll never know—hell, I'll never know—just how good you are until your backs to the wall and some boyo's trying to make you look like an idiot. I think you could go all the way—doesn't that mean something?"

"I'm not interested in the nationals, George. You knew that when I agreed to compete in the regionals."

George eyed Jeff silently for a few moments. "No argument there, but where do you go from here? I don't have much more to teach you. Ask yourself this: why have you been working with me? What's the point if you don't intend to take it as far as you can go? You need to find out what you're made of, Jeff. That means competing in the nationals."

The noise level out in the gym abruptly dropped to nothing. They jumped to their feet and hurried from the room.

"Shit, I'll bet that asshole Bugwit is at it again," George spit out in a disgusted snarl. "He's going to destroy this club yet."

Once onto the main floor they immediately noticed a crowd surrounding Hathwaite and Carl. They were standing nose to nose. Even from a distance Jeff could see that Carl's face was flushed with anger.

"You've been a loudmouth jerk as long as I've known you, Hathwaite. Jeff Friedrick happens to be a friend of mine, and this crap you're spouting is more than I am willing to tolerate. You, sir, have gone too far."

Elbowing his way to the center of the ring, Jeff stopped by Carl. "Hathwaite, this matter appears to concern me directly. Since I have not been privy to its origins, I must have the opportunity to review the circumstances with Mr. Jorgenson. By your leave, sir?"

Favoring Jeff with a mocking smile, Hathwaite bowed. Accompanied by George, Jeff guided Carl to an area of relative privacy.

"What in hell is going on?"

Carl's usual response to stress was cynical humor. On this occasion his expression simmered with anger.

"As you might expect, Bugwit was really laying it on thick with his toadies in full attendance. ..." Carl paused and shrugged. "You may as well hear it all. I think Sarah was egging him on, or at least her presence was, and he pulled out all the stops with that crap about Warsaw."

"Let me guess. Mike sort of helped things along."

"Yeah, you could put it that way, George."

"Al and Harold are here, why didn't they step in? They've been around long enough to know the score. That's why we elected them."

"Damn it, they tried, Jeff, but you know Mike. He just wouldn't shut up! Then he really got cute and asked Hathwaite how often he tripped over his spurs."

"That would do it," George stated. "Someone needs to pound some sense into Mike's head."

"It was more than enough," Carl shot back. "Hathwaite really came unglued. I thought he was going to challenge Mike, but instead he started tearing you apart, Jeff."

"Sarah."

"Maybe that was part of it," Carl replied doubtfully, "but don't forget the regionals. Whatever, I was trying to get out of earshot when he implied that, unlike him, you were avoiding competing in the nationals. He did everything but call you a coward." Carl looked directly into Jeff's eyes. "Do you really think I would stand still for that?"

Jeff tasted bile, and thought, Why do they single me out? Is it just because I'm good with a saber? Jeff recalled his confrontation with Gado; his repeated attempts to provoke a duel. Jeff's features went icy calm and golden-green eyes glinted like polished stainless steel.

"No, I do not. Thank you for intervening. This is now my affair." He turned to George before Carl could protest. "Do you concur?"

"I see no alternative," George replied with a fatalistic shrug. "The insults, expressed as they were in public and in the presence of a close friend, leave no option that I am aware of. I have no doubt you could take him, Carl, but that's not the issue."

"No, it isn't," Jeff said in a flat tone of voice. "It's time to kick ass." He paused for a moment to exchange a level gaze with George. "Let's go."

Hathwaite saw Jeff coming and turned away from Sarah with an expression of smug satisfaction.

"Can't find a way out, Friedrick?"

Anger tried to break free but Jeff shoved it aside. "Hathwaite, you've seen fit to make statements that question my courage. Mr. Jorgenson has fully related their content, and I find them offensive. Before this goes any farther, I must know if you wish to withdraw from your position. The future of this club may be at stake."

"What I said earlier stands, Friedrick. I don't think you have the guts to face real competition." Hathwaite paused dramatically and swept his eyes around the circle of intent faces. "As to the club, that's just an excuse. The dean isn't going to shut it down. You're going to have to run."

The cynical challenge in Sarah's eyes and Hathwaite's comment stoked cold anger to a bright flame.

"Mr. Jorgenson is correct. You're a braggart and incompetent fool. I will have satisfaction tonight, Hathwaite—sabers to first blood."

"Sure you're up to it?"

"Either give me a civil answer or it's all the way."

Hathwaite looked around the crowd again. "Do we see a touch of courage? Marvelous! I accept. A contest with sabers, no limit except resignation."

"Agreed." Jeff stared at Sarah. "Make sure you bring the bitch. I want her to see you get cut."

The city park Carl and Hathwaite's second settled on had been maintained better than most. It still had a few lights that worked. Jeff, Carl and George rode together to the designated area.

"Dueling is out of hand," George reflected quietly. "What? Eight or ten a month on the news? And that's just the tip of the iceberg. But that idiot simply left no option."

"He didn't intend to. He's an asshole. That aside, what do you know about Hathwaite's ability, George? I've never seen him do much except talk."

"I watched a few of his matches during the regionals, Carl. Decent talent, no discipline and poor conditioning." George glanced over at Jeff. "Besides those factors, Hathwaite's major weakness is his temper. He barely qualified for the nationals because of it. It'll work in your favor, Jeff, but never forget it might also lead him to try and kill you. Don't count on him following any conventions."

Jeff had dropped into a black mood and just shrugged

"The only redeeming factor is the timing," Carl observed after a period of silence. "Scheduling it this evening, any publicity will be limited to rumor."

No one spoke the rest of the way, each reflecting on how the media would hype the duel given a moment's notice. Carl groaned when he turned into the park entrance.

"The damn thing's full! There weren't that many cars at the gym!"

"The boys and girls have certainly been using their 'magephones," George concurred, "but I don't see any news floaters. Park on the grass."

Al Grady emerged from the crowd and walked toward them. At thirty-seven, he was the oldest club member and widely respected. He had also agreed to act as monitor. George hurried on ahead to meet him.

They chose a location to speak that offered privacy as well as an overview. Two groups were pitching open beer cans back and forth, prompting bursts of laughter.

"Looks like a party, Al."

"It's not a good scene. Hathwaite's boyos are milking it, but no peripheral challenges to this point."

"Let us only hope."

"Amen, brother. What's the situation with Jeff? Any room to move?"

"I doubt it. Hathwaite didn't leave him much."

Al nodded and examined George's expression. "No, he didn't. You know Hathwaite's likely to go for the kill, don't you?"

"Figured he would."

"Just needed to make sure you were up to speed. I don't want Jeff to be unprepared."

"We've talked about it. Thanks for the time, Al, but I don't want to compromise your position. This needs to be very clean."

"You can count on it." Al clapped George on the shoulder and moved off.

A good share of the crowd surrounded Hathwaite when they walked up. He had an arm around Sarah's shoulders.

"Glad to see you could make it, Friedrick. Thought you would be halfway to Portland by now."

Picking up trash from the area he had selected for the duel, Grady abruptly stood up and hurried over to Hathwaite.

"This is a troubling affair. Your behavior in forcing this issue has discredited our club. We will soon understand where courage resides." He motioned Jeff over. "I must ask you both to reconsider your positions and attempt to seek a solution that exempts combat."

Ignoring Sarah's presence, Jeff stared fixedly at Hathwaite and said nothing. Meeting Jeff's gaze with a contemptuous smile, Hathwaite turned away to share a witticism with his cronies.

Grady had expected nothing more and went in search of a baton. Jeff stripped down to sweat bottoms and tee shirt before kneeling to re-lace his gym shoes. Carl watched with a concerned frown.

"You still warm?"

Testing his sword arm with a few experimental passes, Jeff replied, "Loose enough."

"Stay centered, Jeff. He won't give you the time of day, and he's sloppy on his thrusts."

"I hear you. Don't worry, Hathwaite had his show back at the gym."

Grady caught Carl's attention with a sweep of his arm. "Let's do it, buddy. Clean cuts, and a lot of 'em."

Jeff gripped Carl's hand and walked toward Grady. Hathwaite strode to meet him, spurs clinking.

"Gentlemen, are you ready?"

At their nods, Grady held a stick out at shoulder height. When their swords crossed over the stick, he flicked it away. The rain had stopped briefly, but once again drifted down in fine drops that showed as a yellow-orange mist in the harsh lighting.

Holding guard position, Jeff made no move to attack. Hathwaite stepped back, pointed his sword at Jeff and sighed dramatically.

"This simply isn't going to *do*, Jeffrey. You're going to have to fight."

Hathwaite waved his sword in an elaborate chicane and stamped forward. Their swords met with a metallic ring then slithered and chimed in a series of parries and feints. Hathwaite picked up the pace but only succeeded in notching his blade. Breath pluming in jagged bursts, he disengaged and retreated. Jeff crouched slightly and advanced, saber extended.

The crowd of fifty or so spectators that surrounded the men changed shape as one or the other advanced with quick steps, swords disappearing into blurs only to come together in a deadly song. Just as quickly, they separated and resumed maneuvering for the advantage.

Some minutes into the duel Hathwaite fell back breathing hard. Jeff suddenly skipped forward, saber winking with speed as he came in high. A staccato clashing of steel and Hathwaite jumped out of harms way with a startled curse. There was no missing the worried look on his face.

Shifting position to follow the match, Carl said, "I think Bugwit wishes he were home in bed."

"Or anywhere but here." George stepped forward to get a better view. "Hathwaite knows he's in way over his head by now. He's spooked and getting tired. Just watch—it's about to go down and dirty."

Hathwaite thought he saw a weakness in Jeff's guard and attacked from low position with a series of quick feints followed by a waist-level thrust. The feints were tapped aside, but the thrust was parried with a flick of Jeff's wrist that nearly ripped Hathwaite's saber from his hand. Stung by the near disaster of his attack, Hathwaite muttered a curse and initiated a frenzy of cuts and thrusts.

Forced to retreat, Jeff's heel caught on a tuft of grass and he stumbled backward off balance. Hathwaite lunged in with a low thrust that sliced open Jeff's sweat pants from knee to ankle but missed skin. The crowd let out an excited shout.

"Say good-by to your ass, peon!"

To avoid falling, Jeff put a hand down and pivoted to the side. As he did so, Hathwaite thrust with all his strength. With a whispering sound, his blade penetrated Jeff's tee shirt and nicked the skin along his ribs.

"Finish him off, Justin!"

Carl spun around looking for the voice. George grabbed his arm. "No! Let it go. This isn't your fight."

Regaining his feet, Jeff beat back another attack. God damn it, he thought, that asshole tried to kill me! His mind did a stutter-step and every sense seemed to expand by a factor of two.

Lips pulled back in a grimace of fatigue and desperation, Hathwaite continued to press hard. As if regulated by a metronome, sabers flickered in four-four time interspersed with ringing arpeggios of sixteenth notes. Still on the defensive, Jeff backpedaled steadily and the match moved into a sparsely wooded area.

Furious with himself for having tripped, Jeff found the rhythm and held his ground in a grotto of trees. Mind and body became one smoothly functioning machine and he picked up the tempo. High and low, thrust and cut, engage, riposte, recover—faster and faster until the bright metallic beating of swords seemed continuous. A roar escaped the crowd.

"Holy shit," Carl breathed. "Look at that arm speed. I can't follow his moves!"

"Now that's how you attack!" George crowed. "I'm finally seeing it! By God, he *is* a warrior!"

Retreating with rapid steps as his guard was compressed inward, the whites of Hathwaite's eyes stood out in bold relief. Jeff's saber slipped by a parry and the tip sank into Hathwaite's sword arm. He cried out and his saber clanged off a rusted barbecue as it fell to the ground.

Stepping back, Jeff gestured with his sword. "Pick it up."

Face writhing with fear, Hathwaite snatched up the sword. Blood streamed down his arm and his breath came in great sobs as he tried to get enough air. Within minutes his shirt hung in two pieces revealing a red furrow on his chest. Lower, a red blotch spread outward from a puncture wound in the abdomen.

At the end of his strength, Hathwaite put everything left into a desperate assault. A furious crescendo of sword strokes and he froze. The point of Jeff's saber was resting against his throat. Hathwaite's face was ghost white and his body was trembling.

"Damn you, Friedrick, just kill me and get it over with!"

Also short of air, Jeff had to talk between deep breaths. "That's all fencing means to you, isn't it? Who kills whom? You fucking idiot. How long do you think the club will survive when word of this gets out? Where you going to go when the dean pulls the plug? Downtown to one of the butcher shops?"

Jeff stepped back and resumed guard. "You've got a choice. Resign or continue."

They stared at each other for several heartbeats before Hathwaite stumbled off through the trees. Grady quickly stepped forward.

"Ladies and gentlemen, honor has been served. I suggest we leave immediately before the floaters arrive. Please speak of this to no one!"

As if on cue, a large hovercraft glided into the park. Painted black, it had the contours and armor of a tank. Spewing grass and debris from under containment skirts, the craft settled to the ground with the sound of decelerating fans. Satellite antennas began to deploy at once.

"Don't talk to those news creeps if you want to save the club! Get out of here!"

The crowd broke and ran for the parking lot, but Sarah seemed frozen. Wiping off his saber, Jeff slipped it into the scabbard and walked past her.

"Good-by, Sarah."

They rode back to the gym in silence and hurried to the showers. Raiding a first-aid kit, George dressed the wound on Jeff's ribs. The silence continued until they were on their way out of the gym. Before he pushed through the doors, George caught Jeff's eyes.

"You've answered any questions I might have concerning your ability. That was a consummate display of fencing skill, Jeff. I'm also impressed by the restraint you showed. Given the provocation and that young woman's presence, another man might have seriously wounded Hathwaite or even killed him."

Jeff shrugged morosely. "It hasn't come to that yet." He laughed bitterly and thrust the door open. "Another night like this, and who knows?"

Outside, Jeff and Carl walked George to his car. As he slid inside, a chorus of wailing sirens knifed through the rain. Jeff and Carl turned to listen, but George looked down at the pavement and muttered, "Goddamed city." He enabled the fuel cell and rolled the window down. "Watch yourselves going home, fellows. This is not a good night."

"We will." Carl patted the car's roof. "Be cool, George."

"Yeah."

The parking lot of an all-night restaurant near the university was busy with vehicles entering and leaving when Carl eased the Ford into a slot. Showing identification to the armed guards out front, they stepped into a box-like entry. Following an electronic scan, the door snapped open.

They ordered a big meal and ate in exhausted silence. Watching Jeff fight, Carl decided, had been one of the most emotionally draining experiences he could remember. He signaled the waiter for a fresh cup of coffee and smiled crookedly.

"One hell of an evening, buddy."

"Yeah, you could say that," Jeff replied. "I've been wondering, though, whether this is the end of it. I've got this feeling that something has been started, not finished. Everything that happened tonight has a sense of the inevitable about it. First Gado, then Sarah and Hathwaite. I must have replayed the whole thing a dozen times, but it still comes out the same. There simply was no way to stop that duel short of walking away."

"Five years ago you could have walked away from it, Jeff. If you had done that this evening, you might as well have kept walking right out of town."

"I know that!" Jeff slapped his hand on the table in frustration. Several customers spun in their seats to check it out, another ducked.

A guard sitting at the counter looked at Jeff with narrowed eyes. "Keep it quiet, or leave."

"I will," Jeff acknowledged, and dropped his voice to an urgent whisper. "I do know that, Carl. That's one of the things that really irritates the hell out of me." He was morosely quiet for a few moments before continuing. "Nothing to be done about it, nothing to do or to be done that would change one damn thing."

"Want to talk about it?" Carl inquired while closely searching his friend's features. "Maybe you better. These last months, you've reminded me of someone about to go over the edge."

"That bad?"

"I'm just your average Joe Psychologist," Carl said with an expressive shrug, "but I get the sense that if someone poked you with the right needle—boom!"

Jeff grimaced and nodded. "Like tonight."

"No, not like tonight. I agree with George. You showed remarkable restraint."

The waiter stopped by with a carafe of coffee. He kept a wary distance from Jeff while pouring. Taking a long drink, Jeff sat back rubbing his forehead.

"If showing restraint means that I didn't kill him, then you're right." Shaking his head, Jeff held his hands up as if framing a picture. "Jeff Friedrick, Cultural Anthropologist."

"Yeah, so?"

"It was that close. Maybe that's the only reason I didn't kill him. I tried to turn my head off and do him, but my training wouldn't let me."

"That's serious shit, Jeff."

"More than serious. It scares the hell out of me just thinking about it."

After a period of silence, Carl said, "And?..."

"Twenty-seven, Carl. Twenty-seven years old and I don't have a clue. I used to believe that I could make life what I wanted it to be by hard work and desire. What a joke. How do you fit in? What's the secret? Slinging bullshit? I just can't make myself do it. Now all I want is to get away."

"I can dig it, but it doesn't sound like you're talking about a vacation."

"No, not a vacation. I want to disappear for good."

Carl whistled and raised his eyebrows. "Anthropology isn't enough to make the difference?"

"Maybe it's too damn much." A speculative look settled on Jeff's face. "While I really love anthropology, thinking about it now it only seems to be a step along the way. Something I have to understand before moving on. But to what?" Jeff let his breath out in a long sigh. "Okay. I'm a specialist in Late Antiquity, right?"

"You mean that European mob scene you've talked about?" Carl replied with a wicked grin.

"Yeah, that's it," Jeff responded with a smile tugging at his lips. "About 300 to 700 AD." A frown creased his forehead. "I was drawn to anthropology like a magnet, and when I discovered Late Antiquity there was no doubt where my future lay. I felt like I was coming home! I've very nearly memorized every reference I can get my hands on, yet it's never enough. Can you believe it? Now I'm into Roman history and the Middle Ages trying to get more insight. The people, the history, their manner of warfare—you name it, I've studied it. What is it I'm looking for?"

"I've seen your apartment. Hardly room for a bed with all those holo cubes. Maybe you're looking for yourself?"

"Maybe," Jeff said doubtfully, "but I don't think that's all of it. Sometimes I feel like I'm studying for my dissertation again; like I'm going to be tested." Jeff paused and smiled. "Although Late Antiquity was a brutal period, it was also an exiting time. So much happening!"

Closing one eye, Carl pantomimed drawing a bow. "Twang!"

Jeff threw his hands up and laughed. "Okay, okay. So I'm atavistic."

"Nah. Not implying that. We've been friends long enough that I know how important that period is to you."

"Maybe it's too important. It isn't only that I'm into archery and fencing, or that I'm absorbed by the peoples of Late Antiquity. Sometimes they seem to be the only real things in life. Maybe if I put some distance between that stuff and myself I'd find a way of fitting in. There has to be a point to life somewhere! God, I hope there is!"

Sitting back in the booth, Carl stretched mightily. "As far as fitting into the system goes, who am I to talk? I don't see anymore hope or purpose in it than you do. Thing is, biology and chemistry make the difference for me." Carl smiled wistfully. "Jeff, if you happen to find a point to life will you let me know?"

"You're on the top of all my lists, buddy. Thanks for being there."

Carl happened to look at the clock near the door and let out a dismayed whistle. "Time goes fast when you're having fun, boyo. Nearly midnight! I have to drop some reference cubes off at the lab or old Benford will have my skin in the morning."

"Go on without me. It's only about ten blocks to my apartment. I've got to walk some of this off."

"You kidding? I think it's more like twenty. Man, you know what it's like out there. No one walks unless he's in a friendly crowd and armed. Ride back with me."

"I do know what it's like, but I can't imagine anything capping that little fling with Hathwaite. No one is even going to see me."

"Bullshit," Carl shot back. "Those gangs have every square inch staked out. This is crazy. No, it's stupid! This is not a good night to walk to your car, much less home. Damn it, Jeff, you heard the report."

Jeff stood up. "I'm walking."

"I think this is a very bad decision. You take too many risks. It's really going to bite you one of these days."

Back at the Ford, Jeff extracted the saber case. Carl started the car and stuck his head out of the window.

"You know what I think. Stay alert, huh?" With a wave, he accelerated into the night.

The restaurant was located a short distance south of the Lake Washington Ship Canal. On adding up the distance to his apartment, Jeff had to ruefully agree with Carl that it was at least twenty blocks.

"You really are a dumb shit, Friedrick. What are you trying to prove?" Zipping his windbreaker against the damp cold, Jeff set off at a brisk walk.

He gave alleyways a wide berth and stayed in deep shadow whenever possible. However, some sections offered no cover and Jeff felt like a spotlight was on him. Six or eight blocks along the way he began to relax. Only three cars had passed, and he had not seen a single person. Even the police sirens were quiet. As he walked, Jeff insensibly slipped back into brooding over the duel and where in hell he was going in life.

Some minutes later a metallic clatter sent him behind shrubbery with a reflexive lunge. A garbage can lid skidded out of an alley and ground to a halt. Two cats streaked into view side by side, digging for all they were worth. Jeff began to shiver but didn't move.

A vicious gust whipped by and sent the lid rolling down the sidewalk, drawing his attention. When Jeff looked back, two shadowy figures had materialized out of the alley's blackness. They jogged south, but a voice drifted back, "See you soon, pilgrim."

Jeff deserted the sidewalk and hurried from tree to bush to shrub. "You had to be stupid one more time. Those bastards are really going to appreciate your need for a walk while they're beating your brains out."

The night had taken its toll, and Jeff stopped to take a breather huddled in the shadow of a battered kiosk. Two streetlights were all that remained to give light, north or south. Two harsh pools of light that revealed nothing except black puddles of water and the never-ending rain.

"Okay smart boy," he muttered, "want to try the park? At least you'll have cover." Jeff stared at the black expanse of Volunteer Park across the street. Trash eddied around his feet while he weighed options and shivered.

A particularly cold blast of air made up his mind. Jeff darted across a Tenth Avenue devoid of life. Vaulting a low fence he dodged into the trees and halted while trying to recall the park's layout. It had once been well manicured. With time and reduced maintenance budgets it had degenerated into small areas of grass and broken tables surrounded by clumps of trash-clotted fir scrub.

Decided, Jeff pushed deeper into the park ghosting from tree to tree. Somewhere near a siren shrieked up the scale and began to warble. Jeff forced himself to remain still as a police car raced by, lights pulsing. As the siren dopplered downscale, Jeff felt like his last hope had disappeared north.

Taking a shaky breath he pushed branches out of the way and ran for the next tree. Jeff had taken only a few steps when he tripped and fell on top of something soft. Choking off a scream, he frantically rolled away to his knees.

There was a dark blur on the ground. It didn't move. Reaching out, he touched smooth skin that was cold as marble. Jeff tried to find a pulse in the carotid artery. Nothing.

He explored downward with a trembling hand: large breasts, wide hips, pants hanging onto an ankle. When he pulled his hand away, it was covered with something sticky and black.

"Shit! Oh shit!"

Wiping his hand on the grass, Jeff threw up with a convulsive heave. The moon found a rift in the overcast and a cool beam of light revealed the waxen face of a young woman. She had a terrified expression on her face, and sightless eyes stared into the night sky. Jeff crouched off at a run dragging the saber case.

He skirted a dilapidated tower and weed-choked pond near the park's southern border before pausing. Breathing heavily, he attempted to sling the case but the strap had broken.

Clutching the case under his arm, Jeff raised his head above marsh grass and sighted the fence. The strip of grass that bordered it was free of trees and the street beyond was empty.

Although the way was clear, abject fear kept him rooted in place. Spurred by thoughts of his apartment and safety, Jeff sprinted into the open, hurdled the fence, and darted into the protection of a building on Fifteenth Street.

Putting a hand against the building for support, he threw his head back and took in breath after shuddering breath.

"Thank God! I'm almost there!"

Taking a new grip on the case, he swung around the corner of the building. At that moment, an indistinct group of people materialized from the darkness of a nearby building.

He whirled around looking for an escape route. His heart started to thud when he saw more gang members close the circle.

"Oh, shit! They've got me!"

A dim figure stepped forward from the group in front of him, whispering mirth.

"Looks like you seen a ghost, puke. Somethin' around here we outta be afraid of?" Laughter and giggles circled Jeff. "Maybe you met our little sweetie off there in the park, eh? Ain't she somethin'? Ya try her out? Should'a. Best piece of ass they ever was. Now c'mon, tell ol' Teacher here what ya got in that case." The circle drew in tighter.

It took several moments for Jeff to realize the man thought his saber case was filled with drugs. He ran his tongue over dry lips and tried to speak. Nothing came out.

"Looks to me you just gotta be a runner for those dumb-bastard Leopards, don't ya think? How much stash you carrying in that case, man? I think we're gonna have to really screw your whole night." The circle closed with a rush.

As had happened in the duel with Hathwaite, time and motion slowed to a crawl. Jeff lunged for what appeared to be an opening. Someone jumped in his path and he swung the case at the man's head with all his strength. The impact of wood splintering against bone shuddered up his arm, accompanied by a wailing shriek.

For a moment he thought he had made it through the circle, only to have his legs kicked out from under him. Rolling to his feet still gripping the broken case, Jeff saw that the circle had closed around him. A dim form lay crumpled beyond the circle looking like someone had dumped dirty laundry on the sidewalk.

"That was dumb, asshole, real dumb. You hurt my man, and now you're gonna get cut real bad." The dim figure speaking gestured around. "No guns. I want this to go slow."

Teacher and another man shuffled forward in the knife-fighter's crouch. Breath coming in quick gasps, Jeff knew that his life was at an end.

"No, goddamit!"

He ripped remnants of the case away and drew the saber. The two gang members halted abruptly when they saw the saber's dull gleam, but too late. Jeff vaulted forward with a hoarse yell.

The saber flashed down in a cross-body cut that sent Teacher's right hand spinning to the sidewalk still clutching the knife. Continuing on, the blade sliced through clothing and flesh. Billows of intestines exploded from Teacher's abdomen as he tumbled to the ground with a wild scream. He thrashed around in circles, severed arteries in his wrist jetting pulses of blood in random arcs.

Face set in a snarl, Jeff pivoted to follow the course of his blade. Thrusting upwards with both hands, he drove the saber through the second man's sternum and lungs, two inches of blade springing out his back.

A shriek bubbled from his mouth and he fell to his knees. Jeff put a foot on his chest and wrenched the saber free. Gang members dashed around in confused patterns and alarmed curses bounced off walls. Something hit his back and Jeff lurched forward. The warble of police sirens suddenly crescendoed.

Squad cars came sliding to a halt and what seemed a flood of uniforms slammed open doors. Taking to their heels in a mad scramble, the gang evaporated into the night. Blinded by headlights, Jeff crouched against the wall for support.

"You! Drop your weapon!"

Jeff numbly wiped the saber on his jeans before laying it down.

More sirens. An aid car pulled up followed by two more, and spectators materialized out of nowhere. An officer bent to examine Teacher.

"Christ, will you look at this guy. Gutted like a pig." A startled grunt. "Jesus. His right hand is gone. Quick, get me a tourniquet!"

"Cuff that one by the wall, Pete. Make sure you collect that sword or whatever it is."

"Hey, Sarge," the patrolmen called out as he pulled Jeff's arms behind his back, "this one's got a big cut on his back. Might want a medic to take a look at it. Don't want him to bleed out on us."

The last thing Jeff heard was, "Shit! There he goes. Hey, give me a hand with this guy."

Two

Strange Dreams

Jeff regained consciousness face down on a towel. As his mind continued to come on line, he picked up on a subdued racket in the background: people talking, the squawk of police radios, and the jingle of equipment. Turning his head, Jeff saw what appeared to be a number of white uniforms and smelled disinfectant.

In a sudden rush, preceding events hit like a hammer blow. Jeff tried to push himself up only to discover that his arms wouldn't move. Quick panic caused him to struggle until he heard someone speak close to his ear.

"Settle down, buddy, there's nothing wrong with your arms. They're tied to the table. You're in the Harborview E.R. You'll be fine." Jeff relaxed and became aware of a tugging sensation on his back.

"Looks like this one is back among the living, Madge."

"Wish he would have stayed down," a tired feminine voice replied. "Nearly ripped the clips out when he jumped. Good thing he was tied off. I'll have this one zipped in a few minutes."

It was still black outside when Jeff awakened in response to someone calling his name. He was lying on a hospital bed. A police officer was leaning over the bed, which explained the insistent voice. Nearby, a gangly figure slouched in a chair, mouth open and snoring. An immense wave of relief swept over Jeff.

"Glory be. It's Carl!"

"What?"

"Sorry, officer. What would you like to know?"

A brief interrogation and the officer left. Awakened by the conversation, Carl scooted his chair over to the bed. Yawning hugely, he solemnly examined Jeff's face. An orderly came into the room with a bowl of soup for Jeff, took pity on Carl and found him a cup of coffee.

After a few sips Carl slammed his cup down on the arm of the chair. "Dammit, Jeff, this has to rank as the most stupid thing you've ever done! When are you going to start using your head?"

Jeff cringed with shame. "Maybe never."

Cursing under his breath, Carl tried to wipe coffee off his clothing. "It's a damn good thing I was cruising south. I'd been kicking myself for not talking you out of walking home, backtracked from the library and saw the collection of gumball machines."

The napkin he was using to sop up the coffee began to shred. Jeff handed him a clean one.

"I think I managed to convince the police that you are who your identification says you are, and a law-abiding citizen. Until they've had a while to chew on it, though, I understand you're on a police hold." Carl held his shirt out to look at it and shook his head mournfully. "My favorite one, too."

"I'm sorry, Carl. I'll buy you another shirt."

"Screw it, just tell me what-in-hell happened. When I arrived they were loading you into an ambulance."

There were large gaps in his memory, but Jeff related what he could. "...And that's all I remember. Think I must have passed out from blood loss."

Carl stared at Jeff in shocked disbelief. "Holy shit!" repeated at regular intervals was the extent of his speech for some time. "I expected something bad, but nothing like this. Be right back. I really need coffee."

When Carl returned with a large container of coffee and settled back into the chair, his expression was grim. "I think, my friend, that I had best get busy on some serious damage control with the police in the morning."

Still feeling acutely embarrassed, Jeff whispered, "Yes. Thank you."

Carl waved Jeff's thanks away. "Also, whether we like it or not the university has to be informed at once. You sure that woman in the park was dead?"

An image of her face flashed into Jeff's mind. Every detail was perfect. Not trusting himself to speak, Jeff nodded.

"Finding her like that must have been pure hell," Carl said sympathetically. "Problem is, publicity on this is going to be fierce and who knows which way those winds will blow? You stumbled on her after she was dead, but what will the media make of it?"

"Probably the worst. Get the most splash they can."

"That's a good possibility." After a pause, Carl asked, "What about the two gang members you wounded? Think they'll make it?"

"Things moved so fast...I didn't hold anything back, Carl. Into the chest of one and opened the other's belly. Maybe—if they got help in time."

Carl observed Jeff's expression closely and read a lot between the lines. Only a few hours ago he had seen what Jeff could do when he *was* holding back.

"We'll find out about them soon enough. That's history. Right now I'm concerned about the university. I don't think you want old Hildebrand to learn about this by seeing it on Death and Destruction News."

Charles Hildebrand was Jeff's boss in the Department of Anthropology. Jeff could well imagine what he was going to say.

"That would not be a good thing."

"Bet your ass it wouldn't be," Carl said, and reached for his coat. "I'd best haul my carcass home. I'll give Hildebrand a call first thing in the morning."

"I've done more stupid things in one night than I care to think about, Carl, and have abused our friendship. Thank you."

"I've got a feeling about you, boyo. I think the time will come when the shoe is on the other foot."

With a parting wave, Carl left the room. Jeff was weak from blood loss and fell asleep almost at once.

The graveyard shift made rounds, drifting up and down dimly lit hallways like ghosts. Satisfied that all was as it should be, they retreated to the nurses' station and pools of brighter light.

Shortly before dawn when heads were beginning to nod, the stairwell door eased open. A man slipped through and darted by the nurses' outpost.

Traffic noise was picking up when Jeff groaned in his sleep. His right arm suddenly lashed out as if holding a sword. Sweat stood out on his forehead, and his features were distorted with fear. A great sigh and Jeff relaxed. Darkness shifted in the chair next to his bed.

Headlights from a passing car briefly illuminated the face of a tall man sitting with chin in hand. When another car passed by a few minutes later, the chair was empty.

Carl stopped by early the next afternoon. "Talked with Hildebrand. Expected him to shout a bit, but he hardly raised his voice. Pretty impressive."

"I have never heard him raise his voice. He doesn't have to. That is one serious man. What did he say?"

"Primarily he was concerned for your health. I think he plans to talk with the chancellor's office and fill in the rest of the department staff. Wouldn't be surprised to see him stop by tomorrow."

Swiping part of a sandwich left on the bedside stand, Carl tried to eat and talk at the same time.

"Going to the police station to give a statement when I leave here. I'll check on your saber while I'm there and see if I can get some idea of what happens next." Carl washed the last piece of sandwich down with a big gulp of water and stood up. "Best run along and get things moving." He gave Jeff an appraising look. "How you doing?"

"Feel a lot stronger. Not so blown away emotionally." Jeff frowned and shook his head. "Really had a weird dream last night, though. Never experienced anything like it before."

The odd tone to Jeff's voice was so intriguing that Carl sat back down. "Like what?"

"Like, I don't know. You've seen some of those holographic travelogues, right?"

"Yeah, so?"

"So that's what the dream reminds me of. It was so real! It was as if I were floating several hundred feet up in the air."

"Are you going to tell me what you saw, or do I have to muss you up?"

Jeff grinned at Carl's impatience. "Sorry to be so vague, but. ..." His voice trailed off. "Holy simoleons," Jeff breathed, "now I remember. It had to be a summer evening. The smells. Lord, it was so beautiful!"

"Whoa. You were aware of smells? That's not only unusual, it's almost unheard of."

"Maybe so," Jeff replied with a stubborn set to his mouth, "but smells were definitely present. I think it must have been an island. Looked like pictures I've seen of England except there were mountains right up against the shore. Maybe more like Scotland. Carl, thinking about it now, it almost seems like I was being given a choice."

"Now, don't tell me this dream had a moderator!"

"No," Jeff said slowly, "It was like the land itself posed the choice: do you really want a new life?"

"Some dream, boyo. Maybe wish fulfillment?"

Spreading his hands in uncertainty, Jeff replied, "Could be, I guess. God knows I wouldn't mind finding a place like that to live. Dream, wish fulfillment or whatever, it was so beautiful and offered hope. Think I might try to get to sleep early tonight."

"Think I would, too. Well, got to run. See you tomorrow."

Although it was a good night for sleep, Jeff was disappointed he couldn't remember any dreams Sunday morning. He toyed with breakfast as long as possible before swinging the communication unit over the bed.

"Let's just get it out of the way. I've got to know." He punched a button. "Seattle Times, Sunday edition, 32325." The set beeped and gave the ready signal. "Initiate."

He rapidly scrolled through the first section. Front page, three columns, no picture. Thank God. Jeff scanned the article again.

"Jesus! You killed both of them!"

Jeff tried to punch in the code for a hard copy, but his hands were shaking so badly he kept hitting the wrong keys. Downing what remained of a cold cup of coffee, he whispered, "Hard copy. Alpha one, beta four." Too quiet, no response.

"God dammit! Hard copy! Alpha one, beta four!"

The console whirred quietly and dutifully spit out the requested parts of the paper. Jeff tried to read it through from start to finish, but his eyes wouldn't pass the paragraph that ghoulishly detailed the coroner's report.

Sometime later, it could have been minutes or hours, Jeff was startled from bitter self-recrimination by a hand on his shoulder. He looked up to find a woman standing by the bed. She was wearing a long lab coat and intently examining his face.

"Terrible way to meet, Mr. Friedrick. I'm Doctor Winston."

Jeff tried to figure out why she looked familiar. The doctor glanced down and saw the hard copy, which had fallen from Jeff's fingers onto the bed. She pushed the console out of the way and sat down.

"Want to talk about it? It doesn't take a shrink to see what this has cost you."

Recognition seeped in. It was the doctor from the emergency room.

"Don't know what to think right now."

"It'll take a while." She gestured at the hard copy. "We've seen those two in the E.R. on more than one occasion. What they would have done to you had you not defended yourself makes this article seem like nothing. Small consolation, but it's a fact."

She reviewed his chart on a hand-held computer then listened to heart and lungs. Removing a slender electronic jack from an inconspicuous module attached behind her ear, Dr. Winston slipped the auditory pickup into a pocket and covered her mouth to hide a big yawn.

"You lost at least two liters of blood, Mr. Friedrick—that's nothing to take lightly. You're going to feel weak for another day or two, but your hematocrit is coming up surprisingly fast and I'm comfortable with letting you go. We'll notify police of the planned discharge. As far as I know the hold has been removed."

At the door, she paused and smiled warmly. "Think about what I said. There's been a lot of talk about it in the E.R. No one including myself can see that you had any alternative except permitting them to kill you."

Shortly after she left, Jeff got out of bed and shuffled into the hallway. He was tired of being in bed and needed to break free from thinking about the men he had killed. Slipping his mind out of that gear, he engaged anthropologist mode. A few steps and he had mentally departed the hospital.

The haven of abstract thought proved such a relief that Jeff was able to objectively examine his close call, and to reflect on the explosive growth of gangs. He could not avoid concluding there was a direct relationship between the stunning advances in technology and rapid failure of social infrastructure.

With a sour grimace, he thought, What infrastructure? What did society have left in its system of reward and punishment except punishment?

One percent of the population controls ninety-eight percent of the wealth, the rest starve or are no better than indentured servants. Unless you start on the inside, know someone on the inside, or have an indispensable skill, forget it.

Jeff reviewed his own prospects at the university. The possibility of becoming tenured was fading rapidly. He had already seen a well-connected instructor junior to himself pass by over Dr. Hildebrand's objections.

I've just got to hang on and socialize more, he thought anxiously. Forcing his mind out of that familiar rut, Jeff examined broader implications.

How many years now since the computer revolution started? How many years since New Age Prosperity for all had been predicted? At least fifty, Jeff concluded, probably more. Fifty years of promises, and nothing to show for it but grinding poverty.

It's not that computers or technology as such are at fault, he mused. Jeff glumly reviewed a cycle that had been played out many times in human history.

Plate armor, gunpowder, the possession of iron versus bronze—all technological miracles that had resulted in the dominance of those who first possessed them. But only so long as they kept the advantage to themselves. And that had become much easier. Less than twenty percent of the population could keep up with modern technology.

"It's just like the Middle Ages," Jeff fumed out loud. "What's the practical difference between a financial kingdom and a geographic one? The end result is the same—serfdom."

He caught strange looks from passing individuals and retreated to inward musing. This can't go on much longer. God help us all when it comes apart. Is that what it's going to take to distribute wealth and access to hope? World War Three? An endless cycle of war until nothing is left except feudal states, disease and mass starvation?

An insistent beeping got Jeff's attention. He glanced at the hospital bracelet's digital readout.

"Well, shit," he muttered.

Somehow he had managed to wander not only off his ward, but off his floor as well. Returning to his room on rubbery legs, Jeff slumped down in a chair. America, he morosely thought, is fucked.

He had not moved when Carl entered accompanied by an austere, gray-haired man.

"My, don't we look cheerful."

Jeff scowled in Carl's direction while rising from the chair. "Professor Hildebrand, I'd like to apologize for this mess. I know it's put you in a difficult position."

Hildebrand looked him over carefully before replying. "That, young man, is something of an understatement."

Taking a seat, Dr. Hildebrand gazed at Jeff with unblinking concentration. As on past occasion, Jeff felt like his every thought was apparent to the man. It was unnerving.

"Well, well. Where were we, Mr. Jorgenson? Oh yes, the police."

At the word, police, Jeff tensed and his heart skipped a beat.

"You are a fortunate young man, Mr. Friedrick. University counsel tells me that no charges are to be brought. It seems the commotion at the scene prompted interest in a local apartment dweller given to late night reading." Professor Hildebrand paused to marvel at that fact, cherished it for a moment, and continued. "His statement convinced the police that you acted not only in self-defense, but to preserve your life." Frosty green eyes gazed steadily into Jeff's. "Let me tell you where I stand."

Jeff's heart stuttered again as he waited for his doom to be spoken. That was the sense he got when being addressed by this stately and occasionally severe man.

"Some members of the department have encouraged me to discharge you. The moral outrage they voiced, however, reflected their lack of professional competence and personal ambitions. Others, including myself, espoused a more balanced, thoughtful approach. In short, Mr. Friedrick, no disciplinary action is planned at the departmental level. You must understand, however, that this matter may yet be taken from my hands.

47

Until I hear from the chancellor's office, this matter will remain open. I expected better judgment from you, Mr. Friedrick. Your decision to walk home smacks of idiocy."

Unconsciously holding his breath, Jeff let it out in a quiet sigh. Professor Hildebrand rose from his chair, giving evidence that his visit was at an end. At the elevator, Professor Hildebrand turned to Jeff with a genuine smile and held out his hand.

"I like your work, Mr. Friedrick. Please be more careful in exposing yourself to criticism."

A brief handshake and he was gone.

"What a class act," Jeff observed in a respectful tone of voice. "That is one impressive man."

"That's not all of it, boyo. On the way up Hildebrand mentioned that as a student he fenced for his university. Then he actually smiled. Lord! It made me shiver to look at him!"

"Because he smiled? It's a strange occurrence, I'll grant you, but it seemed nice to me."

"You should have seen it," Carl replied with a vigorous shake of his head. "I felt like hanging cloves of garlic around my neck. Anyway, he smiled and said he had to, and I quote, 'admire the efficiency with which Mr. Friedrick dispatched his assailants.'"

"Well, I will be twice damned."

"I think he's pissed, though, so if I were you I would be just the teeniest bit careful. He also mentioned that the final word ought to come down in about a week."

Jeff started getting organized. He assumed he would be discharged as planned. It wasn't long before Dr. Winston confirmed that assumption.

THREE

Good-bye

It seemed to Jeff that life resumed as if his brush with death had never happened. Publicity was gone as quickly as it had come, replaced by juicier and more current gobbets of news.

For several days his students were determined to draw him out during classroom discussions, but Jeff refused to take the bait. While most students attended by way of the Classroom Holographic Network, those who were present in the flesh made things hot for a number of days. It was one of the reasons they attended.

However, it was an advanced class and finals were just around the corner. Personal concern for academic survival soon diverted questions toward picking his brain in search of test questions.

Gang violence had been increasing around town, some said because of milder weather. Those with a more sanguine view of society reserved their opinion and prepared for worse to come.

Unemployment rates nationwide averaged 30%, but the Dow Jones was expected to break twenty thousand any day. Food banks in major cities were empty and death by starvation, if not commonplace, accepted. In Washington, a coalition of congressmen on the radical right introduced a bill that would reinstitute indenture law.

Roaming a private beltway party they had crashed, reporters overheard a group of elderly senators far to the left discussing the need for insuring continuity in government by making some positions hereditary.

When asked to confirm their conversation, the senators expressed shock that anyone would suspect them of saying such a thing.

Although Jeff read the press releases, he felt detached from outside events. Since the gang attack his interests had withdrawn inward. While he couldn't put his finger on it, something had changed

Life on campus seemed hazy, and his sleep dominated by alien dreams that were crystal clear. The overall effect, Jeff thought more than once, was to make him feel more at home in his dreams than in reality. Two weeks after discharge, Jeff was called into Professor Hildebrand's office.

The door to Jeff's apartment was standing open. That was not only unusual and dangerous, but also frightening. Panic-stricken by what he might find, Carl hurried inside. Jeff was sitting on the edge of his bed staring at the floor. Dark spots stained the carpet at his feet. As Carl watched, a large tear gathered on Jeff's chin and dropped away to join those on the floor.

Feeling crushed with sympathy, Carl set about making a pot of coffee with more noise than was necessary. When he offered a hot cup to Jeff, it was ignored.

"Come on, buddy. Please. Professor Hildebrand called and told me what happened. He's devastated."

Jeff walked over to the window and stared out. "They didn't give him any choice. It's all over, Carl. I'm finished in anthropology."

"Because you showed poor judgment and decided to walk home?"

There was no expression on Jeff's face when he glanced at Carl. "That was just the excuse. One of the regents has a niece that needs a job. Turns out she's an anthropologist."

"Those bastards!"

"It doesn't matter. I think I've known all along that my days in the department were numbered. Who do I know? It was sheer luck that I got the job in the first place. Tell me, what do you think my chances are of being lucky again?" Jeff looked down at the floor. "Why is this happening to me, Carl? What have I done?"

With passing weeks Jeff began to accept what had happened. He had been fired. The days never seemed to end and his mood continued to spiral downward.

Before going crazy from worry, Jeff decided to get away from the city. He had not been able to find a job in anthropology, maybe never would, but he could hike into the mountains.

After talking it over with Carl, Jeff decided to go for it and unearthed his collection of topographical maps. Backpacking equipment was scattered around the apartment when Carl walked in carrying a duffel bag.

"Glad to see you decided to get off your butt, Jeff. About time." Setting the bag down, he leafed through a stack of maps.

"No shit. Have to do something. Can't even leave the apartment without feeling like a trespasser. About the only place I feel comfortable is down at the marina. Sure wish it wasn't too early for the racing season."

"From what you've said about it, sailing might be just the thing you need. Maybe you can get a berth for one of the long distance races when you get back from your hike, say from here to Hawaii. A total change of environment might do the trick. You've been crewing for what? Three or four years now?"

"About four years, and it's a good idea. What you said about needing a change of environment really rings a bell. A week or two in the mountains will be no more than a good start. There doesn't seem to be any point to life anymore except to survive from one day to the next. I don't think I've ever felt so lonely."

"They really hung you out to dry, buddy. Wish there was something I could do to help." Carl unfolded a map. "So, where do you think?"

"Ordinarily one mountain would be as good as another," Jeff replied, looking up from the small campstove he was inspecting, "but this early in the season I think I'll stay low in case a storm moves in. I'm going to head for Black Pine Lake and see if I can work my way over Sawtooth Ridge into the wilderness area."

Carl let out a surprised whistle. "That's low? Little ambitious, isn't it? The Sawtooth area is rugged, even in high summer. Shoot, it's a three-day hike from the lake just to get there. Something goes wrong and you're dog meat. How about something closer and lower down?"

Bent over the stove fiddling with the pressure pump, Jeff gave no evidence he had heard a word. Carl watched him for a period and was reminded of someone in a trance.

"Where you at, man? Space city, it seems to me. You going to be okay for this hike?"

"I'll be fine once I get into the woods." Jeff put the stove aside. "I checked with forest service HQ earlier today. They reported an unusually small snowpack." He kneeled by his sleeping bag and unrolled it. "Funny how the Sawtooths popped into my mind while I was looking at the maps. I really want to go there."

The tone of Jeff's voice and memories of their earlier conversation in the diner sent a prickling sensation along Carl's spine. This was not the Jeff he was familiar with.

"Where do you really want to go?"

Jeff looked up with a confused expression on his face. "To the Sawtooths. Why? What did I say?"

"It isn't what you said, it's how you said it. Jeff, I am truly worried about you wandering around in the woods."

"I'm not going to do anything stupid. The Sawtooths just feel right."

"Like walking home?"

It was a shrewd comment, and meant to be. Jeff winced and studied the deep concern on Carl's face.

"I won't take that kind of chance again. If it looks bad, I won't attempt the ridge." Jeff noted Carl was opening the duffel bag. "Goodies?"

"Sort of. I figured you would decide on some harebrained plan, so I brought a few things from my gear that might come in handy." While speaking, Carl laid pieces of equipment on the table.

"Whoa. Crampons and an ice ax. Snowshoes? I don't think things will get that tense!"

"I don't think so either, but this time of year, as you pointed out I might add, a few precautions are justified."

"You're right, and thanks."

Carl placed the items with other equipment Jeff was assembling. Sitting on top of the pile was a revolver and two boxes of ammunition. Carl picked the weapon up to examine it.

"I've seen that little .38 special you keep by your bed, but I've never been introduced to this baby. For as old as it seems to be, it's in great condition. .357 magnum?"

"Yeah. Colt Trooper. Bought it at a private estate sale I lucked into. The stainless steel tooling was so good I couldn't pass it up. I figure it dates from the late sixties or early seventies."

"Pretty heavy, isn't it?" Carl observed, hefting the pistol several times. "The .38 and a few extra rounds ought to do the job."

"It isn't the dirtbags I'm worried about. Bears are coming out of hibernation about now. Introducing grizzlies may have been a good idea, but they're taking the place over. If I have to tangle with one of those mothers, that .38 would be worthless."

"Okay, you need the Colt. Now answer me this: why two boxes of ammunition? Those babies weigh a ton. How many bears do you expect to meet?"

"What do you mean?"

Carl handed him the boxes.

"Where were they?"

"On top of the pile next to the Colt, Jeff."

"I have no idea how they got there. You're right—I don't need more than ten or twelve extra rounds."

Carl watched in silent amazement as Jeff walked over to the stack of camping gear and set both boxes down on top.

"Jeff, what are you..." Carl stopped and decided to let it go. The ammunition was not a critical issue.

Continuing to sort equipment as if nothing had happened, Jeff looked at Carl with a hopeful expression.

"Going to join me for a few days later on?"

"I'll try. Let's set a meeting time and place. How about west of Hoodo Pass four days before the end of your trip? If I don't show, you'll know I couldn't cut free of my project."

"Sounds good. I'll make a smoke above the treelike so you'll have a marker."

Carl left and Jeff spent the rest of the evening packing. Ready for bed, he happened to glance at the backpack. Perched on top was his saber. Muttering to himself, he padded over to the sword.

"I know I didn't put it there. If I didn't, then who did?" The sword's position clearly indicated careful placement. "Maybe Carl was fooling with it."

Jeff knew Carl had not touched the sword. He reached down to pick it up. The instant his hand brushed the scabbard, Jeff knew that if he did not take the sword it would mean his life.

It might have been ten or fifteen minutes. Jeff would never be sure how long he stood there. Every resource was focused on that decision, about that sword, concerning his life. He had never experienced any feeling that even came close to the awful sense of conviction that prevented him from touching the sword.

Slowly pulling his hand back, Jeff continued to stare at the saber which silently, patiently sat there. An instrument of death, it seemed at that moment to symbolize life itself. Jeff collected himself with a shudder and slipped under the covers.

"I will take that sword and the weight be damned, even if I have to leave something else behind."

Sunshine flooded the apartment when he awoke. Sitting up with a start, Jeff looked at the bedside alarm clock and saw it was already ten o'clock. He looked over at the camping gear.

Perched on top of the pile, the sword was illuminated by a shaft of sunlight. Morning traffic outside posed a sharp contrast to a quiet watchfulness that permeated the apartment.

"Okay, okay, I said I'm taking you!"

Throwing on clothes, he hurried out to the ancient Dodge pickup that served as transportation and coaxed it to life. He didn't want to take time to eat, so Jeff grabbed some cheese and apples on his way out the door with the backpack. The Dodge promptly died when he let out the clutch.

"Oh no you don't, you old bastard," Jeff chortled. He had learned its every dirty trick years ago and teased it back to life. "And away we go!"

They were well north on I-5 and settled in for the haul before the Dodge was convinced that everything was going to be all right. Lulled by the sonorous thunder of the truck's exhaust system, Jeff slipped on sunglasses and bit into an apple.

Near the city of Everett he turned east on US 2 and into the Cascade foothills. At the summit of Stevens Pass he backed off the gas to give the truck a breather on the down slope. With each mile that passed, Jeff felt tension and resentment fade.

"Damn, it's good to be out of Seattle. What a relief!"

They rolled through the Methow Valley over packed snow with the transmission in four-high. The roads were nearly empty, the sun was bright—it was a perfect day to drive on and on.

Still, it was late in the afternoon and there was a special restaurant in Chehalis that called for a pit stop. Later, they were well up Gold Creek on a gravel road when Jeff snapped on the headlights.

"Must be two feet of snow," he worried out loud. "C'mon, baby, get me there one more time."

The headlights picked out the campground entrance near the tail end of dusk.

"Thank God!" Jeff broke into a grin.

Slapping the gearshift lever into second, he locked up the drive train and tramped down on the accelerator. Engine screaming its thrilling song, exhaust pipes bellowing, the Dodge bucked around the off-season barrier, four wheels spraying rooster tails of snow and dirt.

"Yee-ha! Sock it to 'em, you old bastard!"

The truck had a fight on its hands, but the engine held on to the fat part of the power curve. When the Dodge made it back onto the road in a flying leap, Jeff was laughing so hard he had to ease his foot onto the brake and stop.

"Son of a bitch! This is the way to live!" He patted the dashboard in appreciation, and intoned, "Long may your rusty fenders wave, old truck."

Letting the clutch out, Jeff idled the Dodge to an inconspicuous nook he was fond of. Belly still full from the late lunch, he made himself comfortable in the cab. Up with the sun, he scrambled a few eggs for breakfast, made a final check of his gear then looked balefully at the sword.

"Well, you wanted to come along so damn bad, how in hell do I carry you?"

As expected, he received no answer. After trying several arrangements he tied it to the back of the pack frame. Heaving the pack on top of a handy boulder, Jeff slipped into the harness. When he stood up and felt the weight, he groaned.

"I am going to die before this day is out. That pack must weigh eighty pounds." He staggered into motion. "To hell with it. Either it'll kill or cure me."

Several days later, about the time Jeff thought he might not die after all, the trail he had been following began to wind a tortuous way up the eastern flank of Sawtooth Ridge. The incline rapidly increased, and he was forced to use Carl's ice ax to pull himself up the steeper parts. Shortly, it started to snow. That was a worrisome development.

Jeff sat down on a handy stump to take stock. Slipping out of the backpack, he unfolded a topographical map that included Hoodo Pass. Wind gusts kept flipping it around, shaking off the snow.

"Decision time, boyo," he mumbled while measuring distance and elevation. "Ouch, that's higher than I thought. Looks like something over 5,000 feet. Pass ought to be lower, though, and I'm already pretty high. Maybe I can ease over that sucker tomorrow." A vision of Carl's concerned face briefly flickered, and was gone.

Late the next day he was nearly at the end of his strength with several hundred yards to go before he made the pass. The wind was full in his face and blowing hard. Leaning forward, he staggered through the pass in snow up to his calves.

Badly in need of a breather, he sought refuge behind a ledge that gave some protection from the wind. Leaning back against the ledge, Jeff looked out across the Sawtooth Wilderness and, some miles farther to the west, the Cascade Mountains.

The overcast had solidified into a slate-gray shroud that skimmed higher peaks. Visible as a white veil, a snow flurry was coming his way. Stretching north and south as far as he could see, rugged mountains dominated the western sky and emanated a sullen power.

Gray, black and white, alive and immortal, jagged peaks brooded coldly in their early spring sleep but missed nothing. Daylight was fading fast, lending such a sinister appearance to one blown-out caldera that Jeff drew back.

"Holy shit! What have I done to you?"

As if in reply, the wind moaned a funereal dirge around the ledge. The effect was so strong that Jeff considered canceling the hike. A sudden clatter made him start.

Released by spring thaw, a large rock bounded by only feet away. Shivering from the sense of threat, Jeff could not help feeling intimidated.

"They know I'm here! I've never felt anything like this before. Why are they angry at me?"

He had never felt so insignificant, and every attempt to reason with himself only made things worse. With more than a little bravado, he muttered, "Screw you, I'm not turning back now whether you like it or not." Jeff settled the pack and set off down the trail toward the comfort of trees and earth.

He was about to enter the forest when a deep rumbling boomed up through his legs. The ground jerked sidewise and Jeff stumbled to one knee, showers of stones rattling off his backpack. Quiet. The world seemed to be holding its breath. Getting to his feet, heart beating wildly, Jeff stood crouched.

The earth was still.

That's it, he thought several minutes later, only a little tremor. Birds tentatively began their evensong, and a single ray of sunshine escaped the overcast. Flipping off the mountains, Jeff hiked into the trees.

Building a fire larger than was necessary, he ate quickly and pulled out his longtime companion, a battered recorder. Jeff stared into the fire and lifted it to his lips. When he returned to the mutual reality of earth and forest, the fire had burned down to a few glowing embers.

Sunshine filtering through evergreens prodded Jeff out of the sleeping bag. He broke camp and moseyed downslope with a jaunty step, whistling off-key. Hiking where the moment's whim took him, days and nights merged into a seamless whole.

One of those sun-dappled days, Jeff stopped early near a rushing creek. While foraging for firewood he ran across a row of fool hens sitting on a low branch. They were large plump birds, and he was unable to resist temptation. Jeff knocked one of them off its perch with a stick and hurried back to camp.

Once cleaned and spitted on a green stick rotisserie, the monotonous duty of turning the bird freed Jeff's thoughts. Carl's questions about his saber came to mind at once.

"I must have been thirteen or so when Grandad gave it to me."

Jeff couldn't remember how he had escaped the grind of planting, but seemed to recall it had been a wet spring and it was impossible to get into the fields. With his father's blessing and a lunch from his mother, he had headed out from their farm near the Missouri border in southeast Iowa for a day's ramble in a nearby forest.

* * * * * * * * * * *

Deep in a thicket of oak and maple, a gangly youngster no longer quite a boy looked around with an irritated expression. He brushed locks of reddish-chestnut hair out of his eyes and listened intently. All was silent.

"Stupid! C'mon, boy!"

Nothing moved, and he could hear none of the usual crashing sounds. "Dumb dog," he muttered.

A wide grin replaced the frown. Whistling under his breath, hands jammed deep into ragged jeans, he continued on his way. Someone familiar with Jeff Friedrick from school would have been surprised at how unreserved he seemed. Although he was well liked by teachers and a good student, there was something about Jeff that puzzled several staff members.

He was there in the classroom, yet he wasn't. He excelled in sports and because of that moved freely among various cliques while devoting his attention to none of them. Jeff was, the teachers decided, an intriguing young man.

Yet he didn't make trouble or demand attention. They were content to leave it at that and did not attempt to draw him out. That he was alone would have surprised no one.

Jeff had penetrated deep into the forest when excited baying broke out some ways off. He paused to listen. The baying slowly faded then abruptly stopped.

"Now, what's gotten into him? Stupid dog probably ran a rabbit into its burrow and is trying to dig it out." He moved out again. Something about the dog's baying bothered him. "That did not sound like he was chasing a rabbit."

Concerns about Stupid disappeared when he ran across a huge oak that had fallen during the winter. Jeff peered under the trunk near the root bole.

While quite realistic for thirteen, he had just finished reading the Hobbit and visions of elvish hideaways flashed through his mind. However, he tramped the woods at every opportunity and understood that mundane creatures with sharp teeth were a more likely bet.

Finding a long stick, Jeff poked around beneath the tree trunk until he was satisfied that no one was home. It was a tight fit, but he squirmed under the trunk and into a roomy enclosure formed by the root bole.

Shrugging off his daypack, Jeff pulled out a sandwich. He had his mouth open for the first bite when he heard something shuffling around outside.

Although he had never encountered one, bears had been sighted in the forest. That didn't make sense, he decided. The sounds were too furtive and deliberate. Jeff quietly moved to the back of the enclosure. The sounds faded to nothing and he completed the bite.

I'm going to have to be real quiet going home, he thought. Wonder what that was? I've never met anyone here before.

A four-legged missile landed square on his chest.

"Yii! Damn you, Stupid!"

Heart pounding, Jeff tried to defend what was left of the sandwich from Stupid's jaws. He was angry at the dog but so happy to have company that he shared the rest of his lunch. When the last morsel was consumed, Jeff stuck his head out of the burrow. The way was clear and he eased out into the open.

Jeff worked his way back north watching every step. He stopped frequently to listen, but the forest was silent. It was too quiet.

"Where are the squirrels?" he wondered out loud. "They never shut up."

A short distance from the edge of the forest, Jeff crept quietly into his favorite glade. When younger he had decided it was enchanted, now he simply felt at home. It was a special place.

Humming under his breath, he threw pebbles at minnows in a small creek running full with spring rain. He had taken the first step to search for rocks to build a dam with when his brain caught up with his eyes. Leaning against a gnarled oak with folded arms was a total stranger.

Jeff was old enough to understand that not all men had friendly intentions toward boys, and felt real fear for the first time in his life. Never taking his eyes off the stranger, he reached down to catch up the daypack.

Thinking, Where is that stupid dog when I want him, he prepared to bolt.

"Hold on, young Jeff, I mean you no harm." The man's voice was so musical and free of threat that Jeff didn't move. "I only want to talk with you for a few minutes. Don't worry about Stupid. He's off chasing a rabbit and will be back shortly."

The man was at least six and a half feet tall, slender, and dressed in muted brown clothes that looked to be made from doeskin. Calf-high moccasins and a sheath knife belted at the waist added to the effect.

What really caught Jeff's eye was the stranger's mop of chestnut hair with red highlights. The coloring was identical to his own hair.

"You're a hard man to track down, Jeff, let me tell you. I've spent the greater part of the day on your trail. May we talk for a few minutes?"

"Who are you?" Jeff was willing to listen, but also prepared to run for it. "How do you know my name?"

"Please call me Gaereth. I know a great deal about you." The man began to speak in a softly modulated, compelling voice.

Jeff awoke on a bed of dry leaves at the edge of the glen. Sitting up, he looked around wildly trying to orient himself. Stupid lay nearby gazing at him expectantly with head between paws. Rubbing his eyes, Jeff tried to remember what had happened.

With a rush, it all came back up to the point where Gaereth had started talking to him. He remembered little of what had been said except Gaereth's fond farewell and a sense that they would meet again. Jeff suddenly noticed that it was nearly dark. He jumped to his feet with a cry of alarm.

"Mom will really be upset if I'm late! Dad will skin me!"

Grabbing his pack, Jeff was gone from the meadow like a shot. Leaves whirled as he faded like windblown smoke through the forest, Stupid loping at his side. Chasing rabbits was fun, now it was time for serious running.

It was something over three miles to the farmhouse. Brighter stars were visible by the time Jeff sprinted into the farmyard gasping for breath. Taking the back steps two at a time he slammed through the screen door, into the pantry, and nearly collided with his younger brother, Stephan.

"Boy, are you in for it! Mom's on the phone and Dad is getting ready to go looking for you." Stephan's eyes grew round. "Supper is ruined, too!"

Gretchen Friedrick rushed into the pantry and hugged Jeff fiercely. Large tears glistened in her eyes.

"Where have you been? We were so worried."

Feeling his mother's pain acutely, as he always did, Jeff was near tears himself when his father arrived on the scene. A tall man given to long silences and short speech, they had nevertheless become close as Jeff became old enough to work in the fields.

He looked at Jeff intently, the concern in his expression slowly giving way to a neutral expression that Jeff had never been able to decipher. Thinking back, however, he did remember times when it had been followed by serious trouble.

"I think we would all be better off if we talked about this after supper."

Other than the clinking of dinnerware and a few comments about the wet spring, the meal was taken in silence. While Stephan was also quiet, he kept glancing back and forth between Jeff and their father with an expectant look on his face. Jeff was really worried about what he was going to say to his parents, but not so worried that he failed to make a mental note to thump Stephan later.

When the moment of truth appeared to be looming over him, Jeff's grandmother and grandfather stopped by and were served coffee and apple pie.

Jeff felt like a condemned man granted a last-minute stay of execution. Although he racked his brain for a sensible explanation, he still didn't know what to say when plates were once again empty. What could he say? That he met a stranger in the woods who hypnotized him? Not likely!

Conversation trailed off to nothing. The old clock ticking away on the mantle sounded like the march of doom as Jeff searched for a way out of his dilemma. When his father took down a battered pipe and began to fill it, Jeff knew his string had run out. Over the years, he had grown to hate that pipe.

"All right, Son. Tell us what happened today."

Jeff glanced at his mother, then, seated next to her, his grandmother. While her expectation that he act responsibly in all matters was immutable, she had also never failed him in a pinch. She nodded slightly at Jeff, and he knew at once that nothing but the truth would do.

"I met a man called Gaereth in the forest, and he talked to me. He told me things that I can't remember but that I will some day, and then I guess I went to sleep."

Hardly able to sit still, Jeff began waving his arms around. "I've never seen a man like him before, Mother. His hair was just like mine, and he knew my name—he even knew Stupid's name. And his clothes were green and brown like Robin Hood!"

In a rush of words, it all tumbled out. While Jeff rattled on, his mother's attentive frown rapidly faded. She looked anxiously at her mother, Regina Gruenwald, for support but was not reassured by her stern expression.

Although close, their personalities were so different that Gretchen had never been able to fathom such rock-hard determination that surrender to any circumstance could not be imagined.

When Jeff wound down his father also turned to Regina. "Well, Mother, I don't like to say it, but I think this one might be down your alley."

"Perhaps. Jeffrey, try and remember how he talked. Tell me again what he looked like."

"Yes, Mam."

Sifting his memory with a fine screen in an attempt to add more bits and pieces, Jeff related his meeting again. When he had finished, his grandmother didn't respond at once.

Sipping on her coffee, she gazed down at the tablecloth and seemed unaware of those in the room. When she did speak, it was in a whisper that Jeff could barely hear.

"Always it has been the same."

She abruptly looked up. "I think it likely that Jeffrey met one of the Old Ones."

Mrs. Friedrick started in her chair. "No! They can't have him!"

Jeff's father took her hand. "Not this time, Gretchen." He said in a grim tone of voice. "I won't let it happen."

Regina nodded to herself in satisfaction at his response. "Whether we wish to believe it or not, Henry, I believe he has been touched. We have discussed the tales; Rudy and I have documented them for seven generations. They are true." Regina forced a smile. "Enough of this. The man was probably no more than a farmer from south of the woods, out for a walk."

"Would someone please tell me what's going on?"

Jeff's grandfather, Rudy, shook his head. "Not tonight, I think. Perhaps one of these days soon."

The rain relented and spring planting got under way with a frenzied rush, submerging other concerns. Between school and long hours in the fields, what had happened in the forest faded into the background. Then one long summer's evening near the solstice Rudy joined Jeff on the front porch swing.

They shared the magenta sunset, cicada melody and twinkling fireflies in companionable silence. Creaking back and forth on the swing, the day's humid warmth slowly relenting, Rudy placed a hand on Jeff's shoulder.

"I brought something I think it's time you had." Rudy held up what appeared to be a sword and handed it to Jeff. "I've kept this for at least forty years, never knowing why. Regina thinks it's time you had it, and I agree."

Pulling the sword from a leather sheath, Jeff caught his breath as light from the parlor window glittered along the blade's smooth curve. Mind dancing with excitement, Jeff thought, Could it be an elvish sword like Glamdring? It has to be! Where did Grandpa get it?

"You be careful now. It's sharp as a razor. That sword was given to me by your grandmother's father, and to him by his father before. That's a saber, boy, one that goes back at least two hundred years. I have to tell you I don't know much about it other than it's been a part of your grandmother's family for a good reason." Rudy chuckled. "Trouble is, Ulrich didn't know why we were supposed to keep it, either. Your grandmother and I think it's possible that some day you will."

Jeff's experience in the forest came back with a rush. "Can't you tell me anything about that man, Gaereth?"

They continued to creak back and forth in the swing as Rudy thought about the question.

"About 1805, things were really bad in Germany what with the wars of Napoleon making a mulch pile out of the whole country. Down south where we come from, a place called Swabia, there wasn't much left at all. Crops all burned, animals drove off to feed the soldiers, young men forced to sign up with this army or that—lot of folks decided to leave.

"Now it seems that some years before, Catherine of Russia had invited farmers to come to a place out east of Germany called the Ukraine. She'd promised good farmland for the taking, so our relatives packed up what was left and started out. Son, that was one tough trip if you can believe the stories, and I do.

"They got caught somewhere in Hungary by winter coming on. One of Regina's ancestors nearly died from the cold, was saved by a nobleman's son whom, they say, she eventually married. That hair of yours? That color's shown up from time to time on the female side of this family for quite a ways back. But here's the thing—there never was any such hair before that trip if you can believe what the women folk say, and I truly do."

"But I'm not a girl!"

"Yep, you got it straight." A chuckle rumbled from Rudy's belly at the look of indignation on Jeff's face. "You're the first male anyone can think of that's had that color hair. Now you can make whatever you want out of all that. What it means to me, is that your dad's family must have picked up some of the same blood. Seems you got it from both sides and Stephan didn't."

"But what about that man I met, Grandpa?"

Rudy smelled hot cherry pie and heaved himself out of the swing. "Your grandmother has kept track of our family all her life and traced folks way back to the Old Country." Rudy hesitated, then shrugged. "It seems some of our relatives live a very long time, Jeffrey."

Rudy hustled inside, leaving Jeff stroking the saber and thinking about elves.

* * * * * * * * * * * *

The smell of roasting grouse brought Jeff back from his reverie. Pulling on a wing, he decided it was done and sliced off a wedge of meat. At the first bite, Jeff thought he had died and gone to heaven. He ate slowly to prolong the moment and wished he had knocked over two fool hens.

While cleaning up he wondered in passing, Why were Mom and Dad so upset? Were they afraid that Gaereth might kidnap me?

A sheet of cirrus clouds moved in from the west creating a beautiful sunset over the mountains. Jeff admired the view and did a mental inventory of warm clothing. He suspected that the unusually long period of good weather was at an end.

Snug in his sleeping bag, Jeff reviewed what a wonderful trip it had been. Let it come, he thought placidly. It's going to take a lot of bad weather to wreck this hike. And Carl will probably show up tomorrow. It's going to be great.

Cirrus clouds were long gone when he arose. The sky reminded Jeff of aged pewter and the temperature seemed to have dropped twenty degrees.

He stared apprehensively at the sullen overcast and decided to fuel up with a big breakfast. Before leaving camp he pulled on a warm sweater. Securing equipment to the backpack with a second set of straps, he stopped to listen.

"Where are all the birds?" he muttered uneasily. "I don't think I've ever heard it this quiet. Must be one hell of a storm coming."

Resigned to the long climb ahead, Jeff set out toward his meeting with Carl near the pass. He wasn't long on the trail when rain mixed with sleet began to fall.

Having grumbled to himself about the nuisance of carrying crampons and snowshoes, it now felt good knowing they were tied to the backpack. As the elevation increased, rattling bursts of pure sleet lashed him.

"This really sucks!"

Jeff arrived at the tree line with light almost gone and in the middle of a snowstorm. Unexpectedly, the wind had dropped to nothing. He felt his way through the heavy snowfall looking for a campsite. Every so often he stopped to listen, something he had done on numerous occasions since leaving camp that morning.

"What is it that's making me so uptight? No doubt it's too damn quiet, but there's more to it than that. It feels like something terrible is going to happen."

Unable to come up with anything other than the snow and unnatural silence, Jeff continued searching for a tree to camp under.

He stumbled across a big fir that was perfect and was about to drop the pack when he paused to listen again. The sense of unease had grown so strong he wanted to shout from the tension.

"What are those goddamed mountains up to? This is crazy!"

It was deathly quiet. No sound at all, not even a whisper of breeze. Just the thick veil of gray-white sifting down around him and a gut-wrenching premonition that the world was going to end any second. Another minute and he was frantic.

"Oh, God! It's coming! I'm getting out of here!"

Before he could move, the ground gave a sharp lurch and began shifting under his feet. Within seconds, the sound had increased to a bass roar that was mind numbing. The motion took on a circular pattern and Jeff was thrown from his feet, his ears buffeted by the crashing roar of trees falling like dominoes.

Earthquake! Jeff's mind screamed.

Sprawled on his stomach, he tried to hang on to a ground that thrashed under him like a beast in its death struggle. Tree limbs, brush, rocks; all were hurtling through the air, some striking him where he lay.

Terrified at the thought of being buried in an avalanche, Jeff clawed downslope on all fours. A wall of something roared by to the side, inspiring a cry of raw fear. The earth lunged and he was rolled downhill, debris pounding his body.

Another wall engulfed him and he lost all sense of direction as he ripped down the mountain head over heels, now buried in snow, now riding the crest like a body surfer.

Tucking into a ball with arms covering his head, Jeff desperately prayed that the quake would end. It did not.

The Pacific Northwest was finally experiencing the big quake that had been predicted for years. The Cascade Mountains rolled and pitched like a sea tormented by hurricane winds with Jeff the merest bit of flotsam on its surface.

Mountains that would stand forever fell like mounds of gravel only to be pitched back into the sky rumbling and roaring protest. Farther north, one slowly collapsed into the reservoir behind Ross Dam.

A tidal wave raced down the reservoir and thundered into the dam, thousands of tons of water spewing over the top. The dam had a large safety factor built into it and held, but was twisted and heaved by the earthquake like it was made of soft plastic instead of concrete and steel.

Sirens screamed their warning and engineers raced to open spillways. They never made it.

With a grinding rumble, the central section split open. In what seemed slow motion, huge concrete slabs broke free to tumble into the river below. A wall of deep green burst through the damn and arced far out over the river before crashing down.

Millions of cubic feet of water surged toward the break as another tidal wave headed west toward drowsing farmland and cities, filling the Skagit and Sauk Rivers with a force that nothing known to man could resist.

And Mount Rainier shuddered.

Over fourteen thousand feet tall and it shuddered like a leaf, opening wide clefts that delved deep. Subterranean fires under high pressure gained nearly instantaneous release. With a gigantic explosion heard as far away as Missoula, the top of the mountain blew off.

Uncountable metric tons of snow melted in an instant under the lash of the pyroclastic flow that bellowed down the west flank of the mountain at speeds approaching two hundred miles an hour.

The superheated blast of gas, plasma and ash began to dissipate after thirty miles, but the damage was done. A boiling cauldron of mud twenty miles wide raced for Tacoma, filling and scouring every ravine. Then, in a chain reaction, Mt. Baker, St. Helens and Adams spewed fiery death into the sky.

Far up in the mountains, Jeff was aware only that he was going to die. Barely conscious, he was spit out by the avalanche and slammed into a tree. A tremendous blow hammered his mind and he felt himself dissolve into nothing.

Four

Belief Dies Hard

A mound of snow shifted, changing into the shape of a man. Struggling to a sitting position, Jeff grabbed his head. The pain was so bad he thought his head would split wide open. Heavy snowfall blasted by in horizontal sheets turning his world into a white cocoon.

Feeling disoriented and shivering uncontrollably, he crawled to the rim of the shallow depression he was lying in. Bracing himself against the wind, Jeff caught brief glimpses of barren snow and rock.

"What happened?" Jeff gazed around in complete bewilderment. "Where did all the snow come from? There wasn't nearly this much on the ground. Where's the forest?"

Memories of a head-over-heels tumble and roaring earth came to mind in a terrifying burst.

"Holy shit. The earthquake. I'm alive!" His teeth were chattering and he unfastened the backpack harness. "Surviving the earthquake doesn't matter a damn if I freeze to death."

Untying one of the snowshoes, he assembled it with shaking hands. Using it as a shovel, he hollowed out a snow cave. Crawling inside, Jeff dragged the pack after him and located the ground cloth. He rolled the sleeping bag out on top and climbed in, clothes and all. Jeff vaguely wondered if he would survive the storm. Screw it, he thought, at least I'm warm.

He awakened in darkness trying to get his breath. Groping about, Jeff discovered that the mouth of the scooped-out cave had drifted over. Punching an opening, he maneuvered the pack so he could see what was left on the outside.

"Where's my sword? Oh, please, not that!"

Jeff tried to drag the pack outside for a better look but it was anchored in place. About to force it, a shred of restraint led him to explore the cause. He traced a strap and his hand fell on the saber. It was trapped under a knee and buried in snow. When he picked the saber up, a lone strap slipped through the buckle without resistance.

"One strap, and that one loose. No way should that saber have stayed with the pack. What a break! I wonder what else is left?"

The crampons and second snowshoe were still tied in place, but the ice ax, two water bottles and his water filter were gone. Protected by his coat, the pistol and survival knife were present and nearly dry.

"I can't believe it. I am really in luck. That roll down the mountain should have stripped everything off. And I've got the crampons and snowshoes. Shit. With all this snow, Carl's really going to need them if he was camped on the other side of the pass."

The possibility that Carl had not survived the earthquake was too painful to contemplate for more than a moment.

Driven by intense hunger, Jeff set up the camp stove in the mouth of his burrow. Scooping snow into a pot, he tried to figure out where it had all come from. It wasn't long before he was shaking his head with frustration.

"This doesn't make any sense! What does an earthquake have to do with snow? I don't see the connection. Even if I was unconscious for an entire day, there's still no way this much snow could have fallen!"

He munched on an energy bar until the water came to a boil, then dumped in a pack of freeze-dried cereal. At that moment, the cinnamon oatmeal tasted as good as partridge. With food in his stomach, Jeff's spirits climbed up from the soles of his feet.

"Doesn't matter where the snow came from, it's here. Just saving my ass is going to have to take top priority." He stuck his head out to check on the weather. The wind was down to a light breeze, and the snow had stopped. "May as well see how much things were torn up," he muttered. "The forest must have really taken a beating."

At the rim of the depression, one glance told Jeff that the overcast was nearly gone. He looked north, stumbled back a step and drew in a strangled breath.

An enormous mountain range dominated the skyline from east to west. Serrated peaks thrust so far into the sky that it seemed they must fall of their own weight and crush him like a fly.

The effect was so overpowering and unexpected that he cried out. The mountains were so high that he had to tilt his head far back to see their cloud-capped peaks. Mountains he had never seen before.

"I don't believe this. It can't be real." Jeff followed the range to the east. He abruptly dropped to his knees in shock and whispered, "God save me."

The mountain filled, blotted out, the southeastern sky and fully half of the horizon. Tier upon tier, it marched into the sky as if there was no ending. Struggling for a comparison Jeff dredged up memories of Mount Rainier south of Seattle, which overpowered everything around it.

"No, not even close. Maybe Everest."

Struggling to come to terms with the mountain's dimensions, he estimated its elevation had to be well over thirty thousand feet and its base a hundred miles wide.

Hell, he thought, that elevation would put its peak in a vacuum!

Completely dazed, he tore his eyes away from the mountain. Jeff exhaled in relief when he viewed mountainous country to the southwest that was not so daunting. Standing up, he searched the terrain in a slow sweep but recognized nothing.

The sun broke free of a cloud lighting peaks to sparkling brilliance, and still he searched. Jeff came to himself feeling terribly lost and sat down in the snow. Try as he might, there was no way he could squeeze these mountains out of the Cascades. They were not only much bigger but ran east and west.

"Maybe the earthquake threw them up?" That made as much sense as anything he had thought of.

Jeff pulled the pack out of the burrow to inventory what food remained. The small pile that resulted frightened him. He was going to need five thousand calories a day just to stay on his feet, and the food left was worth no more than four or five hikes.

"Shit! The Dodge is within reach, but I don't have a prayer of getting to it through those mountains. Probably nothing left of it, anyway." He glanced to the southwest. That was his only hope.

Packing up as quickly as prudence allowed, Jeff fitted the crampons to his boots, strapped on the pack and hiked southwest into a westering sun.

An hour later his eyes hurt so badly from snow glare he could only squint. Cursing his stupidity, Jeff fished out sunglasses. When he couldn't force himself to take another step and made camp, the tip of one ear was numb and his face painfully sunburned.

Setting out next morning he sank to his knees in soft snow. He strapped on the snowshoes and trudged off. Wherever he looked there was no sign of life or green, only the blinding expanse of endless snowfields and intimidating mountains. He closed his mind to that fact and concentrated on not falling.

No more than a dot lost in a wasteland of snow, Jeff snaked down an ice-caked moraine. He picked his way around boulders with head down, resolved only to find enough strength to take a step and yet another.

Seared by sun and frostbite, the skin on his cheeks had blistered, cracked open and was crusted with ooze. Picking at bits of food frozen in a stubble beard, Jeff tried to remember how many days he had been walking. He thought he had pitched the tent six times.

Something wasn't right. He stared at his legs and wondered why they wouldn't move. He eventually concluded he had entered a snowfield and they were buried to the knees. Perched on a boulder, he made the switch from crampons to snowshoes then thought he might rest for a while longer. It felt so very good just to sit. When he decided to take a longer break, Jeff was surprised to find that he was on his feet and walking.

Unable to fathom how that had happened, he concentrated on taking the next step in a world that had constricted to the patch of snow in front of him.

Dusk was at hand when a snowshoe caught on an obstruction and he fell forward onto his face. Breathing heavily, Jeff lay there and debated whether he had tried hard enough now so that he could rest.

On the verge of losing the debate for the first and final time, Jeff heard a voice in his mind that was both real and compelling.

"*Lift your head and live. It is not your time to surrender.*"

He gazed around stupidly for a few moments before becoming aware that he lay sprawled in a copse of trees. Somehow he had inserted himself well into a scrub forest before a snowshoe snagged a fallen limb. Hope discovered a foundation and sprang to life. The thought of a fire spurred him to tear at the snowshoe bindings in his haste to find tinder.

By nightfall the tent was assembled. He heaped wood onto the fire until it was roaring, yet it never seemed hot enough. When he could function again, Jeff set a pot in the coals to heat water. He found one packet of food at the bottom of the backpack.

Fool hens have to be around somewhere, he thought. The memory of his feast in what seemed like another life set his mouth to watering.

The water came to a boil and he stirred in the packet of food. When he had scraped the pot shiny-clean, he sank down on a log near the fire and stared into the flames. Sometime later Jeff awoke lying on his side.

A degree of vitality had returned by morning. Holding his hands over new flames, Jeff attempted to piece together the last six or seven days. He was about to mark it off as a lost cause when a shot of anxiety hit him. He still had not seen one feature of the land that was familiar. Jeff felt like yelling with frustration but was too tired.

"I don't care how big an earthquake there was," he savagely said, "it couldn't be big enough to create that mountain chain in one throw. And what about that big bastard?"

Tired or not, he couldn't hold it in. "Screw this place! Screw the goddamed mountains!" He felt better after that. "What I have to do is keep heading southwest. There has to be a highway somewhere nearby. Someone must be moving around by now."

The thought of seeing another human set him in motion. Although he felt stronger, Jeff moved cautiously. He had encountered numerous grouse earlier in his hike, and there was also the chance he would run across a porcupine. With grouse in mind, Jeff picked up a stout limb.

As the day passed he saw no evidence of grouse, porcupine or any other game. As fatigue and hunger mounted, so did his worry concerning food.

Jeff had been following a ravine for some time. While nothing more than a shallow gully that morning, it had spread out and become deeper during the day.

Snow levels gradually decreased until there was more bare ground than snow, and he gratefully removed the snowshoes. Trees that had been sparse and short were growing tall and so thickly that he used the ravine as a natural highway.

The ravine eventually broadened into a narrow valley that meandered along to the south. Deep in the valley, Jeff could not see much of the surrounding land until it abruptly took a sharp turn to the southwest and opened up.

"Now that is some kind of country," he breathed.

Viewed from his perspective in the valley and still at high elevation, mountainous forestland spread out in a vast wedge. While the scale of the land was familiar, the scope was not. It faded toward the horizon with no indication that it would ever end.

Jeff gazed around for a spell, enjoying the declining sun's warmth, the view, and the return of all the forest smells. He stiffened and studied the terrain with an eye to detail.

"What the hell? There's no sign of an earthquake!"

Forest cloaked the land, and the only bare rock appeared to be weathered and above the tree line.

"Not even logging clear-cuts. Is that possible? And where are the Cascades? There has to be *something* left that I can recognize." Jeff blanked out for a moment. "This just doesn't make any sense!"

Whipping out a topographic map, his eyes flicked back and forth between it and the terrain.

"Nothing. Not one bloody landmark matches." He searched the immediate area. "Shit. Not even a beer can or scrap of plastic. That is *not* possible!"

Search as he might, Jeff discovered no evidence of human presence. Not a smoke column or vapor trail from a jet, much less a highway. Optimism that had been making a comeback earlier in the day failed completely.

Slumping to the ground, Jeff stared off across a forest wilderness that truly seemed to have no end. The wind sighing mournfully through the trees as if to say, "You're all alone, all alone," and the sun neared the horizon, casting long shadows across the land.

The magnitude of the forest, the scale of the mountains behind him, and the lack of anything to pin hopes of redemption on threatened to crush him. Taking no note of the time, Jeff waged a losing battle with a primal sense of desertion.

Just inside the trees to his right, an indistinct form the size of a pony observed the slumped-over figure. Motionless as a statue, the form seemed a part of the forest. In the blink of an eye it was gone.

When it became dark enough that Jeff could no longer avoid thinking about what he was going to do for the night, he levered himself upright with his staff and trudged down the valley. Two or three steps along the way, a mournful howling came drifting across miles of shadowed forest. Jeff stopped to listen.

Although a powerful song, the eerie wailing nearly overwhelmed him with despair.

It was hard to see when he noted a ravine opening into the valley. Jeff hiked into the ravine where he discovered a creek meandering along the base of a rocky bluff. Snow cover had essentially disappeared, and it took only a few minutes to set up camp.

Extracting cartridges from the Colt, Jeff pulled a scrap of oil-damp cloth tied to a piece of string through the barrel and cylinder bores. Reloading, he held the Colt in the palm of his hand to look at it.

"This is the only thing that stands between me and starving to death. I don't know who runs things, but God or whoever, I could use some help." Testing his small camping flashlight, he hiked up the ravine.

It was a dark night but he used the flashlight sparingly to avoid scaring off game. Happening across what looked like a game trail, Jeff found a seat cushioned by pine needles and slipped into the spell of silence that was on the land. Gradually, he became aware of every sound.

In spite of that awareness, he missed a clinking sound on two occasions. Some inner sense was more alert and brought him to attention. When he heard it again, Jeff felt a surge of excitement.

That sounds like pebbles rolling down the hill, he thought, or maybe hooves!

Saliva pooled in his mouth and his body trembled with anticipation. Shortly he sensed the presence of a darker, slowly moving mass. Jeff raised the revolver to arm's length. He had his finger on the flashlight button when something kicked a rock loose right behind him with a loud clatter.

"Oh, God, don't!"

Jeff flopped around onto his back and flicked on the flashlight. No more then ten feet away, a large buck was staring at him with lowered head and setting a hoof down. Very slowly.

"Jesus!"

Nearly back-to-back, two orange spears of light pulsed followed by muzzle blasts that boomed and echoed in the narrow ravine. The buck shuddered at the first impact, his head snapped back at the second and he collapsed onto his side. Jeff heard crashing sounds and caught a brief glimpse of bodies hurtling by. He was breathing so hard he hyperventilated, and had to lie there to calm down.

"What the hell was he up to? Something is not right. Oh bullshit! Something is fucking wrong!" Hunger took over and he grabbed the deer's antlers.

Dragging the buck back to camp, Jeff frequently stopped to flash the light around. The forest seemed empty of life. He arrived exhausted by the pull and deeply troubled by something he couldn't put his finger on.

Hastily building a fire, Jeff crudely skinned a rear leg, hacked out a piece of meat and held it over the flames on a stick. The smell of roasting venison and the hiss of fat flaring in the fire drove his hunger to the point of frenzy.

Ripping the charred piece of venison from the stick, he tore off a mouthful. The meat burned his hands and mouth, his eyes teared up from the pain, but he crammed more in. Juice and blood ran down his chin and shirt without notice. Jeff stopped when he was on the verge of throwing up.

With a full belly for the first time in what seemed to be months, Jeff dozed off repeatedly. After nearly toppling into the fire he decided it was time to turn in. He tried to get up but was so tired he collapsed. Giving in to exhaustion, he crawled to the tent.

In the small hours of the morning when even night creatures had found their burrows, a line of ghostly shadows filed through camp. They stopped to sniff around the tent then faded into the night like a whisper that is not heard.

The sun was well above the trees when Jeff crawled out of the tent. He felt such a sense of comfortable well-being that he decided to lay over another day. Got to gather strength and save as much of that deer as I can, he reasoned. Now that I have food, what's the hurry? What am I going to do? Lose my job?

The ground was covered with a thick bed of pine needle duff. It was wet, but from long habit he had scraped duff well back from the fire pit. Passing the fire pit on his way to tackle butchering the deer, Jeff stopped abruptly to stare at the moist earth.

"Oh, boy. This is not good."

Stooping, he spread his hand to cover a paw print. His hand was larger by only a small amount, and the impression was over an inch deep. Standing up, Jeff continued to stare at the print.

"Maybe it could be a dog or wolf print, but whatever made it must be really big and heavy. With my luck it probably belongs to a mountain lion or small bear." Suddenly, Jeff groaned. "Oh, shit! The deer! It must have been after the deer!"

He ran to where he had left the carcass, maybe thirty yards upstream from camp. It was untouched, although he noted more prints.

"Now this simply does not make sense. What carnivore is going to pass up a free meal?"

Jeff reviewed his experience with the buck the former evening, as well as his observations while trekking down from the snowfields.

"None of this makes any sense. Where the hell am I?"

The day was getting on and he put his questions aside to attend to business. It was a great relief to tackle a practical task.

Jeff had never butchered a large animal although he had seen his grandfather do it, and cussed under his breath while making a hash of it. His hands and clothing were caked with old blood by the time he remembered the system. He had no more than grabbed a rear leg to turn the deer over when he let go.

"That's odd. This is not a mule deer. I suppose it could be a white tail, but I didn't think there were any in the Cascades." Jeff examined the deer with an eye to detail. "No, not even close to the pictures I've seen. Ears look like a cat's, muzzle's too broad, and the antlers aren't right." Jeff felt the tip of a prong and let out a startled grunt. "That sucker is sharp!"

He stepped back to get a better perspective.

"Holy shit. Will you look at that?" Jeff stooped down and picked up a front leg. "That's not even a hoof. Three toes plus one hell of a dew claw." He noticed something sticking out of the deer's mouth and dropped onto his heels so he could pry it open. "I don't believe this," Jeff breathed. "This is crazy!"

He knelt and ran a finger over sharp, conical incisors and the tip of a long canine tooth.

"That's what I saw last night! That son of a bitch had his teeth bared!" He jumped to his feet and searched the woods. "He was stalking *me*. Maybe they all were!"

There was no sign of motion or anything else in the woods that might suggest a threat, and he resumed butchering.

Although the task became easier as he learned how to skin, Jeff took no pleasure in it. He muttered under his breath while searching for an explanation that would tie together all the discrepancies that had accumulated. As before, nothing came to mind. By the time he had removed all the venison he could pack, Jeff was feeling a bit foolish.

"Here's the intrepid voyager exploring a new planet!" He laughed at himself. "No such thing as a meat-eating deer. Got to be a mutation or something. Carl will really go nuts when I tell him about this critter."

He stuck the knife in a tree for later cleaning and carried a load of venison to the fire.

"Just cure the meat and keep your shit together, boyo."

While the venison slow-roasted on a circle of spits, Jeff dragged the carcass a good distance from camp.

On the way back he thought sourly, Some damn bear jumping on top of me in the middle of the night would really put the finishing touch to this day.

"Bear? What manner of creature is this?"

Jeff spun around. "Who said that?" No one was standing behind him as he half expected. "Get a grip, Friedrick. Now you're hearing voices. Man, I think I've had enough for one day!"

Frost covered the ground when he emerged next morning, but the sun was over the trees promising warmth. Wrapping the meat in plastic he had brought to cover his backpack in wet weather, Jeff hiked into the valley gnawing on a piece left from the prior evening.

"Highway, here I come!"

Over following days he worked his way down into more heavily forested land but saw no smoke, ran across no highways, and encountered none of the offal of civilization. However, he was packing a good supply of food and shrugged it off.

"Sooner or later I'll hit a highway."

Sitting by the fire one night thinking about nothing in general, Jeff noticed the glow of a moon about to rise. That really seems bright, he thought. Probably a full moon.

He decided to go have a look but checked the Colt before leaving camp. Whatever made the big paw prints had visited his camp on several more occasions. Entering the valley, he climbed a hill to get a good view.

"Son of a gun, those moons are beautiful. And they're both full. What a night." Jeff did an incredulous double take. "Two moons? There can't be two moons!"

Immobilized by shock, Jeff watched with jaw agape as the smaller moon rapidly caught up with the larger. All the discrepancies he had been collecting came together and out into the open with a mental shout that nearly brought Jeff to his knees.

"This can't be Earth! It isn't Earth!"

Some time later he glanced at his watch and realized he had been standing there for well over an hour. Turning every so often to view the moons, Jeff stumbled back to camp in a daze. He truly was lost.

Badly needing the moral support of a good blaze, he stirred up the coals and threw on an armload of wood. Jeff thumped down by the fire and followed both moons as they moved higher in the sky. The smaller moon was quite bright and seemed to race by in front of the larger.

He was tempted to pinch himself to see if it was all a dream. Instead, he drew aimless patterns in the dirt with a stick.

A sci-fi addict in his youth, Jeff recalled a book by Heinlein. Okay, he thought, viciously attacking the dirt with his stick, so a nuclear blast blew this guy's fallout shelter into an alternate future. Welcome to the club. Jeff jabbed the stick into the dirt and it broke with a dry snap.

"Oh, bullshit! It's probably no more than my imagination and just the space station."

The argument raged back and forth while he fed the fire. Frequent glances at the smaller moon revealed it was not his imagination, nor could it be the space station. It was far too large. Reason and emotion battled in a no-holds-barred match that covered the entire mental landscape.

While there was no escaping the scalpel-sharp persuasion of higher logic honed by years of academic training, the power of ancient drives proved equal to the task. Reason concluded he was no longer on Earth. Emotion—fear—rallied anger and scorned such a conclusion. It was down and dirty. Hours passed without resolution.

Jeff jumped to his feet, grabbed a rock, and heaved it at a tree. "This whole thing is a bunch of crap! Damn it, this is Earth! That goddamed earthquake has totally fucked me!"

He threw more rocks and kicked the dirt, but all it did was make him want to cry from loneliness. The thought that there might not be anyone within thousands of miles proved so unsettling he sought escape in sleep.

It was a restless night of unsettling dreams and Jeff got up before the sun. He paced and sat, paced and sat, the knowledge that he could not possibly be on Earth chipping away at doubt only to retreat in the face of angry denial. Hunger would not be denied and he spitted a piece of venison on a green stick.

The smell of hot food, the warmth of the sun—both provided a pleasant timeout to put his head back together. It was also challenging to reheat the meat without burning it. When the venison was done to a turn, not charred black, Jeff took a cautious bite but burned his tongue anyway.

For the first time he noticed how flat the meat tasted and sprinkled it with a light dusting of salt.

"Not much left," Jeff muttered, hefting the salt container. "Without salt this diet could really get old, quick."

That kicked off a chain of associations. Okay, he thought, let's accept that at the very least you're no longer in the Cascades. I'm here, wherever that is, and nothing is going to change the fact that I'm lost, but good. Until I can figure out what the score is or hike out, I'm going to have to conserve everything that can't be replaced from what is at hand. I can only use the Colt for self-defense unless there is no alternative.

A cluster of neurons in the memory cortex fired off.

"Wait a minute!"

Diving into the backpack, Jeff pulled out two boxes of ammunition. "I don't remember packing these and should not have brought them. More importantly, why didn't I notice them days ago?"

He opened one of the boxes to make sure it wasn't a dream. Holding a silver cartridge up to the sunlight, he gazed at an enigma.

"Was I really that far gone?" Jeff pursed his lips and nodded. "Yep, I was. No other explanation." He tossed the cartridge in the air and grinned. "Let's hear it for confusion. Loaded for bear, not to mention cheeky deer!"

Having arrived at a livable compromise, Jeff's train of thought continued beyond the deer to include the paw prints. The animal that made them continued to be a mystery. Bear, mountain lion—there was no way of knowing. At least he had seen the deer and knew what to expect.

Stowing the cartridge boxes, he chuckled. "Shoot, maybe it's no more than a large coyote on the prowl. I'm probably spooked for nothing."

The instant an image of a coyote formed in his mind, Jeff was hit by such a blast of outrage that it was physically painful. He had been about to take a seat but sprang upright in alarm.

"Now where did that come from? It couldn't have come from me, could it? Shit, it feels like something is screwing with my head! Am I losing my mind?" Growling, "I have to get out of this damn wilderness before I go entirely over the edge," he hurried to the task of breaking camp.

Since the valley still offered the easiest path, Jeff continued to use it as a highway. While a part of his mind stubbornly refused to accept that he was no longer on Earth, he examined his surroundings with new eyes. At the same time, his thoughts kept drifting back to Seattle.

Memories of familiar haunts came to mind. Mom and Dad, Carl, the fencing club—they all flowed through his thoughts leaving a deep sadness that threatened to drag him down. He was not going to run across a highway, catch a ride, and soon be back in Seattle.

Days passed and acceptance made headway as Jeff cataloged more discrepancies. One day he stopped to run his hand over the bark of a giant evergreen.

"Sure looks like a Douglas fir," he mused, "but the bark's way too smooth."

With the drop in elevation, clumps of aspens had made an appearance. A close examination revealed that the leaves were far too broad to be aspen. The rabbit he scared up looked for all the world like a snowshoe hare, its mottled white and brown spring fur clearly evident as it bounded away. Then he thought about the deer teeth.

Jeff decided to stop for the night when he ran across a meadow carpeted with lush grass and bisected by a wide creek. He pitched tent inside a copse of the aspen-like trees and scouted the area for wood he could fashion a bow out of. Two boxes of ammo or not, something told him it was going to be a long hike.

Selecting several likely varieties, he spent the afternoon being alternately frustrated and encouraged. Putting his knife away, Jeff delved deep into the backpack in search of a length of synthetic line to fashion a bowstring with.

"Well," he said, looking down at the gnarled contraption in his hand, "I don't know how long this thing will last, but it will have to do until I have time to cut and cure a better piece of wood."

Arrows, likewise, were makeshift. He would have to learn how to knapp arrowheads from flint or obsidian. Laying the arrows aside near dusk, Jeff decided he could afford to shoot another deer. He sneaked down near the creek and lay quietly until a large buck came to drink.

Watching the deer graze, Jeff felt immense relief. *At least they aren't pure carnivores,* he thought. *Or at least this one isn't.*

One shot did the trick. The pull back to camp was hard going, and he decided to dress out the deer after only a few steps. Just as he dropped the antlers, Jeff caught movement out of the corner of his eye. He was startled then alarmed when he saw gray, ghostlike shadows gliding through the woods at the border of the meadow.

"If those mothers are coyotes, I'm a dwarf!"

That comparison did nothing for his peace of mind. He grabbed the antlers, back peddled with all his might and brought the deer skidding along. The glow of the campfire seemed the most cheerful thing he had ever seen.

Frequently peering into the circle of darkness, Jeff butchered the deer as fast as he could. His imagination did the rest.

"I can't leave the carcass here, but those things were big! Oh, shit!"

He set an armload of venison on a handy boulder and took hold of the antlers. While the deer was much lighter to pull, it still seemed like an anchor. Although he had never been afraid of the dark, Jeff discovered foot by foot that he wasn't too old to learn. He had not gone far when he couldn't stand it and dropped the carcass.

"I'm outta here!"

Jogging back with pistol in hand, he fully expected *something* to take a crack at him. When he trotted into camp, Jeff already heard sounds of a commotion in the direction of the carcass. While it wasn't loud like lions quarreling over position at a kill, Jeff knew without doubt that the deer carcass was being torn to shreds.

Hurrying to gather extra firewood, he muttered, "Polite carnivores?" The idea was absurd.

The commotion eventually settled down to an occasional loud pop that sounded like bones snapping.

"No sleep tonight, that's for sure."

Jeff dropped a final armload of wood on the pile then occupied his time touching up the edge of his saber. The sword and pistol were very reassuring. Eventually all he heard was the creaking of insects. The recorder filled more time, but his heart wasn't in it. He knew that something was out there. Jeff threw more wood on the fire and imagined a big thermos of coffee. It didn't help. Found out by the day's stress, his head slowly drooped and he nodded off.

A snapping in the fire awakened Jeff with a start. Horrified that he had fallen asleep and allowed the fire to burn down to coals, he grabbed a piece of firewood. Something moved on the other side of the fire, and he froze.

"Oh my God! They're here!"

A number of inkblot shadows were grouped on the opposite side of the coals. Glowing orbs of green and red seemed to hang suspended in the shadows, giving the impression of monstrosity.

Tossing the piece of wood on the fire, Jeff moved back against the tent. It was a big piece of wood and a vortex of sparks shot into the air. Fighting a nearly irresistible urge to take off running, he yanked the saber free.

Illuminated by the slowly growing firelight, six creatures that looked as big as Shetland ponies took shape. Sitting motionless, they stared at him with unblinking intensity. Another minute and they still had not moved. Jeff relaxed a fraction.

"Okay, they haven't jumped you yet. Maybe their bellies are full and they're only curious. Let us hope!"

The piece of wood was full of pitch and flared up.

"Shit they're big," Jeff breathed. "They look like wolves, but I'll bet they run at least two hundred pounds and stand four feet."

Jeff figured his prospects in a free-for-all and knew he wouldn't have a chance, pistol or no pistol. He tossed more wood on the fire, the wolves turning their heads as if linked together to follow his every move. Several let tongues loll out of partially open jaws that looked big enough to swallow a rabbit whole. That and they way they were looking at him really irritated Jeff.

"Those bastards are enjoying this!"

Easing tense muscles and grimly clamping his jaw, Jeff focused on the biggest of the lot. "All right, bucko, this seems to be your game. What's it going to be?" He shifted the saber to his left hand and unsnapped the holster.

"Greetings, two-legged brother."

His mind lurched and Jeff jerked upright like he had been kicked in the rump. Pain lanced through his brain like a red-hot poker.

"God, that hurts!"

Letting the saber fall to the ground, Jeff grabbed his head and groaned. His mind lurched again and was suddenly flooded with alien thoughts racing around inside of it. Opening and closing his mouth spasmodically, Jeff gasped for breath.

"This can't be telepathy," he moaned between clenched teeth. "No way am I hearing their thoughts. Get your shit together before they decide they're hungry."

Another packet of alien thoughts caromed into his mind, sending Jeff reeling backward. "They're laughing at me!"

He wanted to take action, but the pain in his head was so severe that Jeff collapsed onto a piece of wood. For a time, it hurt so bad that being eaten seemed the lesser of two evils. While struggling to master the pain, Jeff felt like the contents of his brain had become a flea market. Clusters of high-spirited thoughts gathered here and there to dig around the merchandise, all the while clucking with mock dismay at the shoddy quality.

Stung by their amusement and tired of the show, Jeff fought off the pain. Getting an idea of how things worked by tracking the wolves around in his head, he kicked them out one by one.

Dusting off mental hands with a sense of satisfaction, he tried to assemble a thought to project. Jeff caught himself as he was about to address the leader as asshole, and reluctantly censored it out of the thought.

"I am greatly surprised by your presence, as you are aware," nodding toward the biggest wolf, *"and do not understand this manner of speech."*

Mirth barely suppressed, the wolf responded with the same diamond clarity as his opening sally.

"We understand that you are new to this world and its ways; that you have never employed this manner of speech. Yet, it is your heritage to so speak.

"We have followed your passage from the high country with great interest. In our turn, we are amazed at your strange manner of hunting with the little stick that makes great fire and thunder. Your bravery in retaining life while in the great snow has also not gone unnoticed."

The leader rose to his feet and walked around the fire to sit back down about three feet from where Jeff was seated. The wolf was so big that Jeff had to look up to meet his eyes. Although not directly illuminated by the fire, they caught enough light to glow a yellow-green. The combined effect was not comforting.

"We have been asked by our brothers to keep watch for one such as yourself, and to be of aid as we might."

Jeff's mind turned inside out once again. *"I must admit confusion. I am expected?"*

The wolf replied with the mental equivalent of a shrug. *"We know only that something has gone amiss, and that you could not be found. You have come to our hunting grounds, we have met. Two suns ago you would have died had we not guarded you from the great shaggy one that does not see well."*

Thinking that one over, it became clear to Jeff why he had not encountered any serious carnivores other than the wolves near his campsites. Maybe the 'great shaggy one' was a bear of some stripe, he mused. Jeff let out a grunt of relief.

"Of course! That must have been the wolves playing with my head a few days ago! Frikking comedians."

Jeff recalled himself to the present situation and found that a reply came naturally to mind.

"I am grateful for your assistance, and pleased that you and your pack shared my kills."

"The eating was good," the wolf acknowledged. *"We will remain with you for a time to help as we may. Call us in need, in the manner you have now become aware of."*

"How are you called?"

"You have seen me, we have shared minds, you know who I am."

The group of wolves arose and trotted off. Their leader briefly turned to emphasize a last thought.

"Be cautious, new brother. One day's march will bring you to lands of two-legs that do not have mind speech and live in fear of that-which-they-do-not-know."

Jeff sat by the fire long into the night and tried to escape the feeling that he was in way over his head.

Five

Battle-ax Remorse

"Shoot, not a single paw print."

Bending over to see better, Jeff circled the campsite again to make sure but came up empty handed. A heavy shower during the night had beaten the dirt flat and left pools of standing water.

Maybe I imagined the whole thing, Jeff thought while groping around in a pocket of the backpack in search of his match container. Really wouldn't surprise me if last night turns out to be no more than a pipe dream. What a bummer that would be.

Although the fire was dead and the wood was wet, dry tinder was available. A kitchen match soon had a merry blaze going. Before capping the waterproof container, Jeff counted how many matches were left. There were eighteen.

"Well," Jeff decided, pouring boiling water over a tea bag, "Either it happened or it didn't, and pipe dream or whatever, my head is not the same. It feels. ..." He laughed. "Okay, why not. It feels like new software has been installed. Question is, if it's there how do I boot it?" Jeff fiddled around in his head to no effect. "Well, shoot. Hello! Anyone out there?"

Jeff chuckled at himself and heated a piece of venison. Still, he knew that something in his head was different. While eating he searched for some concrete change that he could identify. It was the first time he had tried to think about thinking, and found it an eye-crossing experience.

He was about to give up when a red and green cube seemed to materialize out of nowhere. The cube had the appearance of a holographic projection hanging a foot or so in front of his eyes.

"Now that's all right! Damn, its beautiful!"

It had to be a program icon. He was sure of it. Suddenly the cube seemed to expand as it rushed straight at his eyes, pulling his perception around in a sharp U turn to follow.

It was a hot chase, but Jeff lost the icon somewhere in his left hemisphere. He stopped to orient himself and realized with a start what he was doing.

Talk about getting inside your head, Jeff thought, and closed virtual eyes until a wave of dizziness passed. This beats the hell out of most head-trips I've been on. Question is, where am I and how do I get out? Damn those wolves.

Although the facility of vision had no meaning, Jeff was aware of every detail. He hiked along a pulsing arteriole and elaborately folded layers of gray matter that enclosed him in a confusing labyrinth.

That little bastard has to be around here somewhere, Jeff thought grimly, and that's my way out. Think it went deep. Guided by a nerve trunk, he angled right and descended.

Creeping about the base of the cerebellum, he spotted a familiar glimmer and crouched behind a prominent brainstem nucleus. There it is! Come to papa.

Jeff jumped out of hiding with mental arms spread wide to prevent escape and maneuvered the icon against a large bundle of neurons. It quivered and glowed like a cube of green and red Jell-O, giving the impression of neurotic uncertainty.

Okay, I've got the little sucker trapped. Now what do I do? Jeff edged closer and made a flying leap at the icon but seemed to pass right through it. With no perceptible transition, he found himself back in the outside world.

"Whoa! What a rush!"

His mind blinked off then on, Jeff fell flat on his face in a puddle of water, and he was abruptly aware of the world from an entirely different perspective. His vision dimmed, but other senses he had never used expanded a hundredfold.

"All right! I didn't imagine it! Connected and running hot!" Jeff got up spitting mud and water. "Damn it feels weird. I wonder what that faint hissing is? Could it be something like a carrier wave?" Phrasing he would never have previously considered leaped to mind.

"Good hunting be with you this day, brothers and sisters."

He let out a whoop of delight when a chorus of greetings bloomed in his mind, even though none of the pack could be seen. With each message, Jeff received a symbol that represented the individual wolf as if he were looking at him or her in the fur.

"Greetings new brother—hunt well." And again, *"Walk silently this day, for danger approaches in the evening."* Standing out from them all was the leader's symbol and message. *"Strength to your arm."*

The connection dissolved in an instant, the effect so shocking that Jeff nearly toppled off the log he was sitting on.

While it didn't take long to pack up, Jeff spent considerable time attaching the saber in such a way that he could draw the weapon by reaching over his head. The greetings he had received were sobering and offset some of the excitement he felt at being able to speak mind to mind.

I wonder what the natives look like? he thought nervously. The wolves are so damn big! I hope to God that doesn't hold true for whatever it is I am about to meet.

He shouldered the backpack and hiked downslope through high grass that was heavy with raindrops.

Late in the afternoon he encountered a peculiar triangle-shaped spine of rock and earth. It lay directly across his path but appeared to terminate a short distance ahead in a massive bluff. Jeff spent a hard two hours clambering up its flank through dense trees and broken scree in the hope that he might get an idea what the terrain held in store for him.

As he climbed, the sky cleared and it warmed up. The trees began to thin out as he neared the top, and were gone by the time he cautiously shuffled out onto a stone parapet.

"Whoa. That's bright."

His sunglasses had become badly scratched, but Jeff put them on and inched toward the edge of the parapet.

"Now that is worth seeing," he murmured. Heavily forested mountains marched away to the limits of vision.

Wishing fervently for binoculars, Jeff shaded his eyes and got the impression of progressive moderation in the terrain. Deep canyons furrowed the landscape between a series of rugged cordilleras, which debouched fan-like into large valleys off toward the horizon.

Although forested with evergreens, the land was dotted with clumps of deciduous trees. Far to the west he caught the glint of a river and followed snatches of its line.

"That has to be a good-sized stream," he mused. "Might feed into a lake."

Releasing the backpack, Jeff sat cross-legged near the edge of the parapet. The scale of the wilderness, its beauty, called for contemplation. He had never imagined anything like it.

The sun was halfway to the horizon, brilliantly illuminating snow-covered peaks. At lower elevations, mists clung to deeper valleys and softened the forest's collage of greens. While a gentle breeze dried the sweat of his climb, Jeff watched what appeared to be a dozen or more large birds circle above the immense area he was viewing. He turned north to view land already crossed.

"Holy shit." For the first time, Jeff got an unobstructed view of the giant mountain.

Even though he was over a hundred miles from where he had first awakened, the effect was not diminished. It did not seem possible that anything could be so massive. Mountains nearby the giant's location seemed no more than hills although he had earlier estimated they must be twelve to fifteen thousand feet high in their own right. Jeff stared at the mountain for some time but simply could not comprehend its size.

Prodded by the fading day to move on, he took a number of bearings with his compass.

By late afternoon Jeff had passed well beyond the bluff he had named Spine Ridge and angled off toward the river noted earlier. Prepared to hide or run at the first sign of danger, he encountered nothing new. He did chance across a large buck taking his ease near a brook.

The buck clambered to his feet when he spied Jeff and stared at him with lowered head. Showing long canines in a carnivorous smile, he advanced with the stealthy motions of a stalk.

"Well, you insolent son of a bitch."

There was no doubt in Jeff's mind that the animal was considering him with dinner in mind. He released the strap over the Colt and walked toward the buck.

"Not today, dipshit. Move on or take the consequences."

The buck stopped and raised his head but gave no evidence of being frightened. Jeff was no more than fifteen yards away when the buck spun around and trotted into the woods like a horse.

Easing the Colt's hammer down, Jeff called after him, "Pass the word!"

Not long afterwards, and still grumbling about the deer, Jeff ventured into a large meadow cut by a small river. He had taken only a few steps when shouts rang out. Almost at once, the shouts were followed by the unmistakable sound of steel on steel.

Dodging back into the forest, Jeff skirted the meadow. "This is it! That sounded like someone shouting a challenge! What are they going to look like?"

The sound level rapidly increased. "Got to be some sort of fight," he muttered. Pushing through underbrush, visions of weird alien forms flitted through his mind. "Hustle it up, man." He moved as close to the noise as he dared and carefully parted foliage so he could see.

"Oh, no way. They look like humans," Jeff breathed.

No more than fifty feet away, a number of men were involved in a battle that seethed around the head of the meadow. At the meadow apex, the river flowed over a broad ledge adding a muted roar to the banging of shields, hoarse shouts and snatches of song.

"This isn't possible!"

Jeff could hardly believe his eyes. He felt like he had been transported again, this time to first century Germany: blond-haired giants dressed in animal furs, leather boots extending cross-gartered to above the calf, most wearing a form of kilt. Battle-axes, crude swords and cudgels made up the bulk of the weapons Jeff could make out. It was the aliens' size that had him shaking his head.

"They're really tall, maybe around seven feet, but they're incredibly massive to boot. I'll bet they weigh over four hundred pounds!" Jeff started to sort out what was going on. "Looks like seven against four," he whispered. "This can't last long."

Moving nervously behind a screen of bushes, Jeff groaned from time to time as the smaller group lost ground. He caught himself taking sides.

"Oh no you don't. You know nothing about these people. This isn't your fight, dumbhead."

The seven pressed the attack until their opponents were forced to the brink of the waterfall. Suddenly, one of the four leaped forward with a wild swing of his war hammer and broke through the semicircle of attackers. The remaining three followed at once. The semicircle reformed and pushed them toward the woods.

"Oh, shit!"

The four men had suddenly turned and were running directly at Jeff's hiding place. He jumped back to do a quick fade, but they stopped at the edge of the woods and fought on.

Although he had drawn back, Jeff was close enough to smell their sweat and blood, to be nearly overcome by the din of ringing weapons and snatches of song roared out between gasps to find air. *They have no intention of running*, he suddenly realized. *They're going to fight to the death.*

The effect was so strong that Jeff felt himself a part of it, felt every blow and parry. He decided to leave on several occasions but couldn't move.

Shortly there was no more singing, only the cries of agony as the men nearest him fought to lift their weapons one more time. A tremendous overhand blow from a battle-ax crashed down on the shield of one of the defenders, sending him backward into the woods. Tripping over a limb, he fell through brush to land on his back at Jeff's feet.

The warrior who had landed the blow leapt into the woods with upraised ax and exultant shout, only to come face to face with Jeff standing paralyzed by the moment. The warrior froze when he saw Jeff. Blank astonishment quickly gave way to what might have been an expression of fear. They stood that way for one mortal moment, allowing the fallen warrior to roll away.

Jeff was utterly stunned by the size of the man, if that's what he was. The giant axe blade rotated and Jeff knew in an instant that he was the new target. Ripping the saber free, he dumped the backpack in one reflexive move.

Shoulder muscles bulging, the warrior let loose a howl fit to defy gods and the ax flashed down.

Dodging aside, Jeff felt a breeze as the ax whistled by to thud deep into the ground. Hoping to escape, he backpedaled into the woods. Instead of returning to the meadow the warrior followed with giant strides. Jeff had to force his way through undergrowth as he retreated, but the warrior moved as easily as a tank.

"Stop! Goddamit, I'm not your enemy!"

The warrior heaved on the axe and Jeff again dived to the side. The ax head became entangled in vines.

"We must talk! You must stop!"

His words only seemed to infuriate the warrior, and he swung the axe in a vicious arc. Jeff fetched up against a tree trunk and barely had time to twist aside before the ax sank into the tree.

"Oh, damn it!"

Jeff finally accepted that words that could not be understood would not serve. Lunging one step, he thrust over the top of the shield strapped to the warrior's arm and skewered him through the neck.

Blood jetted in a thick stream, but the warrior lifted his ax for another blow. At the top of his swing, the saber fell on his neck and cut halfway through. The ax tumbled from his hands and the warrior toppled to the ground like a felled tree.

Breathing heavily, Jeff was overcome by what he had done and by the stench of blood and bowels evacuated in death. Sprawled in a patch of yellow and orange flowers, the warrior's eyes were blue as a morning sky and filled with profound sadness. Jeff shuddered with self-loathing

"Did you have to kill him?"

Yanking out the Colt, he ran into the meadow, pointed it in the air and fired. Combatants dropped to the ground as if they had been poleaxed. Some dived behind boulders, others tried to disappear in the thick grass.

Stepping over several warriors, Jeff picked up a broken sword and strode between the opposing factions.

"That makes three you've killed. Why not just blow them all away and do it right?"

Savagely jamming the broken blade into the ground, he traced a deep furrow. Nine pairs of eyes followed every move. Pulling the Colt, Jeff waved it at one group then the other. Warriors dove in all directions to get out of the way. He pointed at several men who had serious wounds, and gestured that their fellows were to assist them.

Convinced they were not to die immediately, the warriors looked to their comrades all the while casting anxious glances in Jeff's direction.

The sun was gone and it was nearly dark. Jeff kicked some wood together, built up a fire and set a pot of water on to boil. Tearing up what toweling he had into strips for bandages, he set to work.

When he had done what he could, Jeff walked into the woods and vomited his heart out. The sight and blood-stench of gaping wounds had been too much.

Feeling weak but calmer, he returned to the battlefield only to find warriors eyeing each other suspiciously and growling what were undoubtedly curses. Restoring order, Jeff took a moment to consider his next step.

If they head home now, he reasoned, most of the wounded will never make it or they'll just start fighting again. Jeff threw more wood on the fire. Some of the warriors were inclined to leave until Jeff unsnapped the Colt.

The night seemed to drag on forever. Pacing up and down between the two groups, stopping only to put more wood on the fire, he tried to figure out a plan for the coming morning but couldn't shake memories of what he had done.

The larger moon sailed above the trees, encouraging Jeff to seek relief in music. He unpacked the recorder and let his mind drift away with the notes as they soared along cool pathways offered by moonbeams.

The fire was nearly comatose, lending an acrid quality to the thick tendril of smoke that found its way up Jeff's nose. He awakened sitting by the fire in the grip of an explosive fit of sneezing.

He didn't remember where he was for a moment but figured it out when he noticed a forest of legs knotted with muscle on either side of him. That and the fact that he was about to topple into a bed of ashes drove him to his feet in an awkward two-step shuffle.

"Real graceful," he said around a big yawn, "I'll bet that impressed 'em."

The warriors were toeing the line he had drawn, but instead of exchanging insults they seemed to be talking excitedly.

Progress? Jeff wondered. Screw progress, all I want to do is dunk my head.

Doffing his hat, he kneeled by the river and submerged his head. It was so cold he would have screamed had it not meant inhaling a lungful of water. Instead, and vitally refreshed, he leaped to his feet with a shout.

Slinging his head to get hair out of his face, Jeff looked around and nearly ducked. A thicket of tree-like arms pointed toward his head accompanied by amazed-sounding exclamations. While the words were unintelligible, he kept hearing one that sounded like alarai. Alarai hair? he thought. Whatever, it's time to get these folks headed home.

Through gestures and pantomime, Jeff conveyed the idea that they could leave. The night before he had discovered that the wolf leader's assessment was probably correct: he could feel their emotions to an extent, but that was it.

He let the group of four leave first, then, two hours later, the rest. They disappeared into the forest singing a multiple part continuo that slowly faded to silence.

Remorse and bone-deep fatigue returned almost at once. Jeff sat around what was left of the fire for some time replaying the battle. No matter how he looked at it, there was no excuse for killing the warrior. He could have run. Jeff got up with the intention of leaving but was so exhausted that sleep came first.

When he awakened late in the afternoon, rested but feeling dirty inside and out, Jeff stripped and plunged into the river before he could think about it. He exploded from the water with a cry of anguish. When he could tolerate the water for more than a few seconds, he used the nubbin of soap that remained to good effect.

Drying off in what was left of a sun being overcome by cloud cover, Jeff donned a spare pair of jeans and went in search of food. He decided to set some snares, but had a hard time remembering how to go about it.

On his way back to camp with a collection of spring greens, he stumbled on a bird's nest in a clump of brush. Nestled inside were five pearly-green eggs of good size.

Mouth watering, Jeff picked up three and left before he snatched the last two. Bedding the eggs in the greens, he hurried back to camp. The eggs proved as good as their promise.

Sitting around experimentally tasting the greens and trying to get sparks from various rocks, Jeff mulled over his encounter from a calmer perspective.

"I must have seemed like something from a nightmare. Maybe a demon. They might even have thought the backpack was part of my body." Jeff remembered blue eyes that would never see again and had to fight back a fresh wave of remorse. "I have got to learn their language, and fast, or it's going to be nothing but one screw up after the other."

Jeff let his mind wander to more comfortable territory and pieced together what he had learned.

If there is any comparison between this world and Europe during the first three centuries A.D., he reflected, the prospects of finding civilization this far north are not good. The terrain and climate are too severe to encourage the development of meaningful agriculture. Without that they're stuck with hunting and no time for anything else. Maybe farther south. Some of those battle-axes were of decent quality. They might represent trade items. If I'm going to find settled communities or even cities, that's were they'll be. Have to locate a village, learn the language, then South here I come.

Not surprisingly, Jeff awoke to an overcast drizzling sort of day. He donned his coat and made a quick round of snares set the previous day. Much to his surprise and delight he had snagged a rabbit.

Holding his breath, Jeff gingerly pried the rabbit's mouth open, then let it out in a gusty sigh. Normal rabbit teeth. He dressed the rabbit, tied it to his backpack and moved out, light rain casting the terrain into misty vagueness.

For most of the day Jeff slogged along through wet grass, pants soaked up to the knees. The air was humid and ground fog clung to the meadows, lending a dreamy atmosphere to the forest. It was a relief to have his world shrink to a smaller scale, and Jeff's thoughts wandered far away.

Automatically dodging around a big tree, he slid to a halt and nearly yelled in fright. Sitting on his haunches no more than a foot away, the wolf leader was nearly nose to snout with him.

"Damn you! Give me some warning!" He took a few deep breaths and counted to ten. "Easy does it, lad, easy does it."

"Good hunting, leader."

The roguish mirth evident in the wolf's thoughts confirmed Jeff's opinion that the meeting ground had been selected for more than convenience's sake. Cheap-shot comedian, he muttered deep inside.

"We are happy to see our brother walking on two legs this day."

"The yellow-hairs were eager to taste each other's blood."

"It is always so when strange packs meet and dispute hunting grounds."

Jeff put his irritation aside and got down to issues. *"This one would search out large numbers of his kind in what are called cities."*

He conveyed images of walled cities and a montage of variations on that theme in the hope they would spark memories from the pack's travels.

"Ah! Our brother desires to seek out places that foul the air and water. Our curiosity is great that you should consider these two-legs your kind."

Puzzled by the last comment, Jeff thought he might have messed up the query and tried again, this time including images of men and women. The wolf leader's thoughts overflowed with the same vast amusement.

"We believe that 'your kind' would be unhappy with such comparison."

"Your humor grows old. Please answer me directly."

The wolf fell silent for a period, a certain respect growing in his thoughts. *"You are related to the two-legs of the south as we of the brethren are related to grassland hunters. From your thoughts we conclude you intend to seek them out in search of understanding, and this is deemed necessary."*

"Forgive my impatience, leader of many, but riddles avail nothing. True knowledge to assist my passage would be of great value."

When the wolf replied, it was in a grave tone. *"Much that must be is not given to this one. Two marches to the south you will find a gathering of the golden-haired ones. There you will learn much."* With that and a brief farewell, he was gone.

"Well," Jeff grumbled, "at least something to shoot for. I don't know what gathering means, but most likely a village. Maybe a big one. So many questions and so little information or answers. It looks like I'm going to have to dig it out for myself."

Totally fed up with what seemed to be nothing but evasive replies, Jeff continued on his day's journey with a vow to keep his own counsel and not be moved around like some pawn in a chess game. It may have been a coincidence, but at that moment a faint howl drifted to his ears and made them burn.

The weather cleared as the day wore on, and Jeff's mood followed suite. "Got to give that wolf a name, symbol or no symbol."

Jeff chuckled and laughed as he considered one unflattering name after the other. In the end he got serious and settled on Balthazar.

Blue skies returned the following day, and he made good time as the land opened up a bit. While still heavily forested, there were more meadows. Hurrying across the smaller ones, Jeff detoured around larger meadows to avoid the risk of being caught out in the open. Not long into the afternoon, he ran across evidence of cultivation.

Putting his experience from the family farm to use, Jeff assessed the weed-grown plot. Maybe something over two acres, it had not been worked for a season. The furrows intrigued him. They were large and appeared to have been turned by a two-bottom plow. That meant draft animals. The men he had seen were giants, but not strong enough to pull such an implement.

"Now where did that come from up here? The village has to be close—I've got to see this place!"

Wary of provoking a confrontation, Jeff moved away from the river. He also did not want to stumble onto a settlement without having a chance to first look it over. By early evening he had located the village, set up a secure campsite and wormed his way into a stand of trees on a promontory that gave a good view of the village. He scanned the area and let out a soft whistle.

"Well, there's my lake," Jeff whispered, "and what a lake."

The opposite shore was not visible. Even though there was no breeze to speak of, good-sized waves curled far up a sandy beach.

A number of children raced back and forth chasing the water, and long-legged birds skittered along the shoreline. No boats were visible, which surprised Jeff. While the lake might be barren of fish or comparable species, that possibility seemed unlikely.

As the sun touched the horizon he counted fifty buildings constructed of squared-off logs, their high-peaked roofs covered with sod. Donning sunglasses, he could see more trailing off into the woods.

"Hmm. Remind me of those Viking lodges excavated in Newfoundland. Really sturdy. Maybe twenty-five feet on the side and no chimneys, just smoke holes. Wait a minute, what's that?"

Peering into shadows now extending over the village, Jeff could almost swear that one lodge did have a chimney, and wood planking on the roof to boot.

The people all seemed to fit the same mold as the warriors he had earlier encountered. He saw children sprinting here and there, roaming groups of what looked like dogs, and clusters of adults talking to one another. Wood smoke sifted through the roofs of many lodges.

Close by his hiding place, a man and woman were busy skinning a deer while conversing in a guttural tongue. Occasionally, one or the other would call out to people in the village or laugh uproariously.

Jeff's overall impression was of a people intent on completing the day's tasks while catching up on village gossip. As the sun disappeared from view, Jeff abruptly turned from his survey in the grip of a devastating wave of homesickness. He had experienced a number of serious attacks since accepting he was no longer on Earth, but always in the presence of other demands that could not be ignored. At the moment there was no threat.

The sight of people engaged in routine, familiar experiences in the company of family and friends reminded him of everything he had lost. Caught unawares, Jeff's heart unraveled. The knowledge that he would never see his family again was no longer a strong possibility, it was fact. There was no escaping it.

All the loneliness he had felt up to that point was nothing compared to the anguish that gripped him. Finding his way to the tent, Jeff curled up in his sleeping bag and let the tears come.

They were not tears of momentary distress, rather an outpouring of grief for what was forever gone—the slender but immensely strong resource of people he loved and who loved him without reservation. The transition to sleep came somewhere around midnight

To his intense relief, Jeff felt drawn but calm the following morning; felt as if something had taken another step on the way to being settled. And those he loved were still there, somewhere in the universe. Jeff smiled when he thought about his grandmother. She would never give him up as lost.

Returning to his observation post, Jeff reassessed the village. While it was quite early, villagers were already bustling about. He watched people stream back and forth from a spot in the woods with growing curiosity.

"Oh yeah! Has to be it. Pit toilets. Now that's impressive."

The streets were dirt, certainly, but seemed to be laid out in a regular fashion. Concentrating on an odd building near the center of the village that was open on two sides, Jeff distinctly saw an orange glow.

"Could it be a forge?" Several minutes later, "I think it is! Son of a gun. Technology rears its ugly head."

Jeff was so excited that he forgot himself and stood up. This is a dream come true, he thought, I have to publish this! The absurdity of the thought was such that it brought him back to reality and behind cover.

"No way, bucko, do you go charging down that hill," Jeff breathed. "You wouldn't get more than fifty feet from this spot before they took you out. Question is, how am I going to make myself known to these folks and stay alive at the same time?"

Thinking it over, Jeff came up with a plan that promised to get him into the village in one piece and conscious.

It took some time to cautiously circle around until he was several miles south of the village. He found a dense grove of trees and set the backpack down when he was well inside. Extracting the recorder, Jeff draped a sweater over the pack and hilt of his sword. He figured the former was truly alien appearing, and the latter just might get him killed.

"Okay, I'm ready. Here goes nothing."

Playing a sprightly tune, Jeff walked into the open and strolled along with what he hoped was a confident gait. He had not progressed far before armed villagers and a pack of barking dogs charged out of the woods to surround him.

Faced with a thicket of spears and axes, Jeff's throat clenched tight. Looking straight ahead, he did not slow down. At the last instant before his chest met a spear, the circle opened and allowed him to continue on. Although many villagers were scowling, they seemed intrigued at the same time.

He crested a rise and the village came into view. A short distance beyond the rise, a man stood with arms akimbo directly across his path. Jeff drew to a halt surrounded by jostling villagers.

Two teenagers grinned at one another and gave a third a hearty shove. He was young but in no way small, and almost knocked Jeff to the ground when he stumbled into his back.

"Shit!"

Jeff felt like he was surrounded by a pack of giant pit bulls, and muttered, "Okay, you wanted to brazen it out as a minstrel, so let's frikking brazen while you have the chance."

He put a big smile in place and held his arms out.

"Greetings, citizens of this beautiful metropolis." Jeff had to stop and cough dry phlegm from his throat. "I have come from a land far to the south," pointing grandly in the appropriate direction, "to spread joy and music. I can assure you that I am alone, but the southern rascals tell me they plan to get up this way soon and break some heads. I come in peace and not a little desperation, hoping you will accept my offerings and not open my veins."

Jeff immediately began playing a medley of tunes while assessing the impression he had made.

A number of villagers still scowled suspiciously, but the majority seemed curious and unsure how to respond. On the periphery, a number of younger men and women were stamping out the time and children were whirling around in maypole circles.

Well, I'm still alive and they certainly like the music, Jeff thought with great relief. The fact that I'm by myself might make the difference.

Turning his attention to the villager confronting him, Jeff was impressed by the cool assessment of risk that seemed to be going on. The man, who looked to be forty or so, issued a string of commands and gestured for him to proceed toward the village. A group of warriors trotted off to the south.

One smart dude, Jeff concluded. Wants to make sure this is not a setup. The man who had confronted him stepped into the building with the chimney. Jeff followed with several warriors immediately behind.

Peering around inside, he noticed the hall had a beamed ceiling with planking laid on top and estimated its dimensions to be about sixty by forty feet. The floor was rammed earth and amazingly clean. Low benches were arrayed around the perimeter. At the far end, two split-log chairs cushioned with furs were set in a prominent position. A fireplace constructed of well-mortared and fitted fieldstones bulked large in one corner.

This has to be a combination community and administrative hall, Jeff mused, continuing to look around with what he hoped would appear to be careless aplomb.

Seating himself in one of the chairs, the man gestured for Jeff to approach closer. This guy is most likely the chief, he decided. If I really lay into it, maybe I can get through to his mind. Jeff was gathering a mental thrust when the chief gestured imperiously. What's he pointing at? My backpack?

Feeling behind his head very slowly, Jeff discovered that the sword hilt had escaped the sweater.

"That does it for sure," he groaned under his breath.

The chief gestured again, leaving no doubt he wanted the saber. Jeff glanced over his shoulder at the doorway to see how far off it was. Leaning forward, the chief shouted a command and held his hand out.

The tension peaked as he reached back to draw the saber. Several warriors crouched slightly and raised their weapons. The saber slid from the scabbard with such a loud rasp that Jeff nearly broke and ran. Instead, he held it across his body and offered it to the chief.

Turning the blade over in his hands to test the edge, the chief inhaled sharply and wiped blood from his thumb.

Well, Jeff thought sourly, that clears up one question about their technology: they're certainly not used to weapons that carry a razor edge.

The other warriors clustered around the saber to get a better look.

"Now I suppose one of them will discover it also has a sharp point," Jeff grumbled.

Within seconds one of the younger men jumped back with a yell, holding his hand.

Jeff shrugged expressively and held his hands out, palms up, in the universal sign of, 'Don't look at me, I didn't do it.'

With a peremptory gesture and command, the chief stood up. The saber looked like a toy in his hand as he advanced.

This is it, Jeff thought resignedly. Either it flies or I'm dead. No more killing.

Watching the saber with intent concentration, Jeff was taken by surprise when the chief snatched off his hat. The move had been so quick and unexpected that Jeff was immobilized by indecision. When everyone jumped back and shouted what once again sounded like alarai, all he could do was stare around in confusion.

The chief let out a bellow that quieted the younger men and returned to a position in front of Jeff, but with a different expression. Try as he might, Jeff could only interpret the look to signify respect. He handed the saber to Jeff and clapped his hands twice. Two youngsters trotted into the hall from a back room. The chief spoke quietly with them and they hurried off. Taking a seat, he waved Jeff to do likewise.

Jeff was so distracted that he stubbed his boot when he tried to sit down in the chair, and nearly fell. The girl and boy returned promptly with large tankards. Jeff cocked a hopeful eye at the foam spilling from the tankard handed him. It looked like it might be beer, but....

Taking a cautious sip, his taste buds were greeted by a smooth ale that could have come from a microbrewery in Seattle. Warmth began to spread from his belly outward after a few swallows.

The tankard was hardly tapped when an old man hobbled into the building, grumbling and muttering as he came. He planted himself and fixed Jeff with a piercing look that contained more intelligence than he had seen since last talking with Professor Hildebrand.

This is my man, Jeff decided.

He was assembling a thought when a powerful probe blew into his mind. Jerking upright in his chair, Jeff thrust the probe back to a mental arm's length.

All right, he thought excitedly, it isn't only wolves that are capable of telepathy. First thing I have to find out what the deal is with this word, alarai. My hair may be different, but it isn't worth this much excitement. Are they referring to me?

"Greetings, Elder, my name is Jeffrey Friedrick. How may I address you?"

The old man let out a startled exclamation. *"I am called Gurthwin, and long has it been since I have spoken mind to mind."*

"I am recently come to these parts from a distant land, and have heard little of the Alarai in the time of my absence. It would please me to be informed of their doings, and of your people."

Favoring Jeff with a piercing gaze, Gurthwin was silent for some moments. *"We will talk later. Now it is time to share meat."*

The chief directed a group of villagers to set up rough-planked trestle tables. Shortly they were covered with steaming platters of meat, rough loaves of dark bread, and baskets of tubers. Torches were placed in iron wall sconces, and logs piled into the fireplace to add more light to the windowless building. Villagers streamed in throughout the process.

Calling to their friends, shouting jests and roughhousing, many villagers crowded close to get a good look at Jeff. Songs were raised in competing melodies; conversations were loud and enthusiastic.

The sense of community that Jeff experienced reminded him of Sunday socials after church service. He moved closer to Gurthwin with a self-conscious smile. It definitely was similar to a church social, and he felt like a kid again.

The chief, whose name Jeff had learned was Halric, raised his arms. The room was immediately filled with a thundering chorus of enthusiastic voices raised in common song. After a few measures a number of men and women broke free to sing in parts. Jeff was walking to the head table with Gurthwin when a countertenor set his voice to soar overall.

Stopping to listen, Jeff let the chorus' measured cadence and sweet harmonies fling his imagination to some onion-domed cathedral in Russia. Jeff was so captivated that he hardly noticed when Gurthwin tugged him back into motion.

He had no sooner taken the indicated seat than buckets of beer were placed on the table and a general attack on the food began. Singing quickly gave way to a torrent of loud conversations and banging of wooden utensils.

Taking his cue from the crowd, Jeff sliced off a piece of venison from a smoking haunch. Taking a bite he sighed with pleasure. Plenty of salt and garnished with herbs. Dipping a fresh tankard of ale from the nearest bucket, Jeff really dug into the food.

As the meal progressed and beer buckets were emptied, the noise level continued to rise. Reflexively jerking his head aside as a piece of venison flew by his ear, Jeff thought, What a rowdy bunch! I could get used to this!

The survival knife excited nearly as much interest as had the saber and made its way around the room. Everyone had to try its edge on what remained of the venison. Jeff winced each time it was flourished. Any minute, he expected an errant finger to be lopped off. The knife eventually wound up in Gurthwin's hands.

Speculatively, he turned the knife over in his hands. Gurthwin noticed the compass embedded in the hilt and watched it rotate as he moved the knife. Turning an enigmatic stare on Jeff, he handed the knife back to him.

"Thank providence the Colt is tucked away under my shirt," Jeff murmured. "This guy is sharp."

He was re-sheathing the knife when Halric stood and called for silence with a casual but immediately effective gesture. He waved toward Jeff and spoke in a serious tone of voice filled with consonant rumblings.

Although Gurthwin broadly interpreted the speech as one of welcome, Jeff wasn't convinced it was as simple as that. After only a few words Halric switched to a different cadence, his voice rising and falling in such a steady fashion that it was hypnotic.

Shifting uneasily in his seat, Jeff suspected the recitation was a saga or an oral history sparked by his presence. He really needed to learn the language, and fast.

Jeff's concern increased rapidly when villagers began darting quick looks in his direction. He queried Gurthwin, who was as deeply involved in the story as anyone.

"Now is not the time to speak of this."

The audience expelled a collective sigh at the story's conclusion, stirring on their benches as they came back to the here and now. In only a short time, the hall was once again filled with roaring conversation.

Three men unlimbered leather-covered drums and an instrument that looked like a cross between a fife and shepherd's flute. The drummers played back and forth until they decided where they were going, at which point the fifer entered with a breathy melody.

Stacking tables against the wall until the central portion of the hall was empty, villagers hurried to form a ring around the musicians. Arms around each other's waists, they skipped forward and back while stepping right and left in a complicated pattern.

Gurthwin nudged Jeff. *"Your strange instrument has charmed us all. I am quite sure Halric will call on you to play before this evening is concluded."*

Villagers who had not been part of the meal streamed into the hall. The hall was packed wall to wall and many more villagers could be seen dancing outside when Halric beckoned. Jeff eyed the crowd nervously as he wormed his way to the center of the hall. Nearly every person he dodged around was a head taller, men and women alike.

"I can't get over how big they are," Jeff muttered, ducking an elbow that nearly caught him on the ear. "Six feet tall, and I haven't felt this short since I was a kid. I don't think half of them even know I'm down here."

He made it as far as the ring of dancers but couldn't find a way through linked hands and arms. The dancers shuffled right, left, then right again for a full revolution, skipping in time to the music.

Before he knew it, Jeff's foot was tapping the floor. That guy on the fife isn't bad, he thought. I wonder. ...

Putting recorder to lips, Jeff waited until he had a solid grip on the tempo and horned in with a quick arpeggio. Crowd noise rapidly diminished, and heads turned to look down. Many seemed surprised to find him standing there. The ring stopped long enough to let him through, then skipped back into action.

The musicians wavered, but Jeff shook his head. Never letting go of the beat, he segued into a spirited folk tune from the Balkans. The drummers liked it and came along, the fifer following suit but frowning at being upstaged. Within minutes he was having so much fun with the style that Jeff let him run with it and was content to take the lead every so often when he faltered.

The music was new, meant for dancing, and concentric circles of dancers soon filled the hall. Clockwise and counterclockwise, stamping out the beat until the earthen floor shook, the dancers faded to a collage of impressions as the quartet moved from tune to tune.

Jeff was really getting down when he was jerked off his feet and flipped toward the ceiling beams like a Frisbee. Thunderous shouts of approval sounded each time he was flung into the air. When they finally put him down, Jeff's head was spinning and his stomach was about to object in the strongest fashion. The fifer nodded at the drummers, and the three of them took off on a Balkan reprise.

Before he could rejoin the musicians, Jeff was pulled into the dancing. The rings gradually broke up into smaller groupings that reminded him of square dancing. Head swimming from the beer, Jeff was spun from partner to partner.

The crowd grew rowdier as time passed, forcing the dancers to weave around fistfights and wrestlers.

The hall became hot from all the sweating bodies, and outer garments went sailing into various corners leaving leather shirts and halters to serve modesty. Some of the women were so tall that Jeff's eyes were nearly at chest level. After a period he began to wonder if there was a small-breasted woman in the house.

Somewhere along the way Jeff found himself dancing with a woman who appeared to be in her late teens. She wasn't much taller than he was, which was a great relief.

He was tired of being thrown around, and she appeared to feel the same way. Jeff discovered her name was Rena about the time the music began to falter and slow. She was intrigued by his clothing and let a hand fall to test the texture of his jeans. Suddenly Rena pulled him out of the dancing. Frowning, she ran a finger up and down the zipper in his jeans.

Before he could react Rena found the tab and pulled it down. Jeff did not know what to do so he opted out and did nothing. Rena paused long enough to smile at his expression and pulled the tab back up. Jeff glanced around in embarrassment. No one was paying attention.

Just relax, man, he thought. This isn't Earth. She's simply curious about the zipper. That proved to be the case, but the zipper was flying up and down so fast that he pulled back to avoid the possibility of a painful incident.

The word did get around later. In defense of modesty and his jeans, Jeff unpacked the windbreaker to demonstrate zipper action. While doing so he had to laugh at himself. Having men work the zipper on his jeans as enthusiastically as the women had proven to be a bit too much.

Beer buckets were constantly replenished and slowly thinned the dancers' ranks as one after the other staggered out the door. When the hall was nearly empty, Jeff gave Rena a goodnight kiss. That called for more kissing, and it was some time before she left with her family and he could wobble out of the hall in Gurthwin's company.

The night was clear with a nip in the air, serving to steady his feet. They wended a circuitous path through the village, their way lighted by a moonless sky so full of stars that shadows stood out in bold relief.

Breathing deeply, Jeff felt a degree of contentment that surpassed anything he had experienced for years.

Six

Horse of a Different Color

Jeff rapped his forehead against a handy upright to distract himself from a pounding headache.

"Enough for the moment. Please!"

He felt stupid with fatigue and his brain was on strike. Gurthwin had goaded him awake early in the morning and was perched in his mind holding what amounted to a list of vocabulary.

Not long into their language lesson, the list took on the aspect of a quiver of lightning bolts as word after word was thrown at him. Handing Jeff a mug of herbal tea, Gurthwin threw another brain-twister.

The headache relented and Jeff plied him with questions about the Alarai, but Gurthwin was feeling crotchety and not to be diverted. Over the course of the session Jeff did pick up a good deal of general background.

The village was called Valholm, which meant Village by the Water, and had existed on the same spot for over fifty years. Periodic moves to escape exhausted soil, Jeff learned, were no longer necessary.

Now where did they get the concept of crop rotation this far north? he wondered. It doesn't fit. Outside intervention?

The population consisted of around 500 people, the majority of whom were related in one way or another. That's enough population to keep inbreeding down to a dull roar, Jeff mused, but not over a long period.

Gurthwin picked up on the thought. He had a surprising grasp of every genealogical line in the village and traced one of them. As he did so, it became clear that youngsters were encouraged to seek mates from nearby tribes. Gurthwin's role comprised a mixture of responsibilities including village historian, counselor to Halric, and spiritual leader.

By the afternoon of the second day Jeff was tired of language lessons. He pressed Gurthwin for clarification of his being identified with the Alarai.

Seated on a pile of hides, Gurthwin settled himself more comfortably and frowned in concentration.

"I was a mere child when stories of the Alarai were given into my keeping by the last old one to have personal knowledge of them. They were a long-lived people by all accounts and had been with us for many seasons. We were all children when compared to the knowledge they possessed and freely shared."

"Where is their land of origin?"

"It is said they spring from a small land far to the east, one that is bounded by waters that have no ending."

An island? Jeff privately thought. Could it possibly be the land I saw in my dreams? I certainly got the impression it was an island.

"I have had visions of such a land. It was given over to rolling meadows and gentle mountains. It might well be they are the same."

"While my people have only stories to remember the Alarai by, no one will forget their red hair and green eyes. I have seen the Alarai in the mind of my teacher, and they are you. Thus if the people are yours, it is likely their land would beckon you in such visions."

"How was it they found you?"

"This is not certain. I do understand that it was only with their counsel that our people survived the coming of southern Iron-shirts many seasons ago."

Iron-shirts? Whoa. Jeff sat up straight and stared at Gurthwin. "The Alarai took your part?"

"Without reservation. Nearly were we all destroyed in those battles. And would have been, had not the Alarai brought all the villages together and taught us, man, woman and even child, the manner of Iron-shirt warfare. Season after season, the invaders fought their way north only to be thrown back. Then, one spring, they did not return." Gurthwin paused, a deep frown creasing his forehead.

"It is not understood why they left. We held them, yes. We defeated them in the forests and hills, but their numbers seemed endless. One day they departed and were not seen in our lands again. This has caused much discussion and troubles me still. We have grown soft with peace and arrogant with safety, remembering the victories but forgetting that we were not victorious."

"Do you recall the appearance of these Iron-shirts?"

"My grandfather said they were small, but fierce and well-ordered in battle. It was this that nearly proved our undoing until the Alarai took up our cause." Gurthwin studied Jeff's face. "My people say the Alarai have returned and rejoice. If this is so, my heart tells me we must also have war and does not rejoice."

The old councilor was called to a meeting with Halric, leaving Jeff to wander the village for the rest of the day pondering what Gurthwin had shared.

"And then there's Gaereth," Jeff said in a frustrated tone of voice. "While I may resemble an Alarai, everything I remember about him fairly shouts that he *is* an Alarai. Were Mom and Dad right? Did he have a hand in my coming here? If so, why did he just dump me in the mountains and never show up?"

It was getting late and Jeff set his feet toward the meeting hall and the evening meal. He had nearly died in the snowfields. The memories were bitter. If Gaereth was responsible, he wanted to know why.

Over ensuing weeks, Jeff became increasingly familiar with the village's daily routine. By the end of the third week he found himself thinking in his new language. Telepathy had proven to be an astonishingly effective teaching tool.

As he gained fluency, Jeff became engrossed in comparing life in Valholm with the Europe of Antiquity. Adding in Gurthwin's stories of the Iron-shirts, the similarities were fascinating.

What emerged strongly reminded Jeff of the fading years of Roman occupation in southern and central Europe. He wondered if a similar empire had reached out its mailed fist to conquer this land, only to be defeated by central rot fueled by decades of self-indulgence.

If that were true, Jeff reasoned, then heading south as intended would likely turn up more advanced civilizations. Certainly, that had been the case in southern Europe. The Romans had destroyed local culture, but also brought education, a body of written laws and the concept of centralized government.

"Question is," Jeff pondered aloud, "do I really want to leave? These people are so wonderful."

At that moment he was standing near a field being cultivated by a horse-drawn, steel-shod plow. Next to it, another field lay fallow.

Watching the team turn twin furrows, he concluded that Valholm definitely had been exposed to outside intervention as earlier suspected. The concept of crop rotation was not simple, and steel plows a late development in most cultures. The intervention might have originated with the Alarai, but it also might have come from the south.

As the plow approached, Jeff's attention was drawn to one of the draft animals plodding along in front. In general, it looked like a horse.

However, whereas Balthazar was earthside wolf in every physical respect except size, every aspect of this animal seemed a little off. The differences were accentuated when Jeff examined the horses he was pulling with. No more than ponies in comparison, they would have passed without notice on Earth.

Jeff cocked his head and frowned as the team approached. "What a strange critter. It isn't only that he's so big. I can't remember any horse that had such a long snout, and his ears are certainly a match. They must be a foot long, and look at the way they arch over his head. How can they be so narrow and stand up at the same time?"

The team was nearly abreast his position, and Jeff could only shake his head. "I can't see over his back! Six feet tall? He's built something like an Arabian, but they're small and he's colored like an Appaloosa. Long legs, and look at those hindquarters! Bet he can really move."

As the team passed, the horse stopped and turned his head to look at Jeff. That was not unusual behavior, but he held Jeff's gaze for moment after moment. That was unusual.

"How could I have missed it? I have to call him something, but this is not really a horse. Not with eyes like that. I don't think I've ever seen that shade of blue-green in any animal or human."

Man and horse continued to stare at one another.

"Son of a gun," Jeff murmured, "he's trying to figure me out. And I always assumed horses had the brains of a chicken." Jeff moved to get a better view. "Wow. That is a big brain cage. This might be one smart critter."

The youngster handling the team raised a switch, prompting Jeff to hold up his hand. Although the right words were hard to find on demand, he conveyed the impression that he wanted to look the horse over. Pleased at the interest, the boy gestured for Jeff to go ahead. He walked up to the animal but was careful to stop out of biting range.

"Hey, big boy, what's new?" he asked, looking the horse square in the eye and receiving a look in return that was equally square. "Is he trying to speak with me?"

Try as he might Jeff could not reach the horse's mind. Yet he got the impression that he should be able to. Growing up on a farm, Jeff had learned to interpret animal body language. It was an indispensable skill when working with bulls. In this case he decided there was something going on that was definitely irritating.

Growling under his breath, Jeff pointed an accusing finger in the general direction of the animal's nose.

"All right, fleabag, don't you give me that smart-ass garbage, too!"

Jeff approached the young man and waved an arm toward Cynic, for so he had named him. "How about that one? Is he difficult to work with?"

"Ever he wishes to follow his own course, and of a morning may employ devious stratagems to avoid the harness. Yet he, when willing, needs little direction."

Throwing what he hoped was an insult in Cynic's direction, Jeff wandered toward the community hall. That evening he listened attentively to a saga being recited by a grizzled villager named Hagwane.

The tale lagged, forcing Hagwane to duck thrown food and a tankard trailing a stream of beer. Dodging back and forth, he picked up the pace.

"...And thus, hearing desperate calls, Tehric quickly slew his adversary. Heart beating with fear, he burst into a lodge all aflame and deadly. There lay a maiden languishing in shackles."

The crowd shouted encouragement and advice; some leaped to their feet in excitement. Not letting his guard down, Hagwane darted glances around the room to make sure no more food was on its way.

"Sundering the sweet maiden's fetters, Tehric did lift her to his arms and win through to the forest's protection. Then did fair Marsa recover her senses and look full upon the strength of her savior."

The audience let out a roar of approval and stamped appreciation.

Back in control, Hagwane paused to leer around the room. "Fiercely embracing Tehric, fair Marsa did fall upon him with grateful abandon, ripping his clothing in her haste to give thanks with her body. Finding her desire, Marsa did grip it most firmly and led Tehric to a soft bed of leaves."

More men and women jumped to their feet, many with ear-piercing whistles.

"Smoldering desire burst into flame and Tehric thrust her to the ground, yet was thwarted by her garments."

A female voice bellowed, "Cut them off. He must use his knife to free her body."

Responding to the crowd, Hagwane improvised the sex scene. From moment to moment, Jeff couldn't be sure who was assaulting whom.

"Holy shit! Are they having sex or trying to kill each other?"

A bawdy song that left nothing to the imagination drowned out the final portion of Hagwane's tale. Although he considered himself inured to a wide range of sexual preferences, the graphic nature of the lyrics made Jeff uncomfortable.

"They certainly aren't sexually repressed!" he laughed under his breath.

Sweating profusely, Hagwane took his seat to a round of table-banging approval and the general uproar resumed. A short while later, Gurthwin turned to Jeff with a sly smile and spoke in a voice loud enough to carry well beyond their vicinity.

"Perhaps you would regale us with an exploit?"

As Gurthwin had anticipated, a chorus of voices immediately called for a tale. Villagers emphasized their desire by pounding flagons on the table.

Bending a sour look on Gurthwin, who only smiled innocently in return, Jeff was soon put in a spot where he could not refuse as the thumping and shouting became general.

Okay, buckos, Jeff thought as he got to his feet, bowing to Halric in the process, let's see what I can do. Hope my vocabulary is up to it.

While making his way to center stage, Jeff dredged his memory in an effort to recall the epic poem, *Beowulf*. He located a few stanzas and recited them under his breath to get the meter and style. Jeff abruptly grinned.

"Let's do this right!" He leaped on top of a table and held his arms up for silence.

Opening with his desperate journey out of the snowfields, Jeff gradually became caught up in the flow of events and new words came in a rush. The barbaric setting in the hall and emotions that had barely settled spurred him to eloquence. The tale unfolded as he struggled south, death and destruction at every hand. Pausing dramatically, Jeff embellished his meeting with the wolves.

In a quiet setting, the battle he encountered a day later would have been difficult to relate. The setting was anything but quiet, and Jeff was so caught up in the tale that he chanted out every detail. The only thing he left out was any mention of the Colt.

"...Then did the sun surrender to the night, stricken warriors and their companions falling asleep where they lay. Long through the night did I pace my solitary way defending their slumber. No solace for my spirit could I find but the moon, no reprieve from sadness but that afforded by sweet music."

The story was complete, his euphoric state dissolved, and Jeff gazed around. The hall was silent. Every eye was fastened on him with rapt attention.

"Oh, no," he groaned under his breath, "what have I done? If those warriors up north happen to be related to this bunch, I might have screwed everything up."

Pandemonium broke. Bellowing Valholm's battle song, villagers lifted Jeff from the table and passed him toward the head table hand to hand. Jeff was flustered beyond words by the time he was set back on his feet, and felt something like a beach ball.

Taking his seat, Jeff was met by a probing look from Gurthwin. There was little doubt he had read more from the tale than Jeff would have wished. Halric was staring at the tabletop with what appeared to be concern.

When the crowd reluctantly cleared out some hours later still singing old ballads, Halric signaled Jeff that he would like him to remain.

"Your tale does you credit, and calls to mind those concerning the Alarai and their manner of viewing the world," Halric observed. "Long has it been since my people have tested their prowess, and you must know that they admire yours. Would you retell the story of your meeting with the warriors? I fear it contains the seeds of concern."

Jeff recounted the tale in a more factual manner, describing as much detail as he could remember or tolerate. Prompted by questions from one or the other, the evening was well along before the last point was settled.

Thoughtfully stroking his beard, Halric said, "The warriors of your tale live in two villages far to the north. Their warring has endured for so many years that its roots have been lost, yet is renewed each season by fresh injury and grievance. That their meeting should occur so near Valholm is what must be pondered. While we have experienced mild winters for several seasons, the last was most harsh. Should hunger be severe and the hunting poor, we must be alert for the coming of their tribes."

"I believe it is past time to inform everyone in this village that peace cannot be accepted as our due."

Halric nodded toward Gurthwin. "I have not discounted your counsel. We will send warriors north to determine the nature of this threat, if any."

Listening carefully to the discussion that followed, Jeff began to wonder if the area was coming out of a glaciation period. He gathered that the two tribes involved were solely dependent on a hunting-gathering economy, and held themselves aloof from tribes to the south.

A bad winterkill of game or pandemic would tip the scales. Living one step away from hunger even in good times, they would have to move south in search of new hunting grounds or starve.

The village was in an uproar when Jeff made his way to the meeting hall next morning. Every able-bodied warrior in camp appeared to be gathered around Halric vying to be included in the group that was to be sent north.

The smithy was working nonstop completing last minute repairs, equipment was being sorted, and food supplies loaded onto several plow horses that had been pressed into service as pack animals.

Jeff felt obscurely relieved that Cynic was not one of them, and smiled at his reaction. The horse was a beautiful animal, but there was something else about him that was appealing. It was puzzling.

The scouting party set out some hours later amid general well-wishing, scampering children, and barking dogs. The following days continued to be hectic as a general mobilization ordered by Halric commenced.

When Jeff wondered out loud if Halric wasn't overdoing it a bit, Gurthwin smiled thinly. "Halric has decreed that the sloth of many seasons be cast aside, that fat bellies and soft muscles be put to work in the common good. As I have already said, it is past time."

Jeff spent many an hour at the forge talking to Sigwane when the busy smithy had time, and lending a hand when he didn't. While unskilled in working iron, Jeff had spent several summers on his grandfather's farm helping with chores and assisting him at an old forge he had inherited from his father. What he recalled got Jeff off to a quick start. It wasn't long before he fell in love with the art of forging steel.

Several weeks passed before the scouting party returned. During that period Jeff poked into many aspects of life in Valholm. In the process, and without being aware of it, he became fast friends with many villagers. Foremost among them was Gurthwin.

In the course of one of their late night talks, Jeff shared his origins with the elderly man he had come to look on as a grandfather. Although Gurthwin did not appear to be shocked or even surprised, he was silent for some time after Jeff concluded. When he addressed Jeff, Gurthwin's expression was animated with intense interest and what might have been concern.

"Tell me of your family."

Jeff described growing up on the farm, his schooling, and life in Seattle. Gurthwin interrupted frequently in an effort to understand American society. His questions became increasingly pointed.

"How is it possible that men and women of your land form union? Is there no tranquility in life? Is there no peace with one another? No common ground to forge deep affection and respect?"

The expression on Gurthwin's face was such that Jeff squirmed with embarrassment. "Man and woman must nearly forgo existence to find repose, for little value is placed on quiet association and that in large part lip service. To answer your question more directly, men and women together, in American society at least, must demonstrate great maturity and resolve to overcome divisive forces that are extreme."

"Do not the strengths of association promise refuge and offer renewal?"

"I cannot reply to that question, for I feel too much anger and would not do justice to it."

Jeff's expression was more sad than angry and Gurthwin felt a wave of compassion. "Perhaps we will speak more of this another time. Tell me of your gods."

"You are speaking with the wrong person," Jeff tersely replied, "and since coming to this world I have had ample reason to question whether I know anything of value."

"That remains to be seen, Jeffrey, and is not ours to casually decide."

"Casually? You believe that I have come to this conclusion casually?" Jeff threw a stick in the fire with enough force to send a column of sparks spiraling toward the rafters.

"Do not confuse casual with frivolous, for a vast gulf lies between them. I am content to hear of your gods as you understand them."

"Damn it, that amounts to nothing! He is a stranger to me! Yes when a youth I was schooled to believe in the existence of a god, but I have experienced nothing as an adult that lends credence to what I was taught. All I found were empty words, ritual, and spiritual leaders that offered no more than banal affirmation of dogma that was so obscure as to be incomprehensible. You live or you die, and no god gives a damn either way. The only thing that matters is wealth. What more do you need to know?"

Gurthwin left the lodge long enough to dip two tankards of ale from a keg he kept outside. He handed one to Jeff and resettled himself without saying a word.

Although the silence was not uncomfortable, it was, Jeff concluded over a period of time, quite pointed. There was no doubt that unfinished business required attention.

"Oh, very well. Since my childish outburst did not dissuade you, let me relate what I recall of the god of my youth."

With no more than a crinkling around the eyes, Gurthwin replied, "I am pleased that you would share this with me."

"He is called Jehovah, or simply God, and sent his only son to Earth to live as mortal men do in the hope that he could persuade the people of that time to repent of their evil ways and open their hearts to salvation. The son's name was Jesus..."

At the end of the story, Gurthwin had little to say for many minutes. He sipped on his ale and stared into the fire with an expression of deep sadness.

"And so Jesus died on this cross for speaking the leaders' sins."

"At the heart of it, yes, and because the leaders feared the following Jesus was developing. I was taught he rose from the dead three days after his crucifixion and will come again at the end of all things to pass judgment. From what I recall of reading the record of his life, Jesus' followers truly believed that he did rise from the dead."

"But you do not."

"In my life I have found only contradiction, confusion, and a great silence. While speaking, I recall the terrible sense of spiritual abandonment I experienced after leaving home. Money rules all. It was a bitter fight before I lost my belief."

"Perhaps more of Jesus remains in your spirit than you acknowledge." Gurthwin noted quick rebellion in Jeff's expression and continued before he could erupt. "Tell me of the other gods. I assume there are more?"

"Many more, but my knowledge of them and their teachings is limited."

Jeff quickly ran out of inventory and was content to work on his ale while Gurthwin cogitated.

"You say these gods do not intervene in the madness you have described. Are you certain? Intervention does not necessarily come like a clap of thunder."

"I can only speak for myself. I have never experienced or been taken with descriptions of direct intervention or divine presence."

"Yet, as I understand it, what you have been taught suggests otherwise. Suggests an interest by the gods."

"There exists a large body of written word for every belief system, but each has been so openly manipulated to set groups apart one from the other, often to murderous ends, that the whole is now suspect.

"And conveniently so."

"Given my own perceptions I cannot deny that. However, as you have asked, why do the gods, if they exist, permit such perversion in their names? I suspect many, many people on Earth would welcome frank intervention, for I must believe their existence is as heart sore as was my own. I know I would have."

After a brief silence, Gurthwin smiled gently. "But you are here, Jeffrey."

They were sitting on opposite sides of the fire and Jeff could do no more than stare at Gurthwin. His words had shattered every thought train. Jeff let his eyes drift deep into the wavering bed of coals in a futile attempt to find the heart of his emotion.

"I was brought here by an earthquake, Gurthwin, not gods. I do so wish that were not the case."

Rather than reply, Gurthwin suggested that Jeff put more wood on the fire. It had burned down quite far and required some nursing. Gurthwin waited patiently until Jeff had regained his composure.

"Please tell me more of yourself."

"There is an event that has long cried out for understanding." Jeff related the forest incident in which he met Gaereth.

The tale startled Gurthwin at first. At the end he was slowly nodding. This common thread, he thought, must be understood. The Alarai are present on two worlds. I perceive this young man to be a binding force that promises to reveal the doom of both. Yet to what end? Good or evil?

"I will think on this matter, Jeffrey, for I am troubled by the portent of your coming. While it is certain that Gaereth is of the Alarai, my heart tells me that much is yet to be revealed."

Some days later a sentinel raced into camp shouting that the scouting party had been sighted and was carrying wounded. Jeff ran from the stable and was invited to join Halric and Gurthwin when he puffed up to the meeting hall.

He did a rapid head count as the troop streamed by and concluded that the sentinel had exaggerated.

While each of the packhorses carried a warrior, neither of them appeared seriously wounded and they were calling out greetings as loudly as the rest. A few others had wounds, but they appeared to be of little consequence.

"Let us converse," Halric said to the expedition leader, and indicated to Jeff that he was welcome to join them.

In the meeting hall, Halric set a foaming tankard in front of Gethric. "Will you tell us what transpired?"

"We moved to the north with great care," Gethric reported, draining half the tankard, "but saw no one for many days. Fearing surprise, a number of warriors were sent out to the east and west ahead of our advance. Those to the west were suddenly attacked. Outnumbered, they were obliged to fall back until reunited with the larger part of our force. Recalling our duty and mission, I urged our warriors to retreat south until pursuit was abandoned."

"They did obey?"

Holding his right fist up, Gethric emptied his tankard with the other hand. Halric chuckled and patted him on the shoulder.

Jeff chuckled as well, thinking that it must have been some kind of urging. What a bloodthirsty lot!

Gethric continued his report from across the hall while getting a refill. "They left ample spoor, and by dint of careful effort we discovered their village. The news is not good, for all that was seen gave evidence of movement to the south. Understanding the import of this, we set out for Valholm apace."

Halric dismissed Gethric to a well-deserved meal and bed. The work of dissecting his report lay ahead for those remaining. By the wee hours they had agreed on a plan.

The tribes involved were small, and they decided to establish an outpost a safe distance to the north that was larger than either. The outpost's leader would be instructed to offer the olive branch of assistance with one hand, and the threat of destruction or starvation with the other.

Four days later the outpost group departed, families included. When Jeff questioned Gurthwin about that fact, he shrugged.

"Where a warrior goes to live, so does his family. If the warrior should fall, his family will die with him."

Over ensuing days Jeff became aware of an inner restlessness, a sense of unease that came to occupy every waking hour. Late one sunny afternoon and badly in need of a break, he retreated to the stable corral and spent some time with Cynic.

Trying to communicate might be a good way to divert his mind. Cynic just stared at him, which was irritating, and within minutes the familiar tension was back again.

"It isn't just that I'm uneasy. This thing really has its hooks into me. What could it be? Shit! I feel like I have to do something or I'm going to explode!"

Jeff forgot the horse and paced back and forth in the corral until he had beaten a hard path. Try as he might, he could make no headway toward understanding. Clasping hands behind his back, Jeff picked up the pace but the tension did not abate. Completely fed up, he kicked a clump of dirt and sent it sailing.

"I've never felt like this in my entire life! What is it about these people? They're primitive, even brutal, but are so generous and open at the same time. You know exactly where they're coming from minute to minute, and never have to worry about looking for a hidden meaning. God that's great, and so are they." Jeff shook his head violently. "Dammit, this is my home. I love these people! I can't let anything happen to them."

Stunned by what he had said, Jeff stood stock-still and let the fact sink in that not only did he love them, but they also loved him. He had become a part of them, and they of him.

"I haven't felt this good since leaving the farm!"

Taking a seat on an old stump, the evening meal forgotten, he wondered at the feeling of wholeness he was experiencing.

Jeff reveled in it for a period before turning his thoughts back to the sense of urgency. Without even trying, the answer jumped out at him.

"So that's what it's all about! It has to be the South. Something is heading our way, and it isn't good. I've got to find out what's going on. I can almost feel the threat."

Jeff jumped to his feet only to find himself nose to snout with Cynic, who was favoring him with an intent cyan eye. Set against a gray and silver hide, the effect was strikingly beautiful.

"Well, what?"

His stomach was growling for attention and Jeff turned to leave. Clear as a bell, a thought bloomed in his mind.

"Are you always so tardy in discovering your mind?"

Thunderstruck, Jeff spun around. *"I have attempted to speak with you for weeks! Have you no manners, or are you simply slow?"*

Chagrined not at all, Cynic responded with a touch of caustic humor. *"I had nothing to say."*

Speechless at such a classic rejoinder, Jeff broke out in gales of laughter.

"I must accompany you, you know. On such a journey there must be someone who has common sense. Besides, plowing with stupid creatures that cannot even pass the time of day grows more difficult by the hour. Soon I must turn and savage the beasts from spite alone."

Cynic's acid comment was about to set Jeff off again when he recalled the time. *"You and I have much to discuss, bucko, but I must put the nosebag on or die of hunger."*

Having made up his mind to head south, Jeff broke the news to Halric and Gurthwin that evening. They raised such strenuous objections that Jeff finally had to interrupt to get a word in edgewise.

"With tribes to the north on the move, can we afford to believe that no threat may visit Valholm from the south simply because for many years it has not? How long would this people endure, caught between such forces unprepared? May we ignore the stories of Iron-shirt invaders, knowing they were not defeated? Yet there is more. My very spirit calls out in warning. I have never felt such compelling force, and am persuaded that if gods exist they even now move me to discover our peril. I *must* go. Do you understand this?"

Gurthwin examined the passionate conviction on Jeff's face and dismissed the objections he had lined up to present.

"You will journey south, for what you relate persuades me that it is your destiny to do so. Were you to remain, the future of this land would be dark." Gurthwin's expression grew severe. "Never doubt the gods' presence and interest, Jeffrey. I have shared your memories of Earth, but be assured that *this* land is not abandoned to the written word and its manifold interpretation by self-serving mortals. Anyone who acts on such presumption faces peril beyond belief." Gurthwin glanced at Halric. "Let us consider what must be done."

Halric examined Gurthwin's expression and simply nodded agreement.

While Jeff and Gurthwin debated alternative plans, Halric seemed to be mulling something over and eventually broke in.

"Of a summer when the sun hangs at its highest point in the sky, we are accustomed to undertaking a trek to the meeting of two rivers far to the south. There we join in moot with kinsmen to renew friendships and, perchance, arrange betrothals. If threat is discovered to the south, many tribes may be so advised at one meeting."

Halric's idea was quickly adopted. The time until the tribes got together was short, but summer solstice didn't occur until what sounded like late July on Earth.

After the meeting broke up Jeff started compiling a list. There were a lot of things to do before he could leave. Finding a horse was at the top of his list and only one came to mind.

There wasn't much sleep that night and he was at the stables when the plowing crew showed up. Those who had taken to farming were uneasy about giving up one of their draft animals. Cynic could be a handful, but he was also smart. The matter was quickly arranged when Gurthwin made his wishes known.

Cynic had never been ridden and the ether fairly boiled as they worked out whether, in fact, Jeff was going to ride at all. Then there was the question of who was going to be in charge of the expedition. More than once, Jeff felt sure it was not going to be himself.

Within several days, however, Cynic allowed Jeff to mount and responded to knee pressure with little training. Now it was time to find a saddle.

Jeff scouted the entire village but came up empty-handed. He considered riding bareback and discarded the idea unless there was no alternative. From what he had learned the moot grounds were far south and the city of Rugen, his ultimate goal, quite a bit farther still.

In fact, Gurthwin had no idea how far south Rugen was. It was going to be a long trip and he needed to carry supplies. He talked with the village tanner about the problem.

The elderly man pulled at his beard for a period then hurried to a nearby storage hut.

Hardly daring to hope, Jeff followed along and helped him dig through a pile of leather gear that had accumulated over the years. The gaffer abruptly let out a snort of triumph. The scrofulous thing he pulled out deflated Jeff's hopes in an instant.

Taking a closer look, he saw that it resembled a western saddle. Its shape wasn't the problem. The cinch strap was so cracked as to be useless, one stirrup was missing, and the leather was covered with a fuzzy crop of green mold.

The tanner took Jeff's arm and led him from the hut with a confident smile. "Return late on the morrow."

Showing up as directed, Jeff stared in disbelief at the now gleaming saddle. "I am overcome," he blurted while fingering the new, intricately tooled cinch strap. In addition to fabricating a new cinch strap, the tanner had replaced both stirrups. "Such beautiful work."

The gaffer was delighted at Jeff's response and helped him lug it over to the stables. It wasn't that late, but Jeff decided to wait until the next day before introducing Cynic to the saddle. He felt an ominous foreboding that suggested he had best get a good night's rest.

When he stepped into the stable next day, there was no doubt in Jeff's mind that Cynic had figured out what was going on. Eyes fastened on the saddle, Cynic projected such a strong mixture of apprehension and profound disgust that Jeff knew he was in for it.

"I have agreed to carry you, must you now torment me?"

"This does not look good," Jeff muttered, studying his mount. *"The saddle will not harm you, and offers a better seat to insure comfort on a long day's journey."* He held up a saddle pad. *"This device will give protection."*

Cynic was not deceived for a second. *"Comfort for whom? My back already aches, anticipating its wounds. I will not consent to such an indignity!"*

"Now look here, a lot of work has gone into this." Jeff unlatched the gate to Cynic's stall. *"How about working with me for a change instead of fighting every suggestion? The saddle is not only for my comfort. It will also assist in carrying food for both of us. You're just going to have to bear up, like it or not."*

"That we shall see!"

Thrusting by Jeff, Cynic thundered out of the stable. He put his rump to the corral fence, reared high and shrilled defiance.

Villagers came running and shouted to attract the attention of others along the way. Perched on the corral fence or hunkered down, they began a round of spirited wagering.

Saddle in hand, Jeff advanced on Cynic. Although concentrating on Cynic, he overheard the betting and winced at the going odds.

He managed to get the pad in place, but Cynic immediately pivoted and knocked him on his rear end. Picking himself up, Jeff dusted off his jeans and advanced with grim determination dragging the saddle. Cynic reared again and bolted to the opposite side of the corral.

Villagers crowded the corral fence until it was on the verge of collapse and cheered one or the other, depending on their wagers. Those who had bet on Cynic thought they had it in the bag.

Cynic pranced, crow-hopped and bucked his way around the enclosure for over an hour, knocking Jeff to the ground on several more occasions. The last time he landed flat on his back and the breath whooshed out of his lungs.

On his feet and still fighting for air, Jeff ignored the saddle. He walked over to confront Cynic, his nose a bare inch from the horse's snout.

"Okay, that's it. You have a choice. Do you want to go with me or not? Either you let me put the saddle on your back or you'll be pulling a plow from now on. Make up your mind, and do it now!"

The crowd silently took it all in. As seemed to happen during such confrontations, Jeff had forgotten himself and spoken out loud as well as telepathically.

Cynic figured he had Jeff on the ropes and ready for the canvas, but was forced to consider his alternatives. He despised plowing with every fiber of his being and could hardly wait to leave the village.

"If I must be tormented by plow or saddle, place the saddle. If I am thus wounded, be assured you will walk."

"If such occurs, I shall willingly do so. Now hold still. Please! I know this is difficult to accept. I would never ask this of you if it were not important."

Jeff finally got the job done and convinced Cynic to accept a hackamore. After venting more of his spleen, Cynic was ready to burn off some energy. He and Jeff spent the balance of the day in the surrounding country getting used to the new lash-up and letting tempers cool.

A round of belly laughs greeted Jeff's hobbling entrance at evening meal, although some sympathetic soul did thrust a tankard of beer into his hand.

Having completed preparations to leave, this was also to be Jeff's last shared meal for some time. The tanner had cooperated with a leatherworking friend to construct beautifully tooled saddlebags, and they were presented to Jeff with due ceremony and speeches.

Halric also gave a speech, as did Gurthwin, each one calling for another round of beer. When it was over, Jeff was reeling from the beer and misty-eyed from the general affection heaped on his head.

He woke up next morning with a throbbing headache and had to saddle Cynic in careful steps. The saddlebags proved difficult to attach, and Jeff asked the tanner for a hand.

While the tanner and a few friends worked with the saddlebags, Jeff secured his saber under the left stirrup. When the saddlebags were tied into place, Jeff was forced to remind his reluctant mount that much of the weight resulted from grain.

The entire village turned out and it took the better part of an hour to make his farewells. Mounting up, Jeff leaned down from the saddle to grasp hands with Halric and Gurthwin one more time. Turning Cynic's head south, they were soon lost to sight.

Seven

Camelot

Jeff flipped the compass open. From what Halric and Gurthwin had said, Jeff knew he ought to run into a large lake by heading due south. The lake's discharge river, he had been told, would lead to the moot grounds.

Sighting along the compass, Jeff wondered how many miles they had left to go. Northern tribes had no system of measurement, and Halric could only tell Jeff that it was 'many walks' to the lake.

Extending the line suggested by the compass, Jeff picked out a towering evergreen some miles away and snapped it shut. Cynic had heard the sound so often that he knew it was time to move on, and did so.

Tucking the compass away, Jeff thought, I don't really know if we are heading due south. Sun rises in the east and sets in the west, but who knows how much magnetic deviation and variation there is? Shrugging philosophically, Jeff clucked to Cynic and he moved into a canter.

Pushing south under mostly sunny skies, they enjoyed increasingly balmy temperatures. Brief but occasionally violent thunderstorms passed from time to time, wild flowers bloomed in every open space, and meadow grass was lush. They encountered many deer, grouse, rabbits and other small game.

While setting up camp one evening it became apparent there were also much larger animals about. Standing next to a tree, Jeff whistled amazement.

"That sucker has to be bigger than a Kodiak!"

Reaching as high as he could, Jeff was still several feet shy of touching the top of claw marks gouged deep in the bark. Shaking his head at the implications, Jeff decided to go over his bow one more time.

He checked the bowstring, wasn't satisfied and replaced it with a spare, pulled the bow to full draw several times, and minutely examined the arrows.

"It's ready," he finally decided, "not that it will do one damn bit of good if we run across something like that."

Upon arrival at Valholm, Jeff had been exposed to much rough humor when village archers saw what he was using for a bow. Taking him in hand they pointed out trees that provided the best material for bows, and showed him how to cut and cure carefully selected pieces of wood.

When he recurved the ends of the bow using an improvised steam bath, they argued fiercely against such heresy.

Jeff shrugged it off and proceeded to laminate the central portion of the bow with thin strips of wood using a combination of animal glue and tightly wound gut. At that point his mentors walked off in disgust.

Disgust aside, when the finished product outranged their best efforts by at least fifty yards, Jeff noticed more than one warrior sneaking off into the woods in search of new bow material.

Tanned nut brown from constant exposure to the sun, Jeff's complexion continued to darken as days passed. He wore the Northman's calf-high boots laced over jeans. A wool shirt and leather vest topped by a floppy hat added the final touch.

Sitting easily in the saddle, bow held ready on his lap, he flipped the compass open for what seemed the hundredth time and took a bearing. He snapped it shut with an impatient twitch of his wrist.

"Where in hell is it that damn lake?"

Cynic sensed how perturbed Jeff was and ambled into motion rather than put his oar into troubled waters. He wasn't particularly concerned about finding a 'lake,' but understood it was important to Jeff. Cynic *was* concerned about dark passages that might hide a bear. The claw-scored tree had made a big impression. While he had no idea what a bear looked like, Cynic most certainly did not want to find out by stumbling into one.

Early one morning they finally ran into the lake. Stirred up by a recent thunderstorm, large waves crashed onto a pebble beach as Jeff vainly tried to pick out the opposite shore.

Muttering, "Everything's too damn big around here," he climbed a tree but still couldn't spot it.

They located the discharge river and continued southward. Confronted with heavy growth forest and brush along the river, progress slowed to a crawl. The heat was stifling, and clouds of biting flies tormented them.

Stopping to listen for the river, Jeff removed his hat to get at the sweat with a shirtsleeve. Shaking his head, he laughed mirthlessly.

"Ain't we havin' fun."

Cynic was in a particularly foul mood. He had been complaining all day about the flies, and swarms of the red insects attacked him the moment they stopped.

"*Are we to remain standing until I am consumed by these creatures?*"

"Been a tough day, old hoss," Jeff sympathized. "Let's do it."

They had not gone far when Cynic stopped abruptly, ears swiveling and nostrils puffing in and out.

"What is it you sense?"

"*I am not certain.*" Cynic continued his search. "*A foul odor fleetingly passed. It was most offensive.*"

"Danger?"

"*Perhaps. Yes. It spoke of great strength and anger. I have never sensed its like.*"

Try as he might, Cynic could not recapture the smell and daylight was running out.

"*We must gain our freedom. A night in these woods will leave us open to attack. Come, let us move cautiously but quickly.*"

Easing through the brush more like a cat than a horse, Cynic's nostrils and ears never ceased their work. Whatever breeze there had been failed with the advent of dusk, the flies doubled in number, and Jeff was running sweat from the oppressive heat.

As light faded, Cynic became so nervous he lathered up and jumped at every unexpected shadow or sound. Still, he smelled or heard nothing out of the ordinary. Jeff was seeing goblins in every shadow himself, and cursed under his breath when they were forced to a halt by an impenetrable barrier of tall thorn brush.

With no room to maneuver, Cynic was forced to back out of the trap. He had no more than started when they heard a crash and the sound of snapping limbs a short distance away. Cynic tried to move faster but wasn't built to back up with any speed.

Jeff had the pistol out when two huge birds blundered by, one of them holding a fish in its talons and the other snapping at his tail feathers.

"Shit! We've got to break out of this crap soon or we're both going to go nuts. It's as bad as logging slash!"

Cynic extracted himself from the worst of it, and they backtracked looking for a way around. Jeff was about to give up and make camp when he saw a brighter window of light.

"About time!"

Intensely relieved, Jeff urged Cynic around the last deadfall in their way. Cynic was as eager as Jeff and broke into a fast trot. Penetrating a screen of trees, they rushed into a meadow. An odor that sparked abject fear immediately hit Cynic's nose. He slid to a halt and reared with a terrified squeal.

"What the fuck? Cut it out!"

A coughing roar jerked Jeff's attention to the opposite side of the meadow. Something loomed like a mountain.

"Oh, damn. Look at that bastard! No bear can be that big!" It stood over seven feet at the shoulder.

Whirling around with astounding speed, the bear rose to its hind legs. Jeff didn't think it would ever stop. In near darkness, the bear seemed a monster. Dropping back onto all fours, it let out a high-pitched roar and charged.

Narrowly avoiding the bear's rush, Cynic spurted to the opposite side of the meadow and spun around. Impenetrable brush and trees blocked escape.

Jeff knew he stood no chance of killing such a huge animal. The .357 would be about as effective as a BB gun unless he could get a head shot from only feet away. To attempt that would be insane. Either they escaped or they were dead.

Getting both feet back in the stirrups, Jeff frantically looked around for a clear exit from the meadow then back at the bear. The beast loomed like a dark colossus as it roamed the meadow searching for them in the last shadings of dusk. Quite abruptly, as if someone had thrown a light switch, twin beacons of red blazed to life.

"My God. His eyes. They're glowing red! What is that thing?"

The bear heard the cry and charged, bawling fury. Jeff picked the most likely spot and booted Cynic at the same instant. Hooves digging deep, he bolted. Protecting his face with an arm, Jeff hung on for dear life when Cynic hit the edge of the forest and launched himself into the air.

They smashed through a screen of saplings and landed in thick brush, but Cynic never let up. He dodged large trees, plowed through smaller ones, and sailed over deadfalls in prodigious leaps that never seemed to end. Scrambling and sprinting like a running back, the miles flowed under his hoofs.

Jeff called a halt when he figured they were a safe distance from the bear. Dismounting, he flipped a stirrup up to get at the cinch buckle.

"Nice job with that bear, buddy."

Although unusually subdued, Cynic replied with spirit. *"You would be nothing but a morsel for such a creature, I would be a feast!"*

Breaking out in laughter, things back in perspective, Jeff poured a generous ration of grain into Cynic's nosebag to commemorate their close escape. Building up a large fire to get some light, Jeff cleaned a number of cuts on Cynic's chest and forelegs. There were quite a few, but fortunately most were no more than scratches.

From that night on Cynic was a fanatic where bears were concerned. Jeff came to implicitly trust his horse's instinct in such matters, never questioning a sudden change in course.

The moot camp was duly encountered at the confluence of the river they had been following, the Vekka, and another flowing in from the northwest, the Farga. Caught as they were by the joining, Jeff decided to ford the Vekka.

He made sure everything was snugly tied to the saddle and urged a muttering Cynic into the water. The river was about thirty yards wide. It didn't appear to be particularly deep, but was swollen by spring runoff and flowing fast.

Midstream, Cynic stepped into a deep hole, lost his footing and fell sidewise with a squeal. Jeff was thrown out of the saddle and swept away head over heels. He managed to find his feet only to be knocked rolling an instant later. Fifty or sixty feet downstream he snagged a projecting rock and half swam, half crawled to the opposite bank.

Streaming water, an obviously alarmed Cynic trotted down the bank to Jeff's location. Having assured himself that all was well, he covered his anxiety with a tart observation.

"How you two-legs have managed to survive stumbling around in such a fashion is beyond me!"

131

Coughing and retching, Jeff was so relieved to be back on firm ground he didn't bother to point out that Cynic had been the first to fall.

The terrain slowly changed as they covered ground south in a timeless world of forest and meadow. While evergreens continued to be dominant, they began encountering large stands of hardwoods and other deciduous trees. Herds of deer were heading north for the summer, and hunting became an easy chore they both looked forward to.

One day while they were chasing down a fatally wounded buck, Cynic pounded over a good-sized hill and a new world appeared. Spread out below them, an unbroken canopy of deciduous trees marched off to the south, east and west.

It was a brilliant-clean sort of spring day, the bright green of newly leafed trees shading to a purple haze at the limits of vision. Jeff searched for evergreens in the ocean of trees that rolled away to the horizon. There were none.

The buck had collapsed a short distance beyond the hill's peak and Jeff dismounted to butcher it. Things were well in hand near sunset, and he sat down to watch the play of yellow-green and gold over the canopy below.

"This is what eastern forests must have been like when Boone moved west," Jeff mused. "I've never seen anything that comes close to it."

Next morning, Jeff pulled Cynic to a halt at the forest edge. He looked with dismay at the dense mass of trees and heavy undergrowth barring the way.

"No way are we going to wiggle through that jungle."

Turning west they jogged along for some time before Jeff spotted what looked like a break in the wall of trees. Climbing down from Cynic's back, he walked into the cut and scuffed leaf mulch aside to discover a trail. It was several feet wide and deeply worn.

"Can't be a game trail. Hasn't been used in awhile, but a lot of horses passed this way. That's our ticket."

Remounting, he clucked Cynic into motion. Ducking his head to avoid a limb, they penetrated the forest perimeter. Once inside the underbrush rapidly thinned out. The canopy of leaves was so dense that little sunlight found its way to the ground. A thick layer of rotting leaves muffled Cynic's hoof beats, giving Jeff the impression they were gliding through the forest. It wasn't long before he began to feel closed in.

The hills they encountered were low, and that along with the thick forestation never allowed an overview. The tracts of mixed deciduous and evergreen trees farther north seemed open by comparison. Yet while heavily shadowed and foreboding, the forest was in no way silent. Warbling music filled the air from sunrise to sunset, and tree boughs rustled with the passage of many-colored birds.

Confronted with a narrow trail and no escape route short of plowing through the forest, Cynic's bear paranoia hit a new peak. His ears were in perpetual motion, reminding Jeff of tactical radar antennas as they continually swiveled back and forth. When confronted by a particularly dark passage, Cynic invariably stopped to check it out inch by inch, muttering darkly all the while.

In the middle of one such passage, a coal-black animal that looked like a gazelle burst across the trail in an effortless leap. Cynic swapped ends so fast that Jeff was still going south while Cynic was charging north. Fortunately nothing came unglued when he hit the ground.

Sitting with his back against a tree, Jeff waited. It was some time before Cynic came creeping along the path radiating embarrassment.

Gradually, Jeff came to feel they were moving through a bewitched land. The forest had such presence that he half expected someone or something to tap him on the shoulder. Likely it was the trees. On the other hand, he worried it could be something else entirely.

On more than one occasion, Jeff caught himself searching for large spider webs. He felt foolish but kept doing it. The fact that he saw none, large or small, was a great relief.

Sitting close to a fire of an evening, it seemed that the trees pressed in with drooping branches. The effect was one of curiosity, not malice, as if they wished to listen and observe. Jeff had never experienced such a sense with evergreens, nor did they project the same aura of great age and brooding wisdom. Taken as a whole, the forest stimulated Jeff to explore reservoirs of musical expression that drew him ever deeper into haunting melodies that lived out of time and far beyond previous skill.

Day by day, as they penetrated deeper, Jeff came to believe that these trees at least were alive and aware. He found himself listening intently to whispers that tickled his mind and sighed like a gentle breeze from centuries in the past, whispers that could not be apprehended except through music. During one quiet evening of pastoral melody and meditation, Cynic bedded down near the fire and Jeff scooted back so he could lean against his side.

Legs folded underneath his body, Cynic attended the lilting notes and fire, finding enchantment new to his spirit in both. Normally given to deep suspicion of anything untoward or new that he could not hang a label on, this night he was content to wonder at the points of light that gathered to dance around the fire until they merged into a whirling galaxy of multicolored sparks.

Late in the evening, Jeff lay the recorder aside and fell asleep with blanket tucked under his chin. As the motes of light had come, so they left. Cynic kept vigil until the last one wandered into the forest and blinked out for the last time. Shortly, all was dark and still.

Somewhere toward the end of a day they emerged into a sun-dappled glade watered by a chuckling brook. The first opening of any size they had encountered, it was carpeted with violet flowers and thick grass.

Jeff let out a sigh of relief and Cynic a snort of anticipation. Stripping him of saddle and baggage, Jeff turned Cynic loose to graze while he set up camp.

Later that evening Jeff wandered around the glade with his eyes to the ground. The combined effect of glade and forest was so magical that he hoped to find a faerie ring. Even though it was still early in the season, the evening air had a comfortable warmth to it and he felt tired muscles relax. Giving up his search, Jeff stripped and plunged into the brook for a long overdue bath.

When he waded out of the brook, a brilliant canopy of stars sparkled and winked overhead. The starfield was so dense that the sky seemed more white than black. Jeff let the soft breeze dry him and breathed deeply of the flowers' delicate perfume.

He couldn't put a name to the perfume, but was reminded of lilacs and peonies brought to full effervescence by a warm spring day.

Lying down in a dense patch of grass, he put hands behind his head and watched the larger moon rise above the trees. Small night creatures rustled through the grass and whispered nervously to one another, serving to accentuate the glade's expectant silence. Jeff propped himself up on his elbows so he could look around.

"What a strange feeling. It's almost like something is supposed to happen." He smiled wistfully. "Don't I wish."

Imperceptibly, the glen's dark shadows gave way to moonlight in glimmering shades of metallic silver and green. Nearby, a bird sang a compline of liquid beauty that reminded and promised before fading in a final prayer. Jeff sighed from the ethereal beauty of it and let his mind drift into elvish paths.

On his way back from that land, memories of his relationship with Sarah and several other women came to mind. While the pain was gone, sadness and questions remained. He had tried so hard. Why had all the relationships failed? Was something wrong with him?

Sitting up, Jeff clasped his knees and searched the glen with longing eyes. Just give me hope, he thought. Even a glimpse will do. Do I have to go through life alone?

The glen was enchanted with cool moonlight, babbling brook and nodding flowers, but no lithe form came singing and dancing into the meadow. Give it up, man, Jeff sadly thought. That's kid stuff. There's no Luthien for you.

A shooting star leaped over the horizon and raced into the heavens, trailing fire. Jeff clambered to his feet and stared.

"That's going in the wrong direction. What could it be?"

He took a sudden breath when the object traced a parabola in front of the moon and merged into a glowing ball that rapidly expanded.

"It's going to hit close!"

He was about to dive for cover when a glittering something streaked into the glen riding a moonbeam. A crystal-faceted globe the size of a basketball came to an instantaneous stop only feet from his head and began spinning rapidly.

Jeff couldn't tear his eyes away, was rooted in place by a compulsion that insisted every flashing facet held a secret that must be understood. Then the globe exploded into his mind, filling it with visions.

Emerging from his synthetic cocoon, Jeff held his arms up to bright sunshine. "What a beautiful morning. Haven't felt this good in weeks."

He pottered around camp whistling under his breath and made a leisurely time of preparing food. When it came time to saddle up, Jeff found it difficult to leave the glen. He recalled that Cynic's mane and tail were matted with burrs.

"I should have brushed them out long ago. No time like the present."

He found the currycomb he had picked up in Valholm and went to work on Cynic's mane. Every so often Jeff stopped to lean an arm on Cynic. Something was nagging at him about the prior evening. It was frustrating when all he remembered was a pleasant evening, yet Jeff couldn't keep a smile off his face.

Once Cynic's black mane and tail were brushed out, Jeff figured he couldn't dawdle any longer and fetched the saddle. He had his foot in the stirrup when a sequence of images rushed through his mind and were gone, leaving vague impressions. Jeff laughed self-consciously. Shaking his head, he swung into the saddle.

"Talk about biting off more than you can chew. Where did that come from? Good grief, I'd give anything to find just one." Sweeping his hat off, Jeff bowed grandly to the meadow. "Thanks for a wonderful evening!"

The forest had no more than swallowed them when Jeff guffawed. "Monster castles and tropical islands? Beautiful women? Sheesh. Settle down to earth, boyo."

An hour or so into the day's ride, Cynic recalled Jeff from amused if titilating reflections.

"May this one learn of Luthien and Middle Earth?"
"Eavesdropping again?"
"Your thoughts were quite strong, horse-brother."
"Yes, I imagine they were."

There was no missing Cynic's interest, and Jeff was intrigued by its intensity. "So he's a horse. So what? It's an outstanding tale, and he's one outstanding horse."

Jeff had to search deep, but was surprised at how much he found and how easily it came to mind.

"The full tale is long and quite sad, yet also contains hope and joy."

"I would be most pleased to hear it."

"Very well. This is the story of Beren, son of Barahir, and of Luthien, named Tinuviel by Beren, which means Nightingale, daughter of twilight."

"What is a Nightingale?"

Jeff directed Cynic's gaze to a bright red and yellow bird that flushed from high grass along the trail.

"Like unto this creature, and given to beauteous song."

Although Cynic's question had distracted him, the story came back to mind quickly, and line by line at that.

"Now we shall begin when Beren seeks the land of the Elves, a most wondrous yet stern and prideful people."

"These elves—they are two-legs?"

"Yes, but please abide me, horse-brother. All will be answered as we proceed. Now, let's see—again!" Jeff took a deep breath and let mind and emotion flow with the words.

"'Terrible was Beren's southward journey. Sheer were the precipices of Ered Gorgoroth, and beneath their feet were shadows that were laid before the rising of the Moon. Beyond lay the wilderness of Dungortheb, where the sorcery of Sauron and the power of Melian came together, and horror and madness walked. There spiders of the fell race of Ungoliant abode, spinning unseen webs in which all living things were snared; and monsters wandered there that were born in the long dark before the Sun, hunting silently with many eyes.'"

"Much like bears."

"Oh, I fear these creatures were far worse, horse-brother."

An apprehensive, or perhaps delicious, thrill rippled backwards from withers to hindquarters. Head down in contemplation of the story, Cynic's eyes glazed over as the action moved south in Middle Earth. Soon, man and horse were lost in another age.

A day later they were still at it. The story of Luthien and Beren was complete and had been thoroughly discussed. In the process Cynic became a Tolkein devotee and Jeff agreed to relate the author's complete ring cycle. He also had to stay more alert and make sure Cynic didn't wander off the trail and hit his head on a tree, as had happened the day before.

When the last book was finished and Cynic had picked the series over with numerous pleas for clarification, his questions stopped. However, Jeff knew that wasn't the end of it as he monitored an intense critique running around in Cynic's mind. Jeff was impressed with the quality of reasoning.

After some time, Cynic commented, *"Truly, Melkor and Sauron were creatures of evil."* Then, a few minutes later, *"Shadowfax was the greatest of all horse sires. This one would have been proud to run with him, much as Arod."*

Jeff ran a hand up and down Cynic's neck. "You must remember, my friend, that this tale springs from myth. Many would say only from the mind of the man who wrote it."

The vehemence of Cynic's reply startled Jeff.

"This is not so! My heart understands that such honor and love as you have described were given to this man, 'Tolkien', to share with us all. This tale springs from truth!"

A day later they encountered a wide creek. Jeff eyed the placid stream with some suspicion.

"Thank God there's no boat moored over there. The similarity between this forest and Mirkwood is uncanny. Not nearly so ominous, but the power of it!"

Cynic cautiously forded the creek with water up to his belly and scrambled up the opposite bank. Jeff immediately reined him to a halt.

"Civilization, here we come!"

They were standing on a grass-covered road roofed by overlapping tree boughs. Touching Cynic with his heels, they cantered off.

"Now, horse-brother, this one still cannot understand how the king of Engmer became such a terrible creature, this 'wraith'."

"The king of Angmar. This is what I remember. ..."

Jeff dismounted when it was too dark to continue on and began untying the saddlebags.

"...And thus the king of Angmar was destroyed by his lust for power and dominion. Having given his every moment to obtaining both, and having abandoned love and charity, in the end his very substance became as nothing and his will, Sauron's."
"Until the end of all things."
"Yes."

The road broadened day by day, changed from grass to dirt, and they began encountering traffic. Most people were on foot, traveling in company, and by and large also heading south. Jeff was relieved to discover that his appearance was not that unusual.

Most were on the short side of average height, brown-skinned and tended to dark hair. Clothing was a mixed bag of coarse linen and leather like his own. Quarter staffs and staves predominated as the weapons of choice, peppered with the occasional dirk or rusty short sword. When the forest finally stopped, it did so all at once.

Rounding a sharp curve in the road, Cynic cantered into bright sunlight. Jeff threw a hand over his eyes. It took awhile before he could look around without tears blurring his vision.

"Grassland, with only a few groves of trees. Yellow Brick Road country, for sure!"

While Cynic wasn't particularly impressed with the terrain, Jeff enjoyed the feeling of being out in the open again and able to feel the breeze.

"Looks a lot like eastern Kansas. Might be good farming country. Now what was the name of that city Gurthwin mentioned? Oh yeah—Rugen. Well, Rugen or whatever it's called can't be too far away."

Excitement beginning to build, Jeff clucked to Cynic and he accelerated to a comfortable gallop. Shortly, the breeze brought smells that evoked wonderful memories: spring planting, the smell of earth newly turned with manure, the mustiness of hay and fodder.

Cynic crested a rise and Jeff pulled him to a quick halt. His face went blank with astonishment then filled with wonder and boyish rapture.

"Oh, no. Not this, too. It can't be real, it. ..."

Lost for words, he guided Cynic off the road and swung down from the saddle without taking his eyes from the large valley spread out below them.

"It has to be real," Jeff breathed. "It just has to be."

Walls soaring high and shining in the sun, pennants snapping in the breeze, a vast city rambled across hills and a sizable portion of the valley.

"Look at those walls," he said in disbelief. "They must be fifty feet high!"

As if on cue, a tenor horn raised its voice followed closely by a distant clanking rumble from within the city. Jeff followed the wall with his eyes until its gap-toothed crenels and merlons curved out of sight.

"How it shines," he whispered. "First Mirkwood, now this." He began shaking his head. "If armored knights trot out of that gate, I'm going to lose it entirely." He laughed delightedly. "What a city! If there was ever a Camelot, it must have looked like this."

Resting an arm on the saddle, Jeff watched people stream in and out of the city. Okay, he reflected, so I was expecting a tree-trunk palisade or maybe earthworks. And why not? There is nothing around here to justify a wall of this size. If it was northern Italy in Barbarossa's time, sure, but who do these folks need to keep out? Gurthwin surely would have mentioned it if there were other cities close by. Has to be connected with the last invasion.

Cynic shifted his weight. *"The sun is warm, the day bright, but are we to so stand until night falls?"*

Brought up with a start from his musing, Jeff gave his horse an affectionate slap on the rump and stepped into the saddle.

"Every man needs a horse like you to keep him straight, buddy."

"Every man does not have such good fortune," Cynic responded with good humor, and trotted down the hill.

"Easy does it, fellow," Jeff chided, reining him down to a walk. *"We need a good cover story or I'm going to wind up in a cell and you will be pulling a plow again."*

Cynic was appalled at such a thought. *"What is this 'cover story' you speak of? Truly I do not again wish to pull a plow."*

It was a difficult subject to summarize. Jeff explained why humans often found it necessary or found excuses to build walls.

"...Thus we must gain entrance and discover if this city poses a threat to Valholm, yet must not rouse suspicion."

"You have a sword, I am a war-horse. Should we not fight together?"

"Out of the mouth of babes," Jeff laughed as Cynic halted at the back of the line of people waiting to enter the city. "Okay, mercenaries we have just become."

The line moved so slowly that Jeff had plenty of time to work out the wrinkles in their cover story and examine the surrounding land. The river they had been following off and on, the Vana, flowed into the city on his left or east through a low archway in the wall. The countryside was divided into neat, checkerboard fields set off by tall hedgerows. Teams of horses could be seen pulling plows, while groups of farmers or serfs appeared to be sowing ground already prepared. What looked like small villages were scattered throughout the part of the valley Jeff could see.

A good distance to the west, he spied a cluster of substantial buildings in a park-like setting.

"Now that could be the residence of a duke or baron," he said under his breath.

While absorbed in his analysis they had moved closer to the gate. Jeff was aroused from his musings by the jingle of harness, angry cries and growing agitation in the crowd that now surrounded them.

Looking over his shoulder, Jeff saw a troop of mounted soldiers forcing their way through the crowd. The troop was enveloped in a cloud of dust that had caught up with them as they slowed down, but Jeff could see they were lashing people in their way with short whips. As he watched, a man was bowled over and fell under the hooves of the lead horse.

The road had progressively risen above surrounding countryside as it approached Rugen. Those on foot, which included everyone except Jeff and the soldiers, scrambled to get out of the way. Some were pushed over the road's verge and tumbled down the stony embankment.

Jeff had his hands full controlling Cynic, who was sidling nervously. He had never encountered such a press of humanity and wanted to get free, but there was nowhere to go.

"All right, big boy, settle down. Let's get over to the side of the road so we can look these troopies in the eye."

It was no more than ten yards to the edge of the road, but Jeff began to wonder if they could make it even that far. At one point a press of people became jammed against either flank. Jeff felt Cynic shift weight to his front feet.

"Cynic, no! Don't kick these people. They can't help being pushed around anymore than you."

They eventually made it, and Jeff took a moment to mop sweat off as he watched the soldiers come on.

"No way am I going to put Cynic over that embankment. He'd break a leg for sure," Jeff growled. He got a good look at one of the whips and pulled his saber. "Weighted ends. Those bastards!"

The lead horseman briefly slowed as he approached. Short, fat, ugly and stupid, Jeff decided. So much for armored knights.

"Off the road, scum."

Jeff was surprised that he could understand the language. Before he could open his mouth to reply the trooper raised his whip to strike Cynic on the nose. No thought was necessary.

The saber flashed up and down in one easy motion. The blade snicked by only an inch or two above the soldier's fist, severing the whip at its base. Startled by the saber whistling close, his horse reared high. The soldier cursed and drew his short sword.

Those on foot rushed north in an attempt to get clear of the fight. Troopers swung their whips in vicious arcs but the crowd flowed against them like a human riptide. Spooked by the press and panicked screaming, troopers' horses began to buck and rear. Those who retained control forced their horses into the crowd in an effort to join the fight. The combined effect stirred up clouds of dust that obscured the road in a yellow fog.

Back in control, the soldier spurred his horse toward Cynic. "You dare challenge Morgat? Your guts will feed the birds this night."

Their swords met with a bright clang as the horses' shoulders thudded together. Cynic's head shot out like a snake and his teeth clacked shut just short of the Morgat's hand. He jerked his hand back with a startled curse.

"Gods and demons!"

What a bunch of crap, Jeff fumed. Just like up north. What good will trying to talk with this idiot do? Just get me killed. Screw it! He turned another blow while trying to find an opening, but Cynic's head kept getting in the way.

Cursing sulfurously, his timing shot to hell, Jeff felt like a novice as he clumsily parried blow after blow. Fighting on horseback demanded reflexes that weren't there. At some distance he heard the cry, "Guard! Guard!"

Gatekeepers had called for backup and passed the buck to higher authority. The rest of the troop had lost their battle with the mob and been swept north. Two of them lost control of their horses and went plunging over the embankment with cries of alarm.

For the first time in his life Cynic was in a real fight. Battle fever flamed hot and he gloried in the power that was his to command. This was living; this was what he had been born to do. Lunging ahead he struck Morgat's horse, knocking it onto its haunches. Shrilling the stallion's falsetto, Cynic savaged the animal's neck with his teeth and reared to strike out at Morgat.

Cynic's charge had Morgat grabbing leather and ducking to the side. His horse just wanted to get up and run for it.

Knee to knee with Morgat, Jeff bellowed, "Yee-ha, Cynic!" and attacked. He beat down Morgat's guard and sliced opened the side of his face. On recovery he sliced Morgat's ear and left it dangling by a thread.

"Got to finish this and get out of here!"

Morgat's face was a mask of blood and he was reeling in the saddle. Jeff rammed the hilt of his sword against the soldier's helmet and knocked him senseless to the ground. At the same moment the city gate swung open.

"Hold now by order of the guard captain. Hold, I say!"

The road was packed with people rushing back and forth like schools of terrified minnows. Morgat's troop was organized and moving his way. Their escape route was blocked. Wrestling Cynic back to the side of the road, Jeff rested the saber across his lap and waited to see what would develop.

While the confused mass of humanity slowly sorted itself out, Jeff waved his hand about in a futile effort to see through the choking cloud of dust. As the dust thinned, he became aware of about twenty mounted troopers drawn up outside the gate with a plainly uniformed soldier at their head.

"The boss has arrived," Jeff muttered. "I'm in deep shit if he's an idiot like Morgat."

Motioning his squad to stay put, the guard captain walked his horse forward sitting ramrod straight in the saddle. Tall and raw-boned, he radiated anger while eyeing the pudgy form sprawled on the ground.

Shaking his head in profound disgust, the guard captain pulled his horse to a stop near Cynic. He rested gauntleted hands on the saddlehorn and eyed Jeff speculatively.

"As you value your life, I am hopeful you will have a most convincing explanation for all of this." Pointing at one of the soldiers in Morgat's troop, he growled. "Retrieve that carrion on the ground. At once!"

The worthy singled out to take charge assisted Morgat to his feet and boosted him onto horseback. Shortly, the crestfallen troop was underway toward the city gate. The guard captain pointed again, this time at Jeff.

"Disarm this man and take him into custody."

Without further comment, the guard captain trotted his horse to the head of the column. Two troopers moved in to flank Cynic while another positioned himself behind. Jeff and one of the troopers eyed each other for some moments before Jeff reluctantly handed over his saber. It was the first time in months that he had been more than an arm's length from it, and he felt totally exposed.

The trooper turned the saber over in his hands several times, the blade shooting mirror flashes as he did so. Jeff stared levelly at the man when he looked up. The trooper felt his skin prickle at the golden-green brilliance of the stranger's eyes.

Holding the saber as if it might burn his hands, he said, "If I may have this weapon's scabbard, I will see that it is quickly given to our captain."

Jeff noted a spark of intelligence in the young man's eyes and extracted the scabbard. As soon as the trooper had the scabbard in hand another swatted Cynic on the rump and they trotted into the city, hooves clattering on cobblestones.

Eight

Politics and Trust

They had no more than passed under the portcullis when Jeff's attention was drawn so many ways at once that he was distracted from fears for his personal safety.

Two story buildings constructed of masonry at street level and wood above crowded the street, blocking the sun with protruding balconies. Roofs were thatched with straw that drooped over the eaves in moldy straggles. What whitewash remained was heavily splattered with dirt. Jostling people dressed in homespun crowded narrow, winding streets and only gave way to the troopers with muttered curses.

Jeff gagged when a putrid stench hit his nose. He traced the smell to a stream of raw sewage running down the center of the cobblestone street, and to piles of fly-infested garbage.

In spite of the smells, Jeff was delighted with everything. Head turning right and left as they moved along, he became absorbed in trying to place the architecture. While it wasn't Medieval Earth, the similarities were tantalizing.

"Let's see," he said while rubbing his chin in thought, "not far enough advanced to be renaissance—more like eighth or ninth century. Still, the design of that building doesn't fit. Umm, about 1100?"

They emerged onto a broad, dirt-covered area that had parade ground written all over it. The guard captain gave his horse to a stable hand and strode into a building without looking back.

When Jeff dismounted his arms were pinioned and tied behind his back. Someone gave him a kick and he stumbled toward the building. Jeff sent a thought to Cynic as he was hustled through the door.

"We may be in serious trouble. I want you to go quietly with that dink holding the other horse. Keep your ears open and find out what these nags know."

"I will do so, but am concerned for your safety."

Pushed down a hallway, Jeff was thrust through a doorway into a simply furnished office. The guard captain had taken a seat behind a dilapidated desk and dismissed the troopers.

145

Jeff heaved an internal sigh of relief when the young man who had taken his sword hurried into the room, saluted and laid it on the desk. Shaking his head ever so slightly, the trooper saluted again and marched from the room.

The guard captain withdrew the saber and examined the scrollwork on the blade. "I am Rengeld, Captain and Commander of the City Guard. Tell me why I should not hang you."

Expecting something along that line, Jeff took a few moments to study Rengeld. About thirty-five or forty, he decided, and hard as nails. No bluster, no dummy, one serious honcho.

"I journey south hoping to find a mercenary unit that needs recruits," Jeff stated with an elaborate shrug. "The last bunch nearly got me killed, so we headed north to rest up and winter over. That fool by the gate would have forced us over the embankment. My horse might have broken a leg. He's worth a better end than that."

"Ah, yes. Morgat. Every captain must have at least one like him to complicate life." Rengeld put the saber down and locked eyes with Jeff. "While your desire to collect a little booty and remain alive while doing so strikes a note I am acquainted with, there are aspects of your person and arrival that I find intriguing." He leaned over the desk with narrowed eyes. "Although I have served in this position for many years, you are the first 'mercenary' to enter Rugen from the north in that time.

"Now, I ask myself, is this not strange? I was many things before becoming guard captain and traveled this country widely in my youth. But not to the north. The yellow-hairs do not welcome travelers from the south, and few return who choose to test their hospitality. Furthermore, these ears have never encountered such outlandish accent."

Holding the saber out at arm's length, Rengeld gazed along the blade then tested the edge. With no more than a gentle push he shaved a thick splinter from the edge of his desk.

"Well, now. And this is a mercenary's sword?" He shook a finger at Jeff and laughed. Dry and rasping, there was no humor in it. "Oh no, my friend. A good tale, but one, withal, lacking credit. Now come, tell me of your homeland, your people and your sword." Rengeld rested his boots on the desk and looked at Jeff with the smile of one ready to be amused.

Maintaining a bland expression, Jeff thought, Now what? He was about to answer with a quick fabrication when Rengeld held his hand up.

"Do not bother—I tire of this game. There is only one people with whom you and this weapon belong, and none have been reported or rumored for over fifty years. When they were last abroad, so was war. Once again the suspicion of war looms large and what am I confronted with? The Redhairs of myth return."

I don't believe this, Jeff thought with amazement. The Alarai again. Has to be! Before he could get his thoughts together for a reply, Rengeld continued.

"You are most fortunate that I am a student of history. Had you encountered anyone else, you would already be dead or in our dungeon's darkest cell."

"I am no more than stated," Jeff ventured. "I have no..."

Rengeld slammed his fist on the desk. "Let us be done with tall tales! What is your mission and intent?"

Thinking furiously, Jeff reevaluated Rengeld. Here's a man who seems to have no brute stupidity about him, and of all things is interested in history! Every historian I've known would go to any length to gather unpublished information, everything else be damned. If he is a student of history, killing me will be the last thing on his mind. The odds of meeting such a person right off are dicey, but what choice do I have?

Before attempting a reply, Jeff toyed with phrasing. While the language was similar to the Northman's tongue in structure, it was much more formal in usage.

"Too rarely do I meet by choice or happenstance with men who understand the importance of history in our daily lives. Yes I am of the Redhairs, but have long been separated from their company wandering strange lands." And that's no joke, he thought wryly.

"Urged south by powerful circumstances that defy comprehension, I seek to discover if the broodings and misgivings that consume me are true: that war once again reaches out in an attempt to crush the North. I have been sent. I am here."

Silence settled over the room along with evening shadow as the two men matched wills and strove to augur intent and integrity. Neither gave an inch. The silence continued until it

147

seemed to permeate the small room. An orderly entered and lighted tallow candles set in wall sconces. The orange light they gave off succeeded only in adding to the tension already present.

Rengeld abruptly let his feet clump to the floor and stood up. "For now, you are my guest. You will remain so until this matter is resolved." With that he left the room.

Jeff was escorted to a small cell on the second floor and his wrists cut free. The door to the cell boomed shut and was audibly locked. Later, a small hatch at the bottom of the door briefly flipped open to admit a platter of food.

The night seemed to stretch on forever. Unable to sleep, Jeff restlessly paced the room.

"Well, at least they didn't find the Colt. So far. Thank God Rengeld has my sword and not some scumbag like Morgat."

He examined the cell but found little that would encourage thoughts of escape unless he used the Colt to blast the lock. Reaching out with his mind, Jeff located Cynic's thought pattern.

"Are you well cared for, old horse?"

His call was rewarded by a mental snort of disdain. *"The stable is clean, the hay may be eaten, the horses stupid."*

"We may have to depart in haste. Be prepared."

"When it is time, call me. I will leave."

Jeff signed off for the night feeling much better. "That's my boy!"

Shortly after dawn, Jeff resumed his pacing. Breakfast of sorts was poked through the door, serving to break the tedium if not the anxiety. He was chewing the last mouthful when a bugle sounded an urgent call.

"That has got to be reveille." Jeff hurried over to the barred window.

Foot soldiers came running from the barracks. Some were still dressing while others stumbled along holding their heads, apparently suffering from too much celebration the night before. Jeff heard shouts and tramping from the stable area. Turning his head in that direction, he saw a line of horses emerge lead by grooms.

While trying to mount, one trooper fell backward and sprawled in the dirt accompanied by a chorus of catcalls. Squads slowly formed and the mounted contingent got themselves in their saddles. Another bugle call and an officer read the Orders of the Day, followed by dismissal.

Stretched out on the straw pallet that served as a bed, hands behind his head, Jeff reviewed what he had witnessed. He shook his head emphatically.

"They wouldn't last fifteen minutes against a Roman force half their size. Some discipline, but still more of a rabble than an organized military unit. There is no way this bunch could be Gurthwin's Iron-shirts."

Jeff was considering the implications when a key grinding in the lock abruptly interrupted his train of thought. Rengeld pushed the door open and strode into the cell. There were dark circles under his eyes and fatigue lines on his face, but no evidence of sloppiness in his dress or carriage.

A sardonic smile brushing his lips, Rengeld said, "I trust you have had a restful night?"

Disdaining to address the obvious, Jeff got to his feet and did no more than levelly meet Rengeld's eyes.

"You must know that our conversation of yestereve led me to solitary pursuits for the balance of the night in search of the truth in this matter. As a consequence, there is a man who wishes to converse with you. Prepare yourself at once." Rengeld snapped his fingers. An orderly brought Jeff's saddlebags and sword into the cell. "I trust you will find your belongings intact."

Well now, Jeff thought with great relief as he hurried after Rengeld. Progress! Getting my sword back is a big step in the right direction. Saddling Cynic took only a few minutes and they trotted into the city.

Narrow streets widened as they moved deeper into Rugen. In addition, buildings were cleaner and showed evidence of regular upkeep. Jeff saw no women, but men were emerging from doorways in a steady stream. A heavy-paneled door swung open nearby. A burly man leaped out in a vain attempt to catch it. The door crashed against the wall drawing loud criticism from inside.

A passerby stuck his head into the open doorway with a wide grin on his face. "Have peace, Helda. Your husband is a lout, but a well-intentioned lout."

Arms thrust out, sending the man stumbling back. A rosy-cheeked woman in her thirties stepped out into the street trying to look angry but laughing instead.

"Take you care, Reggie. Lout he may be, but withal mine to hold."

The man in question swung a friendly blow at Reggie, then they ambled down the street in close conversation. Rengeld had drawn ahead while Jeff observed the exchange. Chuckling under his breath, he gave Cynic some slack to catch up.

"These folks seem so much happier than those I saw yesterday. Nothing of the serf mentality about them." Jeff nodded firmly. "Got to be freemen—maybe in the trades and crafts—and that means a middle class."

The residential district rambled on for some time before the street, now quite narrow again, wound up a hill in hairpin switchbacks. The hill was so steep and the street so narrow, no more than steps chiseled out of living stone, that the men dismounted to lead their horses. A pocket garden occupied the peak of the hill and Jeff stopped to take in the view. Rengeld tied his horse to a bench and joined him.

"A most lovely view of Rugen, Captain."

Rengeld did not respond but also made no attempt to hurry Jeff away.

It was a humid morning and moisture softened early sunlight into a misty glow, lending an impressionistic sense to buildings that rambled over lower hills. Jeff followed the course of the Vana River as it cut through the city in broad curves. Even though shops and residences crowded the banks, he could see slender boats plying the river.

At other points boats queued up abreast waiting their turn to pass under bridges that swooped across the Vana in high arches. A round lake of good size surrounded by wooded parkland occupied a central location.

The air was still, allowing smoke from brick chimneys to rise straight up with delicate whorls until the columns dissipated, forming a bluish disk. To Jeff, it seemed he was suspended in a childhood fairy tale. Rengeld indicated it was time to leave by unhitching his horse.

As they descended, the homes gave way to a district of shops that seethed with activity. Broom-wielding men and boys were sweeping debris away from shop fronts while calling greetings to other shop owners doing the same thing. Jeff caught a flash of reflected sunlight. He reined Cynic closer to the shop that had drawn his attention.

"Well, son of a gun," he blurted out. "Glass, and good-sized panes at that. Not distortion-free by a long shot, but still pretty damn good. Now that takes some know-how."

Rengeld frowned over at Jeff. "You appear quite taken with amazement, but I fear I am unable to comprehend your speech."

"Please forgive my rudeness. Yes, I am so captivated by Rugen that my native tongue asserted itself." Jeff waved an arm around, its sweep taking in the array of shops and noisy crowd. "A most industrious scene."

"Industrious, but also troubling."

Searching in the direction Rengeld was pointing, Jeff saw two men flailing away at each other with their fists. Look like drunks, he concluded. He noticed a sign displaying a beer barrel suspended above the brawl and shook his head. Yep, has to be a tavern. Lord, some things never change no matter which planet you're on.

Bushy eyebrows coming together in a scowl, Rengeld urged his horse to the tavern side of the street and spurred him into a trot. The crowd cheering on the drunks scattered with cries of warning. Rengeld's horse plowed into the men and sent them sprawling. One of the drunks staggered to his feet with dirk in hand. Reining his horse around, Rengeld stared down at the man.

Hardly able to stand, the drunk seemed to be having a hard time focusing on Rengeld. He was wearing a filthy smock caked with what looked like dried vomit. The man's rheumy eyes popped wide open.

"Run fer it, Herk! It's tha guard!"

Herk wobbled to his feet and both took to their heels. Unable to resist temptation, a bystander stuck a foot out to send one crashing to the cobblestones. Rengeld stood up in the stirrups while the man scrambled away on all fours.

"Disperse at once. This event is closed."

Rengeld glared around until the crowd scattered, growled something under his breath, and nudged his horse into motion.

As they continued on their way, Jeff was convinced he saw Rengeld's lips twitch into what might have been a smile.

Passing through an area of large houses, formal gardens and neat rows of trees on either side of the street, they trotted onto a wide bridge spanning the river. Hooves boomed on wooden planking, and they were across. Rengeld pulled up in front of a blockish building with groups of plainly garbed people bustling in and out.

Oh ho, Jeff thought. Paper pushers. Got to be. That means some form of organization to this hodgepodge.

Rengeld dismounted. "The horses will be seen to."

Looping the hackamore over a hitching rail, Jeff admonished Cynic to behave himself and hurried after Rengeld. Upon entering the building Jeff decided his first impressions were correct. Brown-robed men and women hurried about carrying scrolls and stacks of parchment while gaudier specimens frowned importantly from behind expansive desks.

Brushing aside pompous demands for authorization to pass, Rengeld strode down a hallway and entered an alcove that had a large door set in the center of a curved wall. He rapped lightly on the door and pushed it open.

Jeff followed Rengeld into a large circular room. It was furnished with a thick carpet on the floor, wooden racks holding scrolls along the walls, and not much else except a table and some chairs. A tall, thin man in his late fifties was seated at the table.

Pushing aside what appeared to be a map or chart, he fixed Jeff with a sharp glance. Neither hostile nor friendly, the glance was so acute that Jeff concluded any attempt at deception might well prove deadly.

"I trust that suspicion has not been aroused?"

Rengeld bowed. "Matters have progressed as designed."

"Excellent." The older man turned his attention back to Jeff. "Your presence has cost Rengeld and myself loss of much sleep, Redhair, but a loss put to good use. How are you called?"

"Jeffrey Friedrick. How may I address you, sir?"

"I am Ethbar, Counselor to Imogo, Sovereign of the Northern Kingdom. I am also, at least for a time, your protector along with good Rengeld. Now, tell me *at length* of the travels that led you here."

Well, Jeff thought, this is it. You're on. It's fish or cut bait time. He met Ethbar's gaze and attempted to fathom risk. In spite of the circumstances of their first meeting, Jeff had to admit that he respected Rengeld. And Rengeld appeared to be on friendly terms with Ethbar. *This guy talks like a straight shooter, but what does that mean when you're dealing with a politician? I really need to check them out.*

That was a forlorn wish, and Jeff knew it. The sense of urgency had not abated in the least since leaving Valholm. If anything it was stronger. There were no viable options and time pressed hard. Okay, Jeff decided, *Let's go with it. This meeting did not occur by chance.*

"I have come to this land from one so distant that I have no words to convey the sense of it. Only recently have I come to suspect that the full circumstances of my arrival speak of power and skill beyond the contrivance of man, whatever their origin. But allow me to relate what I learned at a village far to the north of Rugen; what I learned of the Iron-shirts..."

As Jeff talked, Rengeld crossed his arms and stared down at the table to focus his attention on every word and not the man. Ethbar rested his elbow on the table and sat with chin in hand. Although he listened attentively, a part of his mind was tuned to the impact of the moment. He had studied the history of Rugen, now he was experiencing it.

"...And so I departed Valholm, driven south by urgency and urged on by a man who walks close to the gods." Jeff paused for effect and crossed his fingers. "Now you have heard my tale and must judge its merit."

Without comment, Ethbar motioned for Jeff to be seated. It was some time before he stirred from reflection.

"It is true," he murmured, "the times of legend have returned and I doubt not that war will soon follow." He stared thoughtfully at Jeff. "You have taken a great risk in revealing what you have. For that I thank you. Your trust will not be betrayed." Ethbar probed Jeff with intense eyes.

"What you have said persuades me that your character is sound and fuels my concern for the safety of this land. Now permit me to reciprocate trust and relate in turn what we have learned through our studies." Ethbar frowned at the table.

"Years ago this city was the seat of much knowledge if one can believe the tales and the writings, which we do. While the records in our possession are incomplete, they do clearly indicate that Rugen was first invaded sixty years ago by a people called the Salchek."

Ethbar got up from his chair and unrolled a crude map on the table. Motioning Jeff over, he pointed out various features as he talked.

"The Salchek entered Arvalia through Arzak which lies here, bordering on the southern and eastern ocean. It is a hot land, and from what little we know of it appears to hold no love for strangers or even its own citizens." Ethbar's finger moved far to the west.

"While Arzak is rumored to be a decadent country, Zomar is cloaked in mystery alone. I know nothing of its policies, form of government, or the nature of its people. I do know that while Arzak's role in the invasion suggests complicity, the warriors of Zomar fiercely resisted the Salchek and were never overcome."

Ethbar stroked his chin in silence while studying the map. "I have often wondered what lies beyond the confines of this feeble thing we examine. Careful study suggests the Salchek spring from a land far to the east of Arzak, and perhaps to the south. Ah, well. Perhaps one day we will know." Ethbar returned to his chair. "Whatever occurred to the south, Salchek armies made their way north virtually unopposed.

"At that time Rugen was little more than a collection of rude lodges protected by an earthen wall and quickly fell. The Salcheks then marched farther north only to be met with fierce opposition by the yellow-hairs, as you reported."

"And had some success for a season or two."

"Yes, the invaders made good progress and crushed tribes one by one for a season or two. At that point it appears the Salchek began suffering a series of defeats that cost them most of the ground they had won in the forest land."

Ethbar paused to refill his mug with water and did the honors for Jeff and Rengeld as well before continuing.

"It was about this time that notes began appearing in Salchek records concerning red-haired, darker skinned warriors with eyes like wolves. Warriors who appeared to be leading the yellow-hairs."

"The Redhairs."

"Or as you report their name, the Alarai. A war of stalemate continued for over thirteen years, during which Rugen was continually reinforced and its present walls largely constructed."

"An invasion seemed to me the best explanation for such sturdy defenses with no cities nearby to pose a threat," Jeff commented. "The walls are impressive. Why did the Salchek leave after so much effort to build them?"

"We do not know. Without forewarning and having suffered no serious defeats, the Salchek withdrew southward leaving the city to its own devices. It was most fortunate that northern warriors did not choose to seek revenge. Shortly, mercenaries left behind contended among themselves and with local warriors for supremacy."

"Civil war and anarchy. It must have been a terrible time for the people of Rugen.

"In some ways worse than the Salchek occupation. A full year passed before a mercenary officer named Bartel gained undisputed control of Rugen and the surrounding countryside, styling himself count. The current ruler, Imogo, is his son and has advanced his title to king."

Ethbar stopped speaking for a period while he sorted memories. It was a comfortable silence filled with reflection.

"I was a mere child when the Salchek departed. They were brutal and caused great harm, yet brought learning as well. The Salchek largely introduced the policies that regulate the city and our lives to this day."

"The other side of the coin," Jeff observed. "Great oppression, yet a system of effective laws that create order out of chaos. May I assume the Salchek built more than the walls?"

"This building, the palace, our bridges—all constructed from their designs." Ethbar gestured around the room. "Every scroll you see, in fact every scroll in our possession, was brought or composed by Salchek scribes. Yet I imagine there are now no more than a dozen scholars in this city that bother to study them, and that number declines by the year. There are no schools to educate our young; no attempt has been made to educate their parents. So much has been lost through negligence."

A look of alarm appeared on Rengeld's face. He hurried to the partially open door, checked the hall in both directions, and closed it. Ethbar acknowledged the service with upraised hand.

"Thank you, Rengeld. The door should have been closed from the outset."

"We cannot afford to expose ourselves for even a moment. If maliciously overheard, your words would be artfully employed against us. A closed door is no sure protection."

"I am aware of the risks in so talking, but risks that are as nothing when compared with what is likely to come." Ethbar glanced at Jeff. "I must also say that the risk our guest has ventured by offering us his confidence is not trivial. In my estimation, it far exceeds ours should my words come to the ears of those incredibly ignorant courtiers who fawn on Imogo and find solace in stupidity."

Rengeld appeared skeptical, but bowed acceptance.

"And so, young Jeffrey," Ethbar said, "can you doubt the Salchek I have spoken of and Gurthwin's Iron-shirts are one and the same?"

"It seems likely they are. To argue otherwise would place a heavy burden on coincidence."

"Just so. The question that might well be large in your thoughts, however, is why we share your belief that the Salchek have returned. Rugen, after all, is quite isolated from the South and rumor."

"Having viewed your map of this land, that thought has indeed occurred to me."

Ethbar shuffled through a pile of parchment and hurriedly moved to another. He carefully extracted a single sheet from the third pile.

"Thank the gods. For a moment, I feared it had been misplaced."

"Evidence of invasion?"

"Perhaps. Certainly this mere sheet of parchment aroused our suspicions. One of Rengeld's scouts happened across remnants of a body some distance south of Rugen. This was found nearby."

Ethbar held the tattered sheet up so Jeff could peer at it. The ink was smeared and the parchment looked like it was ready to fall apart.

"It is composed in Salchek script."

Jeff whistled low. "Yes, that would do the trick."

Ethbar raised his eyebrows in query.

"Forgive me. As Captain Rengeld discovered earlier, amazement leads naturally to my native tongue. To be sure, I can well understand that such a discovery would inflame suspicion. Have you succeeded in deciphering its content?"

Ethbar indicated Rengeld should reply.

"We believe the man was returning south when he was slain. All that remained were bits of moldy clothing, scattered bones, and a leather pouch. This single sheet is all that survived within the pouch, and that barely. It is one page of what can only be a scouting report."

Jeff and Rengeld shared a long look. "A scouting report having to do with Rugen, I presume?"

"This lone page has no reference to Rugen," Rengeld drawled. "Considering the other cities located close by, I feel confident in concluding that Rugen was the subject of this report."

That's a good way of putting it, Jeff thought with a smile. There were no other cities, close by or otherwise.

"And then I arrived, speaking of a mission to determine threat."

"Indeed. Once again, shall we argue coincidence?"

When Ethbar looked up from tracing idle patterns on the tabletop, his expression was frustrated.

"My scholarly regrets notwithstanding, Imogo has done well by Rugen and the Northern Kingdom. Yet now he risks it all. If only he would acknowledge what this scrap of parchment implies! He *must* come to realize this threat is real or his son, Torget, will never rule." Ethbar stared into his mug and brooded in silence

Rengeld arose to wander the room, his face a dark study. Some minutes later Jeff's drawn-out sigh broke the silence.

"Now my way is clear. I must journey farther south and discover the truth. If the Salchek have not returned, a subject state or ally might have. It is my duty."

"I believe you have been marked for this task." Ethbar found his feet and extended his hand. "We are well met, Jeffrey Friedrick. Let no one persuade you that chance contrived it."

Releasing Jeff's hand, Ethbar walked to the door with a young man's step. "We will talk again on the morrow. Much remains unsaid." He glanced at Rengeld and chuckled. "Please be so kind as to see our young guest to more suitable quarters."

Upon leaving the building Jeff and Rengeld retrieved their horses from a nearby stable. Well rested and fed, Cynic was in a feisty frame of mind and delighted in testing Jeff's seat. He cavorted, sidled, did stiff-legged hops and generally raised hell. Cynic was only having a little fun, but his timing was terrible.

"Blast you, not now!"

Kicking his legs up, Cynic replied with an equine version of the Bronx cheer. At the show's conclusion, Rengeld and a few onlookers gave them both a round of applause.

Rengeld chuckled off and on as they trotted along. "Your mount appears to be quite spirited. He is also most unusual in appearance. What are his origins?"

"He is, indeed, most spirited and also quite stubborn," Jeff replied with fervor. "I have not yet discovered where he was foaled, having come across him in the North fully grown. As to his breed, I am at a loss. Perhaps we will learn more in the South."

"I would be surprised if you did learn more. I have traveled that land widely yet never encountered such an animal."

They became so involved in discussing the merits of various horse breeds that the return trip seemed to take only minutes. When they dismounted, Rengeld gripped Jeff's hand warmly and bid him good evening.

Examining his new room, which was furnished with a real bed and small writing desk, Jeff found it to be a marked improvement over the cell. Drawn by tantalizing smells and hunger pangs, Jeff found his way to the mess hall. Once inside he was attracted by a particular aroma that led him to a cast-iron kettle suspended over a glowing bed of coals on a hook and chain. He leaned close and breathed deeply.

"May the saints be praised," he murmured. "Not coffee, but smells as good."

While eating, Jeff started getting acquainted with other residents in the Bachelor Officer's Quarters. The men were given to rough humor, but Jeff gave as good as he took. Compared to Valholm humor it was pretty mild stuff. With food in his stomach, the day's roller-coaster emotions found him out and he nearly nodded off at the table. Excusing himself, Jeff turned in early.

The night was not an easy one. He arose well before sunrise, driven from bed by restless dreams and worry. The kitchen bustled with cooks and was noisy with the clatter of pots when Jeff entered. Humid from cooking, the air was laced with the smell of herbs, baking bread and pastry.

Gingerly holding a hot roll, Jeff dipped a mug of what he decided to call coffee. Back in his room, he pulled a chair over by the bed and propped his legs up. Half a mug later his mind was coming on line.

Some things never change, Jeff reflected. No matter where you are the same patterns seem to endlessly repeat. Doesn't matter if it's a tavern brawl or political intrigue. Still, maybe he could make a difference here, or at least enough of a difference to help a few people. Jeff smiled. Not just a few people, but also my people. He marveled at that thought before mentally ticking off what he had learned.

Number one: the Salcheks came much like the Romans and had about the same experience with northern barbarians. Then they left, but no one seems to know why. Recalling Rome's final decades, Jeff pursed his lips and nodded. Most likely internal strife at home. Possibly a war of succession or an uprising.

Number two: the scrap of parchment. The habit of empire was a deep one, and even deeper was the need for raw materials of every kind from furs to minerals. Materials that had to be pumped into the empire's rotting interior to keep it going a bit longer.

Number three: if the Salchek invaded, his people would be totally unprepared to take them on. Fifty years without war inevitably would and had led to dissolution of wartime intertribal bonds. A drifting apart into tribal units that got together once a year or so like Valholm's moot.

Jeff shuddered as he considered what would happen if tribesmen came up against a disciplined army of veterans. They would be cut to pieces then defeated in detail as the invaders ground north.

Nope, he thought, crossing his legs on the bed, can't let that happen. His mind slipped into neutral and Jeff drew the saber.

Examining the blade without really seeing it, his thoughts drifted back to the prior day's meeting.

What do I really know about Rengeld and Ethbar except what they've told me? I've only been around Rengeld two days, and Ethbar for a matter of hours. Are they as open and sincere as they seem? That was one intense meeting! Maybe everything is moving too quick. I walk into that room not knowing whether I would survive the day, and walk out with stars in my eyes. It's possible they're playing games at levels I can't possibly be aware of as a newcomer. How do I know the writing on that piece of paper is Salchek; that there even is such a people?

Laying the saber on the bed, Jeff jumped to his feet and paced a tight circle. "Who are these courtiers Ethbar spoke of? What's their game? I know nothing about the power plays at court! Shit. This is all too much. I feel like a babe lost in the woods."

The pacing worked its charm and Jeff began to relax. Everything Ethbar said about the Salchek invasion dovetails with Gurthwin's tale of the Iron-shirts, he thought, and their Redhairs can be nothing but Alarai. Even the timeline is close.

Ethbar's schedule has the Salchek hanging on for three or four years longer than Gurthwin's does, but so what? It's not unreasonable to imagine the Salchek were hoping for reinforcements and didn't want to give the city up. I think Ethbar and Rengeld are what they seem to be, and God knows I still feel driven to find out what the hell is going on!

The commotion of breakfast in the mess hall was loud enough to intrude on his thoughts. Sheathing the saber he looked to his appearance. On the way to the mess hall he thought wistfully of hot showers, toothpaste and Band-Aids. The last item made him laugh, and he entered the mess ready for whatever the day would bring.

Jeff had already grown fond of some of the young officers. He greeted them by name while collecting a platter of meat and what appeared to be gruel. The trooper who had taken possession of the saber brought a circle of friends over to Jeff's table. As breakfast progressed he let them pass the saber from hand to hand. Excited question flew so fast that he barely had time to eat.

Damn, he thought, I feel like an old man around these kids. Jeff was turning that thought around in his head and finding it amusing when he spotted Rengeld. Washing down the last mouthful of gruel, he made his excuses and hurried from the building.

They took a different route than the previous day and Rengeld informed Jeff they were going to conference at Ethbar's residence. Rengeld carried on a decent conversation along the way, showing no evidence to Jeff's mind of anything but concern for the future of the city.

Rengeld dismounted in front of a large two-story building with spacious lawns, carefully manicured flowerbeds and elaborate courtyard. Talk about a townhouse, Jeff thought.

"Most impressive. Salchek construction?"

A cloud of strong emotion passed across Rengeld's face. "Yes. This was the home of a Salchek officer."

Ethbar was waiting with a fresh pot of the same brew Jeff had encountered in the mess hall. While drinking the first mug, Ethbar's observations concerning palace courtiers never let up. They were so dryly scathing that Jeff found it hard to do no more than chuckle appreciation. On several occasions he felt like roaring laughter.

While pouring a second round, Ethbar spared a quick glance for Jeff. "I must confess that what you told me of Gurthwin has lighted intense fires of speculation. He seems most astute. Will you share his tale of these Iron-shirts again?"

"I would be happy to."

As the day wore on, Jeff never stopped looking for contradictions or other discrepancies. It was a great relief when he found none of significance. In addition, Ethbar and Rengeld proved relentless in cross checking Gurthwin's history of the invasion with their own. As a result, papers lay scattered around the table in disorderly piles.

Ethbar noticed the sun was shining directly into his study, which faced west.

"Enough. Let us be done for this day." He began shuffling papers together but stopped and smiled at Jeff with twinkling eyes. "What questions you must have concerning the two of us."

"That is surely truth," Jeff replied. "I know nothing of this city, its policies, or yours. In addition, I am new to this land and must confess that its customs further confuse my efforts to divine intent."

161

"As a stranger to Rugen I am sure it has been difficult."

"Most difficult. I am, however, indebted to you both for the courtesies extended me. Were a greater span of time allotted us to deepen acquaintance, I have no doubt that a fuller state of trust would come to exist. Yet that time has not been allotted, only the same abiding urgency that gives no rest."

As he spoke, Jeff realized that his doubts about the two men had evaporated for good. Rengeld was about to reply when Jeff cut him off.

"My apologies, but allow me to continue for a moment. Our fears concerning the Salchek must be addressed at once. If they are coming this season it must be within the next three months or snow will force a delay until the following spring. Forgive my frankness, but from what I have seen of Rugen's defenses a determined siege would see its fall within a short span of time. And that leads me to an issue that is central in my thoughts." Jeff paused for effect and eyed the two men.

"What I must know is where you both stand—where the city will stand—defense or welcome if an army does arrive. I am sure you know the North will fight."

"A courageous question and one that is indeed central," Rengeld said in a deadly serious tone of voice. "I am honored that your trust has extended so far as to permit such welcome frankness."

While Rengeld's voice held no censure, it had a quality that spoke of barely restrained emotion.

"I sense the urgency you see in this question of the Salchek," he continued, "and concur totally. Furthermore, your assessment of Rugen's defenses is not far from the mark. But will we fight? Consider this.

"The Salchek built Rugen on the backs of its people. How many deaths do you imagine these great walls and buildings cost? They were built in only thirteen years! Such an endeavor normally would occupy three decades or more! How many babes starved in winter's cold because their food was sent south or north? How many fathers died in a war not their own, conscripted into service and ripped from their families? How many mothers and daughters were forced into brothels for the mighty Salchek?"

Rengeld stopped and struggled to master himself. When he spoke again, it was in a whisper that seethed with hatred.

"Such a mother was my own, taken shortly after my birth never to be seen again. I will fight, and foreswear this city should it choose not to."

Lost in his own memories, Ethbar shook his head as if to clear them from his mind. "The majority of this city's people were touched by tragedy in one fashion or another during the Salchek occupation. With leadership their descendants will resist, without leadership they will panic and give the city away.

"Imogo is a mercenary's son and experienced none of what has been described. But he stands to lose a throne, whatever its worth is judged. More importantly, his head and the heads of his entire family will be forfeit if the Salchek mount a successful invasion. The difficulty we face with Imogo is not whether he will fight, but whether he will come to believe that the threat is real in time to prepare." Ethbar looked pointedly at Jeff. "If in fact it is."

Ethbar paused to gaze out an open window at a slender tree bending and sighing in the breeze.

"There are many things I do not claim to understand in this world. First among them is the manner in which we three are met. It defies all likelihood and expectation, yet leaves no doubt in my mind that such was meant to be.

"You have spoken of your duty, Jeffrey, and I concurred. You have spoken of the sense of urgency that drives you, and I concur. Therefore, you must not dally. Time is, indeed, our great enemy."

A period of silence ensued. Jeff sipped cold coffee but didn't mind. He was at peace with his decision to trust Ethbar and Rengeld. The balance of the afternoon was spent poring over a collection of maps.

It didn't take long to decide the objective of his trip south would be Chaldesia. When Ethbar described Chaldesia, a country of rolling grasslands and farms to the north of Arzak, it became clear to Jeff that its capitol, Khorgan, was actually a city-state. Situated 500 or 600 miles to the south and somewhat to the east of Rugen, Khorgan was Chaldesia's only center of commerce.

Considering its central location on the map, the city would have to be captured or neutralized before an invasion force could proceed north. Daunted by the distance, nearly all of it open prairie, Jeff laboriously copied the most legible map.

The following day, supplied with a pouch of local coinage by Ethbar, Jeff set out for the craft quarter. Leading Cynic he wandered crooked, hilly streets in a delighted daze for much of the morning.

He dawdled at a smithy, chatted with cabinetmakers, admired colored jars in the window of an apothecary, and fingered clothing in a tailor shop. While watching a butcher apply his saw, Jeff found it hard to believe that it was real and not some elaborate set for a holo production.

Arranging to have a new quiver made at a leather shop, Jeff found his way to an armorer recommended by Rengeld. He described the arrowheads he wished forged in minute detail. Words and drawing pictures in the air proved insufficient. The design was radically different from anything the master smith was familiar with.

"May I have a scrap of parchment and a stylus?"

The master became intrigued as the design emerged, as were several journeymen who stopped to view the drawing. After spirited discussion they settled on a final design. The experience was so enjoyable that Jeff wanted to stay longer. However, he had another task to accomplish and had put it off as long as possible.

With great reluctance, even dread, Jeff mounted up. It was time to seek out the farrier. Threading through crowded streets, he tried every trick in the book to convince Cynic that he must be shod. There wasn't a chance that his hoofs would stand up to the rough and likely rocky terrain they would have to cover. He would inevitably pull up lame, stranding them both.

Cynic was totally unconvinced by every argument. *"First you must place this saddle on my back. Now you would force me to accept things of steel driven to my hoofs with deep-biting nails. You ask too much! I will not submit!"*

On the verge of losing his temper, Jeff pulled up, leaped out of the saddle and confronted Cynic eye to eye. Pointing a finger that trembled with terminal frustration, he forgot himself as usual and spoke out loud as well as mentally.

"You *are* going to have shoes fitted. You *are* going to stand still while the farrier does his work. You are *not* going to kick him in the head. And by all that's holy, if you choose to resist I'll have you strung up off the ground like a side of beef and put a bag over your head myself until you come around."

Much like an infuriated sergeant, Jeff paced back and forth in front of Cynic. "You wanted to come along; you *insisted*. No more pulling a plow, you said. And where is the common sense you spoke of? What do you imagine will happen to us when one of your hoofs is injured by a rock? Just use your head and stop shoveling manure at me!"

Jeff stopped his pacing and looked Cynic square in the eye. "You must tell me again—did Shadowfax and Arod once roam Middle Earth, or do they live in myth alone?"

In spite of his stubborn fortitude, Cynic was taken aback by the ultimatum and Jeff's mention of Shadowfax had struck deep.

"Always it is, 'Cynic' do this or that or you will pull a plow. How much more awaits in the name of this cursed plow? If I must, I must, but not willingly!"

"Well, thank God for a lick of sense. You have never been lamed and I will not see it happen now. What is a horse to do if he cannot run?"

Turning away from Cynic, Jeff was startled to find a ring of spectators looking on. As usually seemed to be the case, the strange sight of a grown man holding a lengthy, heated and apparently one-sided conversation with a horse had attracted them.

Standing with arms crossed and heads tilted to one side, they had followed every nuance and were awaiting an encore. Flushing with embarrassment, Jeff hurriedly mounted.

At the farrier, Jeff held Cynic's hackamore to make sure he didn't so much as wiggle. When his temper cooled, Jeff felt growing sympathy. He had never witnessed the process of shoeing a horse. The noise was considerable and the smell was foul as hot shoes sizzled against Cynic's hooves while being fitted.

"Thank you for agreeing to be shod, horse-brother. This is not an easy thing to endure."

Trembling with anxiety, Cynic turned his head to watch the farrier pick up a front leg. It was time to nail the shoes in place.

"I shall trust your judgment that it was necessary."

Although he knew that fitting shoes was necessary and that no pain was involved, Jeff winced when the farrier banged home the first nail. When all four hooves were finished, man and horse were both emotionally exhausted.

With each step away from the farrier, putting each hoof down as if it would break, Cynic regained more of his usual frame of mind. They had not gone far when he noticed that the cobblestones no longer hurt his hooves. In fact, he had not realized there was a problem until the pain was gone. It was a great relief, but an insight he intended to keep tucked away.

The last day in town was rushed. Jeff purchased a stock of durable foods and picked up the various items he had ordered the day before. The armorer had delivered the new triple-bladed arrowheads to the fletcher as promised. Examining the torque-free shafts and precise fletching, Jeff felt like he should frame the arrows rather than shoot them. Securing them in the new quiver, he headed across town for his last meeting with Ethbar and Rengeld.

Days were becoming hot, the nights short. Although summer solstice occurred about a month later than on Earth, Jeff figured the seasons came and went about the same. Counting days, he decided it had to be the equivalent of early June.

Considering the trip he was facing, Jeff did not think he had a prayer of making it to the moot by late July. Khorgan was far to the south and by all accounts a large city. It would take weeks just to learn where the power lay.

When he arrived at Ethbar's residence, Jeff reviewed his concerns. In the end they decided to send a messenger to the moot if Jeff had not returned by a certain date. Rengeld was solemn as he went over everything he knew about the southern plains.

"Trust no one, Jeffrey. Secret your evening camps. Do not be lulled by the grassland's rolling vastness, assuming safety in the absence of forest. Brigandage thrives in its many hidden valleys."

In contrast to Rengeld, Ethbar radiated confidence. "As I have said before, we did not meet by chance and now set out on tasks that must be accomplished. Who can say what price must be paid? That is not at issue. If we pursue that which must be, what is in our hearts, success will follow."

Taking their leave, Ethbar pressed another purse into Jeff's hand. "May the forces that guide our lives be with you, Jeffrey. Do not be concerned about us. Rengeld and I are masters of rumor and will deal with the courtiers."

Rengeld grasped Jeff's hand. "Be assured that I will post scouts to the south near the time of your expected return to lend what assistance they may. Take you care, my friend."

Nine

At Home on the Range

A blustery wind from the north had cleared the air when Jeff left the barracks lugging his saddlebags and other gear. It was early enough that no one was up and about. He had planned it that way. It was hard enough to leave without saying more good-byes.

The stable was quiet except for the sounds of horses champing hay and stomping to shake flies loose. A few stable hands were about, but they were dozing. Although he had saddled Cynic so many times that he could have done it in a few minutes, Jeff took his time. Leaving Rugen was proving difficult.

On the way south from Valholm he had been exasperated at not knowing how far it was to the moot grounds. That, Jeff now realized, had been a blessing in disguise. If you didn't know, there was no way to set up a schedule or to worry about the distance involved. Each day was a journey in itself. Now he had a good idea of what lay ahead. 500 or 600 miles of open prairie.

Rengeld had assured him there were many streams to provide water, and Cynic would be surrounded by grass at its peak, but what about himself? Did he have sufficient staples packed? Although the saddlebags were stuffed, was it enough?

Shrugging in resignation, Jeff wiggled the saddle to make sure the cinch strap was tight enough and began loading. When everything was securely attached he led Cynic to an artesian well that gushed water in a cold freshet. After filling water skins there was nothing left to do but mount up and leave.

While sunlight had not penetrated city shadows, the sky overhead was a limpid blue and free of clouds. They trotted through empty streets, the clatter of Cynic's newly shod hooves echoing hollowly off buildings. As they passed under the gate's portcullis, Jeff's somber mood evaporated.

"Well, horse-brother, we're on the road again. Who knows what new adventures await us?"

"*That such will occur I do not doubt,*" Cynic sent back with an accompanying mental snort. "*I am concerned only that we survive them.*"

Jeff affectionately slapped him on the neck. *"Have we not always done so? You were meant for these great open spaces. Now you will truly be free to run."*

For three or four days the road was busy with traders, tinkers and loads of produce heading for market. By the end of the first week the road had dwindled to a trail, they encountered few travelers, and those they did meet made every effort to avoid close contact.

Having traveled through Kansas and Nebraska on numerous occasions, Jeff found the open prairie comfortably familiar and his concerns dwindled. Although Rengeld had said nothing about animals that inhabited the prairie, Jeff was confident that with so much beautiful grass around they would run across plenty of grazing animals to hunt. It was nearly certain they would also encounter predators.

Days were hot and clear, towering cumulus clouds soaring overhead to cast elaborate shadows onto the prairie. The days were so similar to one another and the prairie so unvarying that Jeff gradually lost track of time.

It seemed that he and Cynic moved in slow motion, one grass-covered hill slowly being replaced by another in endless variation. Lulled by the syncopated rhythm of Cynic's unvarying hoof beats, Jeff let his mind roam wherever it would.

Nights they searched out convenient gullies for concealment. Turning Cynic loose to graze on belly-high grass starting to turn yellow with summer's heat, Jeff generally started a clean-burning fire with dung scavenged from the prairie. There was a lot of it, further convincing him that finding food should not be difficult. After heating the evening ration and maybe brewing a cup of coffee, he bedded down with the saddle for a pillow.

They spotted a few solitary animals that were of good size, but always at a distance. One afternoon they stumbled onto a large herd. From a position on top of one of the hills, Jeff gazed over a seething ocean of backs that covered the prairie in every direction he looked. Nothing like buffalo, they resembled wildebeest. Rumbling along, the herd stirred up a miles-wide dust cloud that rose high enough to turn the sun orange.

Dismounting to give Cynic a break, he squatted on his heels to watch the show. When the herd declined to stragglers, Jeff remounted in a sober state of mind. He had started by counting individual animals then resorted to block estimates. When the count passed 10,000 he had given it up.

Roasted by the sun, Jeff's tan turned to mahogany. Shaving was a bother and used precious water so he let his beard and hair grow long. Never fat, Cynic leaned down until he was all muscle and sinew. He rarely complained and fell into the same silent rhythm that ordered Jeff's daily existence.

They weren't far into the prairie when Jeff learned he could turn the day's ride over to Cynic. He simply pointed Cynic in the direction they wished to go and gave him his head. Muscles bunching and stretching smoothly under his skin in their own hypnotic rhythm, Cynic flowed through the sea of tall grass that rippled and sighed in the never-ending wind.

During one of the seemingly endless golden afternoons, Jeff spotted what appeared to be mountains or hills on the horizon. Day by day they gradually rose higher and appeared to be a range of vast hills.

On the day Jeff concluded the range might be within reach before nightfall, he noticed something moving well behind them. Selecting an unusually high hill, he stopped to discover who or what it was. Cynic had been nervous the evening before. Feeling the same foreboding, Jeff had strung the bow and added extra arrows to the quiver before leaving camp.

The moving dots slowly grew larger and resolved into what appeared to be a pack of animals about the size of wolves. No doubt about it, Jeff decided, they're tracking us.

"Now it is time to run, old horse; to test yourself against those who are foolish enough to pursue."

Cynic needed no further urging. He picked his way down the hill and accelerated to a gait that varied between a fast canter and loping gallop. Not wanting to tire Cynic prematurely, Jeff let him set his own pace. Although the predators were out of sight, he had no doubt they were coming on. With passing hours the hills continued to soar higher, giving hope of refuge and a defensible position.

Never had they moved together so well as they did throughout that long, hot afternoon. The sea of grass lost substance over time until it seemed a virtual ocean of green, and still Cynic never dropped off the pace. Nor did the pursuers. The prairie was their home and this was their game. Slowly but surely they narrowed the distance until Jeff could get a good look.

Not wolves, he thought with detached interest, turning his attention back to the prairie in front of them. Look something like hyenas. May as well call them that.

By late afternoon the hills were within reach. Momentarily rising in the stirrups, Jeff viewed the last stretch of ground they had to cross. It was quite flat. The hyenas had continued to close the gap and were less than a hundred yards behind. Cynic was running strongly but covered with lather and working hard to get his breath.

"I am loath to ask this of you, horse-brother, but now you truly must fly so we may find refuge and seek revenge for this day's work."

"Then prepare yourself."

Shifting his entire weight to the stirrups, Jeff leaned forward nearly onto Cynic's neck. Gathering himself, Cynic burst into an all-out gallop that took Jeff's breath away with its power and speed. He risked a quick glance over his shoulder and saw that the hyenas were running flat out but losing ground.

That's what he had hoped for. They needed time to prepare a defense. As they thundered along, Jeff angled Cynic toward a rocky promontory that looked like it might have a spring at its base.

Still a quarter mile to go, foam flew from Cynic's mouth in white streamers and he was laboring. Suddenly, he stumbled.

Positioned so far forward, Jeff's face smashed against the back of Cynic's head and he was nearly pitched off. Cynic's agony was palpable as he exerted every ounce of remaining strength to stay on his feet. Catching himself, then almost falling; doing it again.

A wailing chorus of triumph from behind spurred Jeff to fight his way upright and to lean far back onto Cynic's hindquarters.

"You can do it! Rise again, Shadowfax!"

New fire burst into Cynic's mind. With a tremendous heaving of muscles, he caught himself. Regaining his stride, Cynic poured his heart into a sprint that tore tears from Jeff's eyes.

Cynic's fight to recover allowed the pack of hyenas to close the gap until they were nearly snapping at his heels.

Pounding into a narrow declivity with a stony wall ahead and a creek to his right, Cynic slide to a rock-spitting halt on his haunches. Jeff leaped from the saddle with a handful of arrows, nocking the first as his feet hit the ground.

With their quarry at bay, the fifteen or so carnivores milled around to take stock. The game had come down to the final moves.

Chittering and wailing eagerness, the pack of hyenas paced continually. Every so often one or the other would make a tentative dash toward Cynic or Jeff while deciding on the best plan of attack. The two-legs would be easy; the horse likely would put up a fight.

Although the animals were nearly as big as a wolf, the similarities stopped there. They had humped shoulders, small ears, and gargoyle heads covered by skin rather than fur. Colored a mottled yellow, they gave off a putrid stench.

The largest of the hyenas stared at Jeff with such intelligent malevolence that he felt his skin crawl. He didn't know whether the creature had mind speech and didn't care. Gathering a mental bolt, Jeff let fly.

"C'mon, you ugly devil! You think you're going to have it easy?"

The hyena abruptly crouched like a coiled spring. His ears shot forward and he raised crimson lips to expose yellow fangs. What slithered into Jeff's mind was so alien, so vicious, that his mind tried to twist away.

"So. Puny two-legs talks. How sweet you will taste! Come to me so your death may be swift."

A wave of command washed over Jeff's mind, but it had little strength and he brushed it away like a mosquito.

"Seek dung for your meal, speaker of filth. Your mind crawls with maggots, your appearance that of long-dead carrion. Leave now, or die."

"This day I will crack your bones to suck their marrow!"

The wailing abruptly stopped and the pack raced in.

Arrow drawn until the triple-bladed broadhead nearly kissed wood, Jeff sighted on the leader and twitched his fingers free of the bowstring. He immediately nocked a second arrow without looking at the flight of the first.

True to its aim, the arrow struck the lead hyena squarely and disappeared into the animal's chest. Emitting a piercing squeal, it gave a tremendous leap and collapsed to thrash on the ground as the second arrow transfixed another's throat.

The rest of the pack seemed confused by the sudden deaths and turned away to mill about again. They wailed like tormented children, the effect doubled by a gibbering quality that inspired horror.

While he was tempted to get off a few more arrows, Jeff didn't want to get caught without a weapon for close-in work. His hand caressed the butt of the Colt for only a moment. That was a weapon of last resort and five rounds might not be enough.

Jeff extracted the saber from in front of the saddle in spite of Cynic's plunging about. Exhausted or not, he was after blood. The creatures came on with a rush.

Darting in and out, attacking in twos and threes, they swirled around man and horse. Jeff put his back to the creek, broke into Valholm's war song, and attacked.

One hyena underestimated the length of the saber and a two-handed stroke decapitated him. Whirling, Jeff backhanded the sword in an upward curve that cleaved halfway through another's body. He had barely recovered when two hyenas launched themselves at the same time.

Ramming the saber into the chest of one of them, he released the haft and grabbed the second animal's neck with both hands as it landed on him. Forced backward, he fell into the stream with the hyena straddling his body.

Fangs snapped shut just inches from his face as he rolled the hyena under the surface. The animal weighed as much as he did and fought clear of the water.

Getting his knees under the animal's chest, Jeff somehow kept the fangs from his throat with one hand while desperately groping for the survival knife with the other. Yanking it out, he rammed the knife between ribs and twisted.

Shrieking and contorting his body, the hyena thrashed the water to red foam. Pulling the knife free, Jeff splashed out of the creek and made a dive for his sword.

Close by, the rest of the pack darted in and out at Cynic. In constant motion, he whirled around with legs plunging and striking out in lightning-quick kicks.

A hyena dashed in going for the hamstrings only to catch both hooves as Cynic ducked his head and lashed out. Such was the force of his kick that the hyena was lofted high into the air gibbering insanely. It fell onto some boulders with an audible crunch and lay still.

The hyenas were so intent on pulling Cynic down that they didn't take note of Jeff until he leaped up behind. Shoulder muscles bulging with the effort, he threw everything into a two-handed cut that whistled down behind the ears of one of them. The severed head went one way, flopping body another.

Retreating to circle and snap, the remaining hyenas whined frustration but were reluctant to get in close. The bow lay nearby and Jeff picked off another. All the heart gone out of them, the hyenas turned tail and ran.

It was after dark before the arrows were reclaimed and Cynic walked until cooled off. Before turning Cynic loose to drink, Jeff plucked handfuls of grass and rubbed him down. Donning gloves, Jeff dragged hyena carcasses well out onto the prairie and set up camp deep inside the rocky defile. The campsite was protected on two sides by cliffs, and by the creek on the third.

Jeff eventually started a fire with brush growing along the creek and prepared a simple meal but a big pot of coffee. While there was little sleep to be had that night as a result, he really could not have cared less.

The following morning Jeff declared a lay day. He figured Cynic needed that much time at a minimum before being saddled again, and a full week of short days and a slow pace to recover. His decision was greeted with enthusiasm.

"Truly it is time to rest and roll in the grass!"

Stripping to the buff, Jeff splashed in the creek's clear waters for some time. Since it was a make and mend sort of day, he dug out dirty clothes for a thorough washing. Spreading a shirt on a flat rock, Jeff kneaded dirt out of the fabric with the help of lye soap.

Nearby, Cynic lay with his legs straight up in the air groaning with pleasure as he rubbed his back. It was amusing to see no more than four legs sticking out of the grass kicking back and forth.

Laying out his clothing to dry, Jeff decided to shave off his beard. Dressed in a pair of shorts, floppy hat and boots, he picked up the bow and set out on foot to see what he could see.

"I will be walking in the hills until the sun is low. Be aware that scavengers may well come to feed on the dead. If they appear and pose a danger, come to me."

Late afternoon he crested one of the hills. Jeff stopped to catch his breath and followed the range's eastern flank as it undulated to the southern horizon.

"These are impressive hills. They can't be anything but the escarpment Ethbar mentioned, and that means we're maybe two-thirds of the way to Khorgan."

Warmed by the sun and caressed by a gentle breeze redolent with grassland smells, Jeff found a nice overlook with a sweeping view to the east and settled in. Sitting cross-legged with hat cocked to one side, he plucked a stem to chew on and watched clouds play shadows across the grassland ocean far below. In the middle distance, three raptors endlessly spiraled up and down coursing the prairie.

"The sun grows tired. All is well?"

Loath to break the spell of silence that embraced him, Jeff stretched mightily and wandered toward camp.

"I come."

Properly chastised upon his return by a revitalized Cynic, Jeff spent some time playing tag with him. Later, Jeff reflected on the changes that had taken place in Cynic since leaving Rugen.

While still given to biting comments, he had matured beyond the coltish intransigence that on earlier occasion had proven so infuriating and embarrassing. His run was nothing short of magnificent, Jeff reflected. Thank God his lungs weren't destroyed. Jeff hugged Cynic's neck.

"You are a mighty horse and friend."

Cynic nuzzled Jeff's shoulder, horse and man standing in tableau while dusk faded to darkness.

Ten

Do or Die

Over ensuing days Jeff skirted the escarpment's eastern flanks. Occasionally he moved higher into the hills looking for evidence of an army on the move such as a large dust cloud. He spotted nothing the least suspicious. When the escarpment took a bend to the west, Jeff angled Cynic off on a southeast tangent.

One blistering-hot morning they cut what appeared to be a major east-west road and turned east at a fast canter. Jeff figured the road might be a trade route between Khorgan and points west. He hoped to join up with a caravan in order to soak up local jargon before being put to the test at Khorgan's gate.

Day after day they encountered no traffic, raising doubt that caravans used the road. A dust cloud some miles ahead supplied the first hint that he might have guessed right. As they drew closer toward evening, Jeff was able to see a plodding line of pack animals. There were only three outriders.

"I'm in luck, and about time. They might be willing to take on an extra hand." Jeff's face split into a dust-caked grin. "Damn. An honest-to-god caravan!"

One of the outriders spotted him, circled back onto the road and waited. Urging Cynic to be alert, Jeff exchanged a careful appraisal with the guard. Short, swarthy and incredibly dirty was his first impression.

Black greasy hair hanging in ringlets was topped with a steel-banded, leather pot helmet. The man was armed with a bow, short sword and the inevitable dagger belted over a chain mail vest. Jeff raised his hand palm out in what he hoped was a peaceful gesture.

"Greetings. I am destined for Khorgan and seek employment. The guard on yon caravan seems slight."

It seemed the man understood at least part of what he had heard, but was silent. Apparently arriving at a decision, he indicated that Jeff was to remain put and wheeled his horse back toward the caravan.

The dust cloud gradually thinned, giving Jeff a better view. He counted ten packhorses in the caravan, plus eight or so ungainly creatures that might result from crossing an elk with a camel.

"Maybe twenty people on foot," he muttered, "plus the three on horseback. Easy pickings for bandits."

The same guard trotted back and motioned Jeff ahead. As they traversed the line of animals and humans, he was struck by their ragtag appearance. One man had his arm in a sling and another was using a staff to walk. Without exception they all looked tired. Jeff concluded they had been on the road a long time and run into trouble somewhere along the way.

The guard stopped by a freight wagon at the head of the column. The man driving it was of average height, wiry, and neither old or young. Salt and pepper hair fluffed around his head, setting off a bushy mustache and close-cropped beard that still had some black in it. Beady eyes sparkling with suspicion, the driver scrutinized Jeff and his gear.

"What is your experience?"

"I am combat trained and travel to Khorgan seeking employment. It appears you are shorthanded."

The man stroked his beard in contemplation. "We are ten days from the city. For that period I will pay you twenty linta, your employment to cease at the west gate."

While he knew nothing of Chaldesian currency, Jeff did know a tightwad when he saw one.

"Forty linta, and you have a deal."

The chaffering continued until they settled on thirty linta and supplies for himself and Cynic. The leader's name was Belstan. He instructed Jeff on his duties, and the caravan resumed its plodding pace toward Khorgan.

Over subsequent days Jeff earned his pay and more. The caravan was still short several guards. Riding night patrol and providing his share of daytime protection left little time to sleep. It wasn't long before he began to question his sanity for signing on. Cynic had no doubts at all.

The other guards had two or three spare horses, but he was stuck with the full load. Still, he didn't complain. The thought of Jeff riding another horse did not sit well.

After several attempts to become acquainted with the mounted guards, Jeff quite trying. They were a clannish bunch and did not reciprocate the effort. That was fine with Jeff. What he really needed was information, and that was easy to come by when tongues loosened around evening campfires.

He learned the caravan was carrying a load of spices from Lugsburg, a city near the western border of Chaldesia on the trade route to Al Harad in Zomar. Three days out, bandits had hit them. The attack was driven off, but they lost two guards and one of the packhorses. Jeff couldn't escape the conclusion that Belstan mourned the horse more than the guards.

Four days from Khorgan and stopped for the night it was time to relax. Farmland was only a day away and bandit attacks were rare. The evening became really mellow when a clay pot of brew that reminded Jeff of rye whiskey was handed around. One swallow proved enough. Downing a long drink of water to quench the fire in his stomach, he volunteered to take first watch.

The party was still going strong when Cynic, then Jeff, grew uneasy.

"What do you sense, my friend? I sense threat, but not its nature."

Cynic tested the air from side to side. "I am also unable to locate it. Perhaps to the south."

"Let us search in that direction."

As Cynic eased across the road, Jeff nocked an arrow. He considered rousing the camp then decided not to until he had more to go on. It was a good party and long overdue. They found concealment inside a stand of scruffy trees that was barely illuminated by a moon about to rise.

Man and horse remained motionless, Cynic's nostrils never ceasing to work the night air. Music and laughter drifted to their ears from camp, but the prairie was silent and nothing moved. Cynic was puzzled.

"This nose has never failed of its task. Perhaps it has gone astray on this occasion."

A flicker of movement in a brushy area off to his right brought Jeff to attention. "It has not."

The moon was about to show itself, and Jeff picked out seven or eight people crouching through the scrub. He selected a target.

"Hold firm while I school them in our presence and warn our companions."

He waited until the last minute to get as much light as possible and let fly an arrow. The shaft flew true to its aim, striking a bandit above the hip. Screaming in shock, he fell spinning to flail about in the dirt. His comrades stood up to look around and a second arrow found its target, sending another to the ground with a cry.

Lanterns flared high in camp followed by Belstan's distinctive voice bellowing orders. Jeff dropped the bow over his shoulder and pulled the saber. Roaring a war cry at the top of his lungs, he put Cynic at the remaining bandits.

Jeff leaned over Cynic's neck with saber extended and impaled the first man they encountered, only to have it jerked out of his hand. Without the wrist thong he would have lost the saber then and there.

The bandits had enough presence of mind to form a circle when they saw that Jeff was alone. Both moons were over the horizon and bathed the land in a silvery sheen of almost light. Wondering where the other guards were, Jeff wheeled Cynic and crashed into the circle of bandits.

A flurry of sword strokes felled another bandit. Throwing down their weapons, they raced helter-skelter through the brush away from camp. Not until that moment was Jeff able to hear the battle cries, clash of weapons and screams of pain from the other side of camp.

"Oh, shit! They split up!"

Cynic heard the commotion at the same instant and sprinted toward the caravan. With no time to circle around, they blew through a herd of bucking packhorses. Jeff spotted the three guards at once.

They were on foot fighting back to back with five bandits a short distance from the caravan. They were hard pressed and about to go under. A quick glance at the caravan revealed two men on horseback and three or four on foot attacking the packers.

His appraisal required only an instant and Jeff guided Cynic's headlong rush toward the ring of five bandits with a shout. His abrupt appearance took them by surprise. They were slow to respond and one bandit lost his head, the saber sweeping it from his shoulders as Cynic thundered by.

Taking heart, the embattled guards went on the attack. Cynic knew where the action was and slid to a haunch-dragging stop. He swapped ends and took off at a dead run toward the two horsemen charging directly at them.

Selecting the rider to his left, Jeff again leaned forward with saber extended. As they closed with a rush, the bandit whipped his sword up for an overhand blow. An instant later the saber sliced along the man's ribs opening his chest to the night air, and he toppled from the saddle with a wailing cry. The stirrup trapped one of his boots and he was dragged bouncing and tumbling into the night.

Cynic leaned hard into a turn but had not straightened out when the second bandit's horse slammed into him. He was knocked back onto his haunches and nearly bowled over. Cynic struggled wildly to find his feet but the bandit's horse kept plowing ahead and he could not.

Half out of the saddle, Jeff clumsily parried a whistling stroke that ripped off most of one shirtsleeve. Cynic was about to fall when Jeff vaulted from the saddle and sprinted off.

"I will draw them away! Regain your feet and come for me!"

The bandit savagely reined his horse away from Cynic and dug in spurs. Jeff stood balanced on his toes and leaped to the side in a diving roll as the bandit thundered by.

The sword whispered close enough to nick one of Jeff's boots. Jumping to his feet, he heard a furious scream and Cynic slid to a plunging halt by his side.

"Mount quickly! I will have revenge!"

Jeff was no more than settled when Cynic bolted. The bandit had his horse turned when Cynic cannoned into them with an impact that nearly unseated both riders. Curses flew and the horses squared off. Cynic was beside himself with anger and flew at the other horse with hooves and teeth.

Although he still found it awkward to fight on horseback, Jeff's encounter with Morgat paid off. He handily parried a two-handed blow aimed at his head and lashed out with a backhand cut that drew sparks from his opponent's sword as they clashed together.

Holding nothing back, both riders tried for a quick kill. Slashing, thrusting attacks almost driving home, but not quite.

"Damn this guy's good," Jeff grunted between clenched teeth as he turned a cut aimed at his neck and counter-thrust.

Sweat running from his face to sting his eyes, Jeff realized he was dealing with a professional. Not only was the man a superb swordsman, he might be more than a match. Unwilling to accept such a possibility, Jeff attacked with renewed fury.

Cynic also had his work cut out for him. The horse he had squared off with was a big stallion and partially armored. Neither gave an inch and hammered away, adding their screams of fury to the ring of swords.

The duel surged back and forth indecisively for some time before Jeff picked up on the bandit's style of swordplay. He landed a vicious blow that glanced off the bandit's helmet, sending him to the ground with a crash of light armor. The chinstrap broke and the helmet went flying.

The bandit lay stunned for a moment before standing up. Long black hair cascaded into view to frame finely chiseled features. Moonlight revealed an hourglass figure and a way of moving that could not be mistaken.

"Oh, shit. That's a woman!"

She saw that Jeff was holding back and leisurely worked the kinks out before sauntering over to pick up her sword. On the way she gave the helmet a kick. Pointing the sword at Jeff, she laughed derisively.

"Come, my warrior. Do you fear to try your skill against a woman? Let us meet on the ground so I may know your true mettle. You have killed the man, but now must face the harder part."

The bandit advanced on foot, teeth bared and gleaming white. Dancing Cynic sidewise to avoid engaging, Jeff cursed in agonized frustration.

Leaping forward, she slashed at Jeff's leg. The blow missed but nicked Cynic's flank. Infuriated by what he saw as an attack on Cynic, Jeff leaped from the saddle.

"Damn you!"

She stood at least six feet tall, long, raven-black hair gleaming in the moonlight.

"Damn us both, man, for nothing awaits but death."

Snarling a curse, she stamped forward with sword in motion.

181

Frozen by indecision, Jeff was forced to backpedal. Concentration had vaporized and one blow nearly gutted him. On the verge of sobbing with frustration, he fought to survive while internally an entirely different battle raged. Black desperation cleared his mind.

"Cut the shit! Fight or die!"

Howling anger at the sky, he counterattacked and picked up the pace until his sword was a blur. Forced backwards by the attack, she countered skillfully and held her ground. Toe to toe, they hammered away at each other until their arms were numb from the impacts.

For one eternal moment they locked guards and were face to face. Chests heaving, they looked into each other's eyes and truly saw death—and something else as well. It was respect and the recognition that one of them would die for nothing but pride. Leaping back, Jeff disengaged.

"Lay down your sword. There is no point to this. Your attack on the caravan has failed. I do not wish to kill you."

She threw her head back and laughed wildly. "Kill me? You have not and cannot. No man will ever best me!"

"I don't want to best you. I want you to surrender. We both know that even if you kill me you will be dead shortly after. Look around." All was silent. Belstan stood nearby with the guards and drovers. No bandits were visible. "Give it up and live."

"Such soothing words! Do you fear to surrender life? Now you shall." Having gotten her breath, she laughed again and skipped forward, sword flashing with regained speed.

He met her advance with quick parries then attacked, the metallic din of combat picking up a tempo that defied human endurance. Illuminated by both moons, their dance of death found its rhythm in stamping, shuffling feet, burning gasps to find air and the bright ring of sword on sword.

Forward and back, whirling around one another, their blades winked and glittered in the moonlight but found no fatal opening. Spectators stood frozen in disbelief, seeming in the moonlight to be demons come to claim a soul.

Although his body and reflexes carried on, Jeff's mind became numb with exhaustion. She split his tunic again, opening a cut along his side. He penetrated her guard and sliced her arm, then again on recovery. Face twisted in a grimace of exhaustion, the bandit's sword drifted ever lower even though she was using both hands to wield it.

Gritting his teeth, Jeff attacked in an all-out attempt to disarm her. He could not and fell back on the defensive. The bandit was so tired she flailed at him like a novice. Bravado and overconfidence had flown, leaving a single-minded desire to win through. To survive. Yet pride would not condone surrender.

Jeff was about to hit the wall. All the signs were there. In spite of that and even though her guard was like a sieve, he could not press his advantage. Deep inside another part of his being free of introspection would not relinquish life on a whim. The bandit gripped her sword and heaved it up.

There was no thought in the smooth thrust of Jeff's arm, only a brief sparkle of moonlight on his blade before it struck home deep in her chest with a grating shudder.

Her sword fell to the ground in what seemed slow motion. Grasping the blade with both hands, she collapsed to her knees. Lifting her gaze from the sword she searched his face with unbelieving, pleading eyes. Her mouth opened as if to speak, but only a dribble of blood came out.

Unable to tear his eyes away, Jeff watched life begin to ebb, watched crimson bubbles froth from her mouth, refused to believe he had killed a woman.

"God, no! What have I done?"

Jeff tried to pull the sword free but it wouldn't come. He screamed agony and wrenched it out. As the point was withdrawn, a foaming gout of blood poured from her mouth and she toppled over. One convulsive heave and her body stilled.

Falling to his knees, Jeff wiped blood from her face and mouth, then gently closed her eyelids. Bowing his head until it touched the ground, one hand caressed silky hair.

No one moved; no one knew what to do. Cynic moved close to nuzzle his shoulder in sympathy. Wiping his eyes with a bloody sleeve, Jeff reached his arms around Cynic's neck and pulled himself up. They stood that way for some time before he crawled into the saddle.

What remained of the night passed in a haze of fatigue and remorse. The wounded were seen to, those who had died buried in a common grave, and pack animals rounded up. One of the guards had been seriously wounded, another broke an arm when he tripped on a rock and fell. Three drovers had been killed.

The caravan got under way well after sunrise to plod through an interminable day of searing heat and choking dust. They reached a small village around sunset and set up camp in a fog of exhaustion.

Security still had to be seen to, but Belstan made arrangements with people he had known for years to help out for the night. Huddled in blankets, Jeff sank into a sleep so deep that not even remorse could penetrate.

He awoke still groggy with fatigue and started to pull a boot on. The camp was quiet and he let it drop. Events of the previous night flooded in, inflicting such an enormous sense of guilt that he groaned from the impact. The sun eased above the horizon and marched into the sky, but Jeff did not move.

Entangled in blankets, head bowed, he tried to make livable sense of what he had done and cared nothing for his mission or anything else. Doubt savaged him as the duel played itself out in his mind over and over.

"Is this what I was brought here for?" he agonized. "To kill and kill? Nothing I do or say makes a difference. And dammit, now a woman! What am I becoming?"

Jeff felt pressure on his shoulder and raised his head. Belstan's face was haggard and drawn, accentuating an expression of genuine concern.

"Food has been prepared and will help."

Roused by the unexpected compassion, Jeff got to his feet. He was about to follow Belstan when he remembered that Cynic had been wounded. The cut was about four inches long and so crusted with dirt he couldn't tell how deep it was.

Silently faulting himself for not having taken action sooner, Jeff hurried to find some clean water and washed the cut.

"Oh, damn, that is not good."

The cut appeared to be at least half an inch deep. He felt around the cut and groaned. The skin was hot and seemed swollen. Spreading the cut a bit he notice some yellow fluid down deeper. Pus. It had to be.

"You dumb shit, Friedrick."

A drover happened by while Jeff was trying to decide what to do. The drover, Garthok, took a good look at the wound and then examined Jeff with a neutral expression.

"It ain't as bad as it looks. Just been sittin' too long."

"Yes, it has."

After a period of silent reproof, Garthok said, "Well, I guess ya gotta learn sometime." He hurried off, saying over his shoulder, "I got some stuff that will fix it up."

Garthok supplied a pot of foul-smelling ointment laced with what looked like strands of fungus or mold. He showed Jeff how to apply it and left without another word.

Breakfast was nothing more than stale bread and cheese. Belstan waited until Jeff had emptied his second mug of coffee before ambling over to sit down.

"I was close witness to your duel, and have lived long enough to know what taking her life cost you. Yet, often do female bandits fight alongside the men." Belstan peered intently into Jeff's eyes. "While there are not sufficient words to console the agony this event has caused you, be aware that given the opportunity she would have killed you without thought or remorse. Yet she could not. I have traveled this land for more years than I wish to remember, but have never seen such sword skill." He paused for a brief moment. "And never have I encountered such an unusual young man."

Jeff experienced a flash of alarm but any response was forestalled by Belstan's upraised hand.

"You owe me no explanation. It is I who owe you more than can easily be repaid, for you have saved both my livelihood and the lives of us all." A crooked smile creased Belstan's face. "Although I am not known for easy generosity, let me say that whatever I can do for you will be done. Given the condition of this caravan, I will be further indebted if you would consent to overseeing its safe arrival at my agent's office in Khorgan."

"Will the men accept my decisions? I am a newcomer."

"They have come to respect you and are concerned that you will leave. We are still two days hard travel from the city. Please think over my proposition."

It required some time for Belstan to recruit replacements in the village, delaying their start until late in the morning. The day went smoothly enough once they were underway, and the time of danger had passed.

Villages dotted the rolling countryside, and most of the arable land was under cultivation. Maturing crops laid out in orderly squares marched to the horizon, broken here and there by rows of tall trees that resembled poplars.

Belstan called a halt before dusk near a lazy river that curved around a good-sized town. The road had widened into a major highway shortly after entering farmland. Heavy traffic bustled by in both directions as travelers hurried to find a night's lodging.

There weren't many good spots left in the grassy area used as a campground, and another caravan was closing up behind.

With a hundred yards to go the following caravan put on a burst of speed and tried to pass. Belstan saw them coming and whistled up his team. The race was on. It was an exciting dash that bordered on a stampede, serving to lift Jeff's spirits.

The caravan was no more than settled for the night when Jeff hurried to the river. Disregarding modesty, he peeled off filthy, blood-soaked clothes and jumped in.

Scrubbing off layers of dirt, he swam out into the river to escape the noise. It was a gently flowing stream, barely cool, and bordered by trees with rich green leaves. Floating on his back, Jeff could hardly take his eyes off them. After days of choking dust and arid conditions, the trees seemed a miraculous creation.

Other caravans arrived as the day dwindled. Although Jeff was sunning well out on a sandbar, the arguments that resulted as caravans squeezed into camp drifted to his ears with volume to spare. Shortly a number of flying bodies plunged into the river seeking relief from the heat and dust.

Jeff felt shy until he noticed that no one else was. Men and women alike, they swam in the nude and beat the water to a froth with their antics. Wading around a particularly spirited water fight, Jeff went to fetch Cynic.

Equipped with a bucket and brush, he enticed Cynic far out onto the sandbar until the water was clear and lapping at his belly. Jeff washed the cut on Cynic's flank, dipped a full bucket from the river and poured it over his back. When Jeff set to scrubbing him with the brush, Cynic's mental sigh of relief and pleasure was so profound that Jeff chuckled.

Exile To The Stars

It was dark when they called it quits. Along the way to camp, lanterns and campfires glowed like giant fireflies illuminating people dancing to gypsy music. Humming in time to the music, Jeff patted the cut dry and applied more of the salve.

Cynic fidgeted when he felt the sting and he hated the smell. Still, the wound was nice and pink and didn't seem so deep. Jeff slathered the ointment on thick. Later, dressed in spare clothing that was worn threadbare but at least clean, he approached Belstan.

"I accept your offer and appreciate the trust you are willing to place in me."

Belstan nodded acceptance. "You could have deserted the caravan without risk when it was attacked. Many would have done so. That you did not recommends your character. The manner in which you then defended the caravan speaks highly of your ability to keep your wits when hard pressed. I could ask for no more."

It was a fine cool morning, and Jeff rode at the head of the caravan next to Belstan's freight wagon. While it was nice to be free of the dust for a period, what Jeff really wanted was more information. Khorgan was only a day away. They passed the time chatting about the city, which Jeff guardedly admitted he had never visited.

"Ah, Khorgan, jewel of Chaldesia. Center of commerce, seat of power, and home to every vice a man might imagine." Belstan's smile disappeared. "It is not a city to trifle with, my young friend, for its bite can be deep and swift. Much of what is good in this world may be found there, but everything that is evil. It is a merchant city run by a council of twelve men and women corrupted by avarice and sated with every pleasure that power can command. Khorgan is also the center of every intrigue that is hatched for hundreds of septa in any direction you might travel." After a brief period of silence, Belstan threw a sly look at Jeff. "Except to the north."

Jeff was caught by surprise, his face showed it, and Belstan laughed with satisfaction.

"Do not be alarmed. Your origins are safe with me and I doubt others in the city will mark your appearance so consumed are they with their own plots. You would be well advised, however,

187

to cut your hair short and," pointing at Jeff's tattered jeans, "purchase clothing not so foreign to this land."

As the day passed and Belstan extolled the virtues and vices of Khorgan, Jeff's interest continued to grow. It promised to be some kind of city. Trying to get a grip on how long a septa was, he asked Belstan to mark it out as the wagon moved along. While no more than an estimate, it appeared a septa was close to a terran mile in length.

By late afternoon it became clear they would not reach the city before sunset. Belstan was not anxious to attempt entry after dark and halted the caravan several hours shy of the western gate. Throughout much of the evening Belstan and other caravan members continued to expand Jeff's knowledge of Khorgan

The overall impression he got was of a walled city three times as large as Rugen surrounded by businesses, crafts and residences that doubled its size. Belstan's agent, whose name was Rogelf, owned a warehouse on the shore of a lake directly across town from the western gate. In order to avoid a long trip around Khorgan, Belstan intended to cut through its center the following day. That night, Jeff cropped his hair short.

They had not been on the road long the next day before entering the fringes of what Belstan referred to as Newtown to distinguish it from the original city. Unconfined by walls, the roads were broad and clear of garbage.

Jeff commented on that fact to Belstan, who shrugged. "It has been thus for many years. A fee is charged, more often than not the refuse taken away. Water is also piped into central areas, again for a fee. Those who seek to avoid the fees are fined and may be imprisoned. Unless, of course, they can afford the bribe."

Everyone, it seemed, was on the take.

Well into Newtown, Belstan stopped the caravan. Motioning for Jeff to follow, he trotted across the street and into a shop that smelled strongly of tanned leather and was lighted by dust-filtered sunlight. The shop's gray-haired proprietor hurried to meet them.

"Belstan, you old thief. I am surprised no one has yet slit your weasand."

"Not for want of trying, Crofel," Belstan replied while clasping arms. "Let us see some clothing for this young man."

When they left the store Jeff had donned a pair of snugly fitting leather pants, a soft leather vest, and new calf-high footwear that reminded him of jackboots. Retaining his floppy hat, Jeff purchased a bright feather to stick in its crown. Belstan waved away his thanks.

"Merely a tithe, my boy. Merely a tithe."

Later that morning the caravan nosed into a large plaza. Leading the way, Jeff reined Cynic over to the side to make way for those coming behind. Belstan stopped his wagon when it was abreast Cynic. He smiled broadly at the look of astonishment on Jeff's face.

"The main bazaar, not to mention the pride of Khorgan."

The plaza was at least two city blocks to a side, Jeff estimated, but the impact of the bazaar was not confined to its size. A babble of voices roared in his ears. Jeff was dumbfounded. He had seen his share of old movies set in one Middle Eastern market or the other, but this was something else entirely.

Shaking his head in disbelief, Jeff clucked Cynic back into motion. "It's full. The whole plaza is full of people. There must be thousands of them. Outrageous!" He caught himself and switched back to northland speech. "I could not have imagined that such a wonderful place existed."

Belstan did not respond. While the bazaar was impressive, it was not that unusual. He pondered Jeff's origins again. He had become convinced the young man was from the North. Now he wasn't sure at all. He had never heard such an outlandish tongue.

The crowd grudgingly made way for the caravan as Belstan maneuvered it close to one side of the plaza where the crowd seemed thinner. Jeff was so overwhelmed by the bazaar that he hardly noticed the change of direction.

Smoke rose from numerous stalls selling food, creating a roiling concoction of odors that were entirely new and smelled so good his appetite went into high gear. Vendors and shills hawking a hundred different shops and services shouted to be heard. Beggars pulled at his stirrup with palm outstretched in supplication. Jugglers, acrobats and sleight of hand artists gathered crowds of people, all the while throwing, tumbling and bellowing their spiels.

Although captivated by the bazaar, Jeff quickly diverted his attention to buildings fronting the plaza. Women dressed in low-cut filmy gowns that hid nothing shimmied and wiggled on second floor balconies along much of the plaza's length. Every so often, one or the other would stop to gesture or call down to someone in the crowd below.

Seeing him staring open-mouthed, one of the women plucked a flower from a rainbow cascade and threw it to him, blowing a kiss as she did so. Jeff laughed shamefacedly and waved. The woman, a stunning brunette, frowned down at him with hands on hips. Jeff laughed again and cupped hands around his mouth.

"You are beautiful. Perhaps another day."

Several streets beyond the bazaar they were confronted by the west gate. Belstan greeted the guards by name and slipped a pouch of coins to the sergeant, who waved the caravan ahead as he tucked it away. Hooves that had been muffled by the packed dirt streets of Newtown abruptly clattered on paving.

Eleven

Redheaded Terror

"Brick streets, and laid in patterns at that. Real sidewalks! This is astounding!" Jeff looked around with delight. "I can't believe this. Khorgan really is some kind of city!"

Angry shouts from up ahead reminded him of his duties. The street was twice as wide as any in Rugen but still choked with traffic. Cynic liked a challenge and hurried through the gridlock with deft moves and some not very discreet shoulder blocks on other horses.

Ignoring the outraged curses that resulted, Jeff guided the caravan through an intersection and immediately turned his attention back to the city.

Brick buildings fronting the street were as tall as three stories. He had seen glass windows in Rugen, but the large display windows they passed would have drawn no criticism in Seattle.

Elaborate signs and colorful bunting sprouted and fluttered over the doors of businesses along the street, drawing Jeff's attention away from wrought-iron lamp standards. Sidewalk cafes, open-air markets, the rumble of traffic and crowd noise— energy filled the air.

Checking to make sure the caravan was together, Jeff studied people on either side of the street. They were dressed in such a bewildering variety of clothing that he couldn't pick out a dominant theme.

Turbans and caftans, soldiers in a wild mix of doublets and pantaloons, portly men dressed in broadcloth suits—the variety seemed endless. While the variety in dress was less among women, the color of their attire ran the rainbow's spectrum. Long hair and long dresses tending to the conservative seemed to be the trend.

Jeff heard the jingle of horses coming up behind and had to give all his attention to maneuvering the caravan to the side of the street. Shortly, twenty or so dragoons passed at a quick trot. When the caravan was moving again, Jeff walked Cynic to the front of the column.

"Belstan, are those troopers part of an army or do they report to the city counsel?"

"Civil Guard answering to the council," Belstan replied sourly, "and a surly lot by and large. Stay clear of them if at all possible, or have gold in your pocket to buy your way free."

The afternoon was well along before they exited the eastern gate and turned onto Marine Way. The lake side of the street was crowded with warehouses but Jeff noticed that only in passing. A forest of masts stretched along the waterfront.

"Holy shit, there must be hundreds of ships!" The caravan moved between two warehouses, providing Jeff an unobstructed view of the lake. "Those aren't waves, they're swells. It must be a real monster."

Driven by a storm far to the east, large swells pounded the seawall with spray bursting over the top. Ships heaved and gyrated at their moorings, singing a dolorous refrain as they ground against piers.

Belstan grinned at Jeff's unbelieving expression.

"Lake Ligura. Impressive, is it not?"

Jeff could only nod agreement.

Lamps were being lighted along the waterfront and the smell of cooking food spiced the air. The crowd was boisterous, largely on foot and filing into taverns along the street. Jeff cocked an ear to listen to music drifting from a nearby inn. It sounded shrill as it wailed through a minor key, but fit in perfectly with the sound of swells as they crashed into the seawall.

It was dark when Belstan pointed to a brightly painted warehouse. "We have arrived."

Jeff let out a piercing whistle and waved his arm in a circle to bunch up the caravan. It had been a long deadly trip and everyone pitched in with a will to see the end of it. The animals were stripped clean in record time. Jeff gathered his crew around.

"Good job, men. Let's get these critters into the holding pen, then, by the gods, it's time to eat."

Whistles and shouts of agreement sounded at once. Jeff found a switch and whacked the strange animals called kalks into motion. On the way by one of them tried to bite him, but he jerked his arm away. Jeff recognized the animal as the same one that had scored on him earlier in the day.

Balling up a fist, he nailed the animal up alongside the head as he had been instructed and it jerked away with a venomous hiss. In passing, however, and at the critical moment, the kalk let out a thunderous fart. Jeff reeled back gasping for air.

"Oh, pig shit! What a smell!"

With the crew howling laughter, Jeff took a running skip and kicked the animal in the rump. It bounded into the holding pen with a bray that sounded quite self-satisfied.

An hour or so later Belstan located Jeff in the stable forking fresh hay into Cynic's manger.

"Will you join us for evening meal? My partner is anxious to meet you."

"With pleasure."

Jeff ran an appraising eye over Rogelf while accepting a cup of coffee. The agent was big in every dimension, with huge arms and massively rounded shoulders. He also had a large belly, but it looked to be as much muscle as fat. About five ten, Rogelf was balding and had piercing hazel eyes. They clasped hands.

"Welcome, Jeefry. May the gods spit on your enemies for saving my old friend's goods, not to mention his carcass."

"It was a near thing, but we got through it."

Rogelf nodded emphatically. "Too near a thing, young man."

He waved Jeff toward a table crowded with food. Overhead, a brass lantern swayed in the cool breeze wafting through open windows facing the lake.

Although his appetite was ferocious, Jeff forced himself to eat at a deliberate pace and with attention to manners. Shoveling food down like he did around campfires would never do.

Throughout the meal, conversation flowed in staccato bursts between Rogelf and Belstan. Rogelf's expression showed real concern when the topic entered the realm of politics.

"The taxes, my friend, the taxes! Shortly after your departure west, the council seemed to go mad. I have lived in this city all my life, but have never been so hard pressed. Import duties, city taxes, export taxes, head taxes, food taxes. There is no end to them!"

Belstan stopped chewing and stared at Rogelf. "Surely the council knows they will destroy their own house if businesses fail? Faced with these new taxes, I am certain that many will do just that."

With a massive shrug, Rogelf threw his hands wide. "How can they not be aware of the danger? Yet there seems to be more than simple greed at the heart of this. My agents report a sense of close-lipped fear among the counselors. But fear of what? Business is good. The piers are filled with ships from the east and south. Caravans pour into the city every day." Rogelf shook his head in perplexity. "While tax revenues must be enormous, to what end? Destruction of the very thing that makes our city great? Its commerce?"

Sighing hugely, Rogelf dished himself another slab of meat and set to work on it while Belstan cogitated. Jeff tried to sort probabilities, but with a full meal in his stomach couldn't do much more than yawn. Rogelf noticed Jeff's condition and had an employee show him to sleeping quarters inside the warehouse.

Jeff was wide-awake shortly after dawn and looking for his boots. When he realized where he was, in Khorgan and not on the trail, it was too late to get back to sleep. Slipping quietly out of the warehouse, he fed Cynic and set out on foot northward along the shore.

Fascinated by the gangs of stevedores, impressed by the huge freight wagons rumbling along wooden piers and enchanted by the haunting calls of sea birds, Jeff soon lost track of time. Drawn like a magnet to the fleet of ships heaving in the swell as they lay moored bow and stern, he wandered from pier to pier.

Along the way he made the acquaintance of an old gaffer, long retired from the sea. Delighted with Jeff's interest, the gaffer took him by the arm and hobbled off toward the nearest ship spinning tales as he went.

Jeff eventually noticed how high the sun was, bought the old-timer a farewell beer and meandered toward Rogelf's warehouse. Belstan was waiting out front anxiously peering up and down the street. He dragged Jeff inside as if he were an errant child.

"Thank the gods! Where have you been, boy?" He waved an agitated finger under Jeff's nose. "This waterfront is not a place to be taken lightly. Before you venture out again, allow me to provide a guide else you be found floating face down in the lake."

Belstan eventually ran out of grisly examples and they sat down for the noon meal.

"Rogelf seemed quite concerned last night. Is something amiss?"

Lost in thought, Belstan silently chewed a particularly tough piece of meat until he got the better of it.

"The council is aroused, even fearful," he said in a puzzled tone of voice, "and that is cause for deep concern when you consider the size of the Civil Guard. When last I had cause to investigate, the city had two thousand well-trained soldiers under arms, and another five thousand militia quickly available."

"That does seem to be an adequate force considering the city is peaceful and we have heard nothing of an outside threat."

"Yet the council is aroused. It is extremely vexing and the tax situation nothing short of ruinous. Rogelf and I considered this for a good portion of last night but found no sensible explanation. While banditry is always of concern, other caravans arriving have not reported unusual activity on that score. Also, having just returned from the West I am aware of no threat from that quarter." Belstan's eyebrows drew together in a frown. "Arzak is never to be trusted, but Rogelf has heard nothing that would rouse suspicion."

"And yet, as you say, the council is aroused."

"To a degree Rogelf has never witnessed before, Jeffrey. This is the heart of our concerns: Rogelf's agents are as good as any yet report only that those serving the council refuse to say anything even when offered large bribes." Belstan muttered darkly, "When a substantial bribe will not loosen jaws in this city, something is seriously awry."

"Any reports of unusual emissaries at council meetings?"

Beady eyes snapping with sudden interest, Belstan stared at Jeff. "Please explain yourself, young man."

Jeff gazed thoughtfully at Belstan while considering options. "As you have already surmised, I am not simply a mercenary looking for work. Before I say more about what I believe is taking place, I want you to think about that and whether you want to have me in your employ."

As he had on prior occasion, Belstan strove to place Jeff's origins. Also as in the past, he failed. Getting up, Belstan paced around the room for a period then re-seated himself and glowered at Jeff.

"I have traded around this country for over thirty years. In that time I have never suffered such confusion as I now do. Suddenly you make an appearance, contrive to save everything I have labored to build, and then present this to me!"

Belstan jumped to his feet and resumed pacing. While not inclined to displays of emotion, he gave the impression of someone who would dearly love to kick some furniture.

Jeff followed Belstan's erratic course around the room while carefully selecting words.

"Yes, I have put you in a difficult position. You have been kind to me, Rogelf openly generous. What I have to do, what I have to ascertain beyond doubt, might well place you and Rogelf at considerable risk. I do not wish to see either of you involved in something that could well be your end."

Having calmed himself, Belstan sat down to reconsider everything he had observed since Jeff joined the caravan.

"It is not every man from the North who employs such words as ascertain. Most of those I have met were barely able to lace their boots. I tell you, young Jeff, I have had a feeling about you from the day we met. Over the years I have learned that to disregard such feelings is perilous.

"There are things afoot here that cause me concern beyond anything in memory. If I am going to listen to what you have to say, and I believe I am, then Rogelf must be present."

It was some time before Belstan returned with Rogelf in tow. The latter ushered them into an inner office and shut the door. Jeff and Rogelf found seats, Belstan remained standing.

"Rogelf and I have worked together for a good share of our lives. We both know in our hearts that some large threat is brewing, something larger than either of us has ever encountered. We must discover its origin before it devours us! You have started something today, Jeffrey. Now we would hear the full tale."

Although having second thoughts, Jeff nodded. "Before I tell you about myself, let me share what I believe is happening in Khorgan. I am many things besides a warrior, and one of those things is a student of history and peoples. These studies lead me to conclude that Khorgan is being forced to pay tribute. Now I ask you, who is mighty enough to force such shame on this city?"

Having finished what he had to say for the moment, Jeff let the men chew on it while he studied them. Several minutes passed before Rogelf sat up straight in outright alarm.

"By the gods, Belstan. Salchesia. It has to be the Salcheks! No other province or city has the power."

Belstan slapped himself on the forehead and groaned. "How could I have not seen this? Yes, yes! It has to be the Salcheks!" He pointed an excited finger at Jeff. "The moment you uttered the word, tribute, everything became clear. Everything we have seen and heard shouts agreement. But the Salcheks! While it has been many years since they left Khorgan, stories of the terror they visited on this city spring to mind afresh. If this is true, it is terrible news."

The traders batted the tribute idea back and forth, serving to deepen their conviction that it was the best explanation for what was going on in Khorgan.

"You have led us to this conclusion quite skillfully, Jeefrey. May I conclude that the Salchek Empire is not unknown to you?"

"Your observation is astute, Rogelf. I believe it time to reveal my origins and intent."

"Please do, lest my mind come asunder with speculation!"

Jeff smiled at Belstan's relieved expression and proceeded to feed information to them in hunks small enough to swallow, starting with Rugen and the scrap of parchment Ethbar had shown him. After brief reflection he decided to say nothing about his ultimate origins. When he was finished they assaulted him with such pointed questions that he discarded that reservation.

"You have referred to me as an outlander, and I am most certainly that. Allow me to give you a better idea of the land I spring from."

Pulling his shirt up, Jeff released the restraining strap and drew the Colt. Opening the cylinder, he extracted the cartridges and laid it on the table.

"With this weapon I have the lives of six men in my hand."

Gazing at the gleaming thing of silver steel lying on the table, both men looked as if they expected it to strike out like a snake at any moment.

"You are among the first people on this planet to view this weapon. Be assured, it is the least of such on my own."

197

They remained closeted for the rest of the day and much of the evening as well. Questions flew thick and fast, especially questions having to do with the word, planet. Mental fatigue took its toll, and the meeting adjourned near midnight. By mid-morning of the next day they were seated around the same table debating implications. Every so often, either Rogelf or Belstan would ask to see "the gun."

Jeff held nothing back. He needed quick access to accurate information that would take months to get on his own. He had probed both men deeply the previous day and concluded that neither of them had telepathic abilities. They were exactly what they appeared to be—sharp-minded traders. Even though he assessed them as savvy men, Jeff had to voice a major concern before the meeting broke up.

"As we value our lives, no word of these deliberations must come to other ears. I believe it safe to say that we all understand the virulence of rumor."

Belstan snorted. "I would sooner talk about having made love to a finmaid while traveling through Borstel, my boy."

The urgency of the situation forced matters along at a furious clip. Rogelf now knew which questions to ask and fanned out agents in hopes of snaring information on just who was in town.

Belstan spent considerable time poring over his collection of maps with Jeff usually hanging over his shoulder. Late one evening, he stabbed his finger onto a map.

"If they are coming, it will be through Lukash, Lugsburg or both."

"Lugsburg is situated close to the ocean," Jeff observed, tracing his finger along the coast, "and accessible by this river. On the other hand, I suspect Lukash will be the first port of call if the Salchek are coming. From what I have heard, it seems likely the Arzak cooperated with the Salchek during the last invasion."

"Without doubt." Rogelf entered and Belstan waved him over to the map before continuing. "While it has been many a year since I traveled to Arzak, I still remember being thankful to have escaped with my life. It is a hateful land, one filled with treachery, deceit and the most vile forms of slavery."

"And Lukash is its capitol city."

Belstan nodded toward Jeff with pursed lips, "Yes, and by extension the center and distillation of all that is evil in that land. That is why I mentioned Lukash as a possible point of entry for an invasion. The ruling families in Arzak have coveted Chaldesia for many years and would make fitting accomplices to the Salchek."

"What is their appearance, Belstan? The Salchek, I mean."

"I was not yet born when they departed, and coming as we do from the South March my family was spared contact. I must admit to a certain curiosity. From what is rumored, one gains the impression of invincible giants."

"Not giants," Rogelf said, "but terrible adversaries. What I know of the Salchek, that is what I feel to be more than rumor, places them as outlanders whose home lies across the sea to the south of Arzak. They are said to be short men of great endurance who prefer to fight from horseback or small carriages. When I was a child, my granny often told stories of their cruelty to make me behave. Sometimes she even succeeded, so terrible were the tales."

Chariots, I'll bet, Jeff thought. Formidable opponents when facing poorly equipped foot soldiers and unskilled cavalry. Shit. Khorgan isn't going to fight, which means Rugen will take the full brunt of the invasion! Jeff felt a burst of angry frustration.

"If history is any guide, the council is likely to believe their gold will purchase safety. My studies inform me they will fail, but only after the Salchek have drained the city of every linta in it. Weakened by the loss of so much of its wealth, Khorgan will fall easy prey to invasion. Once established in this city and Lugsburg, the way north is open."

Belstan's expression overflowed with contempt. "And the council will discover that gold is not a sovereign specific while being marched to the scaffold."

"Yes," Jeff replied, rubbing tense neck muscles, "but not until thousands of the innocent have perished. Let us pray that our suspicions are unfounded."

It was a sober trio that split up that evening, each bent on separate errands. Accompanied by Rogelf's son, Ostfel, Jeff had been cruising military hangouts in search of information. On the way out of the room, Rogelf took Jeff's arm.

"I have given Ostfel other tasks this evening. My younger child has returned from visiting family in the farmlands and will accompany you." Rogelf hurried off.

Jeff looked after him with a puzzled expression. "What odd phrasing, and why is he in such a rush?" Shrugging, he ticked off goals for the night's effort while walking from the warehouse.

Rounding a corner, he slammed into someone who was nicely padded. Jeff caught himself but the woman couldn't save it and crashed to the floor. He extended his hand to help her up.

"My apologies. I should have been more careful."

The redhead slapped his hand away and leaped to her feet.

"You incredible, stumbling oaf! Which barnyard did you escape from?"

"No harm was intended, I have apologized. Good day."

Jeff stepped aside to pass. As luck would have it, she stepped in the same direction and they nearly collided again.

"You are an imbecile devoid of breeding. Get out of my way!"

Staring levelly into green eyes brilliant with anger, Jeff said, "You have legs."

For a moment he thought she would try and hit him. Instead, the woman brushed by with a parting curse and disappeared down the hall.

"Son of a bitch," Jeff muttered, watching her out of sight. "What a banshee! I wonder if she eats nails for breakfast?"

He had stepped outside in search of his partner for the evening when he heard footsteps behind him. "Oh shit I hope it isn't her." Jeff groaned under his breath when the redhead emerged from the warehouse.

Fists on hips, she looked him up and down in utter contempt. "It would seem I must endure your presence this night. Keep your stumbling frame a safe distance downwind."

Jeff smiled pleasantly. "Tell me, what rock did you crawl out from under?"

"How dare you to speak to me in such a fashion!" The redhead seemed genuinely shocked. "You are...you are naught but a common buffoon and the son of a churl!"

"And you, lady," Jeff said in a coldly level voice, "are a spoiled child and possess not the slightest degree of civility. Furthermore, I find your reference to my father so offensive that I will have satisfaction if you ever express it again."

The redhead's complexion flushed to a tint that matched her hair. "*My* father owns this warehouse and has agreed to suffer your presence. Should I do so this evening, I would not be able to show my face in Khorgan again. You are fit only to shovel filth from stables." She spun around and marched into the warehouse.

Memories of confrontations with Sarah had made a strong comeback. Jeff had forgotten what it was like. It made his guts twist.

"God dammit. Just when I was starting to think I had left that shit behind. Say whatever they want without fear of being called out. No more."

Jeff whirled when he felt a hand on his shoulder. It was Belstan.

"Zimma is a most difficult, hot-tempered young woman. You must not take her insults to heart, for they are a common occurrence and widely applied. I am only grateful that Rogelf was not present to hear them on this occasion. Now come, I will accompany you."

Ostfel was back on the job next evening. Over ensuing days Jeff caught glimpses of Zimma, but she was of minor concern to him. Matters were coming to a head. A huge bribe paid to a counselor's personal secretary confirmed that tribute was in fact being paid, and in an amount that staggered Belstan and Rogelf.

One of Rogelf's agents spotted what he thought might be an Arzak entering city hall. Other information confirmed an Arzak presence in council chambers. No one reported sighting a Salchek.

That fact was of little importance to Jeff. He was now convinced that, if an invasion was planned or already underway, Arzak would be a likely agent-state for the Salchek and on the take from both sides.

One step remained to confirm their worst fears. Were Salchek present in Arzak, or not? It was tempting to intercept a courier from Arzak, but Rogelf considered that too dangerous an undertaking. Instead, he organized a trading expedition to the origin of the Megaal River at the southern extremity of Lake Ligura.

Although there was no city as such at that location, Jeff learned a trading post had come into existence some years previously. More importantly, the post was known to have close ties with Lukash.

Scandalized at the thought of wasting a perfectly good opportunity to make a linta or two, Belstan insisted the expedition be an all-out legitimate trading effort. Sleep became a precious commodity in days following as trading goods were organized and stowed on board a trading vessel. In addition to the crew required to handle the craft, an eighty-foot schooner, it was decided that Belstan and Jeff would constitute the trading team.

The night before they were to set sail, Rogelf, Belstan and Jeff were working late trying to put some order to the mission's paperwork. Trade goods were stowed on the Baktar, but there had been no time to organize bills of lading. The office they were working in was quiet with the exception of an occasional frustrated curse.

At the sound of approaching footsteps, the men stopped their paper shuffling and shared a perplexed look. It was close to midnight and Ostfel was out of town. Jeff pushed back from his desk so he could watch the door.

When Zimma walked in wearing a long gown of silken green festooned with ropes of jewelry, he had to choke off a curse. From the way she wobbled on spike high heels, Jeff suspected Zimma had been drinking heavily. Curling his lip in disgust, he vowed to keep his mouth shut regardless of what she might say.

Swaying unsteadily, Zimma gazed around the room. Her eyes passed over Jeff as if he were not there.

"I have deshi...decided to accompany you, Belstan. The south shore of the lake is new to me, and I wish to see it."

Belstan didn't say anything until he had his irritation in hand. "This trip is likely to be fraught with peril, Zimma. I know you to have good sword skill, but you are also young and comely. That fact is likely to pose serious difficulties in Tradertown where there are few if any women. Would you risk compromising our mission?"

Although Zimma had a hard time focusing her eyes on Jeff, the scowl seemed to come naturally.

Exile To The Stars

"If this clumsy oaf is to shail...go with you, I feel certain that my presence can only be an ashet. I am coming."

It was hard, but Jeff kept his jaw tightly clamped and eyes fixed on a manifest. Bloody drunk, he thought. As soon as Zimma had opened her mouth, the smell of alcohol and another odor he was unfamiliar with had permeated the room.

Rogelf had turned away to stare fixedly out a window, but every aspect of his posture indicated painful embarrassment.

Belstan knew Zimma was the apple of Rogelf's eye. She also frequently had him on the verge of despair. While Belstan wanted to say no very badly, the voyage would give Zimma a chance to dry out. He was convinced she was deeply into alcohol and kalheesh. Beyond that reason, he had to try one more time for Rogelf's sake.

"Very well. You may accompany us on one condition: you must agree to follow my orders and not debate or oppose every decision."

Nodding curtly, Zimma threw a triumphant sneer at Jeff and turned to leave. On the way out she collided with the doorjamb. Jeff figured that whatever his feelings, Rogelf's were ten times as bad.

The morning of departure, a crisp breeze was blowing from the southwest giving it an offshore slant. The Baktar was moored with her bow facing the lake on the lee side of the pier. The bow line was let go and the foresail and outer jib hoisted in a rush of thundering canvas.

As the bow pivoted away from the pier, the crew raised the mainsail and let go the stern line. Her booms well off to port, the Baktar gathered way and settled onto a broad reach.

Jeff strolled aft from where he had been standing behind the quartermaster and leaned his elbows on the stern rail. He watched the city recede with a smile of contentment.

Since arriving in Khorgan he had haunted the sailing ships at every opportunity. Yacht racing on Puget Sound was exciting, but the big gaff-rigged schooners were a whole new world that had captivated him.

The breeze picked up as the ship moved farther out onto the lake. When they had made their easting, all hands were called to heave in the sails until they were nearly flat as boards. The captain turned the Baktar south and she went hard on the wind, heeling well over to port.

Taking station in the bow, Jeff hooked his elbows over the weather rail. Breathing deeply of the tangy air, he admired the spirals of birds soaring around the ship. Blue and white, resembling cormorants, their plaintive cries called his imagination south to tropic shores.

Some time later Jeff reluctantly went below to attend a strategy conference with Belstan and the ship's captain. When he entered the captain's cabin, Jeff paused abruptly. He had completely forgotten Zimma was part of the team.

What a bummer, he thought. Why did she have to come? Just one more self-centered bitch. Jeff stared at her for a moment then found a seat.

In the one instant their eyes were locked together, Zimma nearly flinched. The extent of Jeff's contempt was such that she could do nothing but look away. Here on the ship, isolated from her usual environment and friends, an inner voice that had been growing stronger for several years had finally broken through and informed her that she deserved contempt.

She wanted to say or do something in reprisal, but instead remembered the look on her father's face the night she had announced she was joining the expedition. The stab of remorse that followed the memory was exquisitely painful and so new Zimma had no defense against it.

Belstan gazed around the cabin to make sure he had everyone's attention.

"Let us be clear about the purpose of this trading mission. While we are making this voyage to gather information, we are traders as well. The Arzak are a suspicious, arrogant people—never forget that.

"Although Tradertown is in Chaldesia, in truth it is no man's land. If the Salchek have returned as we suspect and conspire with Arzak, agents we encounter are likely to be provocative." Belstan looked directly at Zimma. "Hold your temper, gather information. Perhaps we will turn a few linta to pay for this trip."

Zimma's temper flared at being singled out. While saying nothing in response, she threw a venomous look at Jeff. Her father was due respect, long overdue she conceded, but this seedy barbarian was something else entirely. He will disgrace us all!

Once on board the Baktar, Jeff had donned his threadbare jeans. One pant leg was out at the knee, and sparks from numerous campfires had burned holes here and there over the rest. Other than the jeans, he was wearing an old tee shirt that had seen better days a year ago.

Wrinkling her nose in distaste, Zimma compared Jeff to her latest male companion and smirked.

The rest of the meeting was spent going over trade inventory and picking the captain's brain for information on Tradertown. Instead of describing the town with words, he sketched it.

"That is a large trading post," Jeff said with surprise. "Nearly a city from the look of it."

"Yes, but no one terms it a city," Belstan replied. "If they did, and since Tradertown is in Chaldesia, Khorgan would have to officially claim and defend it. Having no army as such, it has been convenient for Khorgan to leave matters as they are—regardless of what occurs, all may deny responsibility."

When Jeff came on deck next morning he found the Baktar idly turning in the occasional breath of wind. It was a hot day and Jeff thought longingly of shorts. Several hours later a breeze filled in from the northwest and continued to make up until it was blowing fresh.

Belstan went below to get out of the wind, but Zimma planted herself in the bow. One hand gripping a stay, long red hair streaming off to the lee, her cheeks were flushed with exhilaration.

"Well, what have we here?" Jeff murmured when he noticed her. "Is it possible the dildo is in a good mood?"

After a hard fight, Jeff convinced himself he should make a stab at patching things up before they hit Tradertown. Halfway to the bow he stopped. On the verge of changing his mind, Jeff squared his shoulders and hurried forward.

Zimma heard footsteps and turned to see who it was. A familiar scowl immediately formed and she turned her back to him. Leaving plenty of room, Jeff leaned against the weather rail and questioned his sanity. There was no point to his being there; no point in trying to deal with a spoiled little rich girl that could get away with murder. He had to do it or leave.

"I can imagine what you think of me, and my opinion of you is likely worse, but I see no way of avoiding each other on this trip. As difficult as it will be, perhaps we can at least feign civility in order to free Belstan's mind from that worry."

The back of her neck turned red with anger, leading Jeff to wonder what Zimma's face looked like. She stared off to the southwest in frigid silence leaving Jeff to watch her hair swirl and twist in the breeze. There were so many shades of red in it that he became fascinated by the play of color. She was also wearing snug breeches.

Jeff just naturally scanned downward with a clinical eye. One look and a muted "My, oh my" sneaked out, followed by a soft whistle of academic appreciation. She was a bitch all right, but a bitch with one fine rear end.

Although the noise from sea and wind was substantial, Zimma just as naturally heard the whistle and knew exactly what had prompted it. Pleased in a way that took her by surprise, she tossed her head to set red hair flying in bright whorls. Jeff had said all he intended to and decided he would not move until she answered.

It was some time before Zimma decided he wasn't going to leave. Turning to face Jeff, she leaned against the lee rail with elbows on the cap and attempted to view him from a more neutral perspective. It seemed a lost cause. The mere sight of him brought a rush of cutting words to mind. Zimma pressed her lips into a thin line to stop an expression of disgust.

"Your statement is accurate. My opinion of you is quite beyond hope, and I recognize your distaste for my person. Also yes, I agree that we must attempt to work together. With careful attention to duty, perhaps we will succeed."

Reluctantly, Zimma held out her hand.

Taking her hand in the spirit it was offered, Jeff intended no more than a simple handshake. Instead, he lifted it to his lips. Their eyes met and neither moved for several heartbeats.

Cheeks flushing in a different pattern, Zimma withdrew her hand. "I must go below to meet with Belstan. I understand your effort in approaching me was no small matter."

The breeze held steady and they sighted the southernmost shore of Lake Ligura late the following day. The captain reduced sail in easy stages as they approached the anchorage, a deep lagoon protected by a spit of land that curved far out into the lake. He settled on a spot that gave ample swinging room, bellowed a string of orders and the Baktar dropped anchor.

Around sunset the breeze died away to nothing, leaving sweltering humidity. A number of crewmen came topsides to find cooler air. Leaning on the rail, they examined other craft idly drifting around their chains. Jeff was doing the same and ambled over. He gestured with his head.

"Khorgan?"

One of the older men was lighting a pipe, and a wreath of greenish smoke lazily curled around his head. It smelled terrible. He pointed a gnarled finger at two of the boats in turn, cackling as he did so.

"Them scows come from Khorgan, and lucky they was to get this far seein' as how the rot's near et 'em up." The old-timer scowled at the other two ships and spit over the side. "Gods-cursed slavers by the stench of 'em—prolly mean ta pick up some poor bastards and sell 'em off at Borgo."

Jeff could only agree that the smell coming from the direction of the two craft was much worse than a barnyard. He heard, or imagined he heard, faint cries for water and examined the shoreline in an attempt to block them out.

Drunken singing drifted from the shore, and the orange glow of bonfires began to appear as night settled in. He was starting a yawn when an agonized scream pierced the night. With utter certainty, he knew that someone had just died.

Twelve

Worse Than Death

A sullen orange globe hanging low in the east greeted Jeff when he emerged from below. The small effort required to climb the ladder had him sweating, and he plucked a light shirt free from where it was stuck to his ribs.

Accompanied by the squeal of pulleys, crewmembers lowered a net full of crates into the ship's launch. When the way was clear Jeff tossed his duffel bag onto a thwart. Belstan and Zimma joined him, and they clambered down into the deeply laden boat.

With fifty yards to go, stroke oar looked over his shoulder and called out, "Lay into it, lads."

Oars bent to a singsong chant, driving the bow onto dry land. Goods came ashore in rapid succession forming a sizable pyramid. Leaving the launch crew to stand guard, Belstan, Jeff and Zimma waded up the sloping beach in ankle-deep sand and steam bath heat.

The men carried rolls of canvas and line on their shoulders; Zimma cradled a bundle of poles in her arms. Jeff expected her to whine about the load but she staggered through the sand without a word, hair hanging in sweat-sodden strings. The few palm-like trees they passed under gave only fleeting shade.

A short distance from the beach they threaded their way through a warren of shanties. On several occasions they were forced to backtrack in search of a way through the maze. The stench of excrement and urine was bad enough, but with their arms full the cloud of biting flies was maddening.

"We must be careful to avoid passing this way at night."

"It would be worth your life to do less," Belstan heartily agreed, and kicked at a dog harrying his ankles.

They located a central area that seemed to be the center of trading. The place bustled with activity as established merchants opened their booths.

"The best locations are taken," Belstan grumbled. "I am afraid we will have to settle for what is left."

He let his load drop and bent to loosen the bindings. Jeff did likewise, saw that the poles in Zimma's arms were about to go every which way, and grabbed on.

"Okay, we got it. Let it down."

With a surprised glance at Jeff, she did so. Zimma didn't know what to say and began sorting through the poles.

"I will return to the launch and see to transporting trade goods."

"That would be most helpful, Jeffrey. Zimma and I will assemble the booth."

Waves of heat shimmered up from the sand, and Jeff took his time. Intrigued by the hodgepodge of people swarming the area, he moseyed from one point of interest to the other. Right out of Treasure Island, Jeff concluded, except this bunch smell like a sewer. Belstan had pointed out Arzaks on the way into town. Jeff counted fifteen before it occurred to him that he had not seen a single woman.

The Arzaks radiated arrogance as they swaggered by in loose silken pants, high boots and multicolored blouses. Dark haired and dark skinned, all were armed to the teeth. Jeff frowned when an Arzak bulled his way past several traders, sending one to his knees.

"This is really going to be sweet. One dildo and a pack of assholes. How in hell are we ever going to protect her?"

At the beach, Jeff sent the launch to fetch more help. When they returned he headed back with arms full of trading goods, cursing the sand. The crew trailed along behind, likewise encumbered and cursing.

Arriving soaked with sweat and short of breath, Jeff gratefully set his load down. Their booth, no more than an elaborate tent with a counter, was assembled. He noticed that several guy lines were loose and went in search of a hammer. Jeff was driving the last peg when two brightly robed merchants wearing spiral turbans approached the counter.

By mid-morning the area was packed. The air was filled with loud, often aggravated bargaining as individuals and groups of men moved from location to location. Adding to the noise, food vendors hawked their wares while wrestling carts through the sand.

After a period of standing around doing very little, Jeff decided to break free of their booth. He was completely out of his element where trading was concerned. The energy and excited wrangling of the crowd had also proven contagious.

Wandering the bazaar, Jeff discovered the booths tended to be segregated by nationality. When he found the Arzak section, Jeff moved from booth to booth fingering merchandise and listening. Before long the trading patois began to make sense. He could communicate.

The glint of steel caught his eye and Jeff hurried to a rambling booth given over to expansive display counters.

"Well, now," he murmured. "A weapons dealer, and it looks like good stuff."

Jeff picked up a curved sword similar to his saber and held it out to gaze along the blade. It was true. Gripping the haft lightly, he found the balance to be quite good. The blade had every appearance of high-grade carbon steel that had been carefully forged and annealed.

While the Arzaks he had seen so far had left a very negative impression, he was impressed with the quality of their forging. Jeff whistled under his breath when the blade cleanly shaved a section of his arm without the slightest drag.

The shop's rotund proprietor watched Jeff flex the blade and try a few passes before sauntering over.

"Interested in good steel, Khorgan?"

"You might say it is a passion of mine."

They debated the pros and cons of straight versus curved blades, hilt styles, and a wealth of other points. The proprietor knew his trade and was also an accomplished salesman. Before he knew it, Jeff decided to purchase a dirk that caught his fancy.

Haggling a mutually agreeable price was a new experience. It became enjoyable when he realized the hand waving and outrage were no more than part of the process. While the man was certainly an Arzak, Jeff found nothing to criticize. By the sale's conclusion they had developed a certain respect for one another and exchanged names.

As the purchase price changed hands, Saafir leaned close to whisper, "Be cautious, Jeffrey. You are from Khorgan. Not all among us are honest traders."

Moving on with a sardonic smile, Jeff muttered, "No shit."

In response to hunger pangs he purchased something that looked vaguely like an egg roll and took a cautious bite. The afternoon was well along when he wandered back to home base.

In spite of the late hour, a number of customers were still waiting to be served.

Ducking through the back and into heavenly shade, Jeff sat down on a crate and toyed with his new dirk. Some time later Belstan bid farewell to the last customer and dropped rattan curtains into place. He poured the day's receipts onto a makeshift table with loving care. Cracking his knuckles to warm up, Belstan proceeded to sort the take with flying fingers.

Zimma joined him and tallied the various stacks. She abruptly stopped and pointed. "That coin is the wrong denomination." Plucking the coin out of a pile, she dropped it in another.

Belstan appeared embarrassed at his mistake.

Those two are cut out of the same cloth, Jeff decided with a grin. What a pair of traders. Realizing he had just had a positive thought about Zimma, Jeff wiped the grin off his face. He figured it was safe to break the intense silence when Zimma began scooping money into a bag.

"A good day, Belstan?"

"A most propitious day. A few more such and all our trade goods will be sold. If our suspicions are found wanting, I can assure you we will return."

Jeff passed on what he had been told while buying the dirk. "Something is going on that has nothing to do with trade. The question is what."

"My observations agree," Belstan replied. "Perhaps one out of three Arzaks have any commercial interest here. However, I have not yet heard or observed anything that is sufficient to explain their presence. I believe we must stay on shore this night and see what may be discovered."

"I see no other option myself. There's risk but also opportunity."

"Considerable risk." Belstan directed his gaze toward Zimma. "Although you will not like my saying this, lass, you must return to the Baktar. While your presence has attracted a great deal of business, I have also had four offers to purchase you. They were polite offers, but what will the night bring?"

Zimma stared at Belstan in open disbelief. "Purchase me? *Purchase* me?"

"This is not Khorgan, Zimma," Belstan replied with an eloquent shrug.

Fire leaped into her eyes, and Zimma gripped the hilt of her sword. "No such man shall ever lay hand on me, lest it be as he dies!"

"Proud words, young lady," Belstan said, slowly shaking his head. "The opportunity for self defense is never given. This night you must sleep on board."

"If I am to spend the night on the Baktar, you will surely have to first truss then carry me there."

After Zimma and Belstan had been arguing for some time, Jeff decided to risk a comment.

"Milady, even during daylight there is no way we can protect you if you wander off alone. At night our position becomes impossible. While I know nothing of the slave trade between Arzak and Borgo, I am familiar with its history in the country of my birth. You are an attractive woman from a small trading mission. Can you not see that this is liable to pose an irresistible temptation to them?"

Her temper was boiling and Zimma whirled on Jeff, but the hot words rushing to her lips were waylaid. She paused to wonder, What does he mean by attractive? Eyes sparking, Zimma stared at Jeff for a moment then abruptly turned back to Belstan.

"Very well. I agree. The risk is real and I do not wish to jeopardize our mission. I will not leave this enclosure unless accompanied by yourselves or members of the crew." Although Zimma was still playing with a particular word, she had made up her mind. "I am, however, going to remain ashore this night."

The defiant tilt to Zimma's chin decided Jeff. He would take his winnings and run.

"Agreed. Let us hope it proves to be quiet."

The night started out with a fistfight nearby. Matters rapidly deteriorated as bonfires were lighted and alcohol started to flow. To a man, the traders that stayed ashore barricaded themselves behind their trade goods. It didn't take long for Jeff and Belstan to give up any notion of poking around. They piled up a bulwark of crates to block the rear of the booth and lighted a lantern.

Zimma watched shadow figures leap and stagger around the nearest bonfire accompanied by instruments that wailed and moaned. Horrified yet also attracted by the grotesque saturnalia, she leaned over the counter to see better.

A slurred shout rang out, "Come play, lettle cunt!"

Even though she was sure they couldn't see her, Zimma hurriedly withdrew. Belstan put an arm around her shoulders and wondered how long it would take to run to the lake.

It wasn't long before they heard the clash of swords from several directions, screams mixing with drunken songs. The larger moon seemed to spring over the horizon, lending enough cool light to pick out the larger brawls.

The moon was about to set and bonfires had died down to coals when a dozen or so Arzaks stumbled out of the darkness swigging on clay bottles. Belching loudly, one of them staggered closer and leered at Zimma.

"That slutch ish too good for you Khorgan scum. Now you will shell her to me, then she will have a man between her legs!"

Reeling back, he jerked out a greasy pouch of coins and slammed it onto the counter. Before any of them could react, the Arzak grabbed the front of Zimma's light blouse and yanked her against the counter.

Jeff's arm snapped into a looping right cross with a lot of muscle behind it. His fist landed square on the Arzak's nose with a mushy thud. The man staggered backward and took several of his companions to the ground in a struggling pile.

Grossly obese, clothing soaked with grease, the Arzak staggered to his feet roaring oaths and spouting blood from his nose.

Another Arzak ran out of the darkness with drawn sword and rammed its hilt against the drunk's head, felling him. Booting two or three more, he sent them on their way dragging what looked like a corpse.

The Arzak watched them out of sight then strolled over to the booth. Without a word, he stared at Zimma's chest. Jeff felt a wave of revulsion and moved to block his view. The Arzak raised his eyes. Jeff was reminded of the first hyena he had killed, and thought, This guy is fucking crazy. He's drooling!

Scooping up the purse, the Arzak stalked off wiping at his mouth.

Things had happened so fast that Zimma was just starting to react. Jeff turned to see how she was.

"Are you..."

The front of Zimma's blouse was gone. One up-tilted breast was fully exposed and gleamed white in the lantern light. As he watched, the other bounced free.

Desperately staring at anything but her chest, Jeff grabbed a towel and draped it around Zimma's shoulders. Only then did she look down.

She gasped, took one look at the blush on Jeff's face, and her own flamed red. "I...I...Oh! Gods and demons!"

Furious at what had been done to her, she also felt such a rush of excruciating modesty that she could hardly lift her eyes from the sandy floor. It was an entirely new experience.

Clutching the towel across her chest with one hand, Zimma took Jeff's with the other.

"Thank you for defending me."

She held his eyes briefly then looked away, blush flaming anew. During that moment, a period that existed in another time and place free of self-deception, some vital thing passed between them that neither really understood.

Letting his hand go, Zimma hurried to the back of the enclosure in search of a spare blouse. When she was clothed, Belstan confronted her.

"You will not spend another night ashore. If necessary, I shall indeed have you trussed and taken aboard."

Zimma was badly shaken and silently nodded agreement. There was little sleep to be had, but customers began to gather shortly after the sun was up and business was business. Jeff paused on his way out of the booth.

"We don't have a lot of time. I'm going to see what I can find on the far side of town."

Belstan did no more than wave acknowledgement. His attention was focused on a customer heading toward the booth. Zimma paused from setting up a change drawer to favor Jeff with a shy smile. He couldn't help thinking that it was a very nice smile.

Sliding the change drawer under the counter, Zimma watched him walk away. She felt so confused by what had passed between them the previous night. Jeff had switched from jeans to snug leather pants, and she followed the movement of his buttocks as he forced a way through the sand.

"Please assist me, Zimma. Customers are waiting to be served."

Jolted back to the task at hand, Zimma put a 'may I help you' smile on her face and turned to the counter.

Making his way to the southern fringe of Tradertown, Jeff slogged around the eastern perimeter in heavy sand and dense foliage. Halfway back to the lake he spotted a large tent with a contingent of Arzak guards posted out front.

Concealing himself in a clump of bushes identical to large palmettos, Jeff's nose was assailed with a familiar stench. Shortly, slaves chained together were exercised.

"There has to be *something* I can do," Jeff fumed under his breath, "But what? Even if I bust them out, where can they go?"

He racked his brain for a solution while continuing to work his way toward the lake. Unless he could somehow spirit them all onboard the Baktar, it was a lost cause. Left to their own devices they would either be recaptured or die in the jungle.

Perhaps two hundred yards from the slave enclosure he encountered another heavily guarded tent. After a period of observation Jeff decided it had to be Arzak HQ. It was the largest tent he had seen and two tents of good size were attached to the main enclosure. Brass, maybe gold, fittings twinkled on supporting poles, and the guards appeared to be wearing dress uniforms. He watched a procession of soldiers enter and leave for a while before penetrating deeper into the jungle.

Impassable undergrowth and stagnant pools of brackish water confronted Jeff at frequent intervals, the insect horde was ravenous, and animals howled and squeaked without pause. He was close to the lake and ready for a break when faint voices sifted through the foliage.

Carefully working closer, he spotted a group of nattily uniformed soldiers in a clearing. Jeff did a double take. The Arzak uniforms reminded him of those worn by German SS troops. They were Arzak, but nothing like he had seen up to that point.

One of the soldiers was pointing north while two scribbled notes. The fourth was drawing a diagram in the sand. The one who had been pointing walked over to the Arzak drawing in the sand, grabbed the stick, and added a few strokes. Thoughtfully slapping the stick against his breeches several times, he gave a curt order and they left.

Allowing plenty of time for them to clear the area, Jeff crept out of hiding to examine the diagram. Although one of the Arzaks had walked through it, what remained was so intriguing that he stood there for some time staring at the mangled lines. They implied so much.

The night passed without incident and with less tension since Zimma was sleeping on the Baktar. Upon arising, Belstan commented that trading was so good he believed they could close shop in another day or so. Rolling up the booth's shutters, he glanced at Jeff.

"What progress?"

"Good, but I'm still unsure what it portends. Today I must attempt to gather all together." He waved to Zimma, who was approaching in company with several Baktar crewmen, and set off to explore the western perimeter of Tradertown.

Passing a shack at the town's edge, Jeff felt something tug at his blouse. It was an urchin of no more than eight years. Pulling his saber, Jeff followed the boy behind the shack. Saafir was waiting. The look on his face brought every sense to the alert. It was that of a terrified man.

"What has happened?"

The Arzak trader gripped Jeff's arm and spoke in an urgent whisper. "You must leave soon if you would live. That pig commanding the soldiers must have your redheaded woman and will kill you all to get her."

Jeff's mind went into overdrive. "When, my friend, when?"

Sweat trails streaked the dust on Saafir's face, and his eyes constantly roved the area.

"I do not know! Rumor, snatches of drunken conversation! It is said the soldiers will leave soon to meet Salchek marching north. It must be this night."

Confirmation had come out of the blue. Jeff was thunderstruck, could hardly believe they finally had firm evidence.

"I am forever in your debt, Saafir, but why do you give warning?"

"Because you love good steel, and the world must know that not all Arzak are craven. Please tell them. You must!"

He and the urchin dodged into thick trees behind the shack and were gone. Jeff waited for a few heartbeats and followed.

"What do I do now? We're going to have to haul ass today, but it isn't even noon yet. Surely they won't attack the booth while it's packed with customers. Shit! I have got to finish checking this place out!" Jeff headed west at a fast walk.

Several hours later and breathing hard he arrived at the beach. Jeff put it all together in his head while hotfooting it back the way he had come.

Glancing at the sun, he decided he had enough time to investigate what appeared to be a major road coming in from the south. He jogged south for some minutes to make sure the road was not a dead end. In fact, it became broader and ran straight as an arrow.

"That's the connection with Lukash," Jeff said. "No doubt about it."

He had been sitting in a spot of shade to catch his breath. Abruptly, he jumped up to listen. The sound was familiar but he could not place it.

"Maybe a column on the move. From what Saafir said it's not likely to be the Salchek this early in the day. Got to be more Arzak."

Jeff's first impulse was to sprint for camp in warning yet something rooted him in place. He listened intently and identified the sound—it was the clanking of leg irons.

"More slaves. That explains why the ones in Tradertown have not been moved out to the ships. The Arzak want to wait until the last group arrives before jamming them into cargo holds. There has got to be something I can do!"

Jogging toward Tradertown he suddenly swerved off the road by a hill. Jumping a ditch, Jeff cursed under his breath.

"What is it that's bothering me? What's the point of this? I've got to get back!"

Worming his way up the hill through thorns and saw brush, he found a spot that allowed an unobstructed view of the road. He sucked on a cut thumb and swatted insects until a column of slaves shuffled into view.

"Ten, twelve, umm—looks like eighteen slaves and six guards."

Jeff scrambled down the hill when the way was clear. He set out in pursuit planning to press on by the slaves. It was getting on in the day and his anxiety for Zimma's safety was nearly intolerable.

217

Drawing no more than suspicious glances when he passed the column, Jeff darted quick glances at the slaves. They were emaciated, showed raw whip scars through caked dirt, had long beards and smelled like a pit toilet. His stomach turned in helpless sympathy.

Disturbingly long shadows reminded Jeff of the need to move, and he increased his pace to a jog. He hadn't gone far when the same baffling sense slowed him to a fast walk.

"What the hell is going on? It might have something to do with those slaves, but they're no different than the others I've seen. I've got to get back before that asshole hits our booth!"

Entering Tradertown, internal conflict had slowed his pace to a crawl again. Snarling, "Dammit to hell!" Jeff turned off the road into some shade and waited for the column to catch up. The first slave was nearly abreast when he took a casual pose.

Slave after slave shuffled by to the clanking of chains and leg irons. He had no reaction to any of them other than excruciating pity. Some gibbered insanity, others pleaded for water, most were silent shells with nothing in their eyes at all. They passed one by one until he could not bear the sight. Turning to leave, a rasping croak stopped him in his tracks.

"Jeff?"

The clanking stopped and Jeff whirled around. Several guards were mercilessly whipping a slave that had fallen. One look at the slave next in line and a firestorm of emotion exploded. Jeff felt lightheaded and leaned against a tree trunk to keep from falling.

God, not him! It can't be him! Not here! Nearly a double, but someone else! Jeff gripped a tree limb hard enough to crack it. A mental probe burned away disbelief. It was Carl Jorgenson.

"Jeff?" Carl lifted his arms in supplication.

His wrists were shackled to a chain around his waist. When his arms stopped, Carl looked down with a confused expression. He tugged at the chain and began to cry.

Jeff experienced a terrible form of epiphany. There was no world or meaning other than the moment and Carl's tears, but he could do nothing. Given to action, drawn by risk, confident of his ability, yet he could not even touch his best friend. The slave that had fallen was on his feet and one of the guards laid a whip across Carl's shoulders with a sickening crack.

"Get moving, dog, or you'll get more. You stop like that again and there's no water tonight."

Carl's eyes went blank and he lowered his head. Emotional agony tore at Jeff's heart. The limb snapped off in his hand, but he did not draw the Colt. Then they were gone.

Hurrying to their booth, Jeff tried to make sense of it. "Carl must have been near Hoodo Pass when the earthquake struck. If I got tossed here, why not him? But how in hell did the Arzaks get him?" One thing was certain. If Carl didn't leave on the Baktar, neither would he.

Only Belstan was present when he entered the booth. "Where's Zimma? On the ship?"

Belstan briefly looked up from counting the day's proceeds. "No, a customer mentioned some trade goods on the other side of the bazaar that drew her interest. She would not be denied. I sent one of the crew as escort rather than have her venture out alone."

"Oh, shit! How long ago? Quickly!"

Jumping to his feet in alarm, Belstan knocked the table over and spilled a pile of coins onto the floor.

"A short span only. Why? What has happened?"

Jeff had the Colt out. He briefed Belstan while slipping the sixth round into place. "I'm going to get Zimma. What you can't carry in one load to the launch must be left behind. Pull away from shore and wait. Their commander will move any time now." Jeff got directions, scooped up spare cartridges and tore out the back.

Tradertown was in deep shadow. Vendors were closing up shop and customer traffic had thinned out to nothing. He frantically searched the location Belstan had given him. It was deserted except for shop owners. The proprietor Zimma had gone to visit recoiled when he saw Jeff's expression.

"Yes, she was here, then was invited to look at more goods over there by someone's servant."

The trader's finger pointed in a direction that made Jeff's heart stop for a second.

"Oh, God help us, that's the Arzak section." He slammed his fist onto the booth's counter, making the trader jump. "Damnation! Why didn't she use her head? Now they've got her, too!" He left at a run.

Darting from shadow to shadow, Jeff kicked himself for not having come back sooner. "But dammit," he fumed, "I would have missed Carl!"

The Arzak section was also deserted, and Jeff felt a blast of panic. Where? he thought. Where would they take her? He remembered the elaborate tent he had earlier concluded must be Arzak HQ.

It was dark when he arrived at the Arzak military encampment. Slipping from tent to tent, Jeff dodged several guards. With the jungle and safe cover only yards away, he was forced to dive for cover. Two Arzaks stopped several feet away.

Inhaling what looked like cigars to an orange glow, they chatted amiably and traded bad jokes. Whatever they were smoking made Jeff's head swim. Come on, move it, assholes! he thought desperately. What have they done to her by now?

He was about to explode when the Arzaks flipped butt ends cartwheeling sparks and wandered off. Ghosting through the jungle toward his goal, Jeff stumbled over an obstruction. Lying at his feet was the mutilated body of a Baktar crewman.

Jeff's mind crossed a threshold and settled into its coldly calculating state where doubt, remorse and pity had no place. He stepped over the body and moved quietly to the edge of the jungle. Ten yards of open ground separated him from Arzak HQ.

Willing his pulse to slow down, Jeff listened intently. Nothing more than harsh snatches of conversation. Laughter filtered through tent walls then faded to silence. Jeff was about to leave when he heard scuffling sounds and a loud order. No guards were in sight. Drawing knife and saber, he dashed to the back of the tent.

Jeff thought he heard cloth tearing but wasn't sure. More laughter and what had to be a ringing slap. A crash as something was knocked over. Listening for concrete evidence of Zimma's presence, his body jerked at a terrified shriek that was quickly cut off. Lips set in a feral snarl he slit a seam far enough so he could see.

Three soldiers were lifting Zimma onto a table. She twisted and thrashed trying to get free, but they laughed and forced her legs apart. She scratched one of them and he backhanded her across the face. Blood shot from her nose and soaked the gag in her mouth. Laughing at the sight, the guards fondled her breasts.

Zimma was naked except for underpants, which were being cut off. Two guards on duty at the tent door looked on with their lust showing and sidled closer. The commander's erection was visible as he spread Zimma's thighs farther and moved between her legs.

One of the guards stared stupidly when a knife blade suddenly pierced the tent wall and slit a seam from top to bottom.

"You son of a bitch!"

Leaping through the cut, Jeff drove his saber through the commander's body. Kicking the writhing body off his sword with a snarl, he swung a roundhouse cut that nearly decapitated one of those holding Zimma. Shouts of alarm rang out as the saber pierced the throat of another guard. Arzaks stationed at the tent door turned to run but bounced off others trying to enter.

Jerking Zimma off the table, Jeff thrust her behind him and shifted the saber to his left hand. The .357 flew into his right.

Five Arzaks started their rush with drawn swords. Jeff dropped to a knee and fired at the nearest one, the crashing ring of the explosion deafening in the confined space. Hit in the chest, the guard was blown backward into the man behind who was also struck by the bullet as it continued its path. Jeff fired a second then a third time, knocking over two more and filling the tent with gunsmoke and blast concussions. The last Arzak turned tail and ran out of the tent wailing terror.

Holstering the .357, Jeff ripped the gag off. Zimma didn't seem to recognize him, just stared blankly and wiped at the blood running down her chin. One side of her face was turning purple, and red handprints were visible on both breasts.

Fury that had been building since he discovered Carl had not been satisfied, but the need for revenge was pushed aside by the sound of thudding boots. Jeff hoisted Zimma into a fireman's carry and staggered out the rear of the tent.

Once into the forest he stopped to get his breath. Zimma was beginning to struggle so he set her down. Pulling her along, Jeff raced to the body of the Baktar seaman and stripped it of trousers and tunic. He handed them to Zimma, but she let them drop.

221

"It's Jeff, Zimma. You must put these on." He held the clothing out to her again. Shouts and screams were hardly softened by screening trees, and a bugle was braying the alarm over and over. "Oh, baby, please! We can't stay here!"

Zimma shook her head violently, spit blood from her mouth and put on the clothing with Jeff's help. Taking her hand, they moved deeper into the woods. When the uproar faded to a faint commotion, he stopped to wipe blood from her face.

It was a simple act of concern that triggered such a rush of emotion that Zimma burst into great sobs of relief. She really was safe. Jeff held her until she quieted.

"It is difficult to ask this of you. There is another person I am going release tonight. I must do this or not return."

After only a heartbeat, Zimma nodded. Anger had overcome terror. Jeff took her hand again and hurried toward the slave tent. This was a golden opportunity to free Carl. In fact, it was now or never.

With infinite care, Jeff sliced open a rear panel of the wall tent that served as a holding pen and peered inside. A single oil lamp did little more than create shadows. Three guards were present. Two were peering out the entrance trying to figure out what was going on. In a central location, the slaves were chained to two massive posts. There wasn't a chance he could silence all of the guards before they raised the alarm. Hopefully there were no more stationed outside.

It suddenly occurred to Jeff that there might be more than one holding pen. Carl might not be in this one. He studied the pile of slaves and exhaled slowly. Curled up in a ball, Carl was sleeping in a tangle of chains.

Jeff whispered, "Ready?" Zimma gripped his hand in reply. Knife at the ready, he stepped inside.

Slipping up behind the nearest guard, Jeff clamped a hand over his mouth and cut his throat. The guards at the entrance noticed the motion and came on with a shout. Coldly unemotional, Jeff shot them both

"The keys! We must find them! We only have minutes!"

"Here they are!" Zimma plucked a ring of keys from the first guard Jeff had killed.

Panicked by the gunshots, slaves clanked around in a confused jumble while Zimma unlocked chains with flying fingers. Jeff reloaded and hurried to Carl. He was looking around with dazed eyes and little comprehension.

"Off your ass, Jorgenson. We've got to move."

Tearing the irons off Carl's ankles, Jeff dragged him to the front of the tent. He stopped at the entrance and held an arm out to prevent Zimma from leaving while slaves ran from the tent in twos and threes. Angry shouts and orders to stop rang out accompanied by the crack of whips. Jeff counted to ten and looked outside.

The larger moon was well up and the smaller above the treetops, serving to reveal Arzaks racing around the area shouting questions, orders and counter-orders. Bonfires were beginning to roar as wood was heaped on, adding dancing orange light to the confusion. Grimly satisfied, Jeff took Carl's hand and they moved at a cautious trot toward the shore.

They made it to the far side of the bazaar before Jeff heard loud commands not far behind. It was still at least three hundred yards to the beach. They would never make it. He stopped behind a booth and took Zimma by the shoulders.

"You must go on and take Carl with you. I think Belstan will be waiting a short ways from the beach. Call him! If he isn't waiting, swim for the Baktar. I must stay and gain time."

"I cannot leave you to face the soldiers alone!"

"What can you do, Zimma? You have no weapon. Someone must get Carl to the beach. Please do this for me."

Zimma wanted to refuse but realized there was little she could do to help. Suddenly they were in each other's arms. Jeff crushed Zimma to him and quickly released her. Turning away, he jogged back the way they had come.

Taking Carl's hand, Zimma pulled him toward the beach. Before fading into the night, she threw an agonized look over her shoulder.

Concealed behind a trading booth, Jeff waited. Shortly he detected a vague group of figures moving cautiously from shadow to shadow in the moonlight. Jeff counted seven in the group and waited with drawn saber. He planned to cut down as many as possible in the first assault, then turn to the Colt.

When they were abreast he jumped out of hiding with sword in motion. Surprise was complete. Before they could rally, two Arzak were down and the rest fell back. He was about to draw the pistol when he was attacked from the side and had to beat off a furious assault.

Unnoticed, a second group of four Arzaks had circled in from his left. Jeff put his back to the booth and held them off, but could not spare even the few seconds it would take to draw the Colt.

It was not many minutes before he began to grow very tired. He knew the end was not far unless he could get at the pistol. Jeff went for it but felt a searing shock in his left leg and nearly collapsed as a blade drove home. Eager to make the kill, more Arzak crowded in on the fight with excited shouts. Within seconds he had taken another cut on his left side.

Numb with fatigue and blood loss, Jeff was only vaguely aware when the pressure of their attack slackened to nothing and Arzak shouts of victory gave way to mortal shrieks.

Standing with his back to the booth holding his side, Jeff slid to the ground in a sprawl. He watched the battle with vacant interest as blood pooled beneath him then all was black.

Thirteen

A Time to Run

Later, Jeff could remember only disjointed scenes and impressions from the first two days after receiving wounds that had nearly killed him. He faded in and out of consciousness, the only consistent picture that of Zimma's face hovering over him. Distantly, he noted the ever-darker circles under her eyes. On occasion Belstan's voice drifted in from the background.

Jeff entered full consciousness swaying in a hammock strung amidships on the Baktar's deck, the sun warming him as he moved from shadow to light and back again. He tried to lift his head but could not. Zimma's face abruptly appeared and looked down at him.

A large bruise on her cheek was turning green, and her lips and nose were badly swollen. He managed a wan smile. Tears fell on his face when Zimma laid her cheek on his. That evening, having been carried below and fortified with a mug of broth, Jeff learned what had transpired after parting from Zimma and Carl.

At the shore, Zimma and Carl had literally stumbled into Belstan. He had indeed left the beach, but only to collect the Baktar's crew and return. Upon hearing what had happened to her and of the death of their fellow crewman, the Baktars were in a fury. They would have rushed headlong into battle had not Belstan organized and led the attack.

Seven Arzaks remained when they arrived. The crew wanted blood and none of the Arzak remained alive after a furious counterattack. While the battle swirled around her, Zimma tried to stop the blood flow from Jeff's leg but could do no more than slow it down. She called for help and one of the older men applied a tourniquet to his thigh above the laceration. The chest wound was not bleeding badly and would have to wait.

Hoisting Jeff on their shoulders, they beat a hasty retreat to the ship with a fresh contingent of Arzaks on their heels. The captain had remained on board to prepare. The launch had no more than settled on the deck when the anchor heaved out of the water and the Baktar gathered way to the north on a fading zephyr.

At that point in the recitation, Jeff broke in with an urgent whisper. "My sword. Where's my sword?"

Belstan chuckled and came over to where he was lying carrying the saber. "Now I am convinced you will heal. I was certain you would ask. We have also put your weapon-of-six-deaths under lock and key."

"How is Carl?"

"He is in the next cabin sleeping." Belstan shook his head in sadness and disgust. "Long have Borgo and Arzak traded in slaves, robbing them of their lives and, much more heinous, their minds. Some, when by chance or circumstance freed, recover their will while others live on as a shadow of what they were or could have been." He smiled and waved an optimistic finger about. "This one, I believe, has good prospects. The spark of awareness and interest in life appear to be returning."

Three days had passed since leaving Tradertown. Considering the fluky winds, the captain estimated they were still two days out. Jeff spent the rest of the trip flat on his back in a cot or swaying in the hammock. His body was so weak he could hardly shift position, but Zimma was always there to help.

The breeze held up long enough for the Baktar to ghost into port. Jeff became aware of their proximity to Khorgan by a string of loud orders and tramping on deck as sails were lowered, followed by a bump as she slipped into her spot at the pier. Jeff and Carl were transferred to a spacious room in the warehouse next morning. Shortly thereafter a physician visited them.

Unceremoniously rolling Jeff onto his right side, the physician muttered over the wounds. After a period of poking, prodding and sniffing, he redressed the wounds.

"You are most fortunate. The suturing leaves much to be desired, but there is no sign of green suppuration." He turned to Carl.

Carl had been scrubbed clean on the Baktar, exposing every wound. Examining wide areas of crisscrossed whip marks and inflamed, oozing sores, the physician cursed the Arzaks in several languages. Each wound brought a new round of oaths until they grew stale, at which point he cleaned and bandaged in silence. Handing a list of instructions to Carl, the physician packed up and left.

Alone in their room, the two friends silently examined each other. Carl got out of bed and kneeled down to gather Jeff into his arms. His body started to shake, and he burst into great wracking sobs.

"I...oh, Jesus—thank you for finding me. God, I love you. I can't...oh, shit..."

Jeff patted Carl's back. "It's done, buddy. We're back together and you're safe."

Carl hung on for life and wept tears of agony. Jeff pulled Carl's head onto his chest and held him. On and on, tears flowed in recollection of the horror and in relief at having been rescued. Jeff found his friend's pain nearly unbearable and held Carl even tighter as if to physically squeeze love into him.

Some time later and exhausted by the reunion, Carl left to find something to drink. He returned with two cups of fruit juice and sat down on the foot of Jeff's bed. Taking a grateful sip, Jeff solemnly looked at Carl.

"Feel up to telling me how those Arzak assholes got you?"

"Think I need to."

As earlier speculated, Carl had been camped east of Hoodo Pass when the earthquake struck. His experience differed only in that he regained consciousness in the South March, Belstan's area of origin. As Carl got into the story, words came in a torrent.

"Took awhile to figure out I was a long way from home, boyo. Nearly starved to death by the time I met up with a group of hunters who took me in. Don't know who was more scared, me or them. Nice folks, though. Sort of worked my way into their tribe and helped the medicine man—after he finally became convinced I wasn't out to replace him, that is.

"We wandered south to do some trading with a village fifty miles or so north of Lugsburg, and were ambushed by slavers. Never had a chance. They killed everyone they didn't want and chained up the rest of us. I can't tell you what it was like, Jeff. I fought it for several months, but after awhile there wasn't much left to fight with. I was about to give up when you found me. That was the hardest part to bear—giving up and hating myself for it."

Jeff patted Carl's shoulder. "It's done now. Time to rebuild our lives. We're with some pretty fine people by any planet's standards. Here, use this." Jeff handed his shirt to Carl

"That we are, bucko, that we are." Carl dabbed at his eyes with the shirt. "Now—fill me in on what happened to you."

"It's a pretty strange story." Jeff didn't get far before Carl interrupted.

"Tell me again how big you estimated that mountain to be. The one you saw to the southeast."

"The only close approximation on Earth is Everest. Thing is, this one was sitting off by itself, not part of the mountain chain. It blew my mind."

"You know we're going to have to see if we can climb it," Carl chortled, "or at least get as high as we can without oxygen. I've got to see that mountain!"

"You're on. But wait until you hear what I ran into a week or so later." Jeff paused for effect. "Finally managed to kill a deer and happened to look at its teeth. Meat-tearing incisors and great whopping canines."

"Meat-eating deer? Nothing like that down south." Carl grinned wickedly. "Be interesting to drop a bunch of them into the Cascades about deer hunting time. I think that would add a new dimension to the term, open season. It must have been something of surprise when you figured it out."

"Yeah, I can tell you it really got my attention. Still thought I was on Earth at that point."

"Until you saw the two moons, right?"

"You too? But what happened next makes the impact those two moons had pale to nothing."

When Jeff finished relating his first wolf encounter, Carl's expression reflected both disbelief and intense excitement.

"Don't shit me, Jeffrey. Telepathy? The real thing?"

"The real thing, and that was just about my reaction when Balthazar hit me with it. That's how I knew it was you under all that dirt and grime back in Tradertown. Nearly got through."

Jeff related the rest of his story in a few paragraphs, then eyed Carl. "See any short, bandy-legged folks sort of like earth's Mongols while you were in Lukash?"

Still caught up with the wolves, Carl nodded vaguely. "Sure. Saw a whole bunch of them. Now that I think about it they did resemble Mongolians, although I didn't notice an epicanthic fold."

They talked for a while longer, but both men were still far from recovered. Jeff was the first to go. He was awake at the start of a sentence and asleep when Carl finished it. Tucking Jeff under a blanket, Carl tottered off to bed.

It was a week before Jeff' had recovered enough strength to attend a strategy conference. Belstan, Rogelf and Zimma were present as well as Ostfel, who was in charge of coordinating their agents. Carl had been included at Jeff's request.

Zimma hurried to meet them when they entered the room. She kissed Jeff on the cheek, led him to the table and pulled out a chair.

"I'm not going to break, Zimma."

"That remains to be seen."

She pushed the chair forward and he plopped into it. Taking a seat next to Jeff, she matter-of-factly picked up his hand.

"We are now all assembled," Belstan announced. "Let us begin. Jeffrey, what are your conclusions concerning Salchek intent?"

While bedridden Jeff had spent hours studying maps and fitting pieces of the Salchek puzzle together. After providing some background he got down to central issues.

"Saafir's mention of Salcheks marching north and those identified by Carl leaves little doubt that an invasion is underway. Tradertown will soon be taken. It is likely to become the staging ground for at least one prong of an attack on Khorgan. I now believe slaves were being shipped into and not out of Tradertown to do the manual labor called for by Arzak and Salchek fortification plans."

"The diagram you discovered in the sand strongly suggests this will take place."

"Yes it does, Rogelf, but the Salchek will soon move north from Tradertown. Lake Ligura offers an elegant highway to Khorgan. Yet I believe invasion by way of Tradertown is only one portion of this city's peril. Even as Belstan concluded, Lugsburg offers easy entry into Chaldesia. It is directly accessible by sea and only three or four weeks' march from Khorgan's gates."

Rogelf reported that tribute continued to flow south, with no evidence that city councilors were attempting to organize a defense.

"Our esteemed leaders have become so corrupted by greed that they now conclude their chests of gold can buy or control anything. Stupid, stupid, stupid and this city will pay dearly for it."

"Without doubt, but let us proceed to the heart of the matter," Belstan said. "Invasion comes. How soon? Only the Salchek are certain, yet from what has been said I believe they will be at Khorgan's gates and piers before fall. We must plan for our survival in what is to come."

"And I suspect our time to do so has been foreshortened," Jeff interjected. "What occurred at Tradertown is by now well known to the Salcheks. I could not avoid using my pistol, and reports of its effects have no doubt been greatly exaggerated in the telling. These reports may serve to speed the Salchek toward Khorgan. I suspect they will be here in no more than five weeks."

"Or less. Perhaps in three weeks." Belstan stood up and leaned his hands on the table. "There is no dealing with the councilors. I believe it will not be long ere they target us for revenge in an attempt to appease the Salchek. I am well known to them and my association with Rogelf has existed for years." With a sigh of regret, he put into words what everyone was thinking. "We must leave, and soon. If word of our Tradertown escapade should arrive before we accomplish this, all is lost."

A general discussion ensued covering every possible alternative, but it was clear from the start that their options boiled down to two: leave or die. In the end Rogelf and Belstan decided the entire trading operation would be moved north to Astholf. Rogelf had a trading station there that would have to serve.

At that point Jeff backed out of the conversation. Moving a large trading operation by ship was far outside his experience, and other thoughts clamored for attention. Fall was not far off, he had completed his mission, and it was time to leave for Rugen and Valholm. To leave for home. Oblivious to the spirited debate going on around him, Jeff turned the word around in his mind. Home. Where is my home?

When the meeting broke up he walked to quarters on Carl's arm in a state of exhaustion. Before falling asleep, Jeff murmured, "No, the North is my home. At least that much is clear."

"This will never do." Belstan and Carl were strolling the length of Rogelf's pier.

"They're working hard," Carl observed. "I don't see how they can go any faster."

"They cannot, but we are nearly out of time." Belstan hurried off.

Lines of stevedores streamed back and forth along the pier. They had been working from first light to well after dark for several days. Trade goods on hand were being transferred to the Baktar, but the pace was too slow if they wanted to get out of town alive.

Shortly, a number of heavy wagons were also rumbling from warehouse to ship. When the Baktar was loaded, overloaded as far as the captain was concerned, it was sent to Astholf with Ostfel on board to make necessary arrangements.

Rogelf chartered two additional ships, and these were soon tied up at the pier being loaded. A fourth ship, one of Rogelf's that had just come in, was reserved for personnel, furniture and livestock. There was no disguising the frenetic level of activity mandated by the evacuation schedule. By the third day of loading, Rogelf and Belstan's trade acquaintances were calling at regular intervals.

Some of those who stopped by were friends of long standing and were briefed after being sworn to secrecy. Rogelf and Belstan were fully aware how short a time such oaths would hold, serving to increase the urgency they all felt. The rest of those that called were dished up bland fare that had no bearing on reality but might serve for a period.

In spite of the interruptions, either Belstan or Rogelf were always on the pier to make sure the pace never slackened.

Although the job of moving seemed to have no end, the cavernous warehouse slowly emptied.

Anticipating surveillance, Rogelf detailed a number of his men to intercept as many council agents as possible. As a result, toward the end of the loading cycle a number of bodies began to wash up along the waterfront.

However, Rogelf was an old hand and knew his men could not possibly eliminate every agent. Other staff members were given the task of spreading contradictory rumors to foster confusion. Of primary importance, a steady flow of bribes insured current information from council chambers.

When he received reports that the councilors were planning to move against him, Rogelf put the evacuation into overdrive and posted observers on all major streets giving access to the waterfront. Despite Rogelf's concern about his strength, Jeff would not be denied and set out on foot to patrol his station.

He had not left the pier while recuperating and was immediately struck by the number of heavily loaded wagons lumbering north and south on Marine Way. The waterfront was often crowded with traffic, but not shortly after dawn. He resumed walking when he realized what was going on.

"Like rats leaving a sinking ship." Jeff imagined what the waterfront would look like by the end of the day. "This is spreading like wildfire," he glumly muttered. "By now the entire city must be infected. Shit, the place is going to come unglued!" He considered turning back but discarded the idea. Belstan and Rogelf were savvy and extremely well informed.

His patrol area was deep within the city. Jeff selected a café with outside tables near a major intersection. A breakfast crowd jammed the Palace, and the gossip mill was in full cry. Although people seemed uptight, Jeff heard nothing that alarmed him. The street was busier than usual for the hour, and many of the wagons were heavily loaded.

A troop of dragoons went by at a fast trot, and he stood up to see better. They were heading into the city not toward the waterfront, and Jeff sat back down. Just as quickly, he stood back up and followed their backs. They're armed with bows, he worriedly thought. Never seen that before. Time to move on.

He strolled deeper into the city but observed nothing of consequence. Jeff stopped to eat at a busy pushcart when his stomach told him it was time. Some of the rumors floating about were impressive. They ran the gamut from marauding gangs to a terrible disease that was racing through the city. Jeff smiled. Rogelf's strategy was paying off and about to hit the explosive stage.

He stayed close to the cart while eating, and figured he had hit pay dirt when two young officers of the guard stopped for a quick bite.

They were trying to keep their voices down but seemed agitated and spoke louder than intended. Jeff eased closer. His attention was riveted on the officers and he failed to note the two men and a woman who moved in concert with him.

"What in Ruzog's name is afflicting our superiors?" mumbled officer number one.

"And should I know more? I was on leave!" snarled number two. "Two days off and I was called back to duty!"

While it was piecemeal information, Jeff was left with the sense that a special formation had been called for the first hour after noon. He gulped down the last of his food.

"Time to beat feet. It's going down."

Jeff wove through the crowd around the cart. Time was short and he had to hurry. He was out of the press when a man wearing a cynical smile blocked his way.

"Did you have an interesting lunch, citizen Friedrick?"

Jeff whirled around. Three of them!

Elbow slam to the throat, duck, spin and up again with rigid fingers into the solar plexus. Two agents were on the ground, but the third gracefully thrust at his stomach with a dagger.

Jeff sidestepped, caught her arm and spun around. She shrieked with pain as long bones snapped and her shoulder dislocated. He kicked her in the head as she fell and took off at a run. Jeff was down to a walk and breathing hard when he made it to the warehouse. He slammed into the back office and cornered Belstan.

"We must leave now!"

"But goods remain to be loaded!"

"Fuck that!"

Rogelf heard the commotion and ran into the office. "What has happened?"

233

Jeff related what he had heard and his encounter with the agents. Rogelf seemed immobilized by indecision.

"Jeef, we just cannot. We must have three more hours."

"If we do not depart at once," Jeff said as calmly as possible, "the opportunity to leave will never come. The waterfront is coming apart, panic will soon take the city, and the guard will be here within the hour. Load the horses and save what is already onboard ship."

The traders had heard similar reports, ignored them, and were inclined to do the same with Jeff's. He was about to go ballistic when common sense finally overcame cupidity. Rogelf spun around and ran out of the office to start the process of loading the horses. Belstan was only a step behind.

"Where's Zimma? Has she returned?"

Belstan slid to a halt. "She is working on the ship."

The men ran out of the warehouse.

The waterfront was in a state of gridlocked bedlam. Overloaded wagons crept along at a snail's pace when they moved at all. Heavily loaded packhorses staggered by led by people, often entire families, who were themselves packing whatever could be carried. Pushcarts, hand wagons, even dogs, had been pressed into service. What had started out earlier in the day as hectic activity had become a full-scale evacuation.

Cynic was agitated by the groundswell of fear present along the waterfront and capered nervously when Jeff led him to the ship. However, he wanted out of the city as badly as anyone and nearly ran up the gangplank.

Tossing his personal gear down the main hatch, Jeff hustled to join the men guarding the pier head. Jeff stumbled to a halt holding his injured side and bent over to get his breath. Carl flashed an excited grin over his shoulder.

"Ain't we got fun?"

"Some fun, bucko. What a day!"

Emerging from the warehouse with his arms full of furniture, Rogelf bellowed, "The warehouse is empty."

The guard force backed toward the ship a step at a time. Frightened people pleaded and tried to bribe their way onto the ship. A band of wharf rats armed with clubs attacked the north end of the line but took to their heels when confronted with swords.

Exile To The Stars

The situation verged on a riot and was deteriorating fast when a young couple confronted Carl and Jeff. The man was bent under a huge load and sweating profusely. His wife was pregnant and leading a sobbing child.

"Oh please, sir. Please."

"We got the room, Jeff?" Carl shouted while thrusting back a richly dressed merchant waving a sheaf of bills.

"Maybe for fifteen or twenty. The ship is already crowded. Families with kids?"

"Got to do what we can."

Carl got a foot behind the merchant and tripped him backwards while simultaneously pulling the woman and child through the line of guards, closely followed by her husband. Pressed harder every minute, the guard contingent retreated. Every so often the line opened and another family raced for the ship.

They still had a ways to go when a troop of dragoons charged out of the city gate, sounding bugles to clear the way. Seconds later, another troop followed.

An inchoate roar of fear raced along the waterfront. People tried to stay clear of the troopers, but there was nowhere to go. Whips cracked up and down the street, and not only over horses.

The rearguard threw caution to the wind and pelted for the ship. No sooner were they on board than her hawsers were let go. No time for niceties of seamanship, the schooner was poled away from the pier and her sails raised with a rush. There wasn't much breeze and she wallowed like a pig stuck in mud.

The captain called out more orders and every stitch of canvas she owned was set. Slowly gathering way she moved out into the lake trailing lines astern, plimsoll mark two feet below the surface.

They were several hundred feet from the pier when the first of the guard thundered onto the wharf. Riders leaped from horses with bows in hand.

Carl called out, "Take cover!" and ran to herd city folk below.

Diving down the main companionway to the sound of arrows whistling overhead, Jeff caught child after child then exhausted mothers and fathers before returning topsides.

Arrows bristled in the sails, masts and on deck. The quartermaster had been forced to remain at the tiller and was

235

writhing on the deck with an arrow sticking out of his back. One of the horses had been hit and was bucking wildly. A handler got the mare under control, but not until she was exhausted.

Jeff was convinced his irrepressible friend had made a full recovery when Carl marched to the stern rail, dropped his breeches and mooned the soldiers on the pier.

The remainder of daylight was required to sort out the shambles on deck. Crates, furniture, assorted baggage—all were piled helter-skelter. Every able-bodied man and woman turned to under the captain's agitated direction. There was no room in the hold for Cynic and three other horses, so several of the crew knocked together temporary stalls on deck. Others threw tarps over deck cargo and tied it down. Without exception, everyone sweated streams in sauna humidity.

Looking off to the northwest during a short break, Jeff understood the captain's concern. Dark, scudding clouds were almost overhead. Close behind, black thunderheads billowed high blocking light from the sun.

As darkness intensified, the captain ordered crewmen to double lashings. Nearly full dark well before sunset, final preparations for the storm were made by ship's lanterns. Whatever breeze there had been disappeared, leaving the Tounae to wallow sluggishly in confused waves. The captain had two reefs tied into the foresail and the mainsail taken in, depending on a staysail run up in its place to provide balance.

The last hatch had just been fastened when a line squall came tearing across the water. It hit with a steam-whistle roar, laying the Tounae on her beams end in a lash of screaming wind and rain driven so hard it hurt. She slowly righted as the quartermaster allowed her to pay off and run with the wind over the port quarter.

One of the horses had fallen when the squall hit and kicked its stall to splinters while trying to get up on the wet deck. Jeff and Carl got her up and were tying the mare to a ringbolt when Carl happened to look south.

"God, damn! Grab onto something, Jeff!"

The wind had changed direction and blasted in from the south. Slamming the foresail across, the force of the wind heeled the Tounae until her port rail was taking green water over the top.

The same horse fell again in a wild thrashing of legs, this time skidding across the deck to fetch up against the port rail smothered in foaming water. Rain came down in buckets along with lightning bursts that seemed continuous, accompanied by deafening thunder rolls.

The storm built in fury until the surface of the lake was churned into a confused cauldron of towering waves that broke on board from every direction. The Tounae buried her bow in waves that submerged her from bow to stern, others swept across her waist in rushing masses of knee-deep water, and still she lived on.

Tying themselves to the mainmast, Jeff and Carl were nearly suffocated by air that had more water in it then oxygen. Forced to their knees by the wind, they hung on.

Jeff knew it was a thunderstorm, not a large frontal disturbance that might take hours to pass. Still, it seemed to his dulled senses that time had stopped and the storm would never end.

When it did and the first rays of a setting sun suddenly broke through, he could hardly believe it was over. The lightning rapidly decreased, the air became breathable and the thunderstorm was gone, racing east.

Through luck alone, the horse that had fallen didn't break a leg. She was corralled and maneuvered into a hastily re-fabricated stall. Jeff was in the middle of that scrum. When it was over, he felt lucky that flying hooves had not stove in his head or rib cage.

Cynic had stood firm but trembled with anxiety and was covered in a lather of sweat. Calming Cynic, Jeff stumbled below in a state of exhaustion. Too tired to change out of wet clothing, he was about to curl up when he was pressed into duty on a bilge pump crew. The pump eventually sucked air, but he kept turning his handle in a stupor until someone shook him.

It was after noon before Jeff found enough motivation to emerge from below decks. The Tounae was making good time to the northeast on a close reach, the main staysail having been replaced with a double-reefed mainsail. The sun was shining in a clear sky and sparkling off the water.

Hanging onto the weather shrouds, Jeff breathed deeply of the cool breeze. I could live on this, he thought, but a bite to eat wouldn't hurt.

The stench of vomit was overpowering when he went below to get some food, and his stomach churned in sympathy. Snatching a hunk of bread and a wedge of cheese, he fled topsides with Carl close behind.

The bow was empty, providing privacy for Jeff to fill Carl in on the situation in Rugen and Valholm. Carl whistled under his breath when Jeff stopped to yawn.

"So you've got a pack of Vandals and Visigoths doing their thing, and a loosely knit collection of feudal types that would like to think they're a kingdom, right?"

"Something like that, wise guy," Jeff laughed.

"Well, hell. You've got yourself a real situation, all right."

The men debated strategy until a crewman nudged them out of the way so he could hang a night lantern.

"Time to eat, squirt, let's head below."

The main cabin had been aired out, swabbed down, and was now inhabited by folks who could do more than throw up. Children were sleeping in every nook and cranny or climbing on whatever was at hand. Parents did their best to supervise, but it was something of a madhouse scene.

The pregnant mother spotted Jeff and Carl at once. She had no words, but hugged each of them and kissed their cheeks.

Following an evening meal taken in shifts, oil lamps swinging overhead, Jeff cornered Belstan. Talking with Carl had focused his mind.

"Rugen must be the center of any defense in the North. I am convinced the king will fight, the city was constructed to be defensible, and I believe there is time to prepare it for a siege. However, that will not suffice.

"Opening meaningful trade with Rugen is vital and must begin at once if there is to be any hope for its long-term defense. It sits near a treasure chest of raw materials, offering great wealth to any trader capable of perceiving the potential. I believe that you and Rogelf have that capability." Jeff folded his arms and waited.

Belstan stirred in his seat after a long silence. "Great wealth or certain death. Roll the bones and take your chance. If Rugen falls to the Salchek, it would mean death or worse for those who assisted in its defense."

"Yes, but..."

Belstan frowned at Jeff and he shut up.

"On the other hand, if Rugen stands any businessman with an early foot in the door could found a trading empire. As I said, roll the bones and take your chance. I will tell you, boy, that your vision intrigues me, but I must think on it and converse with Rogelf." Belstan patted several children on the head and went in search of his partner.

"Well, I gave it my best shot, Carl," Jeff said with a doubtful expression. "Now we'll have to wait and see what comes of it, if anything. Whatever the outcome, I'll be heading north shortly after we land at Astholf. How about you? Where do you want to fit into all of this? If you even do, of course."

Carl had been cogitating on that very question since they had started their conversation in the bow earlier in the day. He frowned in concentration and spoke slowly.

"It's not often that a person has the opportunity, can choose, to be part of something like this. We're talking a major historical event here, Jeff, not some tribal scuffle." He lapsed into a contemplative silence.

The 'swish, swish' susuration of water coursing along the starboard side of the hull they were leaning against formed a soothing background.

"Rugen could really benefit from your training. From a public health perspective, it's a disaster."

"Doesn't surprise me." Carl began nodding. "I've got to be part of this. I want to put my training to use in a practical way that I could not even dream of back in Seattle." He smacked a fist into his palm. "I have this gut feeling we can whip the Salchek, or at least drive them back south if the right pieces can be put together in time. While you haven't said it in so many words, I know you are going to try and weld the northern tribes into some form of confederation. You are best suited for that job, you have been called to do it, it must be done." Carl narrowed his eyes as if listening to some inner voice.

"I feel, I sense that my place is in Rugen working to make it stronger through what I know. A chance to make a difference." Carl sat up straight, his eyes gleaming. "Damn, what an opportunity. What a time! I wouldn't have missed this for the world."

In Jeff's experience, Carl had never committed to anything other than his work and fencing. Of course, neither had he. There had been nothing on Earth worth committing to.

"You've just said it all, man. A chance to really make a difference. I can't tell you how good it will be to have you at my back in Rugen when I head north. We got us a real team going here."

"Like yea, bro."

Fourteen

Appearance Isn't Everything

Deep in the Tounae's hold, Rogelf watched Zimma closely. Since leaving Khorgan, in fact since her return from Tradertown, she had been so quiet that he had become concerned. Observing her potter about in a distracted fashion, Rogelf thought he had a good idea what was going on in Zimma's mind. In reality, he understood only a fraction of her turmoil.

The shock of seeing Jeff lying unconscious in a pool of blood had been so devastating that Zimma had yet to recover. She had seen seriously wounded men before—that wasn't the issue. It was the role she had played in putting him there.

First she had insisted on joining the expedition in spite of the risks her presence would pose, then repeatedly stood in opposition to every suggestion that would have reduced those risks. As a result, a Baktar crewman had died and Jeffrey had come so close she still found it hard to believe he had survived.

Watching his blood pour onto the sand as she desperately tried to staunch the flow, she knew with clairvoyant certainty that if he died her own life was forfeit.

She had endlessly reviewed her life prior to that one terrifying event, and each time cringed away with self-loathing. The wild, drunken parties. Smoking kalheesh until she didn't remember or care which man she had slept with, or how many. But that was only part of the shame. It was the look of stark fear on her father's face each time she stumbled home, and of contempt on her brother's, that had truly haunted every waking hour and much of her dreaming since escaping Tradertown.

When there were no more tears to cry, the exquisite pain deep in her soul remained. Now, far out on Lake Ligura, the worst of that agony had relented and she was free to focus on an issue that had been endlessly running around in the back of her mind.

Leaning against a stack of trade goods, Zimma called up an image of Jeff when they had first spoken on board the Baktar. A question took shape: what would life be worth without him?

Jolted by the question and not ready to deal with it, she picked up a bale of clothing that had come adrift and found a secure niche for it. Dusting off her hands, Zimma's cheeks grew hot when she remembered the look on Jeff's face when her blouse had been torn off. And the next morning when he walked away in those leather pants. ... Zimma felt something stir that had nothing to do with guilt.

Snatching a block of wood left sitting on a bale, Zimma heaved it at the dim shape of a spubak scuttling across the aisle. The squeak and scrabbling of claws that followed was deeply satisfying.

She sat down on a crate of spices and tried to imagine what it would be like to get up each morning and not feel a rush of excitement at the prospect of seeing Jeff again. To get up each morning and know she would never see him again.

Zimma felt such a stab of fear that she jumped to her feet and couldn't stop a little cry. Then, quite unaccountably, her mind abruptly changed course. For the first time in her life she thought about babies; what it would be like to carry and give birth to a child.

Graphic images of women she had seen in various stages of pregnancy flashed through Zimma's mind. Always before she had thought them ugly and swollen. Now she recalled the radiance that virtually glowed from their skin, and a special kind of contented wisdom in their eyes that had made her feel resentful.

Zimma envisioned herself far along in pregnancy and thought how envious other women would be. Yes, they would be! Jeffrey would put a baby in me such as this world has never imagined!

Breathing hard, eyes flashing, Zimma felt such a rush that she put a hand out to steady herself. With that thought, a line of reasoning closed to form a circle and she knew without doubt what she wanted, and whom she wanted to spend her life with.

The insight was so strong that it staggered her, and was immediately followed by a burst of fear that made the first one seem like nothing. What if he doesn't want me? Why should he? Why would any man want a woman who has treated him so badly? He is going to leave me. I know he is. I'll never see him again. Standing in the dark aisle, Zimma burst into tears.

Rogelf hurried up the aisle and pulled her into his arms. "What is it? Please, little one, you must tell me."

"It is Jeffrey, Father. I am going to lose him. He hates me."

Belstan trotted from the other direction in time to overhear. He was not burdened with the restraints of fatherhood, yet accorded the affection of a favored uncle.

"Look at me, Zimma."

She released Rogelf and turned to face him with downcast eyes. He lifted her chin.

"There is no hate in Jeffrey. You are attempting to hate yourself. Since returning from Tradertown, and for the first time in years, I am proud of you. Now you have come into your own and will either seek what you would have or cast opportunity to the wind, perhaps forever. It is life, Zimma. I know Jeffrey is very fond of you. It is in your hands to discover if there is more."

The uncompromising, even stern, tone of Belstan's voice settled Zimma down at once. She did not need to reflect on his words to understand that they conveyed the stark truth. Choking back a sob, she drew herself up.

"I will have him."

"Then it is time to be done with talking and tears. Go. Discover your destiny."

Zimma kissed Rogelf, hugged Belstan, and fled down the aisle. She missed the corner, slid into some bales, ricocheted back and was gone. Looking at each other, the men let their breaths out together. Belstan waved for Rogelf to follow him.

"I believe this moment calls for a pot of ale."

"Oh, where is he?" Zimma had searched for Jeff from the crew's quarters near the bow to the captain's cabin in the stern.

Heart beating a rapid tattoo, Zimma ran up the main companionway ladder, skidded to a halt on deck and looked around. Even though land was out of sight, she knew a moment of panic. *He is gone!* At that moment she spied Jeff leaning on the weather rail staring across the water, tousled hair blowing in the fresh breeze.

"Thank the gods."

Wishing she didn't smell of sweat and look like a fishmonger, Zimma straightened her clothing. She did a quick mental inventory of her clothing and jewelry. Perhaps some perfume. ...

Zimma shook her head savagely, and thought, No! I have behaved like a whore, but that is done with forever. If he does not want me as I am, or because of what I have been, then it was not meant to be. Gathering resolve for what she must do, Zimma walked over and leaned on the rail next to Jeff.

Startled out of worried reflection, Jeff smiled at Zimma and put a companionable arm around her shoulders. At his touch Zimma knew it was right, had been right for many weeks. She rested a hand on his arm and moved closer so their hips were touching. There was no need for words. The body contact and shared presence was worth more than a volume. Yet there was unfinished business. After a period she disengaged Jeff's arm and turned him from the rail.

"I have yet to thank you for saving my life and freedom, Jeffrey. Still I awake of a night in the grip of deep terror from those hours while a captive. I do not believe my spirit would have long survived, had you not come for me." Captured by those memories again, tears gathered in her eyes. "But you did, and nearly died as a result." Zimma paused and looked down. When she looked up her face was resolute.

"And now there must be a reckoning. These past weeks have afforded barely sufficient time to consider my life in all its shallow and hateful manifestations. I have apologized to my father, yet only time will permit me to compensate him for all he has endured in the name of love."

"Zimma, please. You don't have to do this."

"Yes! Yes I do! I must rid my soul of this burden so that love and charity may find a home." Zimma gripped Jeff's arms so hard it was painful. "And you. You who I called oaf and buffoon, whose very father I termed a churl, rescued my spirit from such degradation as cannot be imagined." Tears streamed down Zimma's cheeks but she would not look away. "Please, will you forgive me?"

Jeff had never encountered such a thing in his twenty-eight years. Zimma had not only apologized, but also given her soul into his hands. Frozen by the moment and lack of even a vague precedent, his tongue was locked in place.

Hope faded as the silence dragged on. It had been too much to expect. Zimma steeled herself when Jeff spoke.

"I...I find myself consumed by such feelings that they threaten to tear me asunder. God, Zimma. You are...I mean. ... Yes, with all my heart. I forgive you. But, you see, I think I...no! I don't think, I know that I...know that I love you."

Zimma watched emotions chase each other across Jeff's face, read the intent of his fractured syntax; understood the meaning. His final words sent her spirit soaring into the heavens.

"Oh, my love."

They came together in one step, bodies molding to one another in a way that knew no hard edges. Their lips met in the first kiss. Long-frustrated emotion found the bridge and rushed between two hearts. It was not a crushing embrace, rather one of true passion that had found release.

When they separated, Zimma looked into his eyes as if seeing him for the first time. She placed a finger on his lips, perhaps to document what had passed between them. Kissing her finger, Jeff wrapped Zimma in his arms. Words had no place in what they were feeling, and they swayed back and forth to the lift and surge of the ship.

They spent the rest of the day holding hands and creating dreams. Jeff's mind had only been waiting for the opportunity to acknowledge what his heart had been promoting for a long time—he loved Zimma without exclusion or doubt. By evening he wasn't sure he would be able to leave her when they arrived at Astholf.

"Zimma, I find my feelings so deeply engaged that I stand in awe. Somehow the word love is not strong enough, complete enough. Yet everything has occurred so quickly, been so life and death centered. How many days do we have to really acquaint ourselves with one another before we must separate?"

"We have this time."

Zimma kissed him slowly and thoroughly, exploring every contour of his lips.

"You are mine, Jeffrey. It is so wonderful to say that." She rested her cheek on his chest. "Yet it is a time of war. I understand that you must leave me for the while, but let us not tarnish the moment with misgivings or doubt. We must grasp that which is possible, not squander joy in anticipation of loss."

Later, as they watched the sun slip below the horizon and turn the water to gold, they shared another kiss; let themselves be consumed by it and each other.

That evening the captain announced they would arrive at Astholf the following afternoon if the breeze held. Jeff and Carl were worried about Belstan. One day to port and still no word. It was a great relief when he approached them with a determined stride.

"You have caused me great distress, young man. Never has my desire to turn a few linta waged such a savage war with my determination to stay alive. It is late, and such serious matters as trade and profit are better discussed at an earlier hour. Rogelf and I will confer with you and Carl tomorrow morning to share our minds on this matter."

True to his word, it was only mid-morning when they were summoned from the main hatchway by an imperious crooking of Belstan's finger. The three of them, Jeff, Zimma and Carl, had been having a wonderful time talking. Zimma shooed them away.

"May the gods preserve you!" She said it with a laugh, but the men were not reassured.

They met in the captain's cabin. Belstan's expression was intense, and his eyes bored into Jeff's.

"Rogelf and I have discussed at great length the part we might play in the supply effort for Rugen. What you have suggested is, to our minds, impossible."

Jeff felt the world spin and was grateful he was sitting down. As Belstan obviously had more to say, he fought back the strong urge to immediately object. Belstan rolled out the inevitable map and waved them over to look on.

"Astholf by itself is nothing. Its strength lies first in its association with Khorgan, and second, with Rugen. It is naught but a pathway for raw material flowing south, and for finished objects flowing north. The great majority of this by way of Lake Ligura. Astholf would have been, has been, the main link in trade with Rugen.

"I must ask you, young men, how long will Astholf's ships remain unmolested on the lake? How long will Khorgan's gates be open to Astholf trade no matter the means of transportation? We believe, perhaps, six weeks. Another six weeks and a Salchek fleet will be tying up at Astholf's piers." Belstan shook his head while continuing to examine the map. "The North has always posed obstacles to trade. You are correct, young Jeff. Rugen does sit near many treasures. But look you where it sits."

Belstan pointed at Rugen's location on the map. "Nowhere! The city is in the middle of this land but close to nothing. It has poor roads when any exist at all. Close by are nearly impenetrable forests and mountains inhabited by warlike peoples. Without Astholf and Khorgan to link with, it is hopeless." Face impassive, Belstan sat down and folded his arms.

After an interval of silence, Jeff quietly said, "Without a reliable source of trade, resistance to the Salchek is doomed to stalemate at first, then defeat. When last they invaded, this land was freed only by the happenstance of their voluntary withdrawal. I believe it foolhardy to once again rely on the intervention of providence."

"The gods expect more of us than that," Belstan agreed.

"Given that," Jeff continued, "I will not pretend to be aloof from your decision, for it is crushing. Yet in spite of that decision the defense of this land remains a duty that cannot be denied or assigned. What must be done, Carl and I will venture to do. Without your help if necessary, but with sadness." Jeff gazed evenly into Belstan's eyes. "Do you, then, counsel despair?"

Belstan's expression was unreadable. For minute after silent minute, he studied Jeff and Carl. Rogelf gave the impression that he was not listening. Instead, he appeared to be examining the cabin floor as if searching for defects in workmanship. Belstan pursed his lips and nodded slowly.

"The substance of your question is basic to this affair and to life. Despair is the resort of fools and the weak. As I said, we have thought deeply on this matter and," waving a finger at Jeff and Carl, "on you both. We are finished in the South not only because of what happened at Tradertown, but by choice."

"Belstan and I understand trade," Rogelf broke in smoothly, "and in doing so have come to some understanding of people as well. Without people of value, nothing of consequence may ever be accomplished. We have both, Belstan and I, come to feel a deep respect for you, Jeefry, and a growing respect for you, Carl."

"Indeed, indeed," Belstan said with firm authority. "Words that lead to action and accomplishment."

One step removed from the interaction's intense emotion, Carl had been watching the traders closely and more objectively than Jeff. These guys are good, he thought admiringly. What a team. Yes! Rogelf's turn!

"Events surrounding the Salchek invasion will likely spin themselves out over the balance of our two lives and a large portion of yours before the outcome is known. What has passed between us today has been necessary so we may decide on a course of action. I am satisfied." Rogelf turned to Belstan with eyebrows raised in silent query.

Totally mystified, Jeff looked to Carl for insight but only got a supportive wink.

Belstan's face broke into a huge smile. "As am I. Despair is for dogs! Rogelf and I will assemble all that remains to us in Astholf and journey to Rugen in caravan as soon as it may be arranged."

Jeff was stunned by what seemed a complete turnabout. He glanced at Carl and got another wink. Looking down, he shook his head and laughed wryly.

"You two are something else. Now that's what I call teamwork."

"Even though our ploy was necessary, I apologize for abusing your trust," Belstan replied, and patted Jeff on the shoulder. "We had to be sure of your steadfastness of purpose. What lies ahead will be no easy thing." Belstan rubbed his hands together. "But such a challenge! To be the ones who open large-scale trade with the North!"

Jeff was feeling very sober and did not respond. It was unsettling to realize that Belstan and Rogelf's decision had crystallized only after grilling him. One immature reaction such as an angry retort might have tipped the scales the other way. So much hanging on a few words, he thought, and I didn't have a clue! Thank God I didn't blow it.

Shortly, Belstan once again had them clustered around the map. "Here is what must be done. As you have implied, Rugen must become the center not the end point of trade routes." Belstan's finger moved around the map.

"For many years to come, Rugen's prosperity will lie not to the south in Astholf, Khorgan and Borgo, but in establishing trade routes to Torsberg and the island of Skene in the east." His finger skipped to the west coast. "Here lies real hope—Jutenberg and Ruun, and to the north, Trunstad and Hochberg."

Rogelf continued the train of thought. "These designs will consume perhaps five years' labor. The challenge Rugen must first meet is surviving the siege that is nearly assured. The supplies we bring will be of value. It is our intention to convert the greater portion of our holdings to products a city under siege will find useful."

Impressed by the scope of the traders' imagination and ambition, Jeff was also aware of the risks they were willing to assume with no promise other than their faith in him and, to an extent, in Carl. That made him uneasy, knowing in his head if not in his heart that he could easily wind up dead in some northern forest.

"In return for all that is proposed and risked, you must be given a charter by the city of Rugen to develop and control these trade routes. You must also be given ironclad guarantees. This will be my first task upon arrival at Rugen."

Belstan and Rogelf were pleased by Jeff's proposal. A planning session ensued and continued for the rest of the day. The first and only really important debate centered on the small matter of survival for the next year or two. The meeting broke up when they received a message that the ship would be tying up at Astholf within the hour.

One look at Astholf while they were tying up and it became apparent that it was a smaller clone of Rugen. That made sense when the men learned that it, too, had been built during the last Salchek invasion.

Anxious citizens eager to hear the latest information greeted the Tounae's crew when they disembarked. Ostfel's arrival, it seemed, had stirred up a hornet's nest.

Jeff and Carl hit the streets early the next day under the guidance of Golfin, one of Rogelf's employees. The few items of clothing that Carl had picked up in Khorgan would never tolerate hard use. It was time to do some serious shopping.

Astholf was a frontier city, and purchasing rugged clothing fit for the trail posed no problem. However, they had no luck at all finding a sword that was both well made and suitable to Carl's tall frame.

"I think it's a lost cause, Jeff. Maybe I can find something in Rugen."

"Not likely. The swords I've seen there are no better. Wish I'd picked up a sword while in Tradertown. The only positive thing I have to say about the Arzaks is that they know how to forge good steel."

Golfin suddenly snapped his fingers. "Thank you, Jeffrey. Perhaps there is yet hope."

Wearing a grin of anticipation, he led them to a seedy shop in a back alley. On the way Golfin explained that the proprietor, a small-time weapons dealer, was deeply in debt to Rogelf and had been dodging payment for some time. More importantly, it was nearly certain he had Arzak dealings through his wife's family. The proprietor winced when they entered.

"All right, Golfin, what will it take to settle."

Golfin smiled toothily and watched Bortog sweat for a few moments before saying, "That's not why we're here. These gentlemen wish to look at swords, good swords and," waving his arm to include everything visible, "not this refuse."

Brightening at the prospect of making a profit instead of having his feet put to the fire, Bortog disappeared into the back of his shop. After a period of dimly perceived activity he returned with an armful of weapons.

"These swords, gentle sirs, are of the finest quality but were forged in Arzak. I would be most appreciative if that fact did not become generally known."

With a sense of relief, Jeff and Carl sorted through a wide selection of weapons that were equal in quality to Saafir's collection in Tradertown. Carl eventually gravitated to a rapier that fit his hand as if made for him.

Stepping outside, Jeff and Carl traded a few passes to test the rapier's balance and length. Both were close to perfect, the action a lot of fun. Although accustomed to a foil, Carl took to the rapier like an old friend.

While Bortog fitted Carl with a sword harness, he picked up and set down a slim poniard so often that Jeff handed it to him for dessert. For his last encore, Golfin guided them to a stable in search of a horse for Carl. It happened to be the one Cynic was quartered in, and Jeff enlisted his help.

It was dark inside the stable so they moved to a corral and inspected horse after horse as they were led by. Cynic rejected each with contemptuous snorts and acid criticism. After a dozen or so had passed, he suddenly shot his head in front of Jeff and brought his teeth together with a sharp clack only inches from the horse trader's arm.

"Gods and demons!" Fishko did a respectable standing broad jump away from Cynic.

"My horse does not respect many two-legs. In this instance, I agree with him completely. You have shown us nothing but wind-broken crow-bait, and most of them lame to boot."

Fingering the haft of his sword, Jeff stared at Fishko until the oily fellow shifted his eyes and feet.

"Either produce horses worthy of the name or you will receive no business from ourselves or anyone we are associated with. If you have no good horses, say so now."

Cursing under his breath, Fishko spat a brown stream and lead them to an adjacent corral. He waved a hand at the horses inside the corral.

"Now don't go gettin' hasty. This yere bunch is good horseflesh."

"Right." Jeff unlatched the corral gate. *"Horse-brother, would you be so kind? If there are any that meet your standards, cut them out so we may view them closer."*

"With pleasure, horse-brother." Cynic trotted into the corral.

Fishko looked on with slack-jawed amazement as Cynic chased, intimidated or provoked every horse in the corral. He settled on two and herded them over so Jeff could get a look.

"Good work, horse-brother. They both appear sound. Which do you prefer?"

Cynic snorted and whuffled a bit before sending a sleek chestnut closer. *"His spirit is good, and I believe he will display courage on a long run."*

"We'll take that one."

"But that is my personal horse!"

"Do you wish to make a sale, or do we search out another stable?"

Fishko writhed, spat, kicked at the dirt and cursed. "He ain't cheap."

Astholf was less than half the size of Rugen, and the number of shops within its walls limited in proportion. Not surprisingly, there were also fewer shops that dealt in quality products. Zimma and Rogelf wandered through a number of food stalls and groceries but found none that were acceptable.

Hope was fading late in the day when she found a grocery that had promise. The building was nicely painted and the walkway in front swept clear of debris.

Entering, Zimma nodded at the sight of youngsters fanning flies away from neat stacks of cheese, dangling rows of summer sausage, and symmetrical piles of fresh produce. Picking up a fruit the size of a grapefruit but blue in color, she found it and others in the display to be almost ripe and not bruised.

"This shop will do, Father. I am so relieved!"

Rogelf found nothing to criticize in the store and just nodded. They wandered the aisles, Zimma plucking items from various displays as they went until the wicker basket she had brought along was filled.

The store's proprietor didn't recognize them, an uncommon occurrence in Astholf, and they chatted while Rogelf paid the tab. It proved such a pleasant experience that Zimma would have talked longer, but she could feel that time was running out.

Arm in arm, they strolled toward the warehouse. Zimma was so happy that every so often she skipped a few steps. Rogelf had not seen Zimma skip since she was a young girl and looked away to conceal his emotion.

It was a soft summer evening and neither of them was in a hurry to see it end. Zimma could not remember the last time she had gone anywhere with her father and felt a stab of remorse. It had been such a delightful afternoon. Squeezing Rogelf's arm, she turned her head to smile at him.

"Thank you for accompanying me, Father. It has been so wonderful having you all to myself that I am reminded of the years when I did not consider such an opportunity worthy of my presence or time."

Rogelf examined his daughter's face while reviewing those heart-wrenching years during which he had helplessly watched her slip away. He patted her hand.

"We are now reunited, my Zimma. Let us never again find ourselves viewing one another across such an abyss."

"It shall never be. I shall never permit it to happen, Father. I cannot find words to express what I have learned of myself through meeting Jeffrey. He is so far within my heart, has filled its every nook to such completion."

"And yet, are you completely sure? As your father I must ask this question. I love Jeefrey as my son and will deny him nothing, including your hand. Yet he is not of our people this land or very world. We know little of his homeland, but what I have heard of it is most disturbing. While he is a courageous, well-thought and honest young man, Zimma, I also perceive he has been deeply wounded. Such wounds of the heart often prevent or subvert true attachment." Rogelf veered to the side of the walkway and stopped.

"I am familiar with many aspects of your nature, Zimma, for they were also present in your mother. Do you understand that, for you, after this night, there is no turning back? That you will be forever tied to and share Jeefrey's destiny? That you will be so tied even though, as an outlander, he might well fail to comprehend and thus fully respect such a binding? In full knowledge of his origins, do you willingly and freely accept this?"

Zimma felt a shiver work its way up her spine. She had never heard her father speak in such a fashion. The finality of his words forced her to review every aspect of her new relationship with Jeff. She did not hurry the process.

"As I have said, I do not have the words to express what I feel for Jeffrey. My life would cease to have meaning were I to discover he was lost to me. Yes, I recognize he is deeply wounded. Having said that, I also perceive this condition springs not from his character but from experiences on this Earth. Was I not troubled, Father?"

Rogelf could only nod. "There is no gainsaying that fact."

"Just so, and severely. Yet I have been salvaged. I do not propose to know all ends of my love for this man or his comprehension of it, only that he is mine and if it must lead us both to a desperate end, even death, then I accept such without reservation. I will have him, I will have his children, I will have his destiny."

Profoundly moved by Zimma's answer, Rogelf bowed from the waist with arm extended. "My heart overflows with gratitude that you are my daughter. May your joining prosper and bear fruit in due season."

In the formal manner of Chaldesia, Zimma duplicated Rogelf's bow. "As the fruit of a gentle summer finds expression in plenitude, so shall our children spring forth and sustain life."

Brushing a tear away, Rogelf placed his hands on Zimma's shoulders just to look at her. In one afternoon, ten years of agony had faded away. The sun was gone when they arrived at the warehouse and Zimma reluctantly dropped his hand.

"I must prepare myself before the Flames of Rishak consume me, Father. Already it has started. Will you see to the food?"

"I would be honored." Rogelf hesitated before saying, "I so deeply miss the presence of your mother. Do you fully understand the Ritual of Testing? That it is no coupling for sport or simple pleasure? It must not go awry! Never forget that Jeefrey is not of our people. If he should..." Rogelf paused to rephrase. "Please, my daughter, do not put your life at risk."

Zimma patted his cheek and smiled. "Aunt Gemma was most dedicated to the task of my education in this matter. Also, and again, I have given considerable thought to Jeffrey's nature. No viciousness resides within him. Now please, Father, be at rest! We will both succeed."

Rogelf relaxed at once. His sister, Gemma, was not one to be diverted from a task she had set her mind on.

"Then test him, daughter, and discover whether his strength is worthy of you."

Zimma's eyes sparked and her skin seemed to glow. "Rest assured that Jeffrey will be tested as no man before him."

Jeff left Carl sorting through his acquisitions and searched for Zimma without success. Apparently she had gone shopping with her father. Tired, feeling melancholy for a variety of reasons and even a bit homesick for the first time in months, he retired to his room. Playing the recorder helped, but his heart wasn't in it and he blew out the candle.

Months of constant exposure to attack while camping out had resulted in a light sleep pattern. One moment Jeff was asleep, the next he was sitting up fully alert. The room was pitch black and there was not a sound to be heard. He was about to shrug it off when a floorboard in the hallway creaked loudly.

"Get serious, boyo," he murmured, "that ain't mice out there." Jeff had his feet on the floor when he sniffed the air. "What is it? Can't smell anything, but damn! I haven't felt this kind of rush since I was thirteen."

A portion of Jeff's mind shouted at him to grab the pistol, but the stronger part wasn't listening. The door to his room opened with a squeak of dry hinges. That did the trick. Jeff shot his hand under the pillow in search of the Colt. Before he could withdraw it, a weight settled on the bed and a hand covered his mouth.

Lips tickled his ear and a low-pitched voice growled, "Be still."

The hand over his mouth was soft and small, the voice feminine. He did not recognize it. Alarm overwhelmed desire and he pulled the hand away, thinking, What the hell is in here with me?

"Zimma?"

Throaty, derisive laughter whispered into his ear and Jeff was thrust onto his back. Before he could react, a body landed on his chest and teeth were fastened to his ear in a hard bite. Within seconds, a tidal bore of desire such as he had never known swept over Jeff and he didn't care who was in bed with him.

The voice snarled, "Take me if you can."

It was Zimma.

Jeff immediately pulled Zimma's head down and crushed his lips to hers. He was sleeping in the nude; Zimma had a thick robe on. Tearing the robe open, he pulled it down over her shoulders and grasped her breasts. Her pleasure was such that she cried out and thrust a hand between his legs.

"Now prove that you will be mine forever!"

Hands and lips explored with painful urgency until Jeff's need was so consuming that he forced Zimma onto her back. Using his weight and arms to hold her down, Jeff attempted to separate her legs with a knee. Laughing disdain, she thrust him away with ease.

Licking blood from his ear, raking his back with her nails, fighting him off again and again, Zimma drove Jeff until he threw her to the floor in frenzy. Zimma's head bounced off wooden planks, leaving her dazed. Jeff tore her legs apart and thrust deep inside with a single stroke.

Shouting triumph and raw exaltation, Zimma clamped her legs around his waist and forced her hips up with a convulsive twist.

Everything faded from Jeff's existence but the thrashing, furnace-hot body underneath him and a single-minded drive to impregnate her that reached beyond the beginnings of humanity. When orgasm exploded, Jeff was only vaguely aware of Zimma's screams of release.

He awoke in bed with his cheek pillowed on a breast and a sense of well being that was euphoric in intensity. When memories of their loving filtered in Jeff nearly bolted upright. Instead, he cautiously sat up and stared down at Zimma as if seeing her for the first time.

As he continued to remember, Jeff thought, What is she? What happened to me? How could anything be so wonderful and terrifying at the same time?

Zimma was sleeping on her back, hair spread out on the pillow in wild disarray and one leg bent out to the side. A brilliant flush on her cheeks swept backward to include the ears, giving them an elfin look. The flush also extended down her neck and between generous breasts in a slender leaf pattern.

How beautiful, he mused, tracing a finger along one edge of the flush. Can there be a touch of green and blue in it? Is that possible?

Letting his questions drift away, Jeff sighed with satisfaction and leaned down to tease a nipple with his lips while caressing belly and thighs. Her eyes opened. Stretching luxuriously, she thrust her chest up and began purring with a throaty rumble.

The pressure of Zimma's eyes was so strong that Jeff released the nipple and raised his head to look at her.

Brilliant green eyes alight with the inner fire of a predator feasted on him; seemed to be judging the right moment to spring. Bright cyan sparks whirled slowly deep within her eyes, drawing him closer to discover new galaxies never imagined.

Zimma sat up, gripped his chin and turned his head with easy strength. When she leaned close to examine his ear, Jeff could feel the heat from her skin. Turning his head back, she raised her lips in a feral smile.

"It was a good bite, do you not think so?"

Whatever they were, whatever the sparks represented, they proved so hypnotic he didn't move or speak. Her gaze softened and Zimma pulled Jeff's head close for a long kiss. When she released him, Zimma sat up straight and bowed.

"First Love's greeting, my Jeffrey. May all our joinings know such rapture."

The formality of Zimma's bow and her wording left no doubt in Jeff's mind that what he had experienced the night before had no analog on Earth. Jeff took Zimma's hand and bowed over it.

"My greetings to you, Lady. I stand in awe of your beauty and the joy of our First Loving."

Placing a hand above her pelvis, Zimma dimpled pleasure.

"The strength of your seed assures me that our children will be strong and numerous."

"I am hopeful I did you no serious injury," Jeff responded. There was a large bruise on her neck and several others on her breasts.

"They are of no significance," Zimma replied with a languid smile. "You were challenged to gain entry and suffered no opposition to that end."

Her eyes came alight with the same predatory glow, with the same brilliant sparks that orbited a point of phosphorescent green. Growling under her breath, Zimma pushed Jeff flat and leaped on top to straddle his hips.

When they awoke the second time, Jeff got dressed long enough to find a jug of water and some bread. They were dehydrated and downed the water at once, but took their time feeding each other hunks of bread. Later, Zimma had Jeff sit on the edge of the cot.

Extracting a damp cloth from the small bag she had brought, Zimma cleaned the bite on his ear. She did it with such careful precision and purred so loudly under her breath all the while that Jeff did not move. He knew it was Zimma beside him, but he also knew it wasn't the Zimma he was familiar with.

Her behavior throughout the night had been so alien to anything he had experienced on Earth that he would not have been surprised to see her transform into a mountain lion. That was it, Jeff decided. She had already transformed and he had no idea what to expect.

Spreading a light coating of salve on the bite, she lay down and held her arms out with a sunny smile. The Zimma of earlier memory had returned. Jeff entered her arms with a great sense of relief.

Before dozing off he reviewed a long list of questions in his mind. Even unanswered the questions urged a conclusion that was unsettling. Brushing the questions away, he smiled and closed his eyes. Whatever Zimma was, he could not imagine life without her.

An appointment at the farriers to replace Cynic's badly worn shoes forced Jeff to get out of bed mid-afternoon. They dressed slowly, reluctant to break the spell of their time together.

"Will you stay with me for the nights remaining to us?"

Brushing her hair to work out the tangles, Zimma turned to Jeff with a matter-of-fact smile.

"Of course. When duty permits, we will never sleep apart again."

The sense of complete finality in Zimma's voice was so strong that Jeff paused to look at her while tugging on a boot. When she grinned and stuck out her tongue, he gave a shout and hobbled over to grab her in an enthusiastic embrace.

At the farrier, Cynic's behavior was beyond reproach. He stood obediently, letting each of his hooves be shod without a single protest. Knowing Cynic, Jeff grew suspicious.

"*Why so cooperative? Are you not feeling well?*"

Cynic responded with what amounted to a sly smirk. "*After mating throughout the night, what more could you stand?*"

Jeff's abruptly stepped back to stare at Cynic. *"My emotions were that strong?"* Cynic was stabled at least a mile from the warehouse.

"Horse-brother, my head still aches! Even were my stable mates disturbed, and they no more than horses."

"Holy shit," Jeff muttered. "I had no idea."

He was still mulling it over when Carl dropped in to have his new mount shod. A grin split his face ear to ear the moment he saw Jeff.

"Glad to see you made it through the night, bucko."

"Damnation! Who told you? Is there some sort of tom-tom telegraph around here?"

That evening, they entered the communal dining hall deep in conversation about the trip north. Jeff and Carl were startled when the fifteen or so people present stood simultaneously and applauded loudly. Jeff didn't know whether to run or maybe do a dance. Carl stepped out of the limelight and joined in the applause, which did not help matters. Entering the spirit of the thing Jeff swept off his hat and bowed deeply, bringing a new round of applause and appreciative laughter.

While gathering food, he glanced at Carl with a bemused expression. "Is there anyone who doesn't know?"

Carl thoughtfully pulled at his chin. "No sir, I'm sure of it. There isn't a single person who doesn't know. Relax, Jeff. These folks are happy for you and Zimma. They think it's perfectly natural, and Rogelf has been grinning around here like a Cheshire cat. First that trip to Tradertown really straightened Zimma out, now it looks like she's found someone to settle down with." Carl erupted in embarrassed laughter.

"Jeff, you and Zimma made so much racket that the whole place was awake. When I ran out here to see what was going on, men and women were discussing it like a football game. Hell, Rogelf threw a party!"

"He threw a party?"

Carl nodded sagely.

"Well, damnation." Jeff laughed in spite of renewed chagrin. "I guess everyone *does* know."

When the worst of his appetite was seen to, Jeff began reflecting on what Carl had said. More questions were added to his list.

"They discussed our lovemaking like a football game, right?"

"Yep, that's what it reminded me of." Carl was so uncomfortable that he squirmed in his chair. "Sort of a play-by-play, I think."

"And Rogelf threw a party in the middle of the night. What kind of party, and with what?"

"Oh, the usual stuff—ale, bread, cheese, sweets," Carl replied with dismissive shrug. "Everyone was congratulating Rogelf and drinking too much."

"Just sort of found all that food lying around, eh?"

Carl examined Jeff with sudden interest. "Now that you mention it, no he didn't. It was all boxed up and ready to go. Pretty fancy stuff, too. What are you suggesting, Jeff?"

"I'm not really sure. Zimma and Rogelf were out shopping yesterday afternoon. I suspect that's where the food came from and why it was fancy. Tying that in with everything I experienced last night and this morning, Zimma's coming to my room was not a spontaneous act but carefully planned."

"That doesn't strike me as unusual, Jeff. In my experience, women usually do plan things pretty carefully. Especially anything having to do with a relationship."

"I'll buy that. On the other hand, do you know of any women on Earth who would go shopping with her father to buy stuff for a party that celebrates visiting a guy in his room?"

"Got me there. Not a chance. Especially a party like the one last night. It was really strange."

"That's a good word. This whole thing is more than strange." Jeff tilted his head in thought. His list of questions pointed in one direction only. "Looking at it now, and as an anthropologist, I cannot avoid the conclusion that I was put to a test as old as Zimma's culture. She isn't human, Carl." He waved an arm around the hall. "None of these people are. Maybe we've forgotten the small fact that we're no longer on Earth."

"Come again?" Carl looked at Jeff in blank-faced astonishment. "You bouncing off the wall?"

"Maybe," Jeff said with spread hands. He turned his head and pointed a finger at the scabbed, semicircular bite mark on his ear. "What do you make of that?"

Carl took a close look and whistled. "One nasty bite is what I make of it, buddy." He pulled Jeff's ear around for a minute inspection. Even though scabbed over, it had the appearance of a serious wound. "A little deeper and you might have lost part of that ear. You telling me Zimma did that?"

"I *am* telling you that," Jeff replied with a decisive nod. "When she came into my room I didn't recognize her voice, and her skin was so hot I thought it would burn me. And strong! She threw me around like a doll! Without going into personal details, let me give you a thumbnail of what happened after that..."

Some time later, "...And then she was back to her old self." Jeff took a long drink and gestured toward Carl. "Okay, tell me what you think."

"I don't know what to think," Carl breathed. "No, what you have just said blows me away! You sure there was some blue and green in the chest display? That something in her eyes actually spun around?"

"The light wasn't good for those colors, but I'm pretty sure," Jeff replied, "and I'm not likely to forget the way those sparks whirled around. The effect was so strong I couldn't look away."

"I think it's high time I kicked myself in the butt, and hard," Carl muttered in a tone of profound disgust. "Me—the young upstart biologist." Carl felt so chagrined he couldn't look at Jeff for a period. "I let myself get sucked into one of the oldest traps there is: the assumption that two phenomena are identical because superficial observation indicates they are."

"I think I get your drift. Since the inhabitants of this world look and generally act like us, we extend that comparison and assume they are the same in every respect."

"That's it."

Pursing his lips, Carl looked at Jeff with an intensely speculative expression. Although Carl blushed easily and frequently, the one spreading across his face like a brush fire set new standards. Jeff nodded judiciously. Whatever was cooking in Carl's head ought to really be good.

"Uh, Jeff, what did Zimma...I mean, you know, did you notice anything different down there, like. ... Oh, damnation!"

Jeff laughed delightedly. "Down there? Nope, and not up there either. She's put together just like a healthy American girl."

Carl grinned, if feebly, and stared off into space for a period. "I suspect you were affected by something like pheromones at

261

first, then may have been injected with more potent agents when she bit you." Carl sat up straight and pointed an excited finger at Jeff.

"Maybe it's reciprocal! From what you've said, it sounds like Zimma actually tasted your blood off and on. I wouldn't be surprised if some of her behavior was stimulated by your body's response to what she injected. I'll bet that's what happens—a positive or negative feedback cycle depending on response. Either the first loving flies or it's all over. I think you were literally put to the test!"

"She isn't a vampire, Carl."

"Settle down, boy," Carl said, making calming motions with his hands. "I'm not saying she is. That vampire shit is rubbish." He drifted off for several moments before saying, "You're right—they aren't human, or at least not entirely so. Nothing in my understanding of human biology stands up to comparison."

Clapping Carl on the back, Jeff stood up. "Or in Anthropology. But then, how do we define human? See you in the morning, buddy. I'm really tired."

"Thanks for the wakeup call, Jeff. It reminds me that I'm a biologist, and also that we've fallen into a wonderful world. There is so much to learn."

"In spades, my friend."

When Jeff walked into his room, Zimma was in bed waiting for him. Compared to their first night together, the second was quiet. While Zimma was passionate and physical, she displayed none of the ferocity Jeff vividly remembered. She made no attempt to bite him, her skin temperature seemed normal, and his desire for her was free of the external compulsion that had driven him into a mating frenzy.

Zimma accompanied Jeff and Carl next morning on a shopping trip to complete their provisions for the trip north. The day passed too quickly as they wandered Astholf. Zimma led them from shop to shop and finally to the food store she had discovered.

Frowning over the sausage, thumping and squeezing the fruit, she personally picked the best foodstuffs. That evening they attended a final conference.

Since everything but a few details had already been settled, Belstan and Rogelf concentrated on major points only. They planned to leave within three weeks. In fact, Belstan noted, they had to leave in that time frame if they wanted to arrive at Rugen before first snow. He estimated they would be on the trail for at least seven or eight weeks.

Rogelf gave a number of letters to Jeff for delivery to businessmen in Rugen he had dealt with in the past. There wasn't much more to talk about, and they broke up early in a somber mood.

Jeff and Zimma spent their last night together holding each other and saying little. They savored every minute, tucking away memories that would have to last for many months. Zimma fervently wished the caravan would arrive at Rugen before Jeff had to leave for Valholm, but she knew the wish was hopeless.

Their lovemaking was intense and slowly thorough, each stroke prolonged until it was hardly bearable in anticipation of the next. It was not until dawn that tears of parting were shared while they assisted each other in dressing. A last, lingering hug that nearly broke their wills and they left for communal breakfast hand-in-hand.

The horses were saddled and waiting when they walked out of the warehouse. Zimma helped him load Cynic and then there was nothing left to postpone departure. Jeff and Zimma walked off a distance so they could speak in private.

Zimma sighed with resignation when Jeff took her in his arms. When she pushed back, Jeff saw something that reminded him of their first night together. Her eyes seemed to glimmer with a light that had no connection to the sun.

"In the short time allotted us, Jeffrey, I have come to understand little of your homeland, this America. Yet withal, my heart is chilled and saddened by the estrangement between men and women that may be perceived. My love, the ways of America are not the ways of Chaldesia." Zimma paused and seemed to be searching for the right words. "There is much that I would share concerning the manner of men and women together in my homeland, on this world, but the telling would be long and such time is not given us.

"I know in part what you will face this winter. That you must travel when others stay warm by their fires, travel even in the great cold of deep winter. The time may come when your spirit threatens to fail and cries for human warmth. If this should occur and you are offered the comfort of another woman's arms, it would greatly please me if you would accept."

"I will not. You..." Zimma put a finger on his lips. "This is our way and is offered to women as well, but I will be among family and friends, warm fires and plentiful food. Jeffrey, I do not fear the loss of your love. That I hold secure in my heart. If the love and warmth of another woman means that you come back to me whole, then I will owe her a debt of gratitude and more. Do not object, my love. Think on it and remember."

"I begin to understand how fortunate I am to have come to this wonderful land. I am blessed in your person. Know that I will return to you." In spite of resolve, they mixed tears in a final embrace.

After a round of farewells with Belstan, Rogelf and others that had gathered to say good-bye, Jeff stepped into the saddle. Wrenching his eyes away from Zimma, he lifted Cynic to a trot and rode out of Astholf with Carl trailing behind.

Fifteen

Words of Wisdom

Carl hung on for dear life. Never having ridden, he had to bend all his concentration on staying in the saddle. Elbows flapping, he bounced from side to side, up and down and in several other directions as well. He thought the first day on the trail would never end.

When Jeff called an early halt to ease the pain, Carl's rear end and thighs were in agony. They hurt so badly he nearly fell from the saddle while dismounting. Very carefully, slowly, he peeled off leather britches.

One look at the oozing blisters on Carl's bright red fanny and Jeff hurried to his saddlebags.

"We have to take care of that right now or you're going to be crippled up by the end of another day. I have just the thing."

"You're going to shoot me, right?"

"Break a leg and I'll consider it," Jeff laughed. "Tell you what, go soak your butt in that creek. Those blisters are ugly and have to be cleaned up. Don't use a lot of soap."

"I know, I know," Carl muttered.

Although Jeff knew it was his imagination, he could swear that steam hissed up when Carl eased down into the creek with a relieved sigh. Jeff located the pot of all-purpose salve, the same compound he had used to treat Cynic's wound. It had worked so well that he now used it on himself.

"Okay, great buffalo hunter. Let's do it."

Before Jeff could apply the salve, Carl snatched the pot from his hand. "What is this stuff? It smells terrible."

"It's supposed to—that's what does the trick."

"No, seriously. Where'd you get it?"

"Down south a ways." Jeff gave him the background.

"Okay, it works." Carl bent over. "Lay on, McDuff, and let the microbes be damned."

Jeff was determined not to take advantage of the situation. He did smile at the way Carl danced around and shouted when he applied the salve.

"Looks real good, Carl. Too bad your butt didn't look like this when you mooned the city guard. You probably would have blinded them as well as pissing them off."

"Anything in the service of a good cause." Carl stood up with a vastly relieved expression. "I suspect there's more in that jar than you think, Jeff. You have the formula?"

"Yep. Made this batch myself."

"I'll want it the minute I can lay my hands on a stylus. The salve base is good, but I suspect the active ingredient is the mold."

"Penicillin?"

"Well, Jeffrey, you did learn something in school!"

Carl picked up his underwear and waded into the creek to wash out blood and serum from the blisters.

"While I doubt the mold is *Penicillium notatum*, I'd be willing to bet it produces some form of antibiotic. Whatever the case, we have a winner and I intend to exploit it."

With summer just over its peak, the night was balmy. Bathed in a warm, fragrant breeze, they strolled away from camp to get the full effect of the night sky unhindered by firelight. Carl wore no more than his boots and walked like a crab to make sure the wind continued to cool his rear end. Although there were no terran-style grasshoppers, an insect chorus of another sort was in good voice.

Head tilted back, Carl tried to comprehend the blazing expanse of stars overhead.

"I wonder where it is. Where Earth is."

"Yes. Even after all this time, it still tugs. Nothing much for us there, but it had so much beauty in it."

"No, nothing much at all. I wonder if we'll ever see it again."

Days and nights gradually fused together in a fashion Jeff remembered so well from his trip south. It was later in the season, however, and the prairie's rolling vastness was now covered with grass that was seared golden brown by the sun. The good weather held and they were blessed with dry, hot days.

While Carl's rear end healed within a matter of days, his skin was another matter. He was quite fair and suffered from the effects of sun and a strong breeze that, to his mind, was tiresome because it never let up.

Carl's riding improved rapidly until sitting a saddle became so natural he stopped thinking about it. In the process he became very attached to his horse, a seven-year-old gelding chestnut he had named Sam. Sam was proving to be sure-footed, showed a good turn of speed in their occasional gallops, and withstood Cynic's attempts to bully him with aplomb.

Well into the second week of their journey, Jeff stopped and unfolded a map Belstan had given him. Carl watched while Jeff frowned over the map and took a series of compass bearings.

"How we doing?"

"I think we're in good shape. I'm hoping to find a spur of the forest that dips south. We should run into it any day now. It's one of the few landmarks that really stands out. We'll cut through the spur, then follow the forest border all the way to Rugen. Question is, how accurate is this map not to mention the scale?"

To his relief, they encountered the forest spur several days later. Near its southern terminus, the forest proved to be more open than farther north and offered cool shade. They were well into the forest when Jeff caught a passing mental image that could mean only one thing. Jeff made sure he had a good seat and spread an image of a wolf in Cynic's mind.

"Horse-brother, have you met these before?"

Cynic jerked to a halt and his ears swiveled rapidly in tactical radar mode. *"Do these creatures eat horses?"*

"Those we will soon greet are friends and would be offended at such a thought. Others we happen across must be approached with caution if their bellies are empty. You are in no danger at this meeting, and I wish for you to speak with 'Sam' on this matter if that may be done."

Reassured, Cynic chewed it over for a while. *"His mind is better than most. I will try."*

Carl was lounging in the saddle and whistling when Sam gave a startled jump. Carl slapped him with the reins.

"Settle down, nutbrain. What's gotten into you?"

Turning his head to hide a smile, Jeff tried to speak casually. "Probably spooked by a rabbit or something."

Casting his mind out like a net, Jeff made contact with one of Balthazar's pack. The rest chimed in and he was swamped with enthusiastic greetings. Balthazar's symbol flashed into his mind.

"We are pleased that our brother has managed to retain life and appears to have prospered. We will come to your fire this night."

As the day progressed, Carl started to get suspicious of his friend's sudden high spirits. It wasn't so much that Jeff was in a good mood. That was nice to see. It was the sly looks followed by bursts of laughter that had him on edge.

Jeff was blandly evasive when questioned, which did nothing to ease Carl's suspicion that he was about to be zinged. Toward the end of the day, they spooked a herd of deer.

"And away we go!" Jeff thumped Cynic with his heels. "Yee-ha! Sic 'em, boy!"

Wild to chase one down, Cynic took off like a shot. Jeff mentally pointed out a buck and Cynic went to afterburner. Trees whipped by in a blur as they cut right and left, Cynic leaning like a barrel racer as he herded the buck away from the other deer.

Sailing through the air in prodigious leaps, the buck rapidly pulled ahead. An old pro at the pursuit game, Cynic was undaunted. When the buck accelerated, Cynic dug into a turn and arrowed off on a tangent. Carl was laughing so hard he almost fell off when Sam leaped a log trying to keep up.

They were waiting in deep cover when the buck came sneaking by. Jeff brought it down with a well-placed arrow and dismounted to butcher it.

"Want to tell me how in hell you knew that deer was going to pass this spot?"

Jeff looked up from his task and smiled at Carl's bemused expression. "I didn't, but I learned long ago that Cynic almost always does. That horse is an artist. First he separates the one I select from the herd, then picks a spot he figures the deer will pass trying to rejoin. It's uncanny."

As Jeff packed up section after section of venison, Carl's suspicion that he was going to be zinged grew by leaps and bounds. It wasn't only the amount of meat that got his attention, but the grin on Jeff's face. He'd seen that grin before.

It was getting late so they made camp near a stream. When Jeff laid out all of the venison he had just packed, Carl knew he was in for it. Suspicion had given way to a certain degree of frank paranoia when he walked over and glared at Jeff.

"What on earth are we going to do with so much meat? And don't feed me any bullshit!"

Jeff smiled innocently as he put steel and flint to work on tinder. "Oh, I'm sure we'll find some use for it."

Kicking a rock, Carl walked off muttering to himself. From prior experience, he figured it was going to be a major hit. Then he smiled and chuckled, remembering some of the setups he had lured Jeff into.

Later, when Jeff set hunks of venison over the fire to roast, Carl brushed his suspicions aside for the moment. This was something new. He hung over Jeff's shoulder with endless questions until nothing would do but to give him a turn handling the spits.

They ate more than they should have, but it felt good to have really full bellies and they lounged around the fire in a relaxed stupor. It was a cheerful cocoon of light, one that played endless variations on the leaves overhead. Jeff pulled out his recorder for the first time since leaving Astholf and attempted to match the fire's dancing rhythm.

While he played, memories of his trip to Valholm from the snowfields filled his thoughts. All of that trip's loneliness and sorrow were now softened by the image of Zimma that glimmered in his mind.

Some time later he was startled from his reverie by a gasp from Carl and snorting, stamping dismay from the horses. Jeff urgently motioned Carl to sit down with a downward sweep of his arm.

One after another, eighteen wolves trotted into the firelight and sat down in a semicircle of three ranks. Lord almighty, Jeff thought, I'd forgotten how big they are.

"May your pack prosper, mighty leader of comedians."

Balthazar was taken back not at all by what he fathomed to be Jeff's attempt at humor.

"We are well met, wolf-brother. From that which is clearly marked in your mind, we are aware that much has occurred since last we spoke. Will you share your experiences with this one more fully?"

Jeff turned to Carl with a smile. "Worth being zinged?" Carl responded with a silent, wide-eyed nod. "Keep an eye on the horses, will you? I've got a lot to talk about with Balthazar."

"Sure, be glad to," Carl replied, "but who's going to keep an eye on me?"

"They're something else, all right." Jeff turned his attention to Balthazar. *"I would be pleased to recount what has occurred, wolf-brother. While we speak, will you and your pack share our kill?"*

"We thank you for such courtesy, wolf-brother. Our way has been long with little time to hunt."

The wolves with Balthazar immediately arose, each expressing their thanks before beginning to eat. Carl watched in amazed silence. There was no growling or squabbling like he would expect from a pack of wolves on Earth.

"If only I were telepathic," Carl murmured with great longing. "What wonderful creatures."

When a pack member dropped a big piece of venison in front of Balthazar, Carl could do no more than shake his head in disbelief.

While Balthazar ate, Jeff recounted the last several months culminating with their discovery of the Salchek and subsequent evacuation to Astholf. When he had finished, Jeff sat back and clasped his knees.

"As suspected," Balthazar commented, grooming himself, *"the invaders have returned and war will soon be on this land again. We conclude you and yours have come to prepare?"*

"It is so."

Jeff proceeded to describe their plans for the coming season and years to follow. As they talked, Jeff got the strong impression that other forces were present in Balthazar's mind. At the end of Jeff's narrative, the wolf turned his head toward Carl.

"This is your packmate?" Jeff affirmed that fact. *"May we speak to this one's mind? We are aware that it is not 'Carl's' habit to so speak, yet possibilities may lie buried that none suspect such as with your companion, 'Cynic'."*

"I will present this to him."

Carl was studying the wolves so intently that Jeff had to jog his elbow to get his attention.

"Balthazar there, the big one in the middle, wants to see if you have latent talent that might be developed. I personally believe you do."

"Yes! Absolutely! I would like nothing better!" Carl's excited expression quickly faded. "As long as there's no big risk that he might burn out my brain in trying, that is. It ain't much, but it works."

Laughing agreement, Jeff reconnected with Balthazar. *"While eager to discover if talent exists, my packmate is concerned that no damage occur in the exploring."*

"A request that will be honored. As you have correctly surmised, we will have assistance in this matter. Advise your packmate that some suffering will be unavoidable. Have 'Carl' indicate when he is ready to begin."

"Now look, Carl," Jeff said with a worried expression, "it sounds like this is not going to be a painless procedure—my first contact certainly wasn't—although Balthazar assures me no damage will be done. Problem is, I have no idea how wolves judge the severity of pain. I'm afraid their threshold might be a lot higher than ours. Still want to go ahead with it?"

"Yeah, definitely," Carl responded after a moment's hesitation. "No pain, no gain, they used to say. I will not pass this up. What do I have to do?"

"Just relax and open your mind as much as you can. When you're ready, raise your hand."

Closing his eyes and breathing deeply, Carl raised an arm. Almost immediately, his body jerked spasmodically and froze in muscular rigidity. Within a brief span, sweat began to bead up on his forehead and his face paled.

Although he trusted Balthazar implicitly, Jeff became concerned as minutes passed and Carl remained frozen. Muscles bunched around his jaw stood out like ropes, and sweat ran in rivulets from his face. Every so often, agonized groans escaped his lips. As concern was growing to outright alarm, Carl relaxed and fell over on his side with a thump.

"He is sleeping and must be allowed to do so," Balthazar said to Jeff. *"He has had a difficult trial, but mastered himself so that we might succeed. 'Carl' is a brave human and worthy packmate. When he awakens, assure him that our work was not damaging."*

While Jeff went in search of a blanket to cover Carl with, Balthazar directed an amused thought at Cynic.

"You have a mind we can appreciate, horse-brother. Do you still believe we would eat you?"

Cynic looked directly at Balthazar. *"I no longer doubt your intent, wolf-who-may-be-brother, but will you speak for all of your kin?"*

After a period of trading slams with Cynic, Balthazar turned his attention back to Jeff. His humorous bent of mind gave way to one that was deadly serious,

"Come into our mind, brother, and learn what you must."

A combination of Alarai minds working with and through the wolf burst into his brain. Forces beyond previous conception filled it to overflowing until Jeff thought his skull would split. At several points the pain was so bad he was afraid it might kill him.

"We are an old people even by our accounting, Jeffrey Friedrick, and have resided on this planet for many ages. Our origins are lost in time, although some relate that we came from the stars in great ships. The machines that still serve us in our travels lend support to this possibility. How it is that many of us also came to live on Earth and labor for its welfare is not documented, and also escapes myth.

"You are descended from these Alarai through your grandmother's line. While intermarriage has diluted such descent, in you our blood runs nearly true. It was Gaereth, the Alarai you met as a child, that uncovered your lineage."

The common voice took on a wry cast. *"Always has Gaereth enjoyed and employed his particular humor, if also always to commendable ends. It is thus not remarkable that we find similar traits in you and in those you associate with, for Gaereth is your grandfather seven times removed."*

Gaereth his grandfather? Jeff's mind went blank with shock. Seven times removed would make him over two hundred years old! That's got to be a fairy tale. Such things just don't happen in real life. Then he thought, You mean, like getting transported to another planet?

The Alarai let it sink in for a few moments before continuing. *"On the day you met in the forest, Gaereth buried in your mind that which led you to Aketti. He understood even then that, given your heritage, you were unlikely to find a place among earth's humans. For the abrupt and destructive manner in which you were ripped from Earth, we apologize, but of needs we were forced* to employ the vast energies of the earthquake. While we had no intention of transporting Carl, and are shamed that he was taken, his presence speaks of more than chance."

A large flag waved for attention in the back of Jeff's mind. "If Alarai remain on Earth, why was it necessary to bring me here? And if it was necessary for some reason, why did you not employ your machines?" A final question that had been jostling for position found expression. "Why was I not given warning or choice?"

The combined Alarai mind pulled back, and Jeff got the sense that an ad hoc conference had been called. Mentally crossing his arms, he nodded to himself and thought, Well now, boys and girls—having a little trouble with that one?

"Forgive our silence. It must seem that we dissemble to avoid revealing motive, but this is not our intent. Rather, there is so much we would communicate and this meeting made so precarious by distance. We find it difficult to select words that will convey fact without implying deception. However and briefly, for we would not do injury to our wolf-brother's mind by prolonged conversation, you were not transported by machine because we were not certain that your mind could be attuned to its function. While you are of the Alarai, your blood is also influenced by many generations that are not. Thus we were forced to utilize the earthquake.

"But our wolf-brother's peril grows. Jeffrey, we sense your unease and distrust. Do you doubt that your life on Earth was desperately unhappy? Or that it would have been otherwise in the absence of your meeting with Gaereth?"

A moment's reflection and Jeff knew the answer to those questions: not a chance.

"Just so. We are, you belong to, an ancient people whose lives have been dedicated to serving others for untold centuries. Now we are few, but duty remains and catastrophe of untold proportion threatens Earth."

Earth? What are they talking about? Jeff felt like his brain had turned inside out. "Then why in God's name did you bring me here?"

Before any reply was possible, the link nearly crumbled and Balthazar collapsed onto his belly.

"Quickly now! We are few, crisis looms first on Aketti, and you must come into full maturity before contemplating a return to Earth.

Always we have been close to the Alemanni, for so we named the yellow-hairs after an ancient people of Earth. You and they discovered each other, now your fates intertwine. Lead them and find your destiny, Jeffrey.

"Finally, given our numbers, can you not understand that we must search out every man and woman of good will whether of the Alarai or not? Can you not see what must be done? You are both Alarai and not!

"In the spring, Gaereth returns to us and will seek you out. Then you will learn much more. Until we speak again, Jeffrey Friedrick, may the gods that look over us all protect and guide you."

The connection dissolved and Jeff tumbled into a pile near Carl. Exhausted by his efforts, Balthazar sprawled onto his side. The remaining wolves curled up to keep watch.

Carl got as far as his knees. Bending over with a gasp of agony, he threw up. Wiping his mouth, he crawled to the woodpile, tossed some sticks in the fire and set water to heating.

"Oh shit it hurts. I've got to learn to keep my mouth shut."

Blearily looking around the campsite, Carl noticed Jeff lying curled up and starting to twitch. The wolves were gone. Carl got to his feet in slow stages, nearly fell down, and had to lean over with hands on knees until his head stopped spinning.

"Coffee," he mumbled, "got to have coffee."

He made it to the saddlebags in short stages, and nudged Jeff with a boot on his way back to the fire with a bag of grounds. Carl stared at the pot, willing it to boil, but had to settle for sniffing the bag.

"If you are going to feed yourself, why not me?"

"Yeah, yeah, give me a minute, will you?" Carl snarled.

He had put the lid back on from checking the water for the umpteenth time when it hit him. Whirling too fast, Carl grabbed his head with a groan and stared at Cynic.

"What did you say?"

The horse just stared at him as if he were a hopeless cretin.

"Okay, okay, let's try this again."

Focusing his mind, Carl directed what he hoped was a thought in Cynic's direction. *"What was that you said, big mouth?"*

Exile To The Stars

"*I think the wolf should have thought longer before he opened your mind,*" Cynic huffed, knowing an insult when he heard one.

His pain momentarily forgotten, Carl let out a jubilant shout. "By, damn! What do you know about that?" Carl grabbed his head again and started dry heaving.

Some minutes later he added coffee to boiling water and in a short while eased the pot from the fire. Carefully decanting a dark brew into metal cups, Carl added a dollop of fruit syrup to both. With the satisfaction of one who does not want to suffer alone, he noted Jeff crawling toward him with his eyes fastened on the cups, groaning under his breath as he came.

Civilized conversation was out of the question. They nursed their coffee and headaches in silence for some time before Carl spoke up.

"Some night, eh bucko?"

"Dammit, Carl, you don't have to shout!"

A few minutes later, grimacing with pain, Jeff grunted belligerently, "Yeah, a hell of a night. I'm glad someone's feeling enthusiastic about it."

Having completed his mental ordeal well before Jeff's, Carl's headache was rapidly diminishing. He was able to smile equably as he poured another cup of coffee for them both.

"Now now, let's not be that way."

By late morning Jeff's headache was gone and he felt capable of polite conversation.

"I've been through something like this before, but compared to last night that first experience was nothing." Jeff related the gist of what he had learned the previous night. "...So, it sounds like I was elected to act as proxy for the Alarai. Sort of a half-breed fill-in."

"I think you may have missed the real point," Carl replied with a vigorous shake of his head. "The Alarai are now so few that they face extinction. At the same time, everything is going to hell on two planets. What was their last comment, again?"

"Something to the effect that I belonged to two peoples."

"Exactly. Pardon my saying it, but they also suggested you use your head and figure it out. It isn't just one world, Jeff, it's two. I think you were brought here as much for training as anything, and thank heavens I happened to be in the right place at the right time."

"They did use the term crisis when talking about Aketti," Jeff reflected, "and catastrophe when referring to Earth. There's a big difference between those terms."

"A very big difference. Maybe it's going to take some folks who are really concerned but have no kinship with the Alarai?"

"Like yourself. Damn. I am so slow at times it makes me want to cringe." There was no humor in his laugh. "They really don't expect much of us, do they? Just get our shit together, whip the Salchek, then maybe recruit some bravos and see what can be done for Earth. You know—a little weekend outing, kick some butt and skip back here. No big deal."

"Yeah, it does sort of take your breath away when you think about it," Carl replied with an appreciative chuckle. "What are we going to do? Shake a finger under the noses of our esteemed leaders while giving them a tongue lashing?"

"Well, we could always threaten them with our bows."

"Yeah, that might work." Carl narrowed his eyes and frowned. "Here's something else to think about—I'm really beginning to wonder if my being transported was an accident. From what you've related, it sounds like the Alarai aren't sure themselves."

"I think it's more a matter of suspecting it wasn't an accident. There is so much that we don't know. If they didn't bring you here, who did? There we were on Earth without a clue, now we've been handed two worlds to worry about and are still in the dark. It's all so confusing I'm tempted to take what Gurthwin said about his gods at face value and invoke divine intervention."

Carl did a little hop and let out a whoop. "Yeah, but what a task. What a time! And divine intervention? Considering everything that's happened, why not? Wouldn't that be something? Nothing to live for back on Earth, now all of this. Damn, it's good to be alive!"

Not wanting to lose any more time in their race with the onset of fall, they hurried to the task of packing up. By evening they had emerged back onto the prairie and were jogging along paralleling the forest border as planned. Carl was delighted with his new ability and used passing weeks to sharpen its control.

While discussing their plans, he switched back and forth between telepathy and normal speech so often and randomly that he nearly drove Jeff to distraction. Cynic wasn't spared, either, and soon threatened rebellion from the frequent teasing he suffered.

When he judged the time was right, Jeff angled away to the west. Crossing farmland, they cut the south road from Rugen.

It was nearly dark when the top of Rugen's wall appeared over the horizon. They picked up the pace, but the gate was locked tight when they arrived.

"Hoy the guard," Jeff shouted through cupped hands.

A voice hailed back, "Who goes there?"

"I can't believe he said that." Carl laughed with delight. "Who goes there? This is great!"

"Yeah, I suppose so. It's after dark and he has to challenge us, but some of the guards I've encountered are bloody idiots. We'll be lucky if he doesn't take a shot at us." Jeff shook his head in resignation, and bellowed, "Jeffrey Friedrick. I am expected and return from the South with important news. Open the gate."

"Begone, ere I call out the guard. The city is closed to…uh, to vagabonds."

"Whoa, this guy really *is* an idiot," Carl murmured.

"Open the fucking gate," Jeff shouted at the top of his lungs, "or I'm going to have your ass!"

"I think that might have gone right over his head, Jeff."

Someone winded a bugle, and they heard what had to be a heated argument followed by a crash that reminded Carl of a cooking pot hitting stone.

"Ouch. That must have hurt!"

"About time. Sounds like the Corporal of the Guard showed up. Maybe we'll get some action now."

Within minutes, one panel of the massive gate opened with a vast groaning of hinges badly in need of grease.

"Welcome to Rugen, buddy."

"Thanks, Jeff. I feel like I'm about to ride into Camelot."

"You are. Khorgan is beautiful, but I truly love this city."

A detachment of the city guard was waiting inside and escorted them to Ethbar's residence. A newly laid fire was taking hold when they were ushered into the parlor and offered a cordial. The chairs were comfortable, the fire started to throw some heat, and Carl nodded off. Jeff poked him awake when Ethbar entered the room swaddled in a voluminous robe.

Getting to his feet, Jeff smiled with pleasure. "It gives me joy to see you again, Ethbar."

"You have returned to us, Jeffrey. I am content."

Rengeld clumped into the room. Striding over, a smile breaking the stern lines of his face, he clasped Jeff's hand.

"Your presence warms this night beyond any expectation, my friend."

Jeff introduced Carl and briefly explained their long friendship while waiting for chairs to be arranged so they could talk. Ethbar indicated they were to sit by doing so, and called for another round of wine.

"Although the hour is late, we deemed your return of such importance, and our impatience of such magnitude, that we contrived a brief meeting this night. I hope you do not find such presumption to be excessive."

"Not at all. It was thoughtful of you both to greet us so cordially." Jeff admired the wine's golden color. Although somewhat acid, it was a welcome change from water. "As you point out, the hour is late. Allow me to draw a few broad strokes this evening to help along discussion on the morrow."

"As we feared, the Salchek threat is real. Even as Carl and I set out for Rugen some six weeks ago, Salchek were moving north in what could only be preparation for the invasion of Khorgan. It will not entirely surprise you, I am sure, to hear that Arzak conspires to profit from the Salchek presence. I must also report that mighty Khorgan whimpers like a cur anticipating the booted heel."

"I am surprised and saddened, Jeffrey. Khorgan is a fabled city." Ethbar shrugged eloquently. "Still, such is the way of all things that ascend to greatness."

Jeff nodded over steepled fingers. "Khorgan's leaders have failed of their duty, and its citizens will pay dearly. I do not, however, bear only sad news. It has been our great fortune to encounter people of worth who have not lost the will to resist. Merchants of great experience and knowledge, I judge they will present themselves in caravan at these gates before the onset of winter."

"That is good news, indeed, and timely."

"Yes, these men will profit Rugen greatly." Hands comfortably clasped across his stomach, Jeff nodded toward Carl. "Before we consider other matters, let me state in what high regard I hold Carl Jorgenson. When shortly I leave for the North to confederate its people in defense of their lands and of this city, Carl will remain to apply his vast experience in arcane studies to the benefit of Rugen. His is a knowledge not yet dreamed of in this land, knowledge which demands the closest attention."

Ethbar smiled at Carl and leaned forward to poke at the fire. "I look forward to long converse, and will lend whatever authority is mine to assist your efforts." Ethbar looked wistfully at his empty glass before handing it to a servant.

"Now, as you have suggested, Jeffrey, the Salchek presence does not come as a great surprise. My heart, however, is reassured beyond expectation by the balance of what you have related. It contains, I warrant, the seeds of hope."

"Regardless of the Salchek invasion, if Rugen is to prosper over the years, men like Rogelf and Belstan will be needed."

"Without doubt, Jeffrey. Years of isolation are not easily overcome."

"How do matters stand now?"

"In your absence, Rengeld and I have also been diligent. Imogo has been fully informed of your mission to the south. While concerned, he remains resistant to final acceptance of the Salchek presence."

"Do you believe he is concerned enough to listen?"

"Moved by love for his family, I believe he is at least prepared to listen attentively to what you might say," a grimace of disgust formed on Ethbar's lips, "in spite of the counsel offered by a cabal of lick-spittle courtiers." He smiled at Rengeld, who had been drumming his fingers on the chair since sitting down. "Perhaps you would relate your part?"

Virtually leaping from his chair, Rengeld clasped hands behind his back to give them something to do.

"In truth, much has been accomplished. Yet much more remains in the balance. As we agreed before you departed,

Jeffrey, Ethbar and I prepared a message and courier against the possibility of your late return. He was dispatched to our northern cousins' moot in a timely fashion. I am hopeful they received him kindly."

"Gurthwin and Halric are given to reasoned thought before raising the battle-ax. He will be given a hearing." Jeff shrugged doubtfully without realizing it.

Rengeld nodded agreement. "Let us pray he is stout-hearted."

Amen to that, Jeff thought. "How do matters progress with the city guard?"

"Although Imogo is not fully convinced of the Salchek threat, his concern has made it possible to increase the garrison. I have been applying myself to that end with great diligence and some success. However, convincing our sovereign that city granaries must be filled has been a more difficult task. He is loath to antagonize beholden duchies by extracting a greater portion of their crop yields. With the news you bring, I believe progress in that area will now be possible."

"I wouldn't be surprised. The kingdom is at stake."

"Indeed it is." Unclasping his hands and rubbing them together with a rasping sound, a huge smile further creased the rough-cut planes of Rengeld's face. "This garrison will soon come to understand the meaning of hard work!"

Ethbar stood up, prompting Jeff and Carl to do the same.

"Our first task in the morning must be to plan a meeting with Imogo that will ensure his full cooperation. I would be honored if you would both accept the hospitality of my home for the duration of your stay in Rugen."

Jeff soaked in a wonderfully hot bath when he got up, but Carl was due for breakfast and he had to cut it short. A servant was setting out steaming bowls of gruel and a tray of glazed rolls when Carl made his appearance looking fresh-scrubbed and rested. It was such a pleasure to eat hot food totally unrelated to venison that they took their time and dwelled over a second cup of coffee.

Comfortably slumped in his chair, Carl looked quizzically at Jeff. "Where did you learn to speak like you did last night?"

"Don't know for sure. It sort of grew on me after being around those two for a while. Can't always find the right phrasing, though, and things come out in a jumble or I glitch entirely. Wouldn't be surprised if the same thing happens to you." Jeff set his mug down with a solid thump. "Well, what do you say we wander downstairs and see what's stirring?"

"About that time."

Ethbar and Rengeld were poring over documents amid a clutter of breakfast crockery when they walked in. Signaling for a servant to clear the table, Ethbar pushed the documents away and motioned for them to be seated.

"I believe a meeting with Imogo can be arranged later this day. Will this give you sufficient time to prepare, Jeffrey?"

"What needs to be said is clear in my mind. I only hope Imogo will be receptive."

Jeff's eyes drifted away from Ethbar and out a tall window that faced north. Recalling memories of ravening hunger and bone-shaking cold, his thoughts leaped far beyond Rugen's walls.

"I must leave within several days, for the task that faces me is daunting and winter long. I would deeply value any advice you might offer."

Jeff was not prepared for the degree of fear that accompanied the memories, and he took a deep breath before continuing.

"I believe you will agree with me when I say that Rugen is the key to a successful defense of the North. Yet, will it survive what is to come without allies to assist in its defense? Rengeld, I am confident your efforts will bear fruit in the form of a well-trained garrison within the city, but we must have means of disrupting Salchek plans outside the walls. Shall we allow them to invest Rugen and assume a leisurely siege that is open to constant resupply from the south? Even with full granaries, how many months, or even granting years, will Rugen stand? We cannot permit these conditions to prevail."

"Ethbar and I have considered this, Jeffrey. With full granaries, Rugen might endure for two years."

"Just so. The yellow-hairs, or Alemanni as I now term them, must come to understand that if Rugen falls their lands will soon be overrun. Much as I was driven south by great urgency, I have come to know it is my task to unite them in common effort. I fear this task yet see no alternative. Shall I wait until warm summer months? Will the Salchek be receptive to delaying their invasion in order to accommodate us?"

It was a rare occurrence, but Rengeld was taken by surprise. He frowned at Jeff as if he could not believe his ears. No matter how courageous, there were some things you just didn't do. Attempting travel far to the north in the dead of winter was one of them. Nervous tension drove him to his feet.

"My friend, what you propose confounds imagination and leads me to fear for your life. Legends spring from deeds much less severe. While it is more than likely that the Salchek will surround this city no later than next summer, are you certain there is no alternative?"

Jeff shook his head with downcast eyes. Rengeld's concern had fueled his fear until it was nearly unbearable.

"There is no option other than rallying the Alemanni. As you have said with different words, time is our great enemy. I also agree that unless the Salchek meet determined opposition in the south we can expect Rugen to be invested no later than next summer. There will be no opposition in the south."

Ethbar winced at what he had to say. "Even as you say, this is your task and must be attempted this winter. Without its completion our outlook is greatly diminished."

Although his expression gave little away, Ethbar felt like he had just signed Jeff's death warrant. He paused to ponder the gods. Why they were using this young man so harshly. There was no answer. No understanding the minds of gods. Ethbar stirred from reflection.

"Come, let us combine our thoughts and hearts to achieve understanding of this task, for you must not perish." Locating a clean sheet of parchment, Ethbar picked up a stylus. "Let us consider clothing..." They only adjourned when the tailors Ethbar had summoned showed up.

Some hours later and standing in front of a tall mirror, Jeff and Carl felt a bit like two musketeers in drag. The fact that the mirror was full of distortions didn't help matters. Baggy pants were stuffed into shiny dragoon boots complete with rowel spurs, all topped by gold-trimmed doublets and wide-brimmed hats with long feathers attached.

The palace was not far from Ethbar's residence near the central lake, so they walked. Boot heels clumping on stone paving blocks, spurs and swords jingling and clinking, the men felt more than a little foolish. As they walked, Ethbar filled them in on court etiquette.

"...Finally, do not be dismayed by the rabble posing as courtiers. Their insolence is a consequence of ignorance, and for a certain number of them something far more ominous. We will confer privately with Imogo following the audience."

The chamberlain kept them waiting in an outer room while he peeked into the audience chamber. Eventually deeming the timing right, he swung the door wide and announced their presence. Ethbar swept into the room and stopped three or four feet from the throne to bow.

"Your Majesty, I am honored to present Jeffrey Friedrick, our emissary just returned from the South. Attending him is his trusted companion, Carl Jorgenson."

As he walked toward the throne, Carl three steps behind as directed by the chamberlain, Jeff surveyed the throne room and its occupants. He was not terribly impressed.

The room was no more than thirty feet to a side with a centrally located dais. Tapestries of modest quality covered portions of stone walls. Even so, the room felt cold. The two objects of obvious quality were the large carpet of intricate weave on the stone floor, and the ornately carved chair that served as a throne.

Jeff's first impression of Imogo was that of a short, somewhat bored, balding man sitting nonchalantly on his throne in a heavy robe. He appeared to be in his late fifties and sported a spade beard dappled with gray. Jeff caught himself staring at Imogo. For the first time in his life he saw truly black eyes. The effect was not so much sinister as compelling.

Although the room was not crowded with courtiers, Jeff estimated there had to be twenty-five or thirty present. He couldn't help wondering how many would like to see him dead or run out of town. Whatever, he decided, from their expressions they sure as hell don't know what to make of us.

Stopping beside Ethbar, Jeff bowed. "Your servant, Majesty."

Imogo sat up straighter and studied Jeff with considerable interest before speaking in a high, piping voice.

"We are pleased to welcome you, Jeffrey Friedrick. Newly returned as you are from southern lands, we anticipate fuller conversation with yourself and your companion. Now we would wish for you to be introduced to the members of our court." Signaling for Ethbar to do the honors, Imogo left the audience room.

Positioning himself between Carl and Jeff, Ethbar guided them toward the largest group of courtiers. As they approached, six or seven pointedly turned their backs and strolled in the opposite direction.

Carl wasn't about to let them off so easily. Jeff couldn't take the risk of being snubbed in public, but he could. Time to get some information. Carl squeezed Ethbar's arm and gestured with his head at the retreating backs. Ethbar nodded and they set off in pursuit, leaving Jeff to his own devices.

Surrounded by courtiers, Jeff caught Carl's move while answering a question about southern commerce. Good move, man, he thought. Go for it.

Casually moving away from Carl's theater of operation, he fielded another question. Although the questions were general in nature, Jeff carefully selected his words to avoid revealing the Salchek presence before Imogo was fully informed. That, he concluded, would be a fatal mistake, perhaps literally.

Taking the initiative, he described Khorgan in detail. The topic proved so exciting to his circle that he never was pushed into the realm of politics. Ethbar and Carl returned unobtrusively and they bowed their way out of the chamber.

Branching hallways echoed their footsteps as Ethbar penetrated deep inside the palace. Stopping at an unremarkable door, he rapped lightly on its panels and entered. Unpretentious and small, the room was comfortably furnished with soft chairs, a table, and thick carpets.

They found Imogo with his feet resting on a stool, robes cast aside and sipping on a glass of wine. Seated next to Imogo was a young man of perhaps eighteen years. Must be his son, Torget, Jeff decided.

With an informal wave toward empty chairs, Imogo indicated they were to sit.

"If you would, Jeffrey, please relate what you observed in the South."

The setting was casual, but Jeff was under no illusion that the circumstances were. Passing over the trip south with only a few words, he described the situation in Khorgan and what he had concluded. When he related the amount of tribute Khorgan was being forced to pay, Imogo's face went blank with disbelief.

"You are quite certain of the amount, Jeffrey?"

"Yes, your Majesty. Eight hundredweight of gold each month. I must say we were all nearly overcome. Such an amount went far to explain the crushing taxation imposed by the city council."

Their trip to Tradertown in search of confirmation was received with an appreciative nod.

"A wise decision. One must never base conclusions on supposition only. Now this Tradertown. A most interesting name. Please continue."

Jeff proceeded to describe everything he had observed and experienced. At the last minute he included Carl and Zimma's rescue. As he had earlier, Jeff concluded with the traders' evacuation to Astholf and decision to trek north to Rugen.

The room was quiet for some time. "The rescue of Carl and your Zimma—you effected their escape unassisted?"

Considering the circumstances surrounding the rescue, Imogo's question was not unexpected.

"Your majesty is most astute. Their rescue would not have been successful against such odds without this."

Experiencing a sense of deja vu, Jeff removed the Colt from under his doublet. Popping the cylinder open, he tilted the pistol up and caught the cartridges as they fell out. Not willing to risk damage, Jeff closed the cylinder and set the weapon and cartridges on the table.

Showing more daring than Belstan and Rogelf, Imogo picked it up. Turning the Colt over in his hands, he marveled at the workmanship.

"Silver steel with no hint of rust," he murmured in a wondering tone of voice.

He set the Colt down with the care usually afforded a delicate object. Imogo gazed at Jeff with a new level of intensity while stroking the metal with a finger.

"There is another story here, it would seem. Would you be so kind?"

"I am not of this world, nor is my companion. We have been brought to this land by my ancestors in defense of the yellow-hairs and Rugen." He let it drop there.

Imogo didn't blink an eye. "The Redhairs of legend."

"Yes, your Majesty."

"We must admit to being captivated, Jeffrey, and are quite willing to accept your alien origin."

Lost in reflection, Imogo gazed into the middle distance. The silence that ensued was not uncomfortable, for it was as if they had ceased to exist. Quite abruptly, Imogo's eyes refocused.

In a series of deft motions, he picked up the Colt, released the lock, swung the cylinder out and plucked a cartridge from the table.

Although taken by surprise, there was no way Jeff would allow the cylinder to be shut with a cartridge in it. Holding the cartridge up to catch the light, Imogo nodded and slipped it into the cylinder. Before Jeff could react, he tipped the revolver up and caught the cartridge in his hand.

"We must assume this smaller device is the actual instrument of death."

Primed to explode into action, Jeff forced a calm reply. "Yes, your Majesty, it is."

Imogo nodded gravely. "Never have we imagined such craftsmanship, or experienced the imminence of death so closely." Setting the cartridge and pistol down on the table, Imogo let his breath out in a long sigh. "Very well. Let us examine matters more closely."

The rest of the afternoon was spent answering questions from Imogo, each one penetrating deeper into southern affairs. It wasn't long before Jeff understood what it was like to be cross-examined by an expert. He was also walking a razor's edge.

Molding each answer to document the need for preparation carried a big risk. Kings did not like to be manipulated, and this, Jeff decided, was one smart king. Several hours later, large sweat circles were visible under his arms. He was outlining plans for the winter when Imogo smiled dryly and broke in.

"Nobly have you withstood this day, Jeffrey. We have learned over the years to discern honesty as well as deceit. That you are honest we have no question. That you are a man of valor and honor we have come to understand. We must dwell on all that you have conveyed."

Everyone jumped to their feet as Imogo rose and left the room, closely followed by his son.

On the way back to his home, Ethbar muttered to himself off and on, "Well, well. Yes; well, well!" He offered no explanations until the evening meal had been consumed.

Gathered near the fire once again, Ethbar finally enlightened them after filling Rengeld in on the day's events.

"You must know that Imogo surprised me today. It was a most refreshing experience. He has never been one to cherish deceit, and can be quite harsh to those in whom it is perceived. Today he found no deceit in spite of dogged effort."

"What surprised you?"

"The full acuity of mind he was forced to employ, Jeffrey. I have not seen it before."

"He's an intelligent man. I have never experienced such intense scrutiny."

"The opposite also being true in the form of your answers. I have rarely enjoyed such a meeting of the minds."

"It was a battlefield of a different sort, all right," Jeff said with a relieved expression. "Glad it's over."

"You did most well, moving carefully between pitfalls astutely put in your path by our Imogo to test your veracity. I believe you have succeeded. It will be most difficult for Imogo to remain uncommitted. Yes, yes! Very difficult!"

"Hopefully, but those courtiers who walked away aren't going to give up without a fight. Am I correct in assuming they're the troublemakers?"

"You have judged them correctly," Ethbar replied with a droll expression, "although it is likely I would have employed a much stronger descriptive term. I look forward to hearing Carl's impressions. It is always helpful to obtain a fresh view." Ethbar winked at Carl and called for the household steward.

"A fresh consignment of makla beans arrived earlier this day. I am told they are a new variety that holds much promise. Let us discover the truth of this matter."

Thankful for the reprieve Ethbar had given him, Carl began ordering his thoughts. The conclusions he had reached were not going to be easy to express.

The makla arrived freshly brewed and was so good that Carl gained an additional period of time while its qualities were debated. Stout without being bitter, it was reminiscent of Colombian Supremo coffee with a spicy taste all its own. Ethbar gestured for Carl to speak when the chatter died down.

"I don't know what I was expecting, but what I heard and observed confirms my belief that some folks will promote their narrow self-interest and personal ambitions until the sword is dropping on their necks, not to mention everyone else's as well."

"You could be describing the councilors in Khorgan."

"A lot like them, Jeff," Carl replied with a quick nod. "The councilors had it all and were willing to sacrifice their city and people in an attempt to keep it. This bunch dream of obtaining such wealth and power and are equally willing to make the same sacrifices to that end. And that attitude, it seems to me, is where the real danger lies. I may be wrong, but I think they know the Salchek are coming."

"Collaborators," Jeff growled, "the worst possible kind of trash."

"Maybe. Please remember that what I'm saying is the rawest form of speculation. There was just something about the way they reacted when we discussed the situation down south. Sort of a smug cocksureness and a 'go fuck yourself and tell us something we don't already know' attitude." Carl said to Ethbar, "Please disabuse me of this opinion. It is a terrible thing to believe of anyone."

Ethbar was impressed with Carl's analysis. "I cannot. Rengeld's agents have carefully documented every aspect of their lives for some months now. They are not only traitors, but relatively stupid traitors." Ethbar raised his eyebrows and smiled ever so slightly. "But then, I suspect this is usually the case and represents a marriage of convenience."

"Right on! I mean, yes, I think that sums it up in one neat package. Oh, hell!"

Ethbar caught the drift and smiled benignly at Carl before turning a more serious expression in Jeff's direction.

"While we discerned some time ago that this group of courtiers was plotting to overthrow Imogo, the full extent of their treason was not revealed. The knowledge you and Carl brought goes far to explain clandestine travel to the south by their agents. Little doubt remains they are collaborating with the Salchek. We cannot move openly, since I judge Imogo unwilling to believe that his cousins would betray not only Rugen but also their own family. Still, you may rest assured they will die quickly and silently when it becomes necessary."

"Imogo's cousins. Should have suspected something like that from the beginning. May I assume they savor thoughts of the crown under Salchek rule?"

"Savor such thoughts, indeed, and quarrel among themselves over who shall wear it," Rengeld replied with a disdainful snort. "Their kingdom will be less elevated and quite dark."

The following morning, Jeff took Carl out to explore Rugen. He also had to purchase clothing and they spent the greater part of the day poking around in one shop or another. They were making their way home when Carl jumped out of the saddle with an exclamation and darted into a shop, leaving Sam free to roam.

Jeff had to capture Sam before he could find out what was so intriguing about the shop. Once inside, he found Carl in animated conversation with the store's proprietor. The men were surrounded on all sides by an intricate cat's cradle of tubing and retorts, some bubbling ominously.

"What a find!" Carl said to Jeff with an excited grin. "This place is a treasure trove. A bona fide alchemy! These guys spend their lives trying to convert base metals like lead to gold, and often blow themselves to shreds in the process. In earth's history at least, they also stumbled across a wide range of potent chemicals but never realized the full worth of what they had. Man, am I going to have fun in here!"

"Would you mind telling me what it was they had?"

"Can't say for sure at this point. I'll tell you one thing, though—by the time you get back in the spring I will, and I think it'll really be dynamite!"

That evening Jeff tried on his purchases to make sure they fit. Among the various items were a fur-lined hat that enclosed his entire head, heavy mittens and woolen undergarments.

289

He would pick up winter boots and leggings at Valholm, as well as a fur coat.

Carl, meanwhile, was muttering over some sheets of parchment he had cadged from Ethbar. Jeff peered over his shoulder to get a better look. The top sheet was covered with chemical equations that might as well have been Greek. In fact, he concluded, they probably were.

Jeff and Ethbar were summoned to the palace the following morning. They were guided to the same room as before, and shortly thereafter were graced with Imogo's presence. A faint smile played across his lips when he addressed Ethbar, but there was a hard edge about him that belied humor.

"Good counselor, we have concluded your strenuous urgings to take up arms have been well advised. We deem it timely to shake off the sloth of peace and set about preserving that which might be. We have dispatched riders to beholden duchies, announcing that all will gather in conclave three weeks hence. You may well guess to what ends.

"Captain Rengeld has served us with distinction, and we are aware you think well of him. He will be given new authority to recruit warriors. He will also be asked to determine the overall needs of the city in regards to its defense. A large responsibility, but one that we believe he will welcome."

"He will do the task justice, Sire."

"We suffer no doubts." Imogo turned his attention to Jeff. "May I assume your northern intent remains fixed?"

"Yes, your Majesty. I will leave Rugen within the next day."

"Your task is a worthy one but fraught with danger, both from the elements and our northern brethren. That which you have accomplished to date, however, leads us to conclude you will meet with success."

Imogo gazed thoughtfully at Jeff for some time. While his cross-examination had been brutal, Jeff found Imogo's steady, coal-black gaze to be equally unsettling. At a practical level, Jeff began to comprehend what he had studied so long and hard: kings were not to be trifled with. When Imogo's gaze softened, the pressure was relieved as if an escape valve had opened.

"We must also express our appreciation for your earlier efforts on behalf of Rugen. We greatly anticipate the caravan's arrival from Astholf, and will greet such valuable allies with due ceremony. But now, what counsel would you offer that will further preparation of the city and surrounding countryside for the advent of Northmen?"

"Your Majesty, I will encourage them to assemble at the southern villages' moot grounds. This lies at the meeting of the Farga and Vekka rivers, a safe distance from Rugen. Once game animals in that area are depleted, the northern warriors must be assured provender whether war ensues at once or a period of waiting must be endured. When battle nears, a camp must then be prepared in the forest north of Rugen."

"This will be done. We also believe it wise to soothe our northern cousins' penchant for bloodshed and rapine by insuring that adequate foodstuffs await them at the moot ground you have spoken of."

"I am relieved, Majesty. Full stomachs will go far toward calming their violent tendencies."

The remainder of the meeting was spent settling details. It broke up early enough to give Jeff time to complete stores. He double-checked everything one more time and took the rest of the evening off to be with his friends. The fire shed cheerful warmth, wine flowed, no word was spoken of the winter to come.

Walking to their rooms that night, Jeff stopped Carl in the hallway. "I borrowed some of your parchment to write a few letters to Zimma. I do not have enough skill with the local script to explain my heart, and have composed them in English. It is a terrible imposition, but would you work with Ethbar on a translation so that Zimma might read them?"

Carl had known Jeff too long to miss the stark fear in his words. "Nothing would please me greater."

Embracing Jeff, Carl hurried into his room to avoid revealing his own fear. The odds against Jeff surviving the winter were overwhelming. Jeff had saved his life, but he could do nothing to improve those odds. It didn't seem right.

The air was crisp and clear as Jeff tied equipment and purchases to the saddle. Cynic was ready to move out. When all was secure, he capered about at the end of the hackamore shooting plumes of vapor from his nostrils. Everything had been said and their parting was silent as Jeff clasped hands with his friends.

Sixteen

Go or No Go

Weeks fled in succession on the way north. They followed the road to what Jeff now thought of as Mirkwood Creek, and picked up the same path they had followed south. This time it wasn't Jeff who was on the lookout for an elf or hobbit in the darker reaches of the forest.

Cynic tried to be coy about the whole thing, which only made his covert searching more obvious and amusing. That it was a horse doing the searching did not seem odd at all, prompting Jeff to reflect on all the changes that had taken place since leaving Earth. Life was so rich now. He could not bear the thought that it was likely to end this winter.

Leaving the deciduous forest behind, they followed the course of the Vana until reaching its origin at the confluence of the Farga and the Vekka. Fording the Vekka, they continued north.

Fall was at hand and accelerated by their passage into higher latitudes. Under other circumstances Jeff would have reveled in the chill mornings and heavy warmth of noon. Leaves were beginning to hint at the riot of colors they would soon display, but he hardly noticed them.

Well into their second week on the trail, Jeff and Cynic had fallen back into the silence of old, solitary habits. Fine clothes left behind he wore the travel-worn leather pants and boots purchased in Khorgan. In addition, Jeff sported a new shirt made of homespun wool. Pulled low over his eyes was the same floppy leather hat, feather rumpled but still waving.

Several days out of Valholm, gray clouds rapidly obscured the morning sun. The temperature plummeted, and by late afternoon large snowflakes danced around them driven by a breeze that smelled of falling leaves.

Jeff shivered while making camp, but not from the cold. Having earlier speculated that a period of glaciation was in retreat, he desperately hoped for a mild winter. That, he knew, was grasping at straws.

They ran across a hunter from Valholm packing a load of venison the next day. He greeted Jeff with great warmth, stirring

293

Jeff to pick up the pace in anticipation of the reunion soon to come. They cantered into the village at dusk. Outposts had spotted them long before.

Cynic had to carefully pick his way to the meeting hall to avoid stepping on one or the other of a swarm of children. The crowd of adults pressing close to call out greetings further complicated the task. A number of musicians snatched the opportunity to perform, adding the sounds of fifes and drums to the uproar.

"Nice to be appreciated, eh buddy?"

Cynic stopped in front of the hall. *"Considering what we have been through in their service, it is the least they could do."*

Chuckling at his mount's comment, Jeff stepped from the saddle and into the crowd. They pushed into the hall with him as he searched for Halric and Gurthwin. While neither man was present, the evening meal was nearly ready and the crowd stayed on to get an early start at the beer barrels.

It wasn't long before matters degenerated into a beer-swigging jamboree. Jeff moved from group to group pounding backs and being hammered in return. At one point he was slapped on the back at just the wrong instant and found himself bent over coughing violently trying to clear a swallow of beer from his lungs.

Halric showed up and shouted a degree of order into the mob before extending his own enthusiastic greetings. The evening was complete when Gurthwin arrived, grumping along as usual.

"It is most gratifying to see you again, Jeffrey. That much has transpired, and still more planned, is clearly written in your thoughts and fears. Do not be ashamed! Your task is large."

Rough humor flew around the room like a summer thunderstorm, but Jeff's return was at the center of most conversations. His alien clothing spurred endless speculation, prompting many to recall old ballads in search of information.

There was no doubt he would be called on for a recitation, and Jeff pushed his tankard away. Villagers were still eating when the expected shouts for a tale grew to a continuous roar. Walking to the center of the hall, Jeff decided to lay it on thick.

When he described their pursuit by the hyenas, the villagers seethed with tension. Cynic's heartbreaking dash across the flats had them on their feet shouting encouragement, then horror when he stumbled. By the time Jeff finished describing the battle, the hall was a madhouse of bellowed war songs and mugs crashing onto tables.

It was impossible to continue, and Jeff took the opportunity to consider the next section. He decided to skip over it. Gurthwin caught his eye and shook his head.

"This has occurred. It must be related."

"I am shamed to have killed a woman."

"The shame lies in another world, the truth will be discovered in this one."

Coming out of his thoughts, Jeff found the hall silently expectant. He soon lost himself in the battle to defend the caravan.

"...And so my sword did pierce her heart, and she fell to her knees at my feet with despairing cry. Then was I fully stricken with the horror of my deed. Yet still she lived and looked into my face with silent plea, asking that death not embrace her, for she was young and strong."

Tears had come to Jeff's eyes, and he looked away for a moment before continuing.

"Yet again, what succor could I offer? What balm to ease death's passage? My cries to the gods went unanswered, and her spirit departed."

Closing his eyes, Jeff fought back a flood of guilt and new doubt. A bass voice pierced his memories, rumbling a sonorous chant. A soprano joined in, singing counterpoint. Then the hall was filled with solemn voices that ebbed and flowed through the Song for the Dead.

Opening his eyes, Jeff gazed around the hall and saw many sympathetic expressions. None displayed blame.

Gurthwin held his tankard high. "To the dead. May her spirit find peace and a new home."

Everyone dived for their tankards and roared out, "To the dead!"

Several rounds of beer later the crowd began settling onto their benches. Feeling a burden had been removed from his soul, Jeff emptied his tankard and picked up the story in Khorgan. The villagers fell silent, eyes wide and heads shaking at so many strange and wonderful things. Breaking into a smile, Jeff described his meeting with Zimma.

Bellowed laughter shook the hall, and a heavily muscled woman jumped to her feet. She grinned around before calling out, "But did you bed her, Jeffrey!"

A chorus of whistles and ground-shaking stamping of feet set Jeff to laughing, and to blushing.

"Her temper reminds me of yours, Gerta, but I won through in the end."

Roaring laughter and another warrior jumped up, staggered, and almost collapsed onto the table.

"You must tell us, Jeffrey—with which end did you succeed?"

Trumpeting laughter, Gerta pounded the man up alongside the head with a friendly blow that sent him to the floor. Grabbing a tankard, she saluted Jeff.

"One end is as good as another, eh Jeffrey?"

Face contorted with laughter, tears streaming from his eyes, Halric found his feet and eventually got everyone back in their seats.

Jeff moved on to Tradertown, his voice ominous as he described Arzaks. Knowing an enemy when they heard about one, a muttering rumble of growls and curses began to swell. Matters came to a head with his discovery of Carl in slavery and Zimma's abduction.

At that point both Halric and Gurthwin had to intervene as calls for revenge and slaughter rebounded. Gerta and her sister, Ingid, were especially outraged. Ingid waved a battle-ax around in such a fashion that those nearby hit the deck. Halric persuaded them to sit down.

"My friends, this is a tale to be remembered, but let us hold our peace so that it may be told!"

His rush through town searching for Zimma had every soul on the edge of their seats. When Jeff described how he stood breathlessly listening behind the Arzak tent, the room became deathly still. What he saw when he cut his way into the tent led outrage and near riot to bloom anew in the crowd. His slaying of the commander and guards was greeted with shouts of approval and a favorite battle song.

Carl's rescue and retreat to the shore had them off the benches once again and fingering weapons. He ended the recitation with his preparation for death, only to be saved at the last minute by Zimma and Belstan.

"...And so, brothers and sisters, I return to you through peril to warn of the Salchek invaders."

The rest of the evening was a blur. Jeff drank far more than he should have and was forced to retell the goriest scenes many times. Later, Gerta and Ingid made it clear he was to stay with them. Gurthwin solved that problem by the simple expedient of taking Jeff by the arm and leaving.

Jeff spent a good share of the following day renewing old acquaintances. That evening he met with Halric and Gurthwin. Throughout the meeting, Jeff was repeatedly struck by the remarkable similarities he perceived in Ethbar and Gurthwin. If at all possible, he thought, I must arrange for them to meet. What a brain trust that would be!

By the time they had chewed his trip down to the bone, Gurthwin was deep in thought and Halric clearly troubled. Jeff emphasized the alliance with Rugen, but nothing could really soften the impact of imminent war.

Halric broke the silence first. "And so you must travel north and do what you may to gather the tribes by spring ere we are ground under the Salchek heel."

"Yes. This must be done."

"You must not bear this burden alone." Gurthwin placed a gnarled hand on Jeff's arm. It was very comforting. "The courier from Rugen arrived, and his message was well received at the moot."

"I am relieved to hear that," Jeff said in a neutral tone. "He was not...uh, overcome with concern?"

Ethbar smiled at Jeff's attempt to be tactful. "No, although it is fortunate that he called on your name early in the meeting."

Now it was Halric's turn to smile, and the three of them suddenly broke out in laughter. Ethbar wiped at a tear in his eye.

"Your Rengeld selected a fine young man, Jeffrey, and he regaled us with the full iron-shirt saga. I can tell you there was strong emotion present at the conclusion of his tale. Many wished to have a part in what is to come.

"Wonderful. A good start, then."

"Yes indeed. Some among our kinfolk will be selected to visit southern tribes we are friendly with but who were not present at the moot."

"I had hoped it would be so. I must venture north and west to those more distant peoples, where as an Alarai it is more likely that I will be welcomed."

"I must think long on what we have learned this summer from the tribes who trekked south," Halric commented. "Much was discussed, and may prove important to your journey. Many tribes we do not know of were mentioned."

The following days were busy as Jeff arranged for a winter coat, leggings and tall boots to be constructed. In between times he worked over the snowshoes and sewed up tears in his tent. It was looking ragged but still had a lot of use in it. Although Jeff really wanted to take the campstove, his last fuel bottle was nearly empty. On the chance it might come in handy to start fires, he tossed it on the pile to go.

The morning that Jeff was to ride out, a solemn crowd of villagers escorted him to the stable. Gurthwin took his arm along the way and spoke in a low voice.

"Do not be ashamed of your fear or regret its presence, Jeffrey, for it speaks honestly of the burden you carry. Open your spirit so it may have its say then find a new home. You will succeed."

Jeff left Valholm under dark skies, fading into the abrupt whiteness of a snow flurry. Some days later, the outpost materialized from a howling snowstorm. The leader of the outpost, Folget, tactlessly waved it away with a laugh as he walked with Jeff to the stable.

"This is merely a promise of what will come. Soon it will start to snow!"

Feeding Cynic and covering him with a blanket, Jeff stomped snow from his boots before entering the lodge used for meetings. While eating a hearty meal of stew near a roaring fire, the wind moaned around the lodge like a dying soul.

On the occasions when it rose to a high-pitched shriek, Folget and others in the lodge looked away rather than meet Jeff's eye. He tried to block it out, but could not avoid the thought that the wind was a living thing and calling to him.

Halric had passed on what he knew about northern tribal connections to Jeff, and this information was amplified next day in talks with Folget. By that evening Jeff had a workable sketch of the surrounding area, villages prominently marked. He also took copious notes on landmarks.

Before he left the hall, Jeff made sure Folget understood that Cynic was to be taken back to Valholm and a warmer stable by the next courier.

Lighting a torch, Jeff trudged to the stable through drifting snow. Gusts tore streams of sparks from the torch, and he had to lean into the wind to keep his balance. Inside, he found a niche that would hold the torch. Circling Cynic's neck with his arms, Jeff rested his cheek against smooth hide.

"Take you care, my friend. I will miss you terribly."

Cynic nuzzled Jeff's shoulder. "*My thoughts will ever be with you, horse-brother. My heart cries out at your peril, but understands that you must attempt this journey. I will await you in patience and greet your return with joy.*"

The stable was a flimsy affair, its loosely-fit planking rattling and shaking with the wind's force as Jeff held on to Cynic. Some time later Jeff kissed Cynic's neck and released his hold.

"Farewell, my brother."

Picking up the torch, Jeff crunched his way to the lodge where he would sleep. It was pitch black and eddies of hard-driven snow stung his face like needles. He felt very alone and frightened in a way that went to the core of his being.

For many hours, Jeff lay awake listening to the storm's frustrated wail as it tore at the lodge. He reviewed the facts that made his trip necessary, found arguments to defeat each of them, and finally whispered, "Why me?"

He had not volunteered to be dumped on Aketti, Jeff reminded himself. He was related to the Alarai, but only distantly after seven generations. Dammit, he desperately thought, why couldn't one of them do it? Why me?

That night as he tossed and turned in his furs, Jeff confronted the difference between facing death in a sword fight thrust on him suddenly and deliberately choosing a path that he had come to believe would kill him.

He fought it, but reason and anticipation told him he didn't have a chance. It was a bitter night of regret and rejection, yet there was no escape. He would go, and likely he would die.

Dawn was no more than black becoming gray. Feeling drawn and tired, Jeff prepared himself for departure. After a large meal and a brief round of farewells, he walked out of the post without looking back under a brooding sky spitting occasional snow flurries.

Seventeen

A Terrible Judgment

Jeff huddled near a fire. Two days out, the forest's whispering quiet felt like it was crushing him. Packing up, he turned back toward the outpost. As he went, Jeff fought a no-holds-barred battle with paralyzing fear. It was several hours before he found enough will power to halt the retreat.

Unable to move one way or the other, face gray as the sky, Jeff dug deep trying to find strength. It was well into the morning when he set his feet in motion toward the west. There was no going back. He was probably going to die on the trail, but his life was finished if he returned to the outpost. It would just take longer. This was his task, and he would do it.

A week or so later, standing high on a stony foothill squinting his eyes against the glare of a westering sun, Jeff feasted on the sight of wood smoke coiling into the sky. Although no more than thin tendrils of blue emerging from the carpet of forest far below him, the smoke was evidence of life. It was a wonderful sight.

Jeff trudged into the village after dark amid surprised shouts and suspicion. He was hustled in front of the chief, but she was more intrigued than hostile.

When he removed his hat, what Jeff now thought of as the Alarai Effect took hold and the reception warmed. He gathered that the chief thought he must be either crazy or sent from the gods to be on the trail in winter. Jeff had expected and was asked to recite his adventures at the communal meal on the second evening.

His tale was received with all the tumult anyone could have hoped for. Later, when talking with the village elder and chieftain, Jeff discovered that they too had heard rumors, and not only of the Salchek. It seemed that his first encounter with the warring tribes had been widely reported. The elder was familiar with the location of the moot grounds and the chief promised to bring warriors.

Before leaving next morning, Jeff swore powerful oaths with the chief to the enthusiastic acclaim of those who had gathered to see him off. He left after procuring directions to the nearest village, thinking grimly, one down and forty-nine to go.

Week by week, Jeff made his way west through heavily forested foothill country and ever deeper snow south of the Bora Mountains. Fear slowly subsided as he adjusted to the wilderness and traveling alone.

Passing over razor-backed ridges and through low passes, new vistas of snow-muffled forest and valley opened to his eyes in unending variation. So terrible were the Boras' presence that he only rarely threw quick glances at them.

Jeff's concern that knowledge of the Alarai and Salchek would fade as he moved west proved groundless. What he had not figured on was the incredibly complex interrelatedness of the tribes. In short, they enjoyed a rumor mill second to none.

He stayed an average of two days in each village, meeting with leaders during the first and mixing with the rank and file on the second. An important part of each day was recording landmarks that would see him to the next village. He was tempted to stay longer on numerous occasions, but it was hard enough to leave after only two days.

Temperatures dropped steadily as fall faded into winter and Jeff moved west. Although snowstorms became more frequent, they tended to be short-lived. Still, over three feet of snow had accumulated and called for continual use of snowshoes. Of an evening, he checked the bindings with obsessive care and repaired the day's damage perched close to a fire.

After one particularly difficult day that included rocky terrain, he wondered how long it would be before he destroyed a snowshoe. He thrust that thought aside and bent to the task of keeping them going for another day. The forest was silent and the air heavy with the promise of snow when he put the second snowshoe down and slipped into his sleeping bag.

When Jeff awoke he found it hard to breathe, and tent walls bulged against the sleeping bag. He dug his way out to emerge into a raging blizzard. The storm confined him to the tent for three days and Jeff struggled into the next village totally exhausted. Digging deep, he found the determination to leave after two days in spite of the chief's worried entreaty to remain longer.

No one in that village or in villages that followed questioned whether he was crazy or a god. They considered him to be something of both with Hero thrown in for good measure.

After many repetitions, his speech, or Telling as villagers referred to it, was memorized and polished to such a glow that it succeeded in inciting to riot every group that heard it. As Jeff learned more of Alemanni motivation, his oaths also improved in delivery and the power to compel.

Shuffling through six inches of new snow one day, head bent into a snowstorm and feeling very lonely, Jeff distracted himself by trying to figure out how long he had been on the trail. Without a calendar there was no precise way of knowing, but days were still getting shorter. That meant it was still fall. Probably late November. The worst of winter lay ahead.

Jeff was picking his way down the backside of a rugged, hog-backed ridge that was thickly grown with stubby evergreens. He grabbed a branch to stop his motion when a large deadfall materialized out of the snowstorm. Jeff felt so tired that he couldn't muster more than a resigned shrug. At that moment, all he wanted was to run across a deer before it became dark. He had not seen a deer in weeks.

Tightening his belt another notch, Jeff belayed himself from tree to tree and skirted the obstacle. He remembered what it felt like to have a full stomach but seemed to have passed beyond the ferocious hunger that had been his constant companion. Villages were now quite far apart and deep snow burned more energy. That night he chewed a stick of venison jerky and dreamed of the real thing.

Cloud cover and snow were gone when he got up, leaving an icy blue sky and deceptive sun that gave little warmth. As the day progressed, a massive high-pressure system from beyond the Boras finished moving in.

Wading through powder snow up to his knees despite the snowshoes, Jeff stopped to catch his breath. The crest of the hill he had been climbing for what seemed an eternity was still a long way off.

"No feeling in my cheeks at all. Temperature must have dropped."

Wrapping an extra fold of woolen scarf around his face, Jeff stepped out again. The risk of frostbite was always there, but he was more concerned about breaking a leg. He was dead if that happened.

Topping the crest, Jeff noticed his fingers were hard to feel and beat his mittens together trying to get some circulation going.

"What's going on?" he wondered, viewing a clear sky. "Sun doesn't get very high, but it can't be that cold." He wriggled his toes and felt immensely relieved that he could feel them. "Those boots have been a godsend."

Consulting his notes, he scanned the countryside. Landmarks were his only hope of finding the next village. They were there. He grunted with relief and heard a popping crackle. Confused by the sound at first, his heart started to race when it happened again.

"You idiot," he muttered, "that's the moisture in your breath freezing the second it leaves your mouth."

As the implications sank in, he felt fear that was only a step away from panic. "Dammit to hell, should have noticed that hours ago. That's why I'm so tired. Not enough food to hold off hypothermia."

The foothill he was standing on towered over its neighbors to overlook an immense bowel-shaped valley. The terrain curved down and away so far that trees on the bottom appeared like blades of grass. The Boras rimmed the valley to the north forming a gigantic wall of gray stone and ice. In their size, they seemed to be the beginning and end of all things. They were magnificent, but Jeff saw no beauty.

He searched for the giant eagles that were often to be seen drawing lazy circles in the sky. There were none aloft or any other birds. For the first time Jeff noticed there was absolutely no breeze. Holding his breath to listen, he heard no sounds at all. The land was deathly, oppressively silent. He rushed downslope at a panic-driven pace.

"I've got to get to the next village before nightfall!" He nearly fell headlong and abruptly stopped. "Cut the shit, Jeffrey. Run anymore and you're dead. Use your goddamed head!"

Dark blue shadows streaked the land when Jeff began to dig into a snow bank. He had hollowed out a good-sized hole before the futility of what he was doing sank in. Breathing hard from his effort but still shivering, he rode out another swell of panic.

"Okay, I'm not even sweating after all that work and temperatures might drop as low as fifty degrees below zero tonight, maybe more. My bag is only good to ten below, and even with everything in the pack piled on and buried in the snow it just isn't going to fly. Not with the hypothermia I've got going. Make a fire, then set up camp."

A mockingly glorious sunset of greens and gold was fading to dark blue when Jeff abandoned his hole and hurried to gather twigs and small tree limbs. Hands shaking with anxiety, he set up the twigs and reached for his flint and wad of punk. Nothing—his fingers were numb. He tried to control his hands by sight but dropped the flint over and over again. When he did hit flint on steel, he was unable to direct the sparks onto the punk.

Wishing desperately for matches that were long gone, Jeff began to realize he might die that night. Blue was turning to black speckled with stars, intensifying the oppressive stillness. The only thing he could hear was his own breathing.

"The stove fuel!" Jeff tore through his pack. He pulled the aluminum bottle out. "It might work. It has to!"

He intended to pour only a capful, but his arms were shaking so that fuel sprayed on snow as well as twigs.

"Please, please," Jeff mumbled and attacked the piece of steel with his flint.

It was no good. Those sparks he managed to land in the right spot would not ignite the fuel.

"I don't want to die! Not like this! There has to be a way to start a fire!"

The wish for matches that had passed through his mind flashed back.

"One chance, that's all your going to have," Jeff whispered.

His lips did not want to work and his cheeks were as dead as a lump of clay. Fumbling a cartridge from the pistol he tried to wedge the slug out but could not.

"Oh, damn it. I have to get it out!"

Jeff opened the cylinder and clamped the shell between it and the receiver. Gripping the slug with his teeth, he twisted the revolver. The revolver moved and the slug between his teeth held firm. His relief was so profound when the slug popped out that he nearly dumped the gunpowder. Bending far over to see, Jeff let the gunpowder trickle into the nest of twigs.

"One chance, one chance."

The larger moon sailed above the horizon lending a fairy-tale aspect to forest and mountains while Jeff repeatedly tried to get a spark. His arms and hands were like sticks of wood and would not work together. He stood there for some time staring at the pile of twigs but seeing nothing.

"And so it's over. I can rest."

Kneeling down with bowed head, Jeff let go of hope and the need to live. Freeing his spirit to begin another journey, steel and flint dropped to the snow in a gesture of final surrender. Pale moonlight set the valley a-glimmer with pure whites and dark greens; illuminated mountains that no longer threatened. The moon sailed higher, nothing moved. All was silent and time passed.

Trees surrounding the kneeling figure whispered. Sighing gently, a warm breeze tugged at Jeff's clothing. Frost had covered his eyes like white patches and melted to run like tears. A squirrel stirred in its nest, moved by thoughts of spring's tender shoots. Somewhere, a bird called out a tentative query. Then, as before, nothing moved. A new silence of contemplation and terrible judgment rested on the land.

And so he kneeled there, and so he was judged.

A jagged splinter of fire burst into life over Jeff's head, flamed to white incandescence and plunged into the nest of twigs igniting the gunpowder. Gone in one brilliant moment, the gunpowder lighted the stove fuel in a slower flare that burned long enough to set the twigs afire.

Staring at the flames from a great height, Jeff smiled at the yellow tongues that waved so cheerfully in the florescent whites and greens of the night.

How beautiful, he thought. I wish I could take it with me, but it's so far away. Can I take it with me? Please? I've worked so hard.

"Yes, you have."

Jeff awoke to his surroundings feeding sticks into the fire, which had grown large enough to shed considerable warmth.

"It's burning! I must have hit one good spark into the twigs!"

Swept by a renewed desire to live, Jeff stumbled around in the trees collecting deadfall wood until he had accumulated a tall pile. Building the fire up to a good blaze, he opened his coat to soak up as much heat as possible. He had set the pot on to melt snow when he heard an explosion and a large limb crashed down nearby.

"Shit!"

Staring at the limb, Jeff gained new appreciation of just how cold it was. The sap had expanded explosively when it froze, severing the limb.

Some time later his face and hands throbbed to life. Chewing a shred of jerky, he sipped hot water and listened. The land was so still he could hear a distant popping like fireworks as more trees shed limbs.

He nodded off several times before unpacking the tent. The thought of going to sleep was terrifying, but there was no choice. Rolling large hunks of wood into the fire, he set his tent up with the mouth facing the fire and crawled into the sleeping bag.

Jeff awoke shivering violently. Teeth chattering, he crawled out of the sleeping bag and from under every warm item he was packing. The fire had burned down, leaving a deep bed of coals. He tossed wood on and new flames sprang to life. When the shivering stopped, his brain began to churn through options.

"All right, time to face it. Somehow you've managed to live through the night, but how much food is left and how far to the next village?"

His heart sank when he pulled out the single stick of jerky that remained. Jeff located his notes and wearily trudged uphill. The landmarks were there; he had located them the previous day. It was the distance to the next village that mattered.

A sense of desperation fought to take over again as he viewed the terrain and consulted his notes. The nearest village was at least thirty miles away. It was too far. He would never make it.

As he tried by force of will to bring the village closer, his gaze fell on the line of mountains towering into the sky. Anger boiled up.

"Screw you. I'm not going to give up now."

By the end of the day he was exhausted beyond anger. He had fallen three times, twisting a knee the first time and hitting it against a tree the third. When Jeff stopped to make camp every step was agony. That night he finished the last stick of jerky.

Well after dark, a shadow figure hobbled out of the forest supported by a rude staff. Three dragging steps and stop. Three more and Jeff stopped longer. Muted gasping sounds gradually faded. Raising his head he sniffed the air from side to side.

Starlight revealed a face that sagged with exhaustion and was so thin that every bone stood out. His clothing was matted with snow from falling, his beard a chunk of ice.

"Smoke. Know I smelled smoke." After a brief silence he sobbed, "Oh Jesus, where is it? I can't do this anymore."

Dragging his damaged leg, three steps at a time, Jeff skirted a number of obstacles but stumbled into another. Circling the mound he continued toward the edge of the clearing, now only a short distance away.

A yellow-orange rectangle of light blinked into existence.

A torch-wielding man cautiously emerged from the rectangle, spear in hand. Vision impaired by the torch, he bumped into the stooped figure. Letting out a terrified yell he jumped back.

Jeff stopped and tried to figure out what the noise meant, failed, and took another step toward the forest. The villager's cry brought others running. Mesmerized, they watched Jeff move in slow motion until he disappeared into the trees.

Casting apprehensive looks into the woods, the villagers hurried to find light and warmth. Inside one of the lodges an elderly man was stoking the fire. He looked up when a younger man entered.

"What has happened? Have the gods visited us?"

"No, Father, it was a demon!"

The old man snorted skepticism. "Tell me of this 'demon.'"

He became alarmed as the tale unfolded. "You are foolish children. This is a man near death, no demon. You must go quickly, Erlik. Gather help and bring him to our lodge."

Erlik ducked out of the lodge with a fresh torch. It was his fervent wish that he would live long enough to duck back in. Rousting out a collection of equally reluctant friends, they edged into the forest muttering terrified oaths at the huge footprints.

Fifty yards into the forest, they found him lying face down in the snow and deathly still. Erlik felt deep chagrin when he kneeled and got a closer look.

"Assist me. Father was right, this is no demon."

Pushing through the door to his lodge, Erlik and two companions lay Jeff on deer hides that covered the floor. A fourth entered and set the backpack down. Quick hands stripped Jeff of clothing. When his hat was removed, the elder drew in a dismayed breath.

"Now will the doom of this village be spoken by the gods. This man is of the Alarai."

Erlik was stricken by his father-in-law's words and took his hand. "Forgive me for having failed you. If such doom should be harsh, it must be mine alone."

The old man, who once was known as Theregrond, shook his head and patted Erlik's hand.

"Are you so mighty as to warrant such responsibility when others were equally negligent? But come, now is not the time to debate guilt. We must begin his warming at once."

Erlik's wife, Lilet, and his daughter had finished undressing Jeff and were cleaning his face of crusted dirt and ice that was beginning to melt. Shortly, they slid him onto a bed of furs near the firepit.

"He is so thin. Will his spirit survive, Grandfather?"

"There is hope, child."

Dropping extra furs by Jeff, Theregrond glanced at his granddaughter. Magda was sitting back on long thighs, hands busy with a rough comb made of bone trying to get accumulated debris out of Jeff's hair.

Magda had intrigued Theregrond as she developed from a quiet, introspective girl into an even quieter woman. While she rarely spoke, he always paid strict attention when she did. Each word seemed to have been picked from a thousand others in order to find just the right one. She participated in village activities and seemed to enjoy them, but never abandoned her emotions to the moment.

Her parents had become concerned that Magda was not showing enough interest in men of her age. Theregrond perceived that concern to be misplaced. He didn't think there was a young man in the village she had not evaluated. She did it without any fuss, and always privately. When Magda made up her mind she would act. He had seen it before.

Magda threw off her clothes and slid under the furs next to Jeff. Lilet did the same and they sandwiched him between them.

"He is so cold."

The tone of Magda's voice and the fact that she had spoken again attracted Theregrond's attention. She had pulled Jeff's head against her neck. Lost on some distant horizon, her eyes were filled with calm certainty. Theregrond glanced at Lilet and found her intently studying Magda's face.

Some hours later Theregrond nodded with satisfaction as Jeff began to breathe deeply and shiver.

"Perhaps the crisis has passed."

Magda said nothing, but closed her eyes and her own breathing took on the rhythm of sleep. Lilet shifted position so she could run a hand along Jeff's ribs, which stuck out prominently.

"He is so wasted from his toil, Father, yet strength remains. It is not his time to leave this world."

"As the gods ordain."

Lilet raised her head so she could view Magda's face from a better perspective. Orange light from the bed of coals illuminated her daughter's features more effectively than full sunlight. Lilet had never been able to understand Magda, for the two women viewed the world from perspectives that could not be reconciled.

While Lilet was comforted by the predictable routine of village life, actively avoided anything unusual, Magda took every opportunity to wander far afield in search of new adventure. Magda, perhaps, understood this better than Lilet. At the moment, however, and sensitized by events, Lilet was taken with prescient insight that eluded the limitations of her tightly ordered life.

The sense of completion to Magda's features, the way she held this man, struck Lilet to the heart. She could not comprehend being attracted to such a person. He had just arrived, was a complete stranger, not of her people, and obviously extremely rash. She saw a future for her daughter that faded far beyond the realm of experience; saw alien landscapes and peoples that frightened her.

Lilet gasped and tears rushed to her eyes. For one brief instant she glimpsed eternity but did not welcome it and shuddered away.

"Oh, Father, I fear for her. What has provoked her to move so quickly? It will be her death to join with this man!"

"Do you doubt a time is come when the gods would walk among us, Lilet?"

"This is a man, no god."

"Yes, he is a man, but will you consider my question?"

"The time is come."

Theregrond nodded. "Then let us be accepting of their will, whatever the import. I believe that, in your heart, you have long known that Magda is a most unusual woman. Perhaps her destiny lies far from this village."

"Thus I fear, for it has been given me to view that destiny and it..." Lilet lay down and placed a hand over Jeff's heart. "I will say no more."

Jeff woke up the next afternoon. He babbled incoherently, took some broth and was quickly asleep again. It was two days before he could stay awake for more than an hour, and six more before he could walk. The skin on his fingers, cheeks and ears blistered from the effects of frostbite. As it became clear over passing days that he wasn't going to lose fingers, Jeff's relief was immense. The swollen knee also began to shrink. Magda was his constant companion during those anxious days.

Never speaking more than a word or two, she always seemed to be there when he needed a hand up or a shoulder to lean on while trying to get his legs working again. His body odor was so offensive that Jeff could hardly bear it, and he was humiliated by what she must think.

Without having to look in a mirror, Jeff knew that his filthy, emaciated body and scabbed face must be extremely ugly. He tried to brush Magda away the first time she gave her hand to assist him. Rather than withdraw, she simply took his arm and pulled him to his feet.

When Jeff was able to stand for more than a few minutes she draped a fur robe around his shoulders and assisted him to the village sauna. Inside, she undressed him like a child and had him sit on a stool. Dipping a bucket of warm water, Magda unceremoniously dumped it over his head. Others in the sauna lent a hand in what became a communal effort.

He could hardly sit on the stool but had enough strength to struggle weakly when Magda scrubbed the worst of the dirt off with a bristle brush. The villagers considered that a positive sign and encouraged him with cries of approval. They did not release their grip. A woman tossed a wad of alkali soap to Magda and she laid into the task.

The village chief and elders visited on a regular basis to keep track of his recovery. When he had gained some strength, Jeff recounted his experiences on the trail in a halting voice. Those assembled hung on every word as the story unfolded. Jeff lapsed into silence after relating what he could remember of the last march.

There was no sound except the fire's crackling as the chief continued to examine Jeff's drawn features and bowed head. Theregrond took the chief aside.

"You must leave now. Life was nearly gone when he was found, and of a night I hear his spirit crying its desolation. We must be patient lest it flies to seek distant refuge."

Nearly the end of December, daylight extended no more than five hours and the deep cold retained its grip on the land. Villagers spent their days constructing new garments, repairing old ones and tending to many other tasks in preparation for spring. Evenings were given over to singing, recitation of ballads and dancing.

It was a pleasant time for the older villagers, but the young set felt confined as winter ground on. Even though game was scarce, they organized hunts just to burn off energy.

Jeff gradually became an accepted part of the village, which he learned was called Fastholm. He visited the meeting hall on occasion during the day, but always withdrew when the real partying began.

One evening, without saying a word, Magda hauled him to his feet and tossed a fur robe at him. When he dallied, she grabbed the robe, threw it around his shoulders and dragged him out of doors.

Taller than Jeff by four or five inches, she had a figure that even his dulled perception had taken note of. Of much greater importance, he always felt comforted in her presence. Jeff thought Magda was the most self-possessed, psychologically poised person he had ever known.

At the hall's entrance, Jeff balked. The commotion inside was overwhelming. Taking a firmer grip, Magda pulled him into the smoky interior and humid warmth. The place was packed with villagers and filled with music and laughter.

"Now you will dance with me, Jeffrey."

They broke into the outermost ring circling the meeting hall. While the pace was fast, the steps were familiar and Jeff was surprised to find that he could keep up. The knee was a problem, but it loosened up after a few times around the hall. The rings eventually broke up into smaller groups. In the process, Jeff was spun away by a woman who was about Magda's age and height. Jeff thought her name was Nilka.

Stopping well away from the dancing, Nilka bent to kiss him. Before she could, a fist flashed past his face to land up alongside her head with a cracking sound. Nilka reeled back, but not far enough.

Magda pushed by Jeff and landed a whistling left cross that dropped the already stunned woman to the floor. Glancing at Nilka to make sure she was breathing, Magda pulled Jeff toward a small group of villagers that had formed into a square.

As the frenetic pace slowed, Magda's body and hands left no doubt she was interested in more than dancing. The hall was quiet except for drunken snores and a lone fifer trying to put two notes together when she lead Jeff to a dark corner and began kissing him.

When Magda slipped a hand under his belt, Jeff called up visions of Zimma much as a priest might hold up a crucifix to ward off temptation and sidled away. Taking his hand, Magda led him back to their lodge.

The evening had been a radical break from morbid brooding. Yet in some ways the merriment had intensified the sense of personal weakness and failure that continually haunted Jeff. The villagers were so full of life and easy confidence that he could hardly bear their presence.

While physically on the path to recovery, a part of his soul had been deeply injured by those last days on the trail. For the first time in his life he had been completely whipped. The sense of fear that hit Jeff each time he thought about leaving was so overpowering that on one occasion he broke down and wept. He had nearly died three times since arriving on Aketti. The last time had wormed its way deep.

Jeff couldn't shake memories of the awful silence and utter loneliness of the land. The beautiful, star-filled night that had sucked the life out of him while trees exploded and groaned their agony. He frequently awoke from sleep bathed in sweat from nightmares of slow death, his body covered with frozen rime, arms reaching out in supplication. But no one was there.

Theregrond and Magda made sure Jeff was not left behind when, late one night, their family trekked to a nearby hill in company with the entire village. Logs were stacked into a tall pile until the whole affair threatened to avalanche down the hill and set afire.

A group of older men and women, including Theregrond, intently viewed the stars as they revolved by overhead. The oldest among them abruptly threw her arms up.

"The sun returns to us. Give joy with the Song of Life."

Individual voices were raised, only to be submerged in a chorus that sorted itself out into a three-part acapella hymn. Although Jeff didn't know the words, he experienced such a rush of emotion that he could do nothing but join in. He also thought, This is it. The Winter Solstice. The longest night of the year. I've *got* to leave.

He intended to get organized the following day but cowered away from even the thought of leaving. Over subsequent days he became moody, even surly, and was given to angry outbursts. It came to a head one night when Jeff awoke with a strangled scream. Everyone in the lodge was awake in an instant and reached for spears, but settled back with sympathetic grunts when they realized it was another nightmare.

Sitting up, Jeff rested his head on his knees and waited for the sweat to cool. He stiffened at a light touch on his shoulder.

"This is not right," Magda whispered in his ear. "Your aloneness will first defeat then kill you. This must not be so, for you are a man of courage and serve us all."

She slipped into Jeff's bed of furs and pulled him down to lie beside her. Taking him in her arms she stroked his body with smooth-drawn caresses. Jeff shuddered from the pleasure of her touch and was reminded of Zimma's, reminded of what she had said.

Throwing his arms around Magda, he buried his face in golden hair and let the tears come. When he awoke she was still there. Jeff felt a wonderful sense of wholeness and drifted into a sleep free of nightmares.

Within a week Jeff began laying plans for his departure. Many hours were spent deep in conversation with Fastholm's leaders. Their knowledge of the land was encyclopedic, leading Jeff to revise equipment and clothing as he learned.

A rough but serviceable sled was constructed to carry extra provisions, clothing and tinder. He adopted the Northman's way of carrying fire buried in a wad of punk that was enclosed in a ventilated earthen jar, devised a liner for his mittens, and constructed a balaclava to protect his face.

Comforted by Magda's arms, his nights were peaceful. Her calm serenity and unwavering persistence in loving him, in believing in him, called forth a depth of passion that first surprised then consumed Jeff. He had surrendered to her, but soon fell in love without really knowing it had happened.

Most of the warriors in the village were eager to join in Jeff's quest to rally the tribes. While cabin fever played a role in their enthusiasm, the threat he reported fueled the larger part. As a result, Thingel, the chieftain, insisted that he send teams out to visit tribes they were related to. Jeff gratefully accepted the offer and estimated that left around fifteen villages to visit.

He had been spending as much time as possible with Magda, could have done nothing else. As the time to leave drew closer, Jeff felt such conflict at leaving her that he began to brood and withdraw. Magda would have none of it. She enticed, pursued and, if necessary, seduced him. In the end she always captured him, sometimes two or three times in a day.

The night before he was to leave Magda silently handed him his furs and, packing more, led him far into the forest. Laying out their bed on the snow, she undressed. Standing tall and ivory in the moonlight, she beckoned to him.

Seeming to come afire, Magda gave him no rest until he didn't want to rest, their cries of joy and pain not ending until shortly before dawn. With sunlight streaking the snow, they walked into the village hand in hand.

Following a tumultuous send-off by the assembled village, Jeff picked up the sled's traces and trudged into the forest. Magda accompanied him until they were alone and could stop for a private farewell. She slipped her hands inside his furs and pulled him close.

"We will meet in the south, Jeffrey. I will not be separate from you, and would hold converse with Zimma."

The absolute conviction in Magda's voice prompted Jeff to step back and look at her. He was reminded of Zimma after their first loving, but what Magda projected had a backbone of steel that surpassed comparison. She appeared radiant, not sad. Deep secrets seemed to lurk in blue eyes that pulled him ever deeper.

Making sure he had scribed every aspect of Magda's features into memory, Jeff studied her face. Yet he could not capture the essence of immutable determination that was such a large part of her being. He thought, How could I have been so fortunate twice in a row? Someone has to be looking out for me.

"You will trek south with Fastholm's warriors as we have discussed?"

Magda smiled, her eyes dancing with hidden magic. "If matters permit, but you must know that I will come."

Jeff tried to decipher what was going on in her head. As usual, he drew a blank. Shortly after meeting Magda, he had learned that she said only as much as intended. When she had said her piece, that was it. There was no point in trying to get more out of her.

"Though pledged to another, I have come to understand in a small way that this world is not stinting with love and will await your coming with great anticipation. My deepest wish is that I not perish in this war before we are reunited."

Shaking her head, Magda smiled softly and kissed him. "I will come, we will meet again. It is the gods' will."

A last lingering kiss and she stepped back, smiled into his eyes and turned away. Jeff watched her walk out of sight and felt like an arm had just been taken off at the shoulder.

The first night was hard. When he awoke without Magda next to him, Jeff felt lost. The effect was so strong that it brought home how deeply he had fallen in love with her. He lingered near the fire after eating to ponder his time with Magda.

For some years he had thought it possible or even likely that he would never find a quality woman to spend his life with. Thought that perhaps something was wrong with him. Now he loved two wonderful women, and even more amazingly they loved him. There was no doubt about it—they did love him.

During long winter evenings, Jeff had related the entire course of his life since being transported from Earth. Magda listened closely, often while sewing new leathers for him or occupied with some other household task. Characteristically she said little, yet Jeff sensed her excitement as events moved south.

When Jeff described his relationship with Zimma, the few questions Magda asked probed deeply. He did not attempt to disguise the conflict that loving two women had created, nor was she surprised to hear he was in conflict.

While she was not telepathic, a synchrony existed between them that in some ways was more powerful. Magda did not attempt to analyze the love triangle, or him, with a flow of words. Rather, she accepted the triangle without the need to rationalize it.

Jeff broke free of his thought train and started packing up. It was getting on in the morning and he had a long way to go. Cinching ropes over the load of supplies on the sled, he decided that he was not going to find any easy answers. Everything he had experienced on Earth spoke against the possibility of loving two women without destroying the relationship with both. But he wasn't on Earth, and it was likely that Zimma and Magda were not human.

Settling the backpack in place and tightening the straps, Jeff reflected on some of his conversations with Gurthwin. Maybe, just maybe, there were gods on this planet after all. What had occurred with Magda, Magda herself, gave strength to that possibility.

Picking up the sled traces, he trudged off with a feeling of strengthened purpose and self-confidence. He had a job to do and was prepared to complete it both from a mental and material standpoint.

In fact, he could now extend his range farther than originally planned. Thingel's offer had opened up possibilities that before would not have been feasible.

Most of the tribes his warriors would visit lay to the south of Fastholm, freeing Jeff to explore farther west. Although Thingel's knowledge of tribes in that area was sketchy, he had warned Jeff about their rumored belligerence.

Considering Thingel's own thunder and lightning personality, that concerned Jeff deeply.

Reassured by the knowledge that he had three week's rations on the sled and another on his back, Jeff fell into step with winter in the mountains. Over ensuing weeks he checked off villages until only one remained to be visited. It was located on the Skola River and called Helstor, or Home of the People.

The last two villages had advised skipping it. Neither village had anything good to say about Helstor. They always went in force when hunting to the west. To be caught out alone would mean your life. However, it was the last village and Jeff wanted to finish what he had started. He would at least attempt to visit them.

It had snowed no more than an inch or two since the high-pressure system had settled in. All moisture had been rung out of the air long ago, and the snow was crusted deep enough to walk on without resorting to snowshoes. The sled skidded along behind so easily that at times it threatened to run up his back.

The terrain he crossed still consisted of rugged foothills with a few high peaks and heavy forest dotted by the occasional meadow. On occasion he heard the rumble of avalanches, but that risk was not new to him. While an avalanche could kill you, so could a broken leg and a long list of other events. Either they did or they didn't.

As time passed Jeff deliberately chose high passes that could have been avoided, for they offered views that demanded comprehension. And so he would stop at the apex of some boulder-strewn passage to while away an hour or two dreaming over the land in its silent cloak of winter.

Silence, white and gray, shades of green, but always silence. Yet he would listen for the silence was palpable; had presence. Over a period of time Jeff came to believe the earth itself was speaking to him, promised understanding.

One day he stumbled across a herd of deer yarded up in a meadow. Stringing his bow, Jeff killed one of the animals and butchered it before the meat could freeze. That night the temperature started to moderate, and by morning a skim of high clouds had moved in. He suspected that an end to the clear weather was not far off. By that afternoon the wind was bowing trees. Overhead, dark gray masses of cloud filled with snow were replacing the high scud.

Jeff stopped to think the situation over. After a brief interval he jerked the sled back into motion.

"Better make camp while I have the chance."

It was getting on in the day before he ran across an outcropping of rock that would serve to protect the tent. Relieved at his find, Jeff was about to drop the sled harness when he heard a commotion somewhere ahead. The wind made it difficult to sort out the exact location or nature of the sounds.

Listening intently, he picked out fragments of a high-pitched snarling that sent goose bumps crawling up his arms. He had never heard such a sound in his life. Jeff was turning the sled to beat a retreat when a deeper snarl came to his ears.

"That's a wolf for sure. Something has that wolf at bay, or I haven't learned a thing about them. What could do that? Maybe a bear? Oh, bullshit." He knew very well what an infuriated bear sounded like from personal experience.

For some time he heard nothing more. "The wolf probably split." Jeff finished turning the sled around. "I'm outta here. That wolf can run a lot faster than me!"

Jeff hadn't gone far when a shriek and telepathic image pierced his heart before both were suddenly extinguished. He tore the revolver free.

"You son of a bitch! That was a cub!"

Once past the ledge he moved cautiously from tree to tree. Momentarily, he broke into a meadow shrouded by gray dusk and the first snow flurries. Maybe seventy feet in diameter, the meadow was splattered with blood.

At the far side a snarling wolf crouched over the body of a deer. Nearby, a smaller animal paced back and forth in front of a still form on the snow. From their mental signatures, Jeff identified them as an adult female and her yearling male cub. The creature advancing in short lunges toward the wolves froze Jeff in his tracks.

Taller than Balthazar by several feet, he guessed it had to weigh at least two hundred pounds more. What was worse, its shape reminded him of a horribly mutated wolverine.

Stunned by its size, Jeff thought, That thing's as big as a black bear! Although it was longer of leg and had shorter fur than a wolverine, its head and overall body shape were the same.

"Holy shit. I've never seen anything that big move so quick," Jeff whispered as the creature advanced with lightning-quick jumps. The larger wolf waited like a coiled spring, snarling defiance and not giving an inch.

With a snow-churning sprint and banshee howl, the monster was on the female. The scene dissolved into a tumbling mass of screaming, snarling fur that moved so fast Jeff saw it only as a blur. Wolf and wolverine sprang apart just as abruptly, once again facing each other across seven or eight feet of snow splattered with new blood.

The female had taken a wound in her hindquarter. It was bleeding copiously, but she crouched back down over the carcass with bared fangs. Waiting for an opening, or for the wolf to weaken from blood loss, the wolverine paced back and forth hissing viciously.

Jeff knew the battle could end only one way.

Maybe a pack of wolves could handle that bastard, he thought, but I don't think they'd even try unless there was no choice. Stricken with fear for the wolves and in terror of the wolverine, Jeff was gripped with indecision.

Looking around as if seeking a way out, he growled, "Why don't I ever have a choice? That devil will eat me alive!"

The wolverine dropped low and inched toward the wolf, a continuous wail rising and falling through bared fangs.

"Oh, dammit it all to hell!" Jeff stripped off his mittens and moved into the meadow.

Colt extended and steadied by his left hand, desperate curses he wasn't even aware of escaped Jeff's lips in a steady stream. Heavy snow flurries whipped around the meadow and light was fading fast, making it hard to see.

The two animals were so intent on each other that he advanced to within about forty feet before the beast whirled to face him and crouched down. Ears shooting up and down in uncertainty, the wolverine emitted a warning snarl. The wolverine's quandary gave Jeff a moment to communicate with the wolves.

"I am a friend of the brethren, wolf-sister. Do not be startled by the loud sounds you will hear when I deal death to this creature."

Jeff had serious doubts and muttered fervently, "God save me, I had better!"

He pulled the hammer back to full cock for an accurate first shot and steadied the sight on the animal's chest. The wolverine made up its mind where the greater danger lay and launched himself at Jeff, snow spewing out behind.

Jeff squeezed the trigger at the same moment.

The wolverine had just pushed off when the slug struck, momentarily stopping his rush. The thunder of the first shot still echoing, the wolverine dug in and charged. The second shot sent him off to the side giving time for a third that either missed or had no effect.

"Die, you son of a bitch!"

Jeff fired the fourth round. He knew it was a miss the moment he pulled the trigger. Dropping to a knee, he jerked the hammer back. Blood dripped from open jaws as the wolverine launched his body and the Colt blossomed fire for the last time.

The slug caught the wolverine at the junction of neck and chest. At a range of no more than ten yards the impact nearly flipped him in midair. Jeff dropped the revolver and went for his knife, but too late as he was knocked over backward.

Struggling wildly, Jeff kicked his way free and pulled the knife. The wolverine lay only feet away.

Shaking badly, Jeff frantically pawed around in the snow until he found the Colt. Not ready to believe the wolverine was dead, he blew snow out of the barrel and reloaded. After dropping three cartridges in a row he slowed down. Snapping the cylinder into place, he poked the wolverine with a long stick. Nothing. It was over.

Jeff approached the wolves in driving snow. The female was sniffing the dead cub and whining. Jeff wanted to leave her alone until she had come to terms with her loss, but it was nearly full dark. If he didn't return to the sled soon he might not find it at all.

"My heart is yours, wolf-sister. May your grief find repose in the One."

The female raised her head. *"In the One lies hope and surcease."*

"Forgive this one's intrusion on your sorrow, but I must soon return to my den. I would know if I may be of assistance. Are you badly wounded, sister?"

"We will recover," she hesitantly replied. *"You are truly a wolf-brother?"*

Jeff sent Balthazar's symbol. *"This is our packmate."*

"This one we know of, for he is held in high esteem."

"He is a mighty leader and friend." Jeff had no alternative but to leave, and set off across the meadow in what he thought was the right direction. *"Darkness is upon us, wolf-sister. Will you and your young one share my den during the great snow?"*

"We will come to you."

Jeff threw a look over his shoulder and saw the female lay down by her dead cub. His path took him by the deer, and he gave it a kick in passing. It had all the resilience of a piece of wood. No food for them there, he concluded. Frozen solid.

While the meadow was not large, light was entirely gone and it was easy to get turned around. He stopped to mentally calculate each step.

"Damn it, I should be there." Jeff was no longer a greenhorn, but still found it hard not to go kiting off in a new direction. "The ledge has to be nearby." He took another step and smacked his nose against rock. "Fuck a duck that hurts!"

The sled was not far from the ledge and he went directly to it. Unfortunately, he found it by falling on top.

"God damn! This day really needs to end! Shit!"

By the time he had a fire crackling under a rock overhang the snow was coming down so thick it looked like a white wall. Lighting a limb full of pitch, Jeff found his way to the wolverine carcass and stuck it in the snow.

The torch was almost used up and his tracks were hard to find when he finished skinning. Jeff was feeling his way through the snowfall when his hand brushed fur.

"Jesus!"

"You are well, wolf-brother?" the female inquired from beside him.

"That is a matter open to debate!"

He dropped the pelt by the fire, loaded on new wood and directed the wolves to a grotto-like niche. When he was satisfied with the fire, Jeff located some stout limbs and pulled them over to the outcropping.

"We will complete your den, wolf-sister."

Jeff propped the limbs over the wolves' grotto. Lashing boughs to the poles, he created a serviceable lean-to.

"Will you and your cub share meat, wolf-sister?"

"We would be honored. Hunting has been lean, and of needs we defended our kill."

Deer meat stashed on the sled was also frozen, but a stick pried open a way to the center where it was not. Jeff knew how much a wolf could eat, and he hesitated.

"Oh, screw it. They must be starving, and sure as hell need it more than I do."

Loading himself with fifteen or twenty pounds of venison, he set it down in front of the wolves. While roasting his own meal, Jeff watched the wolves choke down theirs.

"Lord, they are hungry," he murmured. "That was no more than an appetizer. All right, Jeffrey, dig out some more and quit being such a selfish schmuck."

The second offering was greeted with intense satisfaction.

He waited until they were grooming themselves before speaking. *"How fares your heart, wolf-sister?"*

"She was ours, now she is at rest. Her courage and spirit will never fade from memory. It is done."

Jeff let matters drop. He understood it was not done, but that the cub's death was accepted without the need to ask why or place blame. The wolves found the campfire fascinating and lay at the mouth of their den to watch it. After a period of comfortable silence, Jeff decided it would not be indiscrete to ask why the female was off by herself with two cubs.

"Your pack is near?"

"We are separated from our pack. A great river of snow fell on us high in the mountains many suns ago. We have not been able to find their hunting."

So much packed into so few words, Jeff thought. Sounds like an avalanche either cut them off from the pack or killed the rest. Finding game would be difficult with only one of them an experienced hunter.

"Do you rest well, wolf-sister? When sunlight comes, I will cleanse your wound."

"We are satisfied and will sleep well. We are grateful for the den and food you have given us."

There was still work to be done before Jeff could turn in. He scraped fat from the wolverine pelt first, then cleaned the revolver. Banking the fire, he wrenched a good-sized plate of stone free from the ledge and set it on top of rocks around the fire pit to keep snow out.

When finally zippered into his sleeping bag, Jeff relaxed with a grateful sigh. It had been one hell of a day. The fire died down to embers and all was quiet on the land as snow drifted around the ledge.

Several feet of snow had fallen by the time a dirty gray morning slowly distinguished itself from night. Freshening the coals with several sticks, Jeff put water on to heat. He let it come to a boil then dumped in snow until it was the right temperature.

The female greeted him courteously when he set the pot down next to her. She lay quietly while he scrubbed debris from the wound, patted it dry and spread salve. When he was done, Jeff admired his handiwork.

As hoped, snow had drifted around the lean-to forming a snug den for the wolves. Snow continued to fall in heavy silence and they spent the rest of the day and night holed up.

"Tough going today," he grumbled while peering out of the tent next morning, "and what am I going to do about the wolves?" The female was wounded, and the yearling too immature to be an effective hunter. Their outlook was not good. "No alternatives I can live with. As usual."

"The sun has returned and I must leave this den. Will you and your cub join this one until your pack is found?"

"We are wounded and will prove a burden. Will you have such a one in this hard season?"

Jeff was moved by her willingness to be left and surely die. "I do not travel quickly. You and your yearling will prove no burden."

"We will join you. We thank you for accepting us."

Back in snowshoes, the going was slow and tiring as Jeff broke trail through soft new snow heaving on the sled. The pace was so slow that the female had no difficulty keeping up. She and the youngster ranged off to either side, disappearing at times as they scouted ahead.

They covered a wide swath of territory in this fashion, and it was not surprising if still good fortune that the young male, whom Jeff named Balko, ran across a herd of deer. Taking a firm hand, Jeff left no doubt in the youngster's mind that he was to wait for them to arrive.

When they did, all three crept in close to take stock. There were five deer yarded up in a meadow.

"Let this one use the sharp stick that flies quickly to bring us a sure kill. When it strikes, attack a different animal."

Sneaking in closer, Jeff selected a deer that appeared to be in reasonable condition for the season and let fly. The deer gave one leap and collapsed. Before it tumbled to the ground, Heideth charged into the meadow and seized a second deer by the throat. Balko went for a third but wasn't sure how to go about bringing it down and it escaped into the forest.

The wolves settled in to eat their fill at the female's kill while Jeff butchered the other deer. The pattern and partnership became set over succeeding days as Friedrick's Pack moved west, the female's wound healing nicely and Balko settling down under Jeff's leadership.

Balko was ranging far ahead when he discovered the first sign of Alemanni in the form of a butchered deer. Jeff stopped at the carcass and found a seat on the sled to consider his next moves. He also took the opportunity to explain what he was trying to accomplish in terms that would fit wolves' tendencies to relate all motivation to serving the welfare of the pack.

"...Thus if two-leg packs do not come together, these lands will be devoured by the invaders."

Jeff glanced at the sun and gave up his comfortable seat. As they moved cautiously along, it was clear the wolves were sorting through what he had conveyed. The female, who Jeff decided he would call Heideth, was first to speak.

"The ways of two-leg packs are strange to us, yet your tale of fierce invaders stirs our concern. We understand that all must come together if any are to survive what is to come."

Relieved that he had gotten his message across, and impressed with Heideth's ability to work it out so quickly, Jeff only hoped that the Alemanni he was soon to confront would be as understanding. He suspected that was an empty wish.

Setting up a secure campsite, Jeff removed the snowshoes and backpack in case things came to a fight. Rather than reveal the saber, he attached it to his belt under the fur coat and they left to find the village.

"These are a strange people to this one, my welcome uncertain. Lie close in concealment and come if my need is great."

Heideth understood what a hostile pack could mean. "We will do this. We will come even as you call."

Located close by the ice-choked Skola, Helstor was much larger than he had expected. Pausing at the crest of a hill overlooking the village, he counted at least eighty lodges.

"Well, here we go. The last village, and probably the most dangerous." Stepping out into the open, he walked down the hill.

No more than half way down the hill, a band of warriors brandishing spears jogged to meet him. Jeff saluted them by sweeping off his hat.

"Greetings from the Alarai, who return as is foretold."

His hair color had little effect. They muttered among themselves for some time, none quite certain about anything being foretold. Several made threatening gestures with their spears and advanced toward him. All but one stopped after a few steps when Jeff made no move to run.

Shouting a challenge to meet in combat and brandishing a battle-ax, the warrior took several more steps in a fighting crouch.

Jeff did no more than cross his arms and stare at the youngster, for she could not have been more than sixteen. Growling curses and shaking the battle-ax, she glared back.

Over the winter, Jeff had gained a deep understanding of the Alemanni. The young warrior would not attack unless he drew a weapon. The battle of wills that ensued was brief and lopsided. Throwing a parting curse that suggested he was a coward, she withdrew to the main body of warriors.

One group wanted to forcibly evict Jeff, but the larger faction would not permit it. If this man happened to be a passing god, their argument went, and they forced him to leave, Helstor might be utterly destroyed in reprisal. That did not bear thinking about. Besides, they asserted, the stranger likely had a good story to tell. If he didn't, well, they could deal with him later. Jeff was escorted to the community hall.

The chieftain emerged from the hall as they approached. Uh oh, Jeff thought. This guy is not only young but also spoiling for a fight.

They eyed each other for some time without exchanging words. Darkly suspicious yet superstitious to a fault, the chief glared uncertainty. Before he could arrive at a decision, the same warrior who had confronted Jeff forced her way to the front of the crowd.

"This is no man, but a coward. It is an insult to me that he was allowed into our village. I demand a trial by combat."

"That is your right," the chief replied at once. He turned away from the woman to stare impassively at Jeff. "You will defend yourself or die."

A woman in her fifties stepped out of the meeting hall. "This is not proper. We are not savages."

"It is Villka's right, Mother. I agree with her. They will meet in combat."

Drawing herself up to stand straight and tall, the elder moved to stand beside Jeff.

"This man is an Alarai! Have you remembered nothing from the teachings of your childhood and youth?" She whirled on the crowd. "Have none of you?"

Jeff bowed to the elder. "I am honored to be in your presence and am humbled by your strength of person. While I do not seek combat, neither am I loath to accept it. A question has been raised that now must be answered by strength of arm."

"Wolf-brother! We sense you are in danger! Shall we come?"

"This pack is indeed hostile. There will be single combat to determine courage. Remain in my mind, see through my eyes, and come only if the pack should decide to attack me."

At Heideth's urgent call, the elder stiffened and stared at Jeff. "You speak mind to mind! It has been so long since I have had this pleasure!"

"May I ask your name?"

"I am called Mellia. Who or what manner of creature sought your mind?"

"I am Jeffrey. My companions are great wolves."

"We shall be destroyed."

"No. I am an Alarai, but no god to make such a judgment. Now, before matters worsen, I must deal with Villka. Perhaps she has given me an opportunity that words could not duplicate."

"As you wish."

Turning away from Mellia, Jeff tossed his coat to the side, drew the saber with a metallic ring and smiled at Villka.

"Shall we dance?"

Shouts of approval sounded from the crowd. The stranger had style! They immediately pressed back to form an arena.

Throwing her coat to a friend, Villka gripped her battle-ax and leaped at Jeff with a mighty swing sufficient to fell a good-sized tree.

At seventeen, and in the absence of war, Jeff thought it likely that Villka would be inexperienced. Her swing was badly timed and he simply skipped back a step and let it whistle by.

The battle-ax's momentum carried it high over her left shoulder leaving Villka exposed. She knew she was dead, but Jeff did no more than give his head a disgusted shake.

"Your technique is terrible. You attack a Salchek like that and he'd spill your guts. Come in slow with short swings."

Regaining her balance if not her confidence, Villka attacked again only to have Jeff duck the blow.

"I said, don't rush in!"

With fluid grace, Jeff thrust lightly. The sword point penetrated her skin by no more than a fraction of an inch. A blood spot appeared on Villka's leather shirt and began to spread.

"Do you want to die in the first battle? The Salchek are mighty warriors!"

Some time later Villka was panting hard and her clothing had collected several more spots of blood. She had also learned caution. Shuffling around Jeff to keep her balance, attacking with short swings that did not leave her exposed, Villka searched for an opening.

"Much better. Do you want to continue, or shall we stop and work on becoming friends?"

Stepping back, Villka set the head of her axe on the ground and leaned on the handle. She took several deep breaths then threw her head back and laughed.

"I would be friends. Either that or I will have to make new clothing." She took a long stride toward Jeff and they clasped arms. "I was wrong to doubt your courage. You could have killed me at the outset."

The chieftain and Mellia approached. "My name is Therkan. Who are the Salchek?"

"They have returned. The Iron-shirts of legend have returned and march north."

Many villagers voiced angry exclamations and war cries, others called for more information. Therkan gestured for silence and glanced at his mother, Mellia.

"Forgive me for doubting your teachings."

"We have been separated from our brethren far too long, my son. Now it is time to come together in defense of this land."

"We shall. Let us consider what must be done."

He stepped into the hall followed by Mellia and a number of elders. On his way inside, Jeff sent a thought to Heideth and Balko.

"All is well. Return to our den. I will call when next the sun rises."

Two days later, Jeff took his leave. The village of Helstor, as reported, was definitely warlike.

The smithy and his assistants were sweating over the forge while a long line of customers clamored to be waited on. Older warriors were supervising weapons drill. Archers had departed in search of material for new bows and arrows. Hunters gathered with the elders to discuss how much food they would have to carry on the long march ahead of them. The village was a beehive of activity, the mood, jubilant.

Mellia and Therkan accompanied Jeff to the outskirts of Helstor. Many warriors stopped to say good-by to Jeff then hurried on their way. There was a war to get ready for, and time was short.

While trudging up the hill toward the forest, Jeff asked Mellia, "Will you accompany the war party?"

Therkan smiled. The Alarai had just put his foot in it. Mellia shot Jeff a look that fairly sizzled with indignation.

"Of course I am! Do you imagine I would miss such an opportunity? Do you consider me too elderly?"

Stopping under an evergreen at the forest verge, Jeff studied Mellia with great satisfaction. What a woman, he thought. This whole village has such fire, and she's responsible for a great deal of it.

"Thank you, Jeffrey. Were I some years younger, you would never leave us."

"And I deeply regret having to do so now. Rarely have I had such pleasure as that afforded by the last two days. We will meet in the south."

Eighteen

Wolf or Human

Jeff called it a day when he caught himself searching for a good spot to cross the river and continue west. It didn't seem possible that his mission had come to an end. He could go home.

The thought of returning to Valholm was exciting, but he had to strain in order to recall images of the village and Rugen. The only person who really stood out was Gurthwin. Jeff was disturbed that his picture of Zimma lacked substance.

"It's really time to get back, and I'm going to have to hustle to make it by spring."

Whittling on a stick to occupy his hands, Jeff debated routes.

Although he had no map, the terrain he had crossed and viewed from high altitude was fixed in his mind. Over preceding months he had developed a sixth sense for direction and location that rarely failed him. While Jeff didn't know where Valholm was in terms of coordinates, he knew exactly how to get there. Yet it wasn't an easy decision.

Fastholm was on the most direct route, but Jeff was troubled about Zimma. It had been nine months since they parted, and her image was vague. On the other hand, he could almost reach out and touch Magda.

"I can't do it. I cannot return by way of Fastholm. I'd never leave until they trekked south."

Tossing the stick into the fire, Jeff walked down to the river. Maybe that would help clear his head. Frozen solid, the Skola was humped with pressure ridges and tumbled ice blocks.

"Looks about the way I feel," he muttered. After a period he shook his head and returned to camp. "Zimma will always be first."

In the end Jeff decided to return by making a loop to the southeast and nip around the lakes, leaving a short leg to the northeast. As far as he knew the route was uninhabited, but that had ceased to be of concern. The wilderness, wherever he happened to be in it, was home.

Days then weeks passed as Jeff, Heideth and Balko worked there way southeast. Never out of mental contact with one another, they hunted together, ate together, and slept together.

Living in each other's minds, speech was unnecessary and Jeff fell silent for days on end. Over time he ceased to speak at all.

Sharing their dreams, he saw lands that called to his imagination and creatures that myth would never consider. In the absence of human contact, Jeff became wolf in spirit. The process was slow at first but rapidly accelerated as three minds meshed into a single entity, the One.

Gradually he stopped thinking about his mission, Fastholm or even Rugen and all they contained for him. Jeff maintained his course to the southeast only because that was as good a direction as any.

His mind continued to open until it was aware of the whole land; that it was alive and could be understood if he listened. There was no future or past, just an all-encompassing present, and he found peace.

As items of clothing wore out, Jeff patched them with crude swatches cut from deer hide. His hair had grown long, and a full beard flowed onto his chest. Nights he bedded down in the open. Wrapped in the wolverine pelt, he curled up with Heideth and Balko to share warmth and dreams in another land.

During the day Jeff began calling to them in growls, and in camp with a broad range of softer sounds. Then, one clear moonlit night high on a mountain flank, he joined his voice to Heideth and Balko's as they gazed over a silver-clad valley, all three singing their joy.

Drawing near Lake Elva late in March, they encountered a pack of wolves working north as temperatures moderated. The meeting was not unexpected. All three had been aware for some days that another pack was coming their way.

It was a sunny, warmish day, and the meadow they were crossing showed signs of spring thaw. The snow was heavily crusted, rotten, and channeled by rivulets of water. Jeff had his head down to survey each step lest he break an ankle when Heideth called a warning. He looked up to be confronted by a pack of wolves at the meadow's opposite border.

Jeff stopped at a comfortable distance and politely greeted them. Heideth was not familiar with the pack, so they stayed close together in case of attack. A large male was seated a few feet in front of the main group of wolves.

"We greet you, and hope that all fares well with the pack. We are unused to such as we now see, and wonder greatly."

The leader's curiosity and that of his pack fairly sizzled in Jeff's mind. The fact that the pack seemed friendly was a great relief, but what was he to say? He tried to remember what he had set out to do. What he was.

Jeff had been a wolf in spirit for only two or three months, but the mental union was so strong that his mission seemed a fantasy. Roaming the mountains, hunting, giving voice to his joy—that was real.

Yet he had given the Telling so many times that it was deeply embedded in memory and could not be extinguished so quickly. It came to mind in bits and pieces, then in big chunks.

He shook his head and growled trying to stop the flow of memories, but could not. Then the process was complete. Grudgingly, Jeff recounted the intent of his winter mission. By the time he finished, a degree of humanity had won a precarious existence.

"During the long storms of deep winter, such tales as you relate have been oft repeated. May this one view your head fur? That which is displayed on your face has aroused great interest."

It was an irritating request. He was tired of having to show his hair, tired of the Alemanni, tired of everything. Jeff thought about shaving his head. Snarling frustration, he shook out hair that fell to the middle of his back. The pack stirred with interest at the sight.

"Ah, it is even as you say. We are deeply troubled by the news you bring of southern invaders, for tales of their ferocity have not been forgotten. We must think on this matter and take counsel." The pack leader's gaze shifted from Jeff to Heideth, then back.

"Your path will soon bring you among many two-legs of the yellow hair. Your she and yearling may join our pack if that is their desire, for we see much merit in them."

Heideth mentally bowed to the leader and moved closer to Jeff. "Your offer is gracious, but our pack, while small, has great virtue. We are one and will not see it broken." Balko's response was equally rapid and to the same effect.

Bowing his respect in turn, the leader rose to his feet. "We admire the strength of your pack. Now we must part. Be assured *that what you have said will be given grave consideration and retold to those we meet on our journey. Farewell, but we may meet again in the south."*

Over succeeding weeks, Balko continued to grow and fill out until his size surpassed even Balthazar's. Wondering at his heritage, Jeff spoke to Heideth.

"Your offspring grows large. Was it so with his sire?"

"His sire was the leader of this one's old pack, and of great size and strength."

Of course, Jeff thought, Heideth had to be the alpha female in order to have cubs. Pride in his pack jumped another notch.

They encountered the northern shore of Lake Elva around the end of April. Jeff considered his options then angled farther south to clear Lake Nordval. It wasn't long before he began recognizing landmarks from prior travels. With a mental jolt, Jeff realized he had subconsciously been heading toward Valholm all the time.

For some days, his conversation with the pack leader had been circulating in Jeff's mind. One thought repeated itself: why must I return? He knew the answer, but each time he looked at it a flash of resentment quickly followed. Several more days and Jeff was again locked in rapport with Heideth and Balko. He grew excited at summer vistas high in the mountains that Heideth shared with them both.

The mental images came complete with full sensory input and were so real that Jeff lost himself high in a hidden valley that teemed with deer and was home to many eagles. It was incredibly beautiful, and his heart yearned to see it. Yet his legs continued to trudge toward Valholm.

When Jeff acknowledged to himself that Valholm was only three or four days away, lupine and human motivations that had been savagely fighting for domination met in a free-for-all. Feeling like his head would burst, Jeff called a halt to the day's march.

Later, sitting by the fire poking a stick into the coals, he concluded there was no option but to see it through if he was going to live with himself. Get in and get out, he decided. Pass on what you must, head them in the right direction and split for the mountains. I've done enough. Come fall, we can trek south for Rugen to see how things are going. I'm just one person. They don't really need me.

He held the stick up to watch the flame. Abruptly, he jabbed it into the snow. That's me, he thought. Burned up and snuffed out. Getting up, he chipped a slab of venison from their supply on the sled.

Heideth had been watching Jeff intently. She had been mentally joined with him long enough that she couldn't help but be aware of his conflict. That awareness was heightened by a synchrony with his spirit that had never been duplicated with one of her own kind.

And just as Jeff had melded with the essence of being wolf, so Heideth had become, in part, human. In doing so, she had come to view the world and human society from a different, larger, perspective. Where in becoming wolf Jeff had succeeded in shedding past and future, Heideth had become subject to both. Now she watched and struggled to understand.

Deeply buried within the roiling matrix of Jeff's conflict was the image of a human. Instinctively, Heideth knew the image to be female and important to Jeff's life. There was such a desperate sense about the image that Heideth reached out a mental hand to pull it to the surface.

"Tell us of this female, wolf-brother. She of the red fur. Is this one a worthy packmate? Will she join us?"

Jeff felt like a bucket of cold water had been dumped over his head. A picture of Zimma flared to near reality, and he dropped the piece of venison he was holding. She seemed to be crying and held her arms out to him. He immediately sensed Heideth's intervention and something snapped, letting loose a torrent of anger that had been building for months.

Raising his head, a howl of savage fury burst from his throat. It came again and again until it was more a shriek than a howl. He whirled on Heideth with bared teeth.

"Am I your wolf-brother or not?"

Heideth crouched down and felt the ruff along her back stir at the fury in Jeff's thought.

"We are one. I am not separate from you."

"Then why do you turn on me! Will you attempt to impose your will on me, too?"

Heideth found Jeff's question totally confusing. Her human referents were simply unequal to the task. She mentally bowed.

"My life is yours."

Snarling under his breath, Jeff stalked out of camp. He found a hilltop free of trees to the south and stood motionless. Had anyone other than a wolf passed by, they would have taken no note other than to remark on the odd formation.

Some miles away, a hunting party from Valholm crowded around a fire throwing wood on at a rapid clip. The howling they had heard was like nothing in experience, but called dreadful tales to mind.

"And have we, then, heard the Ruckthor?"

The woman who spoke, a youngster on probation to the hunting team, had tried to pose the question in a casual fashion. The way she gripped the shaft of her spear argued otherwise.

Turning her back to the fire, Gerta tried to pierce the darkness. "What do you know of the Ruckthor, Bernik?"

"Little of worth, my leader."

"That is correct. You are no longer a child. Reserve childhood tales for your own family if you should be so blessed."

Accepting the reproof as her due, Bernik bowed. Inside, Gerta knew she had been too severe.

"Never forget the call, Bernik, for the beast which proclaims this anger has not been heard or named. But enough—Walther and Henretta, you will stand first..."

Soaring high, an utterly desolate wail struck them to the quick. Gerta held her spear at guard but knew she was defenseless, for the Ruckthor lived on.

"Oh gods, preserve us this night," she whispered.

It came again and again, growing in strength until warriors would have fled had it not been for pride and loyalty. In the end, the last wail faded in a forlorn diminuendo that left them bereft.

Spring thaw hit with a vengeance. Most of the snow was gone, and what remained was no more than slush. It was time to abandon the sled that had served them so well.

Gratefully dropping its traces for the last time, Jeff packed up what could be carried.

Valholm was several long walks away when they encountered the first villager. Poised to run, he stared at them as they drew closer. Although Gerta's tale had inflamed superstition in Valholm to critical mass, it was daylight and his legs had never failed him. At the moment, Hafnor was quite sure he could fly. He feared demons, suspected treachery, hoped for the gods, but was rooted in place by subliminal recognition.

Balko was on the point as usual. That's where the action was. Jeff was the only two-leg he had seen, and the one drawing closer was quite intriguing. He was considering a tentative dash to see if the two-leg would run when the stranger let out a startled cry and raced north. Balko watched him skim over the ground with considerable admiration.

Some distance back, Jeff thought, And so it starts. If Zimma means so much to me, why do I feel so mixed up about returning? Heideth and Balko are more committed to following through than I am. The thought of Heideth made him cringe with shame. How do I make it up to her? I had no right to question her loyalty, but she was totally justified in questioning mine. A loving thought intruded.

"We are one. I am content."

On the day they were to enter Valholm, villagers streamed out to meet them. A wolf pacing on either side, Jeff stalked along head swinging back and forth. When someone got too close his lips flickered up and down in warning. It was the automatic warning response of a wolf, and he was not consciously aware of his behavior.

Such was the effect that the warriors kept their distance. Wolves were never to be taken lightly, but Jeff's savage behavior and appearance were in the twilight zone of experience. They were inclined to believe the gods were at work, but like Hafnor weren't entirely sure.

Old friends of Jeff's muttered to one another and began a slow chant as they marched along. Warrior after warrior picked up the measured cadence and clashed spears against shields between stanzas. Rising and falling in stately rhythm, the chorus found its heart and flowed over meadow and forest.

When the procession arrived at the meeting hall, the area was packed with people. There were many that Jeff did not recognize. Gurthwin stood in front of the hall supported by his staff, Halric at his side. The chorus swelled to a mighty shout and stopped.

Gurthwin advanced a step. "Your return brings joy to our hearts, Jeffrey. Long have we feared for your safety during winter's cold."

Villagers pressed close so they wouldn't miss anything and one of them stumbled into Jeff's back. He whirled with raised lips and a snarl that rumbled from deep in his chest.

The man, well known in the village for crowding to the front of any line, leaped backward with a terrified oath. Balko didn't like his looks and jumped at him with exposed fangs, completing the rout.

When the space that opened up was satisfactory, Jeff held his arms out for silence. He opened his mouth to speak. The words were there in his mind, but what came out was a growl.

Those closest to him pushed back farther with wide eyes. Anger at what had been asked of him, anger at himself for having come down from the mountains, anger at the Alemanni reaction exploded in a howl that raged up the scale.

The circle of villagers surged backward with cries of warning. The crowd's response goaded Balko to make a dash at them, and a section of the ring broke and ran. Superstition blowing intellect to tatters, Gurthwin gripped his staff with both hands to control his shaking body.

"Wolf-brother, we must not fail at this pass!"

Heideth's thought knifed through Jeff's anger. He clamped his mouth shut but for occasional rumbles and called Balko to his side. Forcing himself to stand still instead of constantly turning in search of threat, Jeff formed a sentence. The first words had a rasping quality, but word by word Jeff sounded more human.

"Our travels have been most perilous, taking us to the gates of death. Yet the task has been accomplished." Balko and Heideth were pressed against either hip as he glared around at the crowd. "Let it be known to all present that we three are one. Whatever is thought of my brother and sister is thought of me, and whoever threatens their welfare threatens mine to their own great peril. This I oath-swear!"

Partially choking back a snarl, Jeff looked around the crowd daring anyone to challenge him.

Gurthwin was shaken to the core and struggled to make sense of what he was seeing. *What had the gods done to this man? Have we driven him to this?* Comparing Jeff's savage appearance with earlier memories, goose bumps ran up his arms. *Surely he will destroy himself or lead us all.*

"Let there be silence!" Halric raised his arms to quiet the shouts of approval. "Let it be known to all that I, Halric, from this time forward do accept Jeffrey Friedrick's brother and sister as kin, like unto my blood. Whatsoever is done to their gain is done to mine, and that which is done to their peril will be answered by my arm and those of my household."

The crowd responded with a shield-banging roar that startled Heideth and Balko. Gurthwin stepped forward.

"Is it not the manner of wolf folk to speak mind to mind?"

Following Jeff's nod, Gurthwin addressed the wolves. *"You are welcome to this village and all that is in it. Our leader has now accepted you as brother and sister to his pack. We are one."*

Heideth's reply was to the point. *"We are gratified, and will do what we may to serve the One."*

Announcing that a Telling would take place the next evening, Halric entered the meeting hall. Gurthwin trailed after Halric, followed in turn by Jeff and the wolves. Jeff took a seat next to Gurthwin.

"How is it that you understand the manner of speaking with wolves?"

"When no more than a youth, I once happened across a pack in my wanderings." The crow's-feet around Gurthwin's eyes crinkled in amusement, and he shook his head in remembrance. "Well it was that I quickly learned to turn my mind to their way, for they were not friendly!" Gurthwin took a moment to examine Jeff's face in an effort to fathom the changes. "Before we discuss what has occurred here, will you share your journey?"

Why should I? Jeff pondered. *I have done what was asked of me. Must I share everything?* As visions of the mountains' winter beauty flashed through Jeff's mind, low growls and whines escaped his lips. Heideth padded over to look into his eyes, golden-green into golden-green. Gurthwin shivered anew and pulled his furs tighter.

"It is time to share what we have experienced and learned, wolf-brother. The winter was ours. Now it must be theirs also."

Jeff put his arms around Heideth and placed his head alongside hers. The feral gleam in his eyes faded.

"Your counsel gives strength and resolve. They shall have the greater part. You must never leave me, wolf-sister."

"We are one." Heideth sat down by his side.

Reluctantly, Jeff recounted the winter's journey. "...While I do not know how many will come, enthusiasm ran high and seemed sincere for the greater part."

"You have shared what is important to our need," Halric observed, "but I warrant much remains untold. I anticipate its hearing, for the great cold of this winter chilled our hearts for your welfare. But that must wait for Telling on the morrow."

Halric and Gurthwin related their doings in Jeff's absence.

Valholm's messengers had been well received, and warriors from nearby tribes were pouring into Valholm. Smiths had also come to assist in the forging of weapons, and were stockpiling a vast store of arrow and lance heads.

"While last summer's harvest was bountiful and hunting has been good," Halric opined, "we must soon begin our journey south lest food become scarce. It would have pleased me to hear from the great city that provender awaits us at the moot grounds, but winter snows were deep and I am not troubled."

"Nor am I," Jeff agreed. "All must soon leave for the south. Let us share our minds on how we are to accomplish this."

What followed for the rest of the evening was a discussion of all the details involved in moving six hundred souls over a hundred miles south to the moot grounds. When they broke up, Jeff hurried to the stable. Cynic was leaning against the side of his stall, half asleep.

"Goofing off again, I see."

Cynic lurched away from the stall, stared at Jeff for an instant, then let out a piercing squeal and reared. The stable roof was low and solid. Cynic's head cracked into a thick beam. After things settled down and they had exchanged a bit of gossip, Jeff sounded him out regarding the wolves.

"We are now four, having a new wolf-sister and brother. May I bring them to you in the morning?"

"I have heard their thoughts and trust they might become friends. I will speak with them."

On their way to meet Cynic next morning, Balko and Heideth wandered from one interesting point to the next. The village seethed with activity, and Jeff spent considerable time answering the wolves' amazed questions.

Rather than cause equine riot in the stable, he left them near the edge of the village and went to fetch Cynic. When they saw him coming, Heideth and Balko jumped to their feet in astonishment. Balko was so excited he was springing up and down.

"What manner of creature are you?"

Staring down his long snout at Balko, Cynic's thoughts were amused. "Two-legs term my kind, 'horses'. While this name is most unsatisfactory, I fear it must be borne. We are swift of foot and mighty in battle, but only rarely do I find a two-leg that appreciates the full extent of our merit."

"Do others of your kind have the gift of thought sharing? I find your mind to be quite intriguing and acute."

Oh dear, Jeff privately thought, don't lay it on too thick, Heideth. There'll be no living with him!

All three of his companions caught the thought. Cynic twitched his hindquarters and sent Jeff stumbling away grinning and chortling. Balko wasn't old enough to understand the humor, but Heideth sent a mild reproach in Jeff's direction while hiding her own amusement.

"I have found none that are so blessed, wolf-sister."

"Just so. Now, horse-brother, this one understands you have traveled widely. Will you share those experiences?"

Shortly, Cynic and Heideth were exchanging travel adventures and finding common ground, Balko good-naturedly tossing in the occasional comment. The wolves were impressed with Cynic's run and stand against the hyenas, while Cynic was unable to disguise his awe at the wolverine and the wolves' willingness to take it on.

341

After a period Jeff decided a good run in the woods was in order to cement what was shaping up to be a great first meeting. It would also get him away from the press of humanity in the village for a while. He hopped onto Cynic's back and the four of them took off, Balko charging into the lead with Cynic hot on his trail.

When they happened across a wide meadow, Jeff called a halt. Enough was enough. Cynic had cut through several dense stands of trees trying to catch Balko, nearly brushing Jeff from his back. Dismounting, he affectionately slapped Cynic on the rump.

"Go and play, horse-brother."

Cynic bolted toward Balko, who lay crouched and waiting. Heideth sat down to enjoy the spectacle of horse and wolf tearing around the meadow.

"Will you join me, wolf-brother?"

Jeff sat down behind Heideth and scooted forward until she was between his legs. Wrapping his arms around her chest, Jeff linked minds and heaved a sigh of contentment.

By the time they returned to Valholm, Cynic and Balko were well on the way to becoming inseparable. Balko was especially excited for reasons that he innocently explained.

"Now we may run! The horse-brother moves swiftly and is also most devious in pursuit."

Heideth's ears dropped in embarrassment at her offspring's lack of tact. Paradoxically, it was amusing to Jeff.

"Our wolf-brother is young and needs to run. It is also true that my sister and two brothers are much swifter than I. Together we will move like the wind in a summer storm."

The Telling would take place outside given the mob of humanity now in the village and growing daily. The evening meal came first, giving Jeff the chance to renew many friendships and further acclimatize.

When those inside the hall recessed for the Telling, they found the assembly area outside packed. A number of warriors had climbed up on lodge roofs so they could see. Halric gave the order and torches were lighted.

Jeff jumped on a stump and gave a Telling that set his audience on its collective ear. Later, with the customary all-night party in full swing, he was forced to continually repeat two segments of the tale.

The first was his long march in the deep cold, the second their battle with the wolverine. It turned out that none of the warriors had ever encountered such a beast except in legend, and they just wanted to be sure it was as terrible as it sounded like.

Anticipating such questions, Jeff had fetched the wolverine pelt. With a group of ten or fifteen warriors gathered around, he let it unroll. They were stunned. For a brief period, no one moved. In the dim light it seemed the creature would spring to life again. When it did not they pressed close and muttered heartfelt oaths as they examined the pelt and judged the animal it had covered.

That group eventually wandered off shaking their heads and thoughtfully stroking beards, only to be replaced by another bunch wanting confirmation.

Heideth and Balko were also the center of much attention and endured it philosophically. What really worried Jeff was that someone would try and pet them, an affront of such magnitude that mayhem was likely. It was a great relief when they escaped the melee without incident.

Images of Zimma intruded into his dreams that night, mixing with those of Heideth and Magda. Jeff awoke in the grip of feelings and memories that provoked a renewed sense of confusion.

What am I? he pondered. What's happened to me? How can I want to take Heideth into the mountains, while at the same time be with Zimma and Magda? Am I that fickle? But, damn it, I didn't seek any of them out!

While the debate ran hot and heavy in his mind, Jeff set patched clothing aside and pulled on a pair of leather pants he had left behind the previous fall. He suddenly realized they were the ones he had been wearing when he and Carl met the combined Alarai mind. Calling a halt to the debate, he took a deep breath.

"This is all too much. I've got to focus on the Salchek invasion and hope to God that everything else will sort itself out as I go." Jeff once again reviewed how he had attacked Heideth. "And I may be fucked up, but that kind of shit has to stop. There's a job to do, and it's time to get outside my head."

Once dressed he absentmindedly began packing. When he woke up to what he was doing, Jeff realized it was time to leave for Rugen and find out what he had become. Heideth and Balko were in need of some serious running, and eagerly greeted his plans for departure.

Having had a small taste of freedom from the stable, Cynic was ready to leave the instant the subject came up. In addition to his desire to hit the trail again, he had also become quite suspicious of the looks thrown his way by the farming contingent. It was time for spring planting and they were short of draft animals.

Walking into the smoky interior of the community hall that evening, Jeff's musings were drowned out by a roar of welcome and a flying piece of venison. He fielded it and ripped out a hunk with a sidewise twist of his head. Toward the end of the evening, Jeff shared his decision to leave with Halric and Gurthwin.

Normal conversation in the hall during a meal amounted to shouting in order to be heard over the general racket. Once the food was consumed, villagers could concentrate on drinking beer and the decibel level rapidly increased. In the middle of the conversation, someone started a fight. Uttering a curse under his breath, Halric hurried off to referee.

Damn, Jeff thought with a broad grin, I really *have* come home.

Halric was forced to dodge and weave in order to stay clear of the two contestants rolling around on the floor. One of the men grabbed a hunk of firewood and tried to brain his opponent. That was considered dirty pool and Halric kicked it away.

Unfortunately, the piece of wood sailed across the room, thumped a warrior and sent her backward to the floor. On the sidelines, spectators shouted encouragement to both contestants.

The two men broke apart along enough to stand up and have a go with their fists. Pretty good footwork, Jeff concluded. He winced when one fellow landed a buffet that snapped the other's head against a beam with a sickening crack. He collapsed like a half-empty sack of potatoes and fell onto a trestle table.

Amid outraged cries, tankards of beer and food went flying in every direction. Halric made sure the hapless villager was still breathing and sauntered back to the head table. Taking a long pull from his wooden tankard, Halric threw an arm around Jeff's shoulders and motioned Gurthwin closer so he could hear.

"I believe your plan to depart on the morrow will serve us all. We must be certain that supplies have been delivered to the moot grounds. If they have not, you must seek out the cause as you journey farther south. It would…"

Dual shrieks of fury rose above the noise, followed by a crash. Two women jumped to their feet, one of them leaped a table and they rushed together with fists flying. Halric sprang to his feet again. Knowing real danger when he saw it, he circled the pair with great caution.

"Looks like Brunhil and Siglin are not on the best of terms."

Gurthwin nodded sagely, burping at the same time. "Siglin refuses to concede young Odik to Brunhil. They are evenly matched, would you not say?"

"They do honor to the village."

Jeff lay a hand on Gurthwin's shoulder and they sat back to enjoy the second event. Thunking their tankards together, they drank deep. The matter was settled—he would leave in the morning. Now it was time to enjoy.

The first days on the trail were taken at an easy pace to condition Cynic. Spring thaw was well advanced, leaving only a few small drifts in the shadow of trees. Flowers carpeted meadows, birdsong filled the air, excitement and renewal overflowed. Feeling spring's enthusiasm, Heideth and Balko ranged wide in search of game and from a simple need to run.

Cynic toughened up by the end of the first week, the terrain was more open, and Jeff let his mount stretch out in breathtaking sprints. When Heideth and Balko happened to be running nearby, they had to get into the fun as well. The meadows were small and only served to whet their appetites. One day they abruptly emerged into a long valley free of trees.

Broadcasting a sudden, *"Let us run!"* Cynic was off like a shot, the wolves digging after him for all they were worth. This time Cynic was not exhausted after a day's chase and he accelerated like a quarter horse.

Caught by surprise, Jeff had to grab leather while getting sorted out. Shifting his weight to the stirrups, he urged Cynic on with a fierce yell.

They tore down that valley, horse and wolves running for the sheer joy of it. Balanced in the stirrups, the wind forcing tears into his eyes, Jeff felt on top of the world. Life was good.

A stream-washed gully rushed to meet them and Jeff was forced to call a halt to the race. By that time all three were satisfied that they were indeed a match for one another. The race had been in doubt to the end.

Days passed in rapid succession, for each was packed with the joy of freedom, companionship, and adventure. Their hunts ranged across many miles, testing wolf and horse as they pursued game through forest and meadow at breakneck speed. The competition was fierce. The only thing missing, Jeff thought more than once, was a hunting horn to wind when the chase was up.

Evenings were filled with good humor as they recalled the day's events around a cheerful campfire. They were not always successful in the hunt, but that was of no matter. And so they passed to the south.

The moot ground at the fork of the rivers Vecka and Farga was not far off when Heideth and Balko raced back from a scouting jaunt. Heideth reported that a pack of wolves awaited them. She was excited, but Jeff also sensed she was deeply troubled about something. Next day, Balthazar greeted them.

Formal and polite as always, his humorous mindset still evident, the big male nevertheless seemed distracted as they discussed the winter's events. Looking around for the source of his preoccupation, Jeff was not long in finding it.

Some ways off, Heideth and another female were circling each other. The ruff on their backs standing up, heads held low and fangs bared, they growled mutual dislike.

In one instant, Jeff felt his world explode.

"Don't do it Heideth! Don't leave me!"

Balthazar was dazed and unaware of the chaos in Jeff's mind. *"Never have I encountered a female such as this. From which pack does she come?"*

Wanting to scream, "From *my* pack. She's mine!" Jeff somehow choked it back. Until that moment, until he experienced the head-on collision of two radically different societies, Jeff had not understood the inherent pathos of his love for Heideth.

He was not a wolf, could never be a wolf. She could never be a human. It nearly tore him apart. All he and Heideth had shared, gone in an instant.

In spite of what he was feeling, the uncompromising nature of his insight forced reality to the forefront and Jeff described the circumstances of their meeting.

"I know of this pack. Great was its leader, and wise. But now, that which has started must be completed. It is our way."

Surrounded by Balthazar's pack, the two females circled in tighter snarling threats. The final challenge was issued and the females came together in a snarling collage of twisting bodies and flashing fangs before springing apart to resume circling.

They came together two more times before Heideth gained the advantage. Holding her death grip on the other wolf's throat for a moment, Heideth stepped back. Rolling onto her belly, the female crouched in front of Heideth with throat exposed.

The event was closed and witnessed. Balthazar's pack had a new alpha female and Jeff felt like a part of his soul had been ripped away. Conflict on the way to being resolved balled up into a violent knot and hit him like a thrown brick.

Clenching his hands into fists, Jeff fought a rush of fury. It tried to batter a way out, but he clamped his jaw and refused to give in. Then it was gone, and he nearly fell to his knees from the shock.

Holding his hands out, Jeff whispered, "Why? Why does she have to go? Have I asked for too much? Damn it, I need her!" Jeff wiped tears from his eyes with a shirtsleeve. "Fuck this shit. Gurthwin and his lousy gods. What a bunch of crap."

Taking deep breaths, Jeff looked for Heideth and found her touching noses with Balthazar. The instincts of countless generations of wolves had ruled the day and determined with absolute authority what must happen. Bonded to Jeff in a way that was beyond breaking, Heideth was nevertheless a young, dominant wolf. From every aspect she was also a perfect match for Balthazar, and had just won the right to pair with him even as he had won the right to lead.

Heideth left Balthazar and approached Jeff. Ears down, her mind boiled with such turmoil that she felt she could not tolerate the agony. Picking up on that thought, Jeff realized Heideth's pain was at least as bad as his. She had been trapped and blown away by the simultaneous advent of spring, estrus and meeting Balthazar.

"You are deeply troubled, even as I am."

"What has happened was destined to be, yet my heart is torn asunder. Now I must leave your side. I have broken the One. I have done this thing!"

There were no words, no thoughts that could make it right. He knelt and placed a hand on either side of her head. Looking into golden-green eyes, he relished the clarity of her thoughts and total absence of hypocrisy. He wrapped his arms around Heideth and held her while both cried in a way that did not require liquid tears.

Heideth pulled back and stared into his eyes. Memories of the past and thoughts of a future without Jeff fueled anguish that was more human than lupine.

"Now you must judge this one's oath-breaking."

Thinking, I judge that I love you, Jeff forced some order into his mind. He knew beyond emotion that he must let her go.

"Judgment has been given—our wolf-sister must be one with the pack she has won her place to run in, and follow the ways of the brethren. Ever has its leader been my brother. You and I are one but now we must part, for your path in the forest cannot be mine. Go in peace, go with my love. May our destinies remain intertwined."

Crystal tears glimmering in her mind, Heideth mentally bowed. *"Your judgment speaks to the wisdom and strength of resolve that I have come to so cherish. It shall be done."*

Heideth nuzzled Jeff's cheek and trotted over to Balthazar's pack. Watching her move into the pack and take charge, Jeff thought, And what of you, Balko? Will you leave me, too?

The young wolf wasn't long in making his position clear. *"Has this one bitten any 'Salchek' necks? We are one."*

"Then let us continue our journey to that destiny." Turning to leave, Jeff bumped into Balthazar.

"Will you hear me, wolf-brother? Forgive my lack of comprehension?"

"We are one. There is nothing to forgive."

"Yet I now perceive the quality of your pain."

"Understanding will be granted over time."

After a period of mental communion, Balthazar accepted Jeff's statements as fact. Through his association with the Alarai and in a way analogous to Heideth's experience, he had come to understand the wide-ranging and often fragile extent of human emotion. But this was his brother.

They shared a long period of mental silence before Balthazar felt comfortable with moving on to pressing business.

"The one named 'Gaereth' has arrived, but has many forests to cross. Here he will await your return from the great city. Food has been provided for the yellow-hairs and is protected by two-legs from the great city. Our presence has lead to a certain unease, and I believe it were wise for you to soothe their spirits. May I conclude their leader has engaged resolve?"

"This is so, wolf-brother. I believe the two-leg pack leader, 'Imogo', will prove a worthy ally in what is to come."

"Let us rely on that belief. It is also in my mind that the brethren cannot be found wanting in this conflict. We must join battle with the invaders. What is your thinking on this matter?"

"On the open plains and in the face of 'Salchek' weapons I would fear for the lives of my wolf-brethren while the sun gives light. During darkness and amidst the forests of this land, there is no more fearsome enemy. Such allies would be welcome."

"We will pursue this matter. This pack at least will come."

Jeff spent a good deal of time talking with the men Rengeld had sent north with the promised supplies. While badly spooked by the wolves, they were committed to seeing things through.

It was still early in the afternoon when the final points were settled. Now it was time to go, to physically part ways. Balthazar planned to trek northwest toward their summer hunting grounds. With Heideth. She stopped for a moment at the forest verge and looked back.

"Never until this day have I wished to be other than what I am, Jeffrey. Know that at this moment my heart cries out that I were a human female. Always will my thoughts be with you."

Casting a last benediction of love, she vanished into the forest. It was some time before Jeff turned his gaze from where she had disappeared. Heideth had called him by name. No wolf had ever done that before.

Nineteen

Forces Converge

Hardly taking note of his surroundings, Jeff forded the Vekka and rode south. Sensing his state of mind, Cynic and Balko increased their vigilance to take up the slack.

Weeks passed, and the impact of Heideth's loss slowly abated to a dull ache. Having found a kindred spirit and credulous mind in Balko, Cynic helped pass the time by gossiping shamelessly about Rugen.

Moving rapidly, they ghosted through the deciduous forest. On the way north the timing had not been right for Cynic and Jeff to camp in their special glen. That was not the case heading south. Man and horse had many fond memories of the glen.

When they broke out of the trees, Balko understood his friend's excitement. Upon viewing the glen he immediately loped off to explore every nook. The glowing report he had received from Cynic was, if anything, an understatement.

The weather was perfectly warm and settled, the water in the brook just the right temperature to splash around in. Besides those factors, every sense at his command indicated that Cynic was right.

Something resided in the glen that went far beyond the mundane. What it was Balko could not say, nor did he worry about saying it. It was simply there to be appreciated. Although he could have used a bite to eat, Balko never considered hunting the glen or surrounding forest.

Once free of saddle and baggage, Cynic joined Balko. The two friends poked around here and there while Cynic related what had occurred when he and Jeff had first camped in the glen. Balko decided it was an astounding tale. It never occurred to either of them that Cynic's memory of events was much more complete than Jeff's.

After sunset the larger moon crept above the trees. While Jeff bathed in the creek, horse and wolf settled in on top of a little hillock.

The flowers were in full bloom and fragrance, the breeze gentle. Lighted by the moon, every color took on a luminous shade that created a world of the spirit. It was not a night given to extraordinary events, rather one of extraordinary beauty.

Once bathed, Jeff joined them with recorder in hand. Although he had played on several occasions since meeting Balko, the young wolf had never heard such compelling music as now flowed from the recorder in gentle progression. It seemed that his spirit lifted free to hover over the meadow.

After a period, Cynic resettled himself in a more comfortable position. *"Now, wolf-brother, I shall relate the story of Middle Earth; a story of great love, great courage, and great evil."*

Once across Mirkwood Creek and onto the road, the trio blew along at a famous pace scattering fellow travelers right and left. Jeff was impressed by the amount of traffic they encountered as the days passed. It seemed to be much heavier than he recalled from the first trip south. They passed load after load of cordwood, carts piled high with game, and herds of domestic animals plodding along.

When they topped the hill that overlooked Rugen, Jeff pulled Cynic well off the road and stopped. Balko's presence had caused a stampede earlier in the day and threatened to do so again. Jeff wearily climbed down, looked out over the valley, and did an amazed double take.

"Now, that is some sight."

Every square inch of land was under cultivation. Scores of farmers, ant-like in the distance, swarmed over the fields. Jeff turned his gaze toward Rugen.

"Holy shit. Will you look at that." The causeway was jammed side to side and backed up to the hill with people and livestock. "Imogo has really put this city on a war footing!"

The sight of Rugen strengthened memories that had been growing stronger by the day since crossing Mirkwood Creek. Zimma and Carl were down there somewhere. Belstan and Rogelf were probably pulling off some business deal at the very moment. It had been over nine months since he left Rugen.

"I have got to see them!" He jumped into the saddle, only to dismount at once. "Damn it! No way can I take Balko down there." Jeff viewed the causeway scene again and shook his head decisively. "It would be a disaster. We'll have to wait."

They found a spot on the hillside that afforded a good view. It was better than a three-ring circus. There were several mini-stampedes, it looked like two bulls were fighting over a female in heat, and, in a side event, a solid fistfight.

In addition to the action, Cynic's steady stream of pithy comments threatened to undo Jeff from moment to moment. Balko was not immune from Cynic's two-leg jokes, either. On one occasion he let go with a howl, creating further problems at the foot of the hill.

Jeff mounted shortly after sunset in a cheerful frame of mind. The crowd had melted away as the afternoon drew on, and the road was nearly empty. Guards formed up as they neared the gate. There seemed to be some pushing and shoving to see who got to stand in the rear. The senior man, an elderly sergeant, wound up doing, or as the case might be, stuck with, his duty.

"State yer business."

"I am Jeffrey Friedrick. We are expected."

Having said all he intended to, Jeff calmly stared at the man. Tongue lolling out, Balko stood nearby laughing his wolf laugh.

The sergeant was in a tough spot. He had seen some strange sights in his day, but never a great wolf at such close quarters. He was dumbfounded and not a little frightened by the creature's size. Still, he was duty bound not to let dangerous elements into the city. The wolf was, he concluded, likely very dangerous. Recalling information announced at reveille several weeks ago, he suddenly brightened and heaved a vast sigh of relief.

"Well now, ya done returned! I mean, yessir, we heerd ya was maybe on the way ta town. Pass on, but if ya don't mind ah'd 'preciate it if ya sorta kept a good eye on that there wolf. Might set folks in the city on a real tear."

A belly laugh tried to form, but Jeff stopped it. He didn't think he could stand one more.

"He might at that. I'll speak with him about it."

Tuned in to Jeff, Balko did a little jig to keep from howling. This had been a day unlike any in his young memory.

Upon entering Rugen, Jeff's thoughts immediately centered on Zimma. He didn't know where she might be staying, but decided to stop at Ethbar's place first. Someone would know. It was hard to believe she was only a couple of miles away. It had been so long. That fact was emphasized when Jeff took note of the changes that had occurred in his absence. They were startling.

Although it was getting dark, streets he remembered as being merely busy in full daylight were still thronged with noisy people. Makeshift standards had been erected along the streets to support crude oil lanterns that shed little light but a lot of smoke. Businesses they passed were still open and crowded with shoppers. Loaded carts jousted for room to pass where there was none. Jeff could hardly believe that so much had changed in nine months.

Farther into Rugen, a company of soldiers marched by on their way to the barracks or duties somewhere in the city. Instead of the disorderly mob Jeff remembered, they seemed well disciplined. Rengeld had been busy.

Something was also different about the streets themselves. They passed several intersections before he figured out what it was. The streets were free of garbage. Jeff rumbled laughter in spite of the pain.

"Carl, old friend, how did even you manage to get this mess cleaned up?"

The unmistakable evidence of his friend's activities fueled Jeff's excitement, and he urged Cynic to a careful trot. City life was so strange to Balko that he stayed close without being told to. However, he did mark a number of interesting activities for later investigation. First on his list were the food stalls they passed.

Entering the courtyard that served Ethbar's home, Jeff felt so charged with energy that he felt like leaping off Cynic and running into the house. Instead, his eyes were drawn to a lanky figure strolling along in the shadows. Head bent as if to examine the cobblestones, his hands were clasped behind his back.

"Damn, it's good to be back," Jeff exclaimed, "and this is too good an opportunity to miss."

Dismounting quietly, he sneaked up behind Carl as he was about to enter the residence. Pulling his hat low, Jeff tapped him on the shoulder.

"Excuse me, sir, could you tell me the way to Tacoma?"

Balko had tagged along for the fun, and was all eyes and ears as Carl turned. At the same instant, Carl saw the shadowy figure of a bearded, travel-worn stranger and a great wolf.

Letting out a startled "Yargh!" he leaped backward and nearly fell. Regaining his footing, Carl's next comment was somewhere between a snarl and a laugh.

"By all that's holy, Jeff, don't *do* that. You nearly gave me a heart attack!" Laughing delightedly, he grabbed Jeff in a fierce hug and danced him around in circles. "Damn it's good to see you again! Shit, I can hardly believe it! Thank God!"

"I can't tell you how good it is to be back, Carl. Nine months! So much has changed!"

"You got that right, boyo."

Cynic remembered all the teasing he had suffered from Carl on their way north from Astholf and expected nothing less on this occasion. Not wanting to disappoint him, Carl flung a sly hello that immediately set the horse's teeth on edge.

"Now, how about introducing me, Jeffrey? I don't recall meeting this youngster."

"Love to. Balko and I have been through a lot together."

Once introductions were complete they moved to the stable. Cynic grumbled about impudent two-legs but was not slow to sweep up a mouthful of grain when Carl poured a generous portion into his trough.

At the door to Ethbar's home, Carl tried to envision the counselor's reaction when a wolf greeted him in his parlor. Carl glanced at Jeff. No, he thought, make that two wolves. He was still trying to come to terms with the changes that had occurred since parting in the fall.

Jeff's beard was dark red and grown to mid-chest level, his hair of similar length and gathered with a leather thong into a ponytail. Although Carl had never seen Jeff with a beard, that wasn't the change he was trying to pin down—there was something else that seemed hard and wild.

They were about to enter the parlor when Carl mentally kicked himself and stopped.

"Wait up a minute." There was something Jeff needed to know at once. "There's no easy way of saying this. Zimma isn't here, Jeff. She and Belstan left over a month ago on a trip to the west coast."

The smile of anticipation on Jeff's face disappeared in an instant. His expression revealed a flash of raw anger then became distant and cold. For an instant Carl saw it again, saw that something in his eyes. ...

Whoa, Carl thought, never seen *that* before. Some max heavy shit must have come down this winter.

"She was really getting excited about your return," Carl ventured, "but Belstan was in a tight spot and she couldn't say no. There simply was no one else with her experience free to go. Rengeld sent a mounted troop along for protection."

"People come, people go." When Jeff looked at Carl, his features had softened. "Scratch that. I really miss Zimma terribly. It's been a tough winter."

"I can see that." Carl gripped Jeff's shoulder. "It's more than good to have you back."

They entered the parlor at the same moment as Ethbar. At the sight of Balko, he stopped abruptly. Although an experienced statesman who by necessity rarely revealed emotion, Ethbar's expression on this occasion was openly shocked.

"While I have greeted many strange and wondrous guests in my home, this exceeds everything that has gone before! How wonderful!"

Insatiable curiosity urged Ethbar toward Balko. Caution stopped him several yards short. He had seen big dogs before, but they seemed no more than puppies in comparison.

Jeff noted Ethbar's uncertainty, understood it completely, and spoke with Balko.

"This one is a wise elder of the two-legs. He does not have mindspeak but is a wolf-brother in his heart. May he touch you in place of speech?"

"This one senses the wisdom you speak of, and feels great respect. He may."

"Ethbar, this young male whom I have named Balko is a part of my heart and gives you greetings. My brother will accept your touch on his shoulder as acceptance into your home."

Confronted with a great wolf and a young man grown wild during his winter's absence, Ethbar gamely drew near. Gingerly, he placed a hand on Balko's back. Somehow not feeling silly at all, he bowed.

"My house is yours."

Stomachs were empty and suitable fare was found for all. Later they took seats by the fire, Balko stretching his six feet of length on the carpet next to Jeff. A few polite questions from Carl and Ethbar distracted Jeff from thoughts about Zimma. He rose to walk around the parlor while putting some order to the winter's events.

"I don't really know what to say, or perhaps how to say it. A Telling is one thing, fashioned as it is for northern warriors, fashioned of the stuff that makes up their lives and dreams. Yet there are things I experienced that they take for granted but will never leave my memory, and other things I have shared with Balko and his mother that they will never know."

Sitting down, Jeff rested his chin on a hand. "The land still holds my soul fast. How do I speak of a silence so vast that one is at first crushed then consumed by a need to understand what it offers? Of a sweep of forest that goes on and on until it fades into mists that have no beginning and perhaps no end? Of the eagle's cry that calls one ever higher to gain comprehension of the whole? And yet I could not comprehend though the risk of falling to my death seemed a small price to pay for such knowledge.

"And the mountains! Their beauty and power were such that my eyes could not long bear their presence. Yet it is the silence that I remember. At first it was a thing to be feared, now I deeply regret its absence. Of a morning, the land was so still I could feel the earth awaken and greet the sun. Be assured that I do not speak figuratively—it did awaken."

Jeff had invited Carl into his mind. He found a seat high on a rock pinnacle that looked over a valley clothed in green and white that was so deep and wide that the trees seemed no more than a lush carpet.

The air was so clear that Carl felt confident that, if he strained his eyes, he might see forever. Following an eagle as it spiraled into the morning sky, he caught his breath when the sun's first rays set it ablaze with light.

"Well," Jeff sighed, "Perhaps all that can be done is to begin and see what comes of it."

One by one, Jeff picked up the threads of his journey and was soon lost in their weaving. The story was long, and his voice drifted in quiet reflection. When he became silent for the last time, the fire had died down to embers.

They sat without speaking for some time. Carl had deliberately lost himself in the hanging valley Heideth had described, and hoped to remain there. Jeff found him picking wildflowers.

"I haven't been here either, buddy. We'll make it one of these days."

Slumped down in his chair, Carl jumped to his feet and hurried to put wood on the fire. He made no attempt to hide the emotion on his face. Ethbar cleared his throat so he could speak.

"The hour is late. Let us go to our rest and meet again on the morrow so that we, in our turn, may relate what has occurred in your absence."

A good night's rest and all were once again assembled. Jeff was still not adjusted to being back in civilization and felt closed in, although a hot bath made up for a lot. Balko, on the other hand, was thriving on the novelty of everything around him.

He prowled the house from one end to the other in a constant state of bemusement. Ethbar had warned the servants, but Balko followed his nose into the kitchen and caught the staff by surprise.

Jeff was chatting with Ethbar when he heard the clang of pots hitting the floor, followed by terrified shouts and shrieks. He flew out of his chair and ran to collect Balko. It was some time before the cooks were tracked down, the mess cleaned up, and what was left of breakfast set on the table.

Ethbar was still chuckling to himself when a disgruntled cook brought coffee. It had been a wonderful morning.

"I am loath to break the spell of high spirits introduced by young Balko, but fear that I must. Rengeld is in the field recruiting soldiers and scouting potential points of resistance to the Salchek. Agents returned from the south report that Khorgan did capitulate as expected, was then sacked and its ruling council executed. Not surprisingly, Astholf fell two months after Khorgan."

"It's a small city. Without Khorgan they didn't have a chance."

"No, and this fact was not lost on Astholf citizens. What will surprise you, I believe, is not that Belstan and Rogelf arrived at our gates, but that a large number of Astholf's merchants and craftsmen accompanied them. Never has Rugen greeted such a caravan, and I can tell you there was much rejoicing in the streets."

Envisioning the scene, Jeff smiled. "Knowing Belstan and Rogelf, I imagine they put on something of a show."

"Yes, indeed. The city was in an uproar for several days. Unfortunately, the gathering of nobility that Imogo arranged was another matter. How they bellowed against the additional crop tithes! Rebellion seethed in their midst! Unbeknownst to those ingrates, however, Rengeld had succeeded in capturing a Salchek scouting party.

"At the height of the most flowery and treasonous speech, one that denied even the existence of the Salchek, Imogo paraded the chained prisoners for all to see. Oh how those 'nobles' scrambled and clawed to reverse themselves!" Ethbar paused to shake his head and chuckle at the memory. "In summary, we now have their complete cooperation. What could be tithed from last fall's harvest, was, and sits in newly refurbished granaries. Crops were seeded at the earliest possible moment this spring. If we are blessed with favorable weather, the greatest part may be harvested in time to escape the invader's sickle. That we shall see."

"What of the traitors?"

"Their designs and hopes were blown away like smoke when the captured Salchek were displayed, Jeffrey. Although prisoners, the Salchek were a proud and cocksure lot. They showed such disrespect for Imogo that it was not difficult for the nobles to imagine their own position should the Salchek succeed. I believe it safe to say that the disaffected faction surrounding Imogo's cousins was forced to reconsider treason as an alternative to creating an estate by hard work."

"But his cousins still represent a threat."

"I am afraid so," Ethbar sighed. "While Imogo grows suspicious, they *are* family. All that can be said at this moment is that we will continue to closely observe what they do and with whom they speak. Perhaps they will choose to openly oppose Imogo, then we will act."

Much more was discussed, but Jeff's primary interest for the rest of the morning was in getting caught up on what had happened in Rugen after the caravan's arrival.

He was relieved to learn that Belstan and Rogelf had succeeded in gaining the assurances they required from Imogo. Rogelf had departed east with the first thaw to set up trading posts while Belstan and Zimma undertook the trip to Borstel on the west coast.

"Zimma was in good health and spirits when they left? The winter was hard."

"Her health was fine, Jeff," Carl said. "Never even caught a cold the entire winter. And her spirits? It was hard on Zimma to leave knowing you would be back soon, but she handled it okay as far as I could see. I think Belstan was really upset that he had to recruit her. As I said earlier, there was no one else to fill the bill."

"Your Zimma is a remarkable young woman, Jeffrey," Ethbar commented. "Be assured that ever were you in her heart and thoughts. The young dandies that attempted to abate her devotion to you were quickly sent packing, I can assure you. A more fiery spirit I do not recall."

Thinking back on their first meeting, Jeff could only smile agreement. At the same time, an image of Magda hovered close in his mind. Unbidden, he remembered their frequent lovemaking in the sauna and forest, or quietly in the lodge while others slept. They were wonderful memories, but also quite uncomfortable ones in light of what Ethbar had related about Zimma.

Carl suggested he show Jeff what he had been up to rather than describe it. Thankful for the opportunity to break free of the house and the guilt he was feeling, Jeff promptly agreed.

Once on horseback, Carl was quick to appreciate the advantages of having a 200-pound wolf tagging along. As they trotted along city streets, a wedge of space seemed to miraculously open in front of Balko.

"How did you do it?" Jeff gestured around the reasonably clean street. "Where's all the garbage?"

"Becoming compost, my friend," Carl responded. He rolled his eyes for effect. "What a mess, pun intended. I finally got Imogo to shake lose some change for a test collection area over in the craft section. Folks really liked having clean streets and weren't shy about saying so, but with all the money flowing out of city coffers in the war effort Imogo just wouldn't go for it citywide. How do you convince someone in a feudal society that clean streets mean fewer deaths and a more productive city? It doesn't make any sense to them."

"I can see that it wouldn't."

"No, so I threw in the towel and quit trying, at which point the craft people got organized and raised hell. By the time it was over, everyone wanted their section clean, too."

"So you got the job done. That's good, isn't it? From your expression I would say you aren't all that happy about it."

"I, my friend, am solely responsible for starting a bureaucracy."

Noting Jeff's look of disbelief, Carl nodded his head. "Yep, a bureaucracy. I will go down in infamy as introducing these poor unsuspecting folks to a garbage collection fee."

"Son of a gun. I'm riding with the Commissioner of Sanitation? Shouldn't you be wearing a uniform or something fancy like that?"

Carl grinned and threw Jeff the finger. "Asshole. Actually, it isn't all that bad. I contract out the collection, which doesn't take a lot of paper work. If I wanted Imogo's approval, it had to be self-supporting. The sewage problem, though, is impossible at this stage since the whole city would have to be torn up."

Arriving at the craft section, Carl dismounted in front of the same alchemist's shop Jeff remembered from his visit in the fall. As they walked in, Carl hollered toward the back of the store, "Hey, Petto, we got any safe samples around?"

A short, round man popped out of the back room. Grinning ear to ear, he gingerly handed Carl a metal canister. Turning it over in his hands, he looked at the canister with a mixture of pride and sadness.

"I'm also in the business of death, and could really use some feedback on this one."

Raising an inquisitive eyebrow as encouragement, Jeff said nothing.

"I started poking around in here right after you left. From hanging around you, reading sci-fi and my background in chemistry, I picked up a good idea of what these folks did for a living. Remember? Lead to Gold?

"One of the solvents Earth's alchemists came up with was called aqua regia, or royal water: three parts hydrochloric acid, one part nitric acid. Sure enough, great minds think alike and there it was sitting in a corner. Only took a few tests to confirm it. All I had to do then was find out where Petto here got the nitric acid fraction from, pound out some plant fiber to get the cellulose, put the two together, and bingo."

"Bingo? What are you talking about?"

"Damn, Jeff, didn't you learn anything in high school chemistry?"

Giving Carl a sly wink, Jeff said, "Well, there was this great blonde I was assigned to work with in the lab section. Now that was chemistry!"

"Shit." Carl knew he was being had but was still vexed. "Forget the tits and ass, bozo. Put nitric acid and cellulose together in the right proportions and you get gun cotton. Want me to spell it out?" He held the canister out to Jeff. "Got a match?"

"Go to hell! That's wicked stuff, Carl. Didn't they use to put that in torpedo warheads?"

"You got it. We had a few near misses, eh Petto?"

"As you said most vocally on the first occasion, Carl, we nearly blew our goddamed asses off." Petto's expression was entirely neutral, but his belly was shaking with silent laughter.

"Way to go, Carl. That's some fancy English you've been handing out."

"Have your fun, Friedrick. You'll get yours. Now, where the hell was I?" Carl frowned, raised a finger and nodded. "Anyway, what it boils down to is this thing in my hand. Stick a fuse in it and stand way back. Toward the end of our test schedule we had stumps flying every which way. The question is, do we introduce this stuff or not? How bad does the situation have to get before we use it? Do we use it now in defense of Rugen and contribute to the deaths of thousands later? Once you demonstrate something is possible, a lot of other folks will figure out how it was done. I've had some sleepless nights over this one, I can tell you."

Moving on, they visited the infirmary Carl had set up. Rather than try to convert old hands set in their ways, he had recruited new staff and trained them in antiseptic technique. While touring the facility, Carl reverted to their former topic of conversation.

"It isn't all bad, though. If I can find a vein of bituminous coal around here, we might be able to knock out some sulfa drugs."

"That salve working out all right for you?"

"In spades. Only problem is finding the right mold this far north. I've got a crew out harvesting whatever there is. That's when it gets hard. Even if they bring back bales of it I still have to find a way to isolate and extract the active ingredient. After that, coming up with a tablet won't pose a problem. Now, developing an injectable form is going to be one tough job."

Jeff smiled at the excited gleam in Carl's eye. "Sounds like fun."

Once outside they noticed that thunderheads had moved over the city. They weren't dressed for rain and hustled home, chewing on the pros and cons of gun cotton as they went.

Dropping their mounts off at the stable, they hurried inside to the sound of thunder and the patter of raindrops. Entering the parlor, Jeff strode to the fireplace with outstretched hand.

"It is such a pleasure to see you again!"

Rengeld stood warming his hands over the fire. While his clothing was proper in every respect, it hung on his frame like a gunnysack. Thinner by twenty pounds or more, his eyes were sunken and highlighted by dark circles. Rengeld gripped Jeff's hand with undiminished enthusiasm.

"Your presence is a gift from the gods, Jeffrey. Were you not standing here I would hardly credit it. Ethbar has related the gist of your winter's journey, and I must tell you it far outpaces those described in legend. Yet you have returned to us with the promise of allies."

"Let us pray the promise is fulfilled."

"Never doubt what the gods ordain, Jeffrey. They will come." Rengeld released Jeff's hand to accept a cup of coffee. "This evening, may I relate the results of the scouting expedition?"

"Considering its purpose, I would be disappointed had you not offered."

Rengeld waved them toward chairs but remained standing. "One detachment of troops was set the mission of enlisting recruits, and of them I will say no more. I led the larger body of scouts south for some days, meaning to keep rendezvous with agents returning from Astholf and Khorgan.

"It was a hard trip from what I see."

"Nothing compared to your own, Jeffrey."

"It was a long winter. Any evidence the Salchek are moving north?"

"No less than a full army from Khorgan."

"It's a shock to hear it, but not surprising. They want to consolidate their hold on Arvalia as quickly as possible."

"Yes, before a defense can be organized." Rengeld's face was animated and his hands clasped and unclasped behind his back. "From what is known at this time, the army's strength is judged to include four thousand Salchek in addition to three or four thousand troops conscripted in Khorgan. Traveling with the foot soldiers are, we estimate, one hundred of their two-wheeled fighting carts and four hundred light cavalry. Should they continue at the pace we observed, I judge they will arrive in no more than nine or ten weeks."

The room was silent as they mentally juggled timetables and a host of other factors.

"What of the army's supply train?"

"An interesting question, my friend. We counted less than two hundred wains and a smaller number of pack animals. The point of your question?"

Jeff carefully reviewed his reasoning. Rengeld was not a man to tolerate sloppy thinking. "As you are aware, I am familiar with lands the Salchek must cross to achieve investiture of Rugen. An amazing and wonderful land, but one woefully lacking in the usual sources of food for an army on the march. There are no cities to plunder along the way, no farms to strip of livestock. Although large herds of grazing animals roam the prairie, they are often difficult to locate. I am sure the Salchek know of these animals, but I doubt they would risk their army on the hope of finding them."

"And what does this suggest to you?"

The narrow-eyed way Rengeld was staring at him made Jeff pause to think it through one more time.

"It is my thought that much damage and great delay would result if the Salchek supply train were disabled or destroyed. It is said that an army does not long march on an empty stomach. While no expert in this matter, the size of the supply train you recount seems adequate to feed such an army for only a short period."

"I find no fault with your reasoning, but come. Let us try conclusions."

"And so I shall. Tales of Salchek arrogance abound, and I believe they are correct. Certainly they have encountered no meaningful resistance to date, and did not during their last invasion until encountering the yellow-hairs. It is my judgment they anticipate quick reduction of Rugen. With that accomplished, the problem of food disappears."

"A man after my own heart." Rengeld bowed grandly to Jeff. "Your assessment further persuades me. Yes! That is where opportunity beckons! I have most carefully weighed the Salchek Army's food requirements, and conclude they will have little remaining upon arrival at these walls. Now to the manner of exploiting Salchek arrogance. Shall we consider it?"

Ethbar put his foot down and insisted they eat a decent meal. Rengeld was nodding off before he finished. Ethbar sent him to get some rest, leaving the three remaining to toss ideas around for the balance of the evening.

What emerged by the time they called it quits for the night was the urgent necessity of mounting a southern campaign. That night after thinking about it a long time, Jeff shaved off his beard and folded away the last of his winter clothing.

Rengeld strode into the dining room during breakfast and presented his plan of attack. Jeff agreed that a force of 200 cavalry would suit their purpose. They would move fast, wreck havoc, and be gone. The forest spur where Jeff and Carl had met with the combined Alarai mind would provide concealment until the time to strike. Throughout the discussion, Jeff struggled with a personal dilemma.

The Salchek were on the way. That meant he had to return to the moot grounds within several weeks and get the Alemanni started south. Yet several ideas had been taking shape since the previous evening that would demand his presence in the expeditionary force. What to do, he thought. There has to be a way to work this out.

That afternoon, Jeff spent several hours in the hilltop park that had given him his first overview of Rugen. It was the perfect location to ponder his north versus south dilemma.

Someone had planted flowers in neat beds, and the fragrance helped to settle his mind. To the west, a rain squall swept over part of the city while bright sunshine warmed the rest. While he watched, a perfect rainbow formed.

Gaereth could probably handle the Alemanni situation, Jeff thought while admiring the colors in the rainbow, but where was he? Had Gaereth arrived at the moot grounds? Jeff left the park late in the day resolved to take action that had been put off too long.

Having communicated his intent to Balko, they sat facing each other on the floor of their room. Joining minds with Balko, Jeff shot their combined carrier wave north. They were getting tired when he caught a tendril of thought that seemed alien and familiar at the same time. His mind boiling with conflicting emotion, Jeff focused the carrier wave.

"Gaereth?" He received an impression of startled excitement.

"Jeffrey? Where do you seek from?"

Memories of their first meeting in a forest unknown light years away and years in the past immediately came to mind. He didn't know anything about Gaereth. Could he really be his grandfather? If so, why had Gaereth left him to die in the snowfields?

"My wolf-brother and I are in Rugen. Matters are coming to a boil so fast that things might come apart."

The connection had grown stronger, and Gaereth's thoughts were clear as a bell. Excitement bubbled at the surface, but underneath lay something else laden with power and a span of time that Jeff could not comprehend.

"I am close on arrival at the moot grounds. Will we meet there?"

Although Gaereth seemed at ease with the connection, Jeff and Balko were straining to hold their end open. Submerging his doubts to attend to business before he lost it, Jeff filled Gaereth in on recent events and his dilemma.

"...And there you have it. I really need to go with the cavalry, but that leaves the Alemanni situation uncovered. If you would start them south and keep watch over things along the way, it would be a great relief. My darkest fear is that some minor quarrel will lead to a general conflict and rupture the alliance. They are an unruly and quarrelsome lot."

Jeff and Balko were suddenly bathed in a glow of good humor. *"Indeed they are. I will be happy to do what I may to keep these wild men of the North in good spirits, and their murderous tendencies in check. I will seek your mind at this time on the morrow. Good rest to you, Jeffrey and Balko."*

As good as his word, Jeff and Balko picked up Gaereth's questing thought pattern the next evening.

"All is well at the moot, Jeffrey. Halric reports some two thousand souls present at this time. We will begin moving south within the week. May I trust that a camp will be prepared for our arrival?"

"A camp is being set up west of the road about two hours ride north of Rugen. Are you well enough provisioned for the trek south?"

"As you Americans say, no problem. To occupy the energies of our Alemanni brethren, I'll organize hunting competitions to feed the troops. They can test each other's mettle by the game tally rather than in camp by breaking heads."

Jeff couldn't help chuckling at that sally. When Gaereth continued, the carrier wave of his thoughts was serious.

"I'm looking forward to greeting you in person. I have much to apologize for."

Gaereth signed off before Jeff could respond.

The expedition planned on leaving in no more than a week, and Jeff had to scramble. Concerned that the Alemanni camp would indeed be ready, he also had to spend considerable time with Imogo and Ethbar smoothing out details.

The expeditionary force assembled early one morning well outside the city. The troopers had been roused before daybreak. To preserve secrecy they had been told nothing of the mission. Like any military organization on the move, the troopers exchanged excited rumors and some close guesses. None doubted that war was at hand.

Rengeld gave the order to march and his captain and lieutenants moved the troops out in column, packhorses bringing up the rear. Jeff rode parallel to the column.

The sight and sounds of 200 cavalry trotting in formation accompanied by the occasional drum roll was exhilarating. Bright unit pennons, the creak and clinking of saddle and harness: no amount of book study could have prepared him for the impact.

Cynic particularly liked the drums and invariably shifted into a high-stepping gait at each passage.

"It appears you are happy to be on the road again, horse-brother."

"It is time to be at the enemy. I am content."

Balko was unreservedly enthusiastic about the opportunities for mayhem that were soon to present themselves. His only complaint was the slow pace of the troop. That complaint supplied Jeff with a solution to the last part of the plan he had been considering.

They had no reserves to fall back on if things went to hell, as things almost always did in battle. Their slash and burn strategy by its very nature ruled out such provision. Jeff thought he had the solution, and Balko's impatience might be a key factor in bringing his plan to the operational phase.

"Wolf-brother, do you sense 'Balthazar's' pack?"

"While it is in our mind that they hunt in our direction, this one cannot hear their voice."

"That has also been our conclusion. We sense that our wolf-brother moves south to provide assistance in battles to come. Can his pack be found and brought to us? Time grows short before we engage the enemy."

The various time demands were complex, requiring a good deal of consultation.

"I believe we might succeed if I were to move quickly and catch their minds, wolf-brother."

"I agree. There is sufficient time remaining but none to waste. This will be your task. It promises to be a difficult run."

"I anticipate it greatly."

Balko's only reservation was that he didn't want to wind up so far afield that he missed the action. Reassuring him there was enough time and Salchek to spare, Jeff double-checked to make sure they were using the same timetable. When he was satisfied, they bid each other farewell and Balko streaked for the forest.

Although he felt optimistic, Jeff decided not to report Balko's mission until it was certain that Balthazar's pack could be located in time.

The troop rounded the southern extremity of the forest spur three weeks after leaving Rugen. Turning north, they penetrated far enough to ensure a safe base camp. Two veteran scouts attached to the cavalry troop left at once to locate the Salchek Army.

The scouts returned several days later than expected. Jeff looked them over with a bemused expression. Dressed in buckskin from head to toe, Taget and Harko reminded Jeff of nothing so much as a pair of mountain men from America's past. All they lacked were Kentucky long rifles to make the picture complete. Their speech was also different.

While of the North, it was so full of contractions and novel idiosyncrasies that at times it was hard to follow. Jeff had not encountered the dialect before and wondered if it was a natural result of long periods alone in the woods.

He had queried Rengeld on the way south, but had learned little about the men's origins. Taget and Harko had simply drifted in from somewhere to the west several years ago and signed on. Although an odd couple, Rengeld made it clear he had come to trust them without reservation.

Shifting from foot to foot in front of Rengeld and Jeff, Taget eyed Rengeld with some trepidation.

"Sir, I'm purty shor yer not gone ta like this one bit. Thar ain't one army out thar, they's two. Me an' Harko near run inta a bunch'a sojers comin' from the southeast what warn't supposed ta be thar. Looks ta me they's comin' from Astholf, sir.

"I sent Harko ta sorter keep a eye on the army from Khorgan whilst I figgered out how many they was. I counted around a thousand sojers on foot, city folk from the look of 'em, and mebbe two hunnerd what was mounted. They was another hunnerd or so a them Salchek runnin' things."

"Two armies." Rengeld looked down and studied the ground for some time. He nodded. "I should not be surprised."

Jeff retrieved a sheet of parchment from his saddlebags and held it out to the scouts along with a piece of charcoal.

"It would be of great assistance if you could draw how close the armies are to each other, and where they are."

The scouts muttered together before Taget pushed Harko to the forefront.

As the drawing took shape it became clear to Jeff that the armies were likely to rendezvous about eight miles south of the forest spur, with the smaller force from Astholf falling in behind. He couldn't stop a grimace, and thought, Bloody supply train is going to wind up protected by two armies. It'll be like pissing up a rope to attack that setup.

Dismissing the scouts, Rengeld invited Jeff to join him for a stroll in the woods.

"It is possible that our plans were discovered," Rengeld mused. "More likely, however, is the simple fact that the force at Astholf was not well scouted. That will be looked into upon our return. We are now confronted with a difficult tactical problem."

"There is little doubt about that."

Rengeld pointed a twig at the supply train, which was situated at the rear of the main army.

"I judge the two forces will merge some distance south and a tithe west of our location within no more than a day. By this evening, they may well be in sight of one another. The combined force will then continue north."

"If we attack the supply train tonight," Jeff observed, "the Astholf force will be in position to flatten us against the Khorgan Army. Yet, if we wait until the armies join they will roll us up from both flanks in a matter of minutes. The risks are extreme."

"Extreme and unacceptable unless our force be traded for the supply train. Such a decision at the beginning of a long campaign would be foolhardy."

"I agree. However there is another option I have been considering that might improve the odds considerably. What if a blocking force attacked the Astholf column before they joined up?"

"Why, then, our original plan is sound. But tell me, Jeffrey," Rengeld said with frustrated sarcasm, "will you divide our small force and thus risk defeat of each inadequate part, or conjure spirits to assist us in this worthy cause?"

Jeff wasn't stung at all by Rengeld's comment. In fact, it was hard to keep an inner smile from showing on his face at such an apt description of a wolf pack.

"The latter option is appealing and does have great merit. I have worked with my companion for some days to achieve this desirable state of affairs."

He could afford to have his little joke. While Rengeld had been assessing their position, Jeff had received a message from Balko that Balthazar's pack was coming at speed. They expected to arrive late in the afternoon.

Rengeld's face started to purple up. However, he had seen Jeff's humor in action several times and reined his temper in. While offbeat and rough, it was never destructive. He strongly suspected there was substance behind the humor.

"Perhaps you would be so kind as to explain yourself?"

Jeff figured he had pushed Rengeld about as far as was prudent, and proceeded to explain the wolf gambit.

"Wolf packs tend to be small, and Balthazar's is no exception. At last count he was leading eighteen adult wolves. On the surface that seems an inadequate force to accomplish anything, much less attack an army. Yet the terror these creatures inspire in humans is unimaginable. That is how they must be employed—to terrify. While it is obvious that eighteen wolves cannot attack the entire Astholf column, panic spreads like wildfire and will accomplish that task for us."

As the picture developed, Rengeld forgot that he had ever been upset with Jeff.

"Now we attack. Now the way is open."

"I believe that it is, yet there is more. Allow me to convey what I have learned from my studies of warfare in other lands. Ours is not a unique dilemma, and the odds might be further improved."

Pulling together bits and pieces of a number of wars, large and small, Jeff described tactics used in guerilla warfare.

"This is unheard of!" Rengeld sputtered when Jeff concluded.

"That depends on the country and circumstances. The tactics I have mentioned are well proven and effective."

"Yes, I can perceive that they would be, but…"

Rengeld choked off further objection. His superb military instinct was excited and clamoring for attention. In the end he was sold on the whole package.

Preparation began that afternoon. Every piece of harness that had metal attached was padded with rags then each trooper was required to shake the harness. If there was any metallic sound, more padding was applied.

All uniform brightwork was covered with mud or carbon black. Horses with light coats or white spots were also attended to. Troopers were warned that if anyone pulled a sword before the word was given or wore spurs, a military career would end. Individuals and groups were assigned tasks, then ordered to repeat them out loud until they were memorized.

When preparations were complete, Rengeld mustered the troop for the final step. Jeff held out a pot for all to see.

"Watch closely. If this is done properly, it may well save your life."

Scooping out a dollop of charcoal paste, he applied it to his face. Those old war movies he had watched as a kid were finally paying off. Jeff wiped his hands on the ground.

"All right, boys, let's mix up more of this stuff and get it done."

One of the troopers grinned at his buddy and reached for the pot. Within a short period, Rengeld had to curb excessive enthusiasm. Looking like a regiment of rogue Green Berets, the troop was ready to roll by dusk. Jeff had previously informed Rengeld that he would have to go with the wolves.

"To a wolf this night's work is a joyful escapade. You must also know that this pack consists entirely of impertinent wolves—what my country of origin would term smart-asses. They may well enjoy themselves too much and be loath to depart battle. I must assist their leader in effecting such departure."

The time came to leave and Rengeld gave the order to move out. The troop had sobered considerably. Without wasted motion or comment, they ghosted into the night without a sound.

Jeff and Cynic headed southeast where they joined with Balthazar's pack. Jeff had no more than dismounted when Heideth hurried over. Jeff kneeled down to greet her, the deep satisfaction he sensed in her mind reassuring him he had done the right thing in letting her go.

She and Balthazar belong together, he thought, just like Zimma, Magda and I. That was an undocumented wish, and he knew it. Zimma had given permission, but did she really mean it?

Balko was happy to see Jeff as well, although he seemed somewhat anxious. When Jeff asked why, Balko replied, *"This one is concerned there are still enemy necks to bite."*

"More than you can possibly imagine, my impatient young friend."

He mounted up and turned Cynic south, the wolves fanning out ahead. Jeff warned them to be careful of lances, throwing spears and swords, but all he got for his efforts were a few off-color remarks.

"*Do not be concerned, wolf-brother.*" Balthazar commented. "*This pack has traveled widely and confronted two-leg weapons on a number of occasions.*"

The Astholf encampment was far enough south that Jeff had sufficient time to think about what was coming. Memories of the last winter surfaced and he knew that it could happen, that he could die. But this feels different, he thought. Why am I not afraid?

Jeff relaxed to the soothing creak of saddle leather and fell into synchrony with Cynic's rocking chair canter. Some time later, he murmured, "I guess that's what it is. Just been scared shitless too many times. Either you live or you die."

With wolves scouting ahead, finding the army was simple. They crouched to the top of a knoll some two hundred yards shy of their target and stretched out to wait. Below their position a vast sea of campfires glowed red.

In the middle distance off to the west, the Khorgan encampment was visible as a large reddish orb that spread toward the horizon. Anticipation prompted younger wolves to belly forward, only to be chastised by a watchful Balthazar and Heideth.

A faint glow on the horizon gradually brightened. A moon was about to rise. Still no sign of wagons burning, not a sound to indicate battle.

"C'mon, Rengeld, let's get it on. Times wasting!"

Jeff was beginning to wonder if something had gone wrong when he heard a faint but distinct commotion. Jumping to his feet, he stared off to the west. Within minutes a bright flare of light rose well above the campfires, quickly followed by more in an expanding ripple.

"*Brothers and sisters, let us attack!*"

To Jeff's mind and perception, the wolves simply disappeared. Balko was so impatient he fairly danced down the hill waiting for Jeff and Cynic.

373

Murmuring, "God help those men and women down there," Jeff mounted up.

Cynic thought Balko was cheating by getting a head start and tore down the hill in pursuit. They were picking up speed when a shriek cut through the night.

Within seconds, wild cries of fear and screams of agony sounded from multiple locations. Then horses added their terror to the din amid shouted questions, commands and bugle calls. When they hit the flats Jeff leaned forward and Cynic really poured on the coal, the cool night air ripping by.

When he was close enough to see panicked soldiers milling around in the moonlight, Jeff turned Cynic toward the rear of the camp and the supply train. Ten yards ahead, Balko was visible only as a dark blur. Tents passed in rapid succession, agitated figures crawling from many of them but visible for only a second as they flashed by.

One second Cynic was running free, the next he was plowing through a group of conscripts. Bodies sailed into the air on either side, and Jeff reflexively ducked a leg that was gone before he knew what it was.

Balko savaged anyone within reach as he forced a zigzag path through the men and women. Those who were able crawled or scuttled away in terror-stricken desperation. They had bargained on laying siege to Rugen and picking up some loot, but not this.

Once through the conscripts, Jeff guided Cynic toward the line of wains. Leaping from the saddle into the bed of a wain, he kicked a teamster over the sideboards. Uncorking a bottle of turpentine, he splashed some around and dumped live coals on top. The coals weren't hot enough.

"Shit!"

He kneeled down to blow with all his might. There was so much noise that he could hardly think, and expected to be run through or brained any second. Something crashed into the wagon.

Jeff jerked his head up to see Cynic complete his kick and dived to the side as a body flipped into the bed. The turpentine caught with a rush and Jeff had to jump for it. Cynic had the idea and took off for the nearest wain with Jeff half in and half out of the saddle. Balko was standing in the wain's bed when they got there.

As several more wains caught fire, torrents of air rushed in to form a tornado of flame that shot high into the night sky. Jeff urged Cynic into the remuda of pack animals and slashed picket lines as fast as they appeared. Time was running out.

"Wolf-brother! Drive the horses out onto the prairie!"

Balko needed no encouragement and set himself at the horses' heels as fast as they were freed. Jeff was well down the line when the guards got organized and came on with a rush.

"We're outta here! Let us run swiftly to join our brothers and sisters!"

They charged back up the line and plunged into the thick of things near the head of the column. Jeff was appalled at the carnage roiling about him. Moonlight and the burning wagons gave enemy troopers a good look at what was killing them. So rapid were their attacks that the pack's eighteen wolves seemed like fifty to men who had never even seen one before.

Panic-stricken soldiers raced around in wild disorder, others screamed briefly as they were pulled down. Trying to escape, many ran blindly out of camp while Jeff saw others burrowing into bedding and tents.

He was horrified by the scale of destruction and death that seethed around him, and by the realization that it was his doing. At that moment he understood the difference between planning a battle and experiencing it.

A bugle repeatedly brayed its call to action, shaking Jeff out of his state of shock.

"We must leave, wolf-brothers and sisters. Do not tarry!"

Wolves leaped away into the night in twos and threes. Jeff slanted Cynic off to the west and stopped a hundred yards out positioned between the two armies.

As feared, a troop of cavalry emerged from the encampment heading west at the canter. All Jeff wanted to do was get away and forget what he had seen, but his core mission was to block any attempt by the Salchek to support the Khorgan Army. He drew the Colt.

The cavalry troop didn't see him until the last minute. Steadying the pistol on his left arm, Jeff blotted out his feelings and emptied the weapon into the troop in quickly measured shots.

Six tongues of yellow-orange fire speared the night one after the other, accompanied by the rolling thunder of muzzle blasts. Three of the leading horses went down in a shrill, screaming pile and those behind cartwheeled on top.

Others avoided the pileup and came on at the gallop but Jeff was long gone. Cynic had never experienced gunfire and was bucking across the prairie like a rodeo horse.

Unable to locate Jeff, Balko raced back with the pack on his heels. The jumble of thrashing horseflesh and men proved irresistible to some of the wolves, while others saw a more challenging opportunity.

Black forms sailed out of the night to strip horses of riders only to bounce from the ground and do it again. The terrified shrilling of the horses was more soul-wrenching then that of the humans. Jeff directed a frantic call at the wolves when he had Cynic under control.

"Return to the forest!"

Before leaving, Jeff had the presence of mind to realize he had a final task to complete. Dismounting he scooped up several Salchek swords. He remounted in a daze and urged Cynic after the wolves. Not far off, a massive bonfire illuminated the western horizon.

There was no evidence of Rengeld's troop when they arrived at the forest. That was not unexpected. They were farther afield by some miles. Jeff removed the hackamore and sent Cynic off to cool down and graze.

The wolves sat around exchanging war stories, and after a time wondered to Jeff when they might be invited to such a fun thing again. While Jeff felt immense relief that quick feet and total surprise had combined to avoid serious wounds, vivid images of the battle refused to fade.

Balthazar heard Rengeld's troop coming and abruptly stood up. They made their farewells as Balthazar loped off, Heideth at his side.

"We have wrought well this night, wolf-brother. We will hunt nearby. Call when we may be of service."

Adding fuel to one of the campfires to heat water, Jeff thought, Yes, we have wrought havoc and death.

When Rengeld's force filed into camp, Jeff counted troopers. The tally stopped at 185. Fifteen horses carried wounded soldiers.

The water was the right temperature and he called for volunteers to help clean and bind wounds. Although many of the wounds were superficial, four of the men were not likely to survive the return trip.

Snugging a knot in the last bandage, Jeff directed anxious comrades to assist the wounded onto horseback. Just a few days to rest, he thought. That's all most of them need. At the same time he knew it was impossible. Their camp was only an hour's ride from either of the armies. Two hundred horses left a trail that even an idiot could follow.

Rengeld spoke with the wounded men. Always reserved, even stern, on this occasion Jeff observed compassion. Yet there were no options. Rengeld ordered the troop to move out. Taget and Harko were left behind to assess damage and report back when it was clear what the armies would do. Come dawn, they stopped well back in the forest to rest the wounded.

The rear guard joined up and reported no sign of pursuit. To make sure this was the case, Jeff asked Balko to make a sweep back to the campsite. It was a mission that perfectly fit Balko's idea of how to spend a morning. Later, he was disappointed to report that he had encountered no sign of the enemy.

When Jeff related this news to Rengeld, he was pleased but not surprised.

"I believe the Salchek will be forced to treat our assault as a prelude to an attack in corps strength. To do otherwise would be both foolish and incompetent. They are neither."

"Thus they cannot afford to detach cavalry in pursuit of ourselves."

"Exactly. Furthermore, we left the supply train in flames and the army in chaos. Surprise was complete, Jeffrey. They did not suspect our presence until we were among them. Our plan worked to perfection! I have learned much this night, and thank you. Lacking the 'camouflage' you so artfully devised, I am certain our casualties would have been much higher."

Jeff handed the Salchek swords to Rengeld. "These lessons were hard-learned in deadly battles on my world. Battles where the enemy was rarely seen. I am pleased they have served well this night on another. You must present these swords to Imogo in full panoply and view of Rugen's people. They must know that the Salchek are not invincible. We must also allow the city ample warning before entering so that a proper reception may be assembled. We will then enter in camouflage. What think you?"

"Jeffrey, my friend," Rengeld said with an admiring shake of his head, "I had not suspected such a complicated, even devious turn to your mind. Yes. A marvelous suggestion."

One day out of Rugen their presence was noted by a patrol. Rengeld took the opportunity to send word ahead to Imogo. A few hours before arriving they applied camouflage and tidied well-used uniforms.

Jeff unfolded a simple triangle of black cloth that he had been working on in secret. Securing the pennon to a standard, he solemnly presented it to Rengeld.

"Rengeld's Raiders have returned."

Mounting, they proceeded in three precisely ordered columns. Jeff and Balko were in the vanguard with Rengeld. Immediately behind, a trooper selected for bravery in the raid proudly displayed the new unit pennon.

Still a mile from the gate, the crowd had spilled onto the road leaving the narrowest of lanes. Nearer city walls, the road was packed twenty deep. Rengeld held the captured swords up and they went wild.

I really underestimated this, Jeff thought. A lot of these folks are damn near hysterical. This has to be related in some way to the last occupation. Maybe they really did believe the Salchek couldn't be beaten.

A roar of approval followed their progress toward the south gate. Somewhere, drums and cymbals pounded and clashed with stirring abandon. By the time they passed under the portcullis, speech was impossible.

Twenty

Revelation

An honor guard escorted the returning troop to the palace. Streets were crowded with people, and overhead balconies filled to the point of collapse. Some balconies were low enough that a few troopers lost their hats. Other troopers leaned down to grasp hands or accept a kiss.

Imogo was standing on the palace steps accompanied by Ethbar when the troop arrived at the main plaza. Jeff stood up in the stirrups and stared.

"By the gods! It's Belstan!"

While Rengeld solemnly presented the captured swords to Imogo, Jeff tried to spot Zimma in the crowd. When he could not find her, he nearly deserted the column.

Many explanations raced through his mind, but there was no shaking the worst one. Jeff was forced to pay attention when Imogo gestured for him to approach. He was so distracted that he never did remember their conversation.

The ceremony was no more than concluded when citizens mobbed the troop. Jeff fought his way through the press toward Belstan. When he was close enough to read Belstan's expression, Jeff was taken with panic.

Please, not Zimma! The thought had no more than entered his mind when someone cannoned into him, and his face was smothered with kisses.

"Oh Jeffrey!" was all she could get out between the kisses.

Jeff held Zimma at arm's length just to admire her. It looked like she had been crying.

"What has happened, love?"

"It is Ostfel. He and father were attacked far to the east, and an arrow struck Ostfel. Belstan and I had returned from the West only days before they entered the city. Carl cannot say whether Ostfel will live or not. He is so ill!"

Retrieving Cynic, Jeff swung Zimma up behind. Cynic felt the urgency and went as fast as he dared. Carl was slumped in a chair when they entered the infirmary. He was unshaven, appeared exhausted, and new worry lines creased his forehead.

He jumped up at the sight of Jeff.

"Thank God. At least you're in one piece."

"How bad is it?"

"I'll show you."

Zimma remained with her father and the men hurried to see Ostfel.

"The arrow struck him in the back about four inches from the spine. When Ostfel fell backward, the arrow shaft broke off flush with the skin. I can't tell how deep it penetrated. At least he isn't coughing up blood, even though I think his lung is collapsed."

"Can you cut the arrow out?"

Carl stopped to consider an answer. "I'm a biologist and chemist, Jeff, not a surgeon. I've studied human anatomy, but only from books and holographs. Ostfel's wound scares the holy shit out of me. Major blood vessels, lungs, heart—they're all right there. If only I knew how and where they fit together!" Carl took a deep breath and exhaled slowly. "Yes, I can cut it out. Just don't know what else I'm going to cut in the process."

"But you would have operated anyway, given the opportunity. What else is wrong?"

"Thanks for the confidence, Jeff, and yes I would have. The trip back nearly killed Ostfel, and I couldn't risk it until he was rested. Now his temperature's so high he's having periods of delirium."

"The wounds infected."

"Badly. If the arrow doesn't kill him, the infection probably will. It's the left lung, Jeff. If the arrowhead penetrated deep, it may be close to the heart."

"Oh, boy."

Throwing his arms out in resignation, Carl resumed walking. "Doesn't matter, though. I'm going to have to operate whether I like it or not. If only I knew more human anatomy, not to mention we're not even sure these folks are put together like we are."

They entered the room that served as an inpatient ward. Ostfel appeared emaciated, was pale, and beads of sweat trickled down his face. Jeff noticed his breathing was shallow and rapid. Carl picked up Ostfel's wrist.

"His pulse rate has increased again—It's running around 120—and he's comatose. Jeff, we've got to operate, and now! If we don't, he won't last another day."

"All right, let's do it."

"I have to speak with Rogelf first. There really are no options, but this has to be his decision."

Jeff and several assistants were standing by with a stretcher when Carl returned.

"We're on."

They moved Ostfel to the operating room, a roomy cubicle with a stout plank table set in the middle. Buckets and side stands were arranged at the head. Deep grooves had been cut in the table to channel blood into the buckets. Jeff was impressed. The room had been whitewashed, the brick floor was absolutely clean, and the table looked like it had been bleached.

They were strapping Ostfel to the table with leather restraints when Jeff looked at Carl with an embarrassed expression.

"Boy, am I dumb. My backpack is over at Ethbar's place, and I think there are some antibiotic pills in that little first aid kit I carry. Would that help?"

Carl dropped the leather strap he was cinching tight and looked at Jeff with something like hope in his eyes.

"Help? Those little pills might just save the day. I suspect bacteria are the same no matter what world you're on."

Zimma hurried into the room at Carl's urgent call, and was gone as quickly when she had directions on where to find the backpack. Carl and Jeff began washing up.

When she returned Carl had succeeded in exposing the base of the bone arrowhead, which was lodged next to a rib. Zimma blocked out the sound of blood plunking into the buckets and peered over Jeff's shoulder to get a better look.

Carl had made his incision, a clean four-inch cut, along the line suggested by the affected rib and directly over the penetration.

The blood-soaked toweling was bad enough, Zimma decided, but the arrow shaft stub seemed to be growing from her brother's back. It was obscene.

Working the razor-sharp knife deeper, Carl flinched when he felt it grate against the arrowhead. He bent lower in order to see better.

Lanterns suspended from the ceiling ringed the table, but it was yellow light illuminating a red field. Carl probed the wound with a finger. He looked up, his face gleaming with sweat and contorted with doubt.

"Can't go any deeper unless I have no other choice. I think I just felt the pleura, the chest-cavity lining. If it is and I go deeper, I'll be into the chest cavity or the lung itself and really spread the infection or cut a major vessel."

Jeff poured sterilized water into the incision to flush out blood and pus from the incision .

"I can see most of the arrowhead. That's a good sign. Let's see if it'll come, right?"

"I tried that once, but it wouldn't budge. Maybe it will now. Here, give me your hand. Now the other one." Carl placed Jeff's fingers on either side of the incision and had him spread the edges apart. "Good. I want you to hold it just like that."

Zimma lifted a lantern from its hook and brought it as close as she dared.

"Thanks, babe. That really helps."

Carl fished pliers from an alcohol bath. Getting a grip on the arrow shaft, he leaned back and pulled. A piece of the wooden shaft broke off with a sodden snap.

"Shit! Knew I shouldn't have done that!" Slinging his head to get the sweat out of his eyes, Carl took a grip on the arrowhead itself. "Now move, you son of a bitch!"

Carl gritted his teeth and heaved. Ostfel surged against the straps and let out a heart-wrenching scream. The arrowhead didn't move.

"Fuck! There must be a barb on that thing!"

Jeff searched his memory with furious haste in an effort to recall the different arrowhead designs he had seen.

"Carl, a lot of northern arrowheads have barbs, but I can't recall any that were offset. Look at how it's lined up! It has enough rotation to hook the rib. Push and turn the arrowhead before you pull."

Carl nodded, sweat flying off in large droplets. "God damn I hope this works."

Taking a deep breath, Carl found a new grip on the arrowhead but couldn't make his hand push.

"You can do it, buddy. Use both hands to control the pliers."

Clamping both hands around the pliers, Carl murmured, "Please God, don't let me kill him," and pushed. Ostfel surged again and cried out like a child.

Whispering, "Oh, Jesus!" Carl held his grip, twisted the arrowhead and pulled. With a faint sucking sound, the arrowhead came free and he stumbled back holding it aloft.

"Thank God! Finally! And the barb's not broken off!"

For a long moment, all three mutely stared at the arrowhead gleaming dark red.

"Filthy thing!"

Carl flung it away and poured a steady flow of sterilized water into the wound to flush out a new flow of pus. Some minutes later the job was done and Carl loosely closed the wound with gut sutures.

"Shouldn't that be closed tighter, Carl? Won't more air get into his chest?"

"Wish I knew for sure, but I don't think so. I took a few stitches down deep near the pleura. That ought to stop any leaking. Also, I can't imagine we got all of the crud out of there. Have to let it drain. I most certainly do not want the infection to spread."

Attendants entered the room with a stretcher at Carl's call, and they hustled Ostfel back to his cot. After washing up Carl crushed three of the antibiotic tablets with mortar and pestle but wasn't sure how to administer the powder that resulted.

Zimma solved the problem by dissolving the powder in a small amount of water and dripping the solution down Ostfel's throat. Rogelf, Zimma and Belstan set up a schedule so one of them would always be close by.

Carl brought a pitcher of water. "We must encourage Ostfel to drink fluids, but only in small amounts. He must not choke!"

The men collapsed on chairs out front.

"I think that operation was one of the most courageous things I have ever seen, Carl."

"Thanks," Carl replied with a wan smile. "I have never been so terrified in my whole life. Now all we can do is keep our fingers crossed. Ostfel is really dehydrated and that could still kill him."

They settled in to wait it out.

Ostfel seemed to be breathing easier the following morning, and was taking sips of water. After listening to Ostfel's chest, Carl seemed satisfied.

"His temperature and pulse are dropping, and I think his lung is beginning to inflate." Carl stared distastefully at the wooden tube he was holding. "This makeshift stethoscope is better than nothing, I suppose. What I wouldn't give for the real thing." He extracted two antibiotic tablets from a small medicine vial. "Lord, I wish we had more of these."

By that night it was clear to everyone that Ostfel had improved. During one of his brief waking periods he even managed a weak smile. Rogelf planned to sit with his son and shooed everyone out to get some rest.

Jeff and Zimma were so tired they just looked at each another when they were in bed. Together and alone for the first time since Jeff had returned. They kissed and were asleep before their lips parted.

It was well into the next morning before Jeff awoke. Magda was dead to world, but it was enough just to luxuriate in the feel of her silken skin. He abruptly lifted his hands. It wasn't Magda lying next to him, it was Zimma.

Rolling over on his back, Jeff stared at the ceiling for long minutes before quietly swinging his legs out of the bed.

Zimma was awakened by the clink of pottery. She sat up on the edge of the bed to stretch and yawn. Sitting down next to Zimma, Jeff handed her a cup of coffee. All right, he thought, you've put it off long enough. Do it now.

"I must tell you of Magda, of what happened between us."

"I would hear the entire story of your winter, Jeffrey."

"Very well, but the telling is long. Will you join me at the table?"

"And so you accepted her arms and body." Zimma set her empty cup down.

"Yes. Fear and dread consumed me before she gave herself to me. When we made love it was as if you were there too, but Magda is not you." What he was about to say made Jeff pause and feel as if his life teetered on the edge of a blade.

"Zimma, Magda is a wonderful woman and I fell in love with her. I don't know how to understand this. My love for you glows like a white flame, but Magda will always be in my heart. She plans to journey south so she may be with me and meet you."

Jeff noticed Zimma's eyes were swimming with tears. *And so it's over. You knew it all along.*

A great sadness, a great emptiness began to seep into Jeff's heart as he waited for the words that would end their relationship. Just as those words had come so many times on Earth. No other outcome seemed possible.

Wiping her eyes with a napkin, Zimma took Jeff's hands. "In Astholf, when I gave you leave to bed another, my heart knew that such a gift might be the only thing that would bring you back to me whole. Even now I feel the pain in your heart from those days. Having given my leave, do you imagine I will now turn you away? I cherish you more for the telling and owe a debt of gratitude to Magda. I long to meet her. I know I will love her too, for she is clearly a woman of value."

Jeff was totally unprepared for what Zimma had said, simply could not believe his ears. He didn't really intend to stare at her, but was unable to do anything else. Jeff's expression was so confused that Zimma smiled. She brushed away a fresh tear.

"Yes, Jeffrey. I do love you."

"Perhaps I am coming to understand what that word really means." Jeff knelt in front of Zimma and took her hands. "I am so honored. Thank you."

Zimma slipped out of her nightgown, moved to the edge of the chair and opened her thighs.

"Come, lover. Let us celebrate our reunion."

Feeling renewed by their lovemaking, Jeff and Zimma hurried to the infirmary. Carl was already there and beaming satisfaction. Without saying anything, he led the way to Ostfel's bed.

Jeff and Zimma were unable to believe their eyes. What only a few days ago had nearly been a corpse was now a young man sitting propped up wolfing down a bowl of soup and grinning at them between mouthfuls.

"Well, I will be damned!" was all Jeff could get out. Zimma hugged her brother, nearly dumping the soup on his chest.

"Yup," Carl said with an enthusiastic nod, "had the same reaction when I came in this morning to send Rogelf off to bed. Getting that lung inflated and removing the source of infection played a big part, but the antibiotic clinched the whole deal. I've got to find time to isolate the antibiotic from that mold!"

They sat around and chatted until Ostfel fell asleep, then went in search of something to eat. A nearby inn looked clean and bustled with a noisy lunch crowd. All the tables were taken, but the atmosphere was so upbeat they decided to wait. Most of the customers were gone by the time they finished. A good share of the racket left with them, allowing Zimma to relate her trip to Borstel.

"Other than finding a way through the mountains, we encountered few serious difficulties. The soldiers Rengeld sent with us prevented attack and made the whole trip possible. If one of them had not been familiar with the Skarpa Mountains and guided us to a low pass we would never have found our way.

"We traveled to Trunstad first. The merchants were quite enthusiastic. When Belstan had traded what he could, we went to Hochberg." Zimma laughed as she remembered the visit. "Hochberg merchants were most anxious to join in trade when they discovered Trunstad's enthusiasm. Belstan was quite gleeful over the whole affair. I believe the merchants were relieved when we departed."

"I can just see him," Carl chortled. "What a trader!"

"It was certainly an education for me," Zimma replied with wry amusement.

"Good trip back?"

"Without difficulty, Jeffrey. Belstan was worried about the passes becoming closed with snow so we left earlier than planned. While many of the merchants we spoke with talked of forming a caravan and journeying to Rugen, Belstan advised caution until we return west. It would not serve our purposes to have a caravan from either of those cities sacked outside our gates."

Mention of the Salchek sobered them, and it was Jeff's turn to relate events. When he finished, they sat in silence trying to come to terms with what was marching north.

Twenty-one

One Man's Portion

Rugen sweltered in August heat, and the air was sticky with moisture from a recent thunderstorm. On the plus side, rain had flushed sewage channels cleansing the smell of fecal material from the city.

Jeff and Carl were only distantly aware of the welcome change as they followed a messenger sent by Rengeld. A scout had returned. They were barely seated in a room at headquarters when the scout was given the go ahead to report.

The redoubtable Harko jittered nervously in front of so much brass. "Sir, me an old Taget sneaked out the night you folks left and sorta scrunched down to keep a eye on them buggers like ya wanted. Taget, he tooked the big bunch which was hit by you. Me, I hunkered down to watch the sojers out east a bit."

Momentarily forgetting his august company, Harko laughed and slapped his leg. "Well, sir, them sojers was stirred up right good. The wagons was still burnin', and the packhorses was nowhere to be seen."

Jeff asked, "What of the cavalry?"

"Sir, them wolves and you done a fine job. A real mess o' them horse sojers was piled up in a heap fit only fer buryin'. Looking off a piece, I could see a couple hunnerd town folk heading home east. Old Taget, he seen the same where he was. Them wagons you fired was burnt to the ground, sir. Taget, he counted only eighty er so fit to be used."

The story came out bit by bit. A semblance of order had not been restored until a full day after the attack. From what Harko reported, it appeared that a contingent of mounted troops eventually headed south toward Khorgan. What was left of the smaller force from Astholf joined with the main army and the combined force resumed its march north.

"Old Taget, he stayed behind to track them buggers and sent me in to report, sir, but not 'til we follered fer a coup'la days. Taget says to tell you he figgers they's pushing them foot sojers so hard that a good lot of 'em ain't never gone to make it this far. Watched quite a few plumb give up and lay down afore I left to ride back."

After dismissing Harko, Rengeld observed, "I believe we may conclude that our mission was a complete success. That it had certain unforeseen consequences is also clear. Moving as they are, I estimate the Salchek Army will arrive in no more than four weeks. On balance, however, I am content with what was accomplished. The army will be in sad condition by the time it appears, even though that appearance will be somewhat sooner than previously estimated."

"The crops must be harvested at once."

"Indeed, Carl, that must be seen to. There is little enough time. All crops must be in city storehouses no later than three weeks from this date. What remains will be burned in the fields. Likewise, those who cannot fend for themselves in the forest must be within the walls in the same time period. Jeffrey, what are your thoughts on how best to accomplish this task?"

Hoisting a heavy burlap bag onto his shoulder, Jeff picked up a canvas grip.

"You coming, Jorgenson?"

Carl appeared from the bedroom lugging saddlebags and another grip plus sleeping bag and tent.

"Cripes, Jeff, Cynic is going to kick your ass out of the stable when he sees all this stuff!"

"Going to be awhile before I get back to civilization," Jeff replied, nudging the door open with a foot. "We don't have far to go."

"Where's Zimma?"

"At the warehouse with Rogelf. Wasn't anymore to be said."

Carl eyed Jeff when he drew abreast outside the house. "I guess there does come an end to good-byes. Sure hope I find a woman like Zimma someday."

"You will. This isn't Earth."

"Aren't you leaving a bit early?"

"Don't think so. Rengeld really knows what he's doing. I'm more worried about those heathens up north."

"From what I've heard, that says it all," Carl said with an appreciative laugh.

"Yep. Say, listen. Let's drop this stuff out of Cynic's sight and feed it to him one bag at a time."

"Smart move."

The ploy worked to perfection. Cynic was saddled and loaded before he figured out what was going on. By then it was too late for active resistance, but he planted his feet when Jeff tried to lead him out of the stable.

"I will not be abused in this fashion. This day you will walk."

"Damn," Jeff muttered, "there's still the burlap bag to go." He examined the load already on Cynic's back. It was far too much.

"Your point is well taken. It was thoughtless of me. I will prepare a pack animal."

"Got you, eh?" Carl chuckled. Balko's grin was as large as Carl's.

"Just give me a hand, wise guy."

The packhorses were dismal creatures, but Jeff picked one out and they began transferring bags. Carl watched Jeff pull the burlap bag from an empty stall. It certainly did not look like it contained food or clothing.

"Taking the kitchen sink, Jeffrey?"

Laughing self-consciously, Jeff lifted the bag to a spot on the pack board. "This bag, my friend, contains a basic ingredient of life."

Puzzled by Jeff's comment, Carl put his nose close to the bag and sniffed. "Son of a gun. I agree, and good thinking. Makla beans."

Tying off the last line, Jeff returned Carl's grin. "Call them makla or coffee beans, but damned if I'm going to leave without enough to get by. Belstan promised to ship a bigger supply before our playmates show up. I figure it won't take many weeks to hook everyone at that camp."

"You got that right," Carl chuckled, and saddled Sam to accompany Jeff part of the way. There was an issue that had to be resolved. They had exited the north gate when the matter was settled.

"Okay, then, we're agreed," Carl said. "We use the pipe bombs only if they'll make the difference in saving the city. If it appears the Salchek may gain or breach Rugen's walls, I will not hesitate to use them."

"That's about as close as we can come to a livable compromise."

Stopping on the hill above Rugen to make their farewells, Jeff arrived at another decision he had been struggling with for some hours.

"Got something I want you to have." He removed the holstered Colt from his belt and passed it to Carl. "Put it to good use, buddy." Jeff handed him a leather pouch filled with spare ammunition. "The city has to survive, and this may make a little more of the difference." Jeff gazed across the valley. "If those bastards make it into the city, would you look after Zimma for me?"

"Be assured I will do that."

They clasped hands and Carl turned Sam back toward Rugen. Jeff clucked to Cynic. The packhorse rolled her eyes at Balko and waited until the lead rope pulled tight before she would move.

The Alemanni encampment was situated two hours ride north on the west side of the road. With the packhorse acting like an anchor, Jeff figured it would take three hours if his arm didn't give out first. There was ample time to consider his imminent meeting with Gaereth. As he did so, a wide range of emotions coursed through his mind varying from excitement to a certain degree of anger.

In spite of what the combined Alarai mind had said, Jeff couldn't shake the sense that his life had been manipulated to allow only one outcome and no choice. He brushed the anger away.

"So what's new about that? How much choice did Carl have when he was dumped into the South March? When does the pursuit of choice become selfishness?" Jeff growled frustration and directed Cynic to pick up the pace. "I have got to get some answers! If only Gaereth would have asked!"

Throwing a scathing comment at the packhorse, Cynic leaned into the task. Jeff was nearly pulled from the saddle when the packhorse balked.

Stopping abruptly, Cynic decided enough was enough. *"Wolf-brother, would you be of assistance? This beast must learn its place."*

Balko was nearly as irritated as Cynic and trotted to the rear. *"I thank you for the opportunity, horse-brother."* Balko snapped his jaws shut with a loud clack. The packhorse gave a jump and nearly ran up Cynic's fanny.

While still a good distance from camp, Jeff began to hear something that sounded like a sack of tin cans clinking together.

"What on earth could that be?" Another fifteen minutes or so and he suddenly grinned. "Blacksmiths! A lot of them!"

They had no more than turned into camp when Jeff pulled Cynic to a halt and stared.

A large area had been cleared of trees, greatly expanding the original meadow. Scanning the campground, Jeff noted that individual tribes were bivouacked in satellite clearings. The central area, about eight or ten acres in size, was packed with craft lodges and shoulder-to-shoulder with hurrying Alemanni. Gaereth had given a number to Jeff, but the reality took his breath away.

A thick haze of wood smoke from campfires hung over the compound, lending a tangy smell to the air. Jeff breathed deeply and listened to the racket of numerous smithies hard at work. The longer he watched camp activity, the more solemn he began to feel.

"God save me. I'm responsible for all of this. I never imagined that trip last winter would pay off in such a big way. These folks keep their promises." Jeff pursed his lip and nodded. "You've started something; you've called them here. Either you follow through or all this, all the death, has been for nothing." He nodded again, but emphatically. "There's no making sense of it. Now it's a matter of doing."

Jeff guided Cynic through the warren of lodges and throngs of warriors. Excitement permeated the air. There was laughter, shouting back and forth between groups, and many voices were raised in song. It was a time of war, a time to gather honor.

Craft lodges were jammed with customers, especially the breweries, and they passed one smithy that appeared to be hosting a workshop. A number of leather-aproned men and women with massive shoulders and deep chests were involved in a heated debate while peering into the forge.

The meeting hall was located near the camp's center, and Jeff guided Cynic in that direction. A vast humming sound pierced the background noise.

Jerking his head around, Jeff caught a brief glimpse of a flight of arrows arching high on their way down range. He suddenly noticed that Balko had disappeared.

"Wolf-brother! Return to me at once! These warriors are not familiar with you and may inflict harm!"

A wave front of terrified exclamations worked its way in his direction, then Balko came shooting around a lodge grinning ear to ear.

"They did not have time to do so, wolf-brother!"

"Stay close, wander no more." The tone of Jeff's thought was severe; his smile gave the opposite impression.

Dismounting at the meeting hall, Jeff tied the lead rope to the saddle horn and entered with Balko padding at his side.

"See to that dumb shit packhorse, will you horse-brother? We passed the stable on the way in. Somebody will be there to unload her and get the saddle off your back."

"I will do this," Cynic replied, tacking on a long-suffering sigh.

While stupid, the packhorse had learned a certain degree of humility under Balko's tutelage. When Cynic headed for the stable at a trot, he didn't even feel a tug on the halter rope.

Taking a seat on a bench toward the back of the building, Jeff listened in as Halric and Gurthwin mediated what sounded like a dispute between two chieftains. The men were red-faced and shouting insults across a table.

Jeff murmured, "Yes, you have them, but that's much less than half the battle."

His eyes adjusted to the dim light and Jeff spied a thatch of reddish hair behind Halric. Craning his neck to get a better view, Jeff tensed. Gaereth rose and skirted the chieftains.

Jeff stood up but did not advance to meet Gaereth. Longing, curiosity, shyness, anger—all fought for recognition. Balko sensed the origin of the turmoil seething in Jeff's mind and jumped to his feet. Crouching slightly, he quivered like an arrow awaiting release. Gaereth stopped a good four feet away from Jeff.

Neither moved nor spoke for moment after moment until the tension became palpable. The chieftains stopped arguing and benches scraped on wooden flooring as they were pushed back. Heads turned to witness.

Gurthwin shivered at the ground swell of emotion that radiated from Gaereth's mind. His pain and need were overwhelming. Shifting his gaze, Gurthwin saw that Jeff's lips were set in a tight, thin line. Muscles along his jaw were bunched and one was twitching. The dim light showed every line on his face, highlighting sharp angles of privation. All softness was gone.

"Gods grant that charity and compassion survive," Gurthwin whispered.

Getting to his feet, he moved a few steps closer and remained standing supported by his staff. Pride and fear mingled, making Gurthwin's heart pound.

"O my gods, please let them find love," he prayed under his breath. "I have served you faithfully, do not abandon my plea."

Chieftains who had been ready to go at it only moments before stood up, crossed their arms and stood shoulder to shoulder. Their differences were trivial compared to what they were witnessing.

Slowly, Gaereth inclined his head. "Grandson. My life rests in the hope that one day you will find your heart open to forgiveness."

Jeff did not respond; was unable to find words to fit the storm of emotions that threatened to tear him apart. Pain and anger finally gave a focus.

"Why didn't you come sooner?" Anguished silence. "You played with my head like I was some damn robot, then just tossed me into a snowdrift and left me to die. I may be needed here, but why would my grandfather do that? Please tell me."

Although Gaereth's expression did not change, Gurthwin noticed a tremor in his hands and felt a blast of remorse.

"I am defenseless against that question. Only excuses remain. We miscalculated the onset of the earthquake and seriously underestimated how strong it would be. I intended to be at your side well before onset, both to allow you choice and to accompany you here if that was your decision. I was at the lake when it started."

"Why did you wait until the last minute? Why didn't you seek me out in Seattle so I could get to know you and have a chance to think about it? Damn it, I would have come!"

"I wanted to, Jeff, and I've thought about little else for the last year. There were times when it was nearly more than I could bear not to pull up a chair at that tavern." Gaereth smiled wanly. "The night you tangled with that nude hologram was one of them."

Memories of Seattle hit hard: Gado, Sarah, losing his job. "Lick and Swallow."

Gaereth nodded, but the smile was gone. "I had to be sure, had to give you time to understand there was no place for you on Earth. Watching you take that beating was one of the hardest things I have ever had to do.

"It was only when I returned to Aketti that I discovered how badly our plan had also miscarried here—that you had not landed on Skene as designed but high in the mountains of Arvalia. At that time we had no idea that Carl had been taken as well. As I have said, excuses only. Whatever your decision this day, I will always live with the knowledge that I was nearly the instrument of your and Carl's death." Gaereth inclined his head a second time and was silent.

One hand soothing Balko, Jeff's thoughts tracked forward in time from Seattle. With distant eyes he scanned endless snowfields and a gigantic mountain, heard the forest's whispering quiet that had nearly unmanned him. Remembered wailing voices singing the sun to a rest that would leave him in darkness.

Those memories abruptly gave way to the vivid image of a woman staring up at him, blood bubbling from her mouth. His sword buried in her chest. Exploding trees, terrifying aloness, dying screams—the memories went on and on. The whirling montage slowed and came into focus.

Jeff gathered a desperate bolt and blasted it at the heavens. Why? Why did it have to be so hard? Why have I had to kill so many people? Tell me! Please!

Gurthwin could endure no more. It had to be stopped. He was about to intervene when a zephyr of air fragrant with the perfume of many wild flowers and a verdant spring wafted into the hall.

Pulsing golden light suddenly flooded the hall accompanied by a single crystal chime of such tonal purity that tears sprang into his eyes. Every nerve tingling with joy, Gurthwin held his arms out and bowed.

The door to the hall slammed open.

Formless yet formed of grace and appalling majesty, male and female yet neither, power so vast it exceeded dread but softened by eternal laughter, gods strode into the hall. Afraid to look up yet compelled to do so, Gurthwin raised his eyes. Time stopped and held its breath.

Outlined and suffused by incandescent gold, three forms of exquisite beauty confronted him. Vaguely human in shape and gowned in flowing raiment, Gurthwin perceived their appearance reflected no more than the moment's requirement. The nature of their faces, although crystal clear to insight and love, defied description. Unable to bear the radiance of their features, Gurthwin lowered his eyes again.

A gentle thought vibrant with power filled his mind. *"You have served the welfare of this land faithfully. Know that your place in our hearts is secure. We understand that you grow tired and fear your strength will fail in death ere this task is complete. Be assured your flesh and spirit will prevail. Peace be with you."*

While the first thought had more of a sense of the male than female about it, there was a distinct female cast to the second.

"Though flawed by deeply ingrained anger and self-doubt, the young man has been selected for this task. While we are aware of his pain and would ease its burden, his search for identity often borders on self-destruction. We would have you give testimony of his spirit, for he must serve this land and yet another."

Gurthwin's face blanched at the responsibility assigned him. "I am only mortal and love Jeffrey. How can I render judgment to the gods?"

Delighted contralto laughter caroled like a thousand silver bells. *"Come now! When have your people, and it must be known the people of Jeffrey's world, been reluctant to do so? We are not immune to the many pleas cast into our realm on his behalf, and your love for him is clear, but open your heart to us. We expect no more."*

Reviewing his conversations with Jeff, Gurthwin lifted his eyes with stern resolve.

"Then I shall do so without stint. This young man has been used most foully by his homeland, yet ever strives to find truth. Yes, he is flawed by anger of such degree that it has slowed maturity. While destructive at times, his is an anger that seeks reprieve from injustice and the repression of meaningless existence.

"Will you argue that he has not been badly used? Cast from his profession and society into this world to live or die? Maneuvered, not asked, to undertake a task that would daunt a lifetime of informed preparation? Wherefore should he experience aught but anger and a lack of self-definition? Yet he has failed no portion of this task though on repeated occasion it has forced him to the brink of death more severe than any which might be self-imposed." Gurthwin paused to consider his next words.

"Yes, I do love him and would not see him destroyed by this conflict. Yet it may well be his destiny. In the end, whether he is to live or die, his spirit is worthy. I would have none other lead us in this time of great peril."

Opening his arms in submission, Gurthwin bowed his head. After a period of intense silence, his mind was caressed as by a loving hand.

"Well spoken, and nobly so. Be assured the burden of testimony we placed on you was necessary. Jeffrey is not to lead immortals, but men."

A third distinct personality emerged. Crisp and lively, its aura seemed unconcerned with gender but overflowed with a type of energy that Gurthwin could only define as mischievous.

"Yes—a worthy young man and fit to lead. He has confronted anger, is open to self-examination, and shows promise of growing beyond the limitations of youth. I greatly anticipate the outcome of such growth."

A brisk wind flowed into the hall, sweeping the three forms into a single iridescent column of golden light filled with sparkles. Rotating rapidly, the column rushed over to surround Jeff. He faded to an indistinct shadow.

While unaware of any unusual presence, different memories eased bitter pain aside: Magda standing like an ivory statue and beckoning to him, Heideth and Balko loping through the forest, the moon's silver pathway, Valholm on a spring day. An image of Zimma standing with arms outstretched and smiling glowed into existence.

A single thought formed a halo around the memories and image: is this not enough?

The reproof was so gentle that its message was crushing. Turning his face up as if to bask in the sun, Jeff closed his eyes.

"*Yes, it is. Thank you for being tolerant of my immaturity. For helping me find the way. I will try and do better.*"

"*We are pleased.*"

Time let its breath out and moved on.

Opening his eyes, Jeff noticed that everyone in the hall except Gurthwin seemed frozen in place. While Jeff watched, they began to move. He walked toward Gaereth with outstretched arms.

"Grandfather."

When Gaereth and Jeff separated, all they could do was grin at one another. Gurthwin took each by an arm.

"Now we must truly celebrate. This day has been blessed by the very gods!"

Leaving Jeff and Gaereth seated with tankards of beer, Gurthwin and Halric shepherded the chieftains from the hall. Gurthwin hesitated at the door to glance back at Jeff then stepped outside singing under his breath.

While Balko and Gaereth were getting acquainted, Jeff attempted to reconstruct what he had experienced. A few hints and it slipped away like a dream. What remained was a clear memory of being cherished, and laughter that eased all pain. Feeling immensely comforted, Jeff turned his attention to Gaereth.

It had been fifteen years since they last met in Iowa, but Jeff could not identify any changes. Gaereth's hair showed no gray, his face was youthful, and there wasn't an ounce of fat on his lanky frame. Jeff thought Gaereth could pass for thirty. Even his attire was the same—tall boots, leather pants and soft leather tunic.

Gaereth finished his conversation with Balko and turned his attention to Jeff. "Still don't know how I lived through that quake, Grandson."

"It was bad. Seemed like the world was coming to an end. Get beat up at all?"

"No more than a few cuts. I don't understand how that could have happened. There wasn't anything left standing around me."

"How'd you get out? The road must have been destroyed."

"It was, and nothing left of my car but flattened sheet metal. Didn't matter, though. It would have been worthless in that mess. Never would have made it if I hadn't run across an old pickup someone had hidden. I couldn't believe it—not a tree or rock had touched it."

"An old Dodge four wheeler?"

Laughing explosively, Gaereth slapped his knee. "That was your truck!"

"Damn right. Haven't thought about that gnarly old beast for too long. What'd you do? Hotwire it?"

Gaereth grimaced and spread his hands. "Yep. Funny the things you pick up here and there."

"Hell, I don't care! Just glad it was there to help out."

"That it did, Grandson. Good thing you had a winch on it, though. Took three days to make the highway and nearly two weeks to work our way to Seattle. Roads were torn up, cites flattened, electricity gone—had to hand pump gas—it was a real fight. Afraid there wasn't much left of your truck by the time we arrived."

"Again, I don't care. If a pickup has to die, that's the way it ought to go."

Gaereth nodded solemnly. "Well, anyway, without knowing how really badly we had miscalculated, only that you had been translocated, I paid a visit to your folks in Iowa. Tried to be clever and picked up some average clothing so I could pose as a distant relative. Your grandmother is one sharp lady, Jeff. There was no doubt in her mind that I was a relative, but she knew right off that I was a *very* distant one."

"She doesn't miss a thing. Never has."

"That's a fact. She also has an astonishing interest in life for her age. A lot of folks in her generation have given up."

"I don't think that's going to happen."

"She never will, Jeff, and that's what opened the door for me to talk with your folks. Your mother took it pretty well when I convinced her you had not been harmed, little did I know. Your dad was a different story. He's quiet, but let me tell you Henry is no man to fool with!"

"No shit," Jeff murmured ruefully, remembering occasions when he had attempted to do so.

"He finally came around, but not until Regina put some strong moves on him. She was so proud of what you were brought here to do that she was ready to burst. That is one fierce lady. She said her only regret was that she was too old to come herself and lend a hand. Stephen made sure that I would let you know he's made up his mind to pursue farming, and that he misses you a lot."

The news from home lifted a weight from Jeff's shoulders. It was wonderful to hear that Stephen had committed to farming. Although he had studied agriculture at the state university, the issue had been in doubt for some years. With Stephan there to help, Henry could keep the farm going.

A question that had been plaguing Jeff for well over a year came to mind. "Tell me, is the Alarai home base on Aketti located on an island like England?"

"Yes," Gaereth replied with a discomfited expression, "our homeland is on an island called Skene off the east coast of this continent. It has always been a safe refuge, maybe too safe. I don't think anyone except myself has left it in the last fifty years."

The look on Gaereth's face brought a smile to Jeff's. "You responsible for those dreams I had back in Seattle?"

"Afraid so. I was at the end of my rope by that time and sneaked into your hospital room. Things were just moving too fast. I had to give you something to hold on to."

"And do what you could to offer choice. It was confusing, but did help." Jeff shifted mental gears. "What's the situation here?"

"There's a lot of tension. Maybe ten or twelve tribes have serious blood feuds. So far we've been able to keep a lid on it."

"Afraid of that. We have to pull them together fast."

"It's going to pop one of these days soon if we don't." Gaereth got up. "Let's take a stroll around camp so they can see us together. Sort of a double threat."

They left the hall arm-in-arm, Jeff briefing Gaereth on the situation in Rugen as they walked. That led to a discussion of tactics, strategy and how to deploy the Alemanni in battle.

The sight of not one but two Alarai moving around camp soon brought scores of warriors on the run. Many recognized Jeff.

Excitement grew by the minute as their entourage expanded. Ballads, war songs, recitations—all were underway at the same time. Conversation was soon impossible. It was clear that a Telling would have to take place that night.

It was after dark when warriors began gathering, some still gnawing on a rib or leg bone. There was a good deal of give and take between tribes while waiting for the Telling to begin. Most of the exchanges amounted to no more than the banter of people getting to know one another. Some were not.

Conditions were crowded in the arena facing the meeting hall, and a number of feuding tribes came into contact. The tension was explosive and might have ignited into open conflict had not leaders stepped in.

Looking out of the meeting hall when he judged the time was right, Jeff nervously gazed across a restless sea of humanity that stretched well beyond the limit of what he could see by the light of torches. The big crowd was bad enough, but he knew that something far more potent than a routine Telling was called for. The future of the tribal confederation, maybe the war itself, was at stake. And it was his baby—sink or swim.

"What can I possibly say that will pull them together?" Jeff anxiously said. "So many bitter rivalries!"

He reviewed century upon century of murderous ethnic conflict on Earth, and the repeatedly fruitless attempts to mediate a lasting peace.

"Words, words! They haven't been effective on Earth, why should I expect them to work here? You kill my people, I kill yours. I want your land, you can't have mine. That's what it always boils down to."

A hand squeezed his shoulder.

"It's going to be a tough sell, Jeff, but you have what it takes."

"Wish I had your confidence, Gaereth. I don't have any idea what to say. What can be said in one speech to heal years of bloodshed?"

"It may be that what must be expressed to them will have to come from the heart, not your head. You know the Alemanni better than any person on this planet. What are the unifying, common threads present in all of their lives?"

"I don't know!"

"Yes, I think you do."

Gaereth lighted several torches from the fireplace and stepped out onto the porch.

"It's time, Grandson. Free your heart to speak what it must."

An excited rumble swept away from the hall when the Alemanni saw Jeff. He stepped into the pool of light searching for words, but his mind was blank.

Crowd noise decreased minute by minute until there was no sound except that of a gentle breeze sighing through the trees. The larger moon sailed into view fully revealing the number of people. The arena was packed.

God help me, I don't know what to say! Jeff thought desperately. I'm going to lose them!

Nearby but out of the torchlight, Gaereth stood with Gurthwin and watched the agony of indecision that played across Jeff's features. Crossing his arms he let his mind drift far back through time to other deep-forest arenas, and was unconcerned.

Torches sparked and died leaving silver moonlight. The silence continued until it took on a life of its own. A grumbling mutter of unease slowly began to build. Alemanni toward the front were shifting restlessly. A wave of emotion emanated from Jeff, and Gaereth smiled. Standing up straight, Jeff held his arms out to the Alemanni and raised his voice.

> "Shall we sing of life and hope, sing of joy and spring?
> Shall we wander in snow and cold, reft of hope in promise foretold?
> Now we sit and groan, winter that grasps and winds that moan.
> But still we know the joy of old!
> Life is strong and shall return, as the sun from long sojourn.
> Let us sing of joy and spring!"

Jeff's voice wavered at first, grew in strength with each line, and steadied into an uncertain bass at the refrain.

Gaereth stepped into the light, tenor and bass melding in two-part harmony.

> "Now we seek our heart's desire, seek the
> hearth and warmth of fire.
> Meet with friends and all be merry, recalling
> life that will not tarry.
> Bless our children, love in holding, faith in
> family ne'er beholden.
> Let us sing of joy and spring!"

Somewhere in the crowd a feminine voice soared to join the Song of Life in a rich soprano, and was joined by others across the arena. Then, as if directed by the fall of a baton, thousands of men and women burst into the next stanza.

> "Feel the promise that moves within, dream of
> all that shall begin.
> Cries of life that greet the day, we sing and dance,
> let all be gay!
> Child and youth, strong and firm, now our
> hope then cherished in turn.
> Let us sing of joy and spring!"

Stanza by stanza, irresistibly, the song caught a strength that Jeff had not heard before. A strength that could not be stayed as it soared over meadow and forest until it disappeared into some realm deep within the star-sprinkled sky.

When the last voice faded away, when the Alemanni came back to the present and realized what they had wrought, the only sound to be heard was that of weeping.

Jeff wiped at his eyes and gripped the porch railing. "The Song of Life! And who did not know the words? And who did not lend his voice to its power?" Jeff drew himself up and pounded his fist onto the railing. "Why, then, do you slay one another! Why do you end the lives of brothers and sisters!"

Some of those nearest the porch recoiled at the anger in his words, many turned to look at unfamiliar faces. Having stepped back from the light, Gaereth saw other warriors doing the same farther back.

"Hang onto them, Grandson," he whispered. "You have them thinking."

"Indeed they are," Gurthwin whispered back. "I am deeply moved by the power of this moment."

Jeff wanted to pace very badly, but would not risk breaking rapport with his audience.

"Now I will ask you—why did you accept me into your villages? Because my hair is not like yours? Because my skin is darker? Is this the difference between life and death? The color of hair and skin?

"You did not despise me! All villages, all tribes fed and clothed me; gave warmth and affection in full measure. Nearly I died in the great cold that crushes the spirit while drawing life from the body. But I did not.

"Sharing your warmth my life was renewed, yet my spirit was defeated. I became lost in despair, unmanned by the sweating fear of death. Yet you did not despise me! Seeing my peril you opened your hearts, shared your warmth; returned my soul from its wandering."

Caught up by memories and emotion, Jeff threw his arms wide. "But tell me, I will have you tell me! Why do you despise brothers and sisters from unknown villages? Why do you war with those who live nearby? Have you never wondered that outlanders refer to you one and all as yellow-hairs? That you speak the same tongue across your land, have the same customs and cherish song? How can it be but that you have sprung from the same seed? What are the differences that warrant suspicion and warfare?"

Some warriors nodded thoughtfully, but many of those Jeff could see clearly were frowning in doubt. Quite a few were scowling and a number of these turned their backs to the porch and walked away.

A group to the side shook their fists and one of them shouted, "We are not of the same family! Blood will be avenged by blood!"

Jeff stabbed his arm out in a broad sweep, and his voice dripped scorn.

"Remember old grievances if you will. Plot revenge and dwell on murder if this is your way. Take joy in the thought of motherless and fatherless children who are like unto your own flesh. Do so and surrender this land to others." Jeff threw his arms up in disgust and stepped out of the light.

"What are you doing, Jeff?" Gaereth muttered under his breath "You're throwing it away!"

Gurthwin patted Gaereth on the shoulder in support. "Have faith in what you earlier said, my friend. He is chancing it all on a throw of the bones, but when has Jeffrey been loath to risk failure? I must also tell you he had no choice in this matter. He does, indeed, understand our people and has placed their future where it must reside—in their hands."

At the far end of the porch, Jeff leaned his arms on the railing and bowed his head. Unease, hoarse mutters, angry voices raised in argument, a scuffle off to one side. A vast groan of indecision swept the crowd.

"No, no, no!"

The voice was so replete with urgency that Jeff raised his head to search for the source. He saw a man forcing his way toward the porch but could not make out his features.

A way was opened, he bounded onto the porch, and Jeff recognized him at once. He was relatively young, somewhere in his thirties, and stepped into the torchlight. Immediately following, a young woman holding a child in her arms joined him.

Holding the child up, she turned from side to side a number of times. She stopped abruptly and cried out, "Behold our children!"

A man at the front began to weep with great sobs as he looked on the child. His emotion was so strong that great tears of love and grief sprang into many other eyes as warriors remembered.

The child became frightened and began to cry. Unfastening a flap of her tunic, the woman put the child to her breast to suckle. Her husband enclosed them with a massive arm.

"Our child! Your child! Our land!" He shook his head. "You do not know me, for my village lies far to the west. For untold years we have held ourselves aloof from all congress, deeming our might and valor above such intermingling. I would have turned on our war leader had he not shown great wisdom and restraint. I demanded that he prove his courage in single combat! A man who would brave full winter to warn us of great peril, and

I questioned his courage! But we have come, and I am humbled. I am humbled! How is it that I dare speak such a thing?"

Although he did not move from his corner, Jeff stood up straight and gazed at the man with a great sense of satisfaction. It was Therkan from Helstor.

"I dare speak of being humbled," Therkan continued, "for I would not again stand alone. I stand here, for I would no longer be separate from my brethren. The power of this people! The strength of our spirit! We have *never* known its like."

"Nor have I!"

A woman no longer a youth, and clearly a chieftain, ran up the stairs to the porch and confronted the couple.

"Coming from lands to the east we do not know of your village, and regret this is so." The chieftain smiled at the young woman. "What is your name?"

"Silfin, my husband, Therkan."

"I am called Farnil. May I share this honor?"

At Silfin's nod, Farnil faced the crowd and methodically slipped an arm out of her leather tunic to expose a breast. Accepting the child from Silfin, she placed him to her breast and inserted the nipple. Still hungry, he began to suckle with renewed vigor. No words were necessary, none were offered, the crowd went wild.

Chieftain after chieftain hurried to the porch and shouted their support over the uproar of singing, drums and fifes that swept the arena. Therkan moved from the limelight to speak with Jeff. Grave yet animated, Therkan inclined his head.

"I am at your service, as are the people of my village."

"You and Silfin will never be forgotten. Your words and actions will be remembered as the force that molded this people into one. Your service is accepted with great pleasure."

"I am honored, but perhaps there is another service to perform this night." Therkan gestured toward the arena. The uproar had not abated in the least. "We have yet to hear of our enemy, and I fear that this will not occur without intervention."

Therkan's toothy smile brought a grin to Jeff's face. "What do you suggest?"

With a massive shrug, Therkan returned to the limelight where he and other chieftains bellowed orders to settle down. Jeff used the time to help Gaereth replace the torches before they set the porch on fire.

"Never seen anything like this, Jeffrey. Never," Gaereth said in a subdued, reverent voice.

"They are a wonderful people," Jeff replied, sticking the last torch into a sconce. "Now I'm going to add the other part they really love."

"Breaking heads."

"You got it, but this time not each others."

"They're getting tired. Better keep it short."

"Short as possible, and very sweet."

Gaereth withdrew, as did the chieftains, leaving Jeff alone in the renewed circle of light. He held his arms up for silence.

"This night you have discovered kinship. This night you have become one people, and I name you the Alemanni. A name of power that the Salchek invaders will learn to fear, for they are here. The Iron-shirts are not a people of myth, they are here! I have fought them! Now listen to the full tale and dream of the part you will play in that which is to come."

Jeff summoned Balko to his side and dropped into the ritual of Telling. Many had not heard the tale, and those who had would listen to it a hundred times given the opportunity.

As he proceeded to the discovery of the Salchek Army moving north, a rumble of anger swelled in the background. A deathly silence settled as he described the trek south, their preparations for the attack, and the coming of the wolves. That proved to be too much. A thundering clash of sound rose from the crowd as they pounded shields and screamed war cries.

"And then we smote them, Alemanni. We fell upon them with vengeance and smote them! Arrogant they were, and lazy in insolence. And we smote them! We fired their wagons and scattered their horses while they screamed their fear into the night! They bled and died did the mighty Salchek, and many still are running. Two hundred we were against their thousands, yet they ran screaming into the night.

"Soon they will be here—angry, hungry, lusting for battle. But they will *never* forget how we smote them. They are many, mighty and would take all our lands. Listen well, my brothers and sisters, for on your honor, your valor, this mighty battle turns. If we fight as Alemanni, victory will be ours. If we fight one another, *we* will die in our thousands. We will die, and the Salchek will take your lands and children, your husbands and wives, fathers and mothers."

Jeff waited until the angry rumbling subsided. "Hearken to my words and remember what has been spoken." He took a deep breath and cried out, "The Song of Life! We are one! Let it never be broken!" Holding his arms out in supplication, Jeff bowed his head.

The silence lasted only a heartbeat before a thunderous roar broke out on a scale that set the porch to shivering. Many warriors were weeping anew, but many more bellowed war cries and pounded spear hafts on shields. It was quite late before order was established and the beer kegs rolled out.

The encampment was quiet next morning as mass hangovers were carefully nursed. The party had set new standards of comparison. Jeff had spent most of the evening speaking with chieftains in the meeting hall and was spared that agony. Mellia, Therkan's mother, had also sought him out, giving Jeff the opportunity to introduce her to Gurthwin. It had been an evening to remember.

Now, inside the meeting hall, Jeff took a quiet breakfast with Gaereth. Sipping coffee, they pondered the effect of the Telling.

"If that speech of yours last night doesn't pull these folks together, nothing will. It was extremely moving, Jeff. Your use of music, and especially the Song of Life, was inspired."

"Don't know where the idea to use music came from, just glad it did." He swung a kettle out from the fireplace with a metal hook. "One thing for sure, though, Therkan and Silfin made the difference." Jeff held his mug up. "Need a refill?"

Smiling reflectively, Gaereth shook his head in response. "Farnil is some kind of woman."

Jeff dipped out enough coffee to keep him going and rejoined Gaereth. "Has it been many years since you've paired up?"

"Am I that obvious?"

"To a degree, but considering how few Alarai are left it's not hard to deduce that you've been on your own for a long time."

"So very many years, Jeff." Gaereth abruptly got up. "Think I will have a splash."

Let it go, boyo, Jeff thought. That degree of loneliness should not be exposed. He set his voice to carry across the room.

"You're right about the importance of last night, though. That was my best shot at getting them to work together. We have to assemble a tribal congress while that speech is still fresh in their minds and before some squabble breaks out. Have to put them to work devising a common battle song, unit colors, and so on."

Gaereth snapped his fingers and hurried toward the door. "Brought that stuff all this way then forgot it. Be right back."

Puzzled and intrigued, Jeff nursed his coffee until Gaereth returned carrying an old leather bag. He spread its contents on the table one by one. Enjoying himself hugely, Gaereth gave a package to Jeff.

Feeling like it was Christmas, he unwrapped it. Tucked away inside were three small, fat books. The first one he picked up was labeled, *Handbook of Obstetrics and Gynecology*, the second, *Handbook of Surgery*, the last, *Handbook of Orthopedics.*

"I spent some agonizing hours picking out those three, I can tell you. The mass we can carry during transport is limited if you want to arrive in one piece, yet I knew how great your need would be for hard medical information."

"You got that right!"

Gaereth shook his head ruefully. "You can't imagine how many libraries and bookstores I searched, how many war stories I listened to in medical hangouts while deciding what to bring."

Turning one of the volumes over in his hands, Jeff knew he was holding treasure beyond anything that existed on Aketti—knowledge. The books represented an enormous endowment.

"Carl is going to go nuts, you know. Hell, I'm going nuts right now. You could not have picked better gifts."

Gaereth smiled with pleasure at Jeff's reaction. Leafing through the books, they discussed the impact such information would have. When he felt the time was right, Gaereth pushed another package in front of Jeff.

It was heavy for its size. Jeff was stunned when he saw what was inside. Speechless, he could only stroke the cool blackness of the holstered Ruger 9mm automatic and fondle the spare clips that were with it. He pulled the last of the paper away to discover four boxes of ammunition and a cleaning kit.

Jeff cleared his throat several times before finding his voice. "Gaereth this is, this is. ..."

Unable to express himself, he lapsed into excited silence. Opening a box of cartridges, Jeff loaded a clip and inserted it into the weapon's butt after seating the rounds with a few taps on his palm. Leaving the chamber empty, he slid the weapon into its holster and buckled it on while Gaereth beamed pleasure.

"I took a chance on that fourth box of ammunition. I knew you had a revolver with you but wasn't sure of its caliber, so I took the middle ground and brought .38 specials. Hope it was a good choice."

"They'll work fine. I left the .357 with Carl back in Rugen—he'll appreciate a good reserve. Have to get these to him before things hit the fan." Jeff noticed an odd shaped packet he had missed peeking from the paper. He picked it up with a puzzled expression on his face.

"Now what could this be?"

"Rare magic, my boy," Gaereth retorted with a big wink.

"Son of a gun," Jeff breathed when the contents were exposed. "Wow. Some kind of magic!" He held up a slender black tube. "Ball point pens. This blows me away!"

"The foundation of society, wouldn't you say?"

"You got that right," Jeff laughed. "How I have wished for even one of these suckers, and you brought five! This calls for a celebration."

He dipped two mugs of beer out of a cask and set one down in front of Gaereth. Jeff uncapped one of the pens and drew satisfying curlicues on a scrap of parchment.

"Getting back to what we were talking about earlier, I want to avoid pitched battles out in the open where Salchek cavalry and chariots can cut them up. The Alemanni are at their best fighting in hand-to-hand brawls."

"Chariots? This is not good news."

"You got that right. Have to stay clear of them. What I would like to do is move down by Rugen with about a third of our force some night early on, pound them good, then retire north as if in retreat. If we can suck them into the woods, we won't have to worry about the chariots. Which reminds me—did you hear anything from our wolf-brothers on your way here?"

Gaereth grinned. "The chief comedian, you mean?"

"That's the one."

"One of these days I'm going to get the last word with that wolf," Gaereth said under his breath. "Anyway, it seems that pack you ran across way up north has stirred up a lot of concern. Balthazar thought we might expect three or four packs to head our way soon."

"Now there's some good news." Jeff got to his feet. "Let's find some lunch, then I've got to contact Carl."

Locating Carl proved to be more difficult than Jeff had anticipated. There was an unusual amount of background noise in the city. It took some time to identify Carl's thought pattern. Gaereth listened in.

"Carl, got something you need to look at up here that's worth a trip. How about swinging by?"

"Jeff, my boy, I am up to my ears. Sure it can't wait?"

"I think I can say with complete objectivity, that if you don't come you may never forgive yourself."

Gaereth and Jeff could feel Carl's struggle as his thoughts flashed through a long list of responsibilities. As Jeff knew it would, curiosity won out.

"You got it, bucko. I'll be up later this afternoon and stay the night."

"You're not going to believe this, Carl. See you later."

Jeff knew his last comment would drive Carl wild with speculation. They were chatting about it a few minutes later when Jeff's hand happened to brush the hilt of his sword. He stood up to draw the weapon, and handed it to Gaereth.

"Can you tell me anything about it? I have no idea how long it was in our family before it was given to me. Grandpa said it's over two hundred years old. There's something about it that keeps nagging at me." Jeff described what had happened the night before he left on his camping trip.

Gaereth listened intently, all the while turning the saber over in his hands. When Jeff was done with the story, Gaereth did not respond for some time. Sitting motionless, his gaze seemed to have wandered light years away.

"I'm not sure, but this saber might have belonged to my father."

Jeff's face revealed his astonishment. "Your father? This is his sword?"

"Maybe." Gaereth lovingly caressed the blade. "Too much time has passed to be certain."

Gaereth's expression was so poignantly sad that Jeff's heart went out to him.

"Why didn't you inherit it?"

"I was quite young when we were separated by war. I never saw my father again."

"I am so sorry, Gaereth. How old were you? It must have been a terrible loss for you and your mother."

"They fought together, Jeffrey. They were both killed."

Silence settled on the room as Jeff tried to comprehend the magnitude of Gaereth's loss. So many years alone. No, he corrected himself, so many centuries alone. All the while surrounded by normal people whose comparatively short life spans would make close attachments an agony as they rapidly grew older and died. Jeff searched for words to convey his deep sympathy, but found none that came close.

"It's been hard for you."

The compassion in Jeff's voice led Gaereth to brush a hand across his eyes. There was only one tear, but it was the first in untold years.

"So much has been lost."

After a brief pause to collect himself, Gaereth said in a soft voice, "The forests, Jeffrey. If only you could have seen the forests of Gaul and experienced the joy our people possessed before the Romans came. I will never forget the music, the dancing; how many of us there were."

Plopping down on a bench, Jeff stared at Gaereth as if he were seeing a ghost. "Just how old are you, Grandfather?"

"I hate that word, old."

"Sorry, it was a poor choice." Jeff had to smile at Gaereth's expression. "Let me put it this way: what was the year of your birth."

"I'm not sure. Calendars haven't been around that long."

"No," Jeff said dryly, "only since 46 BC, nearly 2000 years, and a lot farther back than that in China."

"In terms of human history that span amounts to nothing. We did not keep track of time in the sense that modern peoples do." Gaereth looked directly at Jeff, and said, "I will not play

411

word games with you, Grandson. My people, your people, have always been technologically sophisticated, although not in the gadget sense of America. Given some time I could probably hang a number on the year of my birth based on the Julian Calendar, but I'm not going to. Not now."

"Okay, I won't press the issue." Jeff folded his arms and sat back. "How about some hints?"

"Our family always has been a stubborn lot," Gaereth replied with an amused chuckle. "All right, I'm comfortable with giving you a general frame of reference."

Gaereth rubbed his chin, wrinkled his forehead, shifted in his seat, and eventually resorted to counting on his fingers.

"Whoa. It's been awhile since I tried to figure this out," he murmured. "Has it really been that long?" When he put his fingers away and looked up, Gaereth's expression was impossible for Jeff to interpret.

"I was no longer a youth when I led a contingent of Alarai in the running battle to slow down Hannibal. When the time is right, we will search backward from there so you may learn your full heritage."

"Hannibal?" Jeff stared at Gaereth as if he were seeing a ghost. "*The* Hannibal of Carthage?"

"Yes."

"My God. You've lived at least 1,700 years. Hannibal crossed the Alps in the first part of the third century, first millennium. You must have seen Rome at the peak of its expansion!"

"Let's just say I experienced Rome at its peak. If you lived in Gaul, Hannibal was simply the greater of two evils at that moment in history. That was a time when there was no winning for losing."

Jeff jumped to his feet, didn't know what to do with himself, and sat down again.

"Shit. This really has me pumped. Rome! And you must have had some contact with the Greeks when they were dominant."

"Yes I did, and they were an arrogant lot. Although Americans think pretty highly of themselves, Greeks of that period put them to shame. Maybe a lesson there somewhere. Now settle down, Grandson. Run around the block or something."

"If there was a block to run around, I think I would!" Jeff let his breath out in a whuff of air. "Okay, now how did you ever locate my family? The European Diaspora went on for centuries."

"Because I only lost contact during the Napoleonic Wars, and I had to if I wanted to remain sane. How many wars do you imagine our people have been through, Jeff? How many wars can one family go through without being wiped out?"

"No more than one or two. Europe was devastated for several generations following World War II. Some authors believe it never recovered."

"Then what about eleven or twelve wars?"

"That's how many you've been through?"

"Yes."

"How did you. ..." Jeff stared at Gaereth in consternation. "It doesn't seem possible that you survived."

"There have been times when I wished I had not. As a people we were destroyed. Your family is all that remains to me in direct line of descent. It took ten years of sorting through genealogical records across a good share of central Europe before I was able to trace their path of emigration to Odessa, and from there to America."

"I can't imagine what it must have been like."

"It was all I had left to hold onto, Jeff. You are indeed my grandson through your mother's line, and a sword much like this one was described in several records. Regardless of who it once belonged to, this saber was forged in what is now Poland by Alarai artisans, using techniques and technology that are to this day unknown on Earth. Tell me—have you ever nicked the edge or had to sharpen it?"

"Not even a scratch, and I touch up the edge for my own benefit not from need."

"There you have it," Gaereth replied with satisfaction. "You will never dull, notch or break this blade, Grandson, and it will never rust."

Standing up, he pushed the saber's point deep into a thick beam and slowly flexed the blade. When it was nearly bent double, Jeff leaped to his feet.

"Stop! That's not a foil!"

"You need to know what you have, Jeffrey. I would never do this to an ordinary saber. Or this." Gaereth released the haft, and the sword snapped straight with an audible hum.

"That scrollwork on the blade? It's not only decorative." Gaereth carefully examined Jeff's face. "Do you want to take the final step with this sword?"

"What do you mean?"

"While I understand nothing of the technology, I do understand that each sword was designed for a specific person's stature, reach, and so on."

"That was common practice from the Middle Ages on," Jeff said with a shrug.

"Yes it was, but Alarai artisans took it several steps farther." Gaereth frowned. "Damn, how do I describe it? Look, each sword was tuned not only to stature, but in some manner also to the individual's personality. There are words of passage on every Alarai blade that permit it to be reassigned. I have no idea how it works, only that it does—maybe harmonics. The sword is imperishable, humans and Alarai are not."

"I want to take the final step and have the sword reassigned to me, Gaereth. There is nothing I would like better."

The excited and determined look on Jeff's face underscored his words, but Gaereth hesitated.

"It's a serious commitment. The words of passage cannot be revoked unless the sword is voluntarily given to someone else. Should there be a conflict between your behavior and what this saber stands for, it could mean your death. Are you sure?"

Sobered by the severe tone of Gaereth's voice, Jeff thought it over again. "I have never been more serious about anything in my life, Grandfather."

Pulling the saber from the beam with easy strength, Gaereth said, "Hold your hands out. Now, rest the blade on your left, grasp the hilt with your right."

When Jeff had done so, Gaereth closely examined the scrollwork, muttering under his breath as he read it over several times. When he spoke, Gaereth's voice was pitched so low that it seemed to vibrate in the air.

"Berold am I called, hear my creed: honor in truth, justice in honor." Gaereth spoke again, but this time the words shattered into Jeff's mind. "Regeth et mora, num sella egath."

A singing tremor worked up Jeff's arms and through his body until his entire being was saturated with ancient power.

"I am so happy for you," Gaereth said with great emotion. "Now it is truly yours. Jeffrey, my grandson."

Shivering violently, Jeff whispered, "What is the power I feel, Grandfather? Is this, then, magic?"

Gaereth smiled softly and shook his head. "No, not as earth legend reports it. No lightning bolts, no humming or singing. Berold is now forged to what you are, to your mind, body and skill. Never forget Berold's creed, Jeff. I do not understand the power, only that it is compelling."

"It's true. I can feel it."

"As I said, it's a life-long commitment. I must also tell you that only time will reveal the full import of your joining. Whoever this sword was forged for, it became yours in part many years ago and will not be left behind. It was you who put it on that pile of camping gear, even though you don't remember it. You couldn't have left it if you wanted to."

Lost in another world and age, Gaereth fell silent. After a period he shook himself and went to fetch coffee.

Jeff held Berold up to a shaft of sunlight and turned it this way and that, the blade shooting beams of light around the room. When Gaereth returned with two steaming mugs, lopsided smile back in place, they set to discussing strategy.

Carl turned Sam into camp late that afternoon. Capitalizing on the Telling, Halric and several other chieftains had organized a songfest to channel energy away from bloodier competition. When Carl entered, warriors from an entire tribe were in the middle of a song.

He drew Sam to a halt so he could listen better, and thought he had never heard anything so beautiful.

The language was different enough that he missed many words, but those he understood were heavy with autumn's reflection. The men and women were singing in parts, and the refrain wrung his heart. It soared then ebbed in a tempo that reminded him of wind sighing through trees and falling leaves.

The day was getting on. Carl let Sam pick his way toward the central hall while he listened. There was a lot of interesting activity in the craft lodges, but it was the music that held him in thrall.

"Now I know why Jeff loves these people. I am so glad I came. It's good to know what you're fighting for."

Jeff and Gaereth heard someone dismount outside and hurried from the hall to find Carl hitching Sam. Suspecting he was about to be zinged, Carl's expression was ripe with suspicion. He looked Gaereth up and down then stuck his hand out.

"Well. Finally! May I assume, sir, that I am greeting an honest to god Alarai?"

Gaereth laughed and nodded while taking Carl's hand. "A solid assumption, sir. Good to meet you, Carl." Gaereth took Carl's arm and guided him inside the hall. "Before anything else is said, I want you to know the Alarai stand forever diminished for allowing you to be enslaved."

"Forever is a long time, Gaereth," Carl soberly replied. "I don't know that I will ever get over what the Arzaks did to me, but everything else considered, where else would I want to be?" Carl looked around the hall. "Where's the coffee?"

While Gaereth filled mugs, Carl rounded on Jeff with a severe look. "All right. It better be good. What's up. "

"Oh, not much, just this." Jeff handed a book to him.

"A book! A medical book! Oh, shit!" Jeff handed the second and third books to Carl. "Three medical books? I can't believe this!" Carl grabbed Jeff and danced him around the room.

The box of cartridges was appreciated, and two of the pens served to ice the cake. Carl thumbed through the books for most of the evening while Jeff and Gaereth talked. He tried to pay attention to the conversation but failed miserably, much to their amusement.

Toward the tail end of evening, Carl tenderly closed a book and held it up. "These are a big dose of what we left behind on Earth. Although I'm not sure I want to know, what's going on there? How much damage did that quake do?"

"You're right," Gaereth replied with a speculative look at Carl. "You may not want to hear it."

"That bad?"

"Probably worse, Jeff." Gaereth frowned. "Thinking about it now, it seems to me that earthquake in the Northwest set a ripple going that may keep bouncing back and forth across the country until everything is gone."

"It doesn't sound like you're talking about seismology."

Gaereth glanced at Carl. "It's all coming apart, fellows."

"What's left of Seattle?"

"The quake must have raised the bed of Lake Washington eight or ten feet, Jeff."

"Holy shit," Carl said in a horrified whisper, "Lake Washington is huge and right in the middle of the city."

Gaereth nodded grimly. "Exactly. When all that water hit the ship canal, it pretty much gutted what was left of central Seattle. The wave front undermined the medical center and collapsed half of it, destroyed the stadium, turned Fremont and Ballard into mud flats, then took out the waterfront. You can imagine what it did to the bridges across the lake, not to mention everything along the lake shore and the rivers that discharge from it."

He thought he knew the answer, but Jeff took a deep breath and asked, "Downtown?"

"Maybe half the buildings survived the quake. Most of those that did survive are no more than shells. I left Seattle about six weeks after the quake—still no power or water, sewage lines were smashed beyond repair, and typhoid was heading north from Portland."

Gaereth tried to continue but couldn't until he had taken a drink of coffee.

"Rainier corked off."

Carl and Jeff froze while their minds reviewed images of the mountain. Even though it was far south of Seattle, Mt. Rainier was still a key landmark. Carl shifted in his seat, and sighed.

"It erupted."

"It blew up. The top one-third of the mountain is gone."

"But Tacoma! I mean, wasn't there some talk about mud flows?"

"Tacoma is no more. Not as a city."

"It can't just be gone!"

"Doesn't matter what you call it," Gaereth replied with a disconsolate shrug. "One hundred and fifty thousand dead and two-thirds of the city under a sea of mud. Mt. Adams, St. Helens and Baker also erupted. You can take it from there."

"I don't want to take it from there!" Carl jumped to his feet shaking his head violently. "There must be several feet of ash covering Washington and Oregon!"

"At least that, and as far away as Nebraska and Kansas. God help them, it reminded me of one of those post-nuclear war movies. Tacoma was gone, and Seattle looked like it had been nuked."

"And the looters moved in."

"Yes. They didn't even wait for the aftershocks to stop. By the time I left, the National Guard was everywhere and martial law had been imposed. Shoot to kill dusk to dawn curfew, even summary executions."

Carl leaned on the table for support. "God, *damn.*"

"Yeah, it's that bad. The Pacific Northwest is in free-fall. Then I headed east. While I'm no sociologist, that quake seemed to hit the entire country right between the eyes. Things started coming apart almost overnight, but that isn't the worst of it.

"Those volcanoes put so much ash high in the atmosphere that it's going to alter the entire world climate. Earth may be in for an ice age, fellows. You can imagine how many doomsday fanatics that brought out of the woodwork."

"Armageddon. The end of all things."

"Among others. Then there are the militias. I don't think anyone realized how many there were. Iowa is stable, law-abiding state, but even there militia groups were carving it up into spheres of influence.

"Your part of the state seems to be holding its own, Jeff. The farmers got organized early on; hell, they had to! Black marketers were raiding crops, not to mention ordinary thugs and hoarders." Gaereth walked over to the coffee kettle. "I understand some of the Alarai on Skene filled you in, Jeff?"

"They were hard pressed to keep the link open, but did manage to give us a thumbnail sketch about the Alarai and what they expect of us."

"Jeff passed it on to me," Carl added, "and I will admit to being overwhelmed. It seems to me that we have an even chance of turning back the Salchek, but Earth! That's a social and political nightmare. Now, after the earthquake, it's really coming apart and there might be an ice age. How in hell are the three of us supposed to even approach that cluster fuck? It seems preposterous."

"There are other problems that don't help the situation. The translocation machinery is about shot. It's worth your life to use it."

"If that's the case, what's the point of even talking about Earth?"

Gaereth held his arms out wide in a gesture of helpless dedication. "We've got to try, Jeff. As a people, we've been working to keep things together so long that I expect it's in our genes by now. Although most of our technicians have been killed along the way, we still have a few who are good with bailing wire and tape."

"Okay, let's stop and back up a few steps." Jeff took a long drink of spring water to buy some time. He really needed to collect his thoughts. "It seems to me we're putting the cart before the horse. I don't know about you guys, but right now my plate is full enough dealing with the Salchek."

"Here, here. Carl, what are your ideas concerning Rugen? Maybe we ought to put our heads together while we have the chance."

"Yes. I have to head back in the morning. I really can't handle thinking about Seattle and Earth anymore."

Weeks disappeared in a blur of strategy meetings and training exercises with Rugen detachments. A messenger service set up between the Alemanni camp and Rugen could not keep up with demand. When the Salchek arrived it would be finished. Their only remaining communication link with Rugen would be Carl. Jeff considered the problem and consulted with Gaereth.

"In my opinion, one of us has to be in Rugen. I think that someone has to be you. Carl is so tied up with responsibilities that he doesn't have a prayer of stretching himself any farther."

"You're right. I have to go. Not only is Carl overloaded with work, he's into medicine not warfare. You and I understand the

Alemanni and agree on how to use them. In Rugen, I'll be able to squash plans that might lead to disaster."

Gaereth was on his way by the close of the day. The following morning he notified Jeff that the first elements of the Salchek Army had arrived.

Twenty-two

Out of the Blue

Worming to the crest of the hill overlooking Rugen, Jeff removed his hat and raised his head. Tongues of fire licked across crops that were too immature to be harvested, generating a dense cloud of smoke that hung over the valley. The sun, a dark orange ball hanging in the west, seemed heavy with malice.

Turning to the city, he groaned at the sight of people still lined up to get inside.

"There must be a hundred or more, and a lot of them are kids. Wait until the last bloody minute then bring everything you own plus livestock!"

Jeff peered south over Rugen but could see no evidence of Salchek or anything else through the haze. He located Gaereth on the wall near the south gate.

"We've got a bunch of folks lined up at the north gate, Gaereth. The Salchek in sight yet?"

"In spades. Can't see much, though. The smoke's really thick. May be some bad news. From the timber I see them dragging along, it looks like they plan to put together siege engines."

There was little breeze to dissipate the smoke and Jeff was no wiser by nightfall. At least everyone had made it into the city. Instead of returning to the Alemanni camp, he decided to sleep in the forest.

A fresh breeze had blown away most of the smoke when he returned to the observation post at first light. Jeff drew in a deep breath.

"Holy shit there's a lot of them!"

They were spread out around Rugen in a vast semicircle from west to east and teemed like a horde of insects. As he watched, tents that had been salvaged from Rengeld's attack were springing up in enclaves.

No siege engines were visible, but Jeff assumed they were being assembled to the south out of his view. Of more immediate concern, a contingent of soldiers was jogging toward the north aspect of the city. Jeff estimated a thousand troops or more were heading his way.

"There they are!"

Under the audible lash of whips, ten two-wheeled chariots burst from the cloud of dust obscuring the main Salchek camp to the south. The lead chariots were in a dead heat and bounced from side to side as they rushed past the infantry.

"Two-man, four-horse chariots with blades on the hubs. Doesn't come much worse than that. We wouldn't have a chance out in the open and on foot. They might as well be tanks."

Evening was drawing on when he and Balko backed away from the knoll. On the way back to the Alemanni encampment, Cynic and Balko did not engage in their usual give-and-take mental gymnastics. They could not recall such a somber state of mind in their brother.

The charioteers had paraded back and forth a safe distance from the north wall for some time, all the while blowing bugles and shouting what Jeff concluded had to be insults. They maneuvered in elaborate chicanes and figures of eight while sunlight winked from hub blades. It had been a consummate display of skill. That night he held a war council with Halric and Gurthwin.

"We must allow the Salchek a short period to become comfortable, to bend all their attention on Rugen, then we will strike a hard blow. However, we will *never* expose our warriors to their sakkas unless by design. The dark hours, stealth and surprise are our allies. Let us consider what must be done." Another possibility came to mind.

"Who among the warriors in this camp has sufficient merit to lead a first attack? If such a one may be found, I will be freed to accomplish another task of importance."

Jeff mentally reviewed the tribal leaders he had met and worked with during the last few weeks. He could think of only one person who would fill the requirements. Halric and Gurthwin had been going through a similar process. Halric seemed especially grave when he broke the silence.

"There are many mighty warriors among the three thousands of Alemanni in this camp. Yet we know little of their leadership skills. That we will determine in battle. Even as you say, the first attack offers great promise that later may not be recaptured. I would have this honor. Do any here doubt my ability to lead?"

Jeff was equally grave in his answer. "Never have I met a warrior I would rather go into battle with, or a warrior with such skill at leading men. I would have none other."

Gurthwin simply nodded and Jeff turned back to their plan of attack.

"Halric, I wish you to gather a force of 800 warriors to attack the Salchek camped near the north gate. When all is in readiness your force must descend as quietly as wolves, only to spring on the enemy with the coming of dawn. You must hold then seem to retreat, drawing the enemy into the forest.

"There, waiting in concealment, a full thousand warriors will fall on them. If the force that pursues is too great in number to overcome, you must draw them ever deeper into the woodlands where they may be finished at your leisure. But you *must not* remain exposed long enough to allow Salchek sakkas or cavalry to come into play."

"As you know, Jeffrey, as a people we are not given to retreat," Halric said while shaking his head doubtfully.

"And yet this is what I expect of your leadership, what I understand you to be capable of. If we fail of this first task, we fail of our promise as Alemanni and will surely be defeated."

Halric held Jeff's gaze. His expression revealed nothing. Gurthwin was sharply attentive but had no intention of intervening. Halric must decide on his own. Yet so much was at stake.

In an abrupt transition, Halric's features became animated with fierce determination. He raised his fist and shook it.

"No!" The fist came down on the table with a loud boom. "No! This people will not be sundered again, nor will we die in our thousands. I will not be remembered in such a fashion! We shall retreat, even though every head be broken to that end."

"I believe this to be true," Jeff said with a deep sense of satisfaction.

"You may depend on it," Halric replied while attempting to straighten the plank he had cracked with his fist. "Let us attend to your needs. How many warriors do you require?"

"No more than fifty. They will accompany me east in the forest border, then south. I plan to attack and fire the engines the Salchek are building to bring down Rugen's walls. Before we discuss my needs father, let us consider how we are to employ the warriors under your command."

Jeff let Halric run with his end of the plan to see what he would come up with. Later, he had to admit he was impressed with Halric's attention to detail. One element, however, was lacking. The concept of holding a force in reserve was as foreign to Alemanni thinking as that of a tactical retreat. It took awhile for Halric to grasp the logic and common sense of it.

"Your plan to hold the balance of our warriors in 'reserve' is understood." Halric let out an explosive laugh and waved a finger the size of a summer sausage at Jeff. "How you do test me!"

Satisfied that Halric had a solid grip on the tactics and was determined to succeed, Jeff communicated the outline of their plan to Gaereth.

"I like it. Halric will be a steady hand at the wheel. Combined with your raid to the south it ought to be an effective one-two punch yet give the Salchek nothing solid to counterattack."

"How are things shaping up at your end?"

"Looks like quite a bit of the crops were salvaged, Jeff, and we've managed to house all the people who came in from outlying farms. Carl's trying to turn the infirmary into a real hospital and making some progress. As you might expect, Rengeld has the city's defense well in hand. I'll take a close look at the siege engines tomorrow morning."

"How did the city stand up to that parade of sakkas? I only saw ten, but I imagine they were out in force south of the city."

"They were. Rengeld's troops are trained down hard and shrugged it off. The civilians were another matter. They sent a delegation to Imogo."

"Let me guess. A delegation of the wealthy, and fat cat merchants. Arrange a truce, sue for peace, hand Rugen to the Salchek."

"Basically, but don't be so hard on them, Jeff. You should remember that Belstan and Rogelf could easily be included in the category of fat cat merchants if you didn't know them. I can only imagine the stories these folks grew up with. The Salchek Army is one tough organization, and by all accounts was utterly ruthless last time in town."

"How did Imogo deal with it?"

"Imogo is a mercenary's son and a king. He put out a hard line, but his cousins never quit trying to stir a revolt so he hung them."

Jeff did an incredulous mental double take. *"His cousins? He hung them?"*

"All of them, plus three of the fattest cats. Their assets will go into the treasury. This is an absolute monarchy, Jeffrey, not a democracy. It's a time of war and Imogo did what he had to. I find no fault with him."

Silence ensued. Jeff had experienced the authority of Imogo on several occasions. It was both impressive and unsettling. Lese majesty, to trifle with kings, was akin to cutting your own throat. He understood that from an academic viewpoint. The reality was something else—the total absence of judicial process set him back on mental heels.

"Let it simmer, Grandson. We'll talk tomorrow about the siege engines. Zimma sends her love. You're a lucky man, and don't forget it."

The first meeting of the Tribal Congress started out tense. Halric was hard pressed to maintain order as chieftains vied to have their warriors included in the initial assault.

Standing next to Halric, Jeff's temper began to perk when two chieftains leaped to confront each other. Nose to nose, they roared insults back and forth until one of them brandished a battle-ax.

"That's it!"

Jeff thrust himself between the chieftains, put a hand on each of their chests and heaved. One crashed onto a bench, the other was caught on his way down.

"Enough! You will all sit down and be silent!"

He glared them back to their seats, but the atmosphere remained charged with anger and suspicion. Jeff paced back and forth until his temper cooled and the hall was silent.

"This is not a small thing we speak of! *Four* tribes must *quietly* creep down near the enemy in the dark and patiently wait *making no sound* until the sun renews itself. With the sun's first light they must attack, but only when commanded by Halric to do so. Then they must withdraw from battle when bloodlust is at its greatest and flee toward the forest as if defeated.

"Let us examine our hearts! As leaders, you know the spirit of our people and how difficult this will be for them. And yet, if we are to be victorious this is what must happen.

"Now, what do I see? You are ready to come to blows with each other! And you are chieftains! Leaders! What will happen with your villagers when they must work together in battle?

"Are you concerned there are not enough Salchek to do battle with? We are three thousand, they are nine thousand!"

Their war leader had a point, and the chieftains knew it. After some shifting of feet they grumbled apologies back and forth. Although half-hearted, they were apologies.

Also, they decided, three-to-one odds were quite respectable. It appeared there were enough of the enemy to go around. Sitting back, they listened attentively.

Jeff pounded away at the need for absolute obedience to Halric's commands, then turned the floor over to him. Jeff's tension gradually drained away as Halric moved into the breech and took charge.

When tactics were settled, deployment of various contingents agreed on and timing understood, Halric described Jeff's mission and the type of warriors he needed. Before closing the meeting, he stood silently until he had the chieftains' undivided attention.

"My brothers and sisters, our destiny beckons. In this battle we will come to understand whether we fight as Alemanni or as tribes. Our war leader has brought us opportunity to gain honor in battle, honor that was denied our fathers. Yet we fight for much more—we fight for our homeland. Let us remember the Telling and not die in our thousands. Your warriors must be made to understand their place and duties. If you fail of this task, they will never see their homes again."

Afternoon shadows had cooled the air when the chieftains filed out of the meeting hall. The man and woman who had nearly come to blows walked with their heads close together, voices hushed and urgent as they conversed.

Other chieftains dispersed shaking their heads as they considered all that had been asked of them. They had gone into the hall thinking only about winning a place in battle, but come out thinking about tactics. Gaereth contacted Jeff later that afternoon.

"From what can be seen, it appears that seven siege machines are under construction. They must be fired before construction is complete. Right now they lie near the periphery of Salchek forces in order to have easy access to the forest and timber. It must be assumed that upon completion they will be wheeled near the walls. Rengeld estimates this will occur in no more than four days."

"He's familiar with siege engines? They're high-tech around here."

"Intimately familiar. I am really impressed by that man, Jeff. From what I've seen so far, Rengeld ranks right up there with the best military minds I've encountered."

"Considering the number of campaigns you've been through, and the men who have commanded them, that's one hell of a compliment."

"And fully intended. Rengeld sees an opportunity developing that he can't pass up. He plans to sally his cavalry corps through the south gate when the engines are fully involved by fire. What do you think?"

"That's his entire cavalry force, five hundred troopers, and one hell of a bold plan. I like it. Hit them hard with everything you have when they least expect it. I think we can count on Rengeld to hold his effort until the Salchek are totally focused on putting out the fires, or to scratch the mission if it falls apart. Timing is going to be our biggest problem. Here's what I have in mind..."

The final disposition of forces was ironed out by the end of the next day. Jeff's unit was also taking shape as warriors reported in. His relief knew no bounds when they all proved to be well seasoned.

"Next, please."

Jeff had been screening applicants for some time. He looked up from scribbling notes and studied a group of three flaxen-haired women. They resembled each other so closely that the effect was stunning.

When Jeff stood up to greet them his eyes were not even with their chins. They seemed amused that he was so short. Jeff had encountered that response so many times it no longer bothered him.

He interviewed them and learned the women were first cousins from related tribes. After they had been inducted into his unit, one of them waited until she could speak privately. She was somewhat taller than the other two, reminding Jeff that her name was Helwin.

"Magda sends greetings. She could not attend this gathering, counting herself too great with child."

Time staggered into slow motion. Magda pregnant? Could the child be his? That possibility had never entered his mind when he was in Fastholm. How could it be possible? Magda likely wasn't human. As Jeff counted months his consternation rapidly mounted.

If the Alemanni gestation period was similar to that of terran females, Magda might well have conceived during his stay in Fastholm. A range of emotions gripped him, varying from exhilaration to guilt. She had shown no interest in other men while he was there.

"Magda fares well?"

"Her strength and spirit were good when we departed. She was quite large although still some months from her time, thus loathe to risk the journey. The decision to remain behind was most difficult to endure, for Magda counts the child as yours and wished to share her joy." Helwin bowed. "You must know she is envied by all the village women."

Jeff's thoughts were elsewhere while organizing his troop. What would Zimma say? Even if he were not the father, would that make any difference in her mind? She had accepted Magda as family, but would she accept this? From what she had earlier said, yes. From everything he knew and had experienced on Earth, no.

Guilt was his constant companion throughout the day. He was not on Earth, the customs and people were not of Earth. He knew that. In meeting Gaereth he had experienced insights that profoundly underscored that fact. And yet he fought a losing battle against twenty-seven years of indoctrination. Helwin's announcement had caught him totally by surprise and blown him back to Earth.

That evening, seated in a chair, he stared into the fire that always burned in the meeting hall. Gurthwin had to shake him in order to get his attention after the hall emptied.

"You must share what has so clearly come to possess your mind this day. What cloud is it that has descended on your spirit, Jeffrey?"

"One of personal responsibility and fealty. Will you hear what I learned this day?"

"If you would speak your heart without presumption, Jeffrey."

"I shall without stint."

Jeff related what he had learned from Helwin. As required by Gurthwin, he let each word be tested by his heart and not his head. Considering his academic background, it was one of the hardest things he had ever done. Prompted by Gurthwin, Jeff backtracked to his stay at Fastholm.

"And so you could not leave. Were defeated."

"I have never before despised my very being."

As he talked and remembered how full of love and care Magda had been, Jeff calmed down. So quiet and steady in her love. So healing. Jeff turned his head away from Gurthwin as tears welled up and rolled down his cheeks.

"They are but honest messengers from your spirit, Jeffrey. Look at me." It was hard, but he did.

"I love Magda with all my heart, Gurthwin. What does this say about my steadfastness in the very thing I earlier professed? To love and cherish Zimma? And yet, searching my heart, I find that I do without reservation. She is accepting of Magda and wishes for her to join us in family, yet I am once again torn by old customs that insist I have betrayed Zimma. Customs that tell me I cannot love two women without betraying both."

"It is abundantly clear you have not won release from your home of origin."

"No I have not, and fear this may never occur. I find that still I am consumed by my former homeland and its ways. On Earth, in America, nothing is freely offered—all things demand purchase. Most especially love and caring.

"There, love between man and woman too often is measured out or withheld day to day in reward or punishment. To me, it seemed no more than a collection of rules that changed on a whim. Seldom could one determine why love was withheld, and thus its offering could only be suspect."

"And life between man and woman perpetually balances on the edge of rejection."

"That has been my experience. You never know, day to day. In the end, I have found it most difficult to retain belief that such love as has been given by Zimma and Magda would not be measured out in like fashion."

"Has their love been measured out?"

"Never. It is not the nature of either woman. Their love is a wellspring, and their words those of true sincerity."

"Just so. And what do you conclude from this?"

"That I have just climbed out of a deep hole!" Jeff laughed in relief. "Thank you, Gurthwin. I really needed to hear myself say those words, true sincerity. Zimma and Magda are wonderful women who live what they speak. I really want that child to be mine! Damn, I can hardly wait until I see them!"

"Your coming to us was timely, perhaps only in time."

"That is surely truth, and I'm afraid there are further battles to wage in this arena. Earth could not be more different than Aketti."

"Still, I have it on good account that matters will turn out well."

Chuckling under his breath, Gurthwin levered himself upright and headed for bed.

Jeff emerged from his lodge whistling a bright tune. "What a relief to be out from under that load! I can't believe it! I'm going to be a father!" He had overslept and jogged toward the meeting hall to attend the final war conference.

The meeting was intended only to reaffirm plans. The fact that it proved to be short bolstered Jeff's confidence. He and his band left camp by the middle of the morning since they had a long forest trek to complete by nightfall. Given the distance, he had scrounged enough horses to mount everyone.

They nearly ran into a crew of Salchek conscripts felling timber along the way, but reached their jump-off spot without being discovered.

It was well after dark when Jeff led his troops out of the woods some miles south of Rugen. Along the way, Balko casually remarked that at least two packs of wolves loosely related to Balthazar's were going to join the Alemanni ambush.

Jeff could tell there was more to it than that. Rather than buy into a setup, he resolved to wait for the other shoe to drop. Balko's association with Cynic paid off and Jeff was the first one to break.

"Yes, and?..."

Balko's jaws parted in a vast wolf grin. *"The pack led by the one you term 'Balthazar' awaits us a short distance from here."*

"Let me guess, wolf-brother. You just happened to mention what we were up to tonight and sort of invited them, right?"

"Would you have it otherwise?" Balko replied, good humor bubbling over into the thought.

Jeff joined the mental laughter and could only agree that, no, he wouldn't have it any other way. It was a great relief to know that Balthazar's ringers would be working with him again and he dropped back to warn the troops. When the moment came and they encountered the dim group of patiently waiting wolves, Jeff heard only a few startled oaths.

With wolves scouting the way, Salchek outposts they encountered never had a chance. When they could penetrate no deeper without risking their line of retreat, Jeff signaled the troop to dismount by doing so. The disgruntled warriors who had drawn short straws and the job of tending the remuda collected horses as troopers climbed down.

Taking the twenty-five warrior reserve force aside, Jeff made sure they understood their responsibilities. When he was satisfied they did, he and Balko hunkered down with Balthazar and Heideth to wait it out.

Somewhere past midnight, Jeff sought and found Gaereth keeping vigil on the south battlements.

"We're jumping off now. Probably take half an hour or so to sneak in."

"Rengeld is ready to roll, and Gurthwin reports that all is well with Halric's command. Good fortune be with you."

Jeff gathered his team of twenty-one warriors and moved out. Three were assigned to each engine: two to soak them with oil and turpentine, one to act as sentry. Wolves would accompany each unit to silence pickets.

If a strong guard was mounted around the siege machinery, Jeff figured they were in deep trouble. He was counting on Salchek ignorance of forces outside city walls and a common tendency to undervalue partially completed items to carry the day.

Visible only as a blur, Balko crept along in a stalking half-crouch several feet ahead of Jeff. Heideth and Balthazar were farther ahead on the point with the rest of the pack patrolling on either side of the column. The warriors followed in Jeff's footsteps by threes.

Five paces and stop to listen, five more. Step by step they penetrated the Salchek perimeter, the night pitch black from overcast.

They had eliminated two sentries when Jeff heard a loud grunt behind him followed by a clank. Shit! One of them must have tripped! Heart racing, Jeff froze in place. A voice suddenly pierced the darkness. It seemed to come from only feet away.

"You hear that, Zed?"

"Don't hear nothing."

Jeff jumped as something shattered, followed by a thump that sounded like a boot hitting flesh.

"I catch you drinkin' again, and yere gone to see the man."

Muttered curses and whines tapered off to silence. Jeff waited for seemingly endless minutes, every sense tuned to the maximum. Nothing more. Breathing deep and exhaling slowly, he sent a thought to Balthazar and Heideth.

"These guards must not give warning."

Something hit the ground and thrashed for a moment. Another brief commotion before all was silent again. The advance continued. Jeff nearly stumbled over a crumpled shape that lay in his path. A few steps more and a greater darkness loomed out of the night.

About time, Jeff thought with great relief. That has to be one of the engines. When they were closer he made out the shape of a large trebuchet. The frame appeared to be complete. Peering intently along the thirty-foot arm projecting vertically into the night sky, he got the impression that the basket had not been installed. Jeff gave the dispersal order.

Led by a pair of wolves, teams crept off in search of the remaining engines. The wolves were tense with anticipation. The attack on the Astholf Army had been fun, but this was a high stakes game much like a stalk. There was nothing they enjoyed more.

It was the first time Jeff had monitored a full pack on the hunt. He was amazed at the continual flow of data between the groups as they dispersed. Each pair of wolves knew precisely where the other pairs were, guard positions were noted and sightings of siege engines passed around.

While listening in, Jeff put his own team to work. Helwin shinnied up the swing arm and trickled turpentine down the wood while others soaked the base.

One by one, five wolf pairs checked in. The sixth pair reported heavy guard activity. They were stymied for a period before finding a way to sneak in. Balthazar had been coordinating the operation.

"All are in position, wolf-brother."

Jeff gave the command to strike fire in a harsh whisper. The other teams had been ordered to wait until they saw clear evidence of fire. Click, click, he heard flint strike steel, followed by a cascade of sparks and small flame. Seconds later the turpentine took off with a rush. Shortly, he saw other fires beginning to flare.

Jeff gathered his crew with urgent whispers. "Hold fast. We must stand firm until the flames cannot be quenched."

Alarmed shouts rang out. Within moments, dim forms could be seen racing toward them in the growing firelight. Shortly, alarmed cries sounded from every quarter, shrill bugle calls split the air, and somewhere a mighty drum began pounding out its call to battle.

Jeff drew Berold with a dry rasp, a thrill shooting up his arm as he did so. Its weight seemed as nothing. A Salchek raced up with his eyes fixed on flames that had raced to the top of the trebuchet. Jeff ran him through, whirled to parry a blow from another Salchek and thrust under the man's guard. He yanked the saber out and ducked away as two more leaped at him with swords in motion.

The soldiers were skilled swordsmen. Jeff had his hands full defending himself while trying to move away from the blistering heat on his back. Desperate to win free before more piled on, Jeff double-feinted, leaped between his opponents and spun. He felled one man, locked guards with the other and slammed the hilt of his sword against the Salchek's head.

One look at the trebuchet convinced Jeff that nothing could put it out. It was engulfed in flames.

"Now! We must leave!" Rounding up his crew, they slipped away.

Groups of conscripts carrying buckets of water rushed by cursing and pointing. Many were partially dressed and none were carrying weapons. They didn't even seem to be aware of Jeff's small unit in their frenzy to get at the fire.

Balko crouched along in front, the rest of the unit following his lead as he darted to one side or the other dodging the larger groups. On several occasions it was a mad scramble to avoid being run over.

They were nearly out of it when Balko sprinted straight ahead instead of dodging. Jeff saw why in a flash.

"Form up!"

The words were barely out when they were fighting back to back, assaulted from all sides by a fully dressed and armed Salchek unit. Sword blows rang out and blades glinted red in the towering ring of fire as Jeff and his unit fought their way toward the horses. Balko charged into the middle of the Salchek and created so much havoc they could not launch a concerted attack.

Worried not at all by the odds, Jeff's warriors were singing battle songs. They had finally found action worthy of the name. The bass drum's sullen pounding never slackened, penetrating through the sounds of battle and crackling fire. It wouldn't be long before more Salchek found them.

Got to get out of this or we're finished, Jeff thought as he parried a blow. He yanked the Ruger out, aimed into the thickest press of Salchek and fired six crashing rounds. As bodies crumpled, the Salchek fell back in shocked disarray.

"Run for it!"

They hadn't gone far when the Salchek unit was on them again. Then it was lunge forward three steps beating out thrust and parry, only to skip back five and do it again. They were about to be overrun when the Alemanni reserve force burst onto the scene shouting for blood.

With the odds reversed, the Salchek were destroyed in a furious exchange. Jeff did a quick head count. The warriors from his team were all present. Thank God. Now if only the other teams made it out.

When they arrived at the jump-off base and he could really take stock, Jeff's heart did a stutter-step. Balko was walking on three legs. Jeff sagged with relief when he found a flesh wound that was more lengthy than deep.

His crew piled onto their horses as ordered and spurred off toward the rendezvous point in the forest. Turning to count how many horses were left, Jeff bumped into Helwin.

"What are you doing here? You should have left with the rest."

A startlingly white grin split Helwin's soot-blackened face. "Magda has the right of it. It seems that someone must insure that you do not fall over your own feet!"

With a fatalistic shrug, Jeff counted horses. Over half were gone. Several teams of Alemanni came running while he counted, two warriors staggering as they carried a third.

Urging them and the reserve force on their way, Jeff trotted back into the Salchek perimeter accompanied by Balko. Several teams were still missing. A rising bugle call pierced through the whistle of fires, its tenor note clear and strident.

"That's got to be Rengeld. He must be starting his sortie. Shit! Where are the rest of those bozos?"

A tremendous shout hammered at his ears and the ground trembled, battered by the rolling thunder of two thousand hooves.

"Time to get out of here!"

He had not taken many steps when a clashing roar washed over him as Rugen's cavalry smashed into the Salchek. Jeff skidded to a halt where the horses were picketed and counted saddles again. Eight remained, not counting Cynic. A faint but urgent cry burned through the noise of battle.

"Captain! Assist me!"

"Where did that come from?" Jeff tensed and stared in what he thought was the right direction. "That sounded like Helwin! What the hell is she doing out there?"

A choking cloud of dust from the cavalry action rolled over him, reducing the firelight to an orange-red blur.

"Screw it!" Jeff took off in the direction of the call.

Although running on three legs, Balko was out in front as usual. A clanging of swords rang out nearby. Balko dug into a turn on all fours and raced out of sight.

Jeff called on a new shot of adrenaline and tore after him. Dim forms locked in combat took shape while another thrashed on the ground with what looked to be a demon at its throat.

"There she is!"

Helwin was holding up a wounded comrade while trying to hold off two assailants. Berold moved in a sullen flash of dull orange. Wrenching it out of the Salchek's chest, teeth bared in a snarl, Jeff whirled on the remaining Salchek. He was on the ground. Balko shook him a last time and released his jaws.

The wounded warrior slipped from Helwin's grip and slumped to the ground. Helwin was so spent she could do no more than gasp for breath. Jeff got the man to his feet, sent Balko ahead to find the way, and they staggered off toward the horses.

"Are you wounded, Helwin?"

"No, Captain, but we must leave soon."

"That's not quick enough. If we're caught in the cavalry battle, we're dead!"

The sounds of battle seemed more distant when they located their horses and the picket guards. The wounded trooper proved able to sit a horse when Helwin boosted him into the saddle.

"That's it, we're out of here. Mount up!"

Warriors were reeling from fatigue when they made it back to camp, and not only from the raid. The forest was alive with Salchek and Alemanni units locked in battle or looking for one another.

On one occasion they had been forced to intervene in a battalion-sized brawl in order to rescue an Alemanni unit on the verge of being annihilated. Jeff was desperate to find Gurthwin and get a situation report on the battle.

Inside the compound, all was confusion. Individuals and groups of blood-covered warriors staggered out of the forest, even as fresh contingents pulled up from the reserve force headed out double-time singing battle songs. Warriors called for assistance while carrying wounded comrades to the first aid station, where cries of agony under the knife rose above everything.

Dismissing the troops, Jeff wearily climbed down from Cynic in front of the meeting hall only to bounce off Helwin again. Too tired to argue, he gestured for her to follow him inside since he knew she would anyway.

Gurthwin was talking with a chieftain, so Jeff collapsed onto a bench and Helwin did likewise. He pointed a grimy finger at her.

"You want to make sure I don't fall over my own feet, eh? Good. You are now my aide-de-camp. That means you get to do all the dirty work."

Helwin was leaning back with elbows resting on the trestle table. Too tired for words, she grinned lopsidedly and raised an arm in acknowledgment.

When the chieftain left, Jeff gave Gurthwin a chance to take a drink of water before moving to his table. Helwin was uncertain whether she should do the same.

"Join us, Helwin. From now on, wherever I go, you go." Jeff waved a hand vaguely in Helwin's direction as she sat down. "Meet Helwin, my new self-appointed aide. How do matters fare?"

Gurthwin smiled briefly and poured tankards of water for each of them. "What I have heard to this time is incomplete, but perhaps enough to draw some conclusions from. As we hoped, Halric's attack achieved complete surprise. The Salchek response, however, was most vigorous and in larger force than we had anticipated. Thus Halric's retreat was more real than deceptive."

Jeff was so upset he fell back on English. "But they did make it to the forest, right?"

While teaching Jeff the Alemanni tongue, Gurthwin had picked up English. "Be at rest. Yes, they did succeed in winning the forest."

"Thank God!"

"Indeed, let us thank the gods. I believe the Salchek are furious to offset the humiliating losses they experienced on the grasslands and seek to destroy Halric. Although it is not clear how many soldiers the Salchek have committed to this point, I believe it to be in excess of four thousands."

"In excess? Jesus!"

Gurthwin sat up and stared at Jeff. "I have come to understand only a small portion of this man's life and works from our talks, but enough that I will not tolerate hearing his name used in this fashion."

Jeff felt like he had been slapped in the face, but bowed. "I will not do so again. Please forgive me."

"You are tired, overwrought, and I do, but never assume that such usage goes unheard." Gurthwin settled his elbows back on the table.

"The second force of warriors that lay in waiting fell on the Salchek to good effect, yet still our numbers were too few. It has been a difficult day, Jeffrey. Throughout the balance of the morning the enemy commander has continued to push new soldiers into the fray, forcing Halric to draw heavily on those held in reserve. Our plan has succeeded beyond expectation. I fear the battle is in question."

"How many remain in reserve?"

Consulting a scrap of parchment, Gurthwin muttered, "Two hundreds remain in camp."

"That's the same as nothing! All of them must be sent out at once. Have the wolves come?"

Gurthwin's expression brightened at once. "Indeed they have. Again the reports are undoubtedly misleading, but a number of packs appear to have joined our effort. Reports of their ferocity in battle have greatly strengthened our warriors, and must be sowing terror among the enemy."

Jeff turned to Helwin. "Rather than my aide-de-camp, I'm appointing you lieutenant. Take charge of our unit, demonstrate leadership, and it's yours to keep. Understood?"

Tired though she was, Helwin jumped to her feet. "I will not fail you, Captain!"

"You have my confidence. Assemble those who are fit from our night's work. We leave for the battle at once. Insure that all are well-mounted and have provisions for one night."

Helwin ran from the hall with a wide grin on her face.

Jeff watched her go with a weary shake of his head. "Ah, youth."

Gurthwin was pouring a tankard of water. At Jeff's comment, he started shaking so hard that water splashed all over the table.

"And you barely into manhood to speak of youth!"

He thumped the jug down, spilling more, and broke into rasping laughter. Bending a sour look on Gurthwin, Jeff poured them both a round and had to smile himself.

When he felt able to walk without the risk of tripping over a crack in the floor, Jeff left to join Helwin.

An hour or so later he inspected the forty warriors assembled. The troops were hollow-eyed, but also exchanging war stories and kidding each other. This bunch still has some fight left in them, Jeff thought with approval.

"We will work together much as we did while returning to camp. You have learned something of mounted warfare, now you will learn more. Any warrior who leaves to pursue his own course will no longer be welcome." Jeff waved Helwin forward. "I have appointed Helwin to be your lieutenant. Her commands are mine."

Jeff wasn't sure what to make of the silence that followed his announcement. However, there was work to be done and he mounted up. Helwin would take charge or he would find someone else.

"Move them out, Lieutenant."

Those were familiar words to Cynic, and he trotted toward the access road. Jeff did not look back but heard Helwin call out commands. Shortly the troop closed up behind. Balko absolutely refused to be left in camp because of his wound and ranged ahead.

They were moving cautiously through a thick stand of trees when Balko called an eager warning. Jeff halted the troop and eased Cynic ahead until the trees thinned. Thirty or forty Salchek were moving laterally in light brush and trees.

There they are, he thought, and here we go. Good thing they aren't mounted. This bunch is not ready to take on a cavalry unit.

There was no room or time to array his troop for a proper charge. Jeff pulled his sword and held it up. He heard an immediate rustle of weapons. Now! Jeff let his sword fall, thumped Cynic with his heels and bellowed a war cry.

The troop crashed out of the trees and fell on the Salchek foot soldiers like thunder, riding them down before turning to finish the job with swords and spears. When the skirmish was finished, Jeff collected his unit.

"Any questions? No?" He eyed them silently for a moment. "You cavalry or foot?"

The term cavalry was new to the Alemanni, but they had it figured out. The troop roared, "Cavalry!"

Jeff nodded and nudged Cynic into motion.

Throughout the afternoon and well into a late summer evening, they fought the Salchek. Jeff tried to locate Halric but failed, the melee swirling through the forest in a confused series of small-unit engagements.

Time and again they aided Alemanni forces that were outnumbered and made the difference, then moved on. They ambushed Salchek forces and destroyed them, only to be taken by surprise and nearly overwhelmed.

By late dusk they were unable to locate more of the enemy in spite of Balko's determined efforts. Jeff moved his troop into a thick stand of trees and had them dismount. Several of those that had been wounded slipped from their saddles and fell to the ground. Others hurried to help but could hardly walk. Ten warriors had died in battle, the rest were nearing the end of their strength.

Jeff walked far enough away so he could listen. The forest was silent except for the occasional birdcall.

"That's it. One way or the other, it's done."

Returning to the troop, Jeff waved Helwin over. "We're going to camp here for the night. That means you have to set up what's called a duty roster. Assign groups of four to guard duty, and replace them every three hours with another group. You can figure it out."

Helwin nodded wearily. "Yes, sir."

When she had made her decisions, Helwin gathered the troop around her and called out assignments. Angry protests rang out at once and a warrior pushed through the crowd to confront Helwin.

It was Elke. Jeff remembered her name because he had been plagued all day by her refusal to stay with the unit. She was the only trooper he planned to separate. While shorter than Helwin, Elke was built like a power lifter. Jeff backed away and watched to see what would develop.

"You will give no commands to *me*." Elke moved closer until she was nose to nose with Helwin. "I will fight and rest as I choose. Go lick your mother's pap."

Elke was from a neighboring village, some years older, and had bullied Helwin at every meeting since she was a girl. Helwin was undecided for only a moment. It had been a very long day. She brought her left fist up and around with every bit of force left in her shoulder. It landed on the side of Elke's face with a sharp crack that sounded like wood hitting wood.

Spit flew, Elke's head swiveled on her shoulders, and she crumpled to the ground. Helwin winced and shook her hand, but did so while calling out the rest of the assignments

Holy shit! Jeff thought. I've seen that left cross before! She most certainly *is* related to Magda.

When Helwin was through handing out guard duty, she recalled something Jeff was prone to shout.

"Dismissed!"

This is it, Jeff thought. Either it flies or it doesn't.

No one said a word. The first shift picked up weapons and left to take up their watch. At that moment Jeff knew his unit had a top gun.

Chilled by the night air, Jeff awoke early and rolled out of his blankets. He immediately stumbled over Helwin, who was bedded down close by. One step and he nearly fell over Balko curled up at his feet.

"Damnation!"

Helwin looked up, bleary-eyed.

"Let's get them on their feet and fed, Lieutenant."

Breakfast consisted of no more than cold venison, and it wasn't long before the troop was saddled up. It took Jeff some time to get oriented, and a longer period of cautious travel before he was convinced the battle was indeed over. He had no idea who had prevailed. It was entirely possible that neither side had. They entered camp ready for trouble.

Even though the day was well along, all was quiet. Smoke from numerous campfires coiled lazily into a clear sky, and walkways were deserted except for the occasional warrior moving about on an urgent mission. The noise and clamor were gone as exhausted survivors slept the day away.

"At least the camp was not overrun," Jeff muttered with relief. He called a halt at the meeting hall. "You are warriors all. I am proud to be your commander. This unit will continue. All who wish to remain a part of it must speak with Lieutenant Helwin. Now it is time for rest and food."

After dismissal the entire troop immediately clustered around Helwin. Shamefaced but determined, Elke elbowed her way to the front. Helwin glanced at Jeff for direction. He did no more than indicate it was her decision.

When Helwin accepted Elke by clasping arms, Jeff nodded agreement. Elke had insisted on standing the last two watches of the night and had stuck to the unit like glue all morning.

Entering the hall, Jeff was relieved to see Halric slumped over a table on his elbows conferring with Gurthwin. That was a good sign they had prevailed or at least come out even. He had a bandage wrapped around his head, but otherwise seemed uninjured. Halric smile hugely when he spotted Jeff.

"Such a battle, Jeffrey! All day we fought and slew them until our arms were like stone. This is a battle to tell my grandchildren of, and to recall around many a winter's fire."

Jeff sat down and accepted a mug of coffee. "Yes. It was a near thing."

"Always were our numbers too few," Halric agreed with a quick jerk of his head, "yet still we overmastered them. We were not long in the forest before we became scattered, as did the Salchek. Many small battles were fiercely contested until by eventime there were few of the enemy to be found. It is my belief that by nightfall we were indeed Alemanni, for tribes became intermixed and fought together as brothers and sisters."

"Were you able to determine how many warriors the Salchek committed to battle?"

"I would not venture to guess, Jeffrey. All was chaos."

"It was that. We'll likely never know. What of our wounded and dead?"

"A count is being taken," Halric somberly replied. "I believe the final tally will number three hundred dead and another eight hundred of wounded. Most of those who fell were lost on the field by the gate, for there the Salchek could bring their numbers to bear on us most cruelly. Withdraw we did, or all would have been lost at the outset."

In spite of his sorrow at the deaths, Jeff was relieved. He had expected twice the casualties reported. They still had an effective fighting force.

Later, Halric and Jeff visited the infirmary to give what comfort they could. Following that they made a round of the tribal enclaves to spread well-deserved congratulations. The sun was nearly gone before they found time to eat.

Halric nearly fell asleep at the table and staggered off to get some sleep. Jeff hung on in order to contact Gaereth, and found him preparing for bed as well.

"That was quite a show your boys and girls put on, Jeff. I was watching from the south wall when the siege engines started lighting up. From what I could see, the Salchek couldn't figure out where the attack was coming from and didn't know which way to turn."

"After the engines lit up, we weren't sure which way to turn ourselves. Rengeld's cavalry charge really stirred things up, but good."

"You should have seen it from up on the south wall! The Salchek were totally unprepared when Rengeld hit them. I have to tell you it was the most awful and moving thing I have seen for several centuries. Our cavalry must have ridden down two or three hundred Salchek before they even got into the fighting. I would be willing to bet the Salchek lost six hundred effectives at a minimum." Concern suddenly colored Gaereth thoughts. *"How did Halric's force do? From what I heard, they took an awful pasting down on the plain."*

Jeff reviewed the battle and his assessment of the outcome. Gaereth gave the mental equivalent of a whistle of admiration.

"That had to really hurt the Salchek, and not only in men lost. What a morale buster, and the second one at that! They're never going to know what happened in the forest and are likely to seriously overestimate the number of Alemanni involved."

"That's what we think up here."

"You feel like you are about to pass out, Jeff. Go get some sleep, and let's chew over our next moves for a day or so before talking again."

Jeff fell onto his cot, clothes and all. At some point during the night he was vaguely aware of something tugging on his boots and clothing.

He got up early in the afternoon with such a ravenous appetite that he trotted to the mess hall. While inhaling food Jeff tried to figure out who had undressed him, not to mention why Balko had not awakened him.

Warming his hands around a mug of coffee, it took some time to find the ambition to search out Halric and Gurthwin. Feeling a level of fatigue that reminded him of his northern journey, Jeff set off for the meeting hall.

Helwin was waiting in front of the building leaning against a hitching post. She looked so fit and ready that Jeff felt envious. Nearby, Balko had found a spot of shade to his liking and was comfortably sprawled out.

"Are you well-rested, Captain?"

"Better than I would have been. You undressed me, didn't you."

"It is my duty to look after the welfare of my captain." Helwin's lips suggested a smile. "Does a woman removing your clothing bother you?"

"No, it does not," Jeff replied, returning her smile. "One of the finer things of life. My thanks for your assistance."

They walked around the compound looking for Halric.

"What is the condition of our warriors?"

"The wounded are resting, Captain, and I believe most will fully recover. Others have taken the opportunity to speak freely with their kin."

"I can only imagine the war stories they've been spreading."

"Yes sir. On my way to our meeting this morning, warriors eager to join our unit detained me at every turn. Some were familiar, many were not. Could we not contrive to form another such unit or enlarge the first?"

"It's a good idea, and we might do so after replacing warriors lost to us in battle."

Jeff stopped so he could face Helwin. She had to look down to meet his eyes but no longer thought of him as short or undernourished.

"Our task is not going to be easy, Lieutenant. From what you said, interest runs high. There are fifty tribes in this camp. What does that mean?"

"Yes sir, I see the difficulty. We must select warriors from every tribe or risk inciting jealousy."

"God forbid. We simply cannot favor one village over another. On the other hand, we will not resort to appeasement."

"We must select only true warriors."

"Or pay the price in battle. It's going to be a delicate task. That said, if many good men and women come forward we will compose a second unit." Jeff looked pointedly at Helwin. "In light of our conversation, how would you go about selecting warriors?"

They had plenty of time to discuss her ideas, for Halric was nowhere to be found. It turned out he had gone to a newly established outpost near Rugen.

As the day passed, Jeff became increasingly satisfied with Helwin's appointment. She was quick of mind and able to grasp, develop, and run with ideas totally new in her experience.

Unusually tall even for an Alemanni woman, maybe six feet seven, she had startlingly blue eyes and appeared to be eighteen or nineteen years old. Helwin's figure reminded Jeff of Magda's, if fuller.

They were about to go separate ways when Jeff's curiosity got the better of him. "In what fashion are you related to Magda?"

Helwin wrinkled up her brow as she figured it out. "We are not of the same village.... Yes. Magda is my father's mother's sister's husband's niece's daughter."

"Well, that certainly clarifies matters!"

Jeff noticed a crisp chilliness to the air as he washed up next morning. Fall was just around the corner. He counted weeks and concluded that it must be the equivalent of early September. *And that means,* he thought with surprise, *that I've been on Aketti for a year and a half. Can that be right?* Jeff knew it was and felt considerably sobered by the realization.

He smoothed his hair in preparation for a working breakfast in the meeting hall. Along the way, Helwin joined him. Halric was relaxing with a mug of herbal tea by the fireplace and waved them over.

"The Salchek are not eager to be taken by surprise again, Jeffrey. They are delving deep to throw up mounds of dirt and rock. And the soldiers! I judge they have doubled them around the north gate!" Halric rumbled with pleasure as he remembered the battle. "I am now fully convinced the Salchek will not attempt to seek us out in the forest."

The kettle of gruel simmering in the fireplace drew Jeff like a magnet. He filled a wooden bowl for Helwin and dished another for himself.

"How far are their fortifications from the nearest point we might approach without detection?"

Frowning in thought, Halric replied with a figure that Jeff interpreted as around two hundred yards.

"That is a distance our best archers might reach with the new bows, do you not agree?"

Halric's grin would have done credit to a wolf. "Yes, Jeffrey, I believe our archers could do this!"

"We must never allow them rest, Halric. The Salchek must always go to sleep fearing they will never awaken, fearing that a horde of Alemanni will descend like the wrath of ancient gods. I want them to tremble in their burrows waiting for an attack that never comes where they prepare for it to fall. Instruct the archers to mark off the distance their arrows must fly. When we are sure the distance is not too great, we will plan. This is how we will overcome the Salchek. Do you perceive the method I am suggesting?" Halric looked doubtful.

"We must torment them. March and countermarch, stinging from all directions, but never, never accepting a challenge where they might crush us. You must not forget what happened in front of Rugen's north gate."

"I shall not. The battle was nearly lost at the outset."

"They will never have such opportunity again. To accomplish our goal of tormenting the Salchek, we will form our warriors into more effective units."

"There is much talk about your cavalry troop."

"So I understand from Helwin. I believe there is much talk because we were successful."

Jeff thought about sending Helwin off to work on troop selection but decided she needed to gain knowledge of military organization as much as Halric. Jeff laboriously and minutely described what he could remember of brigade organization from his studies.

"...So, then, yours will be Headquarters Company, and the rest of the warriors will be divided into regiments under their own captains and lieutenants. If possible, include members of two or three tribes in each regiment to insure that they continue to work together."

"Perhaps from unrelated tribes?"

"As far as possible, although we must avoid mixing tribes that have not overcome their hostility to one another."

"I will consult with tribal leaders."

"That's the way to do it. The Tribal Congress is a perfect setting." Jeff paused to consider. "I would like you to gather the archers from every tribe to form what is termed an auxiliary unit. Depending on how many are assembled in this unit, you may choose to further divide them."

"And assign the archery units to work with various regiments depending on mission."

"Exactly, Helwin."

When they called it quits, Helwin and Halric had a solid grip on brigade organization. It was another crisp, clear day, and Jeff felt the need to soak up some sun while shifting mental gears.

"Will you walk with me while I debate an inner conflict, Helwin? It represents an issue of consummate importance that must be quickly resolved."

"It is a pleasant day, Captain. I would be honored."

Jeff set off across the compound at a leisurely pace, Balko trotting along well out in front on four feet instead of three. Head down, hands clasped behind his back, Jeff wandered along deep in thought. Helwin decided it was going to be a long walk.

Some time later, Jeff was startled from his thoughts when Balko crashed out of the woods chasing a rabbit.

"Where are we? Where's the camp?"

The look on Jeff's face was such that Helwin couldn't help smiling. "We have been walking north on the road, Captain, and are perhaps two miles from camp."

"Damn. I really drifted off." Jeff noticed the smile on Helwin's face and grinned back. "Thank you for keeping track of me. At times like this I might indeed fall over my own feet." Taking Helwin's arm, he wheeled them around. "It's just as well we're away from camp. What I have to say is for your ears only. We're going to have to leave."

"Leave our camp and Rugen?"

"Yes."

They strolled along arm-in-arm, Jeff falling silent again. Breathing deeply of the tangy air, Helwin admired leaves that were showing the first signs of autumn and was content to enjoy the day.

Jeff halted abruptly and turned Helwin to face him. "Lord Gaereth has informed me that the Salchek are also entrenching to the south of the city. What bothers me deeply is that they are advancing salients in a most leisurely fashion. With winter nearly upon them and short of food, why would they do this? Even while speaking, I recall that a number of Salchek rode south after we attacked them on the plains. The Salchek may be arrogant, Helwin, but they most certainly are not stupid."

"The Salchek expect supplies from the south."

"Yes. Both heart and mind tell me a caravan is on its way to Rugen." Jeff stepped out again.

Thinking about another winter journey brought back memories, and not the good ones. He had nearly been destroyed, physically and spiritually. Would have been destroyed except for Magda.

Those memories in combination with the bone-deep fatigue he had been fighting for several weeks lighted a sense of dread that was hard to keep at bay. After going over it two or three times trying to find a way out, he still didn't see any alternative.

"If we succeed in forming another cavalry troop it cannot be assigned to Halric as I had originally planned. I believe it fair to say we are going to need them both. This means you must oversee two troops of cavalry rather than one. Do you wish this responsibility?"

They were into the camp's outskirts and approaching a number of warriors, but Helwin didn't need to think about her answer.

"I find that I enjoy this 'organizational' work, and am well fitted to the task. I thank you for the opportunity."

That afternoon they really dug into the paper work. While Helwin needed some coaching, Jeff quickly discovered she did in fact have a head for organizational work, and figures as well. Not long into the, to him, odious task, Jeff held out one of the ballpoint pens.

"You will need this."

Helwin turned it end for end with a puzzled expression. When Jeff pulled the cap off to scribble a few words she snatched it back.

"How wonderful!" Helwin laughed like a girl and drew complicated designs. "This comes from your home?"

"My former home. Now it is yours. Do use it sparingly, for we only have three."

"I shall cherish it! I am so honored!"

By that evening Jeff thought they would be able to form a second troop if they could speed up the selection process. There was a lot of interest, but not enough seasoned warriors were applying. Jeff smiled as he recalled the excitement generated by the ballpoint pen. To northern warriors, the pen might as well have been a magic wand.

At the end of the day Helwin contrived a leather pouch so she could hang it around her neck. In a very important way, Jeff concluded, the pen was a more potent symbol of her authority than any title or weapon.

Before turning in, Jeff and Helwin split up to pass the word around various satellite camps. It was time to do some serious recruiting.

When Jeff approached the meeting hall early next morning, he nearly groaned. A double line of warriors snaked around the building and out of sight. He needed recruits, but not this many! Muttering, "Bloody paperwork," he entered the hall. Helwin was waiting. She greeted him with hot coffee and a rueful smile.

"I am hopeful that bloodshed will not result by the end of this day, Captain. Anticipation runs high."

Jeff just shook his head and sat down at a table while Helwin summoned the first warrior.

That evening he located Gaereth and communicated his decision. The meeting hall had quieted and was empty except for Gurthwin, who was seated nearby in a chair similar to Jeff's.

Balko lay stretched out in a position designed to soak up as much heat as possible. Seemingly deep in thought, Gurthwin stared into a fire that cast wavering shadows about the hall and over his face.

"We've been knocking the same possibility around here in the city, Jeff. Rengeld is extremely concerned but doesn't see how he can afford the troops it would take to break out of Rugen. If the Salchek are going to attempt resupply, the caravan will have to already be heading north or never make it before deep snow. It's going to have to be a big one, and probably well defended. While I doubt they can field another army this early on, it will still be a rough go for you."

"It hasn't been an easy decision. Things are beginning to mesh here, but it's still pretty fragile. If Halric wasn't such a competent leader and so well respected by the other tribes, I'm not sure I could justify leaving...."

Jeff's thoughts trailed off to be replaced by such a sense of dread and emotional fatigue that Gaereth had to force alarm into the background.

"Want to talk about it?"

"I feel so empty inside, so very, very tired. Coming down out of the mountains last spring, I almost turned back for good. I just don't know how much more I have to give...." After a long pause, "The nightmares are back, Grandfather. As soon as I knew I had to go, they came back. I can't bear the thought of dying like that. Not again."

Gaereth felt Jeff's pain like a knife in the heart. "Will you tell me about it? We haven't talked much about last winter."

The imagery and emotions conveyed by telepathy left nothing to the imagination. The sense of abandonment and spiritual desolation was so powerful that Gaereth felt like he had been punched in the stomach. He reviewed every leader at the Alemanni camp searching for a substitute but knew it was futile. He also knew in his heart that a Salchek resupply effort was moving north.

Feeling a wave of bitterness, Gaereth pulled farther back from the link. *And now must I sacrifice my grandson on the altar of war? So many have died! How can I tell him he must go?*

"I'm sorry if I let you down, Grandfather. I'll do my best."

Emotional floodgates straining to hold back centuries of loss burst. Remorse, sorrow and guilt flooded Gaereth and his head bent to his knees.

Carl was seated nearby working on a training program for his hospital and heard a gasp. A moment later he was inundated by Gaereth's emotion. Frantically wondering what had happened, Carl hurried over to throw an arm around Gaereth's shoulders and immediately picked up on Jeff's state of mind.

The double impact was so severe his knees nearly gave way. Long-repressed memories of his enslavement by the Arzak were released. Caught unprepared, some of them were more than he could bear. Some were unspeakable.

Gurthwin had been keeping close track of Jeff from under bushy eyebrows. He knew that Jeff was exhausted, and the state of his mind when he and Helwin returned from their walk had been alarming. Gurthwin caught Jeff's last thought and unabashedly tuned in. The emotional turmoil present in the three men hit with the blunt force of a hammer.

"Peace and love be with you, brothers. Attend me."

Opening his mind totally, and by his example accepting nothing less from the others, Gurthwin searched their minds one by one. So stern but loving was his examination that Jeff and Gaereth felt peace steal across their minds. Carl quickly sat down before he collapsed from relief.

"*Gaereth, Jeffrey and Carl—embedded in life as it is, there is no salve or potion that will serve to erase the suffering you have experienced. Yet, do you believe all that has come to pass, and the manner of its fashioning, was contrived by happenstance? Can you not comprehend that the very gods oversee these affairs?*"

Gurthwin mentally sat back and let them mull it over. In a cooperative effort, the three men compared notes and ticked off events. The timing meshed so closely that using coincidence as an explanation grew stale. More than a few events were either inexplicable by any device or frankly amazing.

"Even so," Gurthwin commented. "*Furthermore, is it given us to foretell the time or place of our death, or to understand what purposes in the greater scheme of things it will serve? Certainly not. Thus also our actions, regardless of motivation. When missions and people so clearly serve the welfare of freedom and peace that the intent of destiny and those who rule us all lie exposed, we as mortals should tremble with humility.*

"Ours is a terrible task, one that may well require all our lives. Again, that is not ours to foretell. We must only and continually search our hearts for the truth, then promote that truth into worthy action.

"Jeffrey, I will not bandy words and cannot soften them—you and young Balko must go. Gaereth and Carl, you must stay. Yet, is there not enough love amongst us to sustain our spirits in the face of whatever is to come? Are we not all of us surrounded by worthy, virtuous people? Come, let us take sustenance from one another and from the task allotted us."

Gurthwin drew their minds into close embrace with his, the nimbus of his love glowing like a halo.

The fire was down to embers and ash when Jeff awoke. Feeling at peace, even serene, he looked over to find Gurthwin fast asleep. He appeared exhausted. Balko was stretched out on his side near the fire and struggled to his feet when Jeff stood up.

Bending over Gurthwin, Jeff kissed him on the forehead and gently picked up his frail body. Carrying him to his bed in a back room, Jeff tucked him into fur robes and walked out of the building.

"Rolfgar, dismount and adjust your stirrups."

Jeff waited patiently while the warrior fought a frustrating battle to lengthen his stirrups. There were no snickers from other troopers. Rolfgar was only one of many who had been called down. They had a lot to learn about riding horses.

After a period, Jeff stepped in and demonstrated how to get the job done. He didn't mind, in fact felt like a new man and fully prepared to put the training schedule into high gear.

Over ensuing weeks, Jeff and Helwin drove the cavalry troops hard. Time passed in a blur of skull sessions and field exercises. Evenings were spent poring over endless lists and devising tactics. One element was missing. They really needed scouts. To solve that deficiency, Balko was sent on a mission to contact Balthazar.

About the time Jeff was beginning to wonder what had happened to him, Balko loped into camp acting as if he had never been away.

"The matter is concluded. 'Balthazar' and his pack will come, as will the one we met in the far north. This one knows where they hunt and will call them when the hour is come."

Halric took the news well. He was firmly in control of the Alemanni and exuded confidence. In Jeff's estimation, Halric was well on his way to becoming a first rank C.O. Gurthwin set every available tanner and leather fabricator to work constructing winter clothing for the cavalry, and added his own lists to those Jeff tried to avoid at every opportunity.

Helwin wearily entered the meeting hall after a particularly long day in the field. Her face was coated with dust where it wasn't streaked with sweat. She hesitated between water and coffee then made a beeline for the water barrel.

Jeff wasn't far behind and removed gauntlets to slap dust from his pants. He accepted a mug of water and collapsed into a chair. Sitting down nearby, Helwin propped her boots up on a bench with a sigh of relief.

"They're still pretty green, Helwin, but we're out of time. We'll complete training while moving south. Now we must make sure that all the horses are sound, including the pack animals."

Finding horses capable of carrying heavy troopers had been a prime headache. Had they not captured a number from the Salchek during the forest battle, it would have been a lost cause.

"I can handle that, Captain," Helwin replied in English.

"Without a doubt, Lieutenant."

Jeff pulled his knife and began cleaning his fingernails. It was either that or grin at her. They had been working in such close proximity over preceding weeks that he no longer had to translate English thoughts into Northland's speech. His first attempts at conveying military concepts that had originated in a foreign culture and different language to a hundred warriors had proven overwhelming.

Within a short period Helwin began picking up English words. Discussing cavalry tactics had proven a good way to expand her vocabulary. As she learned, they split the task of schooling the troops. Now it was late September and the time to leave had arrived.

"As much as I despise that pile of lists we've collected, let's pull them all together for a final review."

They enlisted Gurthwin's help and by late evening the last item on the last list was checked off. Everything was in place. Capping his pen, Jeff gave Helwin the order for assembly at first light.

The compound was crowded with relatives, friends and chieftains when Helwin summoned Jeff from the meeting hall. There were few tears to be seen, but many loud conversations and laughter. Partings were never easy.

Halric and Gurthwin joined him on the way out. The air was still and heavy with the scent of fall. Although the sun was not up, the sky promised a beautiful day. Helwin had assembled the company a short distance from the hall. Gurthwin stopped on the porch.

"You will return to us, Jeffrey."

"Perhaps, but whatever the outcome of our mission you must know that I will not fail in the effort."

"You have not thus far, and I trust such effort will suffice. The gods require no more of us."

Jeff clasped hands with Halric. "Give the Salchek no rest, my friend."

"They will have none. This land is not theirs."

There was nothing more to say. Jeff hugged Gurthwin and walked away. Helwin drew herself up straight in the saddle.

"At-ten-shun!" A number of warriors were conversing with relatives and were slow to react. "Look alive or pull KP, boots!"

The Alemanni did not have an official band, but musicians from the various tribes had formed a drum and fife corps for the fun of it. Drums roared an exhilarating beat and fifes skirled as Jeff mounted. Arching his neck, Cynic pranced sidewise toward Helwin.

"All present and accounted for, sir!"

Jeff returned Helwin's salute. "A smart looking company, Lieutenant."

"Yes, sir! Ready to kick butt and take names, sir!"

The company was drawn up by troop in four ranks. Jeff walked Cynic to the center. After a period of silent examination, he called out, "What do we do!"

A hundred and one voices roared, "Cavalry rules!"

Jeff pumped his arm up and down, then up again. When he dropped it and turned Cynic, Helwin sang out, "By the troop in three columns, the First Cavalry will move out! Forward, ho!"

Newly fashioned pennons snapping on their standards, drums pounding out their stirring rhythm, Eagle and Bear troops clattered into motion onto the road south in a cloud of dust.

Twenty-three

Guerrilla Action

The need for secrecy dictated that the first day's march take place within the forest. Come night, it would be safe to make the transit to open prairie without trekking farther south in the forest as they had for the attack on the siege engines.

Although farmland with associated villages nearly abutted the forest east and west of Rugen for some miles, Jeff felt certain the Salchek did not have enough manpower to occupy real estate that was of little tactical concern.

Before leaving cover, Jeff contacted Gaereth. *"We're ready to haul out of here. I don't know how long we'll be able to stay in contact, but I would think for at least a week or two. Anything new?"*

"What you might expect. The siege engines are being rebuilt, but it will be some time before they can be put into action. Carl and I will handle the pipe bombs on the south wall. Officers Rengeld has selected will handle the others. Morale is good. We're ready. Gods speed and protect you, Grandson. All our thoughts and love are with you."

"And mine with you all, Grandfather. Please take care of yourself. Give my love to Zimma and Carl."

Hazy layers of pungent smoke hung over fields as they filed by on rutted paths. The only light came from stars, but that was enough to reveal acres of black stubble. Glowing hotspots that had been smoldering for weeks peppered the landscape wherever they looked. The villages they circumvented were silent and dark. Some had been burned. No dogs barked, no children called to one another.

The empty desolation brought home another aspect of war to the Alemanni. It required little imagination to foresee what would happen if the Salchek were allowed to march farther north. They were well to the east and south of Rugen before dawn.

As promised, Balko had contacted the two wolf packs. They were moving south in the forest. Days then weeks passed without incident. The wolves made an appearance, traveled with the cavalry for a number of days, then left to take up position ahead of the troopers to the east and centrally. Both packs were excited about the prairie and eager to learn its ways.

One evening, Balthazar and Heideth unexpectedly showed up at Jeff and Helwin's fire. Their fur was disheveled and appeared to be missing hunks here and there. Both radiated intense self-satisfaction. It wasn't difficult to figure out why they had visited camp.

Although Jeff found them to be even-tempered and given to careful thought, he had never met a wolf that did not have such a deep sense of probity that it was dangerous to contravene.

"It would appear you have had a busy day, wolf-brother and sister. The horse-brother and this one are grateful."

Balthazar licked a cut on his paw in a contemplative fashion. *"We are more than pleased to have been of service, my brother. Those carrion-eaters we schooled were not of the pack that attacked you and our horse-brother, yet justice has been served. I believe it safe to say that others of their breed will shortly come to know caution. While their mind speech is primitive, it is sufficient to convey warning. They are most vile creatures!"*

Five weeks into the journey south, Jeff walked Cynic through belly-high prairie grass that stretched to the horizon in every direction. Burned golden by autumn's heat, it rustled dryly in the wind. A few clouds hovered to the west, and the sky was a color that defined the word, blue.

The two troops were strung out behind in two columns, warriors lounging in the saddle while conversing with their fellows. At the sound of a horse moving at the canter, Jeff turned to see who it was. Helwin reined her horse close and saluted.

Returning Helwin's salute, Jeff admired the beautiful tan her skin had taken on. Hair coiled under a broad-brimmed leather hat that resembled his own, she wore leather pants tucked into tall boots. A short leather tunic much like a jacket completed her uniform.

They jogged along side by side for a while before Helwin broke the silence.

"Our warriors show good progress, Captain."

"They are ready for battle," Jeff replied with a cautious nod. "Most have mastered their horses and are rapidly gaining competence in changing formation. They have also profited from nightly weapons drill. Seven weeks of training is little enough, but they were well seasoned to begin with."

Reviewing their trip south, Jeff allowed himself a degree of satisfaction. Thanks to the wolves and telepathy, feeding the troops had proven less a problem than anticipated. The Wildebeest-like herbivores were trekking south for the winter, and the wolf packs kept a running tally of herd locations.

When it was time to hunt they would cut out a number of animals from the closest herd. That was the part they seemed to enjoy the most—it was good sport—but driving them toward a prearranged ambush was also appealing and had taken on aspects of a game.

As the animals passed their hiding place, troopers would charge out and usually bag five or six. The whole affair had become so popular that both groups often had more food than they knew what to do with.

Then there's the Salchek, Jeff anxiously thought. Where in hell is that caravan? Five weeks and no sign of it. He allowed himself only a brief moment to dwell on the delicious thought that maybe there was no Salchek resupply caravan. Damn it, I know they're coming! Could we have missed it? What if they're coming up the west side of the prairie? If the resupply caravan had taken the western route they would miss it for sure.

Nope, he concluded, letting anxiety drain away, too far. No way do they have the time for that big a detour. Their only hope to beat the snow is a hole-shot straight up the middle or to the east, and we have those routes covered. Four days later he received a call from Balthazar.

"Many wagons and soldiers on horseback pass below us, wolf-brother."

Most wolves had no interest in figures, but Balthazar had proven to be a notable exception.

"What are their numbers?"

"They are beyond this one's counting, wolf-brother."

Hurriedly setting up a base camp and turning command over to sergeants, Helwin, Jeff and Balko departed. Try as he might to suppress it, Balthazar's reply never stopped bouncing around in Jeff's mind.

They met the wolves two days later and camped near a high knoll that overlooked an area the supply caravan should pass the following day.

They were in position shivering from the cold when the sun peeked over the horizon. Late morning they spotted the first wains. Hour after hour, the triple line of wains continued to lengthen. When lead wagons had passed their location, the far end of the column still could not be seen.

Close enough to hear drover's whistles and the cracking of whips, Jeff and Helwin counted wains as they creaked by in a cloud of dust. Jeff was both awestruck and dismayed.

"That is one *big* caravan. They must have stripped Khorgan!"

Late in the afternoon they compared figures and looked bleakly at each other. They had counted three hundred pack animals and four hundred wains.

Assessing the caravan's escort proved a more difficult task. It wasn't until dusk that they had any confidence in their figures. As near as Jeff could estimate, three cavalry companies and the equivalent of four battalions of foot accompanied the caravan. They stuck around until the caravan laagered up for the night.

Jeff fell into a black study on the return trip. He tried to visualize how his force of one hundred troopers plus the wolves could even make a dent in the caravan, much less stay alive in the process. They were nearing base camp when Jeff pulled up and dismounted. Helwin followed suit.

"Let's try and put some order to our thoughts before we hit camp."

"Yes sir. No sense spooking the troops because we're uptight."

"Right on, Lieutenant." He scuffed a patch of prairie grass down to bare dirt.

"Okay, it's clear we have no hope of achieving success by frontal assault. The attack would fail, we would all likely die, and the caravan would continue on its way. Our best hope is to sow confusion and slow progress north. If we are successful, winter may do the rest."

"If we are to sow confusion and slow progress," Helwin observed with slow thoughtfulness, "our primary objective must be the pack animals and draft horses."

"Correct, Lieutenant. Never the soldiers. It may happen that we take out some of the wains, but only if doing so serves our primary objective. If you were in charge, how would you assess our advantages and use them to plan the first attack?"

Dropping onto her heels by the patch of dirt, Helwin scratched out a diagram with her dagger.

"Our advantages are two, and not insignificant. We are blessed with a high degree of mobility, and if we are cautious may effect complete surprise. Now, the wains travel in three columns during the day. While camped they increase that to six. The packhorses trail behind during the day, but are picketed in the center of a large square of wains for the night still at the caravan's southern end."

Helwin fell silent and seemed to be contemplating her drawing. When she looked up her expression was embarrassed.

"Captain, I did not observe where the draft animals are herded for the night."

"Individual teams were picketed near the wains," Jeff commented after a sufficient period of silence to indicate that she should have noticed. "That isn't surprising when you consider there are over two thousand draft animals to care for. It would be impossible to find your team in such a large herd."

"In light of that arrangement, Captain, I believe it likely the draft animals will be guarded by foot soldiers. If that is true, the number of troopers we counted is not sufficient to provide protection in depth. The length of the caravan is too great. Their cavalry will likely be deployed to patrol the perimeter."

"I concur. These are assumptions, but solid assumptions."

"Yes sir." Helwin put the finishing touch to her diagram. "Here is how I would make our first attack..."

It was late in the day by the time a plan emerged that Jeff felt had a chance of success. Commanded by Helwin, Eagle Troop would attack the large square of wains that contained the pack animals, stampede the horses, and burn what they could before withdrawing.

At the same time, Bear Troop would attack the front of the caravan causing as much confusion and destruction as possible. The assaults fore and aft were bound to draw off at least some of the foot soldiers from their duty. At that point the wolves would race in from both sides driving off as many draft animals as possible. They were quick and might be able to work the entire line before the Salchek could regroup.

The enemy cavalry posed the largest and potentially the most deadly problem. There was no way to predict where they would be at the time of the attack. Still, Jeff felt a degree of renewed confidence. Not only was it a good plan, but both troops had a clear path of retreat.

While debating tactics, Helwin and Jeff had taken seats on either side of their ersatz white board. Getting to his feet, Jeff wiped out the diagram with a boot.

"I like the way you use your head, Lieutenant. Let's get back to camp."

"Thank you, sir, and yes sir." Helwin released her horse from the picket stake. "My stomach's fighting a losing battle with my backbone."

Jeff swung into the saddle shaking his head and chuckling. "Out of sight, Lieutenant. Out of sight!"

The Alemanni First Cavalry broke camp and trekked southeast. They were within striking distance of the caravan when they ran across a convenient arroyo that would serve to conceal their camp. The arroyo had a stream running down its center and enough scrub trees to provide firewood.

The second pack of wolves joined up with Balthazar's, and the combined lupine force tracked the caravan throughout the following day.

Blooded by combat, the troops were quiet while preparing for the attack. They knew what was coming. The odds were sobering even by Alemanni reckoning. There was little horseplay while padding harness and applying carbon black to their faces. Following a final skull session, Jeff drove home several points that had already been stated several times.

"If you wish to return to loved ones, do not venture off alone. Heed recall at once and move quickly to assembly points."

They were close to the caravan when Helwin angled her troop off to the south. Guided by two wolves, she set a course to circle around to the rear of the caravan.

Jeff continued on until Balko warned of Salchek outposts. Bear troop dismounted and tended their horses while nervously awaiting the message from Helwin's wolves that they were in position to attack.

* * * * * * * * * * *

"We shall leave on patrol momentarily, my commander."

Lingol Bollit acknowledged the nattily attired officer's crisp salute by touching his campaign hat, a wide-brimmed cap.

"Do not allow your patrols to bunch up. They grow careless. Should I discover they seek entertainment among the women at the rear of the column as they have done in the past, they and most likely yourself will be afoot tomorrow."

"Yes sir. It has been an uneventful trip to date."

Bollit stooped to ignite a slender wand in the campfire. The fire, a lackluster affair fueled by dung, illuminated a face weathered to the consistency of old leather by constant exposure to the elements and many wars. It was also a troubled face.

A globe of fire ignited at the end of the wand and Bollit set it on top of his pipe. He puffed sindar weed alight and drew in a satisfying lungful before returning his attention to the sub-lieutenant.

"This is not an academy exercise, Heskelit. Do not assume that matters will progress according to plan. Our adversaries have proven themselves competent and professional far beyond what past experience would indicate. Their attack on our army's supply train was as well planned and smoothly executed as any I have commanded or participated in."

"They are northern rabble, sir."

"They are not!"

"Yes sir. I deeply regret I was not present to greet them."

You young, foolish idiot, Bollit thought. You were not there. That supply train was savaged. A Power has risen in the North and they saddle me with green snot-noses. And this one! Fresh from the academy and of noble family!

"Do you know what a wolf is?"

Sub-lieutenant Heskelit wondered if his boss was losing his nerve. "Some form of dog, Commander."

"Were a wolf to stand on its hind legs you would have to look up to see its head. If one of these creatures was willing, you could throw a saddle on its back. Think about that while you are on patrol."

"Yes sir. Perhaps they will attack us when we draw near Rugen. My family would be proud were I to return with a wolf head."

"Dismissed. Mount your patrols and maintain intervals."

Heskelit saluted and hurried off. Bollit watched him fade into the darkness. Somewhere in his mind he was composing the letter he would have to send to the young man's family when he was killed in action.

Regretfully knocking dottle from his pipe, Bollit wondered who would write his. He had never had such a thought before and gazed at the heavens in search of guidance, but saw only unfamiliar constellations that offered nothing.

* * * * * * * * * * * *

The tension grew steadily as minutes ticked by. It seemed an eternity before one of the wolves with Helwin put out a general call.

"The yellow-hairs have arrived. They are ready."

Balthazar and the leader of the second wolf pack reported they were also in position. They would hit the front of the caravan and work south, stripping draft horses as they went

Ordering his men to mount up by doing so, Jeff sent the attack order to Helwin's wolves. She would take her cue from them. He nudged Cynic into a walk. Ears laid back in preparation for action, Balko crouched along in front.

"Ready for a little dust-up, brothers?"

"When have we not been?"

Balko was so intent on the caravan that all he did was fling a mental growl.

As they advanced at the walk, a wide band of glowing campfires emerged from the night. Set against a star-filled sky, the band wound south and became a ribbon of light that gradually narrowed as it approached the horizon.

His body charged with adrenaline, Jeff maintained the slow walk. "Come on Helwin!" he muttered. "Let's get it on!"

Cynic was jerking his head with impatience and lathering up when Jeff heard a faint commotion from the south.

"That has to be it! If it isn't, screw it!"

Drawing Berold and letting internal pressure blow out his lungs, Jeff screamed an Alemanni war cry and booted Cynic.

Bellowing battle cries, hooves pounding on the prairie, fifty warriors and horses descended on the head of the caravan like a storm. A confused mob of teamsters boiled out of their bedding in random patterns as Bear Troop charged into their midst.

Unable to see anything in the dark, their frightened questions turned to cries of pain as swords thudded home. Cynic trampled several as Jeff guided him toward the closest wain, their screams lost among the others.

Splashing turpentine on the wagon, Jeff dumped live coals from a pot and blew them to life. A dim shadow reared up in the wagon bed and Jeff ducked as a club whistled by his head. Thrusting with his saber, he felt it grate across ribs. The shadow tumbled down to sprawl over Cynic's withers. Jeff flipped the body off with a desperate heave and fanned the small blaze with his hat until it took off with a whoosh.

Lighting a torch from the fire he urged Cynic toward the next wagon, swinging his saber in vicious arcs as hostlers and teamsters pressed close. Balko leaped into the thickest bunch, bearing several to the ground and scattering the rest. Alemanni troopers holding blazing torches seemed to be everywhere to Jeff's fevered eyes, some leaping their horses over wagon tongues in their haste to find another target.

Then the wolves came charging in on either side of the caravan. They blew through depleted guards and attacked draft horses up and down the line. Rearing and thrashing about in an agony to gain their freedom, many broke loose and stampeded through the battle trampling anyone in their path.

Confused groups of men and women ran from point to point trying to rally as fire after fire sprang up and bathed the area in a hellish glow.

Feeling like an hour had passed, Jeff fought his way from wagon to wagon setting fires as he went and wondering where in hell the Salchek cavalry was. Seeming to be everywhere at once, Balko made the difference time and again.

Jeff hacked his way out of a group of teamsters who were trying to drag him from the saddle and took a second to look around. Those of his troop he could see were hard pressed. This is getting too tight, he thought. Leave while you can!

Putting horn to lips Jeff blew three mighty blasts, let out a rebel yell and charged into a pack of teamsters that were in the way. He was almost through when his leg was hit a tremendous blow. Jeff screamed with pain, and Cynic nearly unseated him when he whirled to trample the life out of a club-wielding teamster. They won free and Jeff sounded the horn twice again to marshal his troop.

His leg hurt so badly it was hard to concentrate, but Jeff thrust it aside. He expected to get hit by the Salchek cavalry at any moment. He ordered his troop into battle formation and sent Balko to reconnoiter. He scouted a wide circle but found nothing of concern.

Dawn was several hours away when they moved out. Jeff calculated that should give them plenty of time to reach the rendezvous point. An urgent call blasted into his mind from Helwin's wolves.

"The female yellow-hair is hard beset! Come swiftly!"

"Dammit, that's where they all are! She won't have a chance against that many!"

Jeff swung Cynic south and set a pace that under other circumstances would have been insane, horses stumbling and sliding in the night. Balko had run ahead when he heard the summons and guided them back toward the caravan. Jeff heard the sounds of a cavalry action.

"Form line!"

They had approached to within several hundred yards of the caravan. There were enough wains on fire to reveal the battle and terrain.

"At the canter!"

Knee to knee, Bear troop brought their horses to the canter and roared out favorite battle songs. Jeff sounded the horn in a mighty blast.

"Charge!"

Bear troop responded with a tremendous shout and put spurs to their horses. When they crashed into the melee, the noise level jumped to the point where thought was blown away.

Engaging a Salchek on either side, Jeff whipped Berold back and forth in an elaborate figure of eight. Cynic took on a horse directly ahead and clubbed its rider out of the saddle. The odds were still more than two to one, and Salchek pressed in from every angle until Cynic could hardly move.

"Wolf-brothers and sisters! Come to me now!"

The call was barely on its way when a wolf sailed by in front of Cynic, stripping a Salchek horse of its rider. Seconds more and both wolf packs had piled into the battle.

Many of the thirty-five wolves leaped from saddle to saddle, clearing Salchek as they went and savaging the horses. The horses bucked and shrilled like mad things as they fought to get away. They crashed into one another, friend and foe alike, while wolves a third as big as the horses scrabbled to keep their balance until they could leap to the next horse.

Everyone knew, Alemanni and Salchek alike, that to fall meant certain death.

Jeff trusted Cynic to deal with the panicked horses and concentrated on keeping a sword out of his back. Cynic had a hard time of it as horses caromed into him from all sides, but kept his feet and carried them deeper into the battle. There was no order or purpose other than to stay alive.

We've got to get out of here. Jeff urgently thought. Won't be long before more cavalry find us. Do it now and screw the ammunition!

Drawing the Ruger, he put the muzzle nearly against an opponent's head and blew half his skull away. Sixteen times an orange spear of flame shot out, muzzle blasts and slugs adding another dimension of terror to the madness.

Withdrawing the dry clip, Jeff rammed a new one home only to find the field clear of enemy. He sounded recall on the horn and shouted for Helwin.

A trooper spurred his horse close to Cynic. "Captain, the lieutenant was last seen near the caravan."

"We must find the yellow-haired she who is my companion. Track back toward the great fire. I will follow."

Jeff put a sergeant whose judgment was sound in charge of both troops.

"Gather as many riderless horses as you can, Wulfern, but do not tarry long. Await me at the rendezvous point."

The trooper saluted and began bellowing orders. Whirling Cynic, Jeff hurried to catch up with the wolves.

"The she is found."

Cynic plunged to a halt by Balthazar. Jeff leaped from the saddle and kneeled by Helwin's side. He probed for the carotid pulse and breathed a great sigh of relief when he found it. The light was poor, but he detected no evidence of blood or open wound except on her head. They were out of time and had to move or die.

Too heavy to lift, Jeff dragged Helwin over to Cynic and somehow manhandled her across his withers. Once in the saddle, Jeff rolled Helwin onto his thighs. Exhausted by the battle and carrying two big people, Cynic staggered off for the rendezvous point.

Tremendous relief swept the company when they arrived. Eager arms lowered Helwin to the ground in the first light of dawn.

His work just begun, Jeff started patching wounds. He mustered the company for role call at full light. The count stopped at 85. Although some had likely become lost and would join up later, Jeff figured he had lost twenty percent of his effectives.

"How many horses did you capture?"

Wulfern looked up from the trooper's leg he was bandaging. Deep lines of fatigue were etched on his face.

"Three hands, Captain."

"I had not hoped for so many. You have done well."

They remounted and headed for base camp, Jeff continuing to carry Helwin. Other warriors were likewise burdened. They stayed well down in the grassland's shallow valleys, wolves working the hills as lookouts. Helwin started to thrash before long, and Jeff was hard put to keep from dumping her.

The sun was well up when they plodded into camp. Jeff groaned relief when troopers eased Helwin off his thighs. As soon as his feet hit the ground, legs long deprived of circulation crumpled and he had to hold on to the saddle to keep from falling.

Waving away help, Jeff hung on until his legs throbbed back to life. When the wounded were taken care of he saw to Cynic and crashed onto his furs.

Jeff crawled out of his nest early in the afternoon. He tried to stand up but injured thigh muscle cramped into a knot. The pain was so intense he clawed at the dirt to keep from screaming. The cramp eventually relented and Jeff was able to limp around camp. Troopers were also moving around and coaxing fires to life.

As predicted, the Alemanni had become hooked on coffee while training north of Rugen. The first pots set to brewing did the trick for those still abed. The two troops mustered under the eye of their sergeants and that of the boss, who was secretly pleased at the initiative being shown.

Handing out assignments, Jeff dismissed the troops then visited the wounded. Helwin was rocking back and forth holding her head when he kneeled by her bed with a damp cloth.

"Tough night, Helwin. You took a hard blow to the head. Hold still."

Removing the bandage, he washed caked blood from her hair and forehead. The wound, a three-inch laceration, started to bleed. A fresh bandage stopped the flow.

"Okay, that ought to do it."

Helwin looked around blankly trying to orient herself. Jeff fetched a mug of coffee to help her come up to speed. By the time it was gone Helwin's eyes were tracking together and she mustered a wan smile of thanks. Jeff gave her a briefing but skimmed over details of her rescue.

"I'm going to head back with Balko and scout results. Get more rest then make sure the troops set up lean-tos. I don't like the looks of this weather. We'll talk when I return."

Helwin set the mug down and fell back onto her furs with a groan. Jeff discovered he couldn't stand and had to crawl a ways toward the remuda before his injured leg loosened up.

"How you doing, big boy? Ready for a little jaunt?"

"I can imagine what little means! But as I have said, this one is always ready."

It was a long, painful afternoon for Jeff and Cynic. Balko had taken a few hits and showed the strain as well. Still, limping or not, someone had to lead the way and it might as well be him.

The weather had been going sour for several days. Jeff looked up at the dark gray clouds hanging overhead and could smell snow coming soon. Winter memories from the far north jumped to mind and sent a convulsive shiver down his body.

When he smelled wood smoke, Jeff turned Cynic loose to graze and follow along at his own pace. Balko was waiting when Jeff bellied up to the rim of a hill that seemed familiar. He removed his hat and cautiously peered over the top. Thirty wains were still smoldering at the head of the caravan.

"Enemy or not, that is one ugly sight."

They worked south from hill to hill, tallying draft horses and dodging the occasional patrol. Dusk caught them only two-thirds of the way down the line.

Jeff slumped to the ground on the backside of a hill. Uncorking a water-skin, he splashed water on his face and took a long pull. Feeling some better, he went over the notes he had taken.

"Can't be more than 1,200 draft horses left," he muttered. "They're going to be down to three or four per wagon. Even if it doesn't snow and we leave them alone, they couldn't make Rugen before year's end."

Jeff wondered how much damage Helwin's troop had inflicted before they were attacked, but it was getting so dark there was no point in going farther. While he knew her troop had fired some of the wains before they were hit, the packhorses were another matter.

A Salchek patrol came winding around a hill to the west, forcing Jeff to beat a hasty retreat. Cynic had enjoyed his afternoon off and loped along without complaint. He had rested a bit, the grass was prime, and his belly rumbled pleasantly. Shortly, leaden skies began to spit snow.

Trotting into bivouac well after dark, heavy flakes had turned the ground white. Leaving Cynic free to graze, Jeff hurried to the nearest fire and the smell of roasting meat. It was a pleasure just to sit and talk about anything except war for a while.

Later, he went in search of Helwin and found her working over damaged battle gear in a circle of firelight. Sitting down next to her on a handy boulder, Jeff warmed his hands over the fire. Snowflakes swirled silently into the firelight, hissing as they fell on coals.

Helwin was occupied redoing a lance head binding, so they shared some minutes of companionable silence. Securing the last turn with a knot, she laid the weapon down on a pile of equipment that had already been repaired. Clasping her knees, Helwin stared into the fire while Jeff related the gist of his reconnoiter. She remained silent for a period after he finished.

"I have learned the complete nature of my rescue. You have saved my life. I thank you."

"You would have done the same for me," Jeff replied with a wave of dismissal. "Any of our warriors would have."

"Any of our warriors did not. You did, and at great personal risk. Do not make light of your effort, for it was no small thing."

Thank you's always made him uncomfortable and Jeff changed the subject. "Were you able to scatter the packhorses before the Salchek cavalry found you?"

The look on Jeff's face was familiar, and Helwin smiled into the fire. Modesty was uncommon among the Alemanni, and it appealed to her.

"We succeeded in winning our way through the wains and were among the packhorses when attacked. I believe it safe to say that while gaining our freedom from the caravan they experienced a certain unease."

Helwin's droll humor brought a smile to Jeff's face, but it was fleeting. He visualized what it must have been like to be assaulted by such a large force while in the middle of such a large remuda.

"Your understatement does you credit, Lieutenant. I think we can count our attack an unqualified success. Now as much as I hate to see this snow for personal reasons, it serves our purpose. Life will be tough for us, but absolute hell for the caravan."

"Mud."

"Lots of mud. It won't be long before those wains are bogged down to their axles. The Salchek aren't going to have any idea how to deal with this weather. From what I know of them, it seems likely they come from southern lands."

"What do you plan, Captain?"

"We will not attack again until I see how they reorganize the caravan. They may have to drop off some of the wains in order to provide full teams for those that remain. Once we see what they decide to do and how they reorder defense, we'll start our attacks again. From now on, however, our method of attack must change."

"Yes sir, I understand your reasoning. The Salchek are warned. Were we to attempt another attack such as our first we would get stomped."

"Nicely put and exactly to the point. Now we must employ hit and run tactics: small groups of archers slipping in close to loose several flights of arrows. Wolves prowling the horses. We must never give them rest. As much as I dislike centering our efforts on the horses, we really have no other option that will prove effective."

Although it was getting late, Jeff was moved for the first time in many weeks to play his recorder. Recalling odd bars of Afternoon of a Faun, he improvised the gaps. Within minutes Helwin was asleep with head resting on her knees.

Jeff tucked the recorder away and smiled softly as he watched shadows play across her face. While asleep, Helwin's features were those of an exhausted young woman with strong suggestions of the girl that still resided within. It was easy to forget she was no more than eighteen or nineteen.

Jeff shifted position, allowing a clump of snow on the collar of his coat to slip inside and down his back. He shivered and got to his feet.

"Gurthwin was right. I don't know how I could do this without her friendship."

Helwin was so groggy when awakened that he gave her a hand up. No more than on her feet and she plopped back down.

"Okay, I can deal with this."

Jeff supported Helwin to her lean-to a few yards from the fire. She nearly fell when he removed his arm.

"Whoa! Steady as she goes! Time to return a favor, Lieutenant. Let me give you a hand getting your clothes off."

Helwin was nearly asleep on her feet and didn't respond other than to lean against him.

"I think that means yes," Jeff said, and chuckled. "We got us a situation here, Lieutenant. How in hell am I going to do this?"

There was some light from the fire, but Jeff had to work largely by feel. The jacket was no problem, but trying to get the woolen shirt over her head proved difficult. Scooting it up, his hands brushed across Helwin's breasts and she cooed in his ear.

"Stop that!"

Helwin was so tired she was tipsy, and just giggled.

"At least hold your arms up so I can get this off!"

"Like this?"

Helwin held her arms up in a languid movement that elevated her breasts to full display. They were gorgeous.

"Oh, wow," Jeff muttered under his breath, "this is cruel and unusual punishment." Keeping his eyes glued to Helwin's chin, he pulled the sweater over her head. "Okay. Crawl into the lean-to. We have to get those wet pants off."

Draping her arms over Jeff's shoulders, Helwin rested her cheek against his head.

"I feel like a babe, Jeffrey."

Helwin was so tall that her breasts pressed against his chest almost at neck level. Jeff carefully placed his hands on her back. It seemed to be the safest place. Helwin's skin was so creamy smooth that he sighed with pleasure.

"Lieutenant, you are definitely a babe. Now come on. Before you freeze and I lose it entirely, let's get you under cover."

When Helwin was stretched out in the lean-to, Jeff pulled off her boots. "Lift your hips so I can get these pants off."

No answer except a soft snore.

"Damn. She can't sleep in those pants—they're soaked. How am I going to get them off? She weighs more than I do!"

Wedging into the lean-to, Jeff straddled Helwin's legs and wrestled sodden leather pants over her hips inch by inch, cursing under his breath all the while. The whole situation abruptly struck Jeff as so ridiculous that he began snickering.

After that, the fact that Helwin was wearing no underpants didn't even bother him. Scooting higher to straddle her abdomen, he dragged her the rest of the way under cover.

Pulling a fur robe under her chin, Jeff touched lips and whispered, "Goodnight, Helwin."

Shuffling through several inches of snow, he made a beeline for his own lean-to. Tucked into sleeping furs, he gathered warmth.

"Oh, damn, this feels good!"

Jeff fell asleep as snow continued to fall with the large flakes of early winter.

Helwin awoke to the muffled quiet of a snow-covered land. Her fur cocoon was comfortably warm and the headache was gone. She drifted in and out of sleep for a period before responding to the nagging call of duty.

Propping herself up on her elbows, Helwin freed a foot from the furs and kicked open the flap of leather that closed her lean-to. The dim light revealed her pants and other clothing folded in a neat pile.

"Jeffrey undressed me. I remember that." She also remembered the feeling of his hands on her breasts. Helwin hurriedly pushed the memory aside. "He is my captain and friend. Were matters otherwise perhaps I would come to know his body and deeper spirit, but they are not." Helwin felt envious of Magda and made a face. "Why couldn't he have come to my village instead of hers?"

Gingerly picking up a spare pair of pants that were merely damp rather than soaking wet, she began dressing. Emerging from the lean-to Helwin noted that the snow had stopped, leaving at least six inches.

A few troopers were up and about trying to find live embers in soggy fire pits. Lean-to's sagged with their load of snow, and some were visible only as mounds. The sky was an even slate gray, although giving promise of thinning as a breeze from the north moved in.

She waded over to a renewed fire to soak up some heat before setting the day's activities in motion. That accomplished, Helwin checked up on Jeff. He was still sleeping and had kicked off his furs. Helwin reached inside fully intending to pull them straight, but his skin looked so appealing that she drew her hand down his abdomen.

The warmth and smoothness proved too much. Surrendering to impulse. Helwin moved her hand between his legs. The sensation was more than satisfying and she dallied for a few moments to feel his response. She quickly pulled her hand away when he moved. It was either that or slip into the lean-to with Jeff. His response had been quick and impressive. Covering him up, she hastily walked away.

When Jeff roused himself and hurried to a fire to get some coffee, the camp was bustling with activity under Helwin's stern eye.

"Time to do it, Lieutenant. Forage and food or it'll be too late. Another snow like this one, and the grass will be out of reach."

Locating the wolf packs, he arranged a hunting expedition that included half of the warriors fit to sit a saddle. He set the rest to digging out fodder for the horses. Jeff and Helwin left camp an hour or so later to scout the caravan.

As they departed, hunting parties were leaving on their own mission. Disgruntled troopers stuck with the fodder detail watched them go with wistful looks but got in quite a few telling catcalls before they were out of range.

By noon the clouds were breaking up, and the sun showed itself now and again. Patrols were out in force, delaying arrival at the caravan until well into a short afternoon.

The caravan was hitched up and moving slowly. Squads of soldiers were slogging through the snow ahead of the wains to break a path. A Salchek sat his horse to the side near the head of the column.

Jeff heard no orders, cursing or other comments that he could assign to the man. A faint cloud of blue-gray smoke seemed to be hanging around his head.

"The guy's smoking a pipe! Now that is coolness."

Whistles of encouragement ran up and down the column along with the singing snap of whips. As they watched, a horse slipped and went down. Before teamsters could get it up the horse had thrashed the wain's harness to ribbons and other horses in the team were bucking madly.

The Salchek on horseback never moved. However, the moment the situation was in hand he reined his horse around. To Jeff's perception it seemed the man looked directly at him.

Lingol Bollit felt an itch along the back of his neck that he had come to recognize and respect many years ago.

"So, my impudent friend, you have come to view your handiwork. And right good work it was. Certainly, Heskelit no longer thinks of wolves as no more than large dogs."

Bollit reined his horse around. He knew exactly where to look and immediately spotted a flash of red.

"And so my worst fears are confirmed. The Tlakish are no myth and bring weapons never recorded." Bollit lifted his hat and flashed a toothy grin. "Yet let it be noted in histories that follow this debacle that Lingol Bollit did not shrink from his duty."

His first impulse was to dodge out of sight, but when the Salchek lifted his hat and grinned Jeff was so impressed that he did not.

"What class. That guy is a real pro." Goaded by the Salchek's panache, Jeff held his hat aloft.

"Captain—the wains!"

Jeff stiffened at the urgency in Helwin's voice and examined the line of wains. "What is it that alarms you, Lieutenant? I see nothing remarkable."

"The teams. Look at the teams!"

"Holy shit. Six or eight horses. How could I have missed it? They must be using what's left of the pack animals."

Helwin nodded glumly. "Yes sir."

A premonition of failure swept over Jeff. Rather than have Helwin see it on his face, he retreated down the hill.

"Nothing more is to be gained from viewing the caravan. Whatever devices the Salchek employ to continue, our duty remains clear."

They entered camp as the sun disappeared, leaving a clear rim of green-blue sky that faded into darker blues and black. Stars flickered into existence between clouds in such numbers that they seemed continuous strips of light.

Warriors waved a greeting then resumed bundling the last of the forage into sheaves. Others were butchering animals around campfires while joking back and forth as they recalled the day's hunt.

Hunks of meat hissed as they roasted, while larger portions had been set over smoky pits to cure. Having decided to visit camp, the wolves were busy worrying their share of the catch.

Jeff did not break the evening's spell of good cheer by reminding anyone it might well be the last one. Winter had arrived.

Memories of that evening faded quickly as sortie after sortie was thrown against the caravan. Yet it seemed to Jeff they were no more than a flea biting an elephant. The caravan continued to grind its way north until he came to hate it as a living thing.

Although he caught glimpses of the Salchek commander from time to time, they exchanged no more pleasantries. The man sat his horse as if exhausted but seemed indomitable.

The snow was soon reduced to slush as temperatures eased above freezing. More than the snow, hub-deep mud slowed the caravan to a virtual crawl. The Salchek abandoned 100 wains, firing them before flogging the caravan back into motion. With full teams of draft horses, the remaining wains broke free of the mud and moved north at a steady pace.

Covered with freezing mud from the waist down, Jeff watched the process but was so tired he couldn't muster any emotion. Slithering backwards, he flipped over and tobogganed down the hill on a mud sluice.

More weeks passed, snowstorms became frequent, and the Alemanni continued to whittle away at the caravan's horses as it crept north. Down to fifty warriors capable of sitting a saddle, Jeff doggedly harried the caravan's flanks as full winter settled in.

Late one bleak and bitterly cold day in January as the troop silently rode back to camp slumped over in saddles from fatigue, dark clouds raced in from the north. Jeff examined the sky and wearily waved Helwin closer. He had to shout in order to be heard over the wind, which was increasing by the minute.

"This looks bad. We're going to have to find better cover."

"Yes, Captain. In the North we would be bringing in extra firewood. Without trees to protect us, the storm will be a total bastard."

The troop straggled into camp leaning into the wind and matted with hard-driven snow. Jeff had to bellow at the top of his lungs to be heard.

"Let's do it this way, Helwin. That hill over there has a big drift on the protected side. Have the troops dig out a deep corral for the horses and snow burrows for themselves. Make sure they have food with them."

Helwin waved rather than try and speak. By the time the corral was ready it was full dark and the wind had picked up to a full-fledged howl, driving stinging sheets of snow horizontally across the ground.

Staggering over to where the horses had been closely bunched for warmth, Jeff checked to make sure picket stakes had been driven deep. When he was satisfied, he made his way through the horses until he found Cynic. Looping an arm around Cynic's neck, Jeff gave him a hug.

"It's going to be tough, old fellow. I will be close by. If you sense trouble with the others, call me."

"What can be done to calm them, will be done. In need, I will call."

Something tugged at his arm and Jeff turned. An indistinct form staggered as a particularly vicious burst of wind shrieked through the corral. Probably Helwin, Jeff decided. He caught her arm.

"Is everyone set? We're out of time."

"All is complete, Captain. I have ordered the troops to share burrows for the sake of warmth, and have taken the liberty of digging a burrow for us nearby the horses."

"Good idea," Jeff replied with his mouth close to her ear. "Let's go."

Taking his hand, Helwin leaned into the wind and pulled him along. Out of the horses' lee they were forced to their hands and knees. In order to maintain contact, Jeff kept his nose close to Helwin's boot and a hand on her leg.

About the time he began to worry they were lost, and his nose was really beginning to smart from the cold and getting kicked, she stopped. Finding his arm, she tugged him along into their burrow. When she fixed a hide over the opening, the sudden quiet was both a tremendous relief and a shock.

Helwin directed a stream of sparks onto a candle made of animal fat until it guttered to life. In the feeble light, Jeff noticed that Helwin had lined the burrow with pelts. They helped each other out of clothing that had frozen into slabs and wormed under a pile of furs.

Shivering violently, Jeff snuffed the candle and pulled Helwin into his arms. It wasn't until he began to warm up that Jeff thought how naturally she seemed to fit. How good her skin felt against his. Sighing with satisfaction, Jeff let a hand play up and down her back. Cupping a buttock, he pulled her hips closer.

When Helwin felt his caress she slipped her hand between their bodies. Feeling Jeff respond to her attentions, deeply reassured by his response, Helwin molded her body to his and basked in the warmth. Within minutes they were asleep in each other's arms and beyond reach of the blizzard that battered at the door to their burrow.

They had not been awake long when it became clear that this was more than a severe blizzard. The door to their burrow fluttered and jerked so hard that Jeff drove more pegs to hold it in place. When he had it tight again, the piece of leather acted like a drumhead and amplified the wind's high-pitched shriek.

He had been in some bad storms, but nothing like this. Jeff listened with bowed head and knew that death was only inches away. He felt such sympathy for the horses that it was painful. Later that day, Jeff dug his way out in response to Cynic's call.

"They are most fearful, horse-brother. You must comfort them, or they will surely relinquish the will to live."

With a line attached to his waist, Jeff fought his way to the corral on hands and knees in the dim grayness that passed for day. Even on all fours he was nearly bowled over. It was hard to breathe in the wind, yet he tried not to because the air was so cold it burned his lungs.

Locating their cache of tightly bundled prairie grass by feel and memory, he hand-fed each horse while petting them. When he was done Jeff spent some time with Cynic. His face and hands were numb and he had to leave after only a few minutes while he could still crawl. Helwin pulled him the last five yards. Inside the burrow, he shivered so violently that he could hardly get undressed.

Teeth clattering like castanets, he crawled under the blankets, into her arms and against warm skin. She pulled him closer to stop the shivering and their lips met in a soft kiss that led to slow exploration.

They slept and awakened, cuddled and fondled one another then slept some more. Time passed without anything to indicate its passage until it was Helwin's turn to check on the horses.

Each repeated the cycle four times as days passed and they waited for the blizzard to blow itself out. There were times when they believed it would not, and dying of starvation seemed likely.

On the third night the wind went insane and ripped the burrow's closure away on two occasions.

After the second time Jeff double-pegged their last free pelt over the entrance and hurried back to Helwin's warmth. Huddling close to her neck he felt something wet and discovered they were tears. Quiet tears, for he heard no sound.

Close to crying himself, Jeff found her lips to give and receive assurance. Tasting salt and sweetness, he responded in kind when they opened and her tongue sought his. Groaning with long repressed need and the need for hope, he moved a hand between her thighs and sought higher. She opened her thighs and placed his hand where she wanted it.

"Come to me, Jeffrey."

When the door was ripped off the burrow's entrance for the third time they could not have cared less. Bodies moving in ageless synchrony, their cries of fulfillment and reaffirmation of life mixed with the shrieking wind.

Miraculously, the blizzard faded to distant moans and light snow. Jeff crawled out of the burrow under clearing skies and stood up to look around.

"Gods save us! Some of those drifts must be forty feet high! I've seen big drifts before in Minnesota, but nothing that approaches this."

Helwin hurried out to join him. Coming from heavily forested land she had never seen really big drifts and gazed around with open mouth. She gasped and whirled to stare at Jeff.

"The horses!"

Two had died during the final day and night of the storm, but Cynic was on his feet and nuzzled Jeff's cheek. He left Helwin to hand out fodder and checked on the troopers. Four had suffocated after their burrows drifted over or had collapsed.

Those who had survived showed little emotion as they lay the plank-like bodies side by side. Their gentle manner and quiet reverence spoke louder than words or tears. There was no fuel to spare for a pyre, so they were covered with furs to offer comfort in a new life.

The ceremony was brief, for every warrior understood that their own lives hung in precarious balance and hard work might improve the odds. Jeff sent his best archers with the wolves on a hunt that promised to be grim business. Helwin took it upon herself to catalog every scrap of food in camp.

Jeff coordinated the hunt for the rest of the day, but they killed only one scrawny bull that was left for the wolves. About the time Jeff noticed the temperature was taking a nosedive, Helwin waded up with a grim expression on her face.

"Captain, with prudence our food will suffice for two days."

Jeff kicked the snow to cover his anxiety. "Every warrior who can walk will have to go out again tomorrow, but we can't expect them to do it on nothing. We'll butcher one of the dead horses and give the other to the wolves. You'll have to organize the hunt, Helwin. I must find a way to the caravan."

It was not easy to leave the burrow next morning. Jeff felt so secure in Helwin's arms that he wanted to stay there forever. It was also the last time they could sleep together. The blizzard was gone, and they were once again captain and lieutenant. While he was looking at her, Helwin awakened and gazed solemnly into his eyes.

"Yes. Duty must be attended to, but not for this last moment."

Throwing the furs aside, Helwin opened her thighs and held her arms out. Although weak from hunger their loving did not suffer. And then, as if their coupling was no more than a dream, they were dressed and left the burrow they had come to think of as home for the last time.

Bundled up in furs, Jeff departed for the caravan with Balko in bright sunshine. Even Balko's can-do attitude was hard pressed as they forced a way through snow that was hip deep in the shallow spots.

Plunging along with giant leaps, Balko disappeared from sight at times. They plowed a serpentine path around behemoth drifts and had to backtrack time and again.

The possibility of getting caught out overnight made Jeff's skin crawl. Not again, he thought. Once almost killed me.

Balko abruptly changed course and took off up a tall hill that was largely free of snow at the top. Jeff swam after him for a look.

"So where is it? Nothing but monster drifts." His gaze happened across what looked like a giant mole trail winding south. "Holy shit. That has to be it."

He stared in disbelieving awe. Drifts had piled up and over the wains, completely burying those that had taken the storm's brunt. Pulling his hat low to reduce the glare, Jeff watched men toss snow from on top of several wains. Other than a blue haze from campfires, there was no other sign of activity.

The broad valley the caravan had been following lay stretched out below. Blinding white in the sun, it was furrowed by giant drifts that resembled swells created by an ocean storm. Some met at odd angles, loose snow blowing off their tops like spindrift.

In spite of how hard he had fought to stop the caravan, Jeff felt sorry for the civilians and horses. He watched the caravan for some time without being able to identify any of those moving about as the Salchek commander.

"I know you're there, and this is the end of road. Maybe for both of us."

Feeling the melancholy of deep winter, his gaze wandered out over a wilderness of snow that stretched to the horizon. Perhaps it was the pristine splendor of the valley or the bright clarity of the air that trapped Jeff's spirit in a tangle of memories. Or maybe the wind's song as it moaned a winter requiem that denied the promise of spring and new life, but offered rest. He lay there as the sun dropped toward the horizon, staring across the valley without seeing and listening without hearing.

"Wolf-brother, attend me! The sun is nearly gone!"

Jeff awoke from his trance to find Balko tugging at his coat. One look to the west and he tumbled down the hill in a frightened rush. Balko was right. The sun was at the horizon.

"Oh gods, Please! Not again!"

Balko went leaping off with prodigious bounds. He was under no illusion that Jeff could survive a night away from his furs. The path they had cut on the way out was largely drifted over and in places was entirely gone. Balko found their trail time and again, but then he could not.

"I must leave to find our way, wolf-brother. Do not wander from where we stand!"

"I will await your coming." Balko porpoised around a drift and was gone.

The wind shrilled its dirge around dark blue drifts and stars winked into being in such numbers that the drifts took on a white glow. Reminded of a glorious sunset far to the north, Jeff knew he once again stood at the crossroads of life and death. He thought about it but felt no panic.

Time was running out but fear no longer had a hold on him. It had grown tiresome. Balko would either find the way or he would not. There was no point in calling. Beginning to shiver, Jeff picked a direction that seemed likely and stepped out.

At that instant Balko suddenly reappeared, grinned at him, and leaped back around the shoulder of a drift. Trying to remain calm but fighting the snow in his haste, Jeff waded after Balko.

Eight or ten drifts later he won through a pass that was chest deep in snow and walked into camp. He took a deep breath and let it out in an explosive sigh.

"Where were you, wolf-brother? I had nearly given up hope."

Balko's ears fell and he radiated embarrassment. *"This one must confess that undue confidence was amply rewarded."*

"You went the wrong way."

"That is perhaps an overstatement, but does reflect the truth of the matter."

"I don't give a shit." Jeff dropped to his knees. *"Come here."*

Balko's ears shot up and he bounded over into Jeff's arms. *"If my eyes do not deceive me, I believe we will fill our bellies this night."*

At least eight wildebeest were being butchered near blazing fires. Hacking out a big slab of meat for Balko, Jeff wondered where on earth they had managed to find so many animals and fuel for such large fires.

A grinning hunter handed him a nicely seared hunk of meat. Before tearing into the food, Jeff posed his questions.

"The wolves discovered them, Captain." The hunter pointed east. "Many animals are wintering in a deep valley not far distant from our camp. Pursuing the animals, we discovered thick stands of trees."

"Was the snow badly drifted in the valley, and did you take note of the grass?"

"While the snow was deep in some portions, it was not badly drifted. A stream flows through the valley's center and likely watered the grass to abundant growth in the warm season. Thus it should be worthy."

What remained of the First Cavalry was packed up and moving early the next morning. They were down to forty warriors and twenty horses. The horses were so thin and weak that everyone walked.

When they arrived, Jeff discovered the valley was closer to being a canyon. He halted the column at the top to look it over. The canyon was oriented on an east-west axis. That would block the prevailing winds.

Jeff let his eyes feast on the heavy growth of timber that wound out of sight along the course of the stream at the canyon's center. They were real trees and not scrub. He cut the inspection short and started down the slope at a cautious angle. There was a lot to accomplish before nightfall.

It was slow, tense work, but they made it to the bottom without setting off an avalanche. Shortly, the sound of battle-axes put to constructive work echoed off canyon walls accompanied by enthusiastic songs. The combined effect set a cornice free to rumble down a sheer canyon wall a safe distance away.

Well before nightfall, smoke sifted through the roofs of crudely fashioned but sturdy lodges. Although the stables weren't much more than elaborate lean-tos, the horses were out of the wind. With their snouts buried in fragrant piles of grass, they were content.

Establishing an outpost near the caravan, they waited three days without a sign of movement. The wind was brisk and the temperature below zero, but their new campsite was well protected. Hunting was good, forage for the horses proved adequate, and camp routine settled into a pleasant rhythm of plentiful food and sleep.

Two more days and the caravan still showed no sign of activity in the caravan. They weren't even digging out. Seated in their lodge, Jeff disassembled the Ruger for a thorough cleaning while Helwin looked on.

"Captain, I am puzzled. Perhaps they are debating what to do?"

"I have no doubt the civilians are. They've lost well over 100 wains and a lot of friends. Now they stand to lose everything."

"They might decide to winter over."

"I suspect that is what their commander is urging them to do, Helwin. He is not a man to give up.

"That much is certainly clear!"

"He is a professional." Jeff methodically checked each part of the Ruger for dirt. "I think we'll see the outcome soon. If they don't head south in the next few days they will winter over. I doubt that is going to happen."

"Of course. The horses." Helwin made a quick grab and snagged a piece of the Ruger that popped from Jeff's hand. She gave it to him. "They are afraid they will lose them all."

"That's part of it." Jeff finished assembling the Ruger and inserted the clip. "They are also exhausted and see nothing but more of the same ahead. They're right. It's called a no-win situation."

"It is sad."

"Yes." Jeff examined the Ruger for several moments and slipped it into the holster. "For all of them."

Next day a trooper from the outpost charged into camp with news that the caravan was breaking up.

Jeff and Helwin provisioned themselves for several days but arrived after dark and had to live with their curiosity throughout the night. Those on duty at the outpost reported what appeared to be fighting.

Dawn told the story. As they watched, several wains straggled out of line and wallowed south leaving piles of cargo behind.

"The civilians have had enough. They're saving what they might and abandoning the rest."

Throughout the day, wagon after wagon pulled out. Although no one spotted a mounted soldier, it appeared that foot soldiers were accompanying the wains.

Just like Napoleon and Hitler's retreat from Russia, Jeff thought. I wonder how many will survive? He strained his eyes in an attempt to spot the Salchek commander, saw several uniforms, but knew with exquisite certainty that the man was dead.

Throughout a two-day period the portion of the caravan they viewed progressively shrank. Since the caravan stretched south for many miles and well out of sight, Jeff and Helwin coursed its length before returning to base camp. The same pattern prevailed.

They made no attempt to hide their presence, and on one occasion stood only yards away as a wain fought through a drift to escape its slot in the line. It was pulled by four painfully thin horses and was nearly empty. The teamster on the wagon seat was so exhausted he didn't even look at them.

"Good fortune. May the gods see you safely home."

The teamster did not respond to the hail, nor did the men and women trudging behind. Jeff realized he must look equally ragged and exhausted, but felt his heart go out to them. Heads bent to watch every step, to conserve every shred of energy, they methodically placed each foot in the wagon tracks.

When Jeff and Helwin were advised that no sign of life remained in the caravan, they rousted out the company and set out under frigidly clear skies. The deserted laager had the eerie quality of a ghost town about it.

Splitting his troopers into teams, Jeff sent them out to make sure. He ordered a wagon broken up for firewood and it made a cheerful blaze, but there was no cheer.

Teams straggled into the bivouac until well after dark with the same story. Deserted wagons, disease and death. Dead horses, dead men, dead women, even dead children. There was no singing or celebration, just silent groups of warriors staring into the fire and taking what food they could stomach.

Jeff had given orders to search the clothing of any body that appeared to be Salchek. Several teams did run across Salchek lying trampled in blood-soaked snow, but their pockets revealed nothing except a few letters that might have been last wishes. Jeff gave them to Helwin for safekeeping. The day might come when they could turn them over to a Salchek representative.

They were sitting on a wagon tongue discussing the only positive find of the day, eight heavy sacks of grain that might go fifty pounds each, when the last team dragged into camp. The team leader, Wulfern, sat down on the wheel next to Jeff and handed him a leather bag.

"We discovered this under the body of a Salchek, Captain."

Jeff extracted a hot piece of meat from the fire and handed it to Wulfern. "An officer?"

"I believe this to be so, although I am not familiar with their custom of dress." Wulfern stopped chewing and looked deep into the fire. "I am moved, Captain. While this man was an enemy and outlander, his spirit will be well received by the gods. I have viewed many faces after death, but recall none that were so composed and gave the impression of such strength of person."

No more words were necessary. Jeff knew who the man was, that his inner conviction was now fact. And it hurt terribly. He was too tired to find anger, too distraught for tears, but it hurt terribly.

"Tell me of his death, for he will be remembered."

"Yes, Captain, this must be so." Wulfern took another bite. His eyes, sunken orbs in dark circles of fatigue and starvation, shimmered with what remained of remorse. "His body was not defiled, for he died by his own hand. While this is not our way, I believe he did so to sustain honor and not fail of his duty. The pouch was hidden under his body." Wulfern shook his head in denial and wiped at his eyes. "Will you share its contents with us?"

"I will do this, but you must understand that I do not have understanding of Salchek writing."

Wulfern collected his team, and others drew near to be part of a ritual of passage that would honor courage. The pouch was lined with silken material of lavender and contained packets of letters in Salchek script.

At the bottom, Jeff discovered a smaller pouch. Inside was a single sheet of parchment bedded on shredded leaf that looked like tobacco. He unrolled the sheet and extracted a curved-stem pipe.

"Oh, goddam this war to hell," and the tears did come. Jeff held the pipe up for all to see. "This was his totem, this speaks of the man."

Murmurs of assent rumbled around the troop while Jeff tried to focus on the sheet of parchment. It was composed in the language of Chaldesia.

"Now you will hear his last words.

"'Greetings from Lingol Bollit, Tlakish. I have come to respect you as soldier, thus the man, and trust these letters to your safekeeping. My family must know I died with honor. The gods understand what we do, I do not, yet duty is complete. Now fill my gomwok with sindar weed and offer smoke to the winds that a better life be opened to my spirit, but do not then cast it aside. I would be pleased to know that this part of me continues. I am saddened that we did not meet in better times, for we would have been friends. May you survive this war.'"

Jeff folded the letter and inserted it into a breast pocket along with the pipe and pouch. Ripping a sideboard off a wagon, he threw it on the bonfire.

"Let us sing for his spirit."

The troop opened their hearts and sang for Lingol Bollit, sang for all who had died, sang for themselves. Jeff filled the pipe with sindar weed and set a red coal on top to light it. It was not tobacco, did not smell or taste like tobacco, but it did not matter.

The Song for the Dead filled his heart as he drew a deep lungful of smoke and exhaled slowly. A brilliant shooting star flashed overhead from zenith to horizon, and he knew Lingol Bollit was at rest.

"How many days march do you calculate we must travel, Captain?"

Jeff concentrated on pulling a bone needle through tired leather. He tugged the stitch down and tied it off inside.

"If it were summer and we were riding well-fed horses, perhaps three weeks to Rugen as the bird flies. Afoot as we are in deep snow, we must first make our way to the forest well south of Rugen. There we will rest and hunt before following its border northwest. I estimate that trek alone will require four weeks. Let us pray to the gods that it snows no more during that time."

"Let me hold it."

Helwin took the jacket Jeff was repairing and held the torn seam together so he could start a new line of stitches. They sat side by side in the small lodge, which was lighted by a tallow candle and a fire that flickered over spent fuel. Wildebeest hides floored the lodge, and beds of fur were placed close to the firepit on either side. Helwin released the jacket after the third stitch and idly tossed twigs into the fire.

"The last hunting party reported that game was scarce. We must leave soon."

"As soon as possible. Troops ready?"

"Yes sir. The horses have gained enough strength to carry our food and theirs, but fuel will journey on our own backs. I have had the wood tightly bound to ease the burden."

"Good thinking." Jeff cut the thread free and laid the jacket aside. "Sleep well, Helwin."

"And you, Jeffrey." Helwin held her lips up and they shared a kiss full of memories.

There were more than a few backward glances as the troop crested surrounding hills and headed north early one morning. The canyon had come to be viewed as home.

Jeff was too preoccupied with the welfare of their horses to spare more than a quick look. Work as they might, they had been able to collect only a modest volume of tightly bundled grass and that decomposing.

Four hundred pounds of grain wasn't much when spread around twenty horses, but he hoped it would make the difference. Wading through the snow beside Cynic, Jeff sighed and patted his neck, relieved that they had any grain at all.

The weather remained clear and below zero for the first week, the snow was crusted hard, and they made good progress north. Then a moist frontal system from the south met the high-pressure cell and it began to snow. No blizzards, just relentless heavy snowfall.

Days were reduced to sodden misery as clothing became soaked, and nights to shaking nightmares that never seemed to end. Day by day they edged north, taking turns breaking trail through snow that was often chest deep. Food for man and horse rapidly dwindled, and the last faggots of wood were burned.

Somewhere along one of those interminable days, Jeff bumped into the horse ahead of him. The horse was so weak it didn't even flinch.

Jeff stared at its tail and wondered why it was there. It slowly dawned on him that the line had stopped and something must be wrong. He waded to the head of the line leading Cynic. There he found a sobbing warrior trying to get her horse off its knees.

"My friend, can you be of any help with this one?"

"He has struggled long and is of good heart, but has no more to give his master. It is his time to lie down and rest. He is very sad to leave us."

Stricken by Cynic's comment, Jeff tried to get the horse up but to no avail. Liquid brown eyes filled with sad resignation and regret, the horse lay down on a bed of snow and was still.

"May I use your knife, Captain?"

Jeff handed the survival knife to Elke. "Would you rather that I did this?"

"No, Captain. Storm was my friend. His spirit has been freed, now he would wish for me to share what remains with us all."

Two more times a horse lay down, and three warriors did not awaken from a night's sleep. Each time a horse died, the warrior who cared for him butchered the animal and distributed the meat. No one suggested that the rest of the horses be killed. To them, it would be the same thing as murder. Since the blizzard, troopers no longer viewed the horses as beasts of burden.

Through it all, Cynic endured with stoic determination. On more than one occasion Jeff was reduced to helpless profanity as he watched his companion grow weaker and so thin he seemed no more than a collection of bones loosely draped with hide.

They stumbled into the forest late one afternoon. By Jeff's reckoning the trip had required nearly five weeks. Stronger warriors supported others who could not walk by themselves. There was no strength left for cheers or chatter. Scraping together the last handfuls of grain, troopers fed the horses and lighted bonfires.

Having made his rounds to check horses and sleeping warriors, Jeff huddled over a fire with Helwin. Her eyes were sunken, and cheekbones stood out like blades.

"We will remain here until all are rested, Helwin. Tomorrow we must send everyone out to hunt. Deer should be plentiful, but finding food for the horses is going to be difficult. If we do not find food we will lose them all."

"My heart is deeply moved by their plight. They are most courageous."

"Yes, but let me tell you something—without your courage we wouldn't have made it. I'm quite sure I would not have made it."

Helwin looked at Jeff solemnly, and thought, He is so thin it seems I might see the stars through his body. Where does he find the strength to lead us? My captain and my friend. ... Helwin felt something else at that moment, but hurriedly brushed it away.

"Our spirits are one, Jeffrey. I no longer think of us in any other fashion. I do not understand this. It surpasses, is not, what I know of men and women together. I am most fortunate to have served under you."

Tired though he was, Jeff quickly looked down to hide a grin. Helwin realized what she had said and laughed quietly.

"As you would say, Jeffrey, ouch!"

They fell silent, content to share the fire and new hope. Helwin's eyes drifted to Jeff's face, trying to fathom what she was feeling.

Why now? she thought. Why do I become aware of this now, with safety and hope only short miles away? Surely he must leave me.

She examined a bony hand and smiled. How strangely does fate beckon desire. Nigh unto death from starvation and still I would know his body. Helwin nodded to herself. Soon you will be lost to me, Jeffrey, but tonight you are mine.

Helwin got to her feet and pulled him up as well. "Let us give added meaning to what has been said, and what we have accomplished. Soon we will return to Rugen and, perhaps, separate destinies. If your spirit and body are willing, I would cherish what has been ours."

Jeff said nothing for a period while he reflected on all they had been through together. Searching his heart Jeff did not find passionate love, rather another form that loomed larger and could not be separated from what he was. Fellow officer, confident, trusted friend, lover and something else that encompassed them all but went far beyond.

"I can think of no more wonderful memorial to these last seven months." Jeff pulled her head down so he could touch lips. "I do not understand my body, only that it would taste of you. Let us discover whether it is capable of such."

Leading Helwin to his bed, Jeff removed her overcoat. Lifting her woolen undershirt, he paused to feel her breasts and test their weight. They were much smaller but also firmer, and in shape gave no evidence of surrender. So like the woman. With a sense of deep satisfaction, he kissed each nipple in turn.

She held her arms up to the moon while he did so, singing softly. When Helwin stood exposed and gleaming in the moonlight, she was smiling into his eyes.

The wolf packs had been hunting the forest for over a week before the war party arrived. Seeing no reason to expose Balko to what he knew the troop must endure, Jeff had sent him on ahead with Balthazar's pack. Balko and Heideth charged into camp early the first morning after the troop arrived in the forest. When they discovered that Jeff and Cynic had survived, they cavorted like cubs.

Throughout the stay, fires were kept burning day and night. Large herds of deer were wintering in the forest and hunting was good. On the other hand, finding food for the horses proved difficult.

Although Cynic was familiar with edible plants in the forest, it was winter. However, spring was not far off and new shoots were starting to bud.

After a round of cautious tasting, Cynic discovered that a number of the buds were quite pleasing. These were harvested along with several varieties of tender bark that proved palatable. While not prime fodder, the bark filled the belly and had some food value.

When troopers and horses had recovered enough to travel, Helwin mustered what was left of the company. She and Jeff looked them over closely during inspection. As they walked along the line of troopers and horses, Jeff sighed internally. They have been through so much, he thought, yet will give whatever is left.

He dismissed the troops and wished for a way to thank the horses. Jeff and Helwin walked into the forest to find some privacy.

"Well, Lieutenant, what do you think?"

Unexpectedly, Helwin grinned. "I think they're keepers, Captain. While still tired, they're ready to march."

Jeff smiled at how well she used English slang, and was impressed all over again at her resilience. His smile softened, remembering. Although desire had required little encouragement, starvation had taken a toll on his body. It was only with Helwin's gentle seduction that his body could do nothing but respond. So like Magda, uniquely Helwin.

"I agree they're ready to march. What other questions must we ask before departure?"

"These are the additional questions that must be asked, Captain: what is the state of the siege, and are the remains of our company capable of fighting."

"As usual, I agree with your thinking. The first question strongly influences the second and that first question cannot be answered at this point. Given that, how would you proceed?"

"Cautiously, Jeffrey, for the answer to the second question is—not a chance."

"No doubt about that. Until the troop has rested for some months I will not expose them to combat unless the need is dire."

"Yes sir. Cannot you employ your gift for speaking mind to mind? Perhaps you might range Lords Carl or Gaereth."

Jeff shook his head. "The distance is still too great."

That was not the truth. Linked with Balko's mind, the distance could easily be bridged. Down deep, something would not let him contact Gaereth or Carl. Some dark mood that grew stronger by the day.

"As you have suggested, Lieutenant, we will proceed cautiously and stay within the forest whenever possible until we understand what awaits us. If the siege is not broken, we will march to our camp north of Rugen."

Neither Jeff nor Helwin could bear to mention another possibility. Rugen might have fallen to the Salchek.

That night, moved by a deep need for the solace of music, Jeff groped around in his gear bag looking for the recorder. Coming up empty-handed and feeling something akin to panic, he feverishly dug deeper.

His hand touched cold plastic at the bottom of the bag. Grasping the cylinder, Jeff snaked it out. And blankly looked at half a recorder, the jagged edges of one end pointing at his heart like a spear.

He was immobilized by a sense of grief that went far beyond the fact of a broken instrument. Jeff could not believe that it was gone, that his music was gone. A tear gathered in each eye and quivered uncertainly. He was holding the mouthpiece fragment, raised it to his lips and blew. A squawking screech cut his soul. Two tears fell into the snow and disappeared.

Thirty-five surviving warriors and seventeen horses filed out of camp in a silent line. Jeff had made his farewells to the two packs of wolves several days earlier when they announced their intent to leave on an extended hunt to rebuild their strength. They also intended to do some recruiting. Both packs had lost three or four wolves.

A week or so after they resumed their journey, Helwin discovered a body sticking halfway out of the snow. Remembering the agony of their trek north, the troop gathered around the frozen corpse and stared.

The body was so emaciated it appeared more a skeleton than once a thing of flesh. It lay on its back with jaw agape and arms thrown wide. Frozen eyes stared into a future they all knew one day would also be theirs. Warriors who had faced death in battle without a thought began muttering sympathy and unease.

"Captain, this is not good. We must leave before fear of such death accomplishes what the living could not."

"I agree, although my heart tells me that worse is to come. I believe we are seeing the answer to the first question."

"Yes sir, but I do not understand this." Helwin gestured at the body. "There is game aplenty in the forest."

"The Salchek conscripted town folk, Helwin. Farmers and tradesmen, not hunters. I also suspect that this man was in desperate straits by the time he deserted. He never had a chance."

From that point on they encountered many bodies. Huddled together in death, strewn among and within makeshift huts, more often they were curled up alone. Some bodies showed evidence of disease, others had been butchered. Jeff shuddered with revulsion as he looked down at a group of three skeletal bodies. A picture he had seen of Auschwitz came to mind, and he hurried away.

With spring only weeks away, a warm front moved in from the south. Sleet rattled down as they formed a skirmish line and moved out into farmland with bowed heads. Entering a burned-out village they passed hundreds of bodies sprawled in filthy sludge. Village after village, the story was the same.

That evening, Jeff wearily led Cynic into a field. "We cannot stop in a village, Helwin. There is no room for the living. We must search out a spot free of death."

Camped in a muddy field, Jeff sat in a huddled knot. His stomach still churned at what they had seen that day. Reason kept demanding that he contact Gaereth or Carl. Unconsciously, steadily, he shook his head.

A tide of sadness such as he had never known fought to consume him, and a sense of guilt growled for recognition. They had seen only a few bodies that could be identified as Salchek.

There is no excuse for killing civilians, he thought. How can I take pride in that? I will not call. Maybe we can slip into the city unannounced.

Helwin had never seen such an expression on his face, and fervently wished there was something to make a fire with. She moved over to sit beside him and draped the fur robe she had around her shoulders over them both.

They had started their last day's march when Helwin spotted a cavalry patrol some ways to the west. As she watched, the patrol abruptly swerved to approach with drawn swords.

The lieutenant in charge was disgusted by their filthy, ragged appearance. He wasn't sure what to make of them, but decided they might be a band of cutthroats out to loot the dead. They wouldn't be the first he had run across.

Making no move to greet the patrol, Jeff stood silently and stared at the ground.

The lieutenant was forming his squad when Helwin advanced. "Be at ease, Franze. We met at the Alemanni camp before the Salchek arrived."

At the mention of his name, Franze Steppord held his arm up to halt the maneuver and dismounted. He walked closer, peered at Helwin and recoiled backward a step.

"Helwin? Is that you?" His face a mask of horrified disbelief, Steppord took several steps toward her. "By the gods, it is! You have returned! But what?..." Lieutenant Steppord hurried back to his squad. He jumped into the saddle and reined his horse close to Helwin. "We return to the city! The king must be informed! You will not be received as beggars! Shall I send assistance?"

"No, Franze. We have come this far on our own, we will finish it on our own."

Steppord saluted Helwin, whistled shrilly and dug his spurs in. His horse leaped off with an angry squeal and the rest of the squad tore after him. Jeff resumed walking but did not raise his head.

By early afternoon the temperature eased above freezing, turning icy fields into quagmires. With each step the calf-deep mud threatened to strip boots, slowing the pace to a crawl. Some slipped and fell and would have lain there had not comrades pulled them out of the mud. After fighting it for a period, several could do no more than stand there and their friends were too weak to help.

As the troops had accepted the horses as comrades, so Cynic had accepted them as worthy of being horses. He suggested to Jeff that they grip the saddlehorn from either side and he would pull. His plan worked and the march resumed.

Sleet pellets once again came driving in from the south. Jeff hunched his shoulders in an attempt to lessen the discomfort, but really wasn't aware of the sleet. Their discovery by the cavalry patrol had been the last straw. The possibility of a quiet entrance into the city was gone. Guilt dug long claws into Jeff's spirit and dragged it down for a leisurely feast.

Reviewing all his perfectly sound motives and well thought out reasoning, he cast them aside. Jeff grasped thoughts of loved ones and safe warmth, what Gurthwin had earlier said, but they slipped away leaving only sorrow.

Somewhere inside his soul cried, why do I live when they are dead? Husbands, sons, daughters—stupid, helpless civilians who couldn't even hunt. And you thought to understand and help people. All you've done is murder and kill.

The refrain went on and on until Jeff unconsciously put hands over his ears in a futile effort to block it out, even as city walls loomed high and intact.

Reminded of his duty by the walls and a commotion he could already hear, Jeff stopped short of the south gate to form up his warriors. He would at least not discredit what they had achieved by having them look like rabble.

The south wall was packed shoulder to shoulder with smiling faces as they neared the gate. Both portals began to open, but were pushed with such enthusiasm that they got out of control and slammed into the stops with a boom. A blast of sound rushed out of the city. Drums and bugles sang an exciting martial air but were nearly drowned out by a multitude of voices.

Entering the city, a roar of greeting hammered them to a stunned halt. It made the reception for Rengeld's Raiders seem like nothing. Humanity surged back and forth, filling the street from side to side. A forest of arms reached through a double line of city guardsmen trying to keep a lane open.

Those that noticed Jeff's silent tears applauded them as joyful, not the expression of a sundered spirit that had given its last effort somewhere on the plains of death.

Twenty-four

Four-sided Triangle

The noise was a sustained bellow. After months of relative quiet it was nearly unbearable.

"This isn't right," Jeff said in a dazed mumble, "there is nothing to celebrate. I've got to get out of here!"

So tired he could barely stay on his feet, Jeff looked at all the smiling faces and felt raw bitterness. Why are they so fat and rosy when everyone else is dead? At that moment he wanted nothing more than to sit by himself in some forest glen free of death until peace should happen upon him, however long that took.

"Captain! Jeffrey!"

Jeff lurched out of his mental haze. "I'm turning the troop over to you, Helwin. I must leave."

"No sir, you will not. It is your honor, and by the gods you will have it! You are my Captain, and I will not permit you to leave!"

The roaring crowd seemed to fade into the background as Jeff took strength from Helwin's defiant eyes.

"Let us finish it, then." Jeff signaled the troop to march, and they wound their way deeper into the city.

Lost in a fog of utter exhaustion and self-loathing, Jeff did not see the freshly repaired gouges on the gate as they passed through. In the city he took no note of buildings beaten to rubble and those blackened by fire.

The king and court were arrayed to greet them when they entered the main plaza, which was packed wall to wall with people. Imogo, Ethbar, and Rengeld were standing at the center. Close by on one side were Rogelf and Belstan. Carl and Gaereth gravely stood with Zimma on the other side.

Both men were in fear of what they would see. The report they had received from the patrol had been devastatingly frank. Hearing the crowd noise swell, Carl and Gaereth shared a troubled look behind Zimma's back. The fact that Jeff had contacted neither of them sat like a lead weight in their minds.

At least Steppord thought he recognized Jeff, Carl thought. Another thought came unbidden: what will be left? Gaereth caught that fragment and slowly nodded, head bowed and rubbing his chin.

As the column forced its way deeper into the courtyard, the crowd threatened to become a mob. They screamed their lungs out and stamped such excitement that the cobblestones trembled.

Zimma drew in a quick breath and a hand flew to her mouth when she spotted Jeff. Neither she, Carl or Gaereth mistook his drying tears for other than what they were, or the starved condition of the few horses remaining for other than what they represented in terms of human suffering as well.

The column drew to a halt in front of Imogo. Ears and brain pounded by crowd noise, Jeff handed Cynic's hackamore to Helwin. Taking the hackamore, Helwin's free hand fluttered toward his face but withdrew. Walking like a windup toy with a bad spring, he slowly advanced toward Imogo.

The cobblestones were slippery with icy mud and Jeff fell, landing on his knees. The pain was so bad that he cried out. Those who could see what had happened gasped in dismay, but no one moved to help. He tried to get up, slipped again, and collapsed in a sprawl. Zimma was nearly frantic.

"I must go to him! I cannot bear this!"

She was about to rush forward when Carl laid a restraining hand on her shoulder.

"No, Zimma. You must let him finish this on his own."

"But he cannot!"

"Yes, he can."

Rengeld watched Jeff shake his head and understood his agony. "Come to us, Jeffrey. You are ours."

The stern, uncompromising tone of Rengeld's voice was such that Jeff braced himself erect and staggered forward. Her vision blurred with tears, Zimma squeezed Carl's hand like a vise as Jeff halted in front of Imogo.

"Your Majesty, we return. It is done."

Imogo was the son of a mercenary and had grown up with endless war stories. He had directed a war but never personally experienced the field of battle. The reality standing in front of him was horrifying. This could not be the same muscular, confident man presented to him at Court.

Caked with mud and filth, Jeff wavered back and forth and peered at Imogo with red-rimmed eyes. While not given to introspection, Imogo felt he was looking on something worse than death. He had prepared a long speech but quickly pared it down.

"Your services and those of your warriors will never be forgotten by us or this city. That its successful defense is due in major part to your efforts is known by us all, and will be heralded for generations to come regardless of what else shall transpire. Be it known to all present that you are named knight of the kingdom and duke of the realm, with all honors and lands ascribed to such position. We are aware that your journey has been most perilous and rest your immediate due. At a later date when all is repaired we will gather in festival."

Imogo embraced Jeff. As he stepped back, the crowd broke out in a roar of delight. They surged through the line of guardsmen to swarm around the troop.

Zimma sobbed with frustration as she tried to fight through to Jeff, only to be thrown back time and again. Gaereth and Carl tried to force a way through with no success. Rengeld noticed their plight and led a wedge of soldiers to open a path.

Running toward Jeff, Zimma was startled by the sight of Helwin and Balko struggling to protect him from the crowd, both with bared teeth.

In a heartbeat, Helwin knew who the approaching woman was. She took Jeff by the shoulders and turned him to face Zimma. As she did so, a feeling of loss hit Helwin that was so deep it was terrifying. She wanted to clutch Jeff to her, not give him up; not give up what they had shared. Instead she whispered, "And so good-by, my Jeffrey." Helwin gave him a shove in the right direction as Zimma ran up to pull him into her arms.

Helwin watched Zimma embrace Jeff and wrap an arm around his shoulders to lead him away behind an escort. Suddenly, Jeff stopped and turned to look at her. Helwin caught her breath in hope and poured her heart into what was much more than a shared glance.

After a period, Jeff broke his eyes away from Helwin and spoke at some length with a blond-haired man. Then he was gone into the crowd. Helwin could not tear her eyes away from where she had last seen him.

Although hemmed in by jostling town folk, she stood alone in spirit. Helwin felt so lonely she thought she must die from the pain. It was several moments before Helwin realized someone was gently shaking her.

Turning her head, she saw a man nearly as tall as she gazing at her with a concerned expression. It was the same man Jeff had spoken with.

One glance and Carl winced inside. Helwin's soul was naked to his eyes and intuition. He viciously thought, Damn this war. This shit has got to stop for a while. No one should have to bear such pain. How did either one of them survive?

"Please excuse my rudeness, Helwin. I am Carl, Jeff's friend. He expressed great concern for you and asked that I be of assistance. Lord Gaereth is seeing to your troopers. You must be at the end of your strength, and it's no easy thing being in an unfamiliar city even when you're rested."

Helwin was so tired and full of pain she couldn't think or speak, and looked like she was drowning. Carl took her elbow.

"Stabling has been arranged for the horses and your troopers are being seen to. Let's find some food for you."

An inn he frequented was nearby. On the way, Carl learned how she fit into the troop. Helwin's platter was still nearly full when she nodded off in the middle of a bite and toppled backward.

It was a small table and Carl lunged across the top to grab her. Dropping a few coins on the table, he got a shoulder under her arm and they staggered out the door. It suddenly occurred to him that he had no idea where Helwin was supposed to be quartered.

Screw it, he thought, Ethbar has more rooms than he knows what to do with.

Ethbar took one look and sent servants flying to prepare a room. Carl was about to turn Helwin over to the servants when he heard her mumble something. He leaned an ear close to her mouth.

"I'm sorry, Helwin, I didn't hear what you said."

Her expression was desperate, and Helwin gripped his hand so hard it hurt. She whispered, "Nothing; it was nothing."

Nothing but your heart breaking, Carl thought. "Let's check your room out and get you in bed. I'll stick around until you're all set."

Helwin never let go his hand as they followed the servants. This is all entirely new to her, Carl thought. May as well have been married to Jeff after seven months together, then wham! He's gone with another woman.

Easing Helwin into a chair, Carl began unlacing her boots. By the time he was done she was sleeping so hard Carl took her pulse to make sure she was all right.

They finished undressing Helwin as a team and gave her a sponge bath. Carl muttered oaths at how thin she was, and the female servant was reduced to tears. Through it all, Helwin never moved or fluttered an eyelid. Carl tucked her in and pulled a comfortable chair near the bed.

Long before they arrived at Jeff's quarters in Ethbar's home, Zimma had discarded all plans for celebration. While helping him wash up she had to fight back tears of horror and grief at the sight of his protruding ribs, thin arms and sunken belly. When Jeff was safely in bed she pulled a chair close and held his hand until he fell asleep. Balko would not be denied and took up his usual position, settling down at the bed's foot.

Helwin awoke disoriented. The room was not only unfamiliar but also totally alien. Relief flooded in when she spied Carl snoozing in a chair and she remembered. She watched him sleep for a while then noticed fresh clothing laid out for her.

While dressing she wondered if Carl had helped bathe her. It felt so good to be clean. She paused to examine him again then resumed dressing. Carl awoke when she thumped a boot on the floor.

"Good morning, Helwin. Would you like to eat?"

"Yes!"

"I thought so," Carl said with a sympathetic chuckle. "Food first then we'll look in on your troops."

"Jeffrey and Zimma live here?"

"They do."

Checking the hall to make sure it was empty, Helwin pulled Carl from the house.

Seeing to the needs of the troop they wandered business areas with Carl showing her the ropes. One day toward the end of the week he noticed the wistful looks Helwin gave passing women, and especially the well dressed ones. He gripped Helwin's arm and wheeled into a clothing shop. She balked inside the doorway.

"Carl, I cannot. I am a simple warrior, not a woman bred of the city."

"You are a beautiful, elegant woman," Carl sternly replied, looking at her from under his eyebrows, "and you are going to purchase clothing that proclaims it to the world. Now, I will hear no more objections. Is that quite clear?"

Helwin saw the steel in Carl's eyes and lowered hers. "Yes, Carl."

They spent the day wandering from store to store shopping for clothes. Carl got her started with color combinations then had to put the brakes on when she got carried away. That night they had their own fashion show. Cheeks rosy with excitement, Helwin jumped from outfit to outfit and she even laughed.

The morning she did not take his hand, Carl felt like the one who was lost. One day Helwin informed him that she would be leading the troop to the Alemanni camp.

"Will you be back soon?"

"In one week. I have learned there will be a Telling that I must attend."

"I will miss you very much."

Helwin studied Carl for several moments. "And I, you. I do not know how I would have survived without your caring."

During Helwin's absence, Carl wandered the streets of Rugen. Hands thrust deep into pockets, chin nearly resting on his chest, he could not escape the image of Helwin in his mind. The feeling of her hand in his. While pacing his room late one evening, Carl admitted to himself that he was falling in love with Helwin.

"Oh, damn it," he muttered fiercely. "Oh, goddamit to hell. Why her? She's in love with Jeff, not me. I don't have a chance."

Helwin finished her business at the Alemanni camp and returned to Rugen as ordered. Carl knew she was in town but felt such aching pain that he moved a cot into an unused room at the hospital so he wouldn't have to see her.

Having finished rounds one afternoon, he sat on the cot staring at the floor. Worried staff paused at the doorway every so often to glance inside. He took no notice. The evening shift came on duty and the hospital settled into its darkened, quiet mood.

Carl heard boots on the floor planking, but only in a distant fashion. He came back from wherever his mind had wandered, wondering who was gently shaking him. He looked up into blue eyes and felt his soul naked to their steady gaze.

Taking his hand, Helwin pulled Carl upright. She held his hand with the same firm grip, looked into his heart and confirmed her own. The pain of loss eased, and the world seemed brighter.

"Will you share this evening with me?"

She didn't wait for an answer, just handed him his coat. When he hesitated she threw it around his shoulders and pulled him from the room. They walked through quiet ice-caked streets and pools of lantern light, neither speaking. Helwin guided Carl to the inn he had first taken her to. She accepted a hot cup of coffee from the waitress. Taking a sip, she dropped her eyes to the tabletop.

"While absent, my heart knew profound confusion. Only while nearing Rugen again did I begin to understand, for perplexion turned to excitement at the prospect of being in your company. When I could not find you at Lord Ethbar's home, I feared that something vital to my spirit had again been lost. I believe I may have resigned from hope at that pass were not the Lady Zimma a most perceptive woman.

"She accepted me whether I would have her or not and was not long in winning me over. Through her heart, and gaining a better understanding of my own, I began to win release from Jeffrey. With her encouragement I came to understand my full peril and sought you out." Helwin looked up, tears shimmering in her eyes.

"Much like Jeffrey's, my spirit has been deeply wounded by this past winter. Will you company such a one? May I seek your friendship, hoping to establish the love I anticipate?"

On the way to the inn Carl had hardly dared hope. Now his heart was singing. He took Helwin's hands.

"Whatever the outcome, whatever the cost, I would not lose your presence. A large part of what I am is in your keeping whether I would have it so or not. Let us begin with friendship and accept love or not as the gods ordain. I would company you."

Blue eyes and blond heads dancing courtship, they ate without seeming to notice that they did. Carl tossed a few coins on the table and they walked out with their arms around one another.

Jeff slept the clock around without moving. Zimma had food waiting when he got up, and was astounded at how much he shoveled down. When the table was empty she offered to get more.

"Thanks, love, but I have to check on the troop."

"Are you well enough? You are so thin!"

He gave her a resounding kiss. "I can't tell you how much better I feel. Just being with you has made the difference."

While still tired and depressed, he could at least hold his own against the guilt. Jeff hurried to the barracks where the Alemanni were quartered.

Most were sleeping and he found those who were awake gathered at a table eating. Jeff indicated they were not to rise but Elke stood up at once, as did Wulfern. Both had been a constant source of strength to the troop. They had shared a burrow during the blizzard and since that time had been inseparable.

"Is Lieutenant Helwin here?"

"She was only moments ago, Captain," Wulfern said while looking around with a puzzled frown. "I am sure she intended…" Elke discreetly poked Wulfern in the ribs.

"Perhaps she left to look in on the horses."

After conversing with the troops for a period, Jeff visited the stable. Helwin had not put in an appearance. Thinking he would catch her later, Jeff returned to Ethbar's residence. There was something of vital importance he needed to tell Zimma. On the way back he reflected that it was also something he was no longer worried about telling her.

Sitting close together near the fireplace that evening sharing a glass of wine, Balko asleep by the bed, Jeff took Zimma's hand.

"I learned from Helwin that Magda has quickened. There is little doubt she carries my child."

Zimma squeezed Jeff's hand and thoughtfully swirled the wine in her glass. "I have contemplated Magda; what you have told me of your time together. Now my conclusions are confirmed. I believe it was her full intent to quicken from your seed. I do not condemn Magda, for I would have done the same in her position."

Looking up from her glass, Zimma searched Jeff's face with brilliant green eyes. Deep within, phosphorescent sparks slowly whirled.

Once the effect had been disturbing, now it was very satisfying. Lost in miniature galaxies, he wondered in passing why he had never seen the effect in Magda or Helwin. Jeff kissed Zimma on the cheek, then the nose. She smiled and held her lips up for the real thing.

"This child is yours, and it is Magda's. But it is also mine. What you have given her has also been given to me, and will bear fruit in due season. You have said that Magda plans to journey south. I pray this is so. If she does not we must seek her out. She is ours, we are hers. Now we are four."

"And I am the luckiest man in the world. I do not know how I could have been so fortunate."

A mischievous smile played with Zimma's lips. "Two women in your bed will pose a challenge, do you not agree?"

Jeff blushed at the prospect, and it deepened at Zimma's bubbling laughter.

"Oh, Jeffrey, my delightful earthling, you are such a joy." Putting her wineglass down, Zimma stood up and held her hands out to him. "Come. This evening I feel it time to put your renewed strength to the test."

The creaking, surging mattress briefly awakened Balko. Dropping head between paws, he closed his eyes smiling a wolf smile.

That night marked a turning point in his recovery. Jeff awoke feeling energized and ready to get on with life. They roamed the city from end to end in company with Balko. Long lunches and shopping, shared laughter over Balko's exploits, slow evening meals and cuddling in front of the fire—it was the first quiet period they had ever had together.

Day by day, Jeff felt himself falling in love with Zimma in a new, deeper fashion. The only frustration in his life was trying to hook up with Helwin. He might as well have been searching for a ghost. Jeff thought he knew the reason.

Ethbar took note of Jeff's return to health and suggested it was time to have a Telling. Zimma and Jeff quickly agreed. They set a date and Jeff sought out Elke and Wulfern.

"I believe it were wise that I not accompany you to our camp. Do you understand why I say this?"

"Yes, Captain," Elke replied. "It has been a painful time for the lieutenant."

"Please give her my greetings and let her know that we will have a Telling one week from this date."

"She might not wish to return, Captain."

"And I appreciate her feelings, yet her presence is required."

"Yes, sir."

On the appointed day, extra chairs were being moved into Ethbar's sitting room when Belstan, Rogelf and Ostfel drifted in. They were early, but by design. Ethbar bustled into the room, pulled them to a table set with coffee cups and picked up a fresh carafe of brew steaming on a charcoal brazier.

The steward was mortified that Ethbar would do such a thing. He hurried over, snatched the carafe from Ethbar's hands and gracefully poured a round. Ethbar winked at the steward before concentrating his attention on Belstan and Rogelf.

"Now then, my friends, I will admit to being intrigued by the trade prospects you anticipate with the West and East. Would you be so kind?..." The trio wandered toward the fireplace deep in conversation.

Gaereth and Rengeld sauntered in some time later, followed by Jeff, Zimma and Balko. It was a raw spring day, the room was quite cool, and the vast fire burning on the grate drew everyone close to warm their hands and backsides. It was the first time they had all gathered at the same time, and enthusiastic conversations filled the room.

While chatting with Ethbar, Jeff frequently glanced at the entryway. "I'm quite concerned about Carl. If he does not arrive soon, I will most certainly drag him here if necessary. He has been so sad of late." Jeff pursed his lips and frowned worriedly. "Come to think of it, though, I haven't seen Carl for well over a week. We cannot have this meeting without him."

"And we shall not." Ethbar nodded toward the doorway.

Jeff turned quickly to see Carl walk in with a stunning blond on his arm. Jeff whistled under his breath.

"What a beautiful woman. Way to go, Carl. That explains why I haven't seen him, but where did she come from?" Jeff did a double take. "It's Helwin! I didn't recognize her."

She was wearing an ankle-length, light blue gown made of winter weight wool, and had a long cape of darker blue picked out with cream embroidery thrown about her shoulders. Helwin's blond hair, which trailed down to her waist, had been brushed until it gleamed and was gathered with a pale pink ribbon. While still quite thin, that only added to the sense of elegance she projected.

Carl and Helwin stopped just inside the room to look around. Carl appeared flustered and nervous, but Jeff hardly noticed. He had not seen Helwin since their return and could not take his eyes off her. Memories of their winter together rushed to mind. They were so strong that Jeff was carried far south by the impact.

Helwin was more than nervous and anxiously scanned the room. Her head stopped when she saw Jeff. Electric blue and yellow-green eyes locked together, forming a conduit for the exchange of memories: bitter cold, starvation, death, shared warmth; loving. The room faded from Jeff's perception as his spirit drank the bitter and the sweet.

Conversing with Gaereth four or five steps away, Zimma turned as Carl and Helwin entered. So did the rest of those gathered, and conversations trailed off to silence.

A hand fluttered to Zimma's throat when she saw the way Jeff and Helwin were looking at each other. Gaereth circled Zimma's shoulders with an arm, and whispered, "What Jeff and Helwin must be feeling is not to be long endured. I am also deeply concerned for Carl. We must intervene before all three come to harm."

One glance at the stark fear in Carl's expression and Zimma squeezed Gaereth's arm.

"I shall see to Helwin and Carl, will you attend Jeffrey?" Gaereth nodded quickly and hurried off.

Zimma walked up to Helwin and hugged her. "You are so beautiful, Helwin. Carl is most fortunate."

When she broke eye contact with Jeff and realized who was holding her, Helwin's cheeks turned a soft rose. She did not avoid Zimma's eyes.

"Thank you for finding a place for me in your heart."

Extracting a square of embroidered linen, Zimma dabbed at the tears in Helwin's eyes and stepped back. They shared a long look that conveyed volumes.

"I feel so fortunate that you were with Jeffrey. Thank you for loving him." Zimma planted a kiss on Carl's cheek. "I was becoming concerned about your solitary life, Carl. I am so happy for you both."

Inserting herself between Helwin and Carl, Zimma led them toward the fireplace and a circle of intense interest. When Helwin had been introduced around, Zimma hurried to be with Jeff.

Letting out a relieved gust of air, Ethbar muttered, "Thank the gods for Zimma and Gaereth. It was a near thing." He raised his voice to be heard.

"Please attend me. I believe a good beginning would be made by asking Rengeld to relate what occurred after Jeffrey and Helwin left for the south."

Everyone hurried to the semicircle of chairs arranged to face the fireplace.

Placing his back against familiar stonework, Rengeld nodded toward Jeff. "You were not gone many weeks before the siege engines had been rebuilt. Shortly they were relentlessly employed to hurl firepots and stones into the city, for having constructed city walls the Salchek knew them to be proof against such assault.

"Two times they attacked and were repulsed, moving siege towers first against the south then the west wall. Sorely had they underestimated our ability to man the walls, losing many lives during each attack.

"However, unbeknownst to ourselves they had constructed a mighty ram protected by thick shields deep in the forest. This they did apply with great vigor to the south gate one moonless night while moving siege towers and many ladders against the east wall.

"Time and again they won their way onto Rugen's battlements only to be thrown back. Yet despite valiant defense they did finally succeed. When their foothold was secure, the Salchek directed large numbers of troops into the city and advanced on the palace, savage resistance notwithstanding. Throughout it all, the ram continued its thunder on the gate and soon its hinges began to weaken.

"It was then that Lord Carl's explosives were employed to devastating effect." Rengeld paused, shaking his head as he remembered.

"The ram's shields were shattered by the first explosion, exposing those handymen left standing to a rain of arrows. Other bombs were hurled to destroy men and machines alike. At the height of Salchek terror, Alemanni warriors descended upon them in main force, called up by the good offices of Lord Gaereth and Gurthwin of Valholm.

"Falling upon their rear like a lightning bolt, this attack forced the Salchek to abandon their assault on Rugen in order to preserve their lives. When the Alemanni withdrew by design, they left the Salchek Army in ruins. The abject fear inspired by our ally's wolf companions can only be imagined, for at least four packs engaged the enemy. And so the Salchek's main thrust was broken, and those who had won entry entirely destroyed.

The several attempts on this city thereafter were paltry affairs of desperation. Although a modest offensive would have forced an unconditional surrender, I was loath to unnecessarily expend more lives. During quiet moments of reflection I have regretted that decision."

Rengeld's face became grim. "Then the snows came. I am a man of war, but sorely was my soul tried as the Salchek began to struggle among themselves. Soon they were dying by the hundreds from wounds and starvation. As they came to understand that the long-awaited caravan was not to arrive, all order disappeared.

"Desertion became rampant as winter deepened, yet to what safe haven could they flee? Disease soon marched among them, and many hundreds more died.

"Unable to endure observing such dishonorable and wretched death, we accepted their pleas and offered succor. Some eight hundreds were all that remained and gratefully accepted." Rengeld bowed and sat down, his face a study in sadness.

Carl gave a brief summary of the city's losses, which amounted to a little more than 400 counting injuries and deaths from stones that were tossed over the walls.

The mood in the room had become somber. Jeff threw a question at his friend that he thought would break the spell.

"How did your hospital work out?"

"Outstanding! I think we must have saved fifty people just from using antiseptic technique. Only had to do two amputations. Those books Gaereth brought really saved the day."

Carl indicated that Gaereth stand and take a bow, which he overdid, leading to a round of laughter and applause.

Ethbar announced a break for lunch and there was a general rush toward the buffet. Jeff lingered behind until he could speak to Zimma with some privacy. First thing, however, he kissed her with such passion that she blushed and pulled away.

"Jeffrey! Think of the people!"

"That's just too bad, sweetheart," Jeff said with a big grin. "Thank you for being so loving and thoughtful. Greeting Helwin in such a generous fashion after having been informed of Magda could not have been easy for you."

"It was not, Jeffrey," Zimma replied, looking down at the floor. "You and Helwin have shared so much, had so much more time together than we have. When first I viewed Helwin upon your return, then again while encouraging her to seek out Carl, I thought it likely she had shared her body with you. Helwin's eyes have now confirmed this and made no apologies."

"She is direct."

"Which I cherish. Helwin is a woman of great character, much as I know Magda to be. Thus I also understand your loving was not frivolous. Yet it was difficult." She abruptly looked up and smiled, but tears lurked in the corners of her eyes.

"Please, Jeffrey—you must avoid being thrown together with any more such women." Tears flooded over and she rushed into his arms.

Jeff held Zimma and rubbed her back while she sobbed quietly. "Your part has been hard and long, sweetheart. One of endless waiting." Jeff gently untangled himself and looked deep into Zimma's eyes. "Your conclusions are correct—our loving was not frivolous or frequent, rather a coming together to sustain life and hope. But know that rather than risk losing my place in your heart, we will leave this day and journey north. There we will be done with partings, done with war, done with grief. I cannot live without you, Zimma."

Zimma's tears brimmed over again. Throwing herself at Jeff, she crushed her lips to his. When she released him, they had to gasp for air and it was Jeff's turn to blush. Glancing around the room, he saw that everyone was pointedly not looking at them.

"Think of the people, Zimma!"

Brushing away her tears, Zimma took Jeff's hand and pulled him toward the buffet.

"How did you phrase that, Jeffrey? That's just too bad? Now come, let us take food. Your place in my heart will never be given up, war must be pursued, and of more immediate importance, our appetites attended to."

Later, Jeff and Zimma strolled out of doors to help the food and emotions settle.

"I need to speak with Helwin before the Telling resumes, Zimma. Will that be all right?"

"Yes, of course you might. She is a lovely woman and perfectly honest." Zimma stopped to face Jeff. "It has been our time apart when you were denied to me that has torn at my heart, not Magda and Helwin. I need you, Jeffrey. Need to grow and share with you. I love you so much."

They turned around and walked slowly toward Ethbar's residence. Arm around Zimma's shoulders, Jeff said, "I have learned so much from the wolves. To them, there is nothing in life that surpasses working for the common good of the pack. They do not even think of themselves as separate entities or assign names. This is all summed up in one phrase: we are one."

Zimma nodded and put an arm around his waist.

When they entered the parlor, Helwin and Carl were conversing in a corner with their heads nearly touching.

Zimma murmured to Jeff, "I believe my tears were shared by another if Helwin's bear testimony."

"This has been a wonderful but trying morning," Jeff commented. "My heart yearns that she and Carl find one another before there are no more tears to cry."

Cocking her head as they walked, Zimma observed, "My eyes inform me they have done so, or are well along that way." Helwin and Carl's lips met in a soft kiss. "A most promising embrace, Jeffrey."

Zimma's tone was so satisfied that Jeff was still chuckling when they stopped by Carl and Helwin. Helwin smiled at Jeff through her tears.

"I find that trials of the heart are more fearsome than those of the sword."

There was no need to reply. Jeff smiled back and was satisfied to admire her spirit from a new more comfortable perspective. He also wanted to hug Helwin, but was afraid he would hurt Zimma or Carl if he did so. Helwin leaned toward him, then back.

"Oh, for heaven's sake!"

Carl put a hand on their shoulders and shoved Jeff and Helwin together. It felt so good to reaffirm their special love in each other's arms that Jeff and Helwin stood there with blissful smiles on their faces.

"What a pair!"

"Yes, and what a wonderful man you are, Carl Jorgenson. Come here." Zimma gave Carl a kiss that was no sisterly affair.

Chairs were starting to fill again, and Jeff released Helwin. Taking her arm and Zimma, Carl's, they strolled toward the fireplace. Jeff sat down next to Helwin.

"I want you to give our portion of the Telling."

A shot of panic flashed across Helwin's face. "But Captain, it isn't my place! I'll blow the damn thing right out the door!"

Snapping his head around, Carl stared at Helwin in amazement. "Jeffrey, what have you taught this woman?"

Jeff grinned but did not divert his attention from Helwin. "Why not? Why isn't it your place to give the Telling?"

Panic receded, leaving a stubborn set to Helwin's mouth. "I have never addressed such a group of people in my life, Jeffrey. It is your honor, you must give the Telling."

"I have all the honor one man can tolerate," Jeff replied with a vigorous shake of his head. "You are an excellent leader, but must learn all of the responsibilities that go along with being one. Besides, I've had to give so many Tellings that I need a break. Let's do it this way. I'll make a short speech to ease your way. The tale then becomes yours until our return, at which point I have something that must be said. Don't worry so! How many winter stories have you heard? Is there an end to them? Recall some you admire and add your own words. Piece of cake."

Outmaneuvered, her flank turned, Helwin resorted to panic again. She needed to walk it off but Ethbar called the meeting to order. Winter tales! I must recall winter tales! Helwin squeezed Carl's hand so hard that he winced.

"Now we must hear what transpired to the south. I say must, for my heart pleads otherwise. This has been a difficult Telling, and I fear that which we are about to hear promises no release." Ethbar smiled down at Helwin and Jeff, then Carl and Zimma.

"What hope I have springs from the love and friendship that has united four people this day—war's sundering has not prevailed." Ethbar motioned Jeff forward.

Walking over to the fireplace, Jeff put chin in hand. "There is no gainsaying that our tale is strewn with terrible loss. Who would argue that war would have it otherwise? Though surrounded by the warmth and comfort of friends, still I feel the cold bitterness that took so many comrades. It must also be said that not all our comrades were human, but wolves and horses as well. Helwin will recount these events, for her part looms large. Lacking her courage we would not have succeeded."

Jeff gave Helwin a hand to her feet, and whispered, "You'll do fine, Lieutenant." He patted her hand and sat down. Carl stood up and raised Helwin's hand to his lips.

"Knock 'em dead, kid."

The insouciant grin on his face banished stage fright. Helwin leaned down to touch lips.

"Thanks, lover, this is a tough one."

There was no need to wait for silence when she arrived at the spot that had become the Station of Telling.

"My captain has given me this honor, and I will strive to do it justice. My courage notwithstanding, all would have come to naught without his leadership."

She stood silent with bowed head for some time, calling those bitter months back from memory's graveyard. Beginning with the decision to head south, Helwin briefly recounted the forming of the Alemanni First Cavalry. She then led them on the southward journey and their contact with the caravan.

As she counted the wains, packhorses, foot soldiers and cavalry, her eyes grew distant. Within minuets she was there again, crouched on top of a hill far to the south.

Jeff glanced around and noted expressions of amazed consternation at the caravan's size. Had it won through to Rugen, the siege would not have been broken.

As the winter's running battle unfolded, Zimma put her arm around Jeff's waist and laid her head on his shoulder. Their march to the forest hit Jeff hard. As Helwin chanted out the deaths of horses and warriors, he started shivering and couldn't stop until Zimma pulled him against her.

"...And so we returned through fields of dead to the loving warmth of friends and hope renewed."

At the story's conclusion Carl leaped to his feet and escorted Helwin to her seat. She wished to be held and they did not sit down at once. Jeff patted her shoulder on the way by.

"That was a Telling to be proud of."

Ethbar had returned to the fireplace but gave way when Jeff approached.

"I won't be long, Ethbar."

"Take whatever time is required. I perceive that what remains to be said is important."

Jeff didn't reply, but his expression was ineffably sad. Ethbar moved off a few steps and waited with crossed arms. A truth was about to be revealed.

"A spirit has passed from this world to the next." Jeff paused and looked at the floor. Not now. Don't lose it now. "His passing will never be forgotten, for he gifted me with insight and bequeathed a cherished possession in remembrance of failed enmity."

Reaching into a pocket, Jeff held up the curved-stem pipe. Extracting the pouch, he dipped the pipe inside and tamped sindar weed into the bowl.

"He was an enemy, was Lingol Bollit, but I came to understand that he did not hate me. A Salchek officer, he was a man of honor who fulfilled his duty to the death. And yet, though I was the instrument of his death, he did not hate me."

Rengeld watched Jeff slowly, somberly, fill the pipe and felt something well up that he thought had been lost forever. A great wave of emotion brought him to his feet and attention. A true comrade at arms had passed on, leaving a hole in the world. An instant later, Helwin joined him.

Dropping to a knee, Jeff pried a splinter of wood from a log and let it ignite in the fireplace.

"We have sung his spirit to rest, we have seen a bright light streak across the heavens, I have breathed smoke from his gomwok to the winds. Lingol Bollit, I salute and thank you for your gift of understanding."

The burning splinter descended to the pipe bowl. As before, Jeff drew deeply and exhaled.

To Jeff, Helwin and Rengeld, it was as if a door opened and they were in the presence of Lingol Bollit. Distant yet imminent, he bowed, flashed a cocky grin and the door closed with a gentle sigh.

Carl knew something had occurred, could feel it, saw the desperate sadness in Helwin as she fought back tears. He glanced at Rengeld and looked again. A large tear rolled down his cheek.

Ethbar was the first to move. Awaiting truth, he had not been prepared for its realization. While he had sensed no presence, he understood they had been visited.

"This has been a wondrous Telling. Wonder fills my heart that Jeffrey and Carl should come among us when they did, and as they did. I wonder at forces beyond my understanding that have brought us all together. As in the past, I am reminded that chance had no part. Our fate, one and all, is in the hands of the gods." He paused until Jeff emptied the pipe and returned to his seat.

"The festival celebrating Rugen's delivery will occur in seven days. The essence of what has been said and experienced here today must be conveyed to all that attend. They must understand the sacrifice and suffering that has been endured in saving their city." Ethbar raised his arms in a sweeping gesture.

"They must understand that what has been done may be done again, and so be sustained in whatever dark hours may be their due in seasons to come."

Jeff and Helwin left for the Alemanni encampment the following day, accompanied by Zimma and Carl. Although still quite thin, Cynic was making a good recovery and insisted on going. Jeff could see he was chaffing at being cooped up and agreed, but saddled another horse and let Cynic run free.

As soon as they were out of the city, Cynic went charging after Balko and the two of them disappeared over the hill. When the foursome trotted over the crest, Carl pulled Sam to an abrupt halt.

"Oh, shit!"

Balko was almost on them and running flat out with Cynic giving it all he had a short ways behind. Balko whizzed by like a blur, but Cynic was no wolf and thundered by with pounding hooves and only feet away from a head-on collision.

Zimma's mare, Pella, reared in fright and tried to bolt. Zimma had no more than settled her down when Balko and Cynic roared back over the hill and chased each other around the horses.

"*Wolf-brother! Horse-brother! That is enough! You will stay ahead of us from now on! Is that clear?*" Wolf and Horse slid to a halt. "*You are far from recovered, horse-brother, and should you become ill from these exertions I can assure you of harsh words and long days in the stable. Now get out of here and keep it clean!*"

Suitably chastened, the two friends trotted into the forest. Jeff watched them go with a shake of his head. He knew their pursuit games would start again the minute they were out of sight.

Balko and Cynic arrived at the Alemanni camp long before their companions. As a result, the place was buzzing with excitement when they rode in.

As expected, it wasn't long before the beer barrels were rolled out and the meeting hall set up for dancing. The warriors had never seen such a small woman and gathered around to be introduced to Zimma. The Alemanni women were as intrigued as the men.

Although Zimma was used to men towering over her, she felt intimidated by the giant size of the women. Helwin was taller than most of them, but there were so many. She felt like a girl, and got a crick in her neck trying to see their faces. However, it wasn't long before she realized they had many interests in common.

Their questions about her hair were so open and excited that she shook it out so they could play with it. Not to be outdone, the men waited their chance and spun Zimma into the dancing. Later that evening they sneaked away to enjoy some quiet time together.

"It appears that you and Gurthwin gave the Salchek no rest, Halric."

Much thinner and more severe in appearance, Halric's good humor had not suffered.

"How we stung them, Jeffrey! We took your counsel to heart and plagued them unceasingly. Never will I forget the night we finally broke upon them in all our fury, scattering Salchek like leaves before the tempest! It was most difficult to withdraw as planned."

Gurthwin was content to study Zimma and Jeff, then Carl and Helwin. He smiled secretly from time to time and every so often chuckled with great satisfaction.

The Rugen contingent, including Helwin, left the following morning after inviting everyone in camp to the festivities.

The foul weather broke, and all greeted the season's first clear and sparkling days with great relief. At Carl's insistence, prisoners were put to work burying and burning decomposing bodies outside city walls.

That accomplished, prisoners not of Salchek origin were released to find their way home to Astholf or Khorgan. Before they departed, each prisoner was supplied with a dowry of food and the means of defense. Although there were less than a hundred Salchek prisoners, their disposition proved troublesome.

Rengeld agreed with Jeff that the enlisted men and junior officers should be released. The number of enlisted was small enough to make no difference as combat elements in an army, and the officers were inexperienced. It was the six senior officers, two of field grade rank, which posed the problem. They understood every feature of the land surrounding Rugen; had taken the city's measure. That, Rengeld observed, posed a danger.

"Okay, let's interview the field grade types and find out where they stand," Jeff said one afternoon during a prolonged debate that was going nowhere. "If we can determine they are men of honor like Lingol, and if they are willing to give their word not to participate in any aspect of this invasion, I think we ought to release them. If they are not men of honor, well, there is ample room in the dungeon for a prolonged stay. As I recall, they are both fluent in our tongue."

They met with the two officers in the dungeon. Rengeld in the lead, they descended several spiral staircases of stone. The air was ripe with the smell of unwashed bodies, smoke from torches, and other odors that, perhaps, spoke of terror.

Entering a stuffy room that reeked of mold and dripped moisture, Rengeld seated himself behind a trestle table and invited Jeff to do the same. The clang of cell doors closing boomed drearily in dissonance with the guards' occasional laughter outside the room. Shortly, the two Salchek officers were ushered inside.

Both men were clean-shaven, in their fifties, and neatly attired in surprisingly intact uniforms. The shorter officer, a lean whippet of a man, casually appraised the room. He bowed and took a seat when Rengeld indicated he could sit. The other Salchek, the older of the two, looked around as if he expected someone to pull the chair out for him.

When no one did he remained standing and assumed a defiant posture. He was florid faced, somewhat paunchy, and to Jeff's mind merely succeeded in appearing pompous. Maybe a prima donna, he tentatively decided. Rengeld had named them earlier. The one in the chair was Bithro Kalmit, the other, Citran Toltek.

"We are presented with a dilemma, gentlemen," Rengeld stated without preamble. "While we do not wish to needlessly imprison you, release is impossible if that means you will rejoin the army of invasion."

"Arvalia is a territory of Salchesia," Toltek shot back. "We are not invaders."

"Call it what you like," Rengeld drawled, "but I would think that events to date indicate we don't agree with you."

Jeff rubbed his eyebrows to hide a grin, and thought, Yes, Rengeld!

Toltek's face took on dark red hue, but Kalmit smiled dryly. "Well put, Commander. I must agree that our reception did indicate a certain difference of opinion on this matter. What do you propose?"

"We have had contact with one of your officers that suggests professionals of the Salchek Army hold honor in high esteem. On your sworn word as gentlemen that you will return to Salchesia and not participate in this war in any fashion, we will consider setting you free."

"May we confer privately, Commander?"

"Of course," Rengeld replied to Kalmit. When the Salchek had been escorted to a cell to converse, Rengeld sat back and looked at Jeff. "Opinions, please."

"Not sure what to think at this point. Kalmit is a cool customer, maybe too cool, and Toltek impresses me as a self-important ass." Jeff twitched his shoulders in a shrug. "Still, those are only first impressions. What has occurred to me is that we know nothing of their customs. Lingol was an honorable man, but how does that virtue relate to Salchek customs of behavior? The two are not the same thing."

"I agree, Captain. It is possible that sworn word means nothing in Salchek society."

"Even if it does, how would that apply to northern barbarians? We are not, you know, of noble birth."

Rengeld snorted. "Thank the gods."

"Amen," Jeff added with heartfelt sincerity. "Do you know which one has the higher rank or more time in grade?"

"Reportedly, Toltek."

"Well, that didn't take long," Jeff said with a surprised look out the doorway. "They're back already."

Toltek huffed into the room and seemed angry, or at least his face gave that impression. Kalmit clicked his heels and bowed.

"I have been asked by Senior Hetlan Toltek to convey his decision. Upon release, we will return to the Homeland and attend to military affairs in theaters other than Arvalia. Although

519

distressed by this decision, the hetlan believes our imprisonment serves no end."

"And the other officers?"

"I'm sure the hetlan will prove persuasive."

Rengeld studied the two men while pondering Kalmit's statement. Sincere in structure, it was evasive in substance. Kalmit met his eyes calmly while Toltek scowled at a wall.

Jeff couldn't put his finger on it, but something was making him uneasy. He found himself pawing at a breast pocket and smiled ruefully. *Two puffs on that pipe and I'm getting hooked.* Jeff abruptly stiffened. *What the hell was that? Did someone just laugh?*

The impression, for it was no more than that, tickled his mind again. He was only puzzled for a few moments. It hadn't been that long since the Telling.

Jeff opened his mind and smiled with pleased amazement as information was arrayed for his perception. The information was both foreign and quite interesting. There was one Salchek custom he was now familiar with.

"I am satisfied the hetlan will persuade the other officers. Before that occurs we will need to have your individual oaths."

Jeff's assumption of authority took Rengeld by surprise. He looked at Jeff with narrowed eyes, but they had worked together long enough that he decided to let matters ride. There was no doubt in his mind that Jeff was up to something.

"I cannot give my word under these circumstances."

Well now, Jeff thought while glancing at Toltek, *what have we here? What is he referring to? Which circumstances? Time to find out.* Jeff drew the gomwok from his breast pocket.

When Kalmit saw the pipe, his mouth moved but no words came out. Toltek rushed to the table.

"You must tell me where you came by this!" He caught himself and bowed. "Please. Please tell me."

Calmly packing the gomwok with sindar weed, Jeff held it out to Toltek. He took it as a revered object.

"Lingol Bollit granted it to me as a last wish far south on the prairie."

Rengeld gripped the hilt of his sword and motioned to the guard. The guard had come to the same conclusion and summoned two of his fellows into the room. Kalmit not only looked like he was ready to explode with fury, his features had in fact transformed into something hardly recognizable as human.

"You stripped his body! This is intolerable! Honor means nothing to you animals!" Kalmit lunged at Jeff.

Action blurred into surreal elements that moved too fast for recognition. When time slowed to its usual pace, Kalmit was thrashing on the floor and his hands were being bound.

"Barbarian swine! Not even a chattel would perform such an act!"

"Perhaps," Jeff said pleasantly. "I can understand your anger, yet I have given Lingol Bollit's smoke to the winds and the Song for the Dead has been sung. We have seen the light of his passage and he is with me now. Will you share the gomwok in memory of a dedicated, courageous man? Will this not reveal the truth?"

The guards hoisted Kalmit to his feet. "I do not share this sacred ceremony with vagabond thieves," he snarled. There was no conviction in his voice and his eyes constantly returned to the gomwok, which Toltek still held.

"May I have the pouch of sindar weed and the loan of your stylus?"

Jeff handed both to Toltek.

Inserting the stylus, Toltek emptied the bowl into the pouch. "Please observe."

Jeff stood up so he could, and received a thorough lesson on how much sindar weed to use, very little, and how tightly to pack it, not very. Toltek handed the gomwok to Jeff.

"You must know that sindar weed is worth more by weight than gold, yet the gomwok far exceeds such value for it is sacred, even as Kalmit has implied."

"Why do you tell me this?"

Rather than answer directly, Toltek said, "Will you tell me of Lingol's death?"

Rengeld had not heard the story and motioned for Jeff to go ahead. At the conclusion, the room was hushed. While Kalmit appeared stunned, Toltek was radiant.

"It is true. You have seen the Light of Passage. Will you tell me of the Song for the Dead?"

It was late, matters were not complete concerning the prisoners, and, more importantly, Jeff was not about to share the words with Kalmit.

"Perhaps later in a more worthy setting." Jeff decided it was time to return the ball to Rengeld's court where it belonged. "Commander Rengeld, my apologies for intruding."

"Given the outcome you have my thanks, Captain." He turned to the prisoners. "And now let us try conclusions. Kalmit, you are senior and have attempted to use an officer junior to yourself as a ploy to avoid giving your word of honor.

"Such an act, to use a man in this fashion, indicates to me that your word is worthless absent the gomwok. Either you share in its smoke or you will certainly remain imprisoned. Hetlan Toltek, I will accept your word as sufficient."

"Lingol Bollit was my friend. I would share his smoke in remembrance." He smiled at Kalmit. "Come, my hetlan, will you not join us?"

In the blink of an eye Kalmit's face transformed again. The changes were so grotesque and horrifying that Jeff and Rengeld leaped to their feet drawing swords.

Words of fury that could not be understood but which were perceived to fly from Kalmit's mouth as virtual objects spewed forth in a chainsaw roar. Heavy with incredible malice, they caromed around the room seeking to extinguish life in murder and madness.

Rengeld and Jeff lunged away to the left and right in a wild scramble. Black foam sprayed from Kalmit's mouth in stinging droplets and he burst the bonds on his wrists as if they were string. Yellow tusks suddenly protruded from open jaws and he sprang at Jeff.

In a brief twinkle of light, Berold flew to meet him with all the strength in Jeff's arm. Penetrating chest wall and lungs, six inches of blade sprang out of Kalmit's back to stand in silver relief. For one brief instant motion stopped. Kalmit's eyes bulged and he emitted a deafening roar of pain.

Now the words were screamed, words of demonic command that blasted water from the walls in steaming vapor and sent furniture tumbling to shatter against stone. Green fluid flowed over the blade in smoking tendrils but could not quench the power of Light over Darkness.

Spittle burned like acid on Jeff's face and clawed hands ripped at his clothing. Gripping the sword hilt with both hands, Jeff braced his legs and forced Kalmit backward.

The body that had been Kalmit's convulsed in great, wracking contortions that flung Jeff from side to side. Berold would not relent and remained entrenched as if locked in stone. And still man and sword endured as Kalmit thrashed on the floor in an attempt to dislodge the blade.

Then Toltek was there and dropped a single shred of sindar weed. Brilliant flames of golden white joined silver steel and neither did they heed the cry of final anguish. So died that which had been born Kalmit.

"Do not withdraw the blade, but release it! Step back! It is not done! The man is gone, not the Yakul!"

Jeff forced his hands to open and jumped back. The sodden body on the floor twitched and slithered about like a serpent while all vestiges of human form disappeared. The face was black, had a pig's snout and curving tusks, and red eyes glared around the room. Hair-covered hands totally out of proportion to the arms wrenched at Berold to no effect.

"Get out of my way!"

Something crashed in the hallway and Gaereth burst into the room with Carl on his heels. Gaereth took one look at the monstrosity on the floor and called out in a deep voice, "Begone, evil that was! Visit this land no more! Salag Toleth!"

Green-blue flames leaped high in actinic display and Berold clattered to the floor, for the creature was gone.

Rengeld picked himself up and slapped at smoldering spots on his uniform. A guard lay sprawled on his back, sightless eyes wide with horror. His chest was split open revealing charred lungs. Nothing was left of his heart except a lump of carbonized muscle. Another guard lay unconscious but breathing in the doorway. The third was nowhere to be seen.

"About time." Carl held his mug up.

An orderly cautiously followed the mug as it shook this way and that. He had become adept at doing so two mugs ago and didn't spill a drop.

Rengeld dismissed the orderly and shut the door to his office. "Will the guard survive, Carl?"

"Yes, he's not seriously wounded. The mental shock is another matter. It will be some months before we know the outcome. It's the other one; the one that died that really shook me up. From what you've said, Kalmit never physically touched him." Carl glanced at Jeff.

"I still can't believe you actually saw words leave his mouth and fly around the room. What were they? I mean, that isn't possible!"

"It might not be possible, buddy, but we saw them. That's what killed the guard. I have no idea what the words meant, or what they might sound like if voiced." Jeff frowned in concentration. "One of the words was short. I think it was…"

"Stop! Don't try and pronounce that word!" Gaereth broke off a conversation with Toltek and hurried to the table where Jeff, Rengeld and Carl were seated. "If you even came close it would probably kill you. Do you understand me?"

This was an aspect of Gaereth Jeff had never seen before. The command in his voice demanded immediate compliance without question. Jeff choked back the word he was about to spit out.

"Close call?"

"Very close, Jeff. I know what happened with Kalmit seems bizarre in the extreme to a twenty-first century mind, but one of those words did in fact kill the guard. Don't ever forget it."

"Lord Gaereth is correct." Toltek joined them at the table. "The words had substance and should never be spoken by our kind." He paused to examine Gaereth, something he had been doing overtly and secretly for some time. Turning to Jeff, he said, "May I examine your sword?"

Jeff looked to Gaereth for guidance. "Grandfather?"

Toltek looked back and forth between the two men in renewed amazement. There was no more than five years difference in age. It didn't seem possible. Questions flew through Toltek's mind at a furious rate.

"Yes. It is permitted."

Accepting the saber from Jeff, the questions faded from Toltek's mind. "This is truly a blade of power. Never have I felt such strength of purpose." He studied the blade closely. The finish was mirror perfect. "To my knowledge, there is no sword in Salchesia that would have come through such an encounter unscathed."

The effect of what had occurred in the dungeon, combined with the host of enigmas, discoveries and apparent discrepancies that followed led Toltek to bow around the room.

"We of Salchesia have long thought that no Power resided in Arvalia. This day that impression stands corrected."

Handing Berold to Jeff, Toltek once again tried to penetrate Gaereth's steady gaze; tried to fathom the display of Power he had witnessed. The longer the silent appraisal went on, the more Toltek became convinced he was viewing a man, if that is what he was, far beyond his experience.

Stirring from reflection, he said, "Few in our land could have banished the Yakul so quickly, for its evil is potent."

Gaereth did not rise to the bait, but Jeff did. "That being the case, why did you so casually provoke it?"

"I did not know it was present, Captain Friedrick. Kalmit was a man of sound reputation and demonstrated considerable military talent over the years. That he was arrogant and supremely self-confident is also true, thus the Yakul found entry. Now, I must ask myself, why did it come to Rugen? Kalmit's reputation was such that he could have chosen any number of assignments with much greater prestige."

"But it wasn't Kalmit that chose. Why do you think the Yakul came north?"

"Wait, Jeffrey, just wait a minute!" Carl held his hands up as much in consternation as to halt the conversation. "Do you realize what you're doing? You're sitting here chatting about demons and spirits as if they were politicians. While I'll grant a certain family resemblance, how about we back up a bit and get some background? I mean, after all! Demons?"

Jeff smiled at Carl's comparison but had to admit he had a point. "You're right, Carl. I've got a few steps on you thanks to Gaereth and Lingol Bollit. This is going pretty fast. Hetlan, if your position permits, will you tell us of Salchesia? I have yet to meet anyone in Arvalia that has traveled there."

"It would be indiscreet of me to discuss any matter that might illuminate military policies, Captain Friedrick. However, I deem your interest lies in a different realm. You are not familiar with the Dark Powers?"

"I am familiar with power, but of a much different sort. Power that would lay waste to Arvalia and Salchesia in a storm of fire such that no living thing would take breath for countless years and leave this world in darkness. Yet this power is of man's devising while what I have witnessed this day springs from another source altogether."

Hetlan Toltek studied Jeff, and to his left, Carl. Their grave expressions left no doubt that what Jeff had said was absolute truth.

"Lord Gaereth and Captain Friedrick, the Yakul came because you are here. Lingol Bollit came because you are here. Both to discover the origin and nature of the Power. One springs from Darkness, the other, Light." Toltek held his hands up to mimic a beam scale.

"Evil and Good, forever at war yet perpetually in balance over time. Thus it has been for untold generations in my land. I do not know where Yakul spring from, only that they and other spirits have always been with us. I am at a loss for words to give further explanation to men who so obviously rely on reason to understand the forces that guide and influence our lives. That was not meant as a criticism, but I believe it to be fact."

"You are correct, and I do not take your statement as criticism. Since coming to this world I have had ample cause to question my basis of understanding."

Gaereth threw a sharp look at Jeff, but the words were out. Toltek did not seem surprised.

"Do not be concerned, for I have divined as much if not to this degree. If released, I can assure you such knowledge will remain in my keeping upon return to Salchesia. To do otherwise would assure a quick and violent death. If I were fortunate. There are forces afoot here that I have never experienced, forces that even now contend for mastery over land and sea. The balance has been destroyed."

"Lingol Bollit was of the White? Belonged to an order?"

"An order?" Toltek shrugged helplessly. "Yes, after a fashion, but it was his destiny."

"Enough. I gather you have arrived at a decision?"

"Yes, Commander. I will eschew Arvalia and return to the Homeland. It is also likely I will resign from the military and seek understanding in our centers of learning. When the officers held with us hear of events, I have no doubt they will hurry to give their sincere word as well."

"Very good. You are free to leave at any time. Your weapons will be returned and food will be provided. If there were horses to spare you would have one, but I am afraid this is not the case."

"Commander, the promise of freedom is sufficient. Each stride toward the southern ocean will be as the breath of life."

Twenty-five

Denouement

The festival was scheduled to begin the following day, Jeff recalled while walking along in a dark study. Thank heavens. Something enjoyable.

Hetlan Toltek and subordinates were well on their way south in possession of Lingol Bollit's personal effects and those of other Salchek. The room in the dungeon had been scrubbed clean and thoroughly disinfected under Carl's direction.

They had decided that only Imogo and Ethbar would be briefed. Certainly not the populace unless rumors from what had occurred gained a foothold. Whatever evil was to come, anticipation and superstition would only make it worse. As Rengeld observed, how did one prepare for the advent of demons?

Yet Jeff had reservations and planned to speak with Gurthwin at earliest opportunity. He needed to understand what they might well confront in the future. Not only evil, but also good. Memories of Lingol's presence and caroling bells were not easily dismissed. He and Carl planned to hold nothing back from Zimma and Helwin.

"Wake up, Friedrick!"

Carl grabbed Jeff by the arm and turned him back toward their favorite tavern. Helwin, Zimma and Gaereth waited by the doorway.

"Let it rest for awhile, my man," Carl whispered. "We're alive, we've lucked into wonderful women, and this promises to be one stomping party."

The Golden Bung was a popular tavern and packed with excited town folk eager to get an early start on the festivities. There were no free tables, but Zimma spied Rogelf and Belstan. They were seated at a table with legs kicked out, celebrating the end of another day with several mugs of ale as was their custom.

Rogelf waved them over and pulled up extra chairs. Assisted by the ale, it wasn't long before a wide-ranging bull session was circling the table. Inevitably, the conversation drifted to matters of war and politics.

It was a relief to talk about such mundane things as massed cavalry attacks, siege towers, and treasonous courtiers. Belstan leaned back with tankard in hand, legs crossed in front of him.

"I have just this day spoken with a trader who bribed his way out of Khorgan and journeyed north by way of Astholf. While this young man appears to be most devious, he is also quite courageous to risk such a journey during wartime and so early in the season." Belstan paused long enough to let loose a satisfying belch. "Now do not take this to heart, but I believe we may have a respite from the war. It is Malchor's opinion that the Salchek will be hard pressed to keep control of what they already have."

"That was a big caravan. The Salchek must have stripped Khorgan of wagons and draft horses."

"According to Malchor they did, Jeffrey. The loss of that caravan wreaked havoc in Khorgan. It seems the Salchek promised payment in gold they did not possess or would not release. Many businesses have failed, and others cannot afford to replace the wagons and supplies that were lost. Gods know where they will even be able to find much less purchase new horses! In short, Khorgan and Astholf are near open rebellion. As I was saying, I believe we may be free of the Salchek for a full year.

"This Malchor. Think his information is reliable?"

Belstan shrugged fatalistically. "As far as one can trust anything a trader says, Carl. Something about this lad I like, though." He pursed his lips and nodded. "Sharp mind; knows how to figure the odds. I believe I will have another long talk with him. Rogelf and I may choose to employ him if all goes well."

Tankards were empty and Rogelf called for another round. Instead of more ale the waiter brought a tray of small cups. One sip and Carl coughed loudly.

"Holy stomach lining! Now that is some fine stuff. Goes down like a single malt scotch."

"In honor of this gathering, Carl," Rogelf replied with a satisfied smile.

A period of silence followed, broken by the occasional appreciative comment. Cheeks were getting rosy when Gaereth reluctantly spoke.

"As much as I hate the thought of leaving, I must head east and north as soon as snow levels drop a bit more. I can tell you I have little enthusiasm for the trip to Skene."

"Any choice in the matter?"

"None, I'm afraid. The Alarai counsel is convening an important conference this summer. In addition, there are vital issues I must discuss with them."

"Amen to that, brother," Carl murmured, then said in a normal tone, "Maybe shake them loose from Skene?"

"It's worth a try, but don't hold your breath. I also plan to visit Earth."

"Status check?"

Gaereth nodded toward Jeff. "Good way of putting it. Basically, I want to monitor the situation in America. I've been hoping the National Guard succeeded in restoring order. Even if they did, it's anyone's guess how long it will hold. Whatever the case, I've got to see where things stand. Other countries will have been hit hard by the climatic changes, but that earthquake brought America to its knees. My greatest fear is that by the time we have things under control on Aketti we'll be facing total anarchy."

"And all the king's horses, and all the king's men..."

"...Couldn't put Humpty Dumpty back together again. Yes, it's that critical, Carl. If America ever splits up it would take fifty years of civil war to rejoin it, but certain foreign powers would exert every effort to make sure that never happened."

"Like the Salchek, they would seek its riches for themselves."

"I'm afraid so, Helwin. The memory of empire never diminishes, and often finds expression in the name of assistance and compassion."

The day had been unseasonably warm, promoting high spirits. With Gaereth's news a gloomy pall settled over the table. Belstan shouted for the waiter, ordered another round of scotch with ale for a chaser, and launched into some improbable tale concerning Zomar.

Within a short span Jeff lost himself in visions of soaring minarets and hanging gardens, turbaned warriors and mermaids. The tale was so outrageous and fascinating at the same time that even Gaereth was captivated.

Exile To The Stars

It was only when Zimma reminded everyone that the festival was to begin the next day that they called it quits and headed home.

The festival was to extend over four days. During the first three, a celebration would be held in a different section of the city each day. The fourth was to culminate with a grand ball cum reception at the palace, and general gala throughout the city.

The warm spell held and city folk streamed into the craft section for a day of food and entertainment. The Alemanni enjoyed a party more than most and came to town in force.

Jeff, Zimma, Gaereth, Carl and Helwin went as a group. Ethbar and Rengeld were tied up with Imogo's official presence and had to decline. Much to their delight, they ran into Halric and Gurthwin.

In high spirits and good voice, Halric gathered other Alemanni as they went. Gurthwin hobbled along aided by his staff, muttering as usual. He didn't miss a thing and proved quite willing to sample local brews.

Some hours later they ran into Ethbar and Rengeld. After a few words of greeting, Rengeld was forced to hurry off in order to check up on troops assigned to patrol the carnival. Upon being introduced to Gurthwin, Ethbar chucked the rest of his scheduled duties.

They stopped frequently to more closely debate this issue or that, and quickly fell behind. Ethbar waved for the group to go on without them, hooked Gurthwin's elbow with his own and led him toward a cart selling ale.

Lamps were lighted as evening drew on, lending an exciting air to the scene. Numerous bands wandering the streets took a deep breath and really laid into it.

To a rhythmic clapping of hands, the crowd formed into lines on either side of streets throughout the craft section. Old-timers called out the dance and the lines skipped together with a shout. Skirts held out of the way, hands on hips, thousands of clogs crashed to the cobblestones in quick time syncopation.

On the sidelines, Zimma gripped Jeff's arm with excitement. "I have never seen anything like this!" She pulled him toward the nearest line. "Come, love, let us join in the merriment."

"Well, okay" Jeff dubiously replied, "but don't be surprised if I fall flat on my face."

Helwin still felt shy around city folk and hesitated when Carl suggested they dance as well. Always more outgoing than Jeff, Carl pulled her toward the action. Within minutes Helwin was laughing and skipping with the best of them.

The bands got their second wind, ale flowed, the night fled. The foursome staggered home shortly before the sun made its appearance. They met for lunch and resolved to be more moderate, but dragged home in a sorry state three nights running.

The morning of the official ball, both couples groaned around their rooms and were even a bit snappish. By the time Jeff and Zimma were ready to leave for the palace, spirits and good temper had revived.

Zimma wore a forest green gown with gold embroidery around the hem, accented by a lighter green sash at the waist. A gold necklace set with bits of emerald glimmered and sparked around her neck. Throwing a light wrap around her shoulders, Zimma paused at the door to stick her tongue out at him and spun from sight.

"Hey! Come back here!"

Jeff snuffed the candles and hurried out the door laughing. "Why is it I always seem to be chasing after that woman?"

Strolling toward the palace arm in arm, Jeff breathed deeply of the fresh spring night and gazed at the milky expanse of stars winking in the night sky.

They were nearly to the palace when he stopped and pulled Zimma into his arms. Music flowed from the entrance, and streams of people hurried across the plaza to join the celebration.

"In my wildest imaginings I never dreamed such a wonderful woman could be mine. I cannot imagine life without you...."

A picture of Magda smiling into his eyes at their parting abruptly came to mind. He and Zimma frequently talked about Magda, but it really hit home that he was a father in the fullest sense. Magda would have given birth to their child some months ago. Jeff could not find any words that would fit the moment or do justice to either woman.

Zimma smiled into serious yellow-green eyes and pulled his head down for a kiss. "Or without Magda and our newborn child.

Yes—I understand this and share your joy. Do you not yet comprehend? I love you for what and who you are, and that shall bind me to you until we are no more. There is no recourse to that love, Jeffrey. Do you, then, imagine there remains a moment-to-moment risk that I will spurn you? No, were Magda and our child present to share this wonderful evening, all would be complete."

Breaking free of his arms, Zimma caroled laughter and pirouetted away with outstretched arms through pools of lantern light. Gown and hair swirling high, her laughter overflowed with happiness.

Spellbound, Jeff watched Zimma and recalled a question asked what seemed many years ago in an enchanted forest. The answer leaped out at him: he was not alone; had not been alone for many months.

True understanding that was much more durable than emotion found a home and opened his heart like a flower to the sun. Jeff threw his head back and shouted laughter. He caught Zimma in his arms and spun around.

"I belong to you and Magda. To our child. To this wonderful world. I finally understand what that means. I really belong!"

Zimma pulled herself up until her eyes were so close that he lost himself in their depths and mystery.

"Yes, of course you do. You have come to us and are ours forever." Zimma smiled. "Welcome home, my Jeffrey."

Closing her eyes, Zimma kissed Jeff softly. Lost in one another, they forgot time, war and death as two moons rose over city walls.

Afterword

Reflecting on the evolution of this book from first draft to final form, I was struck by the number of people who have wittingly and unwittingly contributed to its substance. In fact, it is certain that *I* am not aware of many of those who have contributed to *Exile to the Stars*. Given the complexity of writing a novel, how does one know for sure?

However, there are several people not mentioned in the Acknowledgments that I wish to comment on at this point. Their input was critical and came at a critical time.

Morris Berman is a published author and at that time (1996) taught writing in Seattle. Just before I left that city to re-establish myself in Minnesota, Morris reviewed the manuscript. In looking back, I now realize how very rough the MS was. Given that, his summary could have been devastating. Instead he concentrated on the strengths and made necessary comments about correcting the weaknesses. His input kept me going for many months and re-writes.

About a year ago I sent out the first chapter of *Exile* to established science-fiction authors hoping to gain comments. I did receive a few, but only one author took the time to make marginal notes. David Brin's comments set off a chain reaction that sparked at least 5 or 6 re-writes. When the dust settled I had a much better product. It totally amazed me, and still does, that a man as well-known as Mr. Brin would take the time.

I want to make it expressly clear that mention of these men's names in no way represents their endorsement of the book. They were commenting on the structure of the manuscript and not the finished product. That's as it should be.

Exile to the Stars does not require endorsement by anyone but the reader. That is the only endorsement that really counts.

Dale B. Mattheis   Northfield, MN; June, 2002

Ardentpublishing

Order Form

If you would like to purchase *Exile to the Stars* for yourself or a friend, please use the order form below, or visit our web site: www.ardentpublishing.com

Fax Orders: 507-645-2227 Use this form
Telephone Orders: 507-645-2228
E-mail Orders: orders@ardentpublishing.com
Postal Orders: Ardent Publishing
            P.O. Box 489
            Northfield, MN 55057
Price: $27.95
Sales Tax: Please add 6.5% ($1.82) for products shipped to Minnesota addresses

Shipping by air(to insure quick delivery)**:**
US: $4.00 for the first book, $2.00 for each additional book

Payment (circle your choices):
Check   Visa   MasterCard   Discover
Number of volumes:____

Card number:_____ Exp. date:___/___

Name on card:_____

Street Address:_____

City, State/Country:_____

Zip/Postal code:_____

(please remember to include this information regardless of how you order. We can't send the book without it!)

Ardentpublishing

Order Form

If you would like to purchase *Exile to the Stars* for yourself or a friend, please use the order form below, or visit our web site: www.ardentpublishing.com

Fax Orders: 507-645-2227 Use this form
Telephone Orders: 507-645-2228
E-mail Orders: orders@ardentpublishing.com
Postal Orders: Ardent Publishing
   P.O. Box 489
   Northfield, MN 55057

Price: $27.95
Sales Tax: Please add 6.5% ($1.82) for products shipped to Minnesota addresses

Shipping by air(to insure quick delivery):
US: $4.00 for the first book, $2.00 for each additional book

Payment (circle your choices):
Check   Visa   MasterCard   Discover
Number of volumes:____

Card number:_____ Exp. date:___/___

Name on card:_____

Street Address:_____

City, State/Country:_____

Zip/Postal code:_____

(please remember to include this information regardless of how you order. We can't send the book without it!)

Ardentpublishing

Order Form

If you would like to purchase *Exile to the Stars* for yourself or a friend, please use the order form below, or visit our web site: www.ardentpublishing.com

Fax Orders: 507-645-2227 Use this form
Telephone Orders: 507-645-2228
E-mail Orders: orders@ardentpublishing.com
Postal Orders: Ardent Publishing
P.O. Box 489
Northfield, MN 55057
Price: $27.95
Sales Tax: Please add 6.5% ($1.82) for products shipped to Minnesota addresses

Shipping by air (to insure quick delivery):
US: $4.00 for the first book, $2.00 for each additional book

Payment (circle your choices):
Check   Visa   MasterCard   Discover
Number of volumes:____

Card number:_____ Exp. date:___/___

Name on card:_____

Street Address:_____

City, State/Country:_____

Zip/Postal code:_____

(please remember to include this information regardless of how you order. We can't send the book without it!)

NORMANDALE COMMUNITY COLLEGE
LIBRARY
9700 FRANCE AVENUE SOUTH
BLOOMINGTON, MN 55431-4399